Hope on the Range

CINDI MADSEN

sourcebooks
casablanca

Published by Sourcebooks Casablanca, an imprint of Sourcebooks
P.O. Box 4410, Naperville, Illinois 60567-4410
(630) 961-3900
sourcebooks.com

Printed and bound in Canada.
MBP 10 9 8 7 6 5 4 3 2 1

To those who give hope, security, and love,
especially to children who need it most.

Chapter 1

A PACKAGE FROM FEDEX WAS RARE AROUND THESE PARTS, since most people in Silver Springs, Colorado, adored the postman they'd had going on forty years and thought any other delivery method was akin to treason.

Didn't matter that Gerald's eyesight was going or that he often mixed up addresses and delivered the wrong mail to the wrong people. Which was why Tanya had been so adamant about using another shipping method. Even in the privacy of her own bedroom, merely placing the order had caused her face to grow too hot. If one of the busybodies in town accidentally ended up with her package, she'd never hear the end of it. Especially since no one around these parts could keep a secret.

Tanya's heart pumped double time, and she barely refrained from snatching the large padded envelope out of the flustered-looking FedEx driver's hands. A jingling bell filled the air as Winston, the three-legged goat Tanya had recently nursed back to health, hobbled over to see what was going on.

The FedEx driver read off her name and, at Tanya's nod, finally extended the parcel her way. "This place wasn't easy to find."

"Real sorry about that," she said, more to be polite, since being off the beaten path was pretty much the point of Bullhead Valley Dude Ranch. Admittedly, she was also distracted, her mind preoccupied with the contents of the envelope and keeping Winston from nibbling on the corner. Thanks to the peg leg she'd fashioned, the lopsided goat could get around well enough, and he mostly used his newfound mobility to eat things he wasn't supposed to.

After she informed the delivery guy that no, there wasn't an easier way back to the main road, he left, and a hesitant sort of excitement rose. Tanya had learned to manage her hopes and expectations, but there was also that saying about desperate times and desperate measures. Unfortunately, that term fit her all too well lately, so this summer, she'd resolved to take back the reins on her own life.

She did a quick scan to confirm she was still alone. Between the guests and the staff, solitude was a rarity on the dude ranch. A family of five had checked out shortly before the FedEx truck had arrived; there would be a new group arriving for a corporate retreat momentarily; and then there was the big-shot CEO who'd booked a cabin for the entire month, starting this evening. Apparently, he'd inherited some land and was thinking of getting into the ranching biz. The guy would undoubtedly change his mind once he discovered visiting a ranch and running one were two very different things. Seeing as how he was willing to pay for the full Cowboy Up package, far be it from her to discourage him from learning that lesson the hard way.

With the coast clear, Tanya lowered herself onto a nearby tree stump. "Shall we have a look?" she asked Winston as she ripped open the envelope. The cardboard tab fluttered in the early-morning breeze, and a stray red curl stuck to her lip gloss. Usually, she wore her hair up and didn't bother with makeup, but these days, she was making more of an effort.

Because she'd lost her mind, as the book she withdrew from the envelope confirmed.

How to Land Your Dream Guy: Tips from Today's Top Dating Expert.

A mixture of embarrassment and anticipation whirled through her as she cracked open the spine. She skimmed the intro, since she'd already read it online, and flipped to the first chapter— "Know What You Want."

Well, that was easy. Tanya continually found herself wanting the one thing she shouldn't—her best and oldest friend, who happened to be her neighbor to the east. Butterflies took flight in her gut as she recalled Brady Dawson's scruffy face and the way his lazy, crooked smile spread across it. Then the groove in his cheek would appear, a perfect little accent she'd been tempted to run her finger over the past couple of months.

Okay, fine. It'd been closer to four months, maybe five. At first, she'd been sure it was some kind of delusional phase, mostly due to the shortage of eligible men and having no time for a social life. After all, she and Brady had sworn long ago never to let anything ruin their friendship. They'd seen it time and time again in their small town. Two people crossed the line, only for friendship to turn to hate.

But they were different, right?

They *had* to be, because the desire that arose every time Tanya was around her best friend wasn't going away. Now she needed to figure out how to get Brady to see her as a viable option. If she managed that, it'd eliminate at least some of the risk so she could broach the subject of crossing lines. Although if she thought too much about confessing her feelings, she was seriously going to puke, so one step at a time.

The screen door to the main cabin where she and her parents lived screeched open, and Tanya slammed the book closed, jammed it into the envelope, and tucked it behind her back. If Mom so much as caught a glimpse, she'd do a praise-the-Lord dance before pointing out the dating tips she thought Tanya should pay extra attention to. Namely any that highlighted acting more like a lady.

"Mornin'," Mom said, squinting against the early-morning rays as she held the steaming cup of coffee in her hands. "Did the Crawfords already check out?"

As if he assumed Mom meant the question for him, Winston let out a loud bleat. His buck teeth gave him a perpetual grin, and affection flooded Tanya as she petted his furry head. "They hit the road right as the sun was rising. They also left their regards and wanted me to tell you how much they enjoyed their stay."

"Good, good."

Winston twisted his head so Tanya could give the underside of his chin attention. Due to her rep as the bleeding heart of the county when it came to animals, she'd gotten a call saying the goat's previous owners were going to put him down in favor of amputating his leg and ended up driving over an hour to rescue him. In spite of Tanya footing the hefty vet bill herself, Pops had been upset she hadn't asked before bringing Winston to the dude ranch. Luckily, the goat was a hit with the guests, although Pops made her promise to rehome him once he was fully healed.

In her mind, "fully healed" meant until his leg grew back—so never. "Ready to go clean up a cabin? No eating the pillowcases this time, though. In fact, it's probably for the best if you stay outside."

"You let him inside the cabins?" Mom asked, exasperation lighting the green eyes Tanya had inherited from her.

Considering she did the majority of the cleaning, Tanya figured it wasn't a big deal as long as the end result was the same. Good thing her parents hadn't caught her sneaking Winston inside her bedroom when he'd first arrived, leaving her feeling like the rebellious teenager her parents had often accused her of being. "Er, I mean you have to stay outside like you always do."

Tanya rubbed the goat's fuzzy ear, her voice more on the cooing than reprimanding side. "Shame on you for even asking, Winston."

Pops stepped out of the house, and Tanya crossed her fingers he hadn't heard the conversation and that Mom wouldn't go and enlighten him. Eventually, she and her parents would inevitably butt heads over Winston staying for good, but she'd point out how much she enjoyed having him tag along as she went about her chores and how good he was with the horses *and* guests, and fingers crossed, Pops would give in. "What's everyone standin' around for? We're burning daylight."

It was the mantra she'd awoken to at 7:00 a.m. countless times throughout the years. Dad was gruff, didn't show any "mushy emotions," and ran things the old-school way. The cowboy way, as he referred to it, and Tanya had been around cowboys enough to know it held true. Even Brady kept most things surface level. Frustration bubbled up, as it often did when Pops acted like she required micromanaging. No matter how hard she worked to prove she'd come a long way in her twenty-nine years, he'd always see her as the rash and slightly wild girl she'd been in high school.

When Mom had been justifiably worried Pops would work himself into an early grave, Tanya gave up the remainder of her hard-earned scholarship and returned home to help keep the dude ranch running. Sometimes she wondered what would've happened if she had stayed for the four years she'd planned on, but it didn't much matter in the long run. Although a part of her still couldn't stop searching for what she wanted to be when she grew up, Silver Springs offered the secure, logical path. Not only was it her home, but Brady was here.

Tingles coursed over her skin as she tucked the envelope containing her new handbook under her arm and stood. As soon as she'd cleaned Cabin Three and made it guest-ready, she planned on diving into the book's pages and formulating a game plan. The local rodeo was at the end of the month, and in addition to the main events, she and Brady always had side competitions going. They talked trash about who was going to place higher, who'd earn the fastest times, and how the team at the dude ranch would totally beat the staff at Turn Around Ranch.

And this year, she'd be embroiled in another lofty battle. A secret one that involved winning over her best friend's heart.

Brady urged the sorrel horse underneath him to go faster as he raced toward the pond and copse of trees that marked the halfway point between his family's ranch and the Bullhead Valley Dude Ranch. It'd been his and Tanya's spot since they were old enough to leave the house unsupervised. Anytime he or the cowgirl next door texted to say they needed a meetup, both of them would do whatever it took to sneak away.

He'd been wrapping up riding lessons for the day and texted Tanya to ask if she could get away for a few minutes. He figured they'd set a time within the next hour or so, but she'd taken it to the next level with her "Beat you there" reply.

One of the best things about Tanya was that she enjoyed a challenge as much as he did. These days, that mostly meant working with the at-risk youth in the Turn Around Ranch program. Don't get him wrong, he loved his job, and watching the teens grow was super satisfying, but ever since he'd decreased the number of rodeos he competed in, he'd been missing this particular brand of adrenaline.

Two distinct profiles materialized in the distance, and Brady cursed himself for not taking the time to saddle up CJ, his buckskin gelding. Poor Bud was getting on in years, which made him perfect for first-time riders. Not so great for racing.

While Brady and his rusty steed drew closer to the gnarled old cottonwood, Diesel and Tanya were coming fast, her red hair flying behind her like a flickering flame. Funny how a friendship so blissfully uncomplicated could push him so hard. It was one of many reasons they'd trained for rodeos together and what had inspired him to put a new spin on this year's local event.

"Come on, Bud," Brady said with a click of his tongue. "Just another fifty yards to an all-you-can-graze buffet." The horse snorted and elongated his stride. Excitement zipped up Brady's spine as he leaned over the gelding's reddish-brown neck, making himself as aerodynamic as possible.

Almost...

Brady swore as Tanya pulled her dark paint horse to a stop at the *exact* halfway spot—an oft-debated topic when they were kids. Dust clouds coated the air as Bud skidded to a stop, his white and pink nose nearly bopping Diesel's black one.

Before Brady could so much as get a word out, Tanya dismounted and began to celebrate her victory. "In case you didn't notice, I won. Oh yeah, oh yeah." Her dance moves were exaggerated and sloppy, her hips swaying from side to side—no music and she still couldn't keep a beat.

"Let me get this straight..." Brady gripped the saddle horn and swung himself off Bud, the leather creaking as he did so. "You rode your rodeo-trained horse while I plodded over here on the old nag we use to train nervous Nellies to ride. Real fair odds right there."

Tanya jabbed a finger to his chest. "It's not *my* fault you brought the wrong horse. Besides, where's the cocky cowboy I grew up with?" She lifted her head higher, a stripe of sunlight illuminating her green eyes. "The one who'd tell people he'd beat them, no matter the course or the horse?"

"Oh, he's right here. He's just also smart enough to realize that when it comes to you, he needs all the edge he can get." Brady tugged one of her windblown curls, warmth winding through him as her familiar smile curved her lips—although the bright shade of pink was new. "And maybe he's getting old but doesn't want to mention it."

Tanya made an offended noise in the back of her throat. "He is not. Because that would mean I am, too, and that's absolutely not true."

After looping Bud's reins over a low branch, Brady patted the horse's flank. "True. All the same, I'm getting ready to pass the torch. The Silver Springs Rodeo is gonna be Aiden's first official competition, and he's been borrowing my horse while his gains the necessary experience. Before you know it, I'll be left with slow-and-steady Bud for good."

"Excuses, excuses," Tanya said, shaking her head and clicking her tongue. "If I didn't know better, I'd say you're already waving the white flag on this year's side competition."

"Oh, you'd like that, wouldn't you? Unfortunately for you, the reason I called you here is to inform you that I'm planning on takin' things to the next level." Brady eyed the pond, thinking a dip might be nice about now. "Wanna go for a swim while we discuss it?"

Tanya's eyes went wide, and while he didn't completely understand why, he got the message loud and clear that she'd rather not jump in the cool water. Come to think of it, in addition to the makeup on her lips and eyelids, her hair was all done up, sleek curls in place of her usual messy ponytail. "You got somewhere else to be this evening? I guess I should've asked how long you've got."

"No. I mean yes." She blew out a breath. "Time's not real pressin', but that CEO who's gonna shadow me all month is set to arrive in about an hour, and I figured I'd try to make a good impression. You never can resist dunking me, and 'drowned rat' isn't an easy look to pull off."

For reasons he couldn't exactly put his finger on, her answer grated on his nerves. Why would she put on airs for some city slicker? Not that Brady paid much attention, but she'd never dressed up for one of her guests before.

Had she?

And since when did she care if her hair got messed up? Half the time, *she* initiated the water fights that led to him dunking her. She'd come up for air, slapping water at him and cursing him out for being bigger and stronger—not that she'd ever say it that way. She'd make an excuse about not being ready or that she'd slipped on a mossy rock.

Maybe that was it. She must want a more level playing field as they tossed their dare-filled gauntlet.

"How about we shoot instead?" Tanya opened the bag of tricks at the base of the cottonwood tree that was technically more of a crudely built box and lifted out their bows and quivers of arrows.

Since they often came on horseback, they'd stashed the essentials. In addition to the archery equipment, there were fishing poles, a tackle box, and snacks that were likely past their prime. Not that he was one to talk, since he'd recently begun to feel he was past his, too.

Lately he'd turned into one of those old men who ranted about too many changes and the state of the world. He also fretted over his parents, his five brothers, and the entire staff at the ranch—not to mention each and every teenager in the program, past, present, and future—more than he ever had before. He continually felt like something was…off. Or maybe just missing. Whatever it was, he couldn't seem to put his finger on it. Sure, his goals had changed quite a bit through the years, but he'd been the one steering, and he was happy with his choices.

With any luck, preparing for their annual small-town rodeo and the new twist he wanted to throw into the mix would help. *See. I can embrace change.*

As long as I'm the one in charge of it.

"Are we shooting or snoozing?" Tanya asked, waving his bow in front of his face and returning him to the here and now.

"Is snoozing an option? Because if it is, I choose that."

Tanya shot him a pursed-lip look that reprimanded him for being boring without saying a word, and he smirked and relieved her of his bow and quiver. As they walked toward the tiny meadow where they'd set up multiple targets, he noted the way her purple V-neck top complemented her red curls and pale skin.

Back when they first began playing together, she'd been a slip of a girl with thick Pippi Longstocking braids and a smattering of freckles. Sometimes he still pictured her like that—the girl who'd gone exploring with him, everything from rickety shacks to rusted-out vehicles that'd hosted nests of mice and other vermin.

While he still saw hints of that girl, fiery waves had replaced the frizzy braids, and her pale, delicate features—so at odds with her personality—made her appear as though she should be slinging drinks in a pub in Ireland instead of cowboying it up out on the ranch. She moved her ear to her shoulder in a stretch that exposed the long column of her neck and tightened her shirt over, uh, other assets he was definitely glancing away from ASAP.

Not like he'd never noticed she had breasts before or that, objectively, she was pretty. Those were merely facts that didn't mean anything besides he had eyes. Problem was, she'd put effort into dressing up for some guy she hadn't even met. Despite what his family thought, jealousy over her dating anyone else had never been a factor.

Well, not in the romantic way they meant it. The two of them just had a lot going on, and now that his oldest brother was engaged, Brady felt the weight of the ranch transferring to his shoulders. Given all that, his selfish side didn't want to share her with anyone else.

Although Brady supposed if she were going to date, some out-of-towner who was only here temporarily would be the best-case scenario.

Immediately, guilt settled in his gut. Of course he wanted Tanya to be happy. But the past year had been full of more downs than ups, and he couldn't handle one more change.

A crack punctuated the air as Tanya laced her fingers together and pushed them out, popping her knuckles. "Best of three."

"Deal," he said, and she gestured for him to go on ahead. Back in the day when he'd insisted ladies always went first, she'd punched him in the arm and told him she wasn't a lady and never would be. Under the guise of equality, she'd insisted he go first, but in reality, she just wanted to see what score she had to earn to best him.

Brady grabbed an arrow and placed it on the rest. He set his grip, drew, and aligned the tip of his arrow with the black, blue, red, and yellow target.

His focus grew hazy when he caught a whiff of Tanya's perfume—one he hadn't smelled in years. He hadn't realized she still wore it, and he was sure he would've noticed. Sultry and a hint fruity, it unlocked a memory he'd repressed, one he immediately bricked back up, but damn if it didn't distract the hell out of him.

The muscles in Brady's arm trembled from holding the string taut, which meant he needed to take his shot.

One shallow exhale, and he released the arrow.

It soared through the air and lodged in the outer circle. Not the bull's-eye he'd been hoping for, however nine points wasn't anything to turn his nose up at. Brady stepped aside, and Tanya placed her much smaller foot into his boot print.

"So I've been wanting to get our current group of teens more engaged," Brady started, "and with the rodeo coming up, I came up with a brilliant idea."

"Calling your own ideas brilliant is the first sign of narcissism. Please call for help if you or someone you love are in danger of being a narcissist." Tanya put a hand to the side of her mouth and stage-whispered, "As soon as we're done here, I'm gonna set up an intervention."

Brady chuckled. "Hear me out, and then you can judge."

She glanced over her shoulder and huffed. "I think you're just trying to distract me."

He inched closer, crowding her the same way she'd done to him, and ran his fingers along his jaw. It drove her bonkers when he fidgeted close enough that she caught the movement in her peripheral vision.

"Too bad for you, it won't work." The strings on Tanya's bow *twanged* as she released her arrow. It soared through the air, a little high…

But at the last second, it dipped and hit dead center. Brady made a half growl, half grunt that got swallowed up by her self-satisfied laugh.

"I've got nerves of steel, don't ya know?"

He did. Back when they traveled the rodeo circuit, he was the one who couldn't eat the day of an event while she wolfed down heaps of junk food, no problem. "That's right. The unshakable Tanya Clayton. She's got fancy saddles and big, shiny belt buckles to match."

She bumped her shoulder into his—well, more like into his biceps, since she was a foot shorter. "Hey, remember how my belt buckle is bigger than yours?"

"Oh, you want to compare sizes?" The question burst out of him before he realized what it'd sound like.

"I'll show you mine if you show me yours," she said. The retort shocked the hell out of him, leaving him standing there like an idiot with his mouth hanging open. Judging from her bulged eyes and the panic bleeding into her features, she'd surprised herself as well.

A strangled chuckle came out, and Brady waved off the accidentally flirty-sounding banter. "Set you up for that one, didn't I? Don't worry. I know you didn't mean it like…" He swallowed, exasperated at finding his throat tighter than usual.

What was his deal today? Regardless of whatever other shit was going on in his life, their spot acted like a mini time-out from any worries and cares.

They'd had all of one awkward encounter ever, during the night of their senior prom. That delicious perfume still lingering in the air had started it, too. The two of them had gone together as friends, but Brady hadn't been expecting the strapless, beaded dress that exposed Tanya's shoulders and made her glitter like a disco ball. The obligatory dancing had practically *forced* him to sniff her neck. The sparkling lights overhead had reflected in her eyes as he gazed deep into them, and in spite of it being nearly a decade ago, residual embarrassment heated his cheeks as he recalled going in for a kiss.

One Tanya hadn't returned, instead smacking his arm and asking what the hell he was thinking. There'd been an accusation of misogyny—something about him only treating her like a girl because she'd put on a dress, even though she'd also yelled at him before for treating her like a girl. Then she'd added that he couldn't just kiss her because she was about to leave for college and he didn't know any other way to express his emotions.

As confused as he'd been about her anger, the lesson he'd learned was how much it sucked to be in a fight with his best friend. So he'd made his apologies and vowed never to do anything so foolish again.

Before awkwardness could creep in, Brady fished out an arrow—right as Tanya reached toward the quiver to do the same— and their fingers brushed.

"What if…?" She batted her eyelids like crazy, and then her right eye twitched and squeezed closed. "I do mea—"

"Do you have something in your eye?" He snagged her wrist, tugged her closer, and instructed her to look up. Tanya stood perfectly still, save the hand she cupped around his elbow to steady herself. All he could see as he peered at her eyeball was a whole lot of white, no trace of dirt or flakes of the black mascara she'd coated her lashes with. "I don't see anything. Does it hurt?"

She shook her head and quietly said, "No. It was just a delusional moment, and it's clearly gone now."

"Well, good. Though I don't think you were delusional. All your blinking probably just got whatever it was out already. But if you screw up your shot, I don't want to hear about how your view was obstructed or some nonsense like that." He retrieved an arrow and handed it to her. "You go first this round."

Her forehead crinkled, but before he could ask why she seemed frustrated by his customary ribbing, she took the arrow and nocked it on her bow. "You mentioned the rodeo and the teens but never did get to the point."

"The brilliant idea, you mean."

There was the smile he'd been after, the slant of her lips easing the tightness in his chest that whispered something was off between them. He couldn't handle that right now. Not with his ambitious plans for the rodeo and a new teenage client showing up at the ranch. Wade was burned out on playing tough cop and hadn't been nearly as effective at it since going and falling in love anyway. Which meant it was Brady's turn to meet the boy's parole officer and take the lead.

"All in all, we've got ten teens. My idea is for you find the same number of locals to train—people with little to no experience in the arena—and we put together a sort of preshow/amateur hour with some of the simpler rodeo events. Turn Around Ranch versus Bullhead Valley. We've been working on getting the town to better accept the teens and the program. Seeing them out in the area, participating in town functions, will show everybody they're good kids at heart. Plus, the townsfolk will show up early and make bets, and it'll make all of Silver Springs feel like they're in on it. Win-win."

The tip of Tanya's tongue came out, signaling that the wheels in her brain were cranking away, and Brady's pulse throbbed faster. He didn't want to have to beg her to play along, but with his idea out in the air, he realized how badly he wanted it. A new, exciting goal, using his years of training to teach the teens new skills, the rush that accompanied the buzzer—all of it. "I'm totally on board with helping win over the town," she said.

"But?"

Tanya sighed. "With everything else I've got going on, how am I supposed to find and train that many people? All within a month and a half at that."

"Put up a couple flyers, and you'll have a team assembled in no time." He pulled out the taunt they were both too old for yet never could resist. "Unless you're chicken."

When they were younger, he'd thrown it out to goad her into going along with his daredevil antics. Not to make her do things she didn't want to do but because he'd been a little scared himself and knew he wouldn't be with Tanya by his side.

With the word *chicken* echoing through the air, Tanya lifted her bow and arrow and fired within a matter of seconds. Impressive, but in her attempt to look like an unintimidated badass, she hadn't aimed very well. Which left enough of an opening for him to catch up. She spun to face him, determination setting the line of her jaw. "I *guarantee* I can put together a team that'll give you and yours a run for your money."

"Oh, it's on." That same adrenaline from earlier came along for the ride, and Brady took a few extra seconds to center himself and aim. This time, *he* was the one to hit the target dead center. "Read it and weep—or should we call it a glimpse of things to come. How'd that celebration dance go again?"

Brady bounced around Tanya, smart enough not to attempt the hip swaying she'd done, although he added a spin so he could shake his ass at her. "Karma, am I right?"

Tanya swore and grabbed another arrow, her face so deadly serious he considered running in the other direction. On horseback, she was fast. On foot, she bolted like a cow from the chute.

Best not say that aloud, or she'll be aiming that sharp arrow tip at you.

At the exact moment her fingers began to loosen their grip, he bumped his elbow into hers. It threw off her shot, the arrow wobbling wildly before dropping low and barely striking the target in the outer circle, one-point range.

"You cheater!" She shoved him with both hands, and he fought against a wobble. Apparently a mistake, one that fanned the flame on her temper. She came at him again, and he wrapped his arms around her, pinning her arms to her sides.

"Okay, I admit that move was a pinch dirty." Brady bent so his nose nearly touched hers. An intense blaze heated her green irises, and he bit back his laughter. This was more like their usual exchanges—a mix of exasperation, dares, and heat. Since he didn't want any of that to turn into full-blown anger, he slowly let go and took a large step backward, lifting his hands in surrender. "Do your worst as I take my turn, and we'll call it distraction training."

His arrow came out of his quiver with a satisfying *zing*, and Brady steeled himself for whatever Tanya threw his way.

The fact that his muscles were already burning proved he was out of practice, but he did his best not to let that show. Still, the redhead next to him sensed weakness and pounced. She jabbed at his side, but he held steady. Her attempt to bump his elbow was met with firm resistance.

"Is that all you got?" he taunted, ignoring the slight tremble in his arm from holding back the string for so long. With the tip of his arrow lined up with the yellow of the bull's-eye, he shut out the rest of the world, the same way he always did before charging into the arena to rope or ride.

Three…

Two…

Tanya's warm breath hit his ear, sending a shiver across his skin, and without him telling them to, his fingers let go.

His arrow landed a good foot short of the target. A faraway part of him was disappointed, but the heat pumping through him pushed it to the background. His heart thundered in his chest, dizziness set in, and he couldn't quite forget the way her breath had wafted over his skin.

It's been a while since I've so much as kissed anyone. That's all.

The lack of action, along with the lack of women to use his charms on, meant he was in a sexual drought. Nothing to go thinking too hard about.

His best friend's smug giggle filled his ear, and fortunately it reset that fuzzy, malfunctioning part of his brain. He spun, grabbed hold of her, and hefted her up and over his shoulder. "You're gonna pay for that." He strode toward the pond, fully planning on tossing her in.

"Brady, don't you dare." Tanya kicked her legs, and he tightened his grip on her thigh. "You said yourself it was distraction training. It's not my fault you can't focus for shit."

"If you think this is the way to talk me out of dunking you, you're sorely mistaken." His boots slid in the mud as he reached the shoreline.

A rush of muffled words filled the air, each one merging into the next. "But remember how I have to welcome the big-shot CEO to the ranch." She squirmed against his iron hold and lifted her arm enough to glance at her watch. Then she shoved the ticking thing in his face. "In *twenty minutes, Brady*! You know how my dad will react if I'm a muddy mess when I go to check the guy in, and I already told you it's important to me to make a good impression."

That drew him up short. Both of them were well acquainted with the extra stress that came along with parental expectations and family businesses. Brady readjusted his grip and lowered her to her feet. "Fine. But you owe me one, and don't think I won't collect."

They slipped their way back through the mud and over to the cottonwood where they'd secured their horses and put away their bows and arrows. Brady unlooped Bud's reins and climbed into the worn saddle that felt like a second home. While he'd agreed to let his teenage brother borrow his horse, the saddle he'd won after taking first place at his last big rodeo was a whole other thing.

"Hey, Yaya," he said, pulling out the name he'd called her when they were young and *t*'s were hard for him to pronounce.

She turned Diesel so they were facing each other. "Yeah?"

"All trash talk aside, I know how busy you are, and I don't want you to feel pressured if you're not up for the pre-rodeo show."

"Oh, I'm all in. I just feel bad that you're the one who came up with the challenge, and my team is still gonna kick your ranch's ass."

"In your dreams, cowgirl." This was exactly what he needed. That odd antsy sensation that'd hung over him the past month or so eased, leaving him hopeful that before long, it'd be gone entirely. Maybe he'd never have his name on a plaque in the rodeo hall of fame, the way he and most of the town had thought he would at one point, but he was far from done when it came to making his mark.

Chapter 2

A CLOUD OF DUST ANNOUNCED THE IMPENDING ARRIVAL OF their new court-ordered "guest," and Brady made his way to the main cabin to take care of that whole song and dance. The beginning was always the toughest part—for the teens and the staff.

The older sedan parked a few yards from the front porch, giving Brady a prime view of the sulking teenager in the passenger seat. About ninety percent of the kids came to the ranch with the same dour expression, and a lot of them were sure they were the baddest thing the ranch had ever seen.

Carl, one of the parole officers Brady was familiar with, climbed out of the car. As a result of the looming threat of prison, sometimes the teenagers who came through the courts were easier to keep in line. Other times, it meant the staff had to keep a closer eye on them to guarantee the safe environment that was vital to progress.

The parole officer barked orders through the open car door. A moment later, the passenger side door swung open, followed by a booted foot—motorcycle, not cowboy. Maddox Mikos had on ripped jeans, a white T-shirt, and a black leather jacket, even though it was eighty-nine degrees. The kid had dark hair, visible tattoos, and rings in his ears and on his fingers. Basically he'd gone to great lengths to broadcast what a tough rebel he was.

After a few signed papers, Maddox was officially in the care of Turn Around Ranch. The ink hadn't even dried before Carl was in his car and backing away, as if he couldn't wait to be rid of the kid.

Jessica, their resident chef who hadn't been able to cook a thing when she first arrived, stepped out onto the porch. She still botched the occasional meal, but everyone loved her—especially his oldest brother, Wade, who'd asked her to marry him a couple of months ago.

Speaking of her fiancé, Wade was making his way over. Dang guy couldn't quite let go of controlling every aspect of the ranch, in spite of Brady insisting he could handle it. Wade already had a scowl in place, while Jess beamed at the new kid and waved as if she were welcoming him to Disney.

"Wow, a whole welcome party," Maddox said, his words dripping with sarcasm. "Don't I feel fucking special."

"Watch your mouth," Wade replied. Brady could tell he was about to launch into his spiel on respect, but then his cell rang.

Brady swung his arm toward the porch. "Follow me into the office and we'll get yo—"

"They *what*?" Wade bellowed into the phone. The stream of profanities that followed made Maddox's seem mild. He hung up and jammed his phone into the pocket of his Wranglers. "One of the kids thought it'd be funny to release all the horses. We've gotta go get them before they make it to the field we just sprayed."

Brady's gut sank. The aphids had been awful this year, so they'd hired a guy to spray first thing this morning. If any of the horses munched on the treated alfalfa, they'd end up severely ill. Maybe worse.

Jessica was already rushing down the steps, sprinting after Wade as he raced toward the stables.

Brady pointed a stern finger in Maddox's face. "You will stand right here next to this corral until I get back, or I'll call your parole officer and you'll be in a world more trouble than you already are. You hear me?"

The kid nodded.

"I need you to say it. Tell me you understand."

"I understand." Under other circumstances, Brady might lecture Maddox on speaking more respectfully. With time of the essence, he snagged the keys to the four-wheeler and fired up the machine.

By design, the ranch was out in the middle of nowhere, about ten miles from town. So even if Maddox did attempt to run, at least he wouldn't get far.

———————

This was hardly Maddox's first time being shipped off somewhere adults hoped other people could manage him, but it *was* the first time cowboy hats were involved. Judging from the manure-tinged air, there were actual cows around here, too.

He'd already spent two hours in the car with one uptight dude, only to be transferred to one with an even bigger stick up his ass.

Shit, maybe he *would* rather go to prison.

The country setting and endless stretches of green made his skin itch. He liked buildings he could duck into. Places to hide and streets and alleys he could zip through on his motorcycle and get away from it all. The cot in the office of the mechanic shop after hours, where he could draw in his sketch pad for a while before crashing out for the night.

At least he only had another three months before he turned eighteen. Then he could go back to working at his buddy's auto shop.

Out of the corner of his eye, he caught movement.

A large, tan horse with a pale mane burst into the corral, its female rider yelling, "Hah!"

Hooves pounded the ground, flipping up dirt as the pair rounded a red, white, and blue striped barrel. The instant the horse made it around that one, it started for the other barrel. The female rider leaned with the steed, her dark-blond hair streaming from underneath her cream-colored hat. Everything about her screamed country bumpkin, but for some reason, Maddox couldn't stop watching until she'd made it around that last barrel.

Is she in this ass-backward program, too?

She didn't look like the type who'd been in trouble a day in her life.

I could change that. It was a stray thought, one he shouldn't indulge in. Boredom often led to bad decisions, though, and he foresaw a whole lot of boredom in his future.

Maddox stepped onto the bottom rung of the wooden fence, and the girl seemed to notice him for the first time.

He gave her a nod, and she glanced around as if he must be nodding at someone else. He choked back a laugh and draped his arms over the top log of the corral. "'Sup?"

"Um, not much," she said. "Just training. I don't recognize you, so I reckon you must be new."

Seriously with the thick twang and old-fashioned words? "You reckon right."

As she studied him, the corners of her mouth tightened in disdain. While literally sitting atop her high horse, she'd judged him as trouble that quickly. Hardly a new sensation, but for some reason, it grated at him more than usual. Must be a side effect of being trapped in the middle of nowhere.

"Hey, I have a question for you," he said.

The line of her shoulders tensed, her hesitation clear, but she trotted closer. Her face was all wide-eyed innocence, making him think she must work here. Probably led the group in singing "Kumbaya" as everyone stood around the fire and preached about how warm, fuzzy feelings had cured all their problems.

What a crock of shit.

She gave him a forced smile. "Shoot."

"What exactly does racing around barrels prepare you for? Do you run into a lot of barrels in real life?"

The plastic smile turned brittle. "I run into things—and *people*—I like to avoid in real life way too often, that's for sure. On a horse or on foot, it's always good to know how to get around them quickly."

Touché. He'd underestimated her. Despite her sweet, good-girl exterior, a little sass lay under the surface. *Messing with this girl is gonna be fun.*

Since she and her horse remained in place, the sound of hoof-beats threw him off for a moment.

"Uh-oh," she said, looking beyond him, and Maddox jumped off the fence in time to see a horse rush between two pickup trucks.

Then it darted in his direction.

His heart thundered in his chest, his feet cemented themselves in place, and wouldn't it be just his luck to be trampled by a horse his first day in the country?

The dark-brown horse stopped short and eyed Maddox warily. It didn't have on a saddle, and for reasons he couldn't exactly explain, he stepped toward it instead of away.

The horse reared, and Maddox held up his hands. "Hey, it's okay." The panicked, cornered animal unlocked something deep inside Maddox. He'd seen that type of fear before. Hell, he'd felt it before, too. "I'm not going to hurt you."

"Hold him there. I'll come over and rope him and then guide him to the stables." This from a cowboy on horseback—the one who'd gotten after him for swearing but then did plenty of his own. Adults were always so hypocritical. Do what I say, not what I do.

Maddox glanced at the horse again. About two-thirds of its face was white, making its right, pale-blue eye stand out. He hadn't even known a horse could have blue eyes. The creature stomped the ground, its long nose swinging one way and the other, clearly wanting to run but afraid and unsure of which direction to go.

"Don't worry, big guy. I know what it's like to feel trapped. If you can get away from this place, I say go for it. I won't stand in your way." Maddox pivoted, flattening himself against the corral, and the horse took the opening, galloping past him in a brown-and-white blur.

The cowboy darted after him on horseback, and Maddox

silently cheered for the beautiful creature to get away. While he might prefer the city, there were miles and miles of prairie land here that led to the Rocky Mountains. Enough space to get lost in for sure.

If he had his Ducati, Maddox would seriously consider joining the runaway horse. His motorcycle was more home than any house would ever be and had come in handy whenever he ended up in a mess he couldn't talk his way out of. But once the shit hit the fan, of course he hadn't been allowed to bring his bike with him.

All because timing was a bitch—story of his life, really.

In a handful of seconds, Harlow managed to unlatch the gate. She nudged Maximus out the opening, wishing for her rope. Without it, she'd have to stick to herding.

"See that stallion?" she asked her horse, who loved the thrill of the chase as much as she did. "Let's help Wade catch him."

The young stallion had been sent to the ranch in hopes that Aiden, the Dawsons' resident horse whisperer, could calm him down and train him. Harlow hadn't heard whether Aiden had had any success, but judging from the way the horse zigzagged and evaded people, she'd go with not so much.

Since Wade was closing in on the horse's left flank, Harlow bolted right, the blood in her veins pumping hot. As soon as she reached the stallion, he veered in the other direction.

Last second, the stallion seemed to realize his mistake, but since this was far from Wade's first rodeo, it was too late. The lasso had been thrown, and the loop slipped over the horse's head. Wade gently secured the rope, and Harlow trotted alongside to help the process go smoother.

"I've got it from here," Wade said once they were within a couple of yards of the stables. "Thanks for your help, though. I was starting to worry he'd make it to the main road before I could catch him."

"Happy to help." Harlow pulled Maximus to a stop, had him complete a one-eighty, and urged him toward the corral.

In the distance, the ranch's giant van turned into the driveway. Harlow squinted in the vehicle's direction and then leaned down to pat Maximus's muscled neck and tell him what a good job he'd done. "Who's a good boy? That's you, isn't it?"

Maximus preened, and Harlow slowed him to a trot.

The boy who'd spoken to her with a hint of condescension before morphing into full-on ridicule with his barrel-racing question stood in the same spot as earlier. He screamed trouble, his leather jacket, piercings, and devil-may-care attitude broadcasting how tough he thought he was.

Ooh, I'm so cool. I don't care about anything or anyone.

Several of her classmates went crazy for that type, but she had far too much common sense to let herself be affected, no matter how hot the guy was.

Even if said guy had dark hair, an olive complexion, and thick, expressive eyebrows. Tattoos crept out the sleeve of his jacket and covered the back of his hand. His jeans were torn, and he hadn't even fully laced the combat boots on his feet, as if he'd gotten halfway through securing them and a more pressing matter snagged his attention.

His eyes met hers, and she fought against the urge to look away. She hadn't been ogling him. She'd merely been…cataloging his features. Yeah. That was it.

While Harlow told herself to pass on by, her mouth had other plans. "Looks like my skills came in pretty darn handy with that runaway stallion. Oh, and since you're gonna be around horses while you're here, you might want to work on not bein' scared of 'em."

He opened his mouth as if to reply, but then snapped it shut and shook his head. The sun glinted off the silver bar that ran through his upper ear and the hoop in his lobe.

A zing of victory sang through her. "What? You can dish it out, but you can't take it? That figures."

The line of his jaw tightened. "You just seem like the crying type, and I'm in enough trouble as it is."

The van pulled up to the main cabin, and while Harlow would never admit it, she was glad, because she didn't have a clever comeback. And she was kinda sorta the crying type. But she was working on becoming tougher.

Stupid jerk. He thinks he can take one look at me and figure out who I am. Well, he's wrong. Right then and there, she vowed never to let him see her cry.

As soon as the van doors slid open, the three-year-old twins Harlow often babysat came running toward her. Their mom, Liza Reynolds, called after them to be careful, and they continued to sprint as fast as their chubby little legs would take them, nearly tripping on the way.

"Harlow! Were you riding Maximus real fast?" Everett was the chatty, opinionated one, and Elise usually took a minute or two to warm up. Her biggest frustration in life was not quite being able to keep up with her brother.

Harlow dismounted and draped the reins over the saddle horn so Maximus could munch on grass while she said hello to the twins. Elise reached for her, and Harlow picked her up and slung her up on her hip. "Hey, Princess."

Everett stuck his lips out in a pout. "I came over first."

"No matter," Harlow said. "I have two arms." She scooped him up and plopped him on the other hip. Now that they were getting bigger, it was more of a challenge to balance them both, but she could manage.

Liza came over, her stern mom expression in place as she glanced from Elise to Everett. "Okay, you two, Harlow can only play for a few minutes. She's here to train, not to play with you. Remember how we talked about that?"

"Just a few minutes, but they'll be good ones," Harlow said. She boosted Everett a bit higher on her hip. "I needed a minibreak after all the excitement anyway." She relayed the story about how the horses had gotten loose and spotted Brady, Wade, and Jessica walking in their direction, so all the horses had to be secured and accounted for.

"I'm gonna consider this my weight training." Harlow spun in a circle, and the twins clung to her and giggled. Bonus, that made it easier to avoid Mr. Too Cool for School's stare.

"Wow, is there a family meeting or something?" Chloe asked as she and Aiden walked into the yard hand in hand. Like most teens, Chloe had arrived pissed off at the world and at Jessica, who'd originally taken the cooking position to pay her daughter's way. Now they were both permanent members of the ranch and the extended Dawson family, which tended to grow by the year. "Please tell me the boring part is over already."

Aiden covered his mouth with his free hand, trying to hide his laugh. The two of them were so cute that Harlow couldn't help being a smidge jealous of their relationship.

Who has time for relationships anyway?

If her mama asked, Harlow's priorities included preparing for the start of senior year. But honestly, every waking minute involved recalibrating her goals and expectations, thanks to her former roping partner.

A pang went through her chest. After two solid months of work, Bianca had suddenly informed Harlow that she'd decided to be part of another team. Which meant saying goodbye to winning the All-Around Cowgirl title awarded to the most successful cowgirl in two or more events.

And if you let yourself think about that, you'll break your other goal of not crying in front of that jackhole.

"Do you guys want to go for a ride on Maximus?" she asked the kids, who were growing heavier in her arms by the second.

The twins erupted with cheers and enthusiastic yeses, and Harlow cringed as she realized she should've checked with Liza first. Too late, she glanced up in search of their mother.

Only her gaze was temporarily snagged by the new guy. He was staring at her, his smirk leading her to believe he was mocking her. He had ridiculously pretty eyes for a dude, a mesmerizing shade of amber that practically glowed, which hardly seemed fair when she'd ended up with boring brown ones.

Harlow lifted her chin. Mama always worried about the type of people she'd be around whenever she came to Turn Around Ranch to train or to babysit, but the Dawsons ran a tight ship. Some of the teens she'd made friends with, and others she steered clear of, but she'd never been *afraid* of anyone on the ranch.

Finally, she yanked her eyes away and addressed Liza. "Sorry. I should've asked first."

Worry lines creased Liza's forehead. "Both of them are a bit much to handle when it comes to horses."

"Aiden and I will help," Chloe offered, and Liza's shoulders relaxed visibly.

Mr. Too Cool for School rolled his eyes at them, too, so Harlow decided not to take his obvious contempt for her personally.

"Come on, Maddox," Brady said, clapping the dude on the back. "Let's get you settled in."

Maddox. *Of course* his name was something mysterious and sexy. *No, not sexy. He undid any chance of that with his personality.*

And he's not my type. After her last experience, Harlow resolved to stick to all-American cowboys, which there were plenty of at school. Although not many she hadn't known for all of forever, but that was a problem for a different day. Right now was for getting herself rodeo-ready so that she could at least beat her turncoat partner in all the single-rider events.

Chapter 3

"YEAH, THE WEBSITE SAID IT WAS ISOLATED, BUT MUCH farther and I'd need a passport to return home," Mr. Eric Richmond, CEO and owner of the software company RichTech said to one of the people from the corporate retreat.

There was a large SUV parked by the office. Due to driving dirt roads, the black vehicle that Tanya's truck could outperform ten times over was now closer to brownish-gray.

She wasn't sure whether the guy meant the remark as an insult or if the slight tinge of irritation she felt was due to rushing home yesterday, only for Mr. Richmond to call two hours later and inform her he'd be showing up first thing the next morning instead. Something about a contract negotiation. All she could focus on was disappointment over the fact that she could've spent more time with Brady.

Admittedly, she couldn't stop rehashing their time together. Not even a blip of a reaction had come from the "neck presentation" move, where she'd tilted her head and exposed her neck to him. So she'd taken it a step further, and her cheeks heated as she recalled her attempt to wink at Brady while delivering a flirty line.

Since it'd led him to think she had something in her eye, Tanya needed to either practice winking or take it off the ways-to-flirt list. A moment earlier, she'd been panicked, afraid the "I'll show you mine if you show me yours" line had been too bold, but Brady hadn't even considered it a come-on.

According to the dating book on her nightstand, the biggest mistake women made was to stop trying. And so, even though taking extra effort with her hair and makeup hadn't done a damn thing for her yesterday, Tanya had dressed up again today. Not only for the first impression thing, which had automatically come out yesterday when Brady asked, but also because she was determined.

"Eric Richmond?" she asked, and he glanced toward her. Then did a double take, reducing her frustrations over the guy and makeup all at once.

An idea popped into her head. When she'd read that hair-flipping was a legitimate flirting technique, she'd rolled her eyes so hard she thought she might've sprained them. But as she swept her curly strands over her shoulder, she added a huge smile, and Mr. Richmond's eyes tracked the motion.

Hmm, guess I'll have to try that one on Brady the next time I see him.

Pops came lumbering out the noisy front door, his steps slow yet steady as he gripped the rail and descended the steps on the porch. At sixty-four, he could still handle a lot of the ranch work, but he'd had a heart attack a few years ago, which had slowed him down—much to his dismay. The doctor wanted him to take on less of the physical labor and lower his blood pressure and stress level, which was when Tanya had been summoned home. Extra fun, since he constantly rebuffed her offers to help with physical tasks, insisting he wasn't helpless, while in the next breath, he would complain about how frail he'd become.

"Beau Clayton," her complicated father said, extending a hand to Mr. Richmond, who requested he be called Eric.

After exchanging pleasantries, the businessman turned to Tanya. She wondered if his button-down shirt and slacks were his idea of ranch wear. If so, he'd learn real fast how badly that thin fabric could stain and tear. His features softened, a light hitting his hazel eyes. "And you are…?"

"The woman you've been corresponding with the past month." The guy had asked about a bajillion questions via email, both before and after booking his stay. Not that she minded. It just made it fairly obvious he had no clue how to run a ranch. It'd made her want to ask why on earth anyone had left land to him, but she'd gotten much better at holding back questions people might consider rude.

"Ah, so *you're* Tanya." Eric said her name as if he were tasting it, and despite herself, she softened. After all, the guy was willing to try, and that was commendable. Even if he looked like he drank kale shakes, bragged about his hefty mortgage, and had an assistant to run errands he wouldn't deign to do.

In fact, watching him deal with livestock and manure was sure to be highly entertaining, and who couldn't use more of that? "That's me. I'll be your motivator, overseer, and most likely the person you want to say goodbye the fastest to by the time this is over."

His lips tilted up at the corners. "I highly doubt that."

"You underestimate how hard I'll push you." Without realizing it, their conversation bubble had shrunk to admit only two, when there was an entire group of people awaiting her orders. She scanned the faces that showed a combination of anticipation and trepidation and raised her voice. "All of you."

"That's why I'm here," Eric said. "I'd rather have my hard lesson now than down the road."

He almost made "hard lesson" sound dirty. It'd been so long since someone had flirted with her that Tanya couldn't be sure that was what he was doing, but the guy was slick, that was for sure.

The key in Eric's hand jingled as he lifted it in the air. "I just got checked in, so I'm gonna go get settled, and then I'll be back."

Tanya glanced at her watch. "You've only got seven minutes until the first activity of the day starts. First lesson of running a ranch is that we keep a tight schedule. Animals don't understand sleeping in, and I'm not handing out special exceptions for individuals. We ride and work as a group. If I assign the last horse and you're not there, you'll get left behind." His eyebrows arched, and Tanya raised hers right back. "I suggest you hustle. The rest of you, follow me."

Brady surveyed the group of students gathered in front of him after lunch on Wednesday afternoon. Despite no longer being part of the program, Aiden and Chloe were in the mix. They attended classes with the rest of the teens so they could finish their schooling, and if they wanted to see a counselor, they were free to do so.

He'd seen such a big change in Chloe since she'd shown up last spring, bitter at her mom and at the world and dealing with anxiety. Sadly, depression and anxiety were nearing epidemic levels in teens, beginning from a younger and younger age, and social media often fed the beast.

Pride swelled as Brady thought of how well his soon-to-be niece had learned to manage it, even though it'd be a lifelong fight.

Chloe slipped her hand into Aiden's, and he beamed at her—Brady had seen a big change in his youngest brother over the past year as well. Like their brother Nash, who'd asked their parents if they'd consider also adopting his kid brother, Nick, Aiden had originally ended up at the ranch due to a court order. In addition to what the program had done for him, working with the horses, along with the realization he'd found a permanent home, had caused the kid to really come out of his shell. The blond at his side was also good for him, same way he was good for her.

"Yo, what we doin' out here?" Desiree asked. Half her dark hair was in its usual super curly style, and the other half was in tiny braids. All the girls had been sporting different hairdos than usual. Apparently Danica had decided she was going to become a hairdresser and was thrilled to have a group to practice on.

"Yo?" Brady said, and Desiree rolled her eyes, but her white teeth flashed against her bronze skin as the corner of her mouth turned up.

"Mr. Dawson, sir. Why are we out here on this fine day, waiting for you to say something?" She saluted him, the smart-ass. Since he was the one who graded her science homework, he also knew she was exceptionally smart, period. "*Sir*."

"Would you rather be doing chores?"

Danica smacked Desiree's arm, and Desiree glared at her before beaming at him. "Nope. Carry on with your silent staring."

Brady would call it "assessing," but that fell under the semantics category. He was confident he had all the pieces to make one hell of a team. He merely needed to figure out where to put them. Allie, who was the school principal, Ma, Liza, and his brothers had agreed to let him do the majority of the rodeo training this year—and to give him the extra time he'd asked for so the teens could be included. "As some of you know, the local rodeo is coming up."

The new kid let out a groan, his head lolling back. "This is what counts for exciting around here?"

"It does, and anyone who decides not to participate can clean the stables instead. Anyone wanna volunteer for that?"

The teens stood straighter, arms down at their sides, as if one small movement might mean accidentally volunteering. Save Maddox, who shrugged as if he were above caring.

Probably because he'd only done cleaned the stables once so far, and it'd been a light day. Not to mention Nick had gotten him halfway through. Maddox's attitude had been set to contemptuous since he'd arrived, and according to Nick, he'd treated his first counseling session like it was a police interrogation and he was determined not to say an incriminating word.

Brady hoped the punk would come around eventually. And not just because he had an athletic build that could sway the rodeo preshow odds in their favor. "This year, we're going to have our own mini competition with the ranch next door before the major events. Anyone who qualifies can also compete in the main part of the rodeo and have an extra hour a few times a week to train for that."

"Hell yeah, I'm in already," Abby said. She was fairly new but

had embraced things almost immediately and a mite too enthusiastically. He had a feeling she might be trying to show them she
was totally okay and didn't belong here, but that was more Nick
and Liza's territory.

Still, Brady made a mental note to keep an eye on her and to ask
which one of them was counseling her. Most likely Liza, because
teenage girls were often uncomfortable with a male counselor.
Unfortunately, too many males in their lives had let them down,
betrayed their trust, and even abused them. If he thought about
that, he'd get angry and want to go full vigilante, so it was one of
those things he let the trained professionals handle.

"All right then." The purr of an engine drifted over, and Brady
glanced at the older black-and-blue Dodge heading their way.

Right on time.

The screen door to the cabin swung open, and Ma emerged
from the house with the whiteboard he'd requested. Since a health
scare and hospital stay last winter, the entire staff had tried to convince her to take it easy. Which was why he'd asked her to have
Wade or Trace bring the board and markers outside once she
tracked them down.

Naturally, she was struggling with the various supplies instead,
attempting to prove she could do everything herself. Brady took
a step toward her to help, but Aiden and Chloe were on it. Aiden
grabbed the whiteboard, and Chloe grabbed the stand.

"Oh, for heaven's sake," Ma said with a huff. "I can carry
something."

"You've got the markers and erasers." Chloe jerked her chin
toward the bag in her hand. "Can't write without those."

Ma tried to maintain her disgruntled expression, but she
melted at Chloe's bright smile. "Bless you, dear."

Doing this outside was causing more fuss than it was worth,
but he never did like being in a stuffy classroom on a nice summer
day. One of the benefits of living near the base of the mountains

was the frequent cool breeze that kept the temperature from getting too terribly hot.

Dundee and Quigley, their Australian shepherd and black-and-white border collie, raced toward their approaching visitor, barking like they were tough guard dogs instead of overgrown puppies who only occasionally herded cattle.

Harlow Griffith climbed out of her truck and gave the dogs the affection they were seeking before heading over to the group. "Y'all get started already?"

"Only on the explanation." Some of the kids' attention had drifted, and Brady snapped his fingers and raised his voice to get it back. "We're going to split up and try out a few events. After we observe everyone's strengths, we'll dole out assignments and replace a couple of your usual outdoor activities with training."

"Not that I'm telling you what to do," Danica said, running her fingers through her brown hair and sweeping it to one side, "but could they replace our chores instead? Or classes—I'm okay with missing either."

Yeah, color him the opposite of surprised. "Not all of them, but we'll shorten a class and maybe skip a chore or two, although we'll have to alternate which ones. Things still need to run smoothly around here, and if I catch anyone slacking and not doing their training, they'll get double the chores. Got it?"

Heads bobbed, all except for Maddox's. No skin off his nose, given that Brady didn't need him to nod. He'd outlined the rules, and if the kid didn't follow them, he'd have consequences anyway.

"Harlow here is gonna help us train," Brady continued. "I want you to listen to her and treat her with the respect she deserves." She was his ace in the hole. Giving her a job made her part of the staff. That meant they had another instructor with experience, and since it allowed her more time to train, it benefited her as well.

Harlow lifted her hand in a shy wave. "Can't wait to get started. I appreciate the chance to help out and the job." Her gaze swept to

Wade, who'd stepped onto the porch sometime during the commotion, and then to Ma, who stood near the whiteboard and had a death grip on the markers—the woman was hell-bent on contributing in whatever way she could.

"Happy to have you, dear," Ma said. "The more we see you, the better. Specially if you promise to let me do some of the heavy liftin' and not treat me like some kind of invalid."

Harlow pressed her lips together, and Wade sighed.

"Ma," he said, and she held up a warning hand.

"Don't you start. Or I'll tell your fiancée you don't want dinner tonight."

"With the way my fiancée cooks, you might be doing me a favor."

On cue, Jessica charged out of the screen door. "Wade Dawson, what was that you just said about me?"

Before meeting Jess, Wade's stoic expression would've remained in place. Instead, a grin split his face as he snagged her wrist and drew her close. "I meant *before*. You make a lot of good dishes now."

A whole lot of PDA was about to commence, so Brady talked as loudly as he could while Ma scribbled the events he wanted to cover on the whiteboard.

Team roping
Calf roping
Barrel racing
Pole bending
Chute dogging (maybe)

On account of not wanting anyone to get hurt or to get sued, they wouldn't attempt bareback or bull-riding competitions in their before-the-rodeo rodeo. That was a bad idea all around, especially without years of training.

Same went for steer wrestling, although that was the event Nash signed himself up for his first year on the ranch. Ma just about had a heart attack. She'd sprinted down the grandstand bleachers, hollering and waving her hands, but it was too late to stop him. Fifteen-year-old Nash had rushed out of the gate on horseback, leaped onto the long-horned steer, and pinned its head to the ground remarkably fast. So fast he'd not only won but set a new local record.

The next year, after the adoption had been finalized, Nash upgraded to riding bulls. Occasionally, during the rougher days on the ranch, Brady experienced a pinch of jealousy that Nash got to be out on the rodeo circuit, living the dream Brady had since he was a kid.

Since what-ifs never did anyone any good, he returned his focus to the items on the board. Chute dogging was a milder form of steer wrestling, one for beginners where they didn't ride a horse and used younger, smaller steers. He'd placed it in the maybe category since most of the teens were too afraid of the steers to wrestle them, and again, Brady didn't want anyone getting hurt.

There was living life and then there was asking for trouble.

That made him think of his best friend, because there was no one who liked jumping headfirst into trouble like Tanya. She was more cautious now, but back in the day, he could hardly keep up with her.

Brady rubbed his hands together, the idea of having a victory to hold over her causing an ear-to-ear grin. With this going on, he could leave the professional rodeoing to Nash. Besides, taking a spill off a horse these days meant ice baths and handfuls of ibuprofen. This plan allowed him to compete without as much pressure while also having a heap of fun. "Desiree and Danica, go with Wade for calf roping."

Once they got the hang of solo roping, Brady planned on letting them team up. They already went everywhere together, to the point the teens called them the Double D's, something he and the rest of the staff never did for obvious reasons.

Brady instructed Chloe and Aiden to start with barrel racing, as he could confidently send them to the corral on their own. Then he sent a handful of the kids who were still learning the ins and outs of horse riding to the stables for pole bending with his brother Trace.

"Which leaves Maddox to go with Harlow for team roping. Obviously today, we'll just start with roping."

Ah, hell. I didn't think this pairing through very well. Brady glanced from Harlow to the kid with the enormous chip on his shoulder. The two were on opposite ends of a spectrum, and he should've held another student or two back so Harlow wouldn't have to deal with Maddox one on one. "You know what? I can switch that up. Maddox can go with me as I—"

"It's okay." Resolve burned bright in Harlow's big brown eyes, undimmed by the shade provided by the brim of her cowboy hat. "If he gets out of line, I'll just pull on his hoop earring to get him to do what I want, same way I'd use the nose ring on a bull." She shot Maddox a saucy grin. "Real handy, that."

In the couple of seconds it took Brady to recover from his surprise, a snort-laugh accidentally escaped. Sounded like Harlow could handle the new kid just fine. They'd all be in fairly close quarters anyway as they made their way through the training areas he'd set up around back, so she wouldn't be completely alone with him.

"You heard the lady," Brady told Maddox, who sighed. Tough guys with their eye rolls and sighs—yeah, real scary. He clapped the kid on the back. "Cowboy up, dude."

Maddox shuffled toward Harlow, taking his sweet time about it. She spun on her heel and charged toward the training course without a word, and he reluctantly followed.

Later, Brady would put away the whiteboard. For now, he circled the main house, grinning at the clusters of kids setting up at the various training stations. A win at the Silver Springs rodeo might not come along with expensive saddles, blingy belts, big cash prizes, and fame, but the more he thought about how satisfying it'd be to accomplish so much with a group of newbies, the more excitement stirred in his gut.

He couldn't wait for Turn Around Ranch to show up ready to take names and show the townsfolk what the teens could accomplish when they put their minds to something. In fact, he supposed it was time for a bit of trash talking.

Brady pulled out his phone and tapped out a text.

> **Brady:** Two minutes into our training, and I'm actually starting to feel bad about the whooping my team's gonna give yours.
> **Tanya:** Liar.

He was about to send a not-so-innocent "Who, me?" reply, but his phone buzzed with another message.

> **Tanya:** You forget that I've been around you when you go into competitive mode, and feeling bad about winning is hardly your MO. Since I haven't even formed my team yet, sounds like I'm gonna have to play a little dirty.

Brady's heart thumped harder in his chest, and for reasons he couldn't explain, the phrase *play a little dirty* flashed through his mind like a neon light. He hovered his thumbs over the keypad and searched his brain for a witty comeback. Once again, Tanya was faster.

> **Tanya:** Speaking of whipping, I think I have a nice braided whip in the tack room. Sounds like I'm going to have to dig it out and teach you a lesson.

Holy shit. Brady's throat went dry, and his tongue stuck to the roof of his mouth. Like her tit-for-tat comment about showing each other theirs, he was sure she hadn't meant for it to come out sounding so…dirty.

Then again, she did say she was gonna play dirty. His mind hovered over the gutter, one wrong stray thought from diving in. Was this a tactic? Using her feminine wiles on him to throw him off his game?

Nah. That wasn't her style. In fact, he'd be in danger of bodily harm if he so much as implied she'd stoop that low. This was his dry spell messing with his head again. Brady exhaled a shallow breath and reminded himself that when it came to *his best friend*, inappropriate thoughts crossed a serious line. Picturing her in a leather dominatrix outfit was also off-limits, and he slammed that mental door shut as fast as he could.

But that blip of the image he'd unintentionally conjured was liable to haunt him for days.

With his brain tiptoeing into dangerous territory, he needed to get his head straight. No letting the heat of competition trick him into contemplating things about Tanya that he hadn't pondered for years. First during that reckless dance at prom, and another stretch of time last year, when they'd been road-tripping along the rodeo circuit and he'd let himself wonder *what if* too many times.

Before promptly shutting the thought down, the same way he was doing now.

Brady pocketed his phone and continued pacing the line of training drills. After some time to cool down, he'd think up a clever comeback. One that didn't have a big ol' undercurrent of perviness to it.

Chapter 4

THE FIRST FEW TRAIL RIDES WITH A NEW GROUP WERE OFTEN the longest. Not in terms of distance but in how long it took the people visiting the dude ranch to ride less than a mile. For a lot of their clients, it was one of their first times on a horse—if not *the* first—so Tanya did her best to keep her patience.

Diesel, however, didn't even try. As a result of their rodeo glory days, her stocky paint horse was used to charging through gates at ridiculously fast speeds. The tight turning skills that'd been honed from years of barrel racing also meant that he'd bolted for Loretta Wilson's apple tree the instant Tanya had loosened her grip on the reins and twisted to check on the dude-ranch crew.

The leather of the saddle creaked as Tanya leaned over the horn to whisper soothing words in his flickering ears. "I know you like to go fast, buddy, but we have to wait for the rest of the group."

Diesel nickered and stomped a foot, heavy on the attitude. If Tanya could get away with that move without looking like a crazy person, she'd do the same. She could hardly lecture Diesel on patience when hers was stretching thinner with every minute that passed without a response from Brady.

About ten minutes ago, she'd been texting away, alternating currents of glee and anxiety making a mess of her internal organs. She was being bold and flirty, and in response, she'd gotten nada. What fun was trash-talk if the other person didn't respond in kind?

Had she been too bold? Sent too many texts too fast? One of the tips in her dating book suggested walking away after delivering a great line. Theory being, the guy's head would keep spinning on it, leaving him wanting.

Either wanting to explore more, which left the ball in his court, or he wouldn't take the bait and that probably meant… A lump formed in her throat.

What am I gonna do if he's completely uninterested? Tanya had tried so hard to shut off any romantic feelings for Brady, to no avail. Now she was thinking she should've never sent that retort involving a whip. She'd giggled as she'd typed it, quickly hitting Send before she could chicken out. That was the nice thing about texting. If she'd had to look Brady in the face while saying it, her mouth never would've followed through.

Tanya lifted her phone and growled at it for not having a message. Man, this dating thing was frustrating and complicated, especially when she factored in the friendship aspect.

But the same as the most formidable competitions at the biggest rodeos, it was better to try than to always wonder what could've been, right?

At the sound of approaching horses, Tanya slid her phone in her pocket. One at a time, the stragglers crested the hill, her coworker Miguel bringing up the back.

Eric sat astride Taffy, one of their older, milder horses. The guy rode super bumpy, bouncing instead of syncing his movements along with the horse, but that took time. Riding also took a toll on the inner thighs if you weren't used to it, and the way he fidgeted suggested he was feeling it.

"How's it going?" Tanya asked as he sidled up beside her and Diesel.

"Fine." Eric relaxed his stiff arms, and Taffy interpreted that as being time for a grazing break. "Ahhh, wait, no!"

Eric teetered forward, the saddle horn digging into his gut and saving him from sliding down the horse's neck. Tanya snagged the reins, tugging Taffy's head back up and giving Eric a chance to regain his bearings.

"I have ridden before," he said. "It's just been a while."

"That explains why you ride like popcorn kernels in boiling oil," she teased. Judging from the scrunch of his blond eyebrows, her joke had gone over his head. "You know. Bouncing and popping."

"Oh, I definitely heard some popping. I'm afraid to climb off the horse and see which part of me it was."

Tanya laughed, and a smile spread across Eric's face. Admittedly, it was a handsome face—something Mom unsubtly pointed out this morning. The polished, clean-shaven, suit-wearing men had never been Tanya's type. Not that it mattered to Mom. Regardless of how long or short their guests planned to stay, if one of them was even semi-near Tanya's age, Mom attempted to play matchmaker. Once with a guy who had a girlfriend, and it'd been super awkward to explain that she understood his need to clarify, but *she* wasn't the one who'd left the flirty note with her number on the nightstand.

Almost as awkward as gathering all your courage to send a racy text to your best friend, only for him to completely ignore it.

"How far should we go today, boss?" Miguel hollered in her direction. "Everyone's gotten a breather, but I'm thinking we should stop at the stream for lunch."

"Sounds perfect."

A groan came from Eric. "I'm afraid to ask and sound like a kid on a road trip, but how much longer is that?"

"About an hour," she said, and Miguel was close enough to overhear and snort. In addition to Winston, Pops occasionally referred to Miguel as one of Tanya's strays. The nineteen-year-old had come up through Turn Around Ranch. As soon as the kids turned eighteen, the Dawsons had to bid them farewell, or then they would have an "adult" with the "kids."

The rules of Miguel's parole stated he needed a job, and since he had experience with livestock and the dude ranch needed more help, Tanya had hired him. Which led to a lecture from Pops on being too hasty and not checking with him first, but now both her parents adored him.

Didn't mean they'd ever rescinded their lecture.

Admiration for Eric set in as he exhaled, lifted his reins, and set his chin.

"I'm kidding," Tanya said. "It's only ten more minutes."

"Thank God." A relieved breath whooshed out of him. "I was about to call up my buddy and forfeit our stupid bet."

Tanya opened her mouth to ask for details, but then her phone buzzed. She whipped it out of her pocket so fast it almost flew out of her hand, like a slippery fish hell-bent on returning to the creek. The edges of the blasted device dug into her hand as she clung on, and she tightened her grip even more when she saw Brady's name on the screen.

Brady: You'll have to show it to me when I come over
         later this week.

A squeal escaped, one that made a couple of the riders glance in Tanya's direction. Diesel snuffled, conveying his dismay they still weren't moving, and she clicked her tongue and urged him forward, only vaguely paying attention to the trail. Diesel knew it as well as she did.

It worked! It worked! Tanya did a jig in her saddle, her excitement pumping as quickly as her heart. *Unless....*

Fingers crossed this wasn't one of those misunderstandings where she was the clueless girl who believed she'd done an amazing job flirting, only for Brady to show up ready to play Indiana Jones, like when they were little.

Every time they'd found an ancient treasure—rusted tractor gears, a shoe that'd been lost for decades, and arrowheads—he got to make up the story of what they were and how the clues tied together. In her frustration, she'd pushed past her fear of snakes and caught one solely to wave it in Brady's face. Then he'd said, "Cool, let me hold it," and she'd had to remind him that *Indiana Jones* was afraid of snakes.

Ooh, maybe there's a let-me-hold-your-snake innuendo in there.
Heat crawled up Tanya's neck, and she decided she'd been bold
enough for one day. But the next time she saw Brady in person,
she'd study how he acted toward her and then judge if and when
she should amp things up another level.

Still, she clung to that glimmer of hope and vowed to spend
the next couple of days devouring and highlighting the book that'd
gotten her this far.

———————

Harlow extended a coil of rope to Maddox, who stared at it like it
was a snake that might bite.

Given his puckered expression, she wouldn't mind if the rope
managed to grow fangs and follow through.

Since the Dawsons had hired her to help, Harlow did her best
to stifle her irritation with the judgmental jerk and put on her
teacher hat. "Do you have any experience with rope?"

Maddox's features morphed into a suave expression that probably worked way too well on most females. "You mean tying girls
to the bed on their request? Because then—"

"*Gag.*"

"I've got some experience with that, too," he said, that stupid
smirk still quirking his lips.

Harlow brought out the hard glare, the one she'd used when
boys at school thought it'd be funny to toss innuendos her way,
as if she were too naive to understand them. The glower had been
pretty successful at getting them to back away.

Maddox didn't exactly withdraw, but he did hold up his hands
in surrender. "Just messing with you, trying to find any entertainment I can get."

"Well, I'm not here for your entertainment." Until Harlow
had said it aloud, she didn't realize she'd quoted a P!nk song, and

residual pride bolstered her. Just because she wasn't going out with a guy every weekend or bragging about how older men always fell for her like it was her cross to bear, the way her ex roping partner did, didn't mean she was a clueless pushover.

With a sigh, Maddox took the rope from her. "We're going to be spending a lot of time together, aren't we?"

"Gosh, I hope not. But it'll probably be more than either one of us would like."

Two creases showed up between his dark eyebrows, as if he couldn't imagine a world where a girl wouldn't fall all over him. Harlow gripped the honda, fed her rope through, and flipped the loop, repeating the move until it was armpit height.

Then she stepped closer to Maddox to show him she wasn't affected by his hotness, and she sure as heck wasn't scared of him. "Here, hold the rope like so…" She expected more pushback, but Maddox did as instructed. "This is called a honda."

"Does it help if I know a lot about the type of Hondas that have four wheels?" he asked, and a misguided flutter careened through her belly as he flashed her a smile that seemed more genuine than sarcastic.

Focus, Harlow. No letting him distract you, because that's what he's really after. She showed him how to swing, calling attention to the way she twisted her wrist.

One thing was for sure: this guy was gonna be trouble. Sure, it was the kind of trouble that'd be fun at first, but falling for his charms meant a painful fall on her butt later.

On the bright side, a little verbal sparring might make training more fun. Lately, she'd lost a bit of her spark when it came to that. It wasn't that she didn't like barrel racing, but her true love was team roping.

Without a partner, she no longer had the same drive she'd had earlier this summer.

What was hardest about letting go of winning the team roping event and securing the All-Around Cowgirl title was that she'd poured everything into that goal. To the point she didn't have a lot of friends or other activities to keep her busy. Because good or not—and she was dang good—couldn't compensate for not having a partner.

It was kind of the entire point of *team* roping.

Maddox couldn't help watching the emotions flicker across Harlow's face. They changed so quickly as she'd demonstrated how to form a lasso and how to throw it, from concentration to annoyance aimed at him. Followed by a flicker of happiness as soon as he'd shown interest in the mechanics of what she was trying to teach him.

"Okay, so I make the loopy thing...?"

"You're holding it in the wrong place." Harlow stepped closer, and as she readjusted his grip on the rope, he studied the freckles on the bridge of her nose. They drew his focus downward, to unique, heart-shaped lips that were thin on top and plump on the bottom.

Maddox's fingers twitched with the urge to withdraw the pencil he always had in his pocket and sketch them. Unfortunately, his pad was in his room, hidden away from prying eyes.

"Are you payin' attention?" Harlow asked, and he nodded, even though he was paying attention to all the wrong things.

Or maybe they were all the right things.

When Brady announced they'd be training for the local rodeo, Maddox had thought *Kill me now*. The last thing he wanted to do was ride horses and chase after cows, much less put on a display for an audience full of strangers.

His instructor pulled at the rope, making the loop bigger. "Once you get the hang of it, you'll see that it's even more fun than it looks."

Give him a souped-up motorcycle and a busy road, and he could show the girl across from him what fun truly was.

Not that Harlow would get on the back of his bike, and she was far from his type, anyway. There was something adorable about her, though, like a happy chipmunk who'd found a discarded Cheeto.

For a blissful second, Maddox hadn't even realized where the memory of the chipmunk had come from, but the instant it hit him, it punched him in the gut.

Camping with his mom. Back when he had one of those. Those had been the simpler days, when he'd thought her spur-of-the-moment adventures were fun instead of a way to avoid people to whom she owed money. Before he was old enough to determine that her being high was what led to poorly planned trips without much to eat.

The stupid squeeze in his heart intensified, so he gritted his teeth and dragged the rope through his palm, focusing on the way the rough fibers scraped his skin. Remembering what it felt like to be loved—even in his mother's fleeting lucid moments—to have a home and a family, wasn't good for him. Happy memories made reality harsher, and how could you get harsher than no motorcycle, on a ranch in the middle of nowhere, away from his job and his friends and his semblance of what family meant nowadays?

"You okay?" Harlow asked, and with her all up in his grill, he noticed the contrast between the caramel-and-honey-colored strands in her loose braid. She looked as if some fairy had perfectly highlighted her hair while she'd been sleeping in the forest—which she probably did.

"I'm fine. I mean, I could use a little breathing room." He lifted the lasso the way she'd demoed the move. "Or did you want me to smack you in the head with the rope?"

Her face fell, and he felt like the ass that he was. He opened his mouth to apologize, but she'd turned away, and it was for the best. This was just another temporary situation with temporary people.

Not sure why the judge thought it would convince him to magically change his ways.

He'd get through it like he'd gotten through the other shitty stops forced upon him. Head down, emotional tap turned off, and minimal engagement as he counted down the days.

Maddox began to swing the lasso again, but shouts cut through his iffy concentration. A calf was charging toward him and Harlow. Aiden and the cute blond he was always with were hot on its swinging brown tail.

"Stop him," the blond shrieked, and Maddox dropped the rope and lunged, tackling the calf to the ground.

It bellowed and mooed, and Maddox craned his neck to check if the cow was okay—he'd wanted to stop it, not hurt it. The calf licked his hand, leaving enough saliva for a hundred envelopes, and seeing no other option, Maddox pulled a face as he wiped the hand on his jeans.

Aiden slid a rope around the calf's head and urged it to its feet. Then he stood there as if he were simply taking his cow-puppy for a walk.

When Maddox pushed to his feet, three pair of eyes were trained on him. Wide, surprised eyes. Harlow's mouth also hung open a few inches.

"What?" he snapped, despite telling himself he wasn't going to lash out at her anymore. It was hard to do when people gaped at you like you had three heads. Was cow saliva like a zombie bite? Would he start mooing soon?

Okay, that's the stupidest thought I've ever had.

But maybe there was a disease. Mad cow disease—he'd heard something about that before.

"How in tarnation did you tackle that calf so fast?" Harlow asked.

His first instinct was to mock her for saying *how in tarnation*, but he managed to bite the comment back. There had to be some middle ground between asshole and disengaged. "Was that impressive?"

"I mean, throw up your hands to signal the judge"—Harlow flung up her arms to demonstrate—"and we'd have our competition in the bag, lickety-split."

Maddox blinked at her. "I don't understand half of what you say."

"In the rodeo? Calf roping?" The tilt of her head conveyed how dense she thought he was being, so he ran with the smart-assness.

"Okay, now I don't understand *any* of what you say."

"I've only been doing this a short while," the blond said, "but that was fast." She looked to Aiden for confirmation, and he nodded.

Harlow placed her hand on Maddox's elbow, and in his determination not to think weird, pussy thoughts about fairies and her hair, he accidentally concentrated on her brown eyes. The rim around her iris was darker than the rest, and were her pupils dilating in time with his quickening pulse?

"Were you a wrestler or somethin'?" she asked.

"Or something." Maddox wiped the back of his hand on his pants again. It still felt sticky. "My little br—" He quickly switched gears, because he'd just ruled against happy memories, and the foster placement he'd had during his freshman year, when there'd been that almost family definitely applied. It was too late to completely avoid the subject, but *brother* wasn't the right word.

Not anymore.

A sharp pain radiated through his chest, the fissure that'd formed in his heart a few years ago shuddering. "This little dude at one of my foster homes used to sprint out the door and be halfway out the gate of the front yard if anyone ever turned their back on him. It was my job to catch the tiny fugitive before he reached the street."

Harlow bit her lower lip, and he focused on the soft, pink fullness of her mouth. "We could use that."

Brady rounded the corner. "You get him?"

Aiden lifted the rope attached to the calf and then gestured toward Maddox. "Thanks to the new guy."

Brady almost seemed impressed, but his stern expression quickly fell back into place. "I think it's time to switch stations." He lifted a megaphone Maddox hadn't even seen at first and bellowed into it. "Everyone rotate right."

People shuffled around, but Harlow put her hand out in front of Maddox, blocking him from moving and addressing Brady. "If I can train Maddox to be even half-decent at roping, I'd like to do the team event with him. I could use his extra strength, since that's the part I suck at. If he can rope the head and slow the steer, I can manage the feet."

The narrowed-eyed stare Brady aimed at Maddox contained equal parts disbelief and suspicion.

Bro, I'm surprised as you are. Maddox licked his lips, the dry air and dust suddenly getting to him. "Do I get a say in the matter?"

"No," Harlow and Brady both said.

Maddox considered pointing out that he could simply refuse to compete, but he was going to have to get through his time here one way or another. In order to survive the awfulness, he could use some form of entertainment, and Harlow was the only person who'd sparked a single ounce of it.

He'd try to be less of a dick, too.

"Are you sure you know what you're doing?" Brady asked Harlow.

She shook her head, her braid swinging back and forth. "No, but it's my favorite event, one I need to compete in to have a chance at winnin' All-Around Cowgirl. It'd also help me qualify for regionals."

Brady sighed. "In order for Maddox to get to an advanced-enough level, it's gonna require a whole lot of roping training. More than I was planning on."

"I can handle that part, too," Harlow said, firing a *You owe me* glare in Maddox's direction. For what, he couldn't figure out, but he kept his trap shut all the same.

"We can see how it goes, I guess." Brady squared off in front of Maddox and crossed his arms. "I didn't hire Harlow to come help us so some punk could let her down during an event she's trained years for." The line of his jaw tightened into a long, unyielding line. "So don't be that punk."

While Maddox had heard plenty of growled threats in his day, this one managed to stir a pinch of fear, although he'd never admit it aloud. "Whatever you say, boss."

Brady continued to sneer, as if he couldn't tell if Maddox was being sarcastic or not—honestly, sometimes *he* couldn't even tell.

Harlow clamped on to his arm. "Let's get you on a horse, Mr. Too Cool for School. And if you even think about runnin' away, just know I can toss a lasso around you and yank you right off the back of that horse in a flash." She grinned extra wide, making it clear she'd enjoy it, too.

Apparently, he'd underestimated the sass.

Chapter 5

"YOU NO-GOOD, SPYING SCOUNDREL," TANYA SAID TO BRADY when she caught him poking his head around the stables. As she stormed in his direction, he had the audacity to conjure up an innocently confused expression.

"I told you I was gonna drop by."

Tanya stuck a fist on her hip. "You're early. And don't even act like you didn't do it so you could check out the competition."

The ragtag group she'd recruited was gathered around the circular corral where Tanya had set up three barrels. Winona, the petite woman from the diner, proclaimed she wanted to take up a new hobby while her son was in town to help run her establishment; the seventeen-year-old who worked at Horsefeathers Western Store part-time clamored for the chance to ride a horse under any circumstances; and then there was a handful of others who'd turned up eager to learn and have a shot at competing in the local rodeo.

They'd about finished their first training meeting, but once Tanya caught sight of the familiar tan cowboy hat, she'd left Miguel to wrap things up for her.

"I got out early for good behavior." Brady strode closer, and the beating of Tanya's heart went wonky on her. In her exasperation at catching him spying, she'd momentarily forgotten about flirty lines and leaving a lasting impression. Honestly, she should still smack him. She would, too, if the way he filled out his lightweight checkered shirt and worn Wranglers didn't cause every nerve ending in her body to misfire.

"Doesn't sound like you," she said with a huff, resisting the urge to smooth her curls. After demonstrating barrel racing for the past hour, her hair had grown frizzy and wild. There was a reason she mostly wore her locks in a ponytail prior to this whole put-in-effort bullshit. The plan had been to freshen up between meetups, and how dare Brady stroll into her day forty minutes before scheduled! "Besides, I thought you were playing the hard-ass while Wade was giving good cop a whirl."

"He's struggling to let go of control."

"Big surprise there." The Dawsons had been like Tanya's second family going on forever. Brady was her age, but she'd grown up alongside Wade and Trace as well. Then, when she was fourteen and Nash arrived at Turn Around Ranch, he and Brady just clicked. Upon hearing the Dawsons were going to adopt Nash, along with his younger brother, Tanya had experienced a whorl of jealousy and worry that she might be replaced. Instead they'd become the three musketeers. Sometimes they purposely didn't ask Wade to go along, on account of him being the voice of reason, which didn't particularly sit well with musketeering.

Idly, she wondered if Brady had heard from Nash in a while, but it could be a sensitive subject, depending on the day. Best to keep focused for now.

"How'd you manage to sneak over without—"

On cue, Dundee barked, directing her gaze to the truck parked in front of the main cabin. The Australian shepherd did his best to behave, mostly because otherwise he'd be left behind, but he usually announced their arrivals with plenty of barking.

"Bribery." Brady patted his thigh, and Dundee leaped out of the bed of the pickup and rushed over to prance around their ankles. His owner rewarded his silence with a dog treat, and Dundee peered up at Tanya with his one blue eye and one brown eye. She never could resist his furry face, so she bent to rub his mottled ears the way he liked.

"Wait. Miguel isn't competing on your team, is he?" With her ducked down, her crew was in full view. "That hardly seems fair."

"Sorta like hiring Harlow Griffith to help you? That kind of fair?" Last night when Tanya had gone to the Silver Saddle Diner to grab dinner and discuss joining the team with Winona, Mrs. Griffith mentioned Harlow was doing the pre-rodeo show as well. "Miguel knows horses and cows but has never competed in a rodeo. Whereas Harlow is not only a local favorite but one of the best ropers and riders in the county."

"So are you," Brady said.

"I *was*. Not anymore." At one point, she'd lived for the buzzer that signaled it was time for her and Diesel to charge into the arena and demonstrate what they could do. College courses had left scant time for training, so Tanya hadn't slept much during those two years as she attempted to juggle everything, including a long-distance friendship with Brady. Her last big win was eight years ago, when she'd snagged the All-Around Cowgirl title for breakaway roping and barrel racing at the Colorado state finals in Montrose. Then her parents had needed her, and she'd decided it'd never get better than that anyway. Now she only competed at smaller local rodeos, much like Brady had done the last few years, for many of the same reasons.

"Guess that makes us even, then."

Tanya pursed her lips, neither confirming nor denying. She stood and waved goodbye to the various townsfolk climbing into their vehicles, and Brady lifted a hand as well. Telling the cowboy across from her that his idea about allowing the townsfolk to see the teens in a new light while also getting them more involved was brilliant would only feed his ego. She'd mention it, though.

Eventually. Say, after she'd beat him at his own game.

"And since we're even," Brady said, as if there hadn't been a break in the conversation, "I need a favor."

"Seriously?" she asked with a shake of her head.

Brady flashed her a puppy-dog expression that she used to be much better at resisting before she'd gone and fallen in love with him. "I need to borrow some of your Smallfry kid ropes."

"What's wrong? You took off the training wheels, only to find you weren't ready for an adult rope?"

He lunged forward and pinched her side, and a squeal accidentally escaped. Since she'd made noise, Dundee took that as his cue to let out a bark, and he circled them, ready to play along.

Tanya expected to have to block or for Brady to lunge again. Instead, he took a large step back and slid his thumbs in the pockets of his Wranglers. Of course it made the mouthwatering line of his forearms stand out. "Actually, some of the teens are struggling with the bigger ropes. They're the ones who need training wheels on their ropes."

Tanya fought the urge to bite her lip, and her voice came out breathier than she meant it to. "Likely story."

"Did you put on sunscreen today?" Brady asked, tilting his head and studying her face with a whole heap of concern. "You're looking a little pink, and I know how easily you burn." He gestured over his shoulder. "I have some SPF 50 in my truck if you're running low."

It was the curse of a redhead—turning pink within two seconds flat, whether due to sun, passion, or embarrassment. Here she was ogling and having lusty thoughts about him, and he was taking care of her like she was a little kid who would end up sunburned and peeling. "I, uh, put on the heavy-duty stuff today already."

"Good, good. Anyway, can I borrow a few?"

The haze in her brain cleared, allowing her to connect the dots and fill in the blank. The Smallfry ropes—right. "Sure. Follow me into the tack room, and I'll see what I can dig up."

"I'd be happy to." His voice dipped low when he added, "You've got that whip in there, too, right?"

Luckily, she'd already pivoted toward the open door of the stables, since she had no desire to be asked about her sunscreen usage. But he'd hinted at the whip, and what the hell did it all mean? Were any of her efforts working? Or was she setting herself up for a future crash?

So far, she'd only made it halfway through the dating book. The last chapter she'd read delved into throwing out flirty lines like bait. Between the corporate retreat activities, the countless questions from Eric about ranching, and forming a team of novices, she'd fallen into bed completely exhausted the past few days.

With Brady at her back as she riffled through drawers, muttering and shuffling around bridles and other odds and ends, the urgency to pore over the knowledge from the book increased. "I swear they were right here," she said, merely for something to say.

Brady jerked up his head, and for one glorious moment, she assumed it was because he'd been checking out her butt. Then she realized she'd skidded in the corral during a demonstration and had mud and manure on the seat of her jeans.

Well, shit. Literally.

The man had seen her dirty more times than clean, so it shouldn't matter. Then again, that might mean she would have to work that much harder to get him to see her as a sexy woman instead of his childhood friend.

Not that she'd ever felt super sexy, per se, but when she made effort, she liked what she saw in the mirror well enough. The real question was if perfectly styled hair, a face full of makeup, and some flirty lines would cause Brady to suddenly think: *There's my dream woman. She was under my nose the whole time.*

Tanya opened a cabinet, her mood deflating a bit. There was optimism and then there was delusion, and she wasn't rightly sure which side of the fence she'd landed herself on. "Ope, there they are." As Brady's fingers brushed the multicolored coils she'd extended his way, she wrenched them behind her back. "Wait. If I let you borrow these so your team can try to beat mine, what are you gonna give me in return?"

There. That was flirty yet not over the top. Cheeky without leaving her cheeks flaming red.

The toes of Brady's boots hit hers. "Tanya." His voice dipped low, igniting a riot of emotions that left her lungs straining for air. "We said we were even. Now, hand over the ropes, and no one will get hurt."

She tightened her grip, her stubborn nature and need to win making it impossible to simply hand over the ropes. "*You* said we were square, not me. Even so, I still haven't heard a good reason to let you borrow *my* training equipment."

He reached around her, his chest bumping into hers. "How about because you love me?"

Too true, although she worked to keep those feelings from creeping into her expression. She glanced at the ceiling, as if she had to do some serious pondering on the matter. "There's love, and then there's shooting yourself in the foot."

"Fair enough." Brady's chest rose and fell against hers, and warmth pooled low in her belly. For one courageous second, she imagined leaning in and pressing her mouth to his to see what he'd do. Just go all in and be done with it. "How about because you love a challenge? The better my team is, the higher the stakes."

Excitement surged, his words playing her like the sucker she was whenever it came to their friendly rivalry. While she hated the *chicken* insult and how often he used it against her in their younger days, she was far too much of one to go for a kiss quite yet. Honestly, she'd hoped she'd dangle the bait and he'd do the biting. "You got me there."

"Then there's my last point—and it's my personal favorite: I'm stronger than you." He snaked an arm around her waist, securing both of her arms down at her sides.

"Don't you dare." She grunted and squirmed, but it only made him tighten his hold. Then he lifted her clear off her feet, which was amazing and torturous at the same time. He pried the rope from her fist one finger at a time, his touch and the friction of their smooshed bodies intoxicating. If she focused on that, she'd melt instead of resist. "Brady, I swear. If you don't put me down right now, I'm gonna—"

"Oh. Sorry to interrupt." The figure was merely a dark profile against the bright light streaming in through the stables, but she could tell by the shape and his voice that it was Eric Richmond.

Dundee placed himself between the CEO and her and Brady, glancing toward them to see if Eric was a welcome guess or not.

Brady loosened his grip, slowly lowered her until her boots hit the ground, and fully turned toward the guy. The arm he'd lifted her with remained around her waist, and he hooked his hand on her hip, the heat of his touch slowly spreading throughout her entire torso.

"Hey, Eric," she said, and her stupid voice betrayed her breath-lessness yet again. "This is Brady Dawson. He and his family run the at-risk youth ranch next door."

Eric extended his hand, and Brady stared at it for a beat. She was about to jab him in the ribs with her elbow for being rude when he finally reciprocated the gesture.

They shook, and Tanya said, "This is Eric Richmond, CEO of RichTech. He's recently inherited some land and is thinking about getting into the ranching business."

Although Brady nodded, he remained in her space and seemed to have no intention of moving. "It's a tough gig. Nonstop, few to no vacations."

"I'm used to that. It took tenacity and a lot of long hours to build a business from the ground up as well."

Was this jealousy? That might be a promising development... As she glanced from Brady to Eric, who also stood taller than usual, chest puffed out, Tanya realized this was less about her and more about the two of them. *Ugh, men.*

"If y'all are gonna just stand here and waste time having a piss-ing contest, I'm gonna get on with my day."

She began to move away from Brady, but he caught her hand. "Hold up. I wanted to talk to you about something else."

Just like that, she was under the spell of his blue eyes, scruffy jaw, and a voice she could point out in a lineup.

She conjured up an image of her behind heavily tinted glass in a police station as the officer asked, *Is this your best friend, the one you're afraid doesn't love you in the way you love him?*

They'd instruct the guy in the other room to speak, and she'd indicate it was the culprit with an affirmative nod.

Focus, Tanya, or he and Eric will see right through you.

There was something about the way Eric the city-slicker CEO looked at Tanya that Brady didn't like. A few minutes ago, he'd been debating whether or not to scold himself for checking out her ass, so call him a hypocrite, but there'd also been bantering, the zing of their ongoing competition, and all that history crowding the air.

Hell, he'd forgotten other people even existed until they'd been interrupted.

In the name of civility and getting the guy to stop checking out *his* Yaya, he asked, "So how are you enjoying your stay on the dude ranch, Eric?"

The guy's gaze returned to Tanya immediately, and a crooked grin spread across his face. "Quite a bit. I was cocky enough to think the one summer on my aunt's ranch qualified me for a month of riding and driving cows, but this one humbled me. I can hardly keep up with her."

This one. The guy had been there all of four days. How much could he tell in that amount of time? That she woke up earlier than his prissy ass? That she was better at roping and riding? Duh.

But instead of rolling her eyes along with Brady, Tanya flashed the CEO a smile, and were her cheeks turning pink? "I appreciate that, but I should probably warn you that so far we've only had easy days. And you might want give Taffy extra grain before our ride this afternoon so he won't try to dump you off to nibble on grass. He's not so persuaded by charming words."

If she hadn't said it in her soft voice, that smile still on her face, it might've sounded like a slam. As it was, it sounded disturbingly like flirting.

Usually, she gave guys who tried pickup lines on her a tongue-lashing. And persuaded by charming words? Did that mean *she* was persuaded? Did she think the guy was charming?

Years ago, Brady slammed the door closed on thinking of Tanya as anything more than a friend—to the point he got downright grouchy whenever his family members poked him about it. Over the past few days, he couldn't stop rereading her texts, and he'd been sure there was a playful undercurrent. One that nudged that door a crack open again. He reckoned he should've just shut it and left well enough alone, but he'd wanted to at least peek at his options.

Now he worried he'd read things wrong and was in danger of making a mess if he went and opened his big mouth.

And if Tanya wanted to flirt with a guy who was completely wrong for her, it was her business. Too bad the toxic churning in Brady's gut made it difficult to believe his own thoughts. Add in his jumbled emotions, and that was definitely his cue to go. "Well, I'd better get to town before the feed store closes. But I'll call you later, okay? Then we can finalize the events and whatnot."

"Okay," Tanya said. "Talk soon. And FYI, I'm charging interest on those ropes." The smile she aimed his way sent another swirl of confusion through Brady, but he couldn't help returning the gesture.

"You know I'm good for it." He considered running with his inner caveman and leaning in and kissing her cheek. Then she'd punch him in front of Eric, and wouldn't that just be the cherry on a shit sundae?

"Come on, Dundee. Let's go." Brady readjusted his grip on the multicolored coils in his hands and strode out of the tack room into the much roomier walkway of the stables where he could get the oxygen he seemed to be missing.

His trusty dog rushed ahead and launched into the bed of the truck.

Brady could hear Tanya and Eric behind him, also exiting the stables, but he didn't linger. He'd said his goodbyes, and Dundee was already prancing around like Brady was taking an eternity. The driver's side door opened with a metallic squawk, and through his dust-covered windshield, he spotted Eric still grinning and talking to Tanya.

Brady roughly shifted into first, the gears grinding at the effort. *It's just my protective instincts kicking in.*

Because he's going to spend so much time with her.

Not because...

Shit, he didn't know anymore, even though he'd been sure for years. No one could ever believe he and Tanya didn't plan on crossing lines. They always wanted to make it into something more than friendship.

But it wasn't.

He just never thought *he'd* be the one struggling to get that through his head.

Maddox walked around the main cabin in time to see the blond cook most everyone referred to as Miss Jessica smack the steering wheel of her late '90s Toyota Corolla, fling open the door, and climb out, only to kick the front left tire.

"Stupid piece of shit," she said to the car that used to be blue but was now more rusty brown. "Why are you being like this? Haven't I loved you and taken care of you, even though you're old and no one else would want you? And still you refuse to start for me?"

Maddox did his best not to laugh. He occasionally talked to the vehicles he fixed, but this was a whole new level. Like shame-fixing.

Unfortunately for her, it wouldn't work in the long run, just like it'd never worked for any of the adults who'd tried that method on him.

The front door of the cabin opened, and Wade took one look at his fiancée and pinched the bridge of his nose. With his other hand, he gestured to a row of Dodge Rams, one older and three on the newer side. "I told you to just take one of the trucks."

Jessica defiantly crossed her arms. "And I told you that I just wanted to drive my little car."

"How's that working out for you?"

The trunk popped open, even though no one was near it, and Jessica threw her head back. Then she shot her car a glare. "Remember this moment when you're wondering why you ended up as nothing more than a pile of spare parts in a junkyard."

A smile Maddox didn't even know Wade was capable of spread across his face, and he shook his head. "Stubborn woman."

"Okay, kettle."

Wade's gaze drifted, and Maddox didn't react quickly enough to keep him from being caught staring. "Where are you supposed to be?"

"I have an appointment with Nick. I was just on my way over." Maddox tipped his head toward the cabin-like offices and managed a step in that direction. Slowly, he turned around, even as he fought against the words on the tip of his tongue. Out they came anyway. "I can fix your car if you want."

"That's okay, it's a pile of junk," Wade said as Jessica said, "Really? That'd be awesome."

The two of them glared at each other for a heated beat while Maddox awkwardly stood there, and finally Wade relented—not who Maddox would've picked to give in, so it was a good thing people around here wouldn't make bets with him the way the guys at the shop did. It'd kept long workdays from getting too boring, and often the money he won was what he used to buy himself dinner.

Now that he'd already offered his mechanic services, he wanted to draw out this conversation as long as possible. Anything to avoid a touchy-feely counseling session. "I've even worked on that model before—it'll run forever if you take care of it. I bet it's the ignition coil or the fuel pump. Happens a lot when they get up in mileage."

He had no idea why the woman was so set on fixing up the car. If he had to pick between the beat-up old car or the trucks, he would've chosen the trucks for their Cummins diesel engine. More horsepower, more torque.

"We'll figure out when you might have time in your schedule to work on the car and get back to you," Wade said, his voice as firm as the gray eyes trained on Maddox. "I'll walk you over to see Nick."

Like he was a damn baby. He wanted to reply that he'd been taking care of himself for years, and he sure as hell didn't need to be walked anywhere. Only then Wade might change his mind about letting him work on the car, and Maddox would do almost anything that'd get him out of classes or training for some Podunk rodeo.

Except that last one would mean I wouldn't get to see as much of Harlow.

Fine. He retracted that last part, but he'd love to miss classes and especially therapy sessions.

Wade dug into his pocket, tossed Jessica a set of keys, and then strode on over. He walked past Maddox, who was obviously supposed to follow like a good little soldier.

Maddox dragged his feet for two whole seconds before the

stern cowboy gave him a knock-it-off look. Within no time at all, they arrived at the counseling office, and Wade was opening the door and ushering Maddox into a room where they'd inevitably want him to cry about his mom and his life.

Regardless of what they asked, he wasn't telling them shit.

Chapter 6

ONLY A FEW NUMBERS RANG THROUGH THE DO-NOT-DISTURB mode that Brady had engaged on his cell last night before tumbling into bed.

The haze of sleep weighed down his limbs as he blindly searched the nightstand with his hand. After nearly knocking off the lamp he hadn't bothered turning on, he felt the ringing, vibrating rectangle that was causing way too much racket.

He squinted one eye open. Tanya's name illuminated the screen, giving him a stronger jolt than a cup of Jess's almost chewable coffee, and he quickly sat up. Ranch work pretty much required being an early bird, but at a quarter past five on a random Wednesday morning, the rooster hadn't even crowed yet. "If this is some attempt to deprive me of sleep and throw off my training schedule, you're playing dirtier than I expected. I'm not sure whether to be impressed or appalled."

"Trust me, I wish that were the reason for my call. Unfortunately, I need your help." The frantic note to her voice had him throwing off the covers and climbing out of bed.

"What's going on? You need to meet at our spot, or—"

"No, I'm on my way to you. I'll be pulling into the driveway in a couple of minutes. I got a call from one of our old rodeo buddies—remember Edgar?"

The name tickled Brady's memory, and then the image of the grizzled old cowboy popped into his head. "The horse wrangler and rodeo announcer with no filter, right? The one the PTA petitioned to remove because he kept swearing over the PA system."

While most people thought it was funny and added an authentic flair, a group of women had been up in arms. They found other like-minded souls in towns across the county, but before the petition had finished making the rounds, Edgar decided to end his last rodeo by retiring and putting as many swear words as possible into his farewell speech. He'd made sure to tell the group where they could shove their petition, too.

That was a handful of years ago, and Brady couldn't figure out if he was struggling to put the puzzle together because he was half-asleep or missing a few pieces. Shuffling noises came from the other side of the line, along with the sound of a diesel engine. "He needs our help rescuing a horse over in Thorne Ridge."

It was a short fifteen-minute drive to the next small town over, although Brady and Tanya used to make it in ten back when they drove too fast and thought they were invincible in that way teenagers often do.

Brady threw open drawers and stepped into a pair of worn Wranglers. "Be right out."

He pulled on a button-down shirt but didn't take the time to button it, focusing on getting his socks and boots on instead. He grabbed his wallet and debated a moment before grabbing his pistol as well. If he'd been alert enough, he would've asked for more details, but this was clearly an emergency. Which led him to believe it was a situation that might get ugly, and he didn't want to be the guy who brought a rope to a gunfight.

With the first rays of sun barely peeking out above the horizon, the air was chillier than expected. Since Brady didn't have time for coffee, hopefully the cool temperature would do the job of waking him up the rest of the way.

He rushed toward the stables and stared at the items in the tack room, wishing again he'd been alert enough to ask more questions. In the event a horse required subduing, they kept handy a bag of basic medicine essentials, antibiotic cream, gauze, wraps, and tranquilizers.

The sound of a growling engine and tires on gravel filtered

through, and time was up. He grabbed the medical bag and a rope and bridle and then hustled over to Tanya's shiny, red F-150 and climbed inside. Usually, he'd give her shit about how bright her truck was or how Dodges were better than Fords, just for old times' sake. But she was already pulling away, driving the way she used to in high school—like a bat out of hell, dirt billowing up behind them.

As she turned onto the road that would take them to Thorne Ridge, she glanced at him. Then did a double take. "Did you plan on flashing those abs in case someone needs extra convincing?"

He looked down—oops, he never had gotten his shirt buttoned up. He went to work on making himself decent as he shot her an indecent grin. "You think it'd work?"

One corner of her mouth turned up. "About as well as your training drills."

"So definitely. Got it." He twisted in his seat, and in spite of the harried situation, his breath caught at the way the rising sun lit up her mess of red curls. He couldn't decide if she looked more like an angel or a woman on fire, but damn she was pretty, au naturel with a bit of bedhead thrown in for good measure.

While he'd meant no makeup, the other meaning of that word—the one that involved no clothes—drifted to mind, and he was derailing that line of thinking right now. For people who lived next door to each other, it was sure hard for them to find time together, and they hadn't seen each other since the middle of last week.

In a few minutes, they'd reach the town limits—which had to be a new record—and the tension that'd claimed Tanya's shoulders and neck meant she was worried about whatever they were racing toward.

"Any details you'd like to share with the class?" he asked, and she cast him a confused glance. "About the horse and the situation?"

They'd stepped in to rescue horses before, on cases involving neglect and abuse, and Tanya had reported people on the rodeo circuit mistreating animals several times throughout the years. But it'd been a while.

"Edgar called three times in a row," Tanya said, "which I thought was a little weird, but he had hip surgery about five months back, and here and there, he calls when he gets lonely. He likes to tell me about the glory days, and I enjoy reliving them with him, so I figured I'd pick up and listen to a story…"

Brady wondered why she'd never mentioned the conversations with Edgar before. Not that she had to tell him everything. It was just another side of her. A softer, intriguing side she rarely showed.

Tanya slowed and squinted at a street sign before speeding up again. "Instead he tells me how he came across a horse that had gotten tangled up in a barbed-wire fence. Even though his bum hip was screaming at him the whole time, he tried to free the mare, but then the owner showed up and threatened to shoot him if he didn't get off his property." A steely edge entered her voice. "Brady, the horse clearly hasn't been fed in a long time, and Edgar thinks she was desperate enough to try to break through the fence to get food."

Brady's muscles turned to stone. "Glad I grabbed my pistol."

"I brought mine, too, but Edgar contacted the sheriff's office right before he called me, so hopefully the police will take care of that part. He apologized for it being so early but said half the town is related to this guy, so he needed someone he could trust and knew I'd be able to keep the horse calm. He also added that he was hoping I'd take the mare home while they sorted out things with the law."

Brady nodded. That made sense. He'd call Tanya, too. Good, bad, happy, sad. She was the best person to have by your side.

Tanya made a sharp left turn while muttering about how they should make the street signs out here easier to read, and Brady braced his hand on the dashboard.

About a half mile down, a pickup truck and a police cruiser were crookedly parked next to the fence, obscuring most of the horse. All Brady caught was a glimpse of a reddish-brown coat. "I'm assuming you brought the fence cutters?"

"You know me. Always prepared and ready to destroy." Tanya reached behind the seat, brought out two pair, and handed one to him. They climbed out of the truck and approached Edgar, the sheriff, and a man in a white wifebeater who was doing his best to keep the redneck stereotype alive.

The guy was yelling up a storm about his rights and his property. The rifle on the ground at the cop's feet had obviously been tossed there, skid marks showing it'd slid a few inches.

Edgar bent to grab the gun. He was definitely favoring one leg—or hip, Brady knew now. He released the magazine and used the lever action to eject the bullet in the chamber.

Tanya's gasp yanked Brady's attention back to her. He followed her gaze, and bile coated his throat as he got his first full look at the horse. So skinny he could see ribs and hip bones jutting through the coat, which was shedding in dull, lumpy chunks. Dark-red blood oozed from cuts where the barbs had dug in, and the horse's body sagged on the fence. The mare gave a weak whinny, no longer seeming to care about the barbs digging into its belly—if it could even be called a belly anymore.

Anger ignited low in Brady's gut and spread, but he clenched his jaw and forced himself to hold his temper in check. Horse first, and then he'd deal with the son of a bitch who'd left her in such a debilitated state.

"We're going to cut her loose," Brady said to the deputy, because he was afraid if he looked at the negligent owner, his rage would take the wheel.

The cop nodded, and the owner released a vitriol of swear words about his horse and his property. He also threatened to shoot them, even though his gun was unloaded and out of reach.

"I warned you that I'd have to put you in cuffs if you didn't calm down," the deputy said, and Brady wondered why he hadn't already.

This is probably why Edgar called Tanya.

Brady left them to sort that out, while he and Tanya approached the horse.

"It's okay," she said in a soothing voice as he got to work cutting away the wires. She let the horse sniff her hand and then slowly moved her palm over its neck. "We're going to get you freed and all fixed up, and I promise you'll never have to go hungry or see that bastard again."

Due to several bad experiences with the teens at Turn Around Ranch, Brady knew the law often had too many loopholes. Sure, in a perfect world, parents would get clean and give their children love and affection and learn not to hit them. They'd feed them and care for them in the way they deserved. Same with animal owners. But he was of the belief that some people had lost their chances.

Take Nash's father. The system gave him chance after chance to beat the shit out of his son. Warnings were issued and ignored. Nothing changed. Even a hospitalization hadn't been enough.

The lid Brady was doing his damnedest to keep on his anger rocked, the steam demanding escape but having nowhere to go.

Tanya continued cooing at the horse while she also cut at the wires around its legs and chest. This type of situation—as well as Nash's case—made Brady want to be a one-strike kind of guy, but he'd also seen second chances that'd changed lives for the better.

Those people had to work at changing, though.

That was what it truly came down to. If people put in the work instead of waiting for a magic fix. Right now, he was choosing to believe in the good. Because this mare was going to get a second chance, and she definitely deserved one.

Eventually, he and Tanya managed to snap the last of the wires. They carefully guided the mare to the ground, and Brady immediately went to work on the biggest cuts.

"…not malnourished," the abusive asshole yelled. "That's how you train a horse. Haven't you heard about how they trained Arabian horses by denying them food and water for several days to see if they'd still obey when their owner rang a bell? It's the sign of a strong horse."

Brady recalled the analogy on obedience and self-control. After days of deprivation, the horse was released with water in view. As soon as the animal began running toward it, the owner would ring a bell. If the horse didn't stop and return, the horse was deemed unworthy.

A mixture of myth and religious indoctrination, most likely. Even if it were true, at that time, the horses were also used for war in the middle of the desert. These days, that kind of training was unnecessary and cruel, and he'd argue it was back then as well. There were much healthier, more effective ways to teach horses to obey.

Each irate throb of his pulse echoed through Brady's head, and in order to maintain his focus, he exhaled, exhaled, exhaled as he treated the cuts the best he could. Meanwhile, Tanya tugged handfuls of alfalfa from the field the horse had been trying to get to and offered the clumps to the mare.

"Hey! That bitch destroys my fence, and now she's stealing my crops! Why don't you arrest *her*?"

Brady shot to his feet and whirled around, fists clenched into weapons of mass destruction. Time was up, the lid blowing clean off his anger. He took a step toward the despicable piece of shit. *Let's see how well* he *likes being trained.*

A small hand wrapped around his upper arm. "Brady, don't," Tanya said. "He's already going in the back of that cop car, and I can't have you there with him. I'm not saying he doesn't deserve for you to rearrange his face, but right now, this horse needs you. *I* need you."

The fury that'd replaced his blood called for retribution, but as soon as he looked at Tanya, her eyes wide and imploring, her fingers around his arm, it calmed to a low simmer. She was right. The horse was more important, and as tempting as it was to give people a taste of their own medicine, it rarely did any good.

The sad truth was that life was full of disappointments, hardships, and inflicted hurts that couldn't be healed quickly and simply. Hating it didn't change things, so sometimes all you could do was put the past where it belonged and take on things one at a time.

Brady supported the mare the best he could as he and Tanya guided it into the trailer. The deputy had forced the lunatic owner into the cruiser, and if Brady ever saw the guy again, he doubted he'd be able to restrain his temper.

The deputy handed Tanya his card, Edgar thanked them for their help and asked to be updated on the horse's health, and then they all headed to their respective vehicles.

As tough as Tanya was, this kind of thing got to her. Brady didn't know many people it *wouldn't* affect. Her face was pale, and now that the horse had been freed, the fight slipped out of her, sorrow rising up instead.

Tears filled her eyes as she studied the blood on her hands and arms. Mostly the horse's, although she'd gotten a few gashes while removing the sharp wires. Brady wanted to tell her it was okay, but it wasn't. Placing a hand on her lower back, he led her to her truck. He opened the driver's side door for her, climbed in behind her, and fired up the engine.

They headed one way, and the cruiser headed the other.

"Why don't you call Doc Mullens's office and ask him to meet us at Bullhead Valley?" It needed to be done, and Brady hoped it'd give her a job to focus on. "I don't want to move the horse more than we have to."

She nodded, over and over, and dialed the number. But when a tinny voice picked up the line, Tanya extended her cell to him.

"Can you? I…" A shaky breath shuddered from her lips, and the tears that'd bordered her eyes broke free.

Brady gave the receptionist the details and confirmed it was an emergency. As soon as he hung up, he wrapped his arm around Tanya, holding her as tightly as he could between driving and shifting.

───────────

Tanya straightened and wiped her cheeks as they neared the ranch. She didn't want to look like she'd been crying, despite shedding plenty of tears. The drive home had been quieter than she remembered a ride ever being with her and Brady in the same truck.

"Pops isn't going to be happy about me bringing home another injured animal," she whispered. Most of the time, she was plenty happy to work with her parents. But having to ask for permission for things like this left her feeling like a stunted teenager, and this was her ranch, too. In theory.

Only her name wasn't on the title. The only things she truly owned were the items in the tiny bedroom she'd never bothered updating, since she'd planned to move into one of the cabins eventually.

At least Brady had held her together for a few minutes so she could get out of the truck and be the kick-ass chick she needed to be. Even if that meant an argument with Pops.

"You missed breakfast," Mom said, and then did a double take at Brady, who extended a hand to Tanya and helped her down.

Brady returned his arm to around her shoulders, and Tanya wanted to close her eyes, shut out the world, and bask in the comfort as they awaited the vet's arrival. If she could do that without crying again, she'd consider it a win. She supposed she had to experience mushy emotions here and there, but why didn't they ever hit at a convenient time?

"Had to see a guy about a horse," she said to Mom. True. Sort of. No reason to delay the inevitable, so she broke free of Brady's grasp and rounded the horse trailer. Metal screeched against metal as she swung open the door.

Dark eyes that held very little life greeted her, but there, way down deep, was a flicker. Tanya planned on taking hold of that spark and pouring love and affection on the mare until she was healthy, happy, and fat as could be.

Brady helped her assist the injured horse out of the trailer. It wasn't like the mare could run, and Tanya didn't want to move her far, so they guided her to a patch of grass where she could rest and munch.

Several of the guests at the dude ranch had come out to see what the ruckus was about, including Eric. He cautiously approached, the expression on his face portraying he was as appalled by the animal abuse as Tanya. "Is there anything I can do?"

"We don't want to spook her, so just stay back," Brady said a bit harshly as he waved him and the other guests away. A fair point, although he could at least pretend to be cordial. She supposed after this morning's hectic venture, a discussion on proper manners could wait.

The screen door opened, and Pops pounded down the steps. "Where is everybody? We've got a lot to get done today, and we're already a half hour behind." The commotion drew his attention, and he charged over, already in one of his moods.

Tanya winced but kept her poker face in place as Pops glanced from her to the horse to her again. "What in the Sam Hill is going on?"

"I got a call about an emaciated horse that was stuck in a fence and needed to be rescued," Tanya said. "Doc Mullens is on his way to check her out now."

Pops ran a hand through his thinning hair, his lips parting with a lecture, no doubt.

"I'll pay for it," Tanya said through gritted teeth. "I'll handle everything, I promise."

Pops sighed, nice and loud so everyone in the vicinity could hear. "I thought you were gonna stop making impulsive decisions. We can't afford to take in every hurt animal in the county. When are you going to learn to think things through?"

The frustration that'd been simmering under the surface rushed forward, bringing years of repression along for the ride. She *had* thought things through. Which was why she'd called Brady for backup.

"Pops, this is different than dyeing my hair or challenging strangers to race for money." She'd lost a couple hundred dollars she didn't have that way, but she'd also been seventeen at the time. And sure, she'd made other errors in judgment, enough so he could probably stand there and list them off until her past mistakes crushed her. But this was different, and it killed her that he didn't see that. "I heard a horse was in trouble, and I acted. Sometimes you have to make an executive decision."

"You're hardly an executive." His loud voice carried over their audience and across to her, where it struck her square in the chest.

"Yeah, because you treat me like a child," she snapped, speaking words she'd only thought before.

"Listen here—" Pops started, but Mom stepped between them. *Finally.* It was about seven years too late, but Mom was actually going to intervene. "That's enough." It was as stern as Tanya had ever heard her mother talk to her father, and by some miracle, Pops listened. Then she turned her scowl on Tanya. "Both of you."

Okay, so she was in hot water, too, and maybe even deserved to be. Still it'd felt good to get that out.

The sound of an engine cut through the tension hanging in the air, and Tanya caught sight of the shiny grill of Doc Mullens's truck. She dropped down next to the injured horse, putting her energy into keeping the mare calm. Then she looked to Brady, not caring that it made her a bit of a hypocrite to criticize him for his lack of tact with their audience and implore him to use it on them minutes later.

Without her having to speak her wishes aloud, he understood. In a low yet firm voice, Brady asked everyone to head to their cabins so the vet would have plenty of room to work.

While Doc Mullens and Brady hooked a horse sled up to a four-wheeler, Tanya quickly cleaned a stall. Once the guys delivered the mare to the stables, she helped them get the horse off the sled and settled in her new quarters.

Doc Mullens immediately started an IV, and as he doctored the cuts, Tanya lightly brushed the horse's coat, removing the tangles of hair she'd shed due to lack of food.

"You need a name, don't you, baby," Tanya said. "A brand-new start."

The horse weakly nickered and turned her nose to Tanya's cheek. There were certain animals she'd instantly clicked with, and right then and there, that connection snapped into place. Just like that, Tanya's heart nearly burst.

Names flitted through her mind, but none of them seemed to fit. *Shiloh, Banjo, Arizona…*

That last one wasn't quite right, but it led her to the perfect name. "How about Phoenix? It's a mythological bird that goes through fire, regenerates, and rises again. How do you like that?"

The horse rested her head on Tanya's lap and loudly exhaled, which incontestably meant she was happy with the new moniker. Tanya's neck prickled with awareness, and she glanced up to see Brady grinning down at her. "Go ahead and tease me about being a softie if you must, but this horse is my new baby."

"Wouldn't dream of it," Brady said, although the quirk of his lips said otherwise. The type of tenderness he didn't normally show came along for the ride, and that made it safer for her to go all-in on the horsey cuddling.

After Doc Mullens had finished his ministrations, Brady extended a hand and helped Tanya to her feet. The doctor told her to start with grass hay and move up to grain and then alfalfa. He gave them directions for the bandages, topical ointment, and how often to change out the IV bag.

With that, the doctor wished them a good day, and then it was just her, Brady, Phoenix, and the rest of the horses.

Exhaustion set in as the impact of everything that'd happened—not just rescuing the horse but also with her father—hit Tanya. As nice as crawling back in bed sounded, she was already behind on her day and wouldn't get a chance to flop onto her mattress until late tonight.

Brady skimmed a knuckle down her arm, and her pulse chased after his touch as he linked their fingers together. He didn't say anything, simply gave her a tiny squeeze to let her know he was there whenever she was ready to talk.

Tanya gave in to the butterflies and his assuring presence, her eyes still fixated on the drowsy horse in the stall as she rested her head on Brady's firm shoulder. "Is this how it feels? With the teens who come to Turn Around Ranch?"

"Which part?" Brady asked, his voice low and raspy with emotion. "Looking at a broken creature and wanting to hurt whoever hurt them? Hoping you can help them recover and live a better life?"

"Yes," she said, because it all applied.

"Yeah. Only most of the time, the teens look just fine. With a horse, at least you can see the injuries. It makes it easier to treat." He dragged his thumb over her knuckles, soothing and riling with such a simple touch. "Not that what you did this morning was easy."

"What *we* did." She tightened her grip on his hand. Admittedly, constantly thinking up witty lines and putting out the vibe had also been exhausting. Being on autopilot for this moment—which had resulted in handholding, so yay—reminded her of the many reasons she'd failed to avoid falling in love with Brady Dawson. "Thank you for being there whenever I need you."

"Always."

Warmth suffused her, and she found herself fighting tears for the second time today. Suddenly, she was questioning being in love with Brady all over again. Not because she wasn't—her heart thumped faster and faster, each beat confirming the fact that she was beyond head over heels—but because what if she lost this?

Then again, what if this could be even better?

Hadn't she already analyzed and overthought all this? It was hardly the time, yet her brain whirred too quickly to stop it. "Do you promise?"

His blue eyes met hers, and the world ground to a halt. "I promise," he said, and she flung her arms around his waist and hugged him for all she was worth.

Chapter 7

"HEY, HARLOW."

Chill bumps skated across her skin at hearing her name in that deep, incomparable voice, and she spun around so fast she smacked into the large side mirror of her truck. "Ouch."

A chuckle came out, and Maddox asked, "You okay?"

She growled in response.

"I'll take that as yes."

When she started away from the mirror, a sharp pain pricked her scalp. She twisted to see why she couldn't move without pain and discovered her hair was caught. Newer models didn't have the large mirrors that stuck out as far as the ones on her older truck. While she appreciated being able to see so much of the road in their reflection, she wasn't ready to lose a chunk of her hair to them.

This is what I get for not braiding my hair today.

She attempted to work the strands free but couldn't quite see whether they were stuck in the crease or on a screw, so it wasn't going great.

"Here." Maddox stepped closer, and with his body nearly touching hers, she caught a whiff of his cologne. Unlike the boys she attended high school with, who used a gallon of Axe body spray—sometimes in place of showering—the subtle hint of citrus and note of pine smelled nice and fresh. Like the forest after rain.

As his fingers combed through her hair, a different sort of prickling tiptoed across her scalp.

Don't let yourself get pulled in. He might be nice for one tiny second, but then he'll do a total one-eighty and you'll end up stung again. As soon as Maddox freed her hair, she widely sidestepped both her mirror and him.

His gaze lifted to the straw cream-colored hat atop her head. "Do you ever take that thing off, or is it glued to your hair?"

Harlow clenched her jaw, justification coming along for the ride now that he'd taken a jab at her fashion choices. "Do you ever pull your head out, or is it permanently lodged up your butt?"

He gaped at her, his mouth gaping like a fish that hadn't figured out why he'd been yanked out of the water. A twinge of regret twisted her chest, even as she told herself to ignore it. Let *him* see how it felt to think they were bantering, only for her to shift gears and snap. "Damn," Maddox said. "Someone's in a mood."

Harlow crossed her arms. "Saying I'm in a mood only puts me in a bad mood."

"Which makes me right."

It was like he enjoyed pissing her off. Did that mean she should hide her anger or keep it on full blast whenever she was around him?

Harlow hefted her gear from the bed of her truck and charged toward the training course. Maddox followed, picking up a coil of rope on his way over to where she was squaring off in front of a bale of hay.

As he posted up beside her, she spared him half a glance and said, "If the next words out of your mouth are rude, or if you're gonna be a smart aleck, I'll give you a demonstration on how they castrate steers."

Maddox winced and stuck a protective hand over his package. "Damn, girl. Also, *smart aleck?* What's that?"

She gritted her teeth. "You should know, since you're the very definition. And acting like you don't is doing the exact thing I just warned you against."

With her blood pressure already rising, Harlow decided the best thing to do was to concentrate on training *and only training*. "Do you remember how to make a lasso?"

The tip of his tongue stuck out as he formed the loop the way she'd instructed him to during their first session.

"Good enough. Now, pay attention to my refresher course on throwing, because I don't wanna keep explaining over and over."

He mumbled something about how he'd salute her if it wouldn't leave his crotch unprotected, but she continued on as if she hadn't heard.

"Arm up, loop nice and open as you swing, get some momentum going as you aim, and…" The movements were second nature, ones Harlow had repeated countless times through the years. "Throw."

Most of the time, she could feel if the toss was right the instant she let go, and that sense of rightness flared. Sure enough, the loop slid over the plastic calf head, and she yanked back on her rope to tighten the knot.

After she'd undone the loop and gathered her line, she glanced at Maddox. "Your turn."

Maddox swung the lasso over his head a couple of times. The momentum was there, but he didn't follow through, even though she'd harped on it when she'd taught him to throw. She probably should've mentioned it again.

His rope hit the ground half a foot short and to the right of the bale, nowhere close to grazing the plastic head. Then he snapped his fingers. "Gosh darn, that son of a gun got away."

———

Maddox had been counting down the hours till he'd get to mess with Harlow again. He'd been pretty bored the past couple days, and her arrival was the only thing keeping him going.

Partially because she wouldn't pry into his past. Wouldn't ask about his family, or if he regretted things he'd done, or force him to attend a class that covered signs of addictions and how to deal with them.

As if the first half of his life wasn't all the experience he'd ever need on that subject. Then there was group therapy, where he sat frozen while his classmates spilled their emotions. Didn't they realize people could use those against them? Not his problem, though.

"What?" he asked when Harlow simply tilted her head, frustration wafting off her in waves. "I didn't swear. I made it all PG, just for you."

The line of her mouth tightened, her full lips practically disappearing.

His shoulders slumped. Apparently, this part of the day would be as shitty as the rest of his time here had been. He'd resolved to just do his time and be done, but eleven days had seemed like a fucking eternity. Two months might as well be a death sentence.

He reeled in his rope, dragging plenty of dirt and grass along with it. "Look, Harlow, I'm really trying here. Not just with the rope but with you."

She dug the toe of her boot into the dirt, focusing on the motion before looking back up at him. As she shifted her weight to her right leg, a beam of sunlight drifted to her eyes. Chocolaty brown, somehow sweet *and* fiery, like those chocolate-covered cinnamon bears his mother used to love. "I tried the other day," she said.

"And I was a jerk. I'm sorry."

She studied him as if she didn't quite buy it, and he supposed he deserved that. Why *was* he even trying with this girl anyway?

So he could disappoint her later?

He opened his mouth to tell her to forget it, but then she said, "Fine. I guess you can have two strikes before I count you out."

"In baseball, it's actually three."

Under the brim of her hat, one eyebrow arched higher than the other. "In Harlow World, it's two."

Maddox bit back his smile. "Oh, I'm in your world now?"

"You'd better believe it, buddy. Look around. You're a long way from skyscrapers and sidewalks full of rude people who believe moving out of someone's way is a weakness. Honestly, I'm not sure you can hack it out here in the country."

"I want to say something hard-core and tough, but I'm not sure, either. I'm getting twitchy without my motorcycle. I miss the days I could go for a drive without fuc—screwing over my future."

Her features softened, but she still pulled off an epic eye roll. "*Of course* you have a motorcycle. Did it come with your bad-boy starter kit, along with your earrings and a bunch of tattoo needles?"

Despite his attempt to smother his laugh, a snicker burst free. "For someone who told me not to be a smart aleck, you're sure walking that line."

He didn't bother explaining he'd designed the tattoos himself. Not that he thought that his artwork would impress a girl like her anyway.

Harlow crowded him in an attempt he was fairly certain was supposed to be intimidating, but all it accomplished was giving him a close-up view of her freckles. She didn't have makeup on, her features natural and bare, showing off her flawless skin. "My world, my rules."

"Guess I'd better learn how to survive in your world, then." He readjusted the honda, which he still thought was a better name for a car than a knot. "It might help if you talked me through the throw. I wouldn't be opposed to you wrapping your arms around me and taking the demonstration a step further. I know it's typically a guy move, but I'm all about equality and feminism." He waggled his eyebrows, and this time when she pressed her lips together, it was because she was fighting a smile.

"You're trouble."

"That's why I'm here, babe."

Her muscles tensed, and she swallowed hard. "Let's make a rule. No nicknames. It's Harlow or ma'am."

"Yes, ma'am," he said as gruff and flirty as he could.

Pink crept across her cheeks, and then she positioned herself behind him, grabbed his wrist, and guided it through the motions.

The heat of her body seeped into his, and he became acutely aware of the press of her curves. She smelled amazing, too, like strawberry vanilla flowers with a hint of grapefruit. Not that that was a thing, and what had she said about the way he should flick his wrist?

Maddox glanced over his shoulder at her. "Hey, I've been wanting to ask you something since the other day."

Her sigh sent her breath across his cheek. "You're not payin' attention. I'm not gonna keep my arms around you for much longer, so stop stallin' and throw the dang rope."

How damn cute was it that she didn't swear? While he'd originally thought she sounded like a country bumpkin, he liked the lilt to her words. The same twang he'd heard in country songs when he'd been surfing radio stations and winced before quickly changing it.

He let go of the lasso, watching as it soared through the air and caught on the plastic ear of the calf head.

Then slid off and hit the ground. *Shit, I missed.*

Harlow grabbed his arm and bounced on the balls of her feet. "That was so close! You're getting better."

Her happiness transferred to him, and a tingly sensation he hadn't felt in a long time spread through his chest.

"Reel in the rope and try again," she said.

What could he do but follow her instructions? After all, he was in her world now.

And surprisingly, in this moment, he didn't mind.

━━━━━━━━━━

Brady surveyed the teens in their various stations. One of the biggest challenges at the ranch was motivating kids to apply themselves. But man, once they did, they certainly caught on quickly.

He'd watched as Harlow instructed Maddox on how to toss a lasso. When she'd wrapped her body around his, Brady had about strode over for closer observation—and by that, he meant to glare until they put more space between them.

Mrs. Griffith trusted him and his family to keep Harlow safe while she was at the ranch. In the beginning of their arrangement, Mrs. Griffith had hesitated to allow her daughter to train and stable her horse at the ranch because of the at-risk teens.

It was the kind of automatic judgment many of them received out in the real world. Sure, some of them had deserved it at one time or another. Plenty of the teens had even gone out of their way to cause trouble before. But once they had a breakthrough, big changes occurred. Seemingly overnight sometimes.

A sense of fulfillment flooded Brady's chest as he recalled the faces and names of kids they'd helped through the years. There was nothing like seeing that change.

Just like there was nothing as hard as growing to love a kid who refused to engage. A handful left the program without ever opening up or learning the necessary tools to fight off and overcome their demons.

Brady worried that Maddox Mikos might end up in that last group.

When teenagers were sent to the ranch because their families were worried about them, it came from a place of love. But when a judge ordered someone to serve time, that made it practically impossible for them not to regard their stay as a mere punishment.

Brady racked his brain for an out-of-the-box idea. The trill of his phone scattered his subpar ideas on the matter, and he glanced at the display and then quickly answered. "Nash. Hey."

"How's it going?"

"Same old same," Brady said into the phone over the sound of Desiree and Danica's cheers. As he'd hoped, the duo was having an easier time with the smaller ropes. They encouraged and razzed each other, the combination of friendship and competition pushing them past their limits. They reminded him of himself and Tanya, actually. "What about you? Where you at today?"

"Hamel, Minnesota."

"Should've guessed. It's Bull Ridin' Bonanza time."

"You know me. Gotta defend my title."

In a lot of ways, Brady knew Nash better than anyone. While he'd felt a bit restless himself lately, Nash rarely felt anything but. He was forever switching up the scenery, upping the stakes, and working to find a bigger rush that didn't involve drugs or alcohol. "When's the last time you talked to Ma?"

"Called her right before you."

The tightness in Brady's chest eased. Wade often grew frustrated over how infrequently Nash called and visited. The longer he went without checking in, the more Ma worried. Plus, there was the whole bull-riding thing. "Good. She's always fretting over the day someone will call and inform her that a bull's speared you with his horn or that you've been stomped on in the arena. Or a handful of other morbid scenarios that keep her up at night."

"Well, I'll make sure that day never comes."

As if it were that easy. Since Brady couldn't leave the teens unsupervised, he paced the training grounds as he talked. Chloe and Abby were setting up a barrel one of their horses had tipped over, and Abby's uncommonly wide grin had him patting himself on the back for pairing her with Chloe. She had experience with the program, much like Aiden, and with her practically family, it was nice to have her involved and helping as well. She was good at breaking through to girls who were shy, depressed, and dealing with some of the same anxiety issues she did.

"How's Nick? You takin' care of him for me?" Thanks to Nash,

Nick had been spared most of their biological father's abuse. Before Nash had driven away to follow his bull-riding dreams, the main thing he'd requested of Brady was to take care of their younger brother.

"Yeah, but honestly, he does a fine job of taking care of himself. And you should see him with the teens. He's a natural at the counselor thing."

"Sounds like Nick, turnin' lemons into pie." Pride echoed in Nash's voice. "I'll always be grateful you guys got him out of there before my dad..." Nash didn't finish; he didn't have to. Shuffling sounds carried through the phone. "Anyway, on to the point of this here phone call. The state fair is in Ogallala this next weekend, and since it's only a four-hour drive, I thought you and Tanya might wanna drive up and watch. For old times' sake."

Unlike most everyone else around these parts, Nash never mentioned Tanya's name with all that hint-hint to it. Probably on account of being around them enough to see they were simply super close friends who happened to be of opposite sexes.

Sex. With Tanya. That could be...

Nope, not going there. Brady blew out his breath, reprimanding himself for letting his thoughts snag on her standing across from him in only her underwear. All those fiery curls against her pale shoulders and spilling down to the swells of her breasts...

His head swam and his heart jackhammered his rib cage at a rapid, almost punishing pace.

"You still there, bro?"

Brady cleared his throat. "Yeah, sorry. There's just a lot going on here." Like, say, him having highly inappropriate thoughts about Tanya. The past couple of nights he'd called to check on Phoenix and Tanya and chat, and ever since that moment in the stables, he swore there'd been a different type of chemistry beyond their strong connection—one with an underlying current of desire.

Could they mix everything together without it resulting in a messy explosion that blew up in their faces, though? He'd driven himself crazy volleying back and forth because he couldn't gamble something so important on a maybe. Not if it ran the possibility of ruining their friendship. "Both Tanya and I are busy getting ready for the local rodeo, but I'll talk to her and see if she can sneak away."

"Cool. Let me know. Also ask her if she has any hot friends she can bring along. Surely a sexy woman or two have moved into Silver Springs since I left."

While Brady didn't pay much mind to all the goings-on in town, he would've heard if the population had grown. He could say for certain that the only sexy woman he'd seen in months was Tanya. Well, he wouldn't say it aloud, but she was in his head all the damn time these days, especially when he fell into bed at the end of the night. "If I say yes, will you make an appearance at the Silver Springs Rodeo?"

"I'll see how things look at the end of the month," Nash said, deploying his expert-level skills at avoiding firm plans. "Lately, it does seem as if I'm reliving the same day over and over, like a version of *Groundhog Day* but with bucking bulls instead of annoying groundhogs. Maybe a change of pace—even a slow pace—would be a good idea."

"Ma would love it." Growing up, Nash hadn't heard he was appreciated, cared about, or wanted nearly enough, so Brady didn't bother holding back. "We'd all love it. Everybody misses you."

"Anyway, I'll let you get back to it." Code for: This is turning mushy, and you're still trying to get me to visit, so I'm going to flee the scene of the feelings.

"Later," Brady said, holding back the *love you*. Not because he didn't love his brother but because it might shut Nash down more.

With a sigh, Brady slid his phone into his shirt pocket, his mind lingering on his conversation with Nash.

Aiden walked by, and Brady gestured him over. All three of the brothers who'd become family in an unconventional way had grown leaps and bounds, although Brady wouldn't go calling Nash completely over his demons. Point was, there was hope, and a lot of a person's progress depended on the work they put in. There was something to be said for individualization, too, though.

"What's your read on Maddox?" Brady asked Aiden.

Aiden kicked at a rock on the ground. "He's confrontational. Mad at the world in general. But to tell the truth, I haven't talked to him much."

"Think you could? See if maybe you could get through to him?"

If it made a difference, Brady would use about any means at his disposal. Not at his youngest brother's expense, obviously, but if Maddox could find a friend here to talk to—particularly one who'd understand him better than most—it might help. "You don't even have to report back. I just think he needs to know someone's on his side, even if he resists at first."

Aiden lifted a hand to shield his eyes—he still wasn't sold on cowboy hats, although he occasionally donned one. "He seems to be happy around Harlow."

"That's what I'm afraid of," Brady said. "The something he needs can't be her, or Mrs. Griffith will have our heads."

Aiden nodded. "That woman is *definitely* on the overly protective side. I'll see what I can do."

"Maybe get him on a horse. Harlow can go along for the ride, but I don't want her alone with him." In fact, Brady was going to do another walk by to remind Maddox he was watching every move. He strode over to the duo and placed his hands on his hips. "How's it coming?"

"He's getting better each throw," Harlow said, shooting Maddox an encouraging smile. It didn't seem flirty. Just her regular upbeat cheer, which was why he'd wanted her help in the first place.

"Good. I spoke with Aiden, and we plan to get Maddox on a horse this weekend and see how that goes."

"You know I'm right here," the kid said.

Brady clapped him on the back. "I'm well aware. I just figured I'd tell Harlow while you were within earshot, so you'd know about it but not feel like you had to give me attitude. Guess that method crashed and burned, so back to the drawing board for me."

He probably shouldn't poke at Maddox, considering he wasn't sure the kid understood teasing or that family and friends often used it on people they cared about. But it was Brady's home base and the best way he'd connected with kids in the past.

Maddox shook out his rope and gave him an almost smile, which was the most he'd gotten out of the teen so far. "Joke's on you. I'm excited to ride a horse, especially with Harlow there to help."

Here Brady was worried about her getting attached, when it appeared Maddox was the one becoming enamored. "With training for her other events, Harlow doesn't have time to teach you from scratch, so you'll be with Aiden for horse-riding lessons."

Every ounce of happiness faded from Maddox's features, and a pang went through Brady. That was the other hard part about working at Turn Around Ranch. He and his family wanted to make the kids as happy as possible, so they'd have good memories mixed in with the ones involving hard work and even harder lessons, but sometimes giving them what they wanted wasn't in their best interest.

"Keep up the good work, though. I'm impressed." There. He'd given Maddox encouragement, too. Nick and Liza were far better at knowing the right thing to say. Ma, too.

With their time ticking down for training, Brady should focus. Instead, his phone burned his thigh, imploring him to bring it out and text Tanya for his next fix. The restlessness he'd been experiencing hadn't been as strong since they'd jumped into preparations for the rodeo, but it wasn't quite appeased, either.

This over-the-phone stuff was for the birds. Without body language and tone, he couldn't properly read her intent, and that left his brain endlessly spinning. Perhaps that was the reason he'd been overly focused on Tanya and what every little thing she said meant.

No big deal. All he had to do was schedule a meetup, broach the topic of the state fair, and scrutinize her reaction. The idea of controlling the situation really should've occurred to him earlier, but as he'd told Nash, things had been busy.

> **Brady:** Hey, wanna grab a drink at the Tumbleweed tonight?
>
> **Tanya:** I can't.
>
> **Brady:** You know what they say about all work and no play. We're both too awesome to end up dull. I'll pick you up at seven.
>
> **Tanya:** Rain check? Eric's insisting on taking me out for dinner tonight so he can ask more questions about running a ranch while getting a break from it. LOL

Out for dinner. With Eric. Brady's gut sank all the way down to his toes, and he sure as hell didn't feel like laughing out loud. Tanya was his person. More than anything, he wanted her to be happy, but every organ in his body protested the idea of her out with another guy. The fact that he'd also read everything so wrong scraped at him. What an idiot he'd been, thinking she was flirting with him out of the blue.

It'd been so long since either one of them had a date that he couldn't remember what typical procedure was. Wish her luck? Go threaten the guy with one of those "If you don't treat her right, I'll break your face, which is something I want to do anyway" speeches? Tell her to break a leg?

After rereading the last text, he decided to focus on what was important. Tanya, and how she felt about herself.

Brady: That guy certainly didn't waste any time asking you out. Not all that surprising, but I'd be shocked if he was good enough for you.

Three little dots formed on his screen as she typed her reply, and Brady hoped she'd say something like, *You know what? You're right. Never mind, I'll meet you at the Tumbleweed.* Maybe even request he call partway through the date so she'd have a way out if she needed one.

Tanya: It's not a date, silly. It's a business meeting. I'll call you once it's all wrapped up and maybe we can get together afterward?

Sure. The classic "business meeting dinner." Countless times through the years, he'd caught men checking out Tanya. Whenever he remarked on all her lust-struck cowboys, she clucked her tongue and told him he was imagining things. Trust him, he wasn't. So naturally, she'd never assume the city-slicker CEO was after more than sharing a meal.

And then what? Brady could have the scraps?

Irritation flared, leaving him itchy inside and out, and he fought the urge to toss his phone in the other direction. As if that'd make the situation any better.

His thoughts had only just begun to wander down the perilous what-if path.

A simple correction, and he should be able to wrangle them back to the spot where they'd veered off in the wrong direction. If only a sense of foreboding didn't rise up and whisper that it might not be quite that easy.

Chapter 8

A STRING IN MADDOX'S CHEST TUGGED AS HE WATCHED THE tiny girl with the giant pickup drive away. There went his entertainment for the next few days. The hours they trained suddenly didn't seem like nearly enough.

Once the coast was clear, he grabbed his sketchbook and pencils from his room and sat on the porch. This afternoon, he'd soaked in every detail so he could get Harlow's heart-shaped face exactly right. Each stroke of gray across the blank white paper calmed him, and he got lost in the slope of her nose, shading the round cheeks that popped whenever she smiled, and the shape of her lips.

Seconds turned into minutes, turned into maybe an hour, until movement near the main cabin caught his eye. He blinked as if awoken from a good dream, noting the fading sunlight and refocusing on the actual scenery instead of staring through it.

Shoot, it was dinnertime, and the staff was a stickler about punctuality.

Maddox darted inside the boys' cabin, jammed his sketchbook under his thin mattress, and then rushed across the property to where the adults were herding his classmates inside. Most everyone was already seated around the oversize dining table.

The blond toddler twins both gawked at Maddox as he approached, and Elise pointed at his arm. "He gets to draw on himself, Mommy. Why can't I?"

"And he has an earring," Everett added. "Aren't those for girls?"

Liza grimaced, but Maddox didn't mind directness—he preferred it. Just cut through the bullshit and say what you mean, no false hope or sugarcoating it. Kids were good at that. He'd been stared at plenty, and the majority of the stares from kids stemmed from a fascination with his tattoos.

"These don't come off," Maddox said, stepping toward Elise and rolling his arm to show off his ink.

Then he realized Liza probably didn't want him so close. That happened a lot, too, mothers pulling their children away. But she didn't seem to mind, and even gestured to his extended arm. "They're tattoos. But you can't get them until you're older."

Elise reached up and fiddled with one of her pigtails. "How old?"

Liza sighed and closed her eyes. "Forty."

"Are you forty?" Everett asked.

Maddox chuckled and ruffled the kid's hair. "Close to it, bud. You've got a great mom. Make sure to listen to her, 'kay?"

"I listen, but Everett doesn't," his sister said.

Everett argued "Do too," to which his sister said, "Do not."

"Okay, that's enough." Liza's mom voice made both of them sit straighter. Then she gave Maddox a friendly smile. "Sorry. They're in that curious, ask-a-hundred-questions-a-minute stage. Or they're bickering. It's nonstop, either way."

Maddox ran a hand through his hair. "No worries. I don't mind questions."

"I'll send them to you, then, and you can play Google," she said with a laugh, and he gave her a cautious smile. He wouldn't mind, but he'd also been around the block enough to know she didn't truly mean it. "By the way, I saw you roping today. You're getting better and better. Harlow's an excellent teacher, huh?"

His muscles tensed. Was this a trap? Had she noticed him staring at his roping tutor in those in-between moments, when he got caught up in the scrunch of her nose and those adorable freckles?

Was the woman upset? Trying to warn him away?

He got it. Guys like him needed to stay away from girls like Harlow. Did Liza think he was stupid? Or had a death wish?

I probably am, and I kind of do.

"I'm gonna go sit down," he said, backing away before the counselor could continue her interrogation.

The door between the kitchen and living room swung open, and Jess walked in carrying a large pan. "I'm sure you all smell the smoke, but don't worry. I just spilled some maple syrup on the burner. Silly me, I forgot to buy syrup when I went grocery shopping, so I made it from scratch. It was a little touch and go for a while, but I think it turned out okay."

She put down a pan piled with pancakes, along with a giant pitcher of steaming syrup.

Everyone began passing around the food and digging in. Forks hit plates and the buzz of conversation filled the air. It was like having family dinner with thirty people. Maddox supposed that, anyway, since he'd never done much of the family-dinner thing.

He groaned when he took a bite of the pancakes and the home-made syrup. It'd turned out better than okay, and several people told Miss Jessica so. He should probably add his two cents about it, but that'd mean opening his mouth and drawing unwanted attention.

Smiles spread from one face to another, the spirit of camaraderie palpable. Most of the other teens had been here longer than he had, and they all seemed…happy. Or at the very least okay with being here.

His skeptical side balked, tempted to declare them all brainwashed. But that didn't ring true. Under other circumstances, he might even think this was nice, the assurance he'd get meals three whole times a day while chatting with people who asked kind questions and teased one another. Back in the city, dinner generally involved greasy takeout in the office of the mechanic shop while he and the foster parents he was supposedly staying with pretended one another didn't exist.

But no matter what, he couldn't get used to this.

It wasn't the kind of thing that lasted.

———————

Brady walked past the deer that would never escape the wooden wall next to the hostess stand—the front half of the animal was on one side, the back half on the other. All part of the charm of the Tumbleweed Bar and Grill. Tourists often took pictures of Bambi, and while he supposed the decor came across as weird to outsiders, Jeb Miller had bagged that buck before Brady was even born. He'd heard the story several times, though. Jeb had been about to give up on his hunting trip, and then he climbed over a ridge and there the deer stood.

As Brady rounded the hostess stand, he nodded at Amy and then let his gaze roam over the myriad vintage signs nailed to the wall. Various speed limits, route markers, and clever sayings like "Gone fishing" screamed from every angle.

Wade and Jess had already claimed a table near the bar. Being a third wheel hadn't been Brady's original plan for the night, but when he'd asked his brother if he wanted to grab a drink, he'd mentioned that Jessica was craving the Tumbleweed's chili.

Irritation scrambled Brady's insides as he eyed the two empty chairs. He already loved Jess like the sister-in-law she'd soon be, but being around her and Wade was only gonna remind him of what he'd truly longed for tonight—alone time with Tanya.

Even though he'd seen her a few days ago, he couldn't rid himself of the feeling she was slipping away. Probably stupid and unfounded, but that was the best way he could describe it. Then again, say that fancy-pants businessman did go and sweep her off her feet? What would Brady do then?

His stomach dipped way down to the toes of his boots. Suddenly, he considered bolting through the nearest wall, the way that deer up front appeared to have done.

Over the past several months, there'd been a handful of changes, and positive or not, the adjustment period was a bitch. Whatever was going on with him caused the same sensation of everything in his world shifting without warning. If Tanya were here, she'd tell him to stop acting like a cranky old man.

If she were here, he'd welcome the razzing.

Jess stood and gave him a hug. "Hey, Brady, glad you could join us," she said. Then her face paled, and she spun on her heel and sprinted toward the bathroom. Wade was halfway out of his chair in seconds, watching her rush off, a worried, helpless expression on his face.

The chair legs scraped the wooden floor as Brady took a seat. "Have you guys told Ma that she's gonna be a grandma yet?"

Wade's head jerked toward him, his eyes wide.

"Oh, come on." Brady rested his forearms atop the table. "You said she was craving chili, and then she just looked at me and bolted for the bathroom. I've seen my reflection in a mirror, and it's not one that causes the sudden need to barf."

"Cocky bastard," his brother muttered.

"A *correct* cocky bastard."

Wade slowly settled back into his chair and exhaled. "No, we haven't told Ma yet. Jessica's just over two months along, and you know how Ma gets. Especially after her miscarriage."

It was a subject they usually avoided. At four months along, their mother lost a baby girl, and in spite of how many kids she and Dad already had—both at home and the teens on the ranch—it'd broken a part of her. Now every time a woman in town was pregnant, Ma fretted on her behalf. It meant she'd be ecstatic about becoming a grandmother but take the doting and worrying to the extreme.

Jess returned to the table, most of the color back in her face and a piece of gum in her mouth.

"He knows," Wade said as she settled at the table.

Jess ran a hand through her wavy blond hair. "Bolting at the sight of his pretty mug did me in, didn't it?"

Brady chuckled. "That's about word for word what I said. Congrats, by the way." He glanced at Wade. "You, too."

Wade and his fiancée beamed at each other. Had a conversation with smiles and raised eyebrows before Wade added, "Besides you, Chloe and Aiden are the only ones we've told so far."

That didn't surprise Brady. Jess and Chloe were the closest mother-and-daughter duo he'd ever met, and Wade considered Aiden his kid. When they'd had to go to court to fight for custody, Wade was the one who'd gone to the mat for Aiden.

Jessica picked up the menu. "We're going to tell everyone else soon, though. Your mom keeps asking why I don't want to set a wedding date, and I don't have the heart to tell her she's not going to get to plan a wedding for another year. I didn't want a shotgun wedding when I was sixteen, and I don't want one now, even though Wade and I would both know it wasn't just happening because I'm knocked up. Silly or not, I want the whole big ceremony and a beautiful white dress that doesn't have to accommodate a pregnant belly."

Brady scratched at his forehead with his thumb. "I get it, but Ma's pretty traditional. Plus, she's dyin' to plan a wedding."

"Understatement," Wade said. "On both those counts."

Jess nudged Brady with her elbow. "I guess the only solution is for *you* to hurry up and get married."

"Ha-ha."

"Let's see…" Jess tapped her lip as if she were deep in thought. "If only there were someone perfect for you right here in Silver Springs. Say a funny, smart, super pretty redhead who's been right under your nose for years."

Brady shot her a warning glare, but unfortunately, those had never worked very well on Jess. "For the last time—"

"We're just friends," she and Wade finished for him, giggling as they made googly eyes at each other.

Yep, the singular empty chair at Brady's side now seemed sadder than ever. Agreeing to this outing might've been a mistake. But at the idea of a niece or nephew, anticipation tingled through him, and he always had enjoyed finding out things before everyone else. Went back to his love of winning, he supposed.

The waitress came by, and they placed their orders. Brady couldn't imagine wanting chili after puking, however Jess meant business when it came to her craving. "Please bring chili in the biggest bowl you have, along with a shit ton of crackers."

The door to the Tumbleweed swung open, and Brady automatically glanced toward it. Because of the motion, sure, but it was practically law to wave at everybody, whether you were driving or crossing paths in one of the town's few establishments.

As soon as his brain registered the couple who'd stepped inside, the rest of his body went on hiatus.

Tanya's out-of-control curls had been flat-ironed, and based on her venting about how long that took, it meant she'd put in effort. Totally unnecessary, since she always looked beautiful.

That thought lodged in his brain, where it blinked and buzzed like a neon sign. Had he ever called her beautiful before? In his head or aloud?

Whenever he saw her, he experienced a heap of happiness and comfort, never giving much thought to her appearance. She just looked like her. His person since forever.

Tonight, she'd turned up the volume, leaving it impossible to concentrate on anything else. Her reddish-purple dress exposed her shoulders, and the short, flowy skirt displayed a whole lot of leg. Even though his brain told his eyes to stop it, Brady couldn't help but gape at his best friend. He could count on one hand how many times he'd seen her in a dress, and his lungs filled with lead as he realized she must really want to impress Eric.

Dizziness set in as he went too long without inhaling or exhaling.

"Did you know she'd be here?" Wade asked. "Is that why you wanted to come? To crash her date?"

The question pulled Brady out of his trance, although his heart continued to thunder inside his chest. "She told me she had a date and couldn't meet me for a drink, but I just needed to get away from the ranch for the night. I didn't know they'd show up here." Now he wished he would've stayed home. It felt like someone had taken a knife to his insides and was slashing away with reckless abandon.

Jess placed her glass down on the table with a *clink*. "Does it bother you?"

"Nope," Brady automatically said, but the word came out too tight. He wished for a menu to hide behind, but since the waitress had taken his away, he wadded his straw wrapper into a mangled knot. "Like I said, I knew about it."

Jess placed her hand on his forearm. "Not trying to be confrontational here, but it's pretty clear it bothers you."

Wade leaned back until two of the legs of his chair left the ground. "Babe, remember the rules? No talking about more than friendship when it comes to Brady and Tanya."

She huffed. "I'm more of a rules-were-meant-to-be-broken kinda gal. I've never understood why your whole family tiptoes around it." Urgency crept into her voice as her fingertips tensed against his skin. "You two have crazy chemistry, and you should see Tanya's face whenever I mention your name. There's longing there, I swear."

Brady shook his head, his throat as dry as after a hard day of riding through a dust storm. "You don't know her like I do. Yeah, we love each other, but we're not *in love* with each other, and we certainly don't go gettin' all mushy and talk about it."

Jessica crossed her arms. "Maybe you should. Does she even know that you love her?"

Yep. I definitely should've stayed home. Too late for that, so Brady excused himself and headed to the bar. He was going to need a stronger drink than the on-tap beer in front of him.

━━━━━━━━

At first, Tanya had hesitated to take Eric up on his offer for a celebratory drink after their business dinner at the Italian restaurant down the street. But he'd insisted, she was all dolled up, and honestly, she'd been hoping to see the very cowboy who'd just sidled up to the bar.

Holy shit.

Unlike the guy at her side, who was wearing khaki slacks and a polo, Brady had on a red-and-blue plaid shirt and a pair of snug Wranglers that called to mind the "Cowboy butts drive me nuts" bumper sticker she'd put on her old truck back in high school. She'd thought it was funny. Her parents, not so much, and one night while she'd been asleep, Mom took a razor blade to it and scrubbed it clean off.

"…for you?"

Great. Less than a minute in the door and she'd already lost the ability to concentrate. She'd like to say it was only because Brady was in her direct line of sight, but even during dinner, her mind had constantly drifted to him. What was he up to? Would she get to see him tonight, and if so, would he notice her outfit and hair? Would that be enough to push past friendship into attraction territory?

"Sorry," Tanya said, placing a hand on her churning stomach and dragging her gaze back to Eric. "What was that?"

"I asked what drink I could order for you."

When Eric had asked poor, flustered Marvin for a wine menu down at the Rialto—the theater they hadn't bothered to rename after converting it into a restaurant—Tanya had stepped in. She explained the bistro had lost their liquor license after they'd been caught serving to minors and now only served soda. She'd added that people around here didn't drink enough wine to need a whole menu for it anyway. It was red or white, and the year was the last one, which they considered pretty darn fancy.

In hindsight, less information was also more.

"Actually, why don't you have a seat, and I'll go grab the drinks?" She backpedaled toward the bar, determined to seize the moment, the way her dating book advised her to do. "What'll you have?"

Eric asked for a Jack and Coke, and Tanya nodded and pivoted around.

And immediately sucked in a sharp breath. Brady's eyes locked on hers, prodding her very soul. He tipped his heavy-bottomed glass at her, inciting a riot of emotions, and by the time she reached him, she felt as though she'd run a marathon instead of walked a couple of yards.

"Hey," she said, her voice coming out ridiculously breathy.

Brady raked his gaze down her body, and a trail of heat followed in its wake. "Check you out. All gussied up and out on the town."

Tip after cataloged tip tumbled through her head.

Stop worrying about what could go wrong and focus on what could go right.

Sparking desire requires extra risk.

Teasing creates intimacy.

Play to his masculinity.

"Me? How about you?" Tanya wrapped her hand around his biceps, affected a slightly ditzy lilt, and squeezed. "All big and strong, over here drinking a cocktail and showing off your giant guns."

Instead of him smiling or tossing out another line, his eyebrows scrunched together. "Cocktail? Come on, you know me better than that."

The damn book never mentioned what to do if a guy *corrected* a flirty line. "Well, pardon the hell out of me, Mr. Technical. I embellished for the sake of the words rolling off the tongue nicer.

I take back what I said about your guns." She began to withdraw her hand, but Brady placed his large palm over the top, securing it once again to his arm.

"Now, now. Don't be too hasty. Looks like you're still on a date with the city slicker, and you're certainly not gonna get a thrill like this from fondling his arms."

Tanya rolled her eyes. "I told you it's not a date. I should put in our drink order, though." She leaned her stomach against the bar and asked Jeb Junior for two Jack and Cokes. When she cast a sidelong glance at Brady, he gave her another scrutinizing expression. "What?"

"You what?"

"Seriously?"

"I asked you first," he said, and she fought the urge to smack him. She'd dangled the bait, shown interest, and done her best to make him feel like a man. So why wasn't his desire switch flipping?

When was he going to take her into his arms and kiss her already? Or was he genuinely uninterested, and all this effort had been in vain? She couldn't put this much time into getting ready every single day until he got it through his thick skull that she was trying to put out the vibe.

"No need to glare daggers at me, Yaya." Brady tugged on the ends of her hair, and a shiver of electricity traveled down her spine. The voltage cranked even higher as his callused fingers drifted across her exposed collarbone. "You look nice is all."

"Nice," she repeated as evenly as she could, but she knew her face was as red as a freshly painted barn.

He rested a hip against the bar, swirled the ice around the cup, and took a casual sip of the amber liquid. "That's what I said."

Normally, getting a bead on her best friend wasn't something she had to work at. *Nice* was such a vague term, and she'd hoped for more. He'd shuttered his features, too, as if they were in the middle of a poker game. "Are you purposely being difficult? It feels like you're accusing me of something."

"Telling you that you look nice is being difficult?"

"No. Yes. I don't know."

Brady snorted. "Well, get back to me once you do."

Tanya whirled on him, fast enough that her skirt flared. Along with an undercurrent of frustration, now she got to worry about whether or not she'd flashed the preacher and his wife, who were eating their dinner at the table closest to her. "Shut it, Dawson."

His mouth dropped open, and he flattened a hand to his chest as faux shock flickered through his rugged features. "Me? I'm just sittin' here, enjoying some moonshine. You see, I don't need to dress up and pretend I'm someone I'm not to impress some businessman from out of town."

A sharp pain lanced her chest, the blunt force of his words expelling every ounce of oxygen from her lungs. "I... That's not even... Of all the jerk things you've ever said..." Anger and hurt twisted through her, and she clung to the fire so she wouldn't give in to the overwhelming urge to burst into tears.

"All this?" She circled her face with her hand. "The makeup and hair and sending flirty texts and doing research to figure out what men want? It wasn't for Eric." She snatched the two drinks off the bar, glad to have something to do with her hands, although it was going to take all her self-control not to toss them at Brady. "It was for you, you asshole."

Chapter 9

MADDOX WAS ELBOW DEEP IN THE UNDERSIDE OF JESSICA'S car when he spotted a familiar pair of brown boots approaching.

Everything inside him jolted, as if he'd touched an exposed wire without being grounded, and his heart thrummed faster in his chest. He told himself it was merely from the exertion of working on the car, even though there'd been no rapid heart rate moments ago.

One second passed.

Two...

Then Harlow crouched to peek under the hood at him. Her hat toppled off, and her honey-colored hair cascaded down around her face. "Hey," she said.

Maddox went to roll himself out from under the car but then remembered he didn't have his shop creeper—a flat scooter with wheels that allowed a mechanic to roll around. The wheels wouldn't work well in the dirt anyway, but without its help, it took a few extra seconds for Maddox to wiggle out from the underside of the Toyota.

Minding the bumper so he wouldn't hit his head, he carefully sat up. "Hey."

He swiped his hands together and extended one to Harlow.

Her eyebrows crinkled, her internal debate clear for a second or two before she took his hand and hauled him to his feet. Electricity coursed up his arm, making it hard to convince his fingers to let go. But when she loosened her grip, he let her hand slide free.

"What are you doing to Jess's car?" she asked.

"Stripping it for spare parts," he deadpanned. "Then I'll sell them to a chop shop."

One of her eyebrows arched higher than the other. He took it as a good sign she didn't believe he'd do something like that. Not unless Ian asked him to—Maddox owed him, after all.

The tools clinked together as he tossed them in the borrowed toolbox. "I'm fixing up her car. Don't worry. I'm a far better mechanic than cowboy."

"That's nice for Jess, but not great news for me, your roping partner."

He cracked a smile. "Guess that means you'd better whip me into shape." He leaned in and lowered his voice. "Do you have a whip?"

Her eyes narrowed, the lips he'd sketched more than once pursing. "I could probably find a riding crop."

"Kinky."

Harlow heaved a sigh. "Why do I bother talking to you again?"

"Because I'm your roping partner."

"Lucky me." Now she was the one using the deadpan voice. She flattened her hands against his shoulder blades and shoved him toward the training area. "Less talk, more training."

While he could've resisted, he let her propel him toward the area with the bales of hay sporting plastic calf heads. Once they were there, Harlow grabbed a rope and extended it to him. Then frowned as she eyed his open palms. "Your hands are covered in grease."

"Uh, yeah. You dragged me out from under a car."

"Because it's time to train."

He tapped her on the nose. "Don't worry. I've been practicing."

She tilted her head, her doubt clear. Honestly, he could hardly believe it himself. But he'd spent a healthy portion of his free time over the weekend training.

For her.

Just so they could do well in the competition. And to make her happy. Because they were…friends? Kind of.

Maddox formed his loop and adjusted the size, the way he'd done enough times over the weekend that he'd ended up with a blister. "Give me some space, will ya? I'm about to blow your mind."

Skepticism filled Harlow's expression, which ratcheted up the pressure. As he swung the lasso over his head, he did his best to block it out.

One, two… Three.

He released the rope, and the loop dropped over the plastic cow head with a satisfying *thud*.

Harlow's brown eyes flew wide, her surprised enthusiasm sending another one of those jolts through him. "Dude. You did it!"

"Dude, I know." He gave her a smirk. "I told you I practiced."

"I thought you were full of crap."

"I am. But I was telling the truth about that."

Her smile grew, inciting a fleeting moment of pure joy before panic rushed in and washed it away. Since he'd inevitably disappoint her in the long run, this was a dangerous game. "Don't get too excited," he said. "There's literally nothing else to do out here."

She bumped him out of the way as she formed her lasso, that infectious smile still curving her lips. "I'm Maddox, and I'm so macho and cool," she said in a low voice he was fairly certain was supposed to be his. "I don't care about anything, I'm *that hardcore*. And I only do nice stuff when I'm bored AF."

Right as she went to throw, he bumped his hip into hers, and her rope went wide. It missed completely, a puff of dirt rising as the rope hit the soft ground.

Harlow gasped and spun to face him. "You did not just do that."

"Nope. Didn't you hear? I'm too hard-core for that. And bored AF? Do you kiss your mother with that dirty mouth?"

She smacked his arm, and he laughed.

"Here. I'll get your rope for you." He reeled it in and handed it over.

"What *do* you care about, Maddox Mikos?" Harlow scrutinized him, and his chest squeezed. Not quite panic—he honestly wasn't sure what it was. Only that it was dangerous.

"I've learned not to care too much about anything." Because then it was gone, and he was never going to end up as the dumbfounded and crushed kid ever again.

"You care about your motorcycle," she pointed out.

"I saved up for a year and bought it. It's one of the few things in my life that's all mine, not to mention it's fast as shit. So yeah, I care about that."

She stepped closer. Batted those long eyelashes. "What else do you like?"

The days when you're here. Working to repress his emotions, he went with a casual shrug.

She studied him, and if beads of sweat began forming, he'd blame the sun that was beating down on him as hard as her gaze. "How about we make a deal? Every time you fail to loop the plastic calf head, you have to answer one of my questions—one hundred percent honestly."

It was a risky proposition. Yeah, he'd made that first toss, but he still missed plenty.

She bounced on the balls of her feet, a mixture of excitement and taunting. "Come on. It'll be fun and amp up the stakes."

He glanced away, because damn, the girl was way too good at that. He dragged his rope across his palm so he could focus on the rough fibers against his skin. "What about you? If I'm going to agree, you've got to risk something, too."

"Like what?"

Yeah, like what? He took her in, the innocent, wide-eyed girl who rode horses, raced around barrels, and roped calves in her spare time—*for fun.* "If I say the same goes for when you miss, it's hardly fair. You've been doing this for years."

Did she move closer or had he? "Okay, so make it fair," she said.

He racked his brain but couldn't come up with anything. "I'll have to think about it."

"Sounds like a stalling tactic to me." She squared off in front of the bale of hay and tossed her rope. For a second, he thought she'd missed. While it wasn't as clean as her usual throws, she managed to get it over the calf head. "Tick-tock."

With her watching so intensely, he missed. Good thing he hadn't made a deal with her yet, because he wasn't sure he was ready for her questions.

———————

In addition to yelling at her best friend for telling her she looked nice—or not finding her hot enough, as it were—Tanya had taken to avoiding him.

A totally adult move that her dating book naturally advised against.

But now Brady knew she was interested in that way, and how could she face him after her outburst? All it did was make her feel like the hot-tempered teenager she used to be, which had her alternatively moping and wanting to dig her head in the dirt like an ostrich.

On Saturday, Phoenix took a turn for the worse, so Tanya shoved her personal drama to the back burner. When the vet visited and claimed there was nothing more they could do to breathe life into the injured mare, Tanya draped a blanket over a pile of straw in the corner and slept next her.

Dark, melancholy eyes peered at Tanya for hours as she hummed and ran a hand over the horse's muscular neck. It was almost as if Phoenix *wanted* to give up, and in addition to breaking Tanya's heart, that attitude ignited a tender yet fierce instinct that nearly consumed her.

Two nights passed that way, but on Monday morning,

something miraculous happened, and Tanya dragged her parents out to the stables so they could see it for themselves.

"See how Phoenix reacts to Winston? How he nudges her whenever her head droops?"

Tanya stepped on the bottom plank of the gate to get a better view of her three-legged goat and recovering horse. "He came in first thing, bleating for attention, so I let him inside with us, and now Phoenix is up on her feet and eating again."

Mom smiled. Pops crossed his arms with a huff.

Neither reaction surprised Tanya. While she had their undivided attention, she quickly pushed on with the idea the animals had given her. While her romantic life might be currently strewn with tumbleweeds she'd set on fire, inspiration for a career had struck and spread. "I've finally figured out what I was meant to do with my life. I want to build another set of stables on the back twenty and start a horse rescue ranch. Maybe other animals, too, but the majority will be horses, since I can do the most good there."

A scowl etched Pops's grizzled face, as if she'd suggested they paint the barn neon pink and force all the animals and staff to wear matching tutus. "Not another one of your harebrained schemes." He shook his head. "It's like the spa idea all over again. As if we want a bunch of sissies here to get their nails done. Give someone a manicure and then they'll balk at riding a horse or throwing a lasso."

For the record, a lot of dude ranches were opening a spa area to attract a wider audience. It appealed to family or coworkers who weren't quite ready for "roughing it," which hardly applied considering the state of the cushy cabins. The spa would also bring in local business to help with the off-season. That hadn't been her dream, though—just a profitable idea that'd been immediately shot down. "This is different. It's something I'm passionate about, and I can do it on the side, so you'll still have my help with the rest of the ranch."

Pops's wiry mustache twitched in dismay. "Let me get this straight. I tell you to stop bringing home strays, and you take that to mean you should open an animal shelter on *my* ranch? The ranch that's been in my family goin' on four generations?"

His ranch. *His* family's ranch. The words gouged, a dull knife he wielded to prove he was the toughest SOB out there. Females couldn't pull as much weight, and woe was him for having a daughter who'd eventually inherit the ranch instead of a son. Tanya had pushed harder and faster, merely to prove she wasn't a detriment, but regardless of her accomplishments, Pops would never change his stance. It shouldn't sting as badly anymore, yet pain radiated from the center of her chest anyway. Perhaps she hadn't been ranching as long, but these days, she and her "other stray" Miguel did the lion's share of the physical labor.

Stomping her foot wouldn't demonstrate maturity, so she resisted the urge. "If you're so worried about the land, I'll pay rent. I'll even take out a loan for the stables myself. I'll do whatever it takes to make this work—that's how badly I want it."

Before Pops could completely shoot it down and end the discussion for all eternity, Tanya appealed to Mom. "I started thinking about all the injured and abused horses out there. The ones people don't think are worth enough effort to heal. Mistreated rodeo animals, and those deemed weaker and then promptly discarded." A lump rose in her throat, so much sorrow and passion piling up that swallowing became impossible. "I could heal the horses, rehome some of them, and make a real difference."

Mom made a *hmm* noise, a flicker of interest lighting her eyes. *I've done it. I've finally gotten through to her, and she's the only one who has a chance in hell of getting through to Pops.* "Please just give me a chance to prove myself. I promise not to let you down."

Mom glanced at Pops, and just like that, the flicker extinguished. "While we appreciate your enthusiasm, Pumpkin, it's not a sound business move for us right now. We simply can't afford to build a new stable and take in every stray."

While Tanya had always admired the fact that her mother would do anything for her father, she also went above and beyond to shelter a man who lit matches with his whiskers. The same man who spared no insults if he deemed you lazy, too slow, or in need of "more motivation."

Pops cast her the admonishing expression she'd been painfully familiar with growing up and said, "Work isn't always fun, Tanya. Dreams are for the independently wealthy, which we certainly are not. Someday you're going to have to grow up and learn that."

With that, Pops stormed out, and Tanya worked at not letting her knees buckle. She'd failed at snagging Brady, but in her excitement over finally knowing what she wanted to do with her life, she'd managed to forget about that for a moment.

Only to be told no, like she was a little kid.

As if they sensed her rising anxiety, both Winston and Phoenix wandered closer. Tanya let her hand roam over the goat's spine and then lightly scratched the white diamond on the mare's nose.

Tears welled, blurring the soothing horsey face. On autopilot, Tanya scooped up salve and smothered one of the bigger cuts on the horse's chest.

Mom stood by, a silent sentinel. Then she lifted a brush and combed through Phoenix's mane. "How can someone do this to one of God's creatures?" Her jaw set, a rare flash of outrage filling her green irises. "How can they see the bones sticking out like that and not do anything about it?"

"I have no idea," Tanya said, "because I had to act. You know it was the right call."

Mom hesitated and then slowly nodded. "I'd have done the same thing."

"Can't you tell Pops that? There are so many horses out there who need someone to save them, and I could use your help convincing him to let me do it."

Her mother's long-suffering sigh was answer enough.

"So you can't admit to Pops that you agree with me about the horse? Can't tell him that I came back from college to help out? Does that about cover it?"

A mishmash of pleading and warning twisted Mom's features. "He's a proud man."

Every muscle in Tanya's body tensed. "Well, you know what they say. 'Pride comes before a fall.'"

"You want him to fall?" Mom asked. "You'd take that away from him now, when he's nearing the end of his career?"

Part of her did. Shouldn't he have to live in the real world like everyone else? He was the one who constantly preached on and on about how harsh it was, as if he'd been preparing her for war from the time she could fit in a saddle.

But it'd crush the mountain of a man, and Tanya did want him to be able to retire on a high note.

She turned to fully face her mother and asked the question she both wanted and didn't want to know the answer to. "After all the work I've put into the ranch, can't you at least talk Pops into giving my idea a chance? If I can come up with a business plan and run facts and figures?"

Mom's face went slack as she hunched up her shoulders, her posture guarded.

Inhale, exhale, inhale, exhale. Tanya had worked so hard on stifling her headstrong nature, on thinking things through and always being ready for anything the elements threw at her, and it hadn't made any difference. Her dream bubble burst right before her eyes. "Is there anything I can do to get him to change his mind?"

Crazy how such a tiny shake of a head could slam into her so strongly. "I'm afraid not."

"But maybe if—"

"Let's go on inside and start dinner," Mom said. In other words, there would be no speaking up on her behalf for her idea.

The lump in Tanya's throat morphed a stopper that didn't allow air in or out.

More than anything, she wanted her best friend. But she couldn't even call him because she'd gone and screwed everything up.

Chapter 10

ONCE A MONTH, TANYA MET UP WITH THE LADIES FROM TURN Around Ranch for a ladies' night at the Tumbleweed Bar and Grill. Usually, it didn't tangle her stomach in knots, but on this particular Tuesday night, she settled at a table in the back corner and gnawed at her fingernails.

What if they asked about Brady? Had they heard about how she'd lost her temper and called him an asshole? Would his mother be upset about that, or would she understand?

Then again, understanding required explaining, and no way in hell was Tanya going to go there. She'd made a big enough mess already, and tonight she got to lie in the bed she'd made.

Customarily she, Kathy, Jess, and Liza rode into town together so they'd always have a designated driver. However, after dinner at the dude ranch, Mom asked Tanya if she'd do the grocery shopping. Worse, she asked her to take Pops along, as if they'd get into a vehicle together and suddenly realize they saw eye to eye.

But Pops had also been in Mom's hair, asking for something every five minutes, in spite of the fact that he'd been reading an outdoor life magazine while Mom attended to the guests. Mom would never refuse him, though, and Tanya's suggestion for Pops do the grocery shopping himself was met with exasperation. The few times he'd gone before, he'd called five times, sent two texts, and still showed up with only half the items.

Sometimes Tanya wondered if he was helpless at those sorts of tasks on purpose. The man could rope and shoe horses and haul bales. He could track animals by their hoof or paw prints, where they'd bedded, and their scat. But he couldn't maneuver a labeled grocery store aisle?

Tanya called bullshit.

The ride to town had been full of grating silence, so she'd made a deal with Pops that she'd let him hang out at the fish-and-bait shop while she did the shopping if he would drive the groceries home. She'd considered using the errand as an excuse to miss girls' night, but the truth was, she desperately needed to talk—not about Brady. But literally anything else.

She was already at the Tumbleweed when Kathy, Jess, and Liza entered, chatting and laughing, and Tanya sat up straighter and propped her lips up in a smile. She stood as they approached the table, and Kathy pulled her into a warm embrace.

"It feels like we've hardly seen you lately."

"I've just been, uh, busy with…" *Learning how to seduce your son and then blowing any chance I had by losing my temper.* Tanya reached up and twisted a curl around her finger. "The dude ranch and getting ready for our preshow rodeo."

"You and Brady. Always with the extra competitions."

His name caused Tanya's heart to stutter, and she forced out a laugh that morphed into a titter. In order to cover her awkwardness, she gave Jessica and then Liza hugs. "How are you gals?"

"I haven't burned anything this week," Jess proudly said.

Liza slumped into the nearest chair. "The twins have been extra rambunctious the past few days. They're egging one another on, and it's like if one makes a mess, the other has to outdo that mess, and I'm outnumbered."

The rest of their group settled into their seats, and Kathy reached across the table and patted Liza's hand. "Why don't you bring 'em on over to me when they're like that, hon? I don't mind givin' you a break."

"You do more than enough. I feel bad about how much you already watch them."

Kathy harrumphed. "If you recall, those were the terms of you taking the job. I provide the childcare."

"Yeah, during the day. Elise and Everett just came without one of those handy 'off' buttons for nighttime. Plus, I feel like I'm neglecting them too much as it is. They're angels for everyone else, and then we get home and it's like, *boom*." Liza slammed a palm down on the table. "Cranky nightmare children. It's been that way since they both cut out their naps. And if they do take one, they have even more energy, so I'm honestly not sure which is worse."

Liza rubbed her eyes and picked up her menu. "Just ignore me. I'm sleep-deprived and being melodramatic."

"No, you're not," Jess said, scooting her chair closer to Liza's and giving her a side hug. "It's overwhelming trying to balance it all, and then the mom guilt comes along for the ride. When I first came to the ranch, Kathy and I talked about how we women are the hardest on ourselves about mistakes, especially mothers. It's a lot of long hours and thankless work."

"And I'm so happy I have them." Liza's voice wavered and she blinked back tears. "I just want a tiny break and a full eight hours of sleep. I'd also love a partner instead of the deadbeat dad they have, but there's no use crying over spilled sperm, right?"

The ladies all burst into giggles.

Growing up, Tanya had felt the need to censor herself around Brady's mother, but during these meetups, Kathy had surprised her, allowing her to lower her guard and be herself. Same went for Liza and Jess, although she wasn't ready to confess to buying a self-help book and having a crush on the guy she'd insisted she was "just friends" with every time the women hinted at their chemistry.

Tanya felt the killer chemistry every damn time she was around him. *He* was the one who needed a hint or a smack upside the head.

Or maybe she needed a reality check.

Vaguely, Tanya noticed the attention had shifted to her.

"You're quiet," Jess said.

"Not a lot to add on the subject of babies. I have helped a few mama horses give birth, but that's about it."

"Whatever." Jess moved the happy-hour tent card advertising two-for-one drink specials out of the center of the table so they could see one another better. "You have all those overgrown baby businessmen to tend to."

Tanya chuckled. "True. Although Eric, the CEO who's been shadowing me, hasn't complained much—even when he came off the back of a horse—and has caught on quickly."

"Isn't that who you were here with the other night?" Jess asked, and Tanya's breath lodged in her throat.

"Ooh, you went on a date with some big-shot CEO?" Liza leaned closer. "I need details. Living vicariously through Jess was fun for a while, but she and Wade are practically an old married couple now."

"Speaking of," Kathy interjected. "We still need to pick a date for the wedding."

Jess winced, and Liza mouthed, *Sorry.*

Kathy was still staring at her son's fiancée intently, her lips pursing more by the second, and Jess twisted toward Tanya. "So about this Eric guy? Tell us more."

Now the eyes swiveled back to Tanya. She gave Jess a look, silently telling her *Thanks for throwing me under the bus.*

In return, Jess gave her an apologetic smile that relayed she was sorry but not sorry enough to take it back. After a few months with these ladies, they were getting the silent conversation down pretty well, although it'd never be as easy with them as with Brady.

Who Tanya was absolutely going to avoid thinking about, despite the overwhelming urge to ask if he'd said anything about that night. This was what she got for following a book with tips instructing her to be confident—as if she would buy a book on dating if she'd been confident in the first place. "It was just a business dinner. He inherited a ranch and wanted to talk logistics. There's nothing else to report."

The smile Kathy aimed Tanya's way didn't quite have its usual high-wattage glow. A hint of sorrow—or maybe regret—crept into the curve. Perhaps Tanya was imagining things, too paranoid they'd take a look at her and sense she was leaving out a big chunk of a story. *You see, I realized I'm in love with Brady, and when my course of action didn't immediately work, I yelled at him. Like a completely sane woman.*

Oh, and since he doesn't love me back, can you yell at him till he does?

Who needed a self-help book when she had access to Brady's mom? Not that Tanya would ever use that method. Come to think of it, if that method worked, she and Brady would be hitched by now.

Luckily, their waitress appeared. They rattled off their orders, one by one, until the waitress reached Jessica.

"I'll just have water," Jessica said.

If they were in a TV show, the record-scratch noise would've played. Not that Jess was a huge drinker, but after becoming a mom at sixteen and raising Chloe alone, she'd learned to let loose once a month. Normally, she ordered two margaritas at a time so she wouldn't have to wait for the bartender to mix another—not a lot of blending went on behind the bar at the Tumbleweed.

Jess fiddled with her dangly earrings and avoided making eye contact. "Hello, I'm the designated driver."

"*Hello,*" Liza said, mimicking her sarcasm and handing her the drink menu. "We'll be here long enough you can have one margarita."

Jess nudged the menu right back to Liza. "I'm fine."

"Well, at least order a pop or a coffee or something."

Jess shook her head. "No thanks. I don't feel like anything but water."

"I told you I'd drive us home, same as I drove us here," Kathy said.

"And I insisted that *I'd* drive us home. I know I popped the clutch last time, but I'm getting better at stick shift now. You can even ask Wade."

"She'll have that new watermelon margarita," Kathy said, and Jess told the waitress to only bring the one. The waitress stared at her motionless pen on the notepad, her expression conveying she didn't know what to do.

"I honestly don't feel like a margarita tonight, ladies. It's no big deal." Jess cranked her neck to address the befuddled waitress. "Can you put lemon in my water so I'm drinking something fancy enough for my friends to stop giving me grief?"

"You got it." Their waitress rushed off, and they talked about this, that, and the other until she showed up with their tray of drinks.

"Oh my gosh, this new watermelon margarita is amazing," Liza said, licking salt off her lip. She pushed the glass toward Jess. "You've got to try it."

Liza nudged it even closer, and Jess exhaled out her nostrils and shook her head. "The smell is just…" Jess shoved it away so fast that liquid sloshed over the side. "No, thank you."

Liza slowly dragged her glass back toward herself, but she kept her narrowed eyes on Jess. "Wait. You volunteered to be DD tonight."

"It's not like I never volunteer."

"Right, but you also volunteered last time."

Jess picked up one of the worn coasters, hyperfocusing on it as if it were profound literature. "You're welcome."

"Yeah, but you're acting weird. Like…" Liza threw her hands over her mouth. Kathy's eyes widened.

Tanya was lost.

"Are you?" Liza asked, her hands coming down as quickly as they'd flown to her mouth, and Jess glanced at Kathy.

Oh. The light bulb popped on in Tanya's head. No alcohol. When one of her cousins was pregnant, she'd also had a heightened sense of smell. Even things that smelled good would often send her running to the bathroom to puke.

"I, uh…" Jessica looked around, like a cow that'd been cornered and was trying to find a way out.

And Tanya was glad she hadn't said that aloud. No woman wanted to be compared to a cow.

Jess lifted her chin. "I'm taking the fifth and cashing in my phone-a-friend lifeline."

Kathy turned steady, interrogation-type eyes on Jess. "Honey, this ain't no game show. There are only two answers. Yes or no."

But Jessica had already extracted her phone and was dialing. Kathy made an excited squeaky noise as she bounced on her chair, making it rather obvious she'd be devastated if Liza had guessed wrong.

"Hey," Jess said, and then she rolled her eyes. "You weren't right exactly." Big sigh. "Okay, fine. But like I told you, they would've been just as suspicious if I didn't come with them tonight."

"I'm going to be a grandma?" Kathy shrieked.

"Did you hear that?" Jess asked into the phone. The entire bar sure had, and pretty soon, everyone in town was going to know. "Putting you on speaker now."

Wade's voice came from the phone Jess placed in the center of the table. "Hello, ladies. Ma."

"I'm a lady too," Kathy huffed, and he chuckled.

"I guess I should just say 'Hello, detectives.' So, big news. Jess and I are gonna have a…"

Everyone at the table held their breath.

"New fence built on the south end of the property," Wade finished.

"*What?*" Kathy barked into the phone, and if Tanya had been on the other end, she would've run, inability to reach through the device be damned.

"Yeah. Bright and early, so I need Jessica to be sober. Between digging holes, driving posts, and attaching rails, she's gonna need her strength."

The bar wasn't known as a quiet place, but in that moment, Tanya was sure they could've heard a pin drop.

A snort-laugh escaped Jessica. Then she said, "You see, once our baby gets here, we're going to need the extra protection so he or she doesn't run into the road."

Squeals erupted, along with a good-natured scolding from Kathy, followed by congratulations. Tanya was already envisioning a little Dawson toddling around the ranch. Naturally, the image in her mind changed to Brady. He scooped up the toddler, tossed the kiddo in the air, and then carefully placed his niece or nephew on a horse.

He'd be so good with kids. Here and there, Tanya had thought about children in the hazy, maybe someday future. She was hardly in spinster range, but she was creeping closer to the end of her twenties. There was still so much she wanted to do, though, and opening a rescue ranch sat at the tippy-top. If she had to go into a lot of debt, that'd be something else to consider, and why was her brain going there anyway?

Probably because she'd spent too much of her life waffling, and she was finally grabbing the reins and taking control. While she loved and appreciated her parents, she'd never be the doting wifey type. Once she managed to break free, the last thing she wanted was to be financially dependent on anyone ever again. Especially not a man. It threw off the power balance and left one party thinking they were entitled to make all the decisions.

Maybe the section of the book she'd rage skipped was right. She wasn't demure or super feminine, and she turned everything into a competition. Apparently everything about her, including her goals and all the trash-talking she did, meant she immediately put guys on the defensive, and that killed the allure.

Naturally, she'd discovered those tidbits while she was

smack-dab in the middle of one of her and Brady's infamous competitions. Since she'd involved several townsfolk who'd put in a lot of work, she couldn't exactly forfeit. Nor could she take back the trash talk. She wasn't sure her pride would allow her to do either, even if she could.

So if that were truly the case, she'd be firmly in the friend zone forever.

Chapter 11

THE BROWN-AND-WHITE-FACED STALLION BACKED INTO THE corner of the stall as Maddox approached. On his first day at the ranch—back when he'd tried to help the wild-eyed animal escape—he never would've guessed he'd pop in for visits.

"I was hoping to talk to you," Maddox said, dangling a carrot over the gate. They'd been doing this song and dance for the past week. While the horse obviously didn't do a lot of replying, there was something about saying things aloud. Somehow it felt less crazy talking to the cagey horse than to himself. Not to mention he had too many roommates and people surrounding him at all times for that.

Each day, it took less and less time for the horse to snatch the bait. Sure enough, the stallion cautiously trod over and nibbled the carrot. The loud crunch filled the air, inspiring the other horses to lift their heads in envy.

"Harlow wants to 'amp up the stakes' of our training with personal questions, and I'm not sure if I should." Maddox curled his hands around the top rung of the gate, nice and slow so he wouldn't startle the horse. "I'm sure you understand rocky pasts and the desire to avoid people who might hurt you. But I'm happier around her, and I want to make her happy, too."

The horse nickered, and Maddox slowly extended his hand. The stallion sniffed at it, but when Maddox tried to gently pet the horse, it backed away.

Right as he was about to declare it a sign he shouldn't play Harlow's game, the stallion came closer again. Almost as if he wanted affection but didn't know how to receive it.

And now he was assigning random feelings to a horse.

But when Maddox stepped down from the gate, the horse stuck its head over the top and sniffed again. He supposed if a wild stallion could take a chance on a guy like him, maybe he could be brave, too.

Less than an hour later, he gathered his courage and knocked on the open door of Nick's office. Ordinarily, he'd avoid the place at all costs, but Brady had come into the stables, and Maddox had run his idea by the guy. Unfortunately, he'd told him that Nick would have to clear it. Not great news, since so far, Maddox had connected more with the cowboy in charge of the rodeo training than with his counselor.

Probably sad considering Brady still eyed him suspiciously and Maddox assessed him much the same way, although he hid it better. At least Brady wasn't as stern as Wade and never pushed Maddox to spill his emotions and details about his past like Nick did.

All that working against him, his heart cranking as fast as a lug nut in an impact driver, and yet here he was anyway. Ready to grovel but trying not to let that show.

"Maddox, nice to see you. Did we have an appointment?" Nick shuffled papers around, moving them off one of those big desk calendars and tapping today's date.

"Nah. I just needed to ask you a question."

"Come on in."

Maddox wanted to say he'd rather not, but that probably wasn't the best way to get what he wanted. All because of a girl, too.

His boots seemed to weigh a hundred pounds each as he took a couple of steps inside, remaining closer to the door than the cushy couch that might lull him into a false sense of security. He licked his suddenly dry lips. "You know how Harlow and I have been training for the rodeo?"

Nick's face dropped, which didn't inspire a lot of confidence.

Might as well charge on with it. "Anyway, she came up with

this… I guess you'd call it a game. If I miss when we're roping, Harlow gets to ask me a question, and I have to answer it honestly."

A spark of interest flickered before Nick's expression morphed into his more neutral, contemplative one.

Okay, he didn't immediately shut me down. That's a good sign. I hope.

Maddox shoved his hands deep into his pockets, keeping his detached facade in place. "I thought I'd have her help me work on Miss Jessica's car. Whenever Harlow misses a part name or what it does, I get to ask *her* a question."

Nick propped his chin on his fist, unblinking eyes locked on Maddox. "I like the thought of you opening up to someone."

Ugh, *of course* he made it all about gushy feelings.

"I'll allow it," Nick said, and Maddox held his breath, "on a few conditions…"

The groan Maddox was supposed to keep trapped inside escaped. That earned him a scowl, so he straightened, as if that would inspire forgiveness. "Sorry. Force of habit."

"You need to start opening up in our sessions, too."

He'd rather jab a red-hot needle in his eye. "What if I say forget about it, then?"

The crooked smirk that spread across Nick's face made it clear Maddox had revealed too much. "I don't think you will."

The guy had him, and he knew it. Maddox's shoulders deflated. "Fine."

"Good. Now, here are the other rules." Nick ticked them off on his fingers. "No roping or working on the car after dark; the car needs to be lifted a few extra feet so you two aren't hidden from sight; and lastly…" A deadly serious edge hardened Nick's features and tone. "Harlow is a sweet girl. You hurt her, and we're gonna have a problem."

As much as Maddox hated rules, those particular ones were for the best. They'd keep him in check. He and Harlow were simply getting acquainted. It wasn't like he wanted to kiss her or anything.

Nope, those pink, heart-shaped lips didn't tempt him in the least. He definitely didn't want to press his mouth to them and take a tiny taste. The temperature in the room rose, and he worked to sustain his stony expression. "All right."

"All right." Nick straightened his stack of papers, tapping them against the desk to line them up. "And I'll expect you to be nice and chatty tomorrow morning."

The things I'm willing to do, all so I can spend an extra twenty minutes a day with a girl I absolutely don't want to kiss.

Chapter 12

Tanya: Meet me at our place?

IN HIS RELIEF OVER HER RESPONDING WITH SOMETHING besides "I need some time," Brady nearly dropped his phone in a fresh cow pie. The runt of a calf that'd been born late in the season circled back around to admire his steaming pile of handiwork, curious as a cat and about as finicky.

After bumbling around with his phone, Brady bit the fingertip of his glove and tugged his hand free of the leather so he could type a return—before Tanya changed her mind.

Brady: Give me five to ten to wrap up my day, and I'll
be on my way.

At least the chores were mostly finished. Maddox had returned to the boys' cabin about five minutes ago, so the kids were all accounted for, too. Trace was on lockup duty tonight, which left Brady free to latch the gate to the field he'd been working in and rush toward his pickup truck.

The sky grumbled, drawing his gaze upward. Roiling black clouds had rolled in this afternoon, turning rain from a possibility to a certainty. The crops needed the moisture, but he pleaded for the weather to hold out long enough that he could at least have his meetup with Tanya. She'd been acting as cagey as that wild stallion since storming out of the Tumbleweed, and Brady had planned on storming the dude ranch this evening if it came down to that. There was giving someone time, and then there was going crazy, and he was mighty close to that second thing.

It was for you, you asshole.

The words had slammed into him, rousing his carnal side. Just like that, the friendship switch fully flipped, desire going from a flicker to blinding in an instant. As if it'd been there all along, and the dam holding it back had finally burst.

His first instinct had been to charge after her, yank her to him, and kiss the hell out of her, but even as his internal organs rampaged, an unexpected amount of fear had frozen him in place. Restraint had never been his specialty, but he didn't want to clamor through one of the most important relationships in his life like a bull in a china shop. He'd seen too many broken people in his day, usually as a result of those who claimed to love them.

The shocks in his truck loudly complained as Brady drove the familiar, bumpy path. He pulled up to the large cottonwood, and his headlights illuminated the redheaded woman leaning against the trunk.

The two years she'd been at college had been the loneliest he'd ever felt—surrounded by a ranch full of people, no less. Back then, he and Nash had competed in about any and every rodeo that'd have them. In the quiet moments, though, he'd felt the gaping absence of her in his daily life.

Whatever you do, do not *screw this up.*

If the band around his chest grew any tighter, it'd snap him clean in half. Brady pushed out the door of the truck, his footsteps loud in the stillness. "No horse?"

"Felt like a walk."

Weirdness choked the air, and this was exactly what he'd feared the most. That no matter which way things went, he'd lose an amazing friendship that went so much deeper they needed a new word for it.

Since Tanya wasn't taking the lead on the conversation—the norm for whoever had called the meetup—Brady inclined his head toward the bed of the truck. At her nod, he opened the tailgate, sat, and patted the spot next to him.

Tanya hopped up, the pickup barely bouncing with her weight, and her scent mixed with the smell of the looming rain.

Once they were settled in place, the crickets picked up their evening melody. Brady listened, counting the chirps as he watched the second hand on his watch. The oncoming storm meant the air was cooler, so their chirps were slower, and he counted until his watch hit thirteen seconds.

"Twelve chirps plus forty means it's about fifty-two degrees," he said, as if it were a normal night and the temperature was the most pressing matter. "When you think about it, crickets have it so easy."

Tanya lowered her eyebrows. "Crickets?"

This was a perfect example of what happened when a bull took the lead, but in for a dime, in for a dollar. "Yeah. The dude just rubs his legs together and *boom*, the females are so impressed at the racket that *they* come to find *him*."

Sputtered laughter erupted from Tanya, dissipating the awkwardness in the air between them. Then she lay all the way back in the bed of the truck, not a care to the dirt and hay dust. Her hair contrasted with the dark plastic lining and, with the extra humidity in the air, her curls were bigger than ever, wild and untamed. His fingers twitched with the urge to plow through all that silky, fiery red. "Human males have it easy, too," she said.

Brady lay next to her, clinging to the normalcy of the move, even though he couldn't help being keenly aware of the brush of their arms and the way her breasts rose and feel with each breath. "How so?"

"Oh, please." The dim light of the moon played across her features, softening one and then the other as the clouds muted its glow. "All you have to do is grin or flex, and females come running."

"And all women have to do is smile and bat their eyes. Maybe add a hair flip."

She rolled to face him and propped her cheek on her fist. "I, uh, tried that. You thought I had something in my eye."

A snort-laugh escaped, and Tanya began to pull away. Brady tugged her to him and guided her head onto his shoulder, and then he secured an arm around her waist to prevent any further attempts to flee. "In my defense, that was eye twitching if I ever did see it. Winking goes more like…"

Brady lifted his head an inch or two and gave her an exaggerated wink.

Evidently, his skills weren't what they used to be, because the muscles in her jaw tightened as she shook her head.

He twisted his neck so they were nose to nose. "Talk to me, Yaya. It feels like you're mad at me."

"I *am* mad at you."

"For which part?" he asked, since he didn't doubt she had a reason to be. Once he learned where he'd messed up, he could apologize for it and then they could figure out the rest—they had to. Honestly, that was the main reason he hadn't even let himself indulge in the idea of more. It was a lot to risk, and that was if he hadn't already gone and ruined it.

"I'm pissed at you for not reading my mind, okay? And I know that's silly. It's just I had all these expectations of you noticing how pretty I looked and that somehow my newfound flirting skills would unlock this, like, secret desire. I guess I sorta hoped that after I'd put in all that effort, you'd read the signs and do the rest."

Brady drifted his fingers down the soft skin on her arm and folded her hand into his. "Is that still what you want? Because I can't read your mind. There's a lot at stake, so I need you to tell me."

Tanya buried her face against his shoulder, causing her words to come out muffled. "I… Now that this conversation is finally happening, I'm trying not to freak out. I get it. It's complicated, and in typical fashion, I made it—and everything really—messier than it should be. That's before I add on a whole other issue that I didn't realize I had before today, even though I really should've."

"Uh, how long till we get to the part where you tell it to me straight?" Patience was for people with time, and he didn't have reserves of either of those things.

The curls obscuring her features fell away as she lifted her head to show him her responding scowl. Instead of taking it personally, he studied the constellations in her eyes. Namely, the two brown freckles in the green of her right eye. Then he upped the intensity of his prodding gaze, silently conveying he could last all night if need be.

Last all night. Best think of another way of phrasing it before my thoughts go to... He worked to temper his body's reaction to the idea of going down that road.

"Okay, so..." Tanya sat up, and he followed her lead. She filled him in on Phoenix and how that experience had unearthed a desire to open a rescue ranch. He flinched as she relayed her father's reaction and experienced a pang when her voice cracked. "For the first time in a long time, I let passion sweep me away and leaped before formulating some grand plan. I should've known he'd shoot it down."

Brady wrapped his hand around her knee. "Hey. You have to keep on trying. Regardless of your dad being a stubborn old bear. Truth be told, I always thought your passion was one of your best qualities. Made you a top competitor, too."

Her lips twisted as several emotions flickered across her face. Was she...? Panic bled through his body. She was going to cry, something he hadn't witnessed since they were kids and it was acceptable to shed tears over scraped knees. Crying women made every one of his internal sensors go berserk. He didn't know how to make it better or if it was something you should or shouldn't acknowledge, and whichever method he tried, it always ended up being the wrong one.

"I appreciate you saying so, but it feels like I'm launching disasters at every turn. I dared to suggest an idea not in line with 'the way we've done it at Bullhead Valley for generations.' After Pops stormed out, I begged my mom to try to talk some sense into him, and her refusal left us both frustrated. As if that wasn't bad enough, I also yelled at my best friend in a bar and made it weird... Sorry about that."

"Eh, I probably deserved it," Brady said. "Seeing you with that guy brought out my caveman side, and it was a dick move to make you feel bad about looking so damn sexy."

"Sexy, even?" Tanya sank her teeth into her lower lip, and then Brady's thoughts turned to closing the gap between their mouths so he could take over the biting for her. "You seriously thought so? Before or after I drew attention to it?"

"Yes to all of the above." He dipped his head, imploring her gaze with his. "For the record, I've always thought you were beautiful. Dirty, clean. Straight hair, curly hair, dresses, T-shirt and jeans, and everything in between."

"Wow," she said on a shallow breath, "that definitely amps up the tug-of-war I'm having with myself. One side is caught up in a cocky yet charming cowboy and the possibility of what might be, and the other side won't stop hitting itself against the wall in an attempt to come up with a genius business plan my Pops can't refuse. It took me way too long to figure out my life's calling, but rescuing horses is it. I feel it in my bones."

"Just build the stables on my property and run it from there." On top of allowing a lot of input, his parents gave each of their sons a cabin with three acres of land on their eighteenth birthday. Tanya's parents expected her to practically run the entire dude ranch operation for meager room and board—while constantly vetoing her ideas. "Boom, problem solved. You're welcome."

The perfect solution—one he'd hoped would prevent

tears—yet Tanya scowled, her upset expression leading him to believe he'd offended her somehow. She'd accused him of over-stepping before, and he reckoned it was about to happen again.

"You can't just offer up your land, Brady. Plus, if we cross lines, there will be all these extra strings."

Offense socked him in the gut. "Extra strings? I'm not offering to help contingent on anything. Is that really the kind of guy you think I am?"

Tanya placed her hand on his cheek, soothing the storm inside, while the wind picked up on the one Mother Nature was ready to unleash.

"'Added pressure' is a more accurate term. Our lives are already so entwined, and not talking to you for a few days shone a big, ol' spotlight on how much I stand to lose if things go badly." One corner of her mouth quirked as she picked at a stray thread on her jeans. "I got so desperate I attempted to discuss everything with Winston, who didn't give a single helpful suggestion and hobbled off halfway through."

"That lopsided punk," Brady said with a laugh, and Tanya's tin-kling laughter joined his.

Time froze again, the heaviness in the air shifting from the ear-lier awkwardness to a hum of acknowledged desire.

Tanya licked her lips, and Brady's rapid pulse roared though his head, loud enough it outdid the clap of thunder. "So *I'll* figure out a way to open a horse-rescue ranch. Honestly, all I want you to do is listen and hug me and tell me it'll be okay, even though that's probably unfair of me to ask of you with everything up in the air between us."

Brady drew her into his arms and lightly pressed his lips to her temple, not kissing but lingering and inhaling and once again working to keep his body in check. Damn, this might be harder than he realized, comforting her while wondering if their connec-tion could get even better. "It'll all be okay. You'll find a way. And I'll be there, giving whatever support you need once you do."

Tanya let herself melt into Brady's embrace. She soaked in the scent of his skin: grass and sunshine and musky cologne.

During the last three hours, her heart had grown heavier and heavier until suddenly she was in the middle of texting Brady. Since hashing things out might mean the end for at least one of her dreams, she'd planned on dragging her feet a while longer. But she'd felt lost without her other half.

Finally, she and Brady were in the same place after five days of not-rightness.

Was she truly ready to leap off the cliff? Right now, she wasn't sure. Not without getting a better look at the bottom. He hadn't exactly been forthright about his feelings on the subject. Sure, he'd called her sexy and beautiful, but he didn't say he was ready for more than friendship. In fact, he'd stated there was a lot at stake before lobbing the ball back to her side of the court with his "I need you to tell me."

Brady had a bit of a hero complex. Always had. In order to make her happy, he might just convince himself into feeling more so he wouldn't let her down. She didn't want pity attraction. It was the real deal or nothing, and as his fingertips skated up and down her spine, she hesitated to do anything that'd put moments like this at risk.

Each corresponding zing that shivered down her core, however, beseeched her not to give up on the idea of them as a couple.

Tanya sniffed and broke the hug. She swung her legs through the air in an attempt to trick her body into resuming proper functions yet again.

Silence descended, leaving just the crickets and their noisy, mate-attracting legs. Tanya stole a peek at Brady… And how dare he look so sexy in his pale-blue denim button-down! It shouldn't go with his Wranglers, but his jeans were a couple shades darker, and his belt and buckle separated all the blue and called attention to how ridiculously buff he was. The fabric made his baby blues stand out, too. He didn't have on his cowboy hat, but she could see the faint indentation of where it'd been.

All those mouthwatering details compiled a rather sound case for closing her eyes and jumping on in. He cracked a smile, and that swoonworthy rivet formed in his cheek. For months, she'd been tempted to touch it, so she indulged, swiping the pad of her thumb over the indentation.

His warm breath whooshed across her wrist, and the world ground to a halt. Pressure built, inside and around them, until her head throbbed with it. Brady's palm drifted down her arm, and her skin hummed under the whisper of his roughed fingertips.

Emotion after emotion whirled through her, the internal tornado leaving her on the brink of insanity.

Rain splatted the top of her head—one drop, then another— and she remained perfectly still, afraid moving or speaking would break the spell. Water splashed her arm. Her cheek. A fat droplet hit her lashes and clung there.

"Storm's starting," Brady said, his voice gruff, and for the first time, she let herself believe that he might be as affected by her as she was by him.

"Just a little while longer," she whispered. If they left the special place that'd belonged to them for as long as they'd belonged to each other, reality would creep in. There'd be overthinking and other variables, and she wanted another minute to bask in the abundance of possibility that hung in the air.

The rainstorm increased its tempo, but Brady didn't budge. He was taking most of the splatters, tucking her head under his chin and acting as her very own human umbrella.

A forked bolt streaked through the inky sky, close enough that static electricity raised the hair on her arms. Thunder boomed a couple of seconds later, and then the gray clouds released every ounce of water they'd been withholding at once.

Water seeped into her jeans, and Tanya let loose a tiny squeak. "What are you waiting for? Let's get inside the truck!"

"*Me?* You said you wanted to stay out here, so I was waiting for you."

Lightning flashed, the world going bright for an instant before darkness reigned once again. Almost as quickly, Brady launched himself off the tailgate. He extended a hand her way, tugged her out of the bed of the truck, and pushed her in front of him. He propelled her toward the driver's side door, and she yanked it open and climbed in, Brady hot on her heels.

The wet clothes made it hard to slide across the vinyl seat, and Brady sat halfway on her lap. She wheezed as her lungs struggled for air. "Oh my gosh, you're heavy."

"And you're slow." He stood as much as he could, but quarters were tight between the low roof and the steering wheel. "Scooch over."

"I'm trying. It's just that—"

Brady yanked her a few inches off the seat, flopped down, and then lowered her until *she* was on *his* lap. Tanya blinked at the water pouring down the windshield in streams, wondering how Brady had managed that maneuver in such a tiny space.

Then the heat of his body seeped into her, counteracting the cold rivulets that dripped from her hair, meandered down the front of her shirt, and slid between her breasts. The glass in front of her fogged, and she eyed the other side of the cab, torn on whether to stay put or move aside.

As if he sensed she might be second-guessing things, Brady's arm snaked around her waist. He secured her tighter to him, his chest bumping her back every time he took a breath. Awareness pricked her skin, and then she was acutely conscious of his solid thighs underneath hers, and… She sucked in a sharp inhale as he spread his fingers, his thumb and forefinger slipping under the hem of her T-shirt.

Had he meant to do that?

A strangled noise came from his throat as she twisted to get a read on him. Droplets clung to his hair and eyelashes, and his shirt was plastered to his chest the same way she wanted to be. She saw the moment he went to shutter his features, but he dropped his walls instead, allowing her a glimpse at the naked passion on his face.

Her heart expanded, and *holy shit*, could he truly want her as much as she wanted him?

His breath wafted across her neck, a stark contrast to the cold rainwater clinging to their skin. "You'd better tell me what you want, because I'm mighty close to crossing a line."

Every one of her organs forgot how to function at once. His lips grazed the shell of her ear, and goose bumps swept across her skin. "Let's maybe try a kiss and go from there?"

Brady caught her chin between his finger and his thumb. "That could be arranged."

He tilted his head and leaned closer, but they'd gone the same way. Or the opposite way. "Wait. You go right? Usually, I go left, so…"

Their faces didn't align well, and this so wasn't how she envisioned their first kiss going. In her head, there'd been fireworks, instinct, and fluidity, as if their lips were always meant to find each other.

"Just go right then," Brady grunted.

Nope. This wasn't how it was supposed to go at all. "Why am I the one who has to change? You go—"

"For hell's sake, woman." Brady slipped his large hand behind her neck and guided her lips to his. He dug his thumb into the line of her jaw, applying enough pressure to tilt her head the way she'd sworn she wasn't going to go. As their hungry mouths moved against each other, her center of gravity shifted, tethering itself to this man, this moment, and the exquisite things he did with his tongue.

The temperature of the cab skyrocketed, the windows going from steamy to a heavy fog.

Brady pressed that unyielding thumb to her pulse point once again, tipping up her chin and exposing her neck to his whiskered mouth. Teeth and soft lips, and Tanya felt him growing hard against her butt. Since he'd used his strength to control her head, she was going to see how he liked it. She pushed against his impressive length, fire igniting low in her belly at his groan.

The next thing she knew, she was on her back on the bench seat, Brady's large body looming over her, forearms braced on either side of her head. He swept her wet curls off her face, his gaze boring into hers for several incredible seconds before he resumed the kissing.

One of his thighs slipped between both of hers and pressed against the bundle of nerves that'd throbbed to life. She arched her hips, craving more friction, more of him. "More."

Brady thrust his tongue inside her mouth, tasting and stroking, and an involuntary whimper escaped as she ground against his muscular thigh. He shifted his weight to his left arm and dragged a thumb over one of her hardened nipples, visible through the wet fabric of her shirt and simple white bra.

He moved to the other breast, plucking and tweaking, and she came clean off the seat.

"Good to know," he said, as if he were cataloging what she liked—which at this point, was pretty much every move he had. He captured her bottom lip between both of his and sucked until dizziness set in.

Cool, humid air prickled her skin as he wadded her shirt in his large hand and dragged it up, up, up. In order to avoid hyperfocusing on the fact that she was only in a bra—and the rain had rendered it see-through—she fumbled with the buttons of his shirt. A week ago, she'd caught a glimpse of those pecs and abs, and yet her breath still caught as she peeled away the damp cotton. Manual labor helped her stay in shape, but it made Brady appear as if he'd been chiseled in stone.

The guy pinning her to the seat had been her best friend for as long as she could remember. He'd seen her through frizzy hair and braces and that one summer she'd decided to bleach her locks—it only half took, so she'd looked like Chester Cheetah. She could also recall the days when Brady's front two teeth were missing and then grew in too big for his mouth. Days of overly gelled hair and too much cologne.

There'd been lanky Brady, optimistically-attempting-to-grow-a-beard Brady. Then he'd filled out and morphed into the rugged, absurdly sexy man he was.

He scrutinized her, perhaps recalibrating things in his brain the same way. Pondering their new...well, not normal. But maybe eventually it would be, and that left her teetering on the edge of hope, unsure whether to embrace the thrill of the fall or slam the brakes.

Torturously slowly, Brady skirted his callused fingertips across her collarbone. "So we tried the kissing." Another swipe had her clenching her thighs. Losing her mind. With his pupils so dark and dilated, they nearly overtook the blue.

In a dreamlike stance, she reached out and touched the center of his chest. Real. Warm. Steady heartbeat. Her Brady, in the way she'd imagined for months. "Is it just me, or are we really good at the kissing?"

One corner of his mouth kicked up. "That's just me."

She smacked him on the arm but failed at stifling a giggle. She ran her gaze over his broad shoulders, across his pecs, and down to the V of his obliques. Then her fingertips traced the path her eyes had taken. Shoulders, chest, down his abs...

His muscles twitched beneath her touch. *Be bold. The meek might inherit the earth, but the brazen will get the guy.* Her stomach had bottomed out as she'd read that chapter, and she'd shaken her head over and over. In the silence of her room, she'd asked if she seriously had to be someone she wasn't to get the guy.

But with the guy responding to every little touch, she found she could, in fact, be both bold and brazen. "Well, if you'll recall, I did promise that I'd show you mine if you showed me yours."

Brady's thick swallow echoed through the cab. "You weren't talking about belt buckles?"

"Nope." Tanya's fingertips strayed to the waistband of his Wranglers, where she glided them back and forth, back and forth. Brady groaned, the bulge behind his zipper growing even bigger. The only reason she'd tell herself to wait after a make-out that hot would be because she needed to get to know a guy better.

This guy she practically knew better than herself. Which gave her an idea. "You should remove my bra." She affected a ditzy front and twisted a curl around her finger. "Unless you're chicken."

At first, she thought he was simply shifting his weight from one side to the other, but suddenly her bra gave away. He gripped it in the center, right over the little bow, and yanked it off.

Her heart hammered at a punishing pace, and adrenaline inundated her system, heightening every sensation. Euphoria was within reach. Finally, she was exactly where she wanted to be, only her worries didn't magically disappear, and she couldn't not address them. "I know I implied you might be yellow, as if I were all badass and ready for it, but I might also be a pinch scared. I don't want things to get weird or to ruin what we have. And yes, I realize I should've said this *before* I ended up having to say it topless."

"Feel free to tell me things while topless anytime." The smile he flashed her was familiar yet new, with a hint of kindness and understanding she'd caught glimpses of whenever he worked with the teens at Turn Around Ranch. "Messing up this"—he gestured between them—"is the last thing I want to do. You're in the driver's seat. Same way you were at prom when I kissed you and you let me know you didn't want that."

"Wait, what?" she automatically responded, even as a memory from a decade ago began to take shape. "Oh, yeah. You totally attack kissed me that night. How'd I forget about that?"

"Ouch. Guess my ego needed taking down a few notches."

"Hey, this is karma for claiming all the credit for how good we are at kissing," she teased, placing a hand on his biceps. "I honestly thought you just didn't know how to say goodbye, so you thought kissing was the way to go. Are you saying…? How long have you felt…whatever you feel?"

He chuckled, and she did her best not to be offended, because if he avoided the question again, she was going to activate the flashlight on her phone and interrogate him. She'd get it on video to later analyze, too. He sat back, and her body screamed *noooo*. "You've never thought of crossing lines before?"

With the conversation going on longer than expected, she felt extra naked, so she sat up and secured an arm over her breasts. "It's all I've thought about for months!" Okay, that slipped out rather ungracefully, but playing it cool had never been in her skill set. "The past five or six months, for the record. I'm not sure precisely when it started. I tried to shut the notion right down, but you're you, and I…" She shrugged. "I couldn't seem to stop it."

"Why didn't you tell me?"

"Why didn't you tell me at prom?"

"You shoved me away. I figured kissing you told you well enough, and you answered right back with a loud-and-clear *no*. Which I totally respect. After that, I deleted you from the list of possibilities. Over the years, yeah, the thought occasionally flickered, but as you're well aware, I'm also a bit of a skeptic about love and the way people wield that word these days."

Every emotion she'd experienced since climbing into the truck completed a full one-eighty. Talk about internal whiplash.

Brady cupped her cheek as she reached for a shirt—his or hers, she didn't care, as long as she covered up her exposed body and emotions ASAP. "*But* I don't want to always have to wonder, either. Better to take our shot in the arena instead of sitting and dreaming on the sidelines. Wasn't that our motto?"

Warmth suffused her, reassuring her frayed nerves. This was another version of Brady. The pro-rodeo companion who'd pushed, validated, and given her pep talks before big events.

She'd already wondered what-if for way too long, and she could kick herself for not saying or doing something sooner.

Then again, sitting in the homey cab of Brady's truck, her heart beating as fast as a hummingbird's wings, the timing felt right. Like maybe it wasn't quite right before. Or maybe there was no perfect time and you just had to seize moments. "I say we take our shot. If that's what you want."

"I do," he said, and relief tumbled through her.

Before she allowed herself to surrender to his magnetic pull, she placed a hand on the side of his face and anchored herself in his gaze. "Just swear we'll remain friends no matter what."

Brady twisted his head and kissed the center of her palm, and her heart melted into a puddle of happy goo. "I swear. Now, do we need to discuss anything else before the intermission comes to a close?"

"I think we've done more than enough talking." She curled her fingers into his waistband and tugged him on top of her until their bodies were flush, shoulders to thighs.

He kissed her lips, along her jaw, and the column of her neck. The tip of his tongue darted out, and her hips automatically arched into his. "Yeah, this tastes like a very good idea." He lightly abraded her skin with his teeth as he undid the button on her jeans, lowered her zipper, and palmed her over her panties.

"Brady." She licked her lips, a thrill going through her when his gaze tracked the motion like a predator waiting to pounce. "If you don't get on with it, I'm gonna accuse you of being chicken again."

His knee slammed into the gearshift as he advanced, the loud *whack* followed by a string of swear words. Tanya giggled, and then they both burst into laughter. This so wasn't how she imagined sleeping with Brady Dawson would go, and yet it was *so them*. At their meetup spot between their two ranches, in the truck they'd driven to countless rodeos and horse sales, the pitter-patter of rain providing a steady soundtrack that drowned out the rest of the world.

She recalled his earlier joke about the crickets. "See? You don't have to work very hard to get into a girl's pants. I didn't even make you rub your legs together."

Brady's ear-to-ear grin caused her heart to skip a couple of beats. "Probably for the best, as the situation in my pants would make it rather painful to rub my legs together anyway."

"Guess I'd better help you with that, then." Due to his insistent erection, undoing the button on his Wranglers required a bit of extra work. He let loose a massive sigh as she lowered the zipper and he sprang free of the tighter fabric.

One by one, his boots thumped to the floor, and then the only sound was the swoosh of fabric as he wriggled free of his jeans. The boxer briefs plastered to his muscular thighs did little to conceal his arousal, and desire thrummed through her until her body vibrated from it.

He yanked off her boots, and poor unfortunate soul that she was, she had to sit up slightly and stare right at his package as he got to work on her pants. The wet denim stuck to her legs, but when Brady was determined, he didn't let anything slow him down.

A stupid thread of nervousness stitched its way through her once only their underwear remained. It'd been a while, and now she was thinking she should've worn sexier underwear. When was the last time she'd even trimmed her bikini area?

Brady ran a fingertip from the center of her chest, down between her breasts, sending those thoughts far, far away to where they belonged. He flattened a palm to her stomach and gazed at her exposed body. "Damn, Yaya. Sexy doesn't even begin to describe it."

Dizziness set in. Oxygen no longer mattered.

She was seriously about to explode from the amount of love swelling within her. She squirmed, unable to wait even one second longer, and let out a pleading whimper.

"Don't worry, sweetheart. I'll take care of you." Brady glided his fingertips the rest of the way down her stomach, taking a quick dip into her belly button, before finally—blessedly—wandering beneath her panties.

His mouth came over hers as he touched the spot that'd been begging for attention since he'd dared to stop touching her. At her strangled noise of pleasure, he increased the pressure and tempo.

With his free hand, he tugged her panties down around her thighs and continued his ministrations until she was a delirious, needy mess. Another stroke, another kiss, and then she was adrift on a sea of bliss, Brady her lifeline.

Slowly and tenderly, he brought her down. Pride radiated off him, and if she could figure out how to get her tongue to work, she'd call him a cocky cowboy again.

He locked eyes with her as his thumb flitted across her lower lip. "You okay?"

"Mm-hmm. Better than okay. Amazing. Reeling. Eagerly awaiting more."

"More, huh?"

Considering how pleased he was with himself, Tanya figured it was time for some sexual retribution. She gripped his arousal over his underwear and applied pressure.

His eyes rolled back, and he thrust into her hand as if he couldn't help himself. A lot of times in her work life, she'd felt powerless. The rodeo circuit was the only place she'd felt completely in control, but this went beyond even that. She'd never felt so sexually empowered, and she found that she really, really liked it.

"What were you saying?" she asked once she remembered she'd been in the middle of proving a point.

"Nothing." He groaned and worked his hips again. "Nothing at all."

"That's what I thought," she said, reaching into his boxers and taking him in hand, no pesky fabric in the way. "I do hope you brought a condom."

"Me too," Brady said, and that effectively popped her smug balloon. He leaned over her, opened the glove box, and shuffled around papers. "Aha. We're in luck. I have three."

"Ambitious," she joked, which was much easier with her libido mollified. She was far too turned on not to have sex with this man.

"This has been a long time coming," Brady said as he rolled on one of the condoms. "I think 'making up for lost time' is a better word for it."

"That's"—she lifted her fingers and counted—"five words."

Brady lowered his head so that his lips brushed hers as he spoke. "If you can still count, clearly I haven't given you enough orgasms." He kissed her hard on the mouth and poised himself at her slick, ready entrance. "Sounds like I'd better fix that."

Chapter 13

LIFE WAS MADE UP OF LITTLE MOMENTS, MOST OF THEM ORDI-
nary and expected. But then there were bigger moments, like that
instant before a roller coaster soared downward after taking you
to its highest point. Holding your breath in the chute at a rodeo
before the buzzer went off and you had to charge into the arena
and lay it all on the line.

Free-fall moments.

Make-or-break moments.

Extraordinary moments that could change everything.

This was all of those rolled into one, and Brady took another
second to marvel at the image of Tanya, naked and underneath
him, her damp curls spread out on the seat of his truck. It was an
image he'd hold on to forever, no matter what happened next.

He pushed inside her, groaning at how incredible she felt. How
right *everything* about this felt. Her lips tempted him closer, and
he lowered his mouth to hers, mimicking the movement of their
bodies with his tongue.

Her nails dug into his skin, testing the bounds of his self-
restraint. Especially after all the buildup and flip-flopping of emotions during their earlier discussion. Since ridding her of her shirt,
it'd been difficult to think of anything besides getting his hands on
her. He palmed one of her breasts, massaging it and pinching one
of her sensitive nipples.

Like earlier, she came off the seat, and he slammed all the way
in to the hilt. Tanya tensed beneath him, and black dots danced
across his vision. It'd be so easy to lose himself to the barrage of
intoxicating sensations, but he held on until she cried out his
name and shuddered around him.

The instant she went pliant underneath him, he let go.

His orgasm ripped through him, fast and hard. His fuzzy vision didn't sharpen immediately, and it took a couple of blinks to realize the fog on the windows was so thick he couldn't see anything outside his truck anymore.

Not a surprise, considering their rapid breaths and the steamy temperature inside the cab. Feeling slowly returned to his limbs, and Brady flopped to Tanya's side. They barely fit on the narrow seat, and he secured an arm around her middle to prevent himself from accidentally bumping her off.

Then he pressed a kiss to the nape of her neck. "Am I cleared of all previous charges if I give *you* credit for the amazing sex? Because hot damn, woman. You and I should've done that long ago."

Tanya spun to face him, her breasts squishing against his chest. "I'll take full responsibility." He lightly smacked her on the ass, and a wanton smile spread across her kiss-swollen lips. "If that's my punishment, I'm afraid I didn't learn my lesson."

She was absolutely perfect for him, and why the hell did it take him so long to see it? Although like he'd said, he'd forced himself to repress it for a while, on account of his mama raising him to respect women and their wishes. In hindsight, he might've gone overboard tuning out that frequency when it came to Tanya. "I reckon it's better this way. My teenage self wouldn't have been nearly as impressive."

"Wow. Your humility lasted for all of"—she glanced at her watchless wrist—"five seconds. Admittedly, if I'm picking and choosing, I'd rather *that* be the super short thing as opposed to your stamina."

Before he could conjure a retort, she planted a kiss on his lips that short-circuited his brain. Sex with Tanya managed to be both incredible and comfortable, the afterglow stimulating yet completely natural.

This could actually work. We take things slow and see how they go, and… The haze that'd obscured reality began to clear, and he wished for it back. "Shit. I just thought of something we probably should've discussed earlier."

She tensed, and he wondered if the thud in his chest was from his accelerating heart rate or hers.

"If our families get wind of this, they're going to be all up in our business and super pushy. Like jump right to wedd—" The word snagged on the way out, and he cleared his throat and tried again. "—big plans kinda pushy. There'll be many refrains of 'I knew it' and 'I told you that you were in love with her.'"

Tanya sucked in a sharp inhale, and hell, had he just implied…? Not that he didn't love her, but being in love with her and confessing that kind of thing was putting the cart before the horse. No matter how many breaths he attempted, his lungs couldn't get their fill.

"Hey." Tanya placed her hand on his cheek, same way she'd done before to center him. "We don't have to pay them any mind. This isn't about them. It's about us."

He nodded. "Okay. That's just a whole other level, and I want us to be able to enjoy the beginning exciting stage."

"I get that. So maybe we just keep it to ourselves for a while?"

"At least until after our friendly rodeo competition. We don't want to end up looking like clowns instead of cowboys." His mind whirred, spinning over how tricky it was to hide anything in Silver Springs. And after he'd experienced how amazing it could be, not seeing her in this capacity wasn't an option. "We should go to the state fair in Ogallala weekend after next. Nash asked if we'd come watch and cheer him on. No one will think twice about us going, and Nash can keep a secret if need be. He's the last guy who'll suggest settling down. Then we can have a weekend away to explore this. Once we open the doors to our family and the town, the complications will be plenty, the peaceful times few and far between."

She wrinkled her nose, and while that was more adorable than it had any right to be, he worried he'd somehow said the wrong thing again. Then he realized he knew this woman better than anybody.

"Phoenix will be okay. Fridays evenings are pretty hectic at the ranch, but we can head out bright and early on Saturday morning and be home late Sunday night. I'll also have Aiden and Chloe check on your mare and send daily reports," he said, and when the nose remained scrunched, he tapped it and added, "Twice a day."

"You have yourself a deal, Mr. Dawson. Pleasure doing business." Despite not having on a cowboy hat, she tipped the invisible brim at him. "Now, if you'll be so kind as to hold me in place so I don't fall while attempting to gather my clothes?"

"Who says I'm gonna let you get dressed ever again?"

Tanya wriggled against him. "It's late. And I'm getting cold."

"I have a solution for the latter that'll convince you to forget the former." Brady hauled her against him, so she couldn't miss that he was well and ready for round two. "Plus, I feel like that jab about using all the condoms was a challenge, and you know I can't back down from those."

"It wasn't a challenge," she rasped as he hooked his hand under her knee and closed that last millimeter of space. Her eyelids fluttered closed as he dug his face into the crook of her neck and nibbled at the silky softness there. "You don't have to win every single time, you know."

"The best thing about tonight is that we're both gonna win."

Chapter 14

ON FRIDAY AFTERNOON, HARLOW TOLD HERSELF TO PAY attention to the words Maddox was saying instead of the way his muscles flexed as he pointed to the parts underneath the car and rattled off their names and functions.

His arm came to rest against hers, evoking that fresh-from-the-roller-coaster feeling. "Are you even listening?" he asked, his low voice booming through her like the steady bass in a hip-hop song.

"Yes?"

He sighed, and even though she never would've thought the word *adorable* could describe someone like Maddox Mikos, there was no other word for him. "What's that part, then?" he asked.

"The radiator pipe thingy?"

"*Ahhhn*, wrong," he said, mimicking the buzzer on a game show. "Looks like it's my turn for a question."

"Wait. How is it fair that I'm the one who suggested this game, and you get to ask the first question?"

"I don't make the rules; I just follow them."

"Both of those statements are false," Harlow said with a shake of her head. She was going to emerge with rocks, dirt, and grass in her hair. Being dirty after a day of roping and riding was hardly new; however, curling her hair *before* she came to train at the Dawsons' ranch was.

Obviously, she'd lost her mind.

Maddox asked for the wrench at her side, and she handed it over. Their fingers brushed, and static electricity streaked up her arm. Either her body was going to get used to Maddox's light touches, deep voice, and nearness, or she'd eventually explode from the combination.

Ending up in rubble should probably concern her more than it did, but as she studied his profile, she thought it might be worth it.

"Who was the guy you were talking about with Chloe the other day while Aiden and I were discussing bikes?"

It took Harlow a couple of seconds to connect the dots. After their last training session, Aiden and Maddox had launched into a discussion on motorcycles, and Chloe had looped her arm through Harlow's and led her over to the porch.

As they'd settled on the middle step, Chloe asked about team roping. Harlow replied that her partner, Bianca, recently dumped her, bulldozing her out of her favorite event in the process. Not to mention ruining a shot at the All-Around Cowgirl title she'd had her sights set on since middle school.

Tears had welled, and Chloe shocked a laugh out of Harlow by asking, "Where can I find this bitch?"

No one had ever threatened anyone on Harlow's behalf, and while she should be above it, it felt nice. So Harlow told her Bianca had also accused her of flirting with her boyfriend, even though she didn't know how to flirt and sure as heck wouldn't pick him since he was a cheater and a jerk.

"Well, she sucks, and so does he," Chloe had replied, and Harlow had raised an imaginary glass to toast to that. Since the boys had finished up their conversation and were drifting closer, they'd heard Chloe when she stood and added, "Oh, and, Harlow? Stick to that no-jerks thing. Trust me, I've dated a jerk, and you don't want a guy like that."

Maddox had asked, "What guy?" and Harlow had kept her response vague, telling him it'd just been a misunderstanding.

In the here and now, those same amber eyes prodded her, causing all the heart palpitations. "Nobody, really."

Maddox made the buzzer noise again, and she nearly jumped out of her skin. "That's not how this game goes, Harlow. Do you want me to give non-answers when it's your turn to ask the questions?"

"No, but—" At his darted glare, she gave in. "My former roping partner, Bianca, told me I was flirting with her boyfriend. Which is ridiculous, because he's a cheating jerkface and therefore *is* a nobody in my eyes."

Maddox grinned at her. Grinned! Why was this guy giving her tummy flutters and tingles again?

She scowled at him. "How is that something to grin about?"

"Jerkface," he said with a soft laugh. "You also used 'therefore' in a totally unironic way. I just like how you talk, especially when it comes to avoiding swear words."

She laughed and shoved his shoulder. "So happy you like it, because I do it just for you, Mikos."

"I'm so flattered and not a jerkface at all."

For the next thirty minutes, Maddox stuck to basics, and she managed to label the auto parts right, along with their functions. What could she say? Maddox was a good teacher and she an apt student.

After she'd named the wrong belt—seriously, shouldn't the fact that she got the belt part right count?—Maddox tossed the wrench in the direction of the toolbox and rolled to fully face her. "Why do you spend so much time here? Don't you have parties to go to and friends to hang out with in town?" Harlow felt her face fall, echoing the dull ache that'd throbbed to life in her chest, and Maddox placed a soothing hand on her arm. "Not that I'm not glad you're around. I'm bored on the days you're not. I was just curious."

Even though she tried to inhale, her lungs remained flat and heavy. "I've always struggled to make friends. And don't say that shocks you in that sarcastic way you do, because..." Her voice cracked, and why was she getting all sappy sad about this? It wasn't a new sensation, feeling like she didn't have any true, close friends.

Maddox's fingertips skated down her arm and drifted over the back of her hand, sending a few stray butterflies to mingle with the self-pity churning through her. "Hey, I'm sorry. And I am shocked, no sarcasm. Who wouldn't want to hang out with you?"

"Right?" she asked, but a half sob slipped out, too. She focused on the comic-book sound-effect tattoo on his forearm with the yellow word *POW!* in the middle. It was one of the few spots of color among all his ink. "I thought Bianca was my friend, but I guess she wasn't. At school, we ran in different circles—as in I had a circle of one and she was super popular—and I told myself she wasn't meaning to ignore me, but…" Harlow pressed her lips into a tight line until she regained control of her emotions. "Deep down, I knew."

The subject of friends amplified her worries about her social life during her upcoming senior year as well. "There's this party next weekend. It's the biggest party of the summer, and most of my classmates are going to be there. I'm trying to get up the courage to go alone, but I'll probably just spend that night talking to my horse or having dinner with my family."

"You have to go to the party, Harlow," Maddox said, his voice quiet but steady. His fingers curled around her palm. "Just to show What's-Her-Face that she was wrong about you and that she doesn't get to decide what you do."

Heavy footsteps invaded the intimate bubble they'd created, and Harlow pulled her hand free from Maddox's right as Brady peeked under the hood. "Time for roping practice."

"Actually," Harlow said, "I was thinking we need to up Maddox's horseback-riding game and move to roping from a saddle."

Maddox's posture tensed, every inch of him screaming *no*. After he'd used her limited knowledge about cars to his full advantage in their game of questions, her smug sense of satisfaction over it being her turn seemed perfectly justifiable.

To keep an eye on him and make sure Maddox couldn't be alone with Harlow too much, Brady had assigned Aiden and Chloe to go along with them. *So much for thinking I've earned some leeway by fixing the car.*

While Maddox did his best to remember his one and only horse-riding lesson, Harlow walked her horse out of the stables to get some water and air. The entire time he saddled a black horse named Licorice, he wished she had two wheels instead of four legs. After he was done, Aiden double-checked the cinches.

"I mean…" Chloe paused to watch and twirled a strand of blond hair around her finger. "Look at my smokin'-hot cowboy."

"Not a cowboy," Aiden said, the grin on his face widening. He drew her close and kissed her cheek, and a whorl of jealousy cramped Maddox's gut.

Not because he liked Chloe but because of her and Aiden's relationship. It clearly went deeper than attraction. While he'd had plenty of girlfriends, they'd never done a lot of talking. Maddox wasn't sure he'd ever had a connection like that. The closest he'd come was with Harlow, and maybe that was where the jealousy came from. Because he couldn't be that way with her.

"Sorry," Aiden said, shaking himself out of his goofy, I-love-my-girlfriend trance.

I'm jealous of sappiness. All of three weeks, and this place is already turning me into a softy who'll get his ass kicked when he goes back home. Or what constituted home, since that word had never held the same meaning for him as most people.

"You're good to go," Aiden declared, patting the black horse's neck and handing over the reins. "We'll lead the horses out of the stables, and then we'll ride to the creek."

"You'll love it," Chloe said, grabbing the bridle of a saddled buckskin horse named Rowdy. "It's one of my favorite places on the ranch." She stopped next to Maddox and gave him a meaning-ful look. "I even liked it back when I thought this place was my own personal hell."

Right. She'd come to the ranch after getting in trouble with the law, too. It was hard for Maddox to imagine Chloe and Aiden had once been in his same place. At first, he thought they must've been brainwashed. After the time he'd spent here, he realized that wasn't true, but he'd never end up like them, either.

Happy to get out of the stuffy, hot stables, he led his black horse outside.

And froze in place at the sight in front of him.

Harlow sat, legs crossed, on the grassy ground. Her tan horse nuzzled her neck, and she giggled and cooed as she scratched his opposite cheek. The horse ate it up, too, Maddox could tell. Another mushy sensation unfurled itself in his chest, one aimed at the girl with the honey-colored hair and easy smile. Less than a month ago, he would've thought she was weird, talking and snuggling with a horse like that. Now he found it cute as hell.

The horse trailed its long nose up Harlow's cheek and knocked her hat to the ground.

"Maximus. What did I say about my hat?" She scooped it up and tugged it back on her head. Then she spotted Maddox and their babysitters. She stood and wiped the seat of her pants, and her horse nuzzled her again.

Shit. Now I'm jealous of a horse.

Maddox doused the feelings the best he could and strode over, his black horse in tow. "Maximus? Like the supervillain from the comic books?"

No idea why he'd spared giving her a weird look for talking to her horse when she had no problem giving him one for asking a simple question. "What? No. I don't know who that is, you nerd." That was the first time he'd ever been called that, for the record, but Harlow softened the light jab with a smile. "It's from *Tangled*. That was Flynn Rider's horse's name, and it seemed fitting for this big guy. Didn't it, my big, strong horse?"

The more she coddled the beast, the harder it was to ignore her magnetic pull. "Why am I not surprised you got the name from a Disney movie? You practically *are* a Disney movie."

Her fiery side drifted to the surface, tempting him closer to the blaze. "Let me guess. You're an R-rated action movie."

"Damn straight."

Harlow laughed, and man, she had a nice laugh. Not a titter, as if she worked at sounding sexy. But a full, unbridled laugh that filled the air and buried itself inside his chest.

"Okay, you big action star, you. Get on your horse, and let's get this party on the trail." Harlow gripped her saddle horn and swung onto her horse with ease, like she'd done it hundreds of times, which she undoubtedly had. Chloe and Aiden had already mounted their horses as well.

A grunt escaped as Maddox heaved himself up, but he'd miscalculated how high to swing his leg. As if that weren't embarrassing enough, Licorice trotted a couple of paces, upping the difficulty level considerably. Sheer determination was the only thing that'd kept him from falling.

The other three stared from astride their steeds, waiting for him to get his act together.

"You okay?" Harlow asked, and Maddox managed to maneuver into the saddle and nod. They fanned out, and once the cabin disappeared from view, Aiden and Chloe picked up their pace, giving Maddox and Harlow a bit of space.

The saddle felt too wide, and he yearned for handles to grip instead of a nub of a horn and some puny reins. "I prefer my motorcycle. I've got my grippy handlebars, and I can control the speed."

"A good horseman controls the speed of their horse," Harlow said.

Maddox cast her an unamused expression.

"What? I'm just saying once you get the hang of it, you'll be able to control the speed. You should get on that ASAP, too, because we've only got a few weeks until the rodeo."

"Wait," Maddox said. "There's a rodeo?"

She whipped toward him, her posture relaxing slightly as she realized he'd obviously been joking. He laughed and nudged his horse along a bit faster so he was right next to her and Maximus.

Harlow glanced at him, her curls swishing over her shoulders. He liked the curls, but he also liked when she styled it straight or in a braid or ponytail. Basically, he couldn't stop thinking about what her hair would feel like slipping through his fingers. "Okay, so what kind of horse are you riding?" she asked.

"A black one."

She made a buzzer sound and gleefully rubbed her palms together. "My turn to ask a question."

"That only applies to roping."

Harlow made the buzzer noise again. "Wrong. You made it all car stuff, so I'm applying our game to all cowboy stuff. Fair warning, I'm going to get some of the big questions out of the way first."

Tension claimed every muscle in his body, and he gripped the reins tighter. Since the horse read that as a cue to stop, he had to loosen his hold and nudge the horse on again.

After glancing at Chloe and Aiden, who were out of hearing distance and about to melt into the tree line, Harlow looked at him. "You haven't mentioned your family once."

Maddox kept his gaze glued on the grassy path ahead. "I think you forgot the definition of a question." He'd attempted to mask his inner turmoil, but the subject was too raw.

"Seriously?" Harlow ducked to avoid some low-hanging branches. "Fine. What's up with your family?"

The scent of pine surrounded them, and Maddox attempted to focus on that as he gave his reply. "I don't have a family."

"Come on, Maddox. I told you about my friend situation, and that wasn't easy for me."

She was right, of course, in that annoying way that she usually was. He exhaled a weighted breath and charged on with it. "My mom was the only family I ever knew. She liked to get high a little too much and, as I got older, a little too often. We'd have these great periods where we'd take these fun, last-minute adventures. Camping or movies or hopping in the car and driving to the carnival the next town over."

The memories he'd worked hard to bury burrowed to the surface. "I missed school a lot, because like her job at the time, she thought going was optional. I thought it was great—after all, what kid *wants* to go to school? But it also meant I was always behind my classmates."

Leaves shivered in the breeze, and the world around them seemed too quiet and too loud. "Eventually, she lost her job. I began to realize our adventures were mostly ways for her to avoid people she owed money to. Then her drug problem got worse and worse. She stopped going to meet the sketchy people and brought them home with her."

Almost done. He just had to spit the last part out. "One night, she got into a screaming match with one of them, the cops were called, and then they found out that I hadn't been fed or dropped off at school in a week or so. I tried to lie, but I wasn't very good at it, and I was so, so hungry."

Harlow gaped at him in horror.

He attempted a shrug, but his shoulders were too heavy with the past weighing them down. Pathetic after all the time he'd had to get over it.

"How old were you?" she asked, her voice quiet.

"Eight."

Her gasp carried over to him.

"It's not a big deal, Harlow. It happened forever ago. Basically, the state gave her a lot of chances to get her shit together so she could regain custody, and she chose drugs, so I was put into foster care. I was shuffled around for most of my life, and right now, I'm"—he made air quotes—"'living' with my last foster family.

The truth is, I sleep on a cot in the office of the mechanic shop where I work more often than not, and we both prefer it that way."

His current foster parents hadn't come to bail him out of jail or shown up at the courtroom. Not that he'd expected them to. It just confirmed what he'd already known. Maddox lifted his right hand, showing off the bird tattoo that flew toward the knuckle of his pinkie. "I got this as a symbol of freedom. Three more months, and then I'll turn eighteen and be truly free."

"I like that," Harlow said in a quiet voice. "I'm super sorry about your family, though."

"Like I said, not a big deal. I'm obviously well-adjusted and all that shit."

She cracked a smile with a hint of pity, which was something he didn't want her to feel. Not for him.

"I think I've got the hang of this riding thing, and we're getting behind," he said. "Let's gallop and catch up."

Harlow slid the bead on the strings of her hat up, securing it under her chin, and nodded. Then they were galloping across the meadow toward the creek in the distance. And Maddox was thinking that these get-to-know-you questions and the opening up he'd promised Nick that he'd do in exchange for Harlow working on the car with him were all a big mistake.

One he'd have to take back ASAP.

While Harlow assumed Maddox had it rough growing up, she didn't expect him to say he didn't have a family. She missed her father and how he'd balanced out her mom, who was strict and often overzealous, but he'd always made it clear he cared. Even though she and her mama didn't see eye to eye and the smothering got to her from time to time, Harlow couldn't imagine a scenario where Mama wouldn't show up. Wouldn't fight for her.

Everything in her wanted to pry, but she'd seen the tightness in Maddox's features and heard the open wound in his scratchy voice. She was going to have to spread out the hard questions.

They dismounted, and she turned to him. "Do you know the breed of my horse?"

He winced. "Um, a mustang?"

She made the buzzer noise, and trepidation filled his expression. "When it comes to rodeo horses, you can pretty much always say quarter horse and be right, even though that's the bare minimum. So there's your tip for the day, and as for my next question... If you could travel anywhere in the world, where would you go?"

His face softened, the hint of a smile quirking his lips. "Greece. Not that I know any of my ancestors, but it's where my roots are." One of his tattoos formed a tree with long, tangled roots that climbed up his left arm. Was that a coincidence or, like the bird, did it have meaning? Funny how each of his answers only brought more questions. "I've also wanted to see the ocean, and they have lots of it."

"I'd like to go there someday, too. While I travel quite a bit for rodeos, it's just mostly around Colorado, Wyoming, New Mexico, and Kansas. When I was younger, I used to beg my parents to go to Disneyland—"

"See? And you acted all offended when I called you a Disney movie."

Harlow pointed a warning finger at him. "Don't even. I'm hardly some princess. Not that there's anything wrong with being one or wanting to, and also, they've gotten more bad-A over the last few decades."

The crooked smile appeared, loosening the knot that'd formed in her heart when he'd told her about his family and she worried she'd ruined their outing. "Sure."

"Don't act like you weren't impressed by how awesome *Tangled* was when you watched the movie."

"No need to act," he said. "I've never seen *Tangled*."

"How is that even possible?"

He shrugged, a much lighter shrug than his earlier one. "Those Disney movies always seemed girlie to me."

Her gasp was over the top, but she couldn't help it. "They're not."

He raised his hands as if he were surrendering.

Harlow walked toward him, and he crossed his arms in front of himself as if he worried she'd show him her best Rapunzel impression and smack him with a frying pan. She clamped on to his arm and led him to the shore of the creek. This time of year, it was about three feet deep and perfect for wading. "Take off your shoes."

Aiden and Chloe stood downstream, their jeans rolled up to their knees. "Should I take off my shirt, too?" Maddox asked, arching one dark eyebrow. "Maybe shuck the pants as well? I wouldn't want them to get wet."

Heat flared through Harlow's cheeks. "Just the shoes."

"Are you sure? If you want, you can take off your—"

She slapped a hand over his mouth and felt Maddox smile against her palm.

"What?" The word came out muffled. "I was going to say your hat."

Ignoring that, she kicked off her shoes. "The hat stays, because otherwise I'll end up with a sunburned nose and bright-red cheeks."

"They're looking a little red as it is," he said, lifting his hand as if he were going to touch her face. For a moment, she couldn't breathe, but then he abruptly sat and removed his socks and shoes, and she did the same.

They slid down the embankment and stepped into the cool water. Harlow slipped a bit on the moss-covered rocks, and Maddox took her hand and guided her to the muddy-bottomed middle. She closed her eyes and inhaled the fresh water-and-pine-scented air. Then she turned to see if Maddox was soaking in the awesomeness.

But he was looking at her.

The heat of his palm soaked into hers, and she realized she was still clinging to his hand. She quickly let go and immediately missed the warmth and sense of security.

Time for a reality check. Maddox was the type of guy who could break her heart without even trying, and if she didn't remind herself of the many reasons she shouldn't fall, she'd be his next victim. "Why did you have to come here?"

"As in you wish I hadn't, or…?"

"No, not at all." She bit her lip. Considered taking it back. But now that it was out there, curiosity got the better of her. "I meant why did a judge order you to come here."

Maddox's dark eyebrows scrunched together. "I didn't miss a question about a horse. Didn't toss a lasso and come up short."

"I can ask a question involving horses or roping that you won't be able to answer correctly, or you could just tell me." While she was big on forgiveness and second chances, there were certain things she couldn't get over. Surely, if he'd assaulted a girl, no one would allow her to be mostly alone with him, Aiden and Chloe barely within view.

Come on, Harlow. You're smarter than this. Bad boys don't change their stripes or their leather jackets or whatever.

Maddox took a step back, and she thought he was going to retreat. But then he squared off in front of her. "I made a car delivery for my buddy who owns the mechanic shop where I work, and it turns out there were drugs in the trunk."

All she could do was blink. She wasn't naive enough to think they were, like, pharmaceutical drugs with valid prescriptions.

Oh, holy crap. The confession made *her* want to do the retreating. *He's a certified drug dealer. Abort, abort, abort.*

"Since I had a fake ID on me at the time," Maddox continued, "along with a previous charge for possession, the judge called it strike three and made an example out of me."

"Possession?" Harlow asked, still scrambling to comprehend what this newfound information meant about the guy in front of her.

"It was so minor, just a tiny bit of weed."

Tiny bit of weed. Harlow didn't have a whole lot of experience, but the potheads at school always downplayed the amount they smoked. They'd go into the school bathroom with their vape pens and come out smelling like they'd just done a line of Fruity Pebbles. "Did you *do* the drugs?"

Maddox's gaze dipped to the water rushing around them before returning to hers. "Not the ones in the trunk. I didn't know they were in there, I swear. Fuckin' Ian didn't let me in on what the job entailed, and I didn't find out until I was neck deep in it.

"Turns out the cops had been watching the house where I delivered it, so I got busted along with the people inside. The cops booked me for possession with intent to distribute, which wasn't my intent, and I argued as much. They told me they'd be more likely to believe me if I'd rat on who'd given me the drugs, but I don't rat."

Harlow's attempt to swallow didn't take away the thickness clogging her throat or the spinning going on in her brain. "So you didn't do the drugs in the trunk, but you have done other drugs?"

A heartbreaking smile, one devoid of joy, crossed Maddox's face as he hooked his thumbs in the pockets of his torn-up jeans. In addition to causing his arm muscles to stand out, it gave him this boyish look and, ugh, she had a huge crush on a guy who did drugs.

Correction—she *used* to have a crush on him.

Mothertrucker. How did you get rid of a crush?

"I drink occasionally and smoke some weed here and there," Maddox said. "Not a lot."

"To me, any amount is a lot."

He slowly nodded. "Yeah, I figured from the horrified look on your face."

Harlow's breaths came faster and faster. What did this mean? Did she try to go on as if nothing had happened? "How could you do that when your mom was an addict?"

Okay, so apparently she wasn't going to act cool about it. She never could fake it, so he might as well get it all out now.

Maddox shuttered his features, and while she hated it and the tightness that crept into her lungs because of it, she did her best to convince herself it was better to hash it out now. "I knew you wouldn't get it," he said. "You've lived in this perfect little bubble all your life. But I have to live in the real world. The poor real world, where things are ugly, and sometimes you do whatever you can to get through the day."

"I'm sure that's how your mom started, too," she automatically retorted.

The hurt that flickered through his eyes shuddered through her as well. That was one of those things she should've kept *inside* her head.

Water rippled around Maddox's legs as he charged toward the shore.

"Maddox, wait." One of her pant legs slipped into the water, but she didn't bother fixing it as she struggled to follow after him. Without a hand to hold, she found the slimy rocks made it that much trickier. "I shouldn't have said that. You answered my question and—"

He spun around so fast that she wobbled, her arms flailing as she toppled backward. She braced herself for hitting the water, but Maddox snagged her wrist, catching her instead of letting her fall on her butt like she deserved.

The instant she was steady, Maddox let go of her. Every ounce of warmth had fled from his features, leaving the hostile guy he'd been on the day they'd met. "And you threw it in my face."

A pit formed in her belly. He was totally right. But before she could even tell him that, he'd scooped up his shoes, climbed onto Licorice without putting them on, and taken off.

Luckily, it was *toward* the ranch, so she didn't think he was trying to escape from the program.

Nope, he was just escaping her.

Chapter 15

THE FLAMES FROM THE BONFIRE WERE DYING DOWN, AND THE scent of roasted hot dogs and smoke hovered in the air. Brady shifted forward in the canvas camping chair to accept the cup of vanilla-and-chocolate swirled ice cream with a wooden spoon on top.

"Thanks," he told Ma, who beamed. Nothing could diminish her happy mood tonight, and her ear-to-ear grin sent happiness through him as well.

For most people, Friday signaled the end of work for a few days, but when it came to the ranch and caring for teenagers, there was no end. Brady's excitement over Fridays came from them being bonfire, hot dogs, and s'mores night. As long as the weather permitted and the kids earned it, that was, and the teens had been extra well-behaved this week. No talking back, only one tardy between the lot of them, and they'd done their chores without having to be hounded.

Their chill Friday night had turned into a celebration when Jessica and Wade announced they were going to have a baby. Brady had acted his ass off, afraid of what would happen if Ma found out he'd heard the news before she did. Now she was passing out celebratory ice-cream cups, and Brady resisted the urge to make a bet over who'd be the first to end up in a sugar coma. Him, probably.

Brady squinted through the fire to where Harlow and Chloe sat side by side. Maddox had come back early from their ride, with the others showing up about ten minutes later. It'd looked suspiciously like Harlow had been crying, and he'd been observing the dynamic between her and Maddox ever since.

I swear, I told that kid to be nice to her. I made myself very clear.

Nick had warned Maddox to behave himself around Harlow as well. This was why Wade was a stickler about never crossing lines and keeping the drama low. The teens already had heaps of drama, so adding to it was like juggling three sweaty sticks of dynamite. One wrong move, one slip, and *boom!* It blows up in your face.

After falling for Jess despite the rules, Wade had become less of a stickler, but he was hardly lax. The only reason Chloe and Aiden were allowed to date was because they'd both graduated from the program. The other teens had crushes here and there, sure, but the staff closely monitored them. Brady had noticed Maddox and Harlow had been spending a lot of their time together chatting and laughing, but it seemed more like a mutual friendship that was good for both of them.

Shit. I'm the one who put them together for roping. Brady had also thought working on the car together would solidify them as a team and give Maddox's progress in the program a boost.

I'd better fix it before it gets any worse.

And if Maddox had threatened or hurt Harlow in any way… Safety was of the utmost importance, and if Brady had to, he'd enforce the harshest punishment. Even if it meant kicking Maddox out before they'd had a chance to break through to him.

The very kid he was ready to smack upside the head for ignoring his and Nick's warnings started past, and Brady stood and hooked him by the collar. "We need to have a chat, Mikos."

"Get off me," Maddox said, smacking Brady's arm away.

He'd only lost his temper with the kids a few times—times he wasn't proud of—and he was dangerously close now. *Deep breath in. Long exhale out.* "What happened with you and Harlow?"

"Nothing."

Brady infused his voice with the simmering rage that'd risen to the surface, needing to get the kid away from the crowd before they both erupted. "Follow me. *Now.*"

They stalked a few yards from the pit, to where they could have some semblance of privacy, the buzz of conversations and crackling fire easily masking their conversation.

"What. Happened. With. Harlow?"

Maddox's stoic expression cracked, revealing an inkling of... agony? "Same thing that happens with everyone. She realized I'm a piece of shit."

Brady clenched and unclenched his hands at his side, checking that he was still in control. For now, he was, but if he lost it after this question, he'd call for one of his brothers. "Did you hurt her?"

"I'd never hurt her," Maddox said, so passionately it calmed the tempestuous storm inside Brady. Being around teens who did their fair share of lying had practically turned him into a human lie detector. Didn't mean a lie never got past him, but he'd bet a million dollars the kid was telling the truth.

Cool relief flowed through his veins. Since he'd been the one to hire her, he already felt responsible. In addition to being a natural on horseback and at roping, Harlow was a bright, happy kid. Although she seemed a bit lonely, which was another reason he'd thought hiring her would be a symbiotic situation. If this was simply a case of minor drama, which was also common in Teenville, it'd be one of those things that was a huge deal today and a blip on the radar in another one or two.

Brady shifted his focus to the self-deprecating kid in front of him. "You're not a piece of shit, Maddox."

"Did you read my file? See everything I've done?"

"I don't have to."

Maddox just stood there, defeat so heavy in his arms that they dangled from his frame. There were bumps along the way with everyone who came to the ranch. Some of the teens they'd treated for addictions even went out into the real world and relapsed.

The entire staff experienced heartache on their behalf, and Brady had gone from pissed to desperate to find a way to fix whatever was going on. Maybe he hadn't given Maddox a fair shake. "What do you need?"

"Nothing." Maddox's steely mask descended. "I'm used to nothing. I'm not saying that in a poor-me way, either. It's the truth, and I'd rather keep it that way. Can I go?"

Brady waited a handful of seconds to see if enough awkward silence would prompt the kid to divulge anything. In these situations, he felt completely unqualified. If he thought it'd do any good, he'd call over Nick. Once someone threw up their walls, though, it was often best to let them cool off and then try again later.

Brady released him, and Maddox plodded toward the firelight. Aiden lifted his head in a nod as Maddox approached. *Cool. Aiden can talk to him, and it'll be better than anything I could say.*

But Maddox shook his head, his impassive facade remaining. He shoved his hands in his pockets and trudged in the direction of the boys' cabin. Right before he melted into the dark background, the kid cast one last glance at Harlow. She stared back at him, an anguished, helpless expression on her face.

———

On Sunday afternoon, as Maddox walked toward the big room where they had group therapy sessions, he dragged his feet a bit. It was far from his favorite place on the ranch, but he'd been told they were having a "fun" movie night with popcorn, and it wasn't like he had many other options for entertainment now that he and Harlow—

The soles of his shoes glued themselves to the floor when Harlow popped up in front of the TV, an empty DVD case in hand. *What the hell is she doing here?*

The rest of his cellmates were milling around the other side of the room, but their presence barely registered once he'd spotted

Harlow. He'd already come up with a handful of excuses for why he couldn't train with her next week, and panic and frustration collided and formed another emotion he couldn't even name. How dare she throw a wrench in his plans by being here when she shouldn't be! Little Miss Perfect didn't *need* to be in a program for troubled teens, and he wasn't in the mood to have that rubbed in his face again.

He was so out of here.

Her gaze latched onto his from across the room, and then his plan to escape became that much more complicated.

"Why don't you come have a seat, Maddox?" she asked, her shaky voice infused with enthusiasm. "It's movie night. I'm hosting and everything."

He remained firmly in place and added crossed arms to his immovable stance.

Despite his attempt to relay that he wasn't budging from this very spot, Harlow rushed over like she thought he might bolt through the nearest exit—and perhaps that would've been a better course of action. "I know you're mad," she said, "and you totally have the right to be, but I…" The lower lip he was semi-obsessed with quivered, and her eyes grew watery. "I set this all up for you as a way to say I'm sorry."

Maddox exhaled, pleading with himself not to soften or get sucked in. Not again.

"So do you forgive me? Can we go back to being friends?" Harlow extended a trembling hand toward him, and he stared at it. Vulnerability flickered over her features, and a mushy sensation began to fill that spot over his heart. "Please?"

Damn it. How could he not give in? He did his best to convince himself she was doing the typical girl thing, using her emotions to manipulate him. But Harlow didn't have a manipulative bone in her body, and he could tell she wasn't faking how bad she felt or how much she wanted them to be okay.

And everything in him shouted to soothe her pain.

Reluctantly, he uncrossed his arms and took her extended hand. "Fine. Friends."

Instead of letting go, she tightened her grip and towed him over to a table covered with bowls of popcorn. They exchanged greetings with the rest of the group, and then everyone else backed away and gave him and Harlow space.

"Before we start the movie, we have to get you a crown." Harlow lifted a pile of the flat, cardboard Burger King crowns he hadn't seen since he was the poor kid in class who'd been invited to a birthday party out of pity. His foster parents at the time were happy to get rid of him for an afternoon, and he was thrilled to have a whole meal to himself. "Don't worry. All the cool kids are wearing them." Once Harlow finished fastening the crown, she tipped onto her toes and placed it on his head. "I stole them from Burger King." She lowered her voice and whispered, "See, I'm a rebel, too."

"Whoa," he deadpanned, aiming the most sarcastic look in his arsenal her way. "I can't believe you lifted a bunch of free crowns."

"*Shhh.*" She glanced around as if the police might bust in to arrest her soon. "I didn't even have any kids with me, and they ask that you only take one, and…" Her brown eyes met his. "Will you for reals forgive me for being a jerkface? You answered me honestly and told me all that personal information, and I did exactly what you accused me of. I threw it back in your face, and I suck, and I can't sleep at night, and I know I'm an awful, judgmental person."

Maddox's arms ached with the urge to wrap them around Harlow and assure her all was forgiven, but one of the adults was likely to step forward with a cattle prod and zap him if he did so. "The fact that you care so much you can't sleep only proves how sweet you are."

"Ah." Harlow batted her eyelashes. "So you're saying I'm a sweet rebel."

A laugh escaped, and after four solid days of gloom, a ray of sunshine broke through and began to thaw his icy heart. Somehow, this girl had become his light source. She had him twisted up to the point he wasn't sure which way was up or down anymore, and he cared a lot less about that than he should. He gestured to the crown atop his head. "I'm not wearing this thing if you're not putting one on."

Her smile suffused him with another swell of that addictive warmth. She proudly plopped a crown on her head, and when it fell down over her eyes, he adjusted it for her.

"How do I look?" she asked with a mock curtsy.

"Cute," he answered honestly. He probably should've lied, but he couldn't help it.

"You look pretty cute yourself, Sir Mikos." She blushed, as if she couldn't believe she'd said that. "Anyway, guess which movie we're watching." She bounced on the balls of her feet. "*Tangled*! Because it's crazy you haven't seen it."

Yeah, his heart was definitely on the melty side now. Not only did she care he hadn't seen the movie, but she'd also told him to guess and then hadn't given him the chance before it'd burst out of her.

Harlow placed her hand between his shoulder blades and nudged him toward the couch. Usually, a hand to her lower back would be his go-to move, but he found that he liked being pushed around more than he'd expected.

Especially if Harlow was doing the pushing.

He took the spot next to the arm of the couch, and Harlow sat beside him. As the others settled in, Maddox draped his arm over the backrest. His hand was a mere inch from her hair, and the desire to wind his fingers through the silky softness called to him. To keep himself from following through, he flattened his palm against the worn fabric.

The movie had just begun when the blond twins made their

entrance in footsie pajamas. They immediately streaked for Harlow, shouting her name.

"Remember," Liza said from behind the couch. "You have to sit still and be quiet if you want to watch the movie."

They both solemnly nodded. Then Elise pulled herself onto Harlow's lap, and Everett frowned and wiggled into the nonexistent spot between her and Maddox. *Sure, buddy, go ahead and help yourself,* Maddox thought with a wry grin.

Because of his painful past, Maddox had kept his distance from the funny kid since that night he and his sister had remarked on his tattoos and earrings. At the same time, he was almost drawn to Everett.

The movie started, and Elise whisper-talked, but she wasn't very good at it. With every question and observation, the volume of her voice rose a bit higher. "Lizards! I love lizards!"

"I know what a horse says," Everett said as a horse appeared on-screen.

"Neigh," Elise cut in.

"Lise! Thass what I was gonna say!"

Harlow lovingly shushed them and patted their blond heads. "You both are so smart. You know all the animal noises. Now, let's be quiet and watch the movie."

In the middle of a scene that included a whole lot of singing, Everett melted against Maddox's side in a way that made him think…

He glanced at the kid's face. Yep, his eyes were drifting shut. A minute or so later, Everett slumped over entirely, his head coming to rest in Maddox's lap.

Just focus on the plot and don't think about the last time you watched a movie with a little kid. An image flashed to mind, one where a character named Hiro hugged a big, blobby white robot. As the credits to *Big Hero 6* rolled up the screen, a tiny voice had said, "Maddox, you're my hero *and* my brother."

The past superimposed itself over the present, and Maddox ran his fingers through the blond hair on Everett's head. While his little brother's hair was darker, the fine strands felt similar. Plus, at three years old, Jaxon Wagner also had rounded cheeks and constantly fell asleep on Maddox's lap. Probably because when Jaxon was awake, he never stopped moving. The kid sprinted everywhere like life was one big race. He climbed and ran—often toward the street—and Maddox had honed his reflexes so he could get to where Jaxon was going before he could.

Then he'd toss him up in the air or put him on his shoulders and offer to take the kid to the park. Mr. Wagner had been deployed, and Linda, the kid's mother, was always exhausted. She would constantly ask Jaxon why he couldn't be more like his calm older sister, and every time she did so, it was harder and harder for Maddox to hold his tongue.

The entire Wagner family had been kind to him, but Jaxon...

Longing and sorrow wrapped themselves around Maddox's heart until they cut off the flow of blood. While the rest of the family had hesitated over titles, Jaxon instantly claimed Maddox as a brother. And Jaxon was his. When he was teaching the kid how to write his letters, they fist-bumped over having X's in their names. "Pretty sure that means we were always supposed to be brothers," he'd told Jaxon.

Stop thinking about it. It'll only hurt. But the gaping hole he'd attempted to stuff with other things returned with a vengeance. After six months of living with the Wagners, they started the adoption process—Maddox could hardly believe he was going to have a steady home with people who seemed to genuinely care about him.

But then Mr. Wagner received PCS orders—a permanent change of station—to go to Alabama.

Linda had pulled Maddox aside and told him she needed to keep her family together and that since his mother had made a half-hearted promise to go to rehab, the judge was giving her another six months to get her act together.

Since they couldn't take him to another state without adopting him and that process had been delayed indefinitely, they… Old wounds ripped open—ones Maddox had done his best to convince himself were fully healed. By now, Jaxon would be six years old and already in school. The kid was so young when Maddox had lived with him that he worried they wouldn't even recognize each other if they crossed paths now.

Maddox clenched his jaw, willing away the lump that'd overtaken his throat.

Attachments made him weak. He had to remember that. He'd slipped a little—especially with the girl at his side, the one who was studying him with her forehead scrunched up. "You okay?"

Painful reminder not to get attached notwithstanding, he rubbed a hand down Everett's back, hoping the kid found it as soothing as Jaxon used to. "Yeah. Just enjoying the movie and worrying about Flynn or Eugene or whatever."

"See." Harlow's smile was the very definition of joy. "I told you it was good."

She was good. As well as supersweet. She had a big heart, and she might even care about him the tiniest bit.

But eventually, she'd forget him, too.

Chapter 16

"OH GOOD, YOU'RE BACK," NICK SAID BY WAY OF GREETING when Brady walked into the main cabin. "I need to talk to you about one of the kids." Nick tipped his head toward the hall. "In the office."

Trepidation tightened Brady's muscles as the faces of the teens whizzed through his head. Which one and why? Good or bad?

Since the only way to find out was to go to the office, Brady dragged himself inside, and Nick shut the door behind him. Of all their brothers, Nick was the quietest and most reserved, yet also ridiculously in tune with people's emotions. Even if he hadn't come to Turn Around Ranch through the foster system, Brady suspected he'd be counseling or assisting people in one way or another. Even as young as twelve, he'd helped some of his classmates as much as the program had.

All that said, he was damn hard to read.

"It's Maddox," Nick finally said, and a rock formed in Brady's gut. After the mistake he'd made last time, he didn't want to assume the kid had done something bad, regardless of most closed-door office talks going like that.

"You've seen how close he and Harlow are getting, I'm sure," Nick continued.

Brady had, and he'd been doing his best to keep a close eye on them. "He knows the rules. I've talked to him, as have you."

Nick perched on the edge of the desk and braced his forearms on his knees. "We both know that occasionally the rules get bent a little. And we have to ask ourselves if the bending is for the best or if it's going to cause a break."

Brady nodded, even though he was a bit lost. "I get the gist anyway. Now how about you get to the point?"

"I'll get there when I'm damn good and ready." Nick casually crossed his ankles. "Unless you want me to turn the tables and talk about how I've noticed a change in you this past week, and I have a theory as to why."

"Prick," Brady muttered.

"Liar, liar, pants on fire," Nick retorted without missing a beat. How the hell could his brother possibly know that he and Tanya had crossed lines? If she'd told anyone, surely she would've mentioned it. His routine hadn't changed in the slightest, save today when he'd gone to Bullhead Valley and helped Tanya set up another barrel training course. After all, Tanya had lent them ropes. But he'd do that for her anyway, friendship or relationship.

Yes, it'd taken longer than he'd expected on account of riding a mile or so into a copse of trees to have a quickie, but again, Nick couldn't discern that with a look. Brady was relatively sure anyway, but who knew what sorts of Jedi mind tricks his brother had up his sleeve.

Since this was clearly going to take a while, Brady dropped into the closest chair. "All right, take your time, princess."

Nick smirked, happy to have gotten his way. "I think Harlow's good for Maddox. At first, I worried he'd take advantage of her sweetness, but she can hold her own with him."

"I agree." Brady grinned as he recalled Harlow telling Maddox she'd use his earring to keep him on task, same way as a nose ring on a bull. Yes, he was concerned about the kids getting too close, but he also took comfort that Maddox had formed a connection, which would lead him to more fully engage in the program.

"During the few days they weren't talking, he backslid. But things smoothed out between them, and do you know what he did this morning while you were gone?"

"What do I need to say to skip the guessing game?"

Nick fired a snide smile at him. "No guessing, then. He put a saddle on that stallion."

The kid had been connecting more and more with the horse, but that went beyond connecting. It took determination and courage and was about as cowboy as it got. "That's impressive."

"I agree," Nick said. "Which is why I want to keep him on the path to recovery. Which leaves me walking a tricky line where I use Harlow as motivation to keep progressing while not pushing too hard or making a mess for either him or her."

"We've all walked tricky lines. That's where the magic usually happens."

"I'd call it hard work, but I agree."

Brady rolled his eyes. "Did you bring me in here to brag, or is there a point?"

"I'm considering saying yes to a proposition I'm not sure I should say yes to." Nick ran his fingers along his jaw. "At the end of our counseling session today, Maddox opened up about his mom. The kid's never had anyone, not really. I'm sure you saw in his file what happened with the foster family that almost adopted him."

A residual pang went through Brady, same way it had when he'd read about the adoption falling through. That'd give most people a chip on their shoulder. Didn't mean he'd let the kid get away with giving him attitude. What several parents and guardians didn't realize was that boundaries showed a kid love, even if he or she fought against them.

Not that he always knew where to draw the line. It'd be easier if it was the same for everyone, but that wasn't the way it worked.

Nick scooted backward, overturning a stapler he glanced at before returning his attention to Brady. "Anyway, he told me there's a party this weekend, and that all Harlow's classmates would be there. He says he wants to be there for her. Said she did something nice for him last week—"

"The movie night," Brady said, and Nick nodded.

"I don't want to be a hypocrite who preaches rules and then basically forces the two of them together, but he claims Harlow's nervous about it. Says she'll probably chicken out if she doesn't have anyone to go with—which I could see. She is sort of isolated from the rest of the kids in town, and we know that's not good for teens, either.

"I could tell that Maddox expected to be shut down, but he decided to ask anyway because that's how badly he wants to help Harlow face her classmates and her former partner. He said he'd do whatever it takes. Do all the mucking, dishes, and even tell me his entire life story, start to finish. He also informed me that I could slap a tracker on his ass, and he wouldn't complain. All that mattered was being there for Harlow."

It was quiet for a beat or two, and then Nick asked, "Thoughts?"

Brady tipped up the brim of his hat a few inches and rubbed his fingers across his forehead, wishing it would help him think better. As it was, he'd probably just smeared dirt across his skin. "Did you ask Wade?"

"You've worked with Maddox more than he has. Plus, the old Wade would've automatically said no, and the engaged Wade is… still quite a stickler but also a mystery. Although he did once allow Aiden and Chloe to go to the diner together when Chloe needed a mini escape, so…"

"That's a good idea."

Nick lowered his eyebrows. "What's a good idea? I don't think there were any ideas in there."

The chair creaked as Brady sat forward. "Let Maddox go. He's protective of Harlow; he's not a flight risk as long as she's with him; and I think it'd be good for the both of them to get a break and have some normal teenage fun. But tell him you'll only agree if Aiden and Chloe accompany them since there's safety in numbers and whatnot." He shrugged a shoulder. "Unless he'd like *me* to chaperone. After all, it's always good for kids to feel like they have choices."

Nick laughed. "See. I knew you'd come up with a brilliant and slightly evil solution."

"Those are my specialty."

"Want to talk about Tanya?"

"Wanna talk about why you haven't gone on a date in over a year?" Brady shot back. He'd feel worse if Nick hadn't started it.

"Touché."

As they walked out of the office together, Brady's mind was already returning to his growing to-do list. "Later," he said to his brother, quickening his pace.

"Wait. Don't you wanna come with me and see the look on Maddox's face when we tell him he can go?" Nick's excitement made it obvious he was fond of the kid, and Brady would be lying if he said he wasn't growing attached as well.

In their line of work, it was important to celebrate the rare moments when you knew you were going to make a kid's day. "I suppose I can spare another minute or two."

Chapter 17

HARLOW COULD HARDLY BELIEVE MADDOX HAD PERMISSION to go to the party with her. He, Chloe, and Aiden would be picking her up momentarily, and Maddox had promised he was going to show her how to actually have fun, even if it got him arrested.

Which he'd laughed at like some big joke, while she'd fought the urge to tell him to behave, same way Brady had when he'd gone over ground rules.

Harlow sat on the top of the staircase in her house, waiting for the doorbell to ring, her dressy embroidered boots tapping the carpeted step underneath her feet. It'd been a couple of years since she'd been to a party, and she still struggled to grasp that she had more than one friend going with her.

O-M-G, what if they realize I'm not as cool as everyone else and ditch me, the way Bianca always did?

That'd suck major donkey balls.

Whoa, brain. Balls?

Evidently, she was more nervous than she realized. She was talking to herself *and* borderline swearing. She glanced at her hands. Although she prided herself on how steady they remained before she bolted into the arena on Maximus, they were trembling now.

Shiitake mushrooms, I forgot to grab my gum. Harlow darted into her room and swiped the pack off her dresser. Not that she thought anything would happen tonight that'd require fresh breath, but she'd rather have it and not need it than need it and not have it. After all, parties were loud and required close talking and…

As she neared her perch at the top of the stairs, she heard her mama ask, "Who are you?"

Mothertrucker. Harlow raced down the stairs, nearly tripping on the bottom step. Mama was frowning at Maddox through the open door. Why, oh why, hadn't she insisted on driving? She should've known Mama would take one look at Maddox and be less than thrilled.

Harlow surged forward to save him. "Remember how I said I was going with friends? Maddox is my new roping partner."

Mama gave him a once-over. With each item of clothing, from his untied military green sneakers to his shredded jeans, black T-shirt, and leather jacket, her eyebrows knit tighter together. Mama assessed the rings in his ears, along with the fat ones on his fingers, and the corners of her mouth turned down as she eyed the tattoos covering the back of his hand. "You don't look like a roper."

Maddox's smile was tight, polite, and a pinch nervous. If the cause wasn't Mama's interrogation tactics, Harlow might think it was supercute that he even got nervous. As it was, she was having trouble not blurting out a comment about how freaking hot he looked.

"I'm more of a mechanic than a cowboy, but thanks to Harlow's training…" His amber eyes drifted to her, his smile turning more genuine, and awareness pricked her skin. "I'm getting the hang of the roping thing."

"Yeah, so anyway, Chloe and Aiden are in the truck. See?" Harlow waved extra big, and they waved back. If her heart beat any faster, she'd pass right on out, and she told it to calm down before it outed her and ruined everything. "Just a fun night with *friends* before school starts."

She went to hook her hand on Maddox's elbow but realized that might be too coupley so she simply shooed him toward the truck like he was some kind of farm animal.

"Bye!" she shouted at Mama, who told her to be home by eleven.

Once Harlow was in the truck, she worked on recovering all the breaths she'd forgotten to take.

"Sorry," Maddox said. "I should've had Chloe go to the door. I was trying to be a gentleman."

"It's okay. My mama is naturally suspicious."

"Yeah, I bet. Especially of guys who look like me."

"Of everyone," Harlow said, which was true, but Maddox had definitely ratcheted up Mama's worry-o-meter. How often did he get judged like that? One quick glance and a snap judgment.

Maddox nodded as if it were no big deal, but the tension in his shoulders didn't say the same.

Guilt settled heavy in Harlow's gut, because she'd done something similar when she'd first seen him. The other day, Chloe shared how she'd come to be at the ranch. In addition to getting into legal trouble with her boyfriend at the time, she'd had awful panic attacks and an anxiety disorder. Even though Chloe admitted to using unhealthy coping mechanisms like weed and alcohol to escape, Harlow hadn't felt the need to chide her like she'd done to Maddox. Not only because Chloe had learned healthier methods, including finding the right medication, but because hearing the story had also deepened Harlow's understanding.

It made her realize she had been rather sheltered and too judgmental in the past—and by that she meant, like, last week. But she was working on it, and she was determined to discover more about the boy next to her so she could better understand him.

Harlow reached over and squeezed Maddox's hand. "I can't believe you talked the Dawsons into letting you come. That shows they trust you."

"Not sure I'd say that, but I can't believe it, either, to tell the truth. Of course we did have to bring some chaperones." He jerked his chin at Chloe and Aiden, their driver for tonight.

Chloe twisted toward them, jaw hanging open. "Hey! We're not chaperones. It's safety in numbers." She toyed with the ends of Aiden's dark hair. "We deserve to get out once in a while, too. I still don't know many of the local teenagers."

"You're not missing much," Harlow muttered. Her leg went to bouncing as her nerves shifted into hyperdrive. Yes, she *had* wanted to go to this party and show off how bold and confident she'd become over the past month. Right now, though, she was reconsidering whether or not it was a good idea. She bounced her leg faster, her nerves coiling and uncoiling, like a snake poised to strike.

Maddox placed his hand on her knee, and every ounce of her blood rushed to the spot where his palm and five long fingers radiated heat. "Relax, girl. I got you." The swipe of his thumb managed to calm and rev her up at the same time, her stomach lifting higher with each pass. She cast him a smile he immediately returned, and major swoonage was definitely happening.

But before she could bask in the giddy awesomeness, they were pulling up to the party. And Harlow hoped Maddox hadn't meant *I got you* in a metaphorical way, because for the second time tonight, she seriously felt like she might pass out.

———————

The party was fairly typical. A bonfire out in the boonies. People flirting. Guys trying to impress girls by pulling stupid stunts. Chicks flipping their hair and giggling to catch the male group's attention. One gay couple who looked like they were glad they didn't have to engage in such antics, and a few outsiders doing their best to appear bored and unconcerned, as if they'd ended up here by accident.

While Maddox didn't see any adults, it was still a milder party than any he'd been to. At first, he'd hung back a bit so Harlow could say hi to people, but then she would shoot him a panicked glance, and he'd step forward and join—and often lead—the conversation.

It was weird, considering he was a complete stranger. But since Harlow relaxed visibly every time he took lead, he decided he could be a social butterfly for the night.

After getting past another mini cluster of people, Harlow tapped her boot to his sneakers. "By the way, what's with never tying your shoes? Maybe I should spend some time teaching you how to tie knots."

"Ha-ha." He glanced down. "I don't see the point." And okay, maybe he thought they looked cooler this way.

"Really? Try to run, and I'll rope you before you can get away."

Maddox put his hands on her elbows, holding her arms in place, despite her not having a rope to carry out her threat. "Try that, and you'll see how scary I can be."

"Ooh, I'm quaking in my boots. My boots that don't need to be tied."

He shook his head but failed to smother his smile. Obviously, none of the people at this party had seen this side of Harlow, and the selfish part of him was glad. He liked their casual banter and how she always gave him shit. An odd thing to like, but there it was anyway.

As they neared the group huddled around the fire, some dude eagerly extended a red Solo cup of what he claimed was "just Coke" toward Harlow, and Maddox shoved it away. Then he gave the guy a glare that made him head in the other direction.

When Harlow told him that it was fine because she'd known the guy forever, Maddox replied that he didn't trust anyone who smiled at her like he couldn't wait to get her alone.

"You're exaggerating," she said with a disbelieving shake of her head.

Maddox fought the urge to wrap his arm around her shoulders and claim her as his. "I'm not. He's into you."

She rolled her eyes. "Dude, we've known each other since kindergarten."

"Like that makes a difference. I don't want you accepting drinks you didn't see poured. If you're thirsty, *I'll* go get you a drink. In fact…" He backpedaled a few steps, his gaze remaining on hers. "Be right back."

He waited until the last possible second to turn away from Harlow's pretty face. After nearly slamming into a group of girls because he wasn't watching where he was going, he strode over to a blue cooler. A keg stood at its side, a stack of red cups on top.

Brady and Nick had shocked the hell out of him by giving him the go-ahead for the party, and Maddox found he actually cared that they'd trusted him. The last thing he wanted to do was screw that up, so he was sticking to the soda and water cooler.

Make that second to last, Maddox thought as he replayed the way Harlow's grin stretched wider and wider as he'd continued walking backward. Alternating currents of desire and affection streaked through him, but a stupid ripple of panic had to come along for the ride. His relationship with Harlow had become so important so fast that it scared him.

A red and silver can caught his eye, and while he'd never spike a girl's drink and wanted Harlow to trust him, he also wanted her to learn to be safe, even in this tiny town. As he was fishing another can out for himself, he felt a hand on his shoulder and turned, expecting the girl who'd been keeping his mind nice and busy.

Instead, a chick with über-blond hair and heavy eye makeup stood next to him. Her smile relayed she was used to getting her way. "I don't think we've met." She batted her eyes and extended a manicured hand. "I'm Bianca."

It took him a second to recognize the name. This was Harlow's former roping partner. "I'm here with someone."

"Me, too," she said, low and suggestive as she leaned closer, making it clear she didn't much care about who she came with.

Maddox quickly scanned the area, his eyes peeled for honey-colored hair. "My girl's the best. Oh, there she is." He raised his voice so Harlow would hear him over the roar of the party. "Hey, Sugar!"

Harlow spun and cocked her head, and he motioned her over. He extended the can of Coke and then took her free hand and slipped his fingers between hers. "Bianca was just introducing her-self to me, and I was telling her that I was here with my amazing girlfriend."

"Girlfriend?" Bianca's eyebrows shot up as a different, faker smile curved her lips. "Harlow! You never mentioned a boyfriend."

Harlow rested her head on his shoulder, and he got a whiff of perfume that had him longing to bury his nose in her neck for the rest of the night. "It's new. And you know, with you so busy and me training by myself now—"

"With me, you mean," Maddox said, brushing his lips across her temple for an almost kiss.

The light from the bonfire played across Harlow's features, highlighting her natural beauty as she blinked up at him. "Right. Maddox is filling your old spot."

"I hope you've got a good partner," he said without bothering to look at Bianca. Then he grinned down at his girl—er, the girl he was pretending was his. "You're going to need one to beat us."

With that, he tightened his grip on Harlow's hand and led her away from her frenemy.

"Sugar?" Harlow asked once they were a few steps away.

"'Cause you're sweet like sugar."

"Nuh-uh." She lifted her chin, attempting a stern expression she couldn't begin to pull off. "I'm tough."

"Right. I, uh, guess I forgot."

She gasped and bumped her shoulder into his, sending them both stumbling a few steps. "I am!"

"But you're also sweet, and I like that about you."

Her cheeks colored, and she glanced at their interlocked fin-gers. "Are you doing this"—she lifted their hands a foot or so—"for my benefit?"

Maddox lifted their arms even higher, all the way up to his lips, and lightly kissed her knuckles. "If it's for anyone's benefit, it's mine."

Harlow set her soda, still unopened, on the nearby tree stump. Then she wound both arms around his waist so they were chest to chest. He held his breath, afraid to move or breath, and he probably should've thought this through. "That's the sweetest thing anyone's ever said to me. Maybe I should call *you* Sugar."

One side of him cheered while the other screeched a warning. This was going to crash and burn, but damn was the thrill hard to resist.

Maddox brushed Harlow's hair off her face and trailed his fingertips down her cheek. "If I'm the sweetest guy you've ever been around, you need to broaden your horizons."

"You sell yourself short. You're a good guy, Maddox Mikos."

He wanted to argue or shake his head, but he just stood there and stared at the awe and affection etched across Harlow's face.

He'd had girls stare at him before, but it was mostly lust, and none of them had known him the way Harlow did. She'd wiggled past his defenses, and while everything in him craved letting her in, that'd only lead to more pain later.

"Harlow…"

"Maddox." She innocently batted her eyes at him, and it was the first time she'd been anything but innocent.

He swallowed hard, finding his words and his thoughts slippery. "Are you flirting with me?"

"I'm doing whatever the step beyond flirting is. I'm telling you that I see you, and I know you. And that I…I like you." She wrinkled her cute little nose, and it brought him right back to those big, brown eyes. "Is that flirting?"

It was like the world had hit the pause button, and he lifted his hand and swiped his thumb across her plump lower lip, desperate to satisfy his curiosity. No matter how good the artist, there were some things you simply couldn't capture on paper. "I like you, too, Harlow. But—"

"No buts." She gripped the sides of his shirt and tipped onto her toes.

He watched, captivated and torn and thinking about how he'd probably burn in hell for taking advantage of such a sweet, innocent girl.

He lowered his forehead to hers instead of kissing her like he longed to.

"I don't have a lot of experience," she whispered. "I was kinda hoping you'd take the initiative with the kissing."

He stepped closer to the flames, twining his fingers in her silky soft hair. "I can't, Sugar." He released a shaky exhale as he summoned every ounce of his control. "Not only did I make multiple promises to take care of you tonight and not to cross lines at the ranch—"

"We're not at the ranch. We have this one night away."

If his chest grew any tighter, he'd be unable to breathe. "You're not making this easy."

"I don't do easy," she said, and his heart nearly leaped out of his chest at the feel of her velvety-soft lips hitting his jaw. With his fingers still tangled up in her hair, the temptation to use his grip to tip her head back and give him full access to her mouth slammed into him.

"Harlow, we can't." The plea scraped his throat on the way out, leaving it achy and raw. "I'm not a good guy. Not the guy you need."

"As I said a minute or so ago, you absolutely are a good guy, and how do you know what I need?"

"I just know it's not me. You're naive if you think it'll end well."

She bristled at the accusation, which was the reason he'd chosen the word. Maybe if he pushed... Except he didn't want to push her away, even after all his lessons in what happened whenever he allowed himself to get too close.

Harlow lowered herself flat to her feet, and his body immediately missed the press of her. "Naive? Let's talk about naive." She crossed her arms in front of her, a protective move, as if her subconscious knew he was going to hurt her. "Like how you can possibly consider someone your friend after he lets you take the blame for *his* drugs?"

Apparently, *he* was the one getting hurt tonight. Kitty had claws, and she'd dug them in deep. "You don't understand. Ian's the only person who would give me a chance. He allowed me to sleep on the cot in his office when I didn't have anywhere else to go."

"No, *you* don't understand. I've never wanted to punch or strangle anyone before, but I've a mind to drive to that mechanic garage and have a not-so-friendly chat with your so-called buddy. How dare he take advantage of your situation and use you! What's he going to do when you turn eighteen? Get a new minor to do his dirty work? Or have you continue to do it until you end up in jail?"

Maddox crossed his arms right back, regardless of it being too late to shield himself. "That's my cue to go."

He spun on his heel, but Harlow grabbed his arm. "Maddox, please. You can't just storm off every time I say something you don't like."

"The 'please' won't work this time, Harlow. This is exactly what I'm talking about. How many times do we have to have the same fight?"

Her fingers slid down his arm to grip his hand, and she tugged until he turned around to face her. "How about till you see that I have a point and how much I care about you."

The words slammed into his chest with scalpel-sharp precision. "You only think you do."

The vehement shake of her head caused a dangerous sliver of hope to rise, one that'd later stab him where it hurt the most. And yet...

No. He couldn't afford to let himself hope anymore. It only lifted him that much higher before he plummeted to the ground and punched on through to rock bottom, and he couldn't survive that again.

"I'll only disappoint you." His voice came out with a rasp, his emotions way too close to the surface.

"If you do, then I'll deal with it. But try not to, okay?" Harlow sidled close enough that he could feel the rise and fall of her breaths. They were hip to hip, too, which he tried not to focus on, but how could he not? "Because I'm not gonna give up." Harlow bracketed his face with her hands, her eyes so steady on his. "Maybe other people have done that, but I'm no quitter. It's the one thing that's gotten me through the ups and downs of high school and losing my roping partner. And I refuse to give up on this—on us—when it's the strongest, realest connection I've ever experienced. Please tell me you feel it, too."

This was his chance to push her away. He could lie and tell her that he didn't feel the same. But she'd let down all her walls... Actually, he didn't know if the girl even had walls. What she'd done was put her heart on a silver platter and extend it to him, and he couldn't shove it away.

"Of course I feel it. I count the hours until I can see you again." He figured she deserved the same honesty she'd given him.

The next thing he knew, Harlow had flung her arms around his neck. She hugged him so tightly it felt like she might actually be able to hold everything that was broken inside him together.

When he pulled back enough to look at her face and reassure himself this was real, the purest, most beautiful smile he'd ever seen spread across her face, even as a hint of vulnerability swam in her eyes. "Who would've guessed that a sassy cowgirl would be just what I needed?"

"And who would've guessed a tattooed and pierced mechanic who never ties his shoes would end up being the perfect guy for me?" She licked her lips, returning his attention to that perfect mouth. "But here we are."

Maddox's heart beat out of control as he lowered his lips toward hers. The instant their mouths touched, the world jolted into motion, spinning faster and faster. He'd expected Harlow's kiss to be as sweet as she was, but she fully threw herself into it, clinging to him as she explored the seam of his lips with her tongue. Then she swept it inside, brushing the tip across his, and he stumbled toward the nearest tree, needing to find purchase before his body gave out on him.

He pressed her back against the bark, deepening the kiss and doing his best to keep his hands in the respectable range. She moved her hands down to his butt and drew him against her, so obviously, she didn't have the same qualms.

"Damn," he muttered against her lips.

"Don't you mean *dang*?"

He laughed, and then he kissed her again, taking advantage of this one perfect moment that would stand out in the mess of shitty ones, long after he was gone.

Chapter 18

"THAT'S IT!" BRADY STOOD ON THE LOWEST PLANK OF THE corral cheering along with the rest of the students as Desiree rounded the last barrel, edging it so closely they collectively held their breath.

The barrel rocked but not enough to tip, and Harlow called out the time as Desiree crossed the finish line. The whistles and congratulatory shouts grew louder, as did the rider's smile.

After she'd high-fived everyone, she sauntered over to Brady. "Do you think there's any chance I could skip my last class of the day to practice? It's not about getting out of schoolwork, I swear. I've got the first turn down, but I'm sure I can shave time off the second barrel. If there are other pointers or videos or something, I'll take any help I can get."

Honestly, a few corrections and she could hit times similar to riders in the main event. Harlow and Maddox were working hard but still had a way to go on their team roping, so he didn't want to ask Harlow to help Dez. It did give him an idea, though. "Let me make a quick call and see what I can do."

"Seriously?" Dez squealed and then waved Danica over. She slung her arm over her bestie's shoulder. "What about my other half?"

"We'll see," he said, since managing expectations was important, as was building trust and sticking to his word, so he never made promises he couldn't keep.

As soon as they'd rushed off and the kids had dispersed for the last class of the day, Brady called Tanya. Any excuse these days to hear her voice was more than welcome. "Hey," he said as soon as she picked up. "Can you spare about an hour to help Dez and Danica fine-tune their barrel-racing skills?"

The line went silent, and Brady tightened his grip on the phone. Then Tanya said, "The set of balls you must have on you, asking me to collude with the enemy."

"Must have?" Brady replied, doing a quick glance around to ensure he was alone. "Don't act like you don't remember them fondly. They're certainly big fans of you."

"I'm trying to come up with something witty, but this week has been way too hectic, and my body might or might not be missing all parts of your anatomy."

"Right back at you. We've just gotta make it to the weekend, and then we'll have three glorious days to ourselves. If it'll sweeten the pot, I'll also promise to make up the favor to you. I'll even let you choose how."

"I'm listening…"

They arranged a time for Chloe, Danica, and Dez to head to Bullhead Valley. Unfortunately, Brady had a date with a tractor. Making hay required perfect conditions. Too damp, and the bales could mold, heat, and spontaneously combust. Too dry, and they'd fall apart. It was best to bale when the dew set, so that left a narrow window.

"Thanks, Yaya," he said, wishing he could reach through the phone, draw her into his arms, and kiss her. "I swear I'll make it up to you."

"You'd better," she singsonged, and he was having to tell himself that they just had to make it to the weekend all over again.

———

Thursday evening, after completing the first round of bed checks, Brady called for Dundee. The dog barreled toward him, and Brady bent to pet and praise him before dragging his tired body toward his cabin.

Dundee kept rushing ahead and then circling back.

"I know, I know. It's been a long day, and I'm plumb tuckered out." Great. Not only was he barely able to walk after the bull wrangling he'd done today, but he'd started pilfering sayings from Ma. To be fair, hers were far safer to say in front of the kids.

Brady shed his boots inside the door and headed straight for his bedroom. He discarded his clothes, everything except his boxer briefs, and had barely settled underneath the cool sheets when his phone buzzed.

With a groan, he reached for it, almost afraid to look. What if Maddox had slipped out or run away and they had to call the cops?

He'd do just about anything to avoid that. Legally, they were required to call it in ASAP, but if he and Wade could find him before he got too far, they could try to bring him back without putting another mark on the kid's record.

When it was Tanya's name that greeted him instead, Brady's emotions did an about-face.

> **Tanya:** I'm all packed and settled in bed, thinking about our trip. If you send me a sexy selfie, I might send one back.

Every nerve ending in his body awakened at once, as if he'd hooked himself up to a car battery. He sat up against his headboard and read the text again, his eyebrows ticking together.

Seriously, a selfie? She *knew* how he felt about those, and he considered texting as much. If he had a dollar for every time he'd promised a teenager they wouldn't die if they had to go a week without being on social media or taking a picture, he'd be a wealthy man.

Funny enough, he'd found himself flipping through the pictures on his phone earlier and frowning at how few he had of Tanya. Their steamy Wednesday night had seemed too far in the past and tomorrow's trip too far in the future.

He scrolled up to see if he'd missed any other texts, which only shined a spotlight on the type of photos he usually sent her. Horse sales and a picture of the beat-up fence on the north side of the ranch. He winced at the picture of the underside of a cow, which he'd sent along with the question "Do these udders look infected to you?"

Not only was he a bit rusty in the romance arena, but he was also now very aware of how little wooing he'd done with Tanya. Somehow she'd seen deeper, but she'd been sending texts and making moves, and that meant he was going to do something he'd sworn never to do—take a fucking selfie.

Because all those other things aside, he *needed* a sexy picture of the woman who'd occupied every dirty thought he'd had over the past couple days.

"I can't believe I'm doing this." Brady aimed the camera at his torso and face, and Dundee lifted his head. One ear quirked as he cocked his head and let out a rather judgmental whimper.

"Not a peep, or you'll sleep on the couch."

With a huff, Dundee settled back down in his doggy bed.

The click of the camera sounded, and Brady lifted the phone closer and then immediately wished he hadn't. The picture wasn't sexy. From the angle he'd used, his torso was distorted and oddly lit, and did he have a double chin?

He put a hand on his neck and wiggled the skin.

Hell. Rolling his eyes at himself, he Googled "How to take a selfie." Since that phrase with "men" tacked on showed up, Brady clicked on it. He chose the first video and flinched at the voice— dude must've recently been punched in the junk.

"I can't believe I'm listening to this guy," Brady said as he noted the tips. Up was better than down. Smile, squint a bit, show off your abs…

Out of the corner of his eye, he caught movement and jumped, a thousand excuses for why he was doing something so lame on the tip of his tongue. But it was only Dundee, who'd put his paws up on the edge of the bed as if he'd come to help.

Since Brady was already down a rabbit hole of weirdness, he paused the video, then patted the bed so Dundee could hop up. "But we take this to the grave, you hear."

Dundee's pink tongue lolled as he happily panted—Brady would wager the excitement came more on account of being allowed on the bed than the video. On-screen, the man discussed angles, holding your breath and freezing, and snapping three in order to have options. A few examples flashed across the screen.

The selfie guy mentioned filters and suggested taking the time to edit. Brady was *not* doing that. There were lines that couldn't be uncrossed, and that was some kind of pretty-boy nonsense. The instructional three-minute video cut off, and then it was time for Brady to put the tips to good use.

After a momentary debate, he climbed out of bed, snagged his dressy cowboy hat from the dresser, and secured it on his head. Then he held up his camera, high enough his rumpled bed was in the background. He squinted and smiled and *click, click, click.*

Brady flipped through the results. *That's more constipated looking than anything. Eyes closed and…almost.*

Another pose, another angle, less squinting and three more selfies down.

"Wow, these ones actually aren't bad."

Dundee nudged Brady's thigh with his wet nose, so he got to see the options, too. Brady's heart quickened as he attached the picture to a text, hovered his thumb over the button, and then quickly hit Send.

Tanya bolted upright in her bed, her hands searching through the covers for her phone. Since the dating book had gotten her thus far, she'd taken a page from one of the later chapters, about how to crank up the desire to obsession.

Not that she thought Brady would ever be obsessed with her, nor did she need that. She simply wanted to keep the more-than-friends vibe flowing. If she got her money's worth out of her dating book, even better.

Finally, her hand found the electronic rectangle she'd drifted asleep clutching. Right before she'd hit Send and felt as powerful as she had in the cab of Brady's truck. The instant the message was gone, her stomach had lurched, and she'd thought she might lose her dinner.

The longer Brady had taken, the surer she became that she'd gone too far. With a guy she'd known forever, had sex with, and hoped to have more sex with tomorrow and the next day and the next…

But the instant she pulled up the photo he'd sent, she decided it was well worth the wait.

"Holy shit," she whispered into the darkness of her bedroom as she zoomed in on various body parts. She'd been prepared to drool, but the pulsing between her thighs was a side effect she hadn't bargained on.

We'll be on our way to the fair in seven hours. Then we'll have time to alleviate all this pent-up sexual frustration.

Brady: That was akin to torture, by the way, so gimme.

Hmm. Someone needed a vocabulary *and* a patience lesson. Tanya flipped on the lamp atop her nightstand, ran a hand through her hair, and took a picture of her shoulder and the super-skinny ribbon that held up her nightie. She wasn't the type of girl to wear fancy pajamas, but luckily, she'd planned for this.

Tanya: I did say I MIGHT send one back. You took your sweet time, too. But here you go. Enjoy. XOXO

She gambled that this time, she wouldn't have to wait as long for an answer.

Sure enough, her phone vibrated, not with a text but with an incoming call. She affected her best sensual Playboy Bunny voice. "Hello?"

"Your shoulder? Is it even *your* shoulder? I can't tell because your face isn't in it, and I call bullshit."

"Did you see the part where I pointed out that there weren't any promises made?"

"If that's what you're going with, I promise I'm going to storm over there right now and take a picture my damn self. I watched a fucking tutorial on how to take a selfie, Tanya."

In the background, Dundee barked.

"Okay, fine, Dundee. I'll let her know you also watched the video and provided feedback."

A giggle slipped out, and she twirled a curl around her finger. As if watching a video to send her a sexy selfie wasn't sweet enough, he'd enlisted the help of his dog? Her insides melted, and if they weren't hours away from their getaway, she'd be banging his door down right now. "A video, huh? Was that hard for you?"

"Damn straight. And speaking of things that are hard, I've got something that's gonna be hard for you all night now. The least you could do is send me a photo to help take the edge off."

Heat pooled in her belly and flared in every direction until her cheeks radiated fire.

"If you want to," he added, the gentleman in him unable to help it, even as his caveman side caused the words to come out grumbly.

"Full disclosure, that was the plan. I just thought it'd be fun to tease you and ensure you're properly anticipating our trip first."

"I'm anticipating it, and there's nothing proper about it. Because there's this thing called payback, and we're gonna see how you like to be teased."

Tanya squirmed underneath her covers, turned on and possibly in over her head. If she could unstick her tongue from the roof of her mouth, maybe she'd think up a witty retort or be able to grab her dating book and see if it provided any suggestions. Instead, she was considering driving over to Brady's and regretting her lack of sleep in the morning.

Then again, there might be a happy medium. She snatched the brazen idea instead of stifling it. "What if I make it up to you?" At the dude ranch, they focused on getting people to disconnect and experience the slower pace of life, but technology did have its uses. Turned out flirting was a muscle, one that became stronger the more she'd used it. "I'll give you a choice. I can send a sexy photo…*or* we can stay on the phone and FaceTime."

The request to add video to their chat was all the answer she needed.

Chapter 19

"How's your preshow team doing, anyway?" Brady asked Tanya as they reached the last leg of their trip to Ogallala. After chatting and, um, taking care of business over the phone last night, the two of them were red-eyed yet giddy and had spent the first hour of their trip alternating between light touches, yawns, grinning, and caffeinating.

The only problem with chasing away the grogginess was that it awoke other parts of her, and were they there yet? She needed to get the guy she'd scooted next to into the privacy of their hotel room ASAP. Tanya took a swig from the bucket-sized Mountain Dew cup they were sharing. "Nice try, but I'm not falling for your dirty spy tactics. You won't get intel out of me just because we're sleeping together."

One of Brady's eyebrows arched higher than the other. "You forget I now know all the right buttons to push." He placed his hand on her upper thigh and slowly drifted it higher. Her pulse zipped faster with each inch, her body not caring she'd taken the edge off last night.

"Pretty sure if we start playing this game"—she wrapped her hand around his thigh and used his own move against him—"you and I will wreck and die before we get to the hotel. Then all that button pushing isn't going to happen."

"That'd be a shame," he said, loosening his grip but not removing his hand.

She couldn't remember the last time she'd been so blissfully happy. Yeah, the horse-rescue ranch stuff was still in the back of her head, but it wasn't going anywhere.

As they entered the city, they hit traffic, which left them

crawling toward their destination when they wanted to sprint. Brady tapped the steering wheel as she jiggled her foot, but at long last, they reached the hotel.

They shot out of the truck like it was on fire, and when she went to reach for her suitcase in the bed of the truck, Brady snagged the handle before she could.

"I can take it," she said.

"I believe you've met my ma. She's about yea high"—he placed a flat hand in the middle of his chest to demonstrate—"and would tan my hide if she found out I let you carry your own suitcase. And that's without being on the up and up about our relationship. If you don't remember my stubborn stance on this, I guess it's been too long since we were on the rodeo circuit together."

Of course Tanya remembered. It'd been one of their biggest disagreements. She'd argue she could do it herself and insist he didn't treat her like some fragile flower. While she'd meant it during that time, she realized allowing kindness spurred more of it, and she also admired his chivalrous side.

"Thank you. I appreciate how you always treat me like a lady." Brady scrunched up his forehead. "Is this a trap?"

"What? No." Tanya smacked his arm. "I'm trying to tell you that I appreciate you. Don't be a jerk about it."

"You've just never thanked me for something like that before. In fact, usually you get pissed if I treat you like a lady."

A pang went through her chest. "I thought I was being strong and independent, not rude and shitty. I'm guessing that makes you feel like I don't appreciate you."

"Hey." Brady cupped her chin and tilted her face to his. "You and I don't have to say those types of things. We just know."

"Oh? What else do you just know?"

He dipped his head and kissed her. "This weekend is going to be amazing, and once we set foot in our hotel room, I'm gonna devour you."

Butterflies erupted, swirling and multiplying as he brushed his lips across hers again. "Not if I devour you first." What could she say? She'd always been competitive, and obviously, he recognized that by now.

They checked in at the front desk, hopped the elevator, and stepped into Room 207.

"Wow. A bed even?" Tanya said as she eyed the king-size bed in the center of the room. "What am I, the Queen of England?"

The *thud* of the suitcases hitting the floor echoed through the room, and she turned in time to see Brady stalk toward her. Heat ignited every cell in her body, and an instinctual squeak came out, even though she had no intention of fleeing this hunter.

He gripped her hips, lifted her off her feet, and tossed her onto the bed. After removing his hat and boots, he crawled over her and rained down pleasure with an intoxicating mixture of coarse stubble and soft lips.

His cell phone trilled, the electronic square vibrating against her hip bone through the pocket of his jeans. He reached back and gripped the collar of his shirt, pulling it up and over his head in a way that would frizz her hair. Then his lips descended on hers again as he fiddled with the buttons on her shirt. One by one, they came undone, and as he dragged his mouth over the swell of her breasts, her nipples puckered in anticipation.

The phone rang again, and Brady sat up. Surely, he wasn't going to answer a call in the middle of their heated make-out session.

Thankfully, he unbuttoned and unzipped his Wranglers and shucked them, phone and all, onto the floor. "Where was I?" Brady raked his gaze over her. "Right. Getting you naked and underneath me." He undid her jeans and tugged them off her thighs. He paused to rid her of her boots, and then her pants joined his on the floor.

As he leaned over her, Tanya hooked her legs around his waist and secured him against her. The warmth of his skin seeped into her, and she rolled her hips, gasping as his erection knocked against her core.

A booming knock echoed through the room, and Brady and Tanya both froze, their eyes going wide.

"Knock, knock." The door muffled the deep, rumbly voice but not enough to prevent her from recognizing it as Nash's. "I called and called, but you must have your phone on silent. I'm gonna tell Ma on you."

"Shit," Tanya said at the same time as Brady did.

"Lucky for you, I was able to sweet-talk the desk clerk into giving out your room number. She said you'd just checked in, too."

Brady leaped off the bed, extended a hand to Tanya, and hauled her to her feet. He scooped up their pile of clothes and shoved her jeans and shirt toward her. "Can you answer the door? My dick doesn't currently fit in my pants."

A giggle burst out, and Brady chuckled as well.

Nash knocked again. "Hello? Have you gone deaf?"

Tanya jerked on her clothes as fast as she could. Brady's T-shirt was on, the button and zipper of his Wranglers undone, and she smacked his ass as she walked past. "Can't wait till later, when we can finish what we started."

"Not helping," Brady muttered, ducking into the bathroom as Tanya went to answer the door.

As soon as she swung it open, Nash wrapped her in a bear hug. "Tanya! I haven't seen you in forever. You look…" His eyebrows drew together. "Flushed."

"Um, yeah, I was on the bed dozing off a bit, and…" She studied him right back, from the angles of his cheekbones to the strong jawline, dusted with blond whiskers. She tugged the ends of his hair, now long enough to brush his shoulders. "Dude. No barbers on the road?"

"Don't act like you're not affected by the sexiness," Nash said, waggling his eyebrows, and she laughed. The guy had the bluest eyes she'd ever seen, but there was a hint of sorrow in the depths that'd never gone away, as if he'd lived three lifetimes already.

"Why do you think I haven't been to Silver Springs in a while. Ma would chase after me with scissors, and I doubt telling her that I'm like that Samson dude who got strength from his hair would do any good."

"It would not," Tanya confidently proclaimed.

Brady stepped out of the bathroom, and she got out of the way as the two brothers strode toward each other. They crashed into a hug in the middle of the room, and Tanya found her throat unexpectedly tight. She wasn't sure of all the reasons Nash stayed away, but she did know Brady missed him terribly.

They clapped each other on the back—presumably because slapping made hugs manlier—and then settled into the two chairs at the circular table in the corner of the room. Tanya sat on the foot of the bed, and they chatted about life and rodeos. Nash made a joke about how he'd won so many buckles and saddles that soon he'd be unable to carry all his prizes around.

"Humble as ever, I see," Tanya teased.

"I'll get right on that after I'm the number-one-ranked bull rider in the world."

"So any day now."

"Give or take."

They all chuckled, and the strings in Tanya's heart twanged. With Brady around, she didn't lament the loss of the "good ol' days" often, but now that the three of them were together again, she could hardly focus on anything else. She'd missed this, but seeing Nash somehow made her miss him even more. It'd be tempting to use this as an opportunity to persuade him to come home. All the Dawsons missed him fiercely. But she'd sometimes resented her lack of options, so she wasn't going to pressure him to fit in whatever box he'd view as a cage.

"Anything else you two want to disclose while we're catching up?" Nash asked, and Tanya and Brady shared a look. Did they fake ignorance? Did they tell? It wasn't like he could just sense it.

Right?

"Yes, I am talking about you two. Tanya, your shirt is crooked, and Brady, the bottom of yours is sticking out your fly."

"What?" Brady glanced down. "Bro, what have I said about staring at people's crotches? It's creepy."

"Nice try, but your reverse psychology tricks don't work on me now that I'm so mature and shit." Nash crossed his arms on the tabletop and narrowed his eyes at them. "How long have you been sleeping together?"

————————

If Brady were being honest, he'd wanted to shout the news from the rooftops for days. He glanced at Tanya again and, at her nod, came clean. "We took things to the next level a couple weeks ago, and we've been fitting in as much line-crossing as possible since, if you know what I mean."

"Nice," Nash said, and they high-fived.

"Um, hello?" Tanya said, waving her arms as if they'd forgotten about her.

"Sorry." Nash scooted the roller chair to the foot of the bed and held up his palm. "High-five." He added his stupidly charming grin, and Tanya smacked his hand.

"No one else knows, and like Brady said, it's new."

"Maybe to you two." Nash snatched the bag of sunflower seeds they'd brought off the TV stand and helped himself. One cheek popped out as he poured the seeds into his mouth. "The rest of us have seen it since always."

"See, this is why we're not telling people," Brady said, and out of the corner of his eye, he noticed Tanya's furrowed brow. "Isn't it?"

"I…" She shrugged. "Something about complications and people in our business. Sounds like everyone's been all up in it since always."

"That's why I got out of town. Silver Springs is a fuckin' fish-bowl sometimes and sadly short on things to do."

"Just don't ever say anything like that to Ma."

"Who do you think I am? The same punk kid who first came to the ranch?" Nash cracked open sunflower seeds with his teeth. "One day, it'll be a great place to settle down. But for me, that day is way, way, *way* down the road."

Tanya tucked her legs underneath her. "Too busy bedding buckle bunnies?"

"Too busy in general. But shame on you, Tanya Clayton, for prying into my love life." Nash placed a hand on his chest and added an overly dramatic gasp, and Tanya threw a pillow at his head.

Nash blocked it with his forearm. "Bro. Control your woman."

With a shriek, Tanya launched herself at Nash, pillow in hand. She smacked him with one end, and they went back and forth, exchanging insults and pillow hits and laughing. Then Tanya moved to Brady's side of the table and sat on his lap, one arm draped over his shoulders.

He snaked an arm around her waist and leaned into the kiss she offered him. With her snuggled close and his brother here laughing and talking, the sense of fullness he'd been missing the past several months settled over him, and he wished he could hold on to it for longer.

"Sorry, lovebirds." Nash stood and raked his hands through his hair. "But we've gotta get going. I'd like to grab lunch before we head to the fairgrounds, because we'll probably have to eat dinner there. Then Destiny awaits."

"Wow. Never thought I'd hear you spouting lines about destiny," Brady said, getting to his feet as well but keeping his arm secured around Tanya's waist.

"Don't worry. I didn't get all deep and reflective on the road." Nash clapped him on the shoulder. "Destiny is the name of the enormous, grumpy-ass bull I drew."

Chapter 20

As Brady sat in the grandstand, holding hands with Tanya, he was on cloud nine. It was fun watching the emotions flicker across his best friend's face as she winced and cheered for the riders—and for the bulls—as they took their spin in the rodeo grounds.

"What?" she asked when she glanced at him, making him realize how intensely he'd been staring with a goofy grin on his face.

"I just… This is nice, being here with you like this." He leaned in and kissed her pinkening cheek.

"You don't miss the rush of the arena?"

"Here and there, sure. I think I tend to idealize the good old days and forget that competing also took a lot out of me. Honestly, I never expected to enjoy sitting in the stands so much, but I was watching you get all riled up, so pretty I can hardly believe you're mine, and it's a different kind of rush. One I could definitely get used to."

At the moment, Brady could hardly remember what the anxious, restless sensation that'd plagued him for months even felt like.

But hearing "Nash Sutherland" across the speakers caused tension to creep along the line of his shoulders. He and Tanya stood, as did the rest of the crowd, because they were up to the heats with the cream of the crop, and every second mattered that much more.

Tanya tightened her grip on his hand to the point he might not have circulation in it for the rest of the day, but he held on to her right back. "He's got this," she said. "He does this all the time, and he's a pro."

"You convincing you or me?"

She sank her teeth into her bottom lip. "I'm not rightly sure. Eeep—"

The sound of the gate swallowed up the tail end of her nervous noise, and Brady's heart beat double time. "The bull's kicking and spinning great."

"Nice height and rotation," Tanya added. "So lots of points there."

Brady winced as the bull cranked at an angle that threw most riders, and Nash's head flung forward, his face missing the sharp end of one of the horns by mere centimeters. Brady's breath whooshed out in relief as Nash corrected, riding parallel to the animal, the arm in the air never touching the bull.

"Six, seven…eight," Tanya said, and the buzzer punctuated her countdown.

They screamed and cheered, as did everyone around them. Nash had built quite a name for himself. Ever the show-off, he out-clowned the clowns, shaking his ass at the bull. Then he sprinted over to the audience, tossed his hat into the stands, and threw up a fist.

The crowd roared, eating up the cockiness and blasé attitude.

Nash was well suited for this career and for the fame that came along. Adrenaline plus adoration without anyone scratching beyond the surface or digging too deep. Occasionally, Brady worried his brother hadn't quite slayed all his demons, but if riding bulls kept them away, he wished Nash a lengthy and successful career. Now he just had to keep that from giving Ma a heart attack—which was why he kept his concerns to himself.

Ma had a saying about the teens who only became angrier if you showed them any kind of praise or affection. "Some people need more love to fill their well, but unfortunately, those who were supposed to keep it primed and full never added anything, so they sealed it and gave up. What we've gotta do is keep on pouring, even if only a couple of drops get through that lid at a time."

She'd also added that water was one of the most powerful forces on earth—second to love, of course.

As the announcer leaned toward the microphone to read off Nash's scores, the crowd collectively held their breath.

"Eighty-seven point nine."

The crowd went wild once again, celebrating the fact that Nash had just taken the lead by a point and a half, with only one more rider to go. Eight seconds could feel like a freaking eternity in so many ways. In the arena. Biding your turn to go. Watching a loved one. Waiting to see if someone else would beat the top score.

The next rider stayed on for eight seconds, but the bull wasn't as tough to manage, and the rider didn't look to be as in control as Nash had been. Sure enough, a moment later, Nash sealed the win.

"We should go find him before this place gets crazy," Brady shouted at Tanya over the racket, and she took his hand. They made their way down the grandstand bleachers and headed around back to wait for Nash by his parked truck.

But then Tanya gasped, and a horse let out an awful noise full of pain, and Brady whirled to find the source. His brain caught up to his eyes a couple of seconds later as he watched a man flog a gray-speckled horse.

Tanya's hand slid from his before he realized what she was doing. She sprinted over and inserted herself between the hysterical horse and the man with the whip, and his heart lurched in his chest, so much panic flooding his body he feared he might drown in it.

———

"Stop," Tanya pleaded. "He's hurt and exhausted—"

"Mind your own business, bitch. He's my horse, and I can do what I please. Now move, or you'll get the whip, too." He cocked his arm, and Tanya lifted her shoulder and ducked her head, bracing for impact.

The man flung his arm forward, but Brady caught the guy's wrist, spun him around, and clocked him in the nose. He fell to the ground, swearing and screaming as blood gushed from his nose.

"Stay down," Brady said in the firmest, scariest voice she'd ever heard him use.

One of the guy's stout cohorts rushed Brady from behind, but then Nash was there blocking and shoving him away. "You're gonna stay back. I just rode an eighteen-hundred-pound bull, so I'm fairly certain I could handle you."

The guy held up his hands and slowly backpedaled.

"Smart move," Nash said.

Tanya's rapid pulse throbbed, everywhere screaming at once—from the confrontation and thinking she was about to feel leather slice her skin and Brady and Nash and the horse. Passing out wouldn't do anyone any good, so she sucked in a deep breath and cooed at the horse as she ran a gentle hand over it, avoiding the lacerations, some old, some fresh with dark-red blood.

Out of the corner of her eye, she caught sight of the abusive owner, lunging for Brady's legs. Tanya opened her mouth to call out to him, but her cowboy was already anticipating the move. With the heel of his boot, Brady kicked the guy flat on his back. He dove on top of him, one hand fisted in his shirt, the other clenched and ready to strike.

Nash grabbed Brady by the arm. "Remember what Ma always says. Doesn't matter if someone else loses their temper, we keep our heads. We have to be better."

"Tell that to his horse. To Tanya—he nearly whipped her."

Other cowboys had obviously seen the altercation and were rushing over, and a police officer was also headed their way, coming from the grandstand area. Seconds before everyone else arrived, Brady straightened.

As various voices shouted and explanations began, Tanya returned her attention to the horse. "You okay, big guy?"

She frowned at the raw skin behind the bronco's front legs—most likely a product of fastening the cinch too tight, and not just today, either. Another mark left her suspecting the guy also used a wire tie-down, which kept a horse's head from lifting too high. An ache burrowed itself deep in her heart and radiated sorrow and indignation through every inch of her body.

Her throat constricted to the point she wasn't sure she could successfully get out any words, and thanks to the ruckus of several baritone voices speaking at once, she had to force her voice louder. "We need a vet, ASAP."

The officer glanced in her direction. "Already on her way. She'll be here any minute."

Tanya nodded, and the abusive owner yelled he'd sue them all and that he was going to press charges and she'd better get away from his horse or he'd have her arrested.

"You're the one going down to the station," the officer said as he bent and cuffed the man's wrists. "Afraid I didn't get the name of the guy who hit you." The officer tilted his head at Brady, hinting for him to get lost.

"Not without her," Brady said, jerking his chin her way.

Tanya cleared her throat so her words would come out as firm as her decision. "It's okay. I'll be fine. You and Nash do a lap or whatever while I wait for the vet."

"I'm here," a female voice said, sticking an arm in the air and waving it around, and the men parted to make way for a dark-haired woman who was *maybe* five foot. She had big, brown eyes and hoop earrings and was unquestionably the youngest, prettiest veterinarian Tanya had ever seen. Judging from the dropped jaws of the cowboys—save Brady, who was still looking at her, and was that hurt in his eyes? "I'm Doctor Camila Rojas."

"Tanya Clayton. I don't own the horse. I just stepped in when I saw the guy whipping him while he was tied to a post." She updated the doctor on what she'd witnessed and the wounds she'd spotted behind the front legs.

Dr. Rojas didn't have to lean down nearly as far as Tanya did to examine the underside of the gelding. She unzipped her medical bag and dug through her supplies. "If everyone will give me some space," she said, and Tanya hesitantly turned to go. It'd be torture not to know if the horse was going to be okay or what was going to happen to him, and this was why she needed to open her rescue ranch. There were too many cases like this, and some of the abused horses didn't have time on their side, which meant neither did she.

Tanya turned to leave, but stopped when Dr. Rojas placed her hand on her arm.

"Mind sticking around and helping me keep the horse steady and calm?"

"Of course. I mean, of course not. I'd be happy to help." Tanya glanced over her shoulder to signal the boys. Brady's flinty expression confused and concerned her, but before she could address it, Nash gave her a look that conveyed he'd take care of it and nudged his brother away from the melee.

———

Brady paced the length of Nash's truck, back and forth, back and forth.

"Bro. Sit down," Nash called from where he was lounging on the tailgate. "You're making me nervous."

"Well, at least one of us has enough sense to worry. If you're going to ride bulls and Tanya's going to take on every abusive lowlife this side of the Mississippi, that leaves me to be the responsible one."

"Nah, that's Wade's job."

Brady whirled on his brother, not in any mood to joke. "He's got other things to worry about. He's engaged, with a baby on the wa—" Too late, Brady caught himself.

"Wade and Jess are having a baby?"

"Dammit." Brady scrubbed a hand over his face. "I was supposed to let Wade tell you. Didn't he call you?"

"He left a message, but I haven't gotten around to returning the call."

"Because you know he'll give you shit for not coming home to say hello to Ma once in a while?"

Nash's usual humor faded, and a muscle flexed in his jaw and cheek. "I get it. I'm the asshole who abandoned the family who actually wanted me. If you don't think I know that, don't worry. I do."

"That's not what I was sayi—"

Nash held up a hand and said, "Don't bother." He scooted to the edge of the tailgate, and then closed it with a loud clang. "I'm gonna go for a walk. Clear my head. Maybe you should do the same."

With a groan, Brady threw back his head. His entire body vibrated with rage, his nerves stretching and fraying, a second from snapping. He was about to take Nash's suggestion to take a walk and cool off, but he spotted fiery-red curls, and his feet quickly ate up the space between them.

"What were you thinking, getting between that asshole and that horse?" He hadn't meant to bellow the question, and the anger that widened Tanya's eyes let him know she didn't appreciate his tone.

"I was thinking I needed to stop him. That's as far as I got."

"That's the problem," he said, keeping his words softer but unable to keep himself from speaking his mind. "You can't go around all half-cocked, flinging yourself in danger's way. Next time, just give me a heads-up. We can make a plan, be smarter about it, and stop it together."

"Smarter about it?" She crossed her arms, the move emphasizing her cleavage and scrambling his brain. "Please, tell me about how impulsive and hotheaded I am. How I don't think things through enough. You wanna call up my dad while you're at it, so you guys can present a united front?"

Brady blew the air from his nostrils, understanding those raging bulls that charged into the arena looking for a target. "That's not fair."

"You sure about that? Or do you want to hear the rest of what I've got to say before you decide?" She stormed closer, and Brady did his best to maintain a neutral expression. "Because that horse needs a place to recover and someone to help, and you bet your ass I volunteered. Unfortunately, that means we're gonna need to cut our trip short." Her voice cracked, and the hard shell that'd formed around him did, too. "But if all we're gonna do is fight, maybe that's a good thing."

He pinched the bridge of his nose, frustrated they'd somehow ended up here when this was supposed to be a carefree weekend *away* from complications. "Look, it just scared the shit out of me. Can't you understand what it's like to see someone you care about seconds from getting hurt? And then have to leave them behind?"

Tanya glanced away, and when her gaze returned to his, unshed tears glistened in her eyes. "Can't you understand that I can't *not* do something? This whole experience proves I can't sit back and wait any longer." A tear slipped down her cheek, and she swiped it away. "I have to do whatever it takes to help. And I have to do it now."

Brady surged forward and gripped her shoulders, unable to stand there and watch her cry without attempting to comfort her. "I do. It's one of the things I love about you. But I'm here. I want to help. But you have to let me."

"I'm sick of everyone telling me what I should do. Of not having a say in my own life."

That stung, and his defenses pricked. Was he included in that "everyone"? He reckoned he could've worded things better. "Let me try again. I want to help. Please let me?"

She hugged him around his middle and dropped her head on his chest. "I don't know why I'm crying. Yeah, it was intense and kinda scary, but I'm"—*sniff*—"fine."

He tucked her head under his chin as he held her. "Adrenaline's awesome, but coming off it after a traumatic situation, not so much."

He felt her nod against his chest, and she sniffed again. "The fresh injuries were bad enough, but the horse has so many scars, and I can't stop thinking of everything he's endured, which is why when they said they didn't have any place that could take the horse right now, I volunteered."

Of course she did. It didn't surprise him in the least, but it didn't bother him, either. He'd seen her with Phoenix, Winston, and every other injured animal that crossed her path. Hell, she'd gotten a reputation in the three counties that surrounded theirs. "Do we need to find a horse trailer?"

"No, I already worked it out with a guy from Loveland. He's gonna put his horse in with a friend's and said he doesn't even mind picking it up from Bullhead Valley because he wanted to do what he could to help."

It probably didn't hurt that Tanya was also a beautiful woman, but saying so and letting his jealousy get the best of him might undo the peace.

Tanya broke the embrace, wiped at her cheeks, and glanced around, her eyebrows ticking together. "Where's Nash?"

"Ah, I pissed him off, too. I'm on a real streak today."

She gave a half laugh, half sob. Then her features grew serious, and he instinctively steeled himself. Days like this, he couldn't help wishing he had a rewind button. Then he could undo and make it right. Although, truth be told, he would've just put himself in the way of harm instead of letting Tanya do it, and that likely would've made her mad, too.

"What does it say about us that we couldn't even make it through a weekend without a fight?"

Brady shrugged. "That's hardly unusual for us. Sometimes it's a playful kind of an argument, or we're talking trash during competitions, or rubbing one another's face in our victories."

"True. I guess I just thought that with us dating, things would be smoother. Since we already know each other and have since forever."

"Hey." Brady cupped her cheek. "We agree on a lot, but we're both stubborn and opinionated, so we've got a few angry fireworks to mix in with the sexy kind." He looped his finger through her belt loop, fervently needing to keep her close and placated so she wouldn't go doubting them already.

She nodded her head, and he hoped that meant she believed him. Crazy how they could go from pure bliss to so much friction and unease in less than an hour. "It might be trickier, and more work than either one of us realized, but I'm all in. Okay?"

One corner of her mouth twisted up, and while he'd prefer her full smile, he'd settle for half. "Okay."

A loud throat clearing announced Nash's approach. "You two get things all patched up?"

"Yeah, and I guess it's time for apology number two," Brady said, turning to his brother. "I was worried and grumpy, and I shouldn't have taken it out on you."

"Ah. Probably needed to be said. I can't exactly explain why, but I..." Nash rubbed his fingertips along his jaw. "I have plenty of good memories at the ranch, but sometimes being there just reminds me of the first fifteen years of my life and of my dad, and then I didn't come home when Ma was in the hospital, and after that, I didn't feel worthy to drop by anymore."

Brady's throat tightened, and Tanya flung her arms around Nash. That belief system Brady was working to shake, about how people broke those they claimed to care about, seemed to be tapping him on the shoulder. Despite all the progress Nash had made, he was still restless and averse to counseling. Ironic, considering

Nick was such an amazing therapist. Not that Nash would see his brother, but there were plenty of good ones out there—for instance, Liza.

"Now, now, I don't need all this," Nash said in a husky voice that belied his statement.

"Your family loves you and always will," Tanya said. "They're also fairly understanding and big believers in second, third, and twentieth chances."

"Twenty?" One blond eyebrow rose higher than the other. "Really?"

"Too low?" Tanya quipped, and Nash laughed full-out, back to his charming, boisterous self. "So not to break up the happy, but we should get that horse loaded."

"That hors—don't tell me," Nash said. "You're gonna rehabilitate it and find it a good home."

"As long as the officer and the law back me up, I'll be able to do it without a big fight. Well, save maybe a fight with my pop."

Nash backhanded Brady's pec as they started over to where the trailer and horse were. "Remember that time she made us stop in the middle of a road for a bird?"

"Oh yeah." Brady smiled as he recalled the day he, Nash, and Tanya had been late for school trying to save the tiny creature. "On her insistence, we were gonna drive it to the clinic, but the poor thing shuddered its last breath."

Nash took up the familiar story, the sense of nostalgia tinging the evening once again. "I tried to put it in a nice patch of grass, but this girl vehemently shook her head."

"Coyotes could've gotten it there," Tanya said, and Brady and Nash chuckled, not because the bird's death hadn't been tragic but because she'd given them big puppy-dog eyes until they'd relented and let her pick a burial spot near the trees.

Brady drifted a hand over her back, this amazing woman who'd always been so fierce yet kind. "So we pulled the shovel out of the back of the truck and got to work, even though the ground was frozen solid. Gave it a proper burial, and for our efforts—"

"Detention," they all grumbled together, as if they were teenagers again. It wasn't the first or last time they'd had detention. Ma used to lecture them on setting a good example and giving the townsfolk hope she could rehabilitate teens instead of proving she couldn't even handle her own kids. Tanya had been part of that, too, as she and her family had always been considered part of theirs.

They talked to the cowboy from Loveland, got the gorgeous blue-eyed Appaloosa into the trailer, and then headed to the hotel to grab their bags and switch trucks. From there, they made their goodbyes.

After one last hug, Tanya told Nash and Brady she was going to give them some privacy to say goodbye and if they needed to clear any of their earlier shit to do so. They both saluted her, earning them a shake of the head and a muttered "smart-ass cowboys" before she climbed into the truck.

Once again, Brady found his throat too tight. Here he was, borrowing a page from Ma again. He didn't know when he'd see his brother next, and with his high-risk career, there was always a chance that... Well, he wasn't going down that road. He hugged Nash and clapped him on the back. "It was really good to see you. I'm not gonna pressure you to visit, but I will say you're always welcome and should never hesitate. The local rodeo's coming up, if that's the only way we can get you there."

Nash grunted, which meant he'd think about it. Or that he wouldn't discuss it. Either way, it was the best he could give. Then he patted Brady hard on the back and headed toward his truck. He abruptly spun around and gestured toward the cab of the truck. "Don't mess that up—you and Tanya. You're good together."

"Trust me, I'm gonna do my best." Brady hadn't been worried

until their fight this afternoon. He couldn't lose rodeo and Tanya on top of everything else, so he sent a wish into the universe that his best would be good enough.

Chapter 21

Tanya stormed out of the office and nearly slammed into Eric. She stuttered to a stop, her eyes and nose burning with the urge to cry. To say the meeting with her parents had not gone well would be a massive understatement.

"Sorry," she choked out. "Did you need something?"

"Sounds like you might. Would you like to go for a horse ride? I might be able to keep up with you—as long as you go slow."

Tanya barely kept her laugh from turning into a sob. "I could use a ride."

Over the past month, Eric's cowboy skills had vastly improved. She wasn't sure he was ready to run a ranch, but sometimes you had to dive in. Unless people insisted on blocking the path, the way her parents were doing.

As if he sensed her distress, Diesel didn't complain about the slower pace. They cantered across the rolling green miles to the top of the hill that provided a stellar view. "See how the valley looks like a bull head, complete with horns?" Eric's brow furrowed, and she trotted a bit closer to him and Taffy and pointed out the shape with her finger. "That's how Bullhead Valley got its name."

"Now I see it. Kind of." His gaze fixated more on her than the view, and judging from the concern crinkling his brow, she'd failed at putting on a happy front. "So full disclosure, I couldn't hear what the fight was about, but it sounded heated."

Tanya put a hand to her face. "How embarrassing and unprofessional. I'm so sorry."

"You forget that I've been in corporate meetings with twenty men who argue and yell and then throw a tantrum if they don't get their way." Eric waved a hand through the air. "That was nothing."

It didn't feel like nothing. More like she'd caught a fragile butterfly of a dream, only to have batted it to the ground and squashed. The business plan she'd spent the last twenty-four hours perfecting twitched, legs up and a moment from death. "I want to start a horse rescue ranch."

"Ah. I saw that you'd brought another pony home."

"Yeah, after I stepped between the horse and the asshole who'd tied it up to beat it"—she gritted her teeth, and she'd been doing enough of it the past couple of days that her jaw ached—"and then Brady was pissed I put myself in danger without consulting him first." As if talking things out ever helped. "Maybe I do have impulse-control problems, but if the other option is to stand by and say nothing, I'd rather embrace my obstinance."

"I'd say it's more compassion, passion, and ambition—all qualities I look for when I hire someone, by the way."

"Well, it doesn't so much matter what qualities I have if I can't get anyone else on board. This part of the ranch is great for grazing, but there's more than enough room to build another set of stables and still allow the horses room to roam. And still, my parents refuse to let me try. I told them I'd start searching for other properties and take out a loan, but it's not like I have a down payment saved. As my dad so nicely pointed out, my credit's not great. I got a bit carried away pretending my credit card was free money in college."

While her scholarship took care of tuition, she'd had to buy a laptop and books and pay rent in one of the most expensive cities in the state. "But I chipped away at it, and I'm working on improving my credit score." Tanya wrinkled her nose. "Wow. That might be the most boring phrase I've ever uttered. Being an adult is so overrated."

"I hope I'm not overstepping by saying so, but that goes double when people don't treat you like one."

That twang in her chest sharpened, and because it hurt too

badly to admit he'd hit the nail on the head, she shrugged. "My parents are old-school. It's their way or the highway."

"Have you ever considered the highway?"

Tanya lowered her eyebrows, trying to figure out what he meant by that. Just walk away from the ranch that'd been in her family for generations? "Did you not hear the part about not having money?"

"Let me back up a bit further, and maybe then what I'm about to say will make more sense. Have you ever gotten in over your head for a bet?"

If Tanya rattled off every time her and Brady's competitions had grown out of control and how far she'd go to win—for instance, her rodeo team was now doing two-a-days—they'd be there all afternoon. "More times than I can count."

"Then you might get a kick out of what I'm about to tell you." Eric braced his crossed forearms on the saddle horn. "When I found out my aunt had left her ranch to me, I was shocked. The summers I spent there were amazing, but I hadn't spent more than a day or two there since high school, and I spent most of that time cursing the slow internet."

This time, her smile came easy. "We finally upgraded a couple of summers ago because every single complaint was about the weak internet connection. People seemed to miss the point about getting away from it all."

"Well, it's easier to do that if you can send a quick email."

Tanya rolled her eyes, nice and big, and Eric laughed.

"But to your point, my reliance on my Wi-Fi connection and phone is probably why my buddy laughed so hard when I told him I was considering selling my business and becoming a full-time rancher. He bet me I couldn't make it a month here, and I was determined to prove him wrong."

"Some of my proudest accomplishments have come from pettiness."

Eric laughed again. "Mine, too. Admittedly, being here this past month also made it clear that I can't run a ranch on my own. I've barely scratched the surface of what I need to know. Which brings me to my comment about taking the highway…"

During his pause, the munching sound of the horses filled the air, along with the light metallic clink of the buckles on their bridles, and a bird soared overhead with a loud caw.

"A buyer is interested in buying RichTech, and I've decided to sell and take on a new challenge. With my company, I've always been comfortable taking bold risks. But with my aunt's ranch, I worry I'll screw it up." His gaze met hers. "You're underutilized here, Tanya. Help me run my ranch, and not only will I take you on as a partner with an equal say on what happens, but I'll build the biggest damn stable you've ever seen for your rescue horses."

For a moment, all she could do was blink at him. "Are you being serious right now?"

He pressed his lips together as if he was trying not to laugh. "I'm one hundred percent serious. I'd already surmised I'd want to hire someone like you, so once you told me about your dream of running a rescue ranch, I saw a way for both of us to get what we want."

Could it really be that easy? No going into debt, no strings, just her dream offered up on a silver platter? "Equal say? As in we listen and talk and then you decide which way we go?"

"What kind of bullshit equality is that? We'll have a small staff, but you and I will run the show. If anything, I'll defer to you because you've lived this life your entire… You get it."

Diesel stepped a few paces to nibble on a new patch of grass as Tanya's thoughts bounced around her head. She knew she needed to ask the next question. She just wasn't sure she wanted the answer. It was something she should've asked before her excitement level had been cranked to ten. "Where exactly is this ranch?"

"Palisade, so not as harsh winters, either."

So about a five-hour drive southwest. Just long enough to make traveling back and forth an ordeal, but not a ridiculous distance that couldn't be done on the weekends. "Can I think about it?"

"Of course."

Tanya exhaled as all the possibilities and consequences and pros and cons whirred through her head.

As soon as she returned to the dude ranch, she sent Eric off with Miguel and a family reunion made up of five different households to do the sorting exercise—basically, they paired mothers and calves and herded them into a corral on the other end, which taught teamwork as well as provided a fun challenge.

After rushing through her chores, Tanya found herself in Phoenix's stall once again. It was amazing how much better the mare looked after a few weeks of eating and healing. The chunks of clumped hair had been cleared away with tender brushing, and the coat was gradually regaining its glossy sheen. Winston bleated, and Tanya opened the gate for him. Half the time, the goat and the mare slept in the same stall. This morning when she'd come in to check on the animals, Winston had been sleeping atop Phoenix, both of them as happy and cuddly as could be.

Tanya cupped grain and let Phoenix eat out of her palms. "You're doing so well, aren't you, beautiful girl? The fire's over, and you're ready to come out stronger than ever." She slapped the few remaining kernels of grain off her palms and petted Winston's knobby head. "Any progress with the new kid?"

Tanya chuckled at her "kid" joke, but Phoenix and Winston had the audacity to act like it wasn't that funny.

"Why don't we see if we can't cheer him up?" Tanya secured the latch behind her and Winston and moved to the stall with the Appaloosa. Pops had been so angry she'd brought another horse home that he'd turned bright red and stormed off before she could even explain.

During their meeting this morning, he'd lit into her, bellowing that they weren't going to *reward* her for disobeying a direct order. If she took Eric up on his offer, there wouldn't be lectures and orders. No more feeling like a teenager who has to ask for permission at work *and* at home…

The idea called to her, but then Brady's face flickered, slamming the brakes on the idea. Going above and beyond with her chores to prove she could handle everything had kept her busy for the past three days. Thanks to the benefits they'd added to their friendship, she was currently suffering from two types of withdrawals—chatting with her best friend and getting naked and sweaty with him.

If she hurried and took care of the new horse, she should be able to squeeze in about an hour with Brady before racing back to work for the fishing expedition. Pops could do it himself, but he'd use it as evidence the injured horses took up too much of her time for her to properly do her job as well.

The Appaloosa stuck his head over the gate and sniffed Winston. The wobbly goat placed his front hoof and peg leg on the wooden stable door and nudged the horse's pink and white nose. The horse gave a half-curious, half-nervous neigh, backing up and then slowly approaching again.

Another sniff. Another nudge.

Tanya opened the stall and brushed the horse's gray dappled side, careful around the cuts and bruises that boiled her blood. Rage, determination, and empathy made an interesting mix, tugging her heart this way and that.

Within a minute or two, Winston had made himself at home, and Mr. Grey—wait, that was probably the wrong way to go with the name. On the other hand, it'd be fun to tell people that Mr. Grey would see them now… Regardless, the gelding didn't seem to mind the company and even bent his neck to nibble at the hay.

With the horse eating and Winston there as added comfort,

Tanya half skipped and half floated toward her truck, thinking of all the ways she could seduce her best friend.

Her boyfriend? She hadn't referred to him as such yet but found she liked the idea. Considering he'd called her his as they'd been snuggled up in the grandstands, surely he wouldn't have a problem with it. Maybe they'd pull a prank on the entire town and announce their couple status at the rodeo.

Another thought hit her, causing a sinking sensation to go through her gut. She needed to talk to Brady about the job offer. She groaned at the idea of delaying sex yet again—they'd never gotten their steamy night in the hotel room, and she'd been frustrated since. Last night, she'd planned on sneaking over to his cabin, but a thunderstorm hit fast and furious, making the gelding so nervous she'd been afraid he'd reinjure himself pacing around and rattling the stable door.

Okay, so it wouldn't be a seductive, fun conversation to have, but given that it involved a total life switch-up—one that left a lot of miles between them—she could use Brady's input. Pressure grew underneath her ribs, crowding her lungs. How could she leave Silver Springs? Especially after finally crossing lines with Brady.

Then again, it'd been a rockier transition than she'd expected. What if she stayed, only for them to discover they constantly bickered and that soured everything else? And the even bigger question: How could she say no to having the freedom to run a ranch the way she wanted, a financial backer willing to build stables without her having to go into debt, and the ability to rescue a whole slew of mistreated horses?

As Tanya neared the main cabin, she slowed her pickup to a crawl. Along with the numerous teenagers, Liza's twins often ran around the unfenced yard, as did a whole mess of animals.

Since Brady's truck was up front and there weren't any tractors in the field, Tanya headed to the stables. And there he stood in the center of the aisle in all his rugged cowboy glory. He gifted her with a heart-melting grin, and everything she'd been contemplating flitted from her brain. The only thing left was how long it'd been since she'd savored those lips and that unbelievable body of his.

Tanya took a few large strides and leaped into his arms. Brady caught her, his hands bracing her butt, and his mouth crashed into hers. "God, I've missed you," he murmured between kisses. His large, capable hands massaged her ass, awakening the kind of desire that consumed and conquered.

"Me too. It's been a madhouse since Friday night."

"I'm guessing your dad wasn't very happy about the horse?"

"You'd guess right." She leaned her forehead on his and sighed, savoring the sense of rightness that came from being in his arms. "And speaking of, I…"

The rest of the sentence faded into oblivion as Brady's lips sucked at her neck. A moan slipped out, and she glanced toward the open doorway. Her fingers dug into his shoulders, pulling him closer, even as she said, "We're going to get caught. I only have about an hour before I have to be back at the dude ranch, but maybe we can head to your cabin?"

"I have a better idea." He released his hold on her, and a rough, strangled noise sounded in the back of his throat as she slid down his body. She gasped as his erection knocked against the insistent, greedy spot between her thighs. "Up the ladder," he gritted out. "There's a blanket in the loft."

She didn't have to be told twice.

While she climbed the ladder, Brady did one last check for witnesses. Then he boosted himself into the loft and unfurled a patchwork quilt, spreading it across the straw that covered the wooden floor. "Is this okay? I'm afraid if anyone sees us on the way to my place, we'll get held up, and I don't think I can wait another minute to have sex with you."

The blood in her veins turned molten, upping her sense of urgency as well. "Not only do I feel the same way, but being up here is adding a whole forbidden, clandestine vibe. Do you need me to—?"

Brady snagged her wrist and yanked her to him. "I need you all right." He kissed her long and deep as he eased her onto the colorful quilt. Thanks to the straw, it made for a softer landing than she'd expected. "I've been thinking about you all day long, and when you walked in, I almost thought I'd dreamed you into existence."

"Maybe you did, and this is just a dream."

"Well then, there are several things I plan on doing before I wake up."

Chapter 22

Maddox was underneath Jess's Corolla, taking care of the last few fixes, when a shadow cut through the stream of sunshine that'd been creeping underneath the car.

His heart thumped harder as Harlow dropped to her knees and peeked at him.

"Afternoon, Sugar," he said. "I was hoping you'd show up soon."

Her smile was brighter than the sun, and so was the happiness flowing through him. The girl who'd told him she wouldn't give up on him tossed aside her hat, flattened her belly to the ground, and rolled until she was under the hood beside him.

One of his exes used to complain if he kissed her without scrubbing his hands or showering first. Harlow, on the other hand, just charged through the dirt and grass like it was nothing.

Desire flickered as she completed another half roll, leaving the front of her body against his side. Her curves pressed into him, and as if that wasn't amazing enough, her mouth drifted to his.

His thirst for her overloaded his system, and he dropped the wrench in his hand—barely missing his face—as he twisted to better participate in the kiss. They probably didn't have long before someone would check on them, so he cut the kiss shorter than he wanted. Since he could kiss Harlow all day every day, it'd always be too short.

Still, her enthusiastic greeting filled him top to bottom with the kind of yearning he hadn't allowed himself to feel in a long, long time. Dangerous, but he couldn't help himself anymore, not after her very convincing speech the other night.

"Hi," she said. "Also, I can't believe you're still calling me Sugar."

"It's sticking... Get it? Sticky like sugar."

She giggled, the sound a balm to his soul.

"Plus, you've got this caramel-and-honey-colored hair." Maddox lifted the strands and slowly let them fall. "Chocolate eyes. Strawberry lips." He leaned in for another peck. "And like I keep saying and you keep trying to deny, you're sweet—sweeter than I deserve for sure."

"Hmm." She skirted his jaw with her fingertips. "If I'm being honest, I sort of love it. Now I just need to think up a nickname for you." She bit her lip. "How about Hot Pants Roping Partner?"

"It's kind of long," he said, running his knuckles down her arm and linking their fingers. "And aren't hot pants basically booty shorts? I'd rather *you* be wearing those."

She blushed and gave his shoulder a shove before using their entwined hands to yank him back to her.

"Okay. Let's go with Sexy-Pants Mechanic Dude—or SPMD for short. Now you sound like a doctor of sexiness." She grinned, so pleased with herself that he didn't bother telling her he might have trouble responding to that, even if she happened to remember the acronym.

The truth was, he'd respond to whatever Harlow Griffith called him.

"Hey, you two." Jess squatted next to the tire of the car, and an orange tabby cat circled her ankles, rubbing and purring. The camp cook didn't strike Maddox as the type to rat them out. However, she was engaged to Wade, who was a stickler about the rules, so Maddox reluctantly let go of Harlow's hand. "I just wanted to say thank you for fixing up the car, so I made some cookies, and this batch actually turned out." She lifted one. "They don't even look like cow pies."

"Do they usually?" Maddox asked without thinking, and Jess nodded.

"They don't taste like them, thank goodness. Winona from the Silver Saddle Diner gave me a no-fail recipe I assured her I could fail at, but these actually turned out super yummy." Jess popped one in her mouth and shoved the bite to one side of her cheek. "Do you guys want some?"

"I never say no to cookies," Harlow said, winking at him before rolling out from under the car.

Maddox followed, doing more of a scoot-drag move that stirred up a cloud of dust. He pushed to his feet and wiped his hands on his jeans before taking one of the warm cookies. Jessica perched on the second-to-bottom porch step and set the plate of cookies next to her. The cat that constantly followed her around leaped onto her lap, and she scratched between its ears. "I feel like I've missed out on all the rodeo training. Are you guys excited for this weekend?"

Maddox almost asked what more she wanted from him than fixing her car. Or if she'd been the one assigned to spy on him today.

But Harlow took the lead, bragging about how good he'd gotten at roping and riding, even though he could barely keep up with her. "In some ways, I want it to be over because I get so nervous thinkin' about it, but the other side of me wants a lick more time to prepare."

Lick. For the most part, Maddox had grown accustomed to Harlow's country twang and odd choice of words, but occasionally, one still struck him funny. In further proof he was a total goner, it made him want to wrap his arms around her and kiss her until both of them were desperate for oxygen.

"I get that." Jess lifted another cookie off the plate. "What about you, Maddox? Excited or nervous? Indifferent?" Two creases formed between her eyebrows. "Wondering why some mom lady is asking you questions, from the looks of it."

"No, I… Well…" He shrugged. "I guess a little of that."

"It's been a quiet day so I'm bored, and like I said, I wanted to thank you for all the work you've put in on my car. But I also care about you guys. I've never been to a rodeo before, either, so I'm super excited. Wade's riding a bucking bronco, and that honestly scares the shit out of me. Add in the baby hormones, and I'm basically a mess of feelings."

Maddox had been warned to watch his mouth, but Jess didn't seem to think twice about swearing in front of him while also telling him that she cared. Maybe if he'd had a mom like her—

Nope. Not going there.

At this point, he figured he might as well speak the truth. Most of the truth anyway. He still had a possible trick up his sleeve, but he wasn't sure he could pull it off. And what if he tried and ended up hurting instead of helping? "I'm afraid I'll screw things up for Harlow, and she'll wish for her old partner, even if she's a backstabbing bit—witch."

"Ah, a bit-witch," Jess said, tapping the side of her nose. "I've dealt with a few of those in my days."

Harlow gaped at him. "Are you for reals? You're not going to screw anything up. Honestly, I don't even care if we place. I just want to show people at school that they can't knock me down. Especially that witch with an actual B, Bianca."

Maddox gave her a quick side hug. Leave it to Harlow to ease his worries when she was the one with so much at stake. "Don't worry, Sugar. I've got you."

"And I've got you."

Jess beamed at them. "I'm glad you two have each other. It's no fun having all the pressure on your shoulders. Take it from someone who took way too long to admit she couldn't do everything on her own. Find yourself real friends who accept you, flaws and all. Not only do they make life a hundred times better, but they're the ones who'll pick you up when you're down."

Harlow patted his leg, and for such a small gesture, he felt it down to his bones. Jess glanced at the car that was a few tweaks away from driving like a dream—a rusty old dream, but it'd get her to where she was going nonetheless.

"No offense, Miss Jessica," he said, "but I've been meaning to ask why you even want that old car fixed. I constantly hear Wade telling you to take one of the trucks, and the road from here to town is so bumpy."

Jess stretched out her legs, steadying the cat, who gave her an offended meow. "Oh, I know all about the road. I got stuck in the mud my first week here and had to have Wade bail me out—despite the fact that he'd told me to take one of the trucks. But I hadn't wanted to admit I couldn't drive a stick, nor did I want him thinking he could tell me what to do."

Harlow laughed. "I bet he was mighty grouchy about that."

"Oh, he was. But we got into a mud fight, and it all worked out in the end." A dreamy expression overtook her features, and then she chuckled. "Anyway, that memory's enough to make me want to hold on to the Corolla, but I also think it'd be good for Chloe to learn to appreciate an older vehicle—as long as she's also safe driving it, which is why I'm so glad Maddox was willing to help."

As she aimed her smile his way, Maddox felt a slight tug of affection for her, too. Who even was he right now?

"But the main reason is, when I was a disowned and pregnant sixteen-year-old, I scrimped and saved while working at a grocery store so I could buy that car. It was an old beater, but I paid for it myself, and I took that to mean I was strong enough to raise my baby by myself, too." She gave them a pointed look. "Don't get me wrong. It was hard and I don't recommend anyone follow the path I did—seriously. Stay in school, use protection, do all the right things."

They both nodded. "Yes, Miss Jess," Harlow added.

"But that car is a symbol of what I was able to achieve during one of the hardest times in my life, and I'm not quite ready to let go of it yet."

"I know what that's like," Maddox said, surprising himself and, judging by the faces of the two women, them as well. "That's how

I feel about my motorcycle. It's fun to drive, but it's also the first thing I worked my"—he decided to keep it PG for the sweet girl at his side—"butt off for. It's one of the few things no one gave me, only to take it away later. Well, till I ended up here, but it's still mine. It'll be there when I go back home."

Harlow nodded, a hint of sadness creeping into the curve of her smile. She was staring at him as though he were a stray puppy she wanted to take home. It wasn't so much pity; more like she cared he'd had such a rough life. It tightened his throat and made it hard to breathe in the best possible way.

"Exactly," Jess croaked out around her emotions.

"I'm almost done with the car." A renewed sense of purpose filled him, too. He was going to make the vehicle run better than it had in years.

"Thank you." Jessica stood, picking up the now-empty plate as she did so. "I'll get out of your hair. But if either of you ever want to talk about anything, I'm here. On top of being a mediocre cook, I've had my fair share of bumpy experiences. Just putting it out there." Jess patted her thigh. "Come on, Ed Sheeran," she said, and the orange tabby cat trailed after her.

The name for the ginger cat made Maddox chuckle. And while he likely wouldn't take Jessica up on her offer, it was nice to know there was one more person who cared enough to treat him like he was decent, regardless of all the mistakes he'd made.

Weird to think that after a month at the ranch, he'd somehow gone from counting the days to wanting to slow them down. Part of that stemmed from everyone in the program being so damn nice—even talking to Nick was beginning to feel more like a relief than a burden—but most of it was due to the girl seated beside him.

The one who accepted him flaws and all. The exact type of person Jess had advised him to hold on to.

After spending another half hour under the car, "helping" Maddox, Harlow dragged him toward the stables. It was high time they practiced roping, stage-rehearsal style.

Harlow loved the way Maddox automatically laced his fingers with hers. The butterflies in her gut drifted in lazy circles, high on his nearness. "I can't think of any more questions, so how about you just tell me something not many people know about you."

Her—dare she say *boyfriend*?—lifted a dark eyebrow. "Wow, thanks for the vote of confidence. You're already so sure I'm going to miss that you're preemptively asking me a question?"

Harlow curled closer, studying the planes of his face, the slope of his nose, and those enticing lips—a handful of stolen kisses and she was already such a goner. "Our time's running out, and I want to know everything about you. I hoped that by now I could ask without having to earn it."

As they stepped into the stables, Maddox glanced around. Then, in an unexpected movement that robbed her of breath, he pivoted her around, pressed her against one of the wooden posts, and slanted his mouth over hers. The rasp of his whiskers sent goose bumps skating across her skin, but before she could fully participate in the kiss, he withdrew and flashed her a devious grin. "You always have to earn it."

At first, she was going to give him her hard glare, but instead she decided to beat him at his own game. "What if I bat my eyelashes and say please?" She leaned in to him and ran a hand down his chest, going so far as to add a pout for good measure.

Right as he touched his lips to hers, she jerked back. "Not so fast, mister. Where's my secret?"

He groaned and shook his head, but then he looped a finger through her belt loop and tugged her closer. "I take it back. Your tactics aren't even a little bit sweet when it comes to getting what you want."

Her grin stretched so wide that her cheeks hurt. Finally, he'd admitted she was tough, although yeah, she was sweet, too. Even better, Maddox made her feel like she could safely show that side of herself without worrying he'd take advantage of it.

A loud throat-clearing popped their intimate bubble. They jumped apart as Brady and Tanya descended the ladder in the corner.

"What's going on?" Brady asked.

Maddox straightened and maneuvered Harlow behind him. "We were just coming to get the horses so we could practice roping."

"And you thought the horses were in each other's mouths?"

Harlow's cheeks burned with the fire of a thousand suns. *Busted.*

But then she noticed how harried Tanya seemed. How she was tugging at her disheveled clothes and all the strands of straw sticking from her red hair. "Looks like we weren't the only ones."

Oops, I blurted that right out.

Tanya and Brady looked at each other, guilty expressions on both their faces. Then Brady rubbed the side of his neck. "We were just, uh, grabbing something from the loft."

Since Harlow had already dug a hole, she figured she might as well keep digging. "Did Tanya fall? She's got a whole bunch of straw in her hair. And your shirt is all catawampus."

Maddox whipped his head toward her. "Catta-what-now?"

"It means crooked." Harlow pointed, even though her mama had taught her better. "See how the buttons don't line up?"

Brady sighed and ran a hand through his hair. "Okay, we're busted, too. But we're consenting adults, and you two are minors who are in my care."

"It was me," Maddox said, stepping forward.

Harlow quickly stepped up beside him, desperate to keep him out of trouble. "No, I'm the one who practically begged him to kiss me. We just…care about each other."

"Brady, I really need to go," Tanya said. "I didn't mean to fall asleep, and I need to talk to you about something, but I only have five minutes to speed to the ranch or I'm gonna be late."

"Go ahead. I'll come by after work." Brady glanced at Harlow and Maddox, muttered something under his breath, and then gave Tanya a heated goodbye kiss.

Harlow focused on the toes of her boots in an attempt to give the two adults their privacy. Fear was also slithering in and taking hold. On account of her being such a rule-follower, she rarely found herself in trouble and had never been much good at being bad. If an authority figure so much as sneezed in her direction, she caved and confessed, her guilty conscience assuming she'd done something wrong.

All the same, Harlow couldn't bring herself to feel guilty about kissing Maddox. He'd needed her and she needed him, and they had a connection that was real and intense and worth taking a risk.

Although right now, she worried they'd never get to kiss again.

As Tanya walked by, she gave Harlow's shoulder an encouraging squeeze. Then she glanced at Brady, mouthed words Harlow didn't catch, and then sprinted across the yard toward her big red truck.

Brady turned his full attention back on them as Tanya drove away, and in spite of the reason they were in trouble, Harlow grabbed Maddox's hand and held on tight.

The cowboy across from her pinched the bridge of his nose. "Tanya urged me to take it easy on you two."

"Can I vote for that option as well?" Harlow asked, swallowing thickly. Maddox stood like a statue by her side, not giving anything away but rubbing reassuring circles across her knuckle with his thumb.

A sigh was their only answer for what seemed like forever but was probably only a second or two. "There's nothing against you two liking each other in the rules, but I've got to bring it to the staff's attention, and that means close supervision from here on out. It's as much for your safety as anything. Like I've said before, I'm responsible for you both. So..." Brady took his phone out of his pocket and checked the time. "Until everyone else gets back, I'll be with you while you train."

Not great, but also not the end of the world.

Harlow cast a quick glance at Maddox, trying to silently assure him it would be okay.

The tight smile he responded with spoke heaps of doubt.

It's all going to be okay. It's all going to be okay. Just as Harlow's screeching pulse was beginning to recover, Brady swung open the gate to CJ's stable. Instead of looking at his buckskin horse, his eyes were on Harlow and Maddox. The grim set of his jaw sent a prickling sense of foreboding through her, and she tried to convince herself it couldn't get any worse.

But then Brady said, "And, Harlow, I'm afraid I'm going to have to tell your mom."

Chapter 23

IT WAS ALL HARLOW COULD DO TO DRAG HER TIRED SELF TO her truck that evening. Brady had worked her and Maddox hard, not in a mean way but in a way that broadcast he was going to push them to keep them in line.

On the upside, she and Maddox were hitting times only a couple of seconds slower than she and Bianca used to during their best rounds.

On the downside, ouch.

Maddox's voice drifted over to her. "...just need to tell her something really quickly. I'll remain at least two feet away and leave my hands in my pockets the entire time."

"Make it three feet," Brady said, and Harlow turned to see Maddox moving faster than she could after their brutal afternoon, which was hardly fair when she'd been training for years.

Maddox stopped way too far away, and she barely restrained herself from reaching out for him.

"I had a little brother once," he said.

"The one you mentioned after you tackled that calf?"

A smile spread across his face, different from any she'd seen before. Happy and sentimental, a hint of the carefree boy he might've been in another life. "Everett reminds me of him. When I was thirteen going on fourteen, I lived with this foster family for six months. I'd been in some bad homes, and I'd expected this one to be like those, but it..." His voice grew rough, his expression bittersweet. "It wasn't. They were nice. Instead of letting my piss-poor attitude shove them away, they embraced me anyway.

"And Jaxon." The smile returned, so bright she felt its glow. "Day one he was calling me his big brother." Maddox swallowed hard. "He was like pure energy. His mom was exhausted by it, so I was the one who raced after him. I'd do things like take him to the park so he could tire himself out."

The muscles along Maddox's jaw flexed, and tears clogged Harlow's throat as she watched him struggle with his emotions. "After six months of living with the Wagners, they asked if I wanted to be a permanent part of their family."

Everything inside her froze, because she knew this story wasn't going to have a happy ending. Maybe she *was* a Disney girl.

"I thought I was dreaming." He gave a sardonic laugh. "In the end, that's what it ended up being. Just a dream. Mr. Wagner was in the military and had received PCS orders to go to Alabama. My mom decided that would be the perfect time to make another attempt to get clean and check herself into rehab, so the judge awarded her more time instead of terminating her rights.

"By that point, I didn't believe she'd ever get clean. And while it sucks that I was right, I also didn't want to have to go back to living with her, which makes me feel like I'm just as shitty at being a son as she was at being a mom." Maddox shrugged as if it was nothing, so much weight on his broad shoulders.

Tears burned Harlow's eyes, growing hotter and hotter as she did her best to hold them back.

"The Wagners *had* to move, and since they couldn't take me across state lines, they left me behind." Maddox clamped his lips, as if he was only now realizing how much of his past he'd spilled. "But that's not the secret I wanted to share with you. I just wanted to tell you that once, I had a little brother named Jaxon and that I loved him. If I turn myself around enough, I'm going to try to find him. He probably won't remember me, but I need to find him and see how his life turned out."

The dam broke, and Harlow's tears ran warm trails down her cheeks. Yeah, it meant she'd broken her promise never to cry in front of him, but she was a different girl than she'd been a month ago, just like Maddox was a different guy.

"Damn, Sugar," he said. "I'm not going to tell you any more secrets if they make you cry."

"I just…" Harlow sniffed. She wanted to hug him so badly that her arms ached as fiercely as her heart. "I'm sorry, Brady," she called in his vicinity. "I have to."

She took two large strides, closing the crappy three feet of distance between them. She gave Maddox a tight, super-quick hug before retreating a step.

He reached out and wiped the tears from her cheeks with his thumbs. Then he quickly dropped his arms, plastering them to his sides. "Goodbye, Harlow Griffith."

It sounded so final, that goodbye. She refused to say it, because it *wasn't* the end. She blew him a kiss. "Good night, Maddox Mikos."

Harlow hopped in her truck and headed toward home. She didn't even make it halfway before another wave of tears hit her. She went ahead and let them pour, crying her heart out for the boy who'd lost a brother and his dreams in one fell swoop.

No matter how mad Mama was or how hard it was to train with adults breathing down their necks, Harlow renewed her vow never to give up on Maddox, no matter what happened after he left the ranch.

━━━━━━━━━━

"But they're so good together," Jess said, perching on the edge of the desk instead of sitting in a chair like the rest of the staff had done.

Brady wasn't a fan of these official meetings where they had to discuss punishment options and how to enforce the rules without losing the progress one or more of the teens had made. Unfortunately, the meetings were necessary to keep everyone on the same page. This one hit him harder, because he'd been the person who'd gotten closest to the teens in question.

It's always the ones you don't expect.

Prior to witnessing the kids' exchange by the truck—before he'd seen for himself the unguarded emotion on Maddox's face as he'd told Harlow whatever he had—Brady most likely would've argued against Jess's point. He might've even suggested Maddox was taking advantage of a sweet girl.

But some things you couldn't fake.

Brady slumped in his chair. "I know."

"Great. Now I've got two softies to deal with," Wade said. Back in the day, he would've said it harsher, with more of a woe-is-me tone. Now he grabbed his fiancée's hand and tugged her onto his lap. "But if we don't keep control—"

"Then what's the point of them being here?" most everyone in the room finished along with Wade. This wasn't their first rodeo when it came to teenage crushes and angst. Each situation was different but the same. No cut-and-dried answers, on account of life being too messy and complicated for that.

"All this might be a moot point once I talk to Mrs. Griffith," Brady said. The lady was fairly strict and had publicly fretted about the teens on the ranch being a bad influence more than once. He knew from experience the local teenagers got into plenty of trouble on their own and were rarely around the teens at Turn Around Ranch anyway. Save her daughter, because *he'd* hired her to be. "Unless someone else wants to talk to her for me?"

Silence descended.

Once the crickets stretched to the uncomfortable point, Ma said, "No matter what Mrs. Griffith says, it's important to have a plan and for you to be able to tell her the precautions we're taking."

As usual, Ma was right.

Jess wrung her hands together. "It's hard for me to remain neutral on this, because as I'm sure you all remember, when my daughter was the one getting kissed, I was pissed. But it's not like Maddox and Harlow went off the property or broke any of the big rules, so I'm going to embrace being a hypocrite and suggest maybe the no-relationships policy needs to be updated."

Jess tipped up her chin so she could peer into Wade's eyes and use her feminine wiles to sway him to her side. He responded with a sigh and a kiss to her temple. "The problem is, relationships often involve sex."

"That's more of a bonus, if you ask me," Jess said, her words on the flirty side. Then her eyes flew wide with panic, presumably because she realized she and Wade were hardly alone. "Oops. Can we delete that from the record?"

Liza snickered and nudged Jess's side with her elbow. "First of all, congrats on all the sex. As your friend, I'm saying it was about time for you. Not so much for the teens, though. And as we've explained before, we don't have a court reporter typing up the transcript."

"Then please just strike it from your memories." She glanced around Brady and the desk and shot Ma an apologetic grimace. "Sorry, Kathy."

"Hey, I'm getting a grandbaby, so you won't see me complaining. In fact, I'm gonna encourage all my boys to do the same." Ma's gaze moved to Brady and then roved over to Nick and Trace.

"Let's get back to the topic at hand," Nick said in a loud, authoritative voice. "I, too, have noticed a difference in Maddox since he and Harlow began spending time with each other. He hasn't had nearly enough people care about him in his life, and you know Harlow…"

Everyone nodded. In addition to being supersweet, she radiated joy and compassion. Honestly, Brady thought she also seemed happier and less lonely these days.

"But we can't have them sneaking off together," Wade said, and everyone nodded at that as well.

Nick stood and began to pace. "I get that, and I agree. But Maddox is finally sharing in our sessions. I'm slowly uncovering what we need to address so that I can give him the best tools to help him heal and succeed. Ban him from Harlow, and I'm afraid he'll shut down again." He glanced at Liza. "Thoughts?"

"We all know that kids will get crushes, and yes, we have to protect every single one of them, and there are behaviors we absolutely can't let them indulge in. But I think a chaperone is plenty. The most they'll have is twenty or so yards and two or three minutes to themselves. No need to make them feel like they're in prison."

Ma allowed everyone a moment to marinate on the idea, and then she scooted to the edge of her chair. "Is everyone in agreement, then?"

One by one they nodded, even Wade.

"Okay. We'll take shifts so they have extra supervision, shake up the timetable on the bed checks, and go from there. And, Brady, you'll call Mrs. Griffith?"

As much as he wanted to beg off, he was the one responsible for Harlow spending so much time with Maddox, and Ma wasn't truly asking but reminding. "I'll handle it."

"Good," Ma said. "Meeting adjourned."

The staff popped up in intervals, like kernels in the popcorn bag that didn't want to be left behind, and Brady bolted for the door. He'd brought the issue to the staff, so on to calling Mrs. Griffith before going to see Tanya. After their steamy escapade in the loft, they'd both accidentally fallen asleep, and immediately after that, he'd been distracted by catching Maddox and Harlow. The more he replayed Tanya telling him she needed to talk to him, though, the bigger whatever it was seemed.

I'm sure I'm just blowing it out of proportion since it's been such a hectic afternoon.

"Brady, hang back, will ya?" Ma asked as he'd reached the doorway. "I'd like to talk to you. I'll make it nice and quick."

As much as he'd like to say *Nah, I'm good*, that would never fly.

Once the rest of the staff had filtered out of the room, he closed the door and sat in the chair nearest her. "What's up?"

Ma tilted her head, a *Come again?* look on her face, and he revised it to "Hello, dearest Mother. What would you like to discuss with your favorite son?"

She clucked her tongue. "Keep it up, Brady Calvin Dawson, and I'll demote you. Then you'll be the only one of my sons *not* tied for first place." An empty threat, but he sat up straighter to maintain the ruse. Growing up, he and his brothers used to argue about who was Ma's favorite, but anytime they went to her for denial or confirmation, she claimed they were *all* her favorite. "Tanya rushed out of here so quickly that I didn't get to ask how she's been doing. I was hopin' you'd pass on my well wishes."

His throat went dry. Years of being around kids who had a tendency to stretch the truth had turned Ma into a lie detector. Or maybe she'd been born with that sixth sense. Whatever it was, he did his best to erase any traces of guilt from his face, regardless of not knowing what precisely he was guilty of.

Except maybe not telling Ma that he was in a relationship with his best friend, but not to get too excited, even though he was already plenty excited himself.

This is probably some sort of spy tactic, and I refuse to break. "I'll do that. She's been real busy between the dude ranch and rescuing those two horses."

Ma's eyes narrowed to truth-extracting slits, and Brady worked to keep his face set. Way slower than he wanted to, he casually pushed to his feet. "Well, if that's it..."

"Unless you have anything else to discuss?"

"I already told you that Nash said hi and sent his best, so I think that's it."

"Would've been nice if you would've taken me along to the rodeo so I could see him for myself, but yes, you did mention as much."

Now he felt guilty for not disclosing his relationship with Tanya *and* omitting the fact that he'd been going to see Nash. If he would've brought along the entire family, Nash would never have given him a heads-up again. Unfortunately, discussing Nash's absence from the ranch often left Ma in a mopey funk, and Brady could see the hint of sorrow in her eyes.

"He's okay, Ma. He's still working out some stuff." Brady would have to have a chat with Nash later, whether his brother liked it or not. It'd have to be next week, though, because he was all filled up on shit to do as far as this one went. He bent and placed a kiss on his mother's cheek.

As soon as he stepped out onto the porch, he made the dreaded call to Mrs. Griffith. Long story short, she was furious. She informed him Harlow would be training somewhere else for the rest of the week and they'd be searching for a new place to stable her horse after the rodeo.

Brady let her yell at him in hope it'd mean less yelling for Harlow, and then he sent a text to Nick updating him on the situation. Poor Maddox probably wouldn't take the news so well, but his brother would handle breaking it to him easier than Brady could.

With that all taken care of, the need to talk to Tanya grew stronger, and he glanced at his watch.

If it were later in the evening, he'd ask if she wanted to meet at their place, but she'd been in a mad rush earlier due to taking the time to come to him, so he decided to drive to Bullhead Valley. That way, he could pitch in on whatever chores she had left for the day, and they could have their talk that much faster.

As soon as he fired up his truck, his mind drifted to those moments in the loft. He hadn't had a second to himself to bask in it, but now that he was alone, the dirty reel began to play. Flashes of Tanya's naked body and how the sunshine had streamed through the slats of wood and sent golden stripes of light across her skin.

Watching her shatter. Climbing over her. Gazing into her familiar eyes and seeing pleasure and passion reflected back at him.

Bursts of torrid heat pumped through his body, leaving him revved higher than the engine of his truck. If he didn't get himself under control, everyone at the dude ranch would see exactly how he felt about Tanya.

Maybe he'd drive slower than usual to allow himself time to cool down.

But when he reached the ranch, he spotted her talking to the city-slicker CEO, and a different type of heat flooded him.

They parted ways, Tanya heading into the stables with the horse Eric had clearly been riding but handed off to her. *What a chump. Can't even put his horse away, and he thinks he can run his own ranch.*

But the prick sure managed to find the time to ogle Tanya's backside. *Yeah, we're gonna have to talk about keeping us a secret.* Around here, secrets never stayed that way for long, and more than that, Brady wanted to make sure that everyone—but especially Eric Richmond—knew that she was his.

His best friend, his girlfriend, just *his*.

Brady blew out a long exhale to calm himself for the second time since hopping into his truck, and then he climbed out and closed the door with plenty of gusto.

Eric glanced his way and gave him a snake-oil grin, one that said he thought he could sell fishing hooks to lake trout. "Hey, man. You're Tanya's friend who lives next door, right? What was it...? Brandon?"

"Brady."

"Oh, that's right."

And you're full of shit.

"Did she tell you the good news?" Eric asked, undeterred by the daggers Brady was glaring at him, so the dude clearly didn't have any common sense or solid survival instincts.

Brady gritted his teeth. "What news?"

"I guess you could say I've made her an offer she can't refuse. I asked her to be my business partner in restoring and running my aunt's ranch."

Well, you can't have her, you pompous asshole.

Even as Brady thought it, doubt poked holes in his assuredness. Surely, when Tanya said she needed to talk, she didn't mean... *She's not actually going to take the job, is she?*

Luckily, he'd just practiced his poker face with Ma, and he held on to it now. First things first, he'd talk to Tanya and get to the bottom of things. Then, when the guy ended up being wrong, Brady would make sure to kindly rub it in his face.

"By the way, I've decided to join in on the rodeo fun this Saturday and signed up to compete in the preshow. Not sure if Tanya told you that part, either."

"Well, you'd better bring your A game..." Brady patted Eric's shoulder, a bit harder than necessary. "Turn Around Ranch certainly will be."

One side of Eric's mouth twisted up in a condescending half smile. "I always bring my A-through-Z game, just to cover all my bases. It's why I invariably get what I want."

Brady's hands curled into fists that longed to punch the smarmy grin off the guy's face. This city slicker thought he could stroll into town, play cowboy, and take Brady's best friend? He acted like he was playing hero, too, swooping in and saving her.

Tanya must've hated that. She'd probably done her best to remain professional, though. Too bad she hadn't told the CEO to shove his offer up his ass so Brady wouldn't have to force himself to be so civil right now.

Fiery-red hair snagged his attention, and Brady glanced toward the open doorway of the stables. There she was, the woman who'd made it clear again and again that she didn't need saving... Hell, she would hardly accept help. For the first time, Brady was glad she'd remained stubborn on that point, despite it occasionally making him crazy and causing a handful of fights.

Brady's eyes drank her in. Everything inside him calmed, making it much easier to ignore Eric and focus on Tanya.

"If you'll excuse me, my girl's waiting for me." Brady strode past the self-important prick and over to Tanya. As soon as he reached her, he pulled her into his arms and claimed her mouth. Yeah, the move landed on the primitive, caveman side of the scale, but he didn't care.

Considering the way Tanya melted against him as he slipped his tongue inside to possessively stroke hers, she didn't mind. But then she clamped on to his upper arms and straightened, coming out of her trance. "Um, are you trying to blow our secret?"

"What if I am?"

She glanced over his shoulder, spotted Eric, and pressed her mouth into a flat line. The pieces were obviously clicking into place, and she wasn't happy about the full picture.

"Don't give me that look," Brady said. "He asked for it."

"Eric asked you to kiss me while he watched, and you thought you should indulge a request like that?"

She wouldn't like his answer, and he needed answers of his own, so he simply shrugged a shoulder. "I figured any excuse to kiss you was fine by me."

Tanya stepped around him and gave the bastard a smile. "Eric, you go on to dinner without me. Brady and I need to have a chat."

Well, if that wasn't ominous sounding, but unfortunately for her, she wasn't the only one who was upset. "Is it going to involve the job he told me he offered you?" Brady asked—more like demanded, because he couldn't hold it in anymore.

Now Eric received an ire-filled glower. "Men. Such big mouths. And I can't believe you two aren't mature enough to skip the pissing contest."

Brady was pretty sure saying *He started it* wouldn't have her believing he was a mature, well-adjusted boyfriend.

Tanya sighed, and despite the frustration deluding his system, Brady's heart tugged, insisting he make it better. "Wanna hop in my truck and head to our place?"

The sad shake of her head further unraveled his nerves. "Not tonight. Let's head to the stables." She charged in that direction, and he followed, the sinking in his gut telling him that things were about to change between them again, and not for the better this time.

Chapter 24

TENSION CROWDED THE AIR, ALONG WITH ALL THEIR YEARS OF knowing each other. Usually their ability to read each other brought about a sense of ease and peacefulness, but the silent walk to the stables meant Tanya was fortifying herself for a difficult conversation. Which didn't lend itself very well to the solid *Hell no, I'm not going to work for Eric* response Brady longed to hear.

Panic drifted up and bound his lungs, but he did his best to keep his worries at bay until he could determine which way to aim them.

Tanya paused in front of the two stalls housing the horses she'd rescued this past month, and the reddish-brown mare and the Appaloosa gelding both stuck out their heads to greet her. The mare nickered at Brady, and he stuck out his palm and let her get a sniff. Then he rubbed a hand down her long nose.

He gritted his teeth through the silence, waiting for Tanya to take the lead, but after a good minute or so, he couldn't hold back anymore. "You're not actually considerin' taking the job, are you?"

Tanya's face crumpled, and suddenly he was wondering if he knew her at all.

"Seriously?" he asked, working overtime to keep his voice steady. "You're gonna leave your home to work for some guy you hardly know? Where even is this ranch?"

"Palisade. Which isn't that far when you think about it."

"Oh, I'm thinking about it right now, and anything that puts that much distance between us is too fucking far. We already had to deal with that when you went off to college, and even though you were only a couple of hours away, I never saw you."

"You did here and there on the weekends, when we met up for rodeos."

A rock settled heavy in his gut. "That was enough for you? You want to go back to seeing each other a weekend a month?"

Tanya's chin quivered. "I'm not sure I have an option. Not if I'm serious about going after my dreams and running a rescue ranch." She turned to face him yet failed to make eye contact, her gaze fixated in the center of his chest instead of his face. "My parents aren't going to budge. It's the best way to get what I want."

"Yeah, it's the best way for Eric to get what he wants, too. He obviously wants to get in your pants." It came out sharper than Brady meant it to, but that didn't make it untrue.

"Gee, thanks. Are you saying the only reason he'd offer me a job is because he wants to have sex with me? That's what you think of my skills?"

Irritation agitated his insides, like a washing machine set to destroy instead of clean, and Brady attempted to remain calm when he felt anything but. "You have more skills than I can shake a stick at, and I have no doubt you'd be good at the job and whatever else you set your mind to. I'm just saying he has ulterior motives."

"Eric sees that I'm capable, good at what I do, and—"

"I see those same things," Brady said, dropping his hand from the horse's face and taking a couple of strides toward Tanya.

"And he'll let me run the ranch my way. No more asking for permission and feeling like a recalcitrant teen who's constantly getting lectured. He offered me a full partnership with equal say. He promised to build a set of stables so I can rehabilitate mistreated horses, and that's not something I'll ever get here at Bullhead Valley. Pops wants these horses out ASAP, and look at them. Where are they gonna go?" Tanya's voice cracked. "Who's going to take care of them? Who's gonna make sure other horses going through this have a safe place?"

Finally, her green eyes lifted to his face, but she'd closed herself off in a way she'd never done before—not to him. "It's an amazing opportunity, Brady. It's everything I hoped to build here and more. So if I have to move five hours away to get that, I'm willing to make that sacrifice. Even if it'll also break my heart a little."

What about my heart? he wanted to say but wouldn't. He hated that he'd even though it, but he could feel the damage deep inside, nothing tough or badass about it. A fissure split the life-giving organ down the middle, yawning wider at the thought of Tanya leaving, allowing misery to ooze out and mix with the rest of his blood. For so long, they'd danced around the obvious, too scared to take a leap. He'd thought they were going to travel this blissful path together, but now the rug was getting yanked out from under him, and he was struggling to find where to land.

"You've barely even tried to start a rescue ranch here in Silver Springs, and now you're giving up. That's not like you." Of all the emotions, he wasn't sure why he chose anger. Probably because it seemed like the strongest and safest route for himself. "Did you hear that the Thompsons are selling their ranch?"

"Yeah, for more money than I could make in two lifetimes of working for my parents. You and I both know I can't buy that place. I don't have enough saved for a down payment, and I guarantee the bank won't lend me that much without collateral."

Brady locked eyes with her, thinking that if he could break through, they could come up with a better option. One that kept her here with him. "If you'd just let me help you—"

The shutters she'd thrown up dropped to reveal a flash of indignation. "I don't need your help. I don't need a man to save me."

His temper flared. "Oh, that's all I am. A man? Yet you let that city slicker you hardly know help you."

"He's not giving me a handout, you ass. He offered me a job and is allowing *me* to make the decision, not declaring he knows best and telling me what I should do, like Pops does with my mother, and you know how much that bugs me."

This situation was getting out of control. Brady sucked in a deep breath so he wouldn't say anything he couldn't take back.

"Tanya, we've been best friends forever. I'm not telling you what to do." His heart beat a savage rhythm, one that screamed it didn't know how to beat without the woman across from him. "I'm telling you that I'd do anything for you, just like I'd do anything for my family. I love you."

It'd burst out of him, but it was the truth.

"I'm *in* love with you." Those feelings had expanded so quickly once they'd taken things a step further. Maybe it was fast, but in a lot of ways, they'd been building to this for their entire lives. They were supposed to work.

They *had* to.

He didn't take it as a good sign that instead of saying it back, Tanya started crying.

———

Tanya was as embarrassed as she was upset. She'd always prided herself on her control over her emotions, and she loathed crying in front of people. Even Brady.

Lately, she seemed to tear up at the drop of a hat. Yet that wasn't being fair to herself, because there'd been a lot of huge upsets this past month. Pops not listening or budging, confessing her feelings for her best friend, and struggling to find a way to balance it all. When she was a little girl, Pops used to tell her that if she was going to cry, he'd give her something real to cry about. But choosing between her dream job and her dream guy seemed pretty freaking real, with a side of unfair. It was also a decision that could affect the entire course of her life.

Brady swore, his expression on the helpless side as he looked at her with the same level of alarm one might give a ticking time bomb. "I'm sorry. I pushed too hard."

"I promise I did try to find a way to stay." She sniffed. "I did my homework, wrote up an entire business plan, and presented it to my parents. It just fell on deaf ears." While she loved the way she'd grown up, she was sick of feeling like she wasn't progressing and never would. "I can't live like this anymore. And while I haven't given Eric a firm answer, mostly because I needed to talk to you first, how can I say no to a huge opportunity? As you and I well know, those don't come around every day. Especially not here."

Her best friend stared at her, not moving or even breathing it seemed, worry and adoration in every line of his face.

"You could come with me," she whispered, already so sure of the answer she didn't dare up the volume of her plea. A few times during high school—predominantly whenever she was grounded for this, that, or the other—she'd asked Brady to run away with her. While it was mostly a joke, he'd always gone and brought logic into it. He'd tick off questions, like how would they get money, what would they eat, and where would they live? Then he'd add that Silver Springs and his family's ranch was home, and he'd live and die here. Still, she had to ask. "Your past concerns would be solved. As equal owner, I could offer you a job. We could rescue and rehabilitate horses together. None of the townsfolk would even know us well enough to meddle, so bonus."

Brady let out a long exhale full of despair and regret. "I can't, Yaya. Every time my ma mentions Nash, I can see how much it breaks her heart that he left behind the home she worked so hard to give him. She already feels like she's lost one son, and with Wade and Jess getting ready to have a baby, they're going to need all hands on deck."

"I know. This place is in your blood." Knowing and being happy about it were two different things. Shallow, rapid breaths sawed in and out of her mouth, and tears stung her eyes once again. "Living and dying for your land is the cowboy way, and you're the very definition of a cowboy."

"You're a helluva cowgirl, too," he said, his voice as rough as gravel. He glanced at Phoenix and the Appaloosa gelding, back to her, and then he ran a hand over the lower half of his face. "I know I'm not gonna win this argument, same way Nash and I couldn't convince you to leave that bird on the side of the road without a proper burial."

She opened her mouth to respond, but he placed a gentle finger to her lips. "Truth is, we could use more people out there like you, stepping in when something ain't right. I'm sure you're going to do amazing things, no matter what path you take, Tanya Clayton."

"I appreciate that." His features blurred as more tears flooded her eyes. She wound her arms around his waist. "And just so you know, I'm in love with you, too."

He cleared his throat over and over, as if he were struggling with the same giant lump she was. "Shit," he croaked out.

"Shit," she echoed. "I realize this situation is far from ideal, and not what either of us planned or hoped for. We barely just scratched the surface on the romantic side of our relationship, and now…"

How did she even finish? She was trying so hard to convey her feelings while walking the right line that would leave their relationship—whether friendship or more—intact. A big part of her wanted to ask if there was any way they could still make things work. But long distance would make everything more difficult, and maybe they'd only end up damaging everything they'd had. "Now I'm feeling conflicted and confused and questioning myself all over again."

Brady grazed her cheekbone with his knuckles. "That's why you need to take me out of the equation."

"How on earth do I do that?" she asked. "You've been part of me for so long I don't know if that's something I can even do."

"You can. I don't ever want to hold you back."

She shook her head. "You've never ever held me back."

"I'm sure I have. Your parents have, too, although they likely thought they were protecting you, same as me. If it weren't for us, you would've graduated from college, found your passion sooner, and would likely already have a rescue horse ranch up and running."

"Maybe. But I wouldn't change the way things happened for the world."

"Me neither. I'm glad we had this last little while, even if it wasn't nearly long enough. Take all the time you need to figure things out." After giving her a sad smile and chucking her on the chin, he turned to leave.

"Wait," Tanya said, snagging his hand. "Where are you going?"

"Home. Not much else to do." The world skidded to a stop as he cupped her chin, much the same way he had the first night he'd kissed her. He used that iron thumb to tip her face to his, and then his lips brushed hers, a light peck she couldn't quite latch on to before he began to withdraw.

But then he dove in again, as if he couldn't help himself. Tanya looped her arms around his neck and kissed him with everything she had in her, doing her best to show him how much she cared.

The kiss turned urgent, and Brady drew it out, as if he were taking his time memorizing the taste of her.

When they broke apart, a horrible truth slammed into her and robbed her of her breath. That hadn't seemed like a to-be-continued kiss.

It felt like goodbye.

Chapter 25

Oh, holy crap.

Harlow pulled up to the rodeo grounds on Saturday, her heart doing a *thump, pump, splat* thing that suggested it'd forgotten how to be a heart. This morning's breakfast threatened to make a reappearance, and suddenly she wanted to turn around, slam the gas pedal to the floor, and hightail it out of here.

But Turn Around Ranch was depending on her, even though she'd been MIA since Monday. Also known as the last day she'd seen or talked to Maddox. Did he think she was mad? Or worse, that she'd given up on him? Had he decided she wasn't worth the trouble?

Life had been rough since Mama received the call from Brady, along with the news he'd caught her and Maddox kissing. While Harlow had known Mama would be upset, she'd had no idea. She'd overheard Mama yelling at Brady about how she'd trusted him, an obvious mistake since he clearly couldn't keep her daughter safe.

As if she were ever in any danger. She'd even attempted to argue that point before her punishment had been delivered. No more training at Turn Around Ranch. No more parties, no phone for a week, and no Chloe and Aiden.

Worst of all, no Maddox.

What there had been more than enough of this past week were tears. Harlow cried over the story Maddox had told her about his little brother and the family who'd left him behind. Regardless of whether or not they meant to, they'd solidified his belief no one would ever truly want him. She cried because she missed him more than she thought it was possible to miss a human. Before this past week, she'd thought that type of longing was reserved for the hours she had to be without Maximus, who'd always been her best friend, sad or not.

Somewhere along the way, Harlow had formed friendships with Chloe, Aiden, and—the most unlikely candidate in the group—Maddox. Hopefully that last dude considered them more than friends, the same way she still did. It'd taken a whole lot of bargaining and a lengthy list of regulations, but she'd managed to persuade Mama to let her finish her job of assisting during the amateur preshow and to allow her to rope with Maddox for the official team roping event. It was the only way she'd still have a chance at the All-Around Cowgirl title, and luckily, Mama understood how much that meant to Harlow.

Her biggest fear was that the second the rodeo ended, Mama would drag her away and ban her from the ranch until Maddox was long gone. Then he'd leave and continue thinking no one cared, and the thought of that didn't just tug on her heartstrings, it snapped them clean in half.

As if all that angsty crapola wasn't bad enough, over the past few days, she'd had to train in the same arena as Bianca. Oh, but it couldn't just end at that level of suckage. Bianca's mother had heard from a friend of a friend about how good girl Harlow Griffith had been caught making out with one of those troubled teens, and in addition to spreading that around, she suggested everyone watch their precious children! As if the teens at the ranch were deviants set on destroying the purity of the teenagers in town. Spoiler alert: They did a good job on their own.

"Now it makes sense a guy that hot went for you," Bianca had said with a snide smile as she'd passed by Harlow and Maximus yesterday morning. "He didn't have a whole lot of options."

Maximus had stomped a hoof as if he wanted to make Bianca pay for it, but Harlow held her ground. Maybe she was as sweet as Maddox claimed—although he might've changed his mind after the mess they'd landed in—but she'd grown stronger as well.

So she'd smiled and said, "You're not gonna have a whole lot of options once we beat you and whatever minion you're ropin' with. What's gonna happen when you run out of people who can actually stand you?"

That'd been the sassier and more confident version of Harlow. Currently, she was wishing she could return to her past self and break off a chunk of that confidence. The annoying thing was that Bianca's words had replayed through Harlow's head enough to leave her wondering if she *had* overestimated Maddox's affection for her. That she'd simply been there.

No. Bianca doesn't get to diminish my connection with Maddox because she's jealous.

Harlow's hand trembled as she reached for the door handle. She didn't recall ever being this nervous for a rodeo, and she should be a pro by now.

She *was* a pro at this.

Which was why she sucked in a breath and climbed out of her truck.

The black, embroidered rockabilly shirt had been a slightly frivolous purchase, but it fit her perfectly, the red roses standing out and the skulls adding that hard-core touch she aspired to.

Harlow ran a hand down her hair and snagged her black felt cowgirl hat from off the bench seat. She slammed the door and placed the Stetson on her head. Another deep breath and she was ready to go find everyone.

And by everyone, she mostly meant Maddox.

Excitement and nausea were a weird combination, one that reminded her of the time she'd eaten too much cotton candy at the state fair, ridden every crazy ride there was, and ended up barfing blue.

Real cheery thought. Why don't you tell Maddox about that first thing so he can run screaming? If he doesn't already want to run away from me.

The familiar Dodge Rams that were ordinarily lined up beside the main cabin at Turn Around Ranch caught Harlow's eye. She walked over to where the staff was putting horses into different gated-off sections.

"Hey," Harlow said as she approached Chloe.

Chloe immediately embraced her in a tight hug. "Girl, you look amazing! I'd be terrified if I was competing against you. Honestly, I'm a bit terrified anyway. I'm afraid I'm going to fall on my face or my ass, and I couldn't even sleep last night, I was so nervecited. How do you do this all the time?"

It took Harlow a moment to sort through the stream of words and realize Chloe had combined *nervous* and *excited*, which was the perfect definition for how Harlow was also feeling. "I guess it's become the norm for me, but I'm still nervecited. Especially today."

"Because Maddox will be here?" Chloe punctuated the question with an eyebrow waggle.

"Maybe. Is he, uh, here already?"

"I came in the first wave with the rest of the girls, but the boys are pulling up now." Chloe clamped onto Harlow's hand and charged toward the giant van Mrs. Dawson was parking next to the trucks. "By the way, sorry you guys got busted kissing. The same thing happened to me and Aiden, and it totally blew. I'm sure it'll get better, though."

Harlow certainly hoped so. *Please,* please *don't let Maddox think I'm more trouble than I'm worth.*

Speaking of Aiden, he was helping Mrs. Dawson out of the van now. The older woman reluctantly accepted his hand, and then the back door slid open. Three guys and Maddox stepped out. The only boy she had eyes for was wearing his usual white shirt, ripped jeans, and... Well, at least his biker boots didn't need to be laced.

A full-body swoon swirled into her tornado of emotions. If she attempted to squish them all together, the way Chloe had done, it'd be more of a mouthful than supercalifragilistic-whatever-adocious from *Mary Poppins*.

Her lungs stopped taking in oxygen as Maddox approached, and they ceased working altogether when he reached up and smoothed the spot between her eyebrows with his thumb. "What's got you thinking so hard?"

"Mary Poppins."

Maddox laughed, the sound so loud and full that it buoyed her, too. "I can't believe I ever suggested you weren't tough."

"Yeah, only tough people think about Mary Poppins. That chick packed some serious heat in her bag."

He laughed again, and then Harlow was in his arms, being hugged so blessedly tight. "God, I missed you."

She fought tears as she returned his embrace. "Right back at you. Are you okay?"

"I am now," he said, and with his arms around her, everything inside her calmed and soared at the same time. Maddox glanced at the group of adults with a sigh and dropped his arms. Then he gave her a bone-melting smile. "Ready to kick…butt?"

One of her hands drifted to his biceps, and she couldn't help copping a quick feel because dang, he was even more ripped than she remembered. "Actually, I'm ready to kick as"—Maddox's eyebrows shot up, and she finished with—"inine people's butts."

Maddox chuckled. "I was about to say, 'Whoa there, Sugar.' Five days without me, and you go and turn into a rebel."

"I didn't mean to leave you alone." She glided her fingertips down his arm and grabbed his hand because she wasn't sure how many more times she'd get the chance.

"I know," he whispered as he laced his fingers with hers, plugging the hole that'd formed in her heart and renewing her confidence.

"Okay, everyone," Brady said, pausing to scowl at her and Maddox's linked hands. Right. Mama had yelled at him and most likely updated him on the list of restrictions: no holding hands, no kissing, and above all, no sneaking off with "that boy."

Reluctantly, they let go of each other and, at Brady's continued glare, put a foot or so of space between them.

They read through the program so they'd be aware of the order and pinned their numbers on their shirts. Halfway through Brady's instructional spiel, Harlow scrunched up her forehead and studied him. Something seemed off. His words were sharper than usual, his temper shorter. Perhaps he was nervous, but then again, he didn't strike her as the type to be easily shaken.

Cautiously, she approached him. "We trained and practiced a lot. Don't worry. We're good to go."

Brady's gaze had drifted toward the other side of the entry area, where Tanya and her group were preparing. He slowly peeled his eyes off them and blinked at Harlow. "Uh, yeah. Thanks again for all your help, and for being part of our team. Sorry about the mess with your ma. I didn't want to tell her, but because it could put the ranch and the program at risk, I didn't have much of a choice."

"It's okay. We all made our choices, and while I'd make them again no matter how much trouble it's landed me in, I get it."

A hint of a smile curved Brady's lips. Then his attention drifted back to Tanya, and every ounce of happiness drained from his face. Harlow suspected something had happened between the two of them, but it wasn't like she could just chat up Brady about it. They weren't close like that, and it would be awkward to discuss relationship stuff with an adult anyway.

Except maybe Jessica or Liza. Harlow wouldn't mind giving or receiving advice from them—possibly because they were women and that made it easier.

A tug on her belt loop had her glancing over her shoulder. When Maddox tugged again, she didn't resist, allowing him to draw her back against his chest. She leaned into his embrace, soaking in the stolen moment.

"I'm going to find a way to make this right," Maddox said, his lips brushing her temple.

"You didn't do anything wrong."

"I don't know about that." The adults were circling back around, so Maddox released her and took a large step back. Harlow immediately missed his warmth and steady strength. Somewhere along the way, the last boy she should fall for had become her center of gravity, the force of their attraction too strong to resist. "All the same, I'm going to try to fix it."

Take him out of the equation?

Seriously? Was the guy on crack when he'd tossed out that suggestion? As if it were honestly that simple.

Over the past week, Tanya had a gaping, Brady-shaped hole in her life. Her − Brady = Sadness. That was the fucking equation.

During their time apart, between working and getting ready for the rodeo, she'd made a pros and cons list, and she still felt like the white handkerchief in the middle of a tug-of-war. She also needed to have a frank discussion with her parents, but they'd been impossible to nail down. Almost as if they sensed she wanted to have a crucial conversation involving the future and they didn't want to deal with it.

Discouraging to say the least.

Sorrow rose up every time she contemplated leaving Silver Springs, but Tanya had meant what she'd said about needing to make her own choices and having a career that allowed her to be in charge of her own life. After the last decade of utter frustration, it was extremely important to her and one of the things she couldn't compromise on.

A chance at an equal partnership on any ranch, much less the ability to rescue horses, would give her the challenge, stability, and independence she craved, and she refused to be the girl who gave up an amazing job for a boy.

Time to grow up and make the smart decision. No more being hasty and just hoping things will all eventually work out. That'd been her method for the past several years, and it hadn't gone so well.

How unfair was it that she and Brady had finally gotten the timing right, only for life to laugh in their faces and rip it away? That wasn't the right timing, it was bullshit, and she wanted to stomp her foot and say it wasn't fair.

Life wasn't fair, though, which was why there was a whole stupid saying about it.

Also not fair: her compulsion to scan for Brady. It'd started the instant she'd entered the rodeo grounds. She longed to see what he was wearing and what he was up to. If he looked okay—well, he'd look smokin' hot, obviously—but she meant emotionally okay. Had he simply shrugged off their tragic, ships-passing-in-the-night situation? Or was he hurting as badly as she was?

She wanted to ask him if he, like she had, kept picking up the phone to text or call, only to feel like he no longer had the right.

"Okay, guys. Are we ready to kick some butt?" Her mock enthusiasm was pathetic, but she didn't have any of the real stuff left. "Karlie, you ready?"

The seventeen-year-old cashier from Horsefeathers Western Store waved at her group of friends in the stands. Based on a couple of conversations, Tanya gathered Karlie's main reason for joining in the rodeo fun had to do with catching the eye of a boy— or roping him if it came to that, as the teenager had joked one day.

Tanya rattled off a few key points for Karlie to remember, and then she backed away to give her and the horse she sat atop enough space.

Once again, Tanya's gaze drifted to Brady's side of the arena. He was hyping up Chloe to take her upcoming turn at roping, his enthusiasm one hundred percent genuine. Chloe nodded, hanging on his every word, and then she slapped his raised hand before moving closer to the gate.

He's so good with those kids. It took a unique set of skills to cautiously dig around for unseen injuries—in people who often fought against it, at that—in order to help them heal and grow. The entire Dawson clan had a surplus, and while Brady always claimed Liza and Nick did the heavy lifting, he cared about every single kid who ended up at the ranch.

With Chloe nearing the gate for her turn, Brady helped Desiree onto a white mare named Moonbeam.

While Tanya would normally jump at the chance to beat Brady, no matter the challenge or venue, she found she wished she was on his side today. That way, she could listen to his reassuring voice, same way she used to before her own turn in the arena. Funny how they could be talking trash one minute and cheering each other on the next.

Naturally, a part of her still craved winning and rubbing the victory in his face. In a teasing way that wouldn't put him on the defensive, so as not to go against the dating book that had helped her win him over. Unfortunately, the dating book didn't cover what to do when you were madly in love with someone but life pulled you in different directions—she'd checked.

The sight of Brady was also tugging her toward staying in Silver Springs.

No matter how many lists she made or how she mapped out the future, staying wasn't an option. Not really. In the end, she would resent being stuck in an endless cycle, unable to earn enough to buy her own ranch or to do anything with Bullhead Valley until her parents passed away. Depressing all around, and why was she rehashing this again?

Maybe a future of being alone was what she got for declaring she didn't need anyone—awesome.

The buzzer sounded, and Chloe burst out of the gate on Rowdy. While she took a second to find the flow with the lasso swinging over her head, she threw the loop with practiced ease. By the time it slipped over the calf's head and held, the calf was already near the other end of the arena, so the time wasn't superfast by any means. Still, Brady jumped higher than a bucking bronco.

Another reason Tanya loved him so damn much. He was passionate about his job, and every time one of those teens succeeded, he celebrated more than he'd celebrated his own wins back in the day.

Didn't she deserve that, too? Rescuing horses would fill up her well in a way nothing else would.

"Let's go, Karlie," Winona hollered, and Tanya jerked her attention to the arena.

The gate opened, and Karlie and her horse took a few extra seconds to charge. Whoops and hollers came from the crowd as the calf rushed to the end of the arena. A quick swing…and a miss.

"So close," Tanya yelled. Even the pros missed sometimes, and she told Karlie as much once she returned.

"It's okay. It was a pretty big rush, and on my way back, I gave Justin a big wave. He told me good job, so…" Karlie squealed, and Tanya smiled. Not that she'd go back to being a teenager in high school for all the money in the world, but she did miss the lack of complications and responsibilities once in a while.

Perhaps that was just her impulsive, rebellious side shining through.

Out of the corner of her eye, Tanya caught sight of the Thompsons. Like most townsfolk, they'd lived here most of their lives, as had their parents. They'd listed their property a week or so ago, and around these parts, they might sell in a day or it could be in three years.

As the teams worked their way through the preshow program, Tanya couldn't stop wondering if the Thompsons had any offers. If they'd laugh at the lowball one she could make. How eager they were to sell and why.

Winona took her turn at barrel racing, which she'd taken to like a fish to water. Her small stature meant the horse could go faster, and she didn't risk falling off as easily since she was already so close to the saddle.

"You got this! One more barrel to go," Tanya called as her entire team cheered Winona on. They clapped even louder when they saw her amazing time.

As soon as the diner owner was back and had been properly congratulated, Tanya pulled her aside. Due to the Silver Saddle being one of three places to eat in town and the fact that Winona often doled out advice and anecdotes along with slices of pie, she knew all the goings-on in town. "Any idea why the Thompsons are selling their ranch?"

"Oh, there are a lot of factors involved. Mrs. Thompson's been trying to drag her husband back to the city, pretty much since the day he moved her here. Their oldest boy, Scott—do you remember Scott?"

Tanya flipped through her mental list. "I think so. He was probably four or five years younger, so I don't know him well."

"He and his wife just had a baby, and Mrs. Thompson wants to be closer to her grandchildren."

Well, that didn't exactly make Tanya feel young, but the brick wall her brain had been hitting itself against since Monday cracked open, allowing for a stream of ideas to seep through. Crazy ideas that would be far from easy, involve a whole lot of people, and perhaps be on the wrong side of possible. "Do you think they'd consider selling it off in lots?"

"Only one way to find out," Winona said, and Tanya blinked at her as she awaited the answer. "You'd have to ask."

"Right." So the answer was a question. Technically, a whole heap of them.

"Tanya?"

She turned toward the male voice. Eric, who also wanted an

answer. While she'd told him she needed to have a meeting with her parents and at least give them a heads-up, he was leaving on Sunday evening, so the clock was ticking down on her time to let him know whether or not she'd be accepting the position.

It would be so much easier if she didn't keep volleying back and forth, attempting to leave her hometown when she still had one foot firmly in place. Though the foot wasn't the real issue; it was her heart.

"We're falling behind," Eric said. "Even with Winona's amazing time. We need to win this next event in order to have a shot at beating Turn Around Ranch." The desire for victory was there in his voice. The guy probably didn't lose a lot.

Speaking of questions, there was one she probably should've asked before. Only she worried that Brady might be right and then she'd be up a creek without a paddle. Better to have all the facts, though, right? "You're not interested in me, like, romantically, are you?"

His eyebrows shot up, his surprise clear. "I wouldn't say I'm exactly uninterested. But before you go thinking that's why I offered you a job, my attraction to you has nothing to do with that. I need someone with your skill set to succeed, and I'm going to do whatever it takes to run my aunt's ranch in her honor and make her proud. As far as you and I go, we can just see how it goes—there's no rush and no pressure."

What did she say to that? "I assumed you knew that I was in love with Brady."

"Praise the Lord," Winona interrupted, sticking her face between them. "You and Brady finally got together? When did this happen?"

"It's complicated, and we already kinda sorta broke up, so…"

Winona heaved a sigh that conveyed she thought Tanya was being impossible.

"Let's just say we're figuring things out, and I'd appreciate it if you could keep it a secret for now."

Winona zipped her lips and headed to help one of their team-mates, and Tanya returned her attention to Eric. "I'm sorry if I accidentally led you on, and if this changes things—"

"It doesn't, and I'm not surprised about you and Brady. But I'm also willing to see what happens once you and I get the ranch up and running."

Well, this might be something she'd have to take to the grave, because if Brady found out, she'd never hear the end of it. More, she couldn't help but wonder if she was going to move her entire life only to discover she still didn't have the complete control she craved.

"I'm sorry, but I actually have to go." Tanya waved over Miguel and patted his shoulder. "Congrats, you're the new coach."

Miguel's mouth dropped open. "Wait. What?"

"I have an important meeting." Anyway, she would have, as soon as she demanded one.

"Aren't you competing later in the rodeo?"

"Not anymore. Something more important came up." Afraid to hope but more afraid of the regret she'd experience if she didn't try, Tanya rushed away from the familiar sights, sounds, and smells of the arena.

And as she climbed into her truck and headed away from the rodeo grounds, she made her first call of many. . .

Chapter 26

FIVE DARK, RESTLESS DAYS.

That was how long Maddox had gone without Harlow. At one point, he'd hatched a plan to sneak out, hot-wire a vehicle and drive to her house, and then break into whichever bedroom was hers. Mostly to see if she was okay, but he might've gone so far as to ask her to run away with him, dumb idea or not. He'd never missed somebody to the point that every inch of his body ached from it. Sure, he'd missed Jaxon and still did, but his pining for Harlow had reached a whole new level this week, one that threatened to consume him.

Maddox perched atop one of the large metal gates and grinned at Harlow as she readied the Double D's for their turn at barrel racing. He'd been afraid she would be mad he hadn't kept his hands and his lips to himself and had landed her in trouble or that she'd realize she didn't need him the way he needed her.

He'd be lying if he said he hadn't considered turning to old vices. If he searched hard enough, he was sure he could find enough alcohol and weed around town to drift toward numb oblivion for a while. But then his worst fear would come true—he wouldn't deserve Harlow Griffith. Part of him thought taking away the possibility of becoming a couple would be for the best. That way, he wouldn't be as hurt if she decided she didn't want him.

Which was a lie, because it'd crush him.

His life had been fairly empty before, but last week, it'd been desolate.

The staff and other students at Turn Around Ranch had tried to keep him occupied, but everywhere he looked, he saw the absence of Harlow. The constant churning in his gut left him nauseated enough to end up in the kitchen one night, as if food would somehow help.

Miss Jessica had taken one glance at him, reached into the freezer and pulled out a carton of ice cream, and demanded he sit. After she got him all hopped up on sugar, he'd spilled his guts, the way Nick had wanted him to from day one.

Best decision he'd ever made, and now he had to bide his time until he could put the plan Miss Jess had helped him come up with into motion. He was also going to apply the go-big-or-go-home method when it came to the team roping event so that Harlow had the best possible shot at that All-Around Cowgirl title.

Maddox jumped into the narrow section next to Desiree and Moonbeam, the white mare she sat atop. He ran his hand over the shiny coat of the horse he'd ridden several times, ducked under its head, and stood beside Harlow, who winked at him.

She was sunshine and oxygen and the best damn thing that'd ever happened to him, and he was determined to find a way to be around her until his time at the ranch was up. Even then, he couldn't imagine going back to life without her.

One thing at a time. It's going to be hard enough to accomplish step one. Or maybe step two, considering the order...

"Okay, just remember, it's better to take the turn a bit wide than to knock over the barrels and get a five-second deduction," Harlow said.

Desiree and Danica, who was getting ready to climb on her horse, nodded. Like Maddox, neither of them had bothered with cowboy gear. Desiree had on her usual jeans, a pale-pink T-shirt that complemented her bronze skin and ebony braids, and Vans. Harlow gestured to her giant earrings. "Need me to hold your hoops?"

"Why? You need me to fight someone? Who messed with you? Just point me to them, and I'll take care of it."

Harlow pressed her lips together in that way that meant she

was trying not to laugh. "I could hug you for being ready to fight on my behalf, but I just meant in case they get caught up in your hair or snag on something."

"Nah, I'm good." Dez gathered the reins in her hands and nudged Moonbeam a bit closer to the gate. "But I'll take that hug once I kick everyone's asses."

Maddox respected how real everyone in the program was. They all had their issues, but they were also protective of one other and didn't mince words. The announcer called Desiree and Moonbeam's names, and Maddox and Harlow backed away. Then Harlow reached out and hooked her pinkie with his, causing his entire body to light up like a fireworks show.

The buzzer sounded, and Harlow leaned along with Dez as she made her way around the barrels, circling one tightly before heading toward the other.

"That's it…" Harlow held her breath, and Maddox wondered how much trouble they'd get into if he snuck a kiss. Wouldn't everyone else be watching the show, which was admittedly more entertaining than he would've guessed? "She's got it, she's got it."

Dez made her way around the last barrel and raced toward the finish line.

The flag went down as she crossed the finish line, marking her time.

Harlow bounced up and down, screaming and clapping as Desiree came back through. "You did amazing!"

Desiree swept her braids over her shoulder. "Yeah, I know."

Had to admire her confidence. The next competitor from the other team did well, but Desiree remained in the lead by one point two seconds.

Danica went next. She tipped one barrel but smoothly circled the others. Her time was the slowest so far, but she seemed completely unbothered by that fact. "Wow, that was a rush. Dez is gonna win, yeah?"

"Bullhead Valley's got one more person left," Harlow said, "so she has a good chance—she'll at least take second place."

The four of them crowded the fence to the arena to watch. One barrel, two… "Too wide," Harlow whispered, and she was right.

As Dez was declared the official winner of the amateur barrel-racing contest, their side erupted in cheers and high fives and a few swears the staff either missed or ignored.

Then the announcer declared it was time for the chute-dogging event.

"What are you doing?" Harlow asked as Maddox strode toward the gated-off section where Brady already stood. "You're not…" She quickened her pace, following hot on his heels. "Maddox, you're not chute dogging, are you?"

He winced. "Brady said you'd be worried about it."

Her voice went up at least an octave. "Worried? I'm more than worried. Hello, those steers have horns." She tapped him on the shoulder, and he dared a quick glance. "Did you know they have horns?"

"The better to hold them with, my dear."

Her fists went to her hips, and the feistiness she reserved solely for him rose to her pink cheeks and fiery brown eyes. "This isn't the time for jokes, Maddox."

Maddox looked to Brady, who gave Harlow an apologetic smile. This past week, as Maddox had been going out of his mind, the cowboy had asked him if he was up for a challenge. Preparing to use the same skills he'd used to tackle a calf to wrestle a steer, along with practicing his roping skills over and over, were the only things that'd kept him semi-sane. "It's not a big deal, Harlow. I'm really good at it, I promise."

Harlow spun and said, "Brady?" Apparently she figured she'd try another method to stop Maddox if she couldn't sway him.

Brady winced the same way Maddox had. "Don't worry. Since the competitors are novices, the steers don't weigh as much as usual, and Maddox has been practicing all week. He's also been ridi—"

"Let's hold off on that news," Maddox quickly said, not wanting to ruin the surprise that could be his undoing, and Brady gave an understanding nod.

Harlow tipped onto her toes and peeked over at their competitors. "Speaking of weight, that CEO who's going up against Maddox has at least fifty pounds on him. Seems mighty unfair if you ask me."

Maddox nudged Harlow with his elbow, attempting to lighten the mood. "You know what they say. It's not the size of the dog in the fight. It's the size of the fight in the dog. And trust me, I've got more fight than some dude who usually sits behind a desk all day."

Maddox frowned at the helmet Brady extended his way. "Do I really have to wear the helmet?"

"Hello, do you want your brains scrambled?" Harlow shrieked. Then she grabbed the helmet from Brady and jammed it onto Maddox's head. While he was smart enough not to say so, he found her exasperation ridiculously cute. It sucked that he couldn't hug her and assure her he'd be right back to kiss those addictive lips.

Harlow yanked on the strap to tighten the helmet, hard enough that she might end up injuring him before the steer had a chance. "I swear. Tryin' to give me a mothertrucking heart attack."

He flashed her his million-dollar grin. "Aww, you worried about me, Sugar?"

"Um, yes. Remember how I care about you?"

Maddox wrapped his hands around her wrists, halting her brusque movements and forcing her gaze to his. "I'll be fine, and you and I will be team roping before you know it." He released one of her wrists and tapped the tip of her adorable little nose. "Also, I really want to kiss you right now, but you insisted on the helmet."

"That's to keep your face safe so that you can kiss me later. And I feel you there staring at me, Brady, but right now, my worries about Maddox outweigh my worries about getting caught kissing again."

How did he get so lucky to have a girl this amazing care about him? Come to think of it, that was probably one of the reasons he didn't feel so much as a sliver of fear. Wrestling a steer was going to be a cake walk compared to what he needed to pull off later.

The CEO dude went first. He dragged the steer across the white line and then struggled to get the cow's giant head down to the ground.

"Come on, fight harder than that, Mr. Steer," Harlow said, and when Maddox cocked his head, she shoved his arm. "I feel mean doing it, but I'm still cheering for him to fail. Happy?"

Maddox reached down and hooked her pinkie, the same way she'd done to his earlier. "Yes."

Eventually, Eric Richmond managed to get the steer's head to the ground, and once that happened, the body followed.

Then Maddox was up.

He carefully climbed into the chute with the steer. He crouched next to the animal and rubbed its muscular black neck. "Hey, buddy. Look, I'm sure both of us are wondering how we got ourselves into this situation."

The steer let out a loud moo as he attempted to escape the same way he'd come, sending Maddox's back against the bars of the chute. But with the gate closed, the steer wasn't going anywhere.

Maddox tried again, talking softer as he petted the beast. "To be honest, I know how *I* ended up here. I'm trying to impress a girl. You know what that's like, right? So once we get out there, I'm just gonna drag you across the line, we'll hit the ground, and then you can run free. Deal?"

"Get a grip on him," Brady said.

Maddox took hold of the horns, the whistle blew, and the gate swung open. The roar of the crowd and pounding of hoofbeats thundered out a rhythm matching his pulse, and every ounce of focus narrowed to that white line…

As soon as he and the steer crossed it, Maddox tightened his grip, one hand on the horn and the other on the jaw. Then he threw his body weight behind the move Brady referred to as the sleeper hold, and the steer went down to the ground, head quickly followed by the body.

The whistle blew again, and Maddox kept his promise to let go so the steer could run free.

"That was fast, wasn't it?" he heard Harlow ask, and he peered through the metal grid that made up the front of his helmet. Wade was next to Brady as well, and they both nodded in answer.

Yes! I did it!

The announcer declared Maddox the winner, and he threw his fists in the air. As the crowd roared, he grinned, soaking up their energy. In that moment, despite the fact that he'd always prefer riding a motorcycle or tinkering under the hood of a car, he totally got the cowboy thing.

Harlow cheered louder than the rest, happiness and relief filling her features as she showed him how much she truly did care. If it wouldn't poke holes in his plan, he'd rush over, fling off his helmet, and kiss her like in the old days when kissing the girl was the grand prize.

But Harlow wasn't a trophy to be won, and he wanted more than a kiss—he wanted a chance at a future.

Which meant he had to go against his nature and be patient for a little while longer.

———

Harlow mounted Maximus and glanced at Maddox. Then she did a double take at his horse—the brown stallion with the half-white face. Even crazier, the horse wasn't bucking him off or acting flighty.

"Oh, this old thing?" Maddox said, patting the stallion's neck. "I just pulled him out of the stable."

Harlow blinked at him. "I… What's going…? Explain."

"He and I've been making friends for a while, haven't we, Bucky?"

"Bucky?"

"Like the Winter Soldier, he was a bit misunderstood. But I speak his language."

"So I guess that makes me Captain America?"

A slow grin spread across Maddox's face, one that unfurled a curl of heat. "I would definitely call you my captain today."

The announcer called their names, and the bottom dropped out of Harlow's stomach. "You ready?" she asked Maddox. It was easier to deflect to him, since suddenly she didn't feel so ready.

Thanks to Dez's barrel-racing win and Maddox's chute dogging, Turn Around Ranch had won the amateur competition, which made Harlow happy beyond reason. A few events ago, she'd set a local record for barrels, beating Bianca by almost three seconds. With her goal of winning All-Around Cowgirl within reach, the pressure built until her insides felt like they were caving in on themselves.

At least she knew her heart was still working because her rapid pulse thundered through her head, leaving her face too hot.

"I'm ready. Don't you worry about me. Bucky and I have been putting in a lot of long hours, and I've got this." Maddox nudged the stallion close enough he could snag hold of Harlow's hand. "You've got this, too, Sugar. I've never seen anyone as amazing on horseback as you are."

"You haven't seen many people ride horses," she joked, although it was also true, so what did that make it? Just an observation that no one was actually laughing at?

"Hey," Maddox said, sterner than she'd ever heard him speak. "Don't do that. Don't underplay how incredibly talented you are."

Warmth flooded her, her lungs inflated with oxygen, and slowly her confidence returned. She'd done this countless times. She was a dang good roper and rider.

Maddox squeezed her hand and locked eyes with her. "We're beating Bianca, you hear me? She doesn't get to win."

Harlow's resolve reappeared and hardened. Bianca and her new partner—a girl from Thorne Ridge—had just finished their turn, coming in half a second faster than she and Bianca used to earn together, which didn't sound like much but meant a lot in the arena, and Harlow was doing her best not to let that mess with her head.

But then she glanced at her partner. Maddox might be less experienced in the arena, but he was also better at pep talks and boosting her self-esteem—not to mention he made her happier than she'd ever been before. He was the best partner a girl could have in more than one way.

Right after the chute dogging, Mama had texted to say she'd seen how cozy the two of them looked on the sidelines and promised—or more like threatened—they'd talk about it later. Surely, she'd known that the text would mess with Harlow's head, which meant Mama cared more about her not kissing Maddox than the goal Harlow had had for an entire year.

Don't let it mess up your focus. Focus on the here and now.

"Hey, Maddox," she said, and he ran his thumb over her knuckles. She smiled at him, affection filling her from top to bottom. "Even if I don't win All-Around Cowgirl, I still win. I made amazing friends this summer, and I'm here with you. So no matter what happens, I'll always remember our time roping and fixing cars and…" Her cheeks warmed.

"And kissing," he said, and she nodded. "Me, too, Sugar. Thank you for believing in me in a way no one else ever has."

If she didn't get herself under control, she'd be roping with blurred vision. She wanted to clear the lump from her throat and tell him that she loved him, but it seemed so huge, and she truly did need to concentrate. *After. I'll tell him after.*

The announcer called their names, and then it was time. Months of training for less than a minute in the arena. Instead of shutting out the roar of the crowd, Harlow basked in it, letting the adrenaline fuel her. She released Maddox's hand and leaned down to whisper to Maximus. "You know what to do, boy. Let's give them a show."

Maximus neighed.

Harlow exhaled and gripped her rope.

The buzzer sounded, and they shot out of the gate to race after the steer. Bucky was insanely fast and tracked the cow like a heat-seeking missile. Maddox swung his lasso over his head again and again, eyes homed in on the steer.

Maddox lifted a few inches off the saddle and took his swing, releasing the loop and letting it soar.

And the lasso slid over the cow's head as if Maddox had been doing this his entire life. *He got it!*

Harlow's attention narrowed to her rope whirring through the air, Maximus's hoofbeats, and the back legs of the steer.

Right…

Now!

She released the lasso.

Held her breath.

And yanked the rope. The steer jerked to a stop, its head and back legs now bound.

"Wow, can these kids rope," the announcer yelled. "Coming in at eight point three seconds!"

Harlow about fell out of her saddle.

That means…

"And not only does this pair win the team roping event, but that makes our local gal Harlow Griffith our All-Around Cowgirl!"

The entire crowd jumped to their feet and roared, and Harlow lifted her hat off her head and waved, her grin so wide it stretched the bounds of her cheeks. She dismounted, searching for Maddox so they could celebrate their win as well as reaching her goal, but he was over by the clown for some odd reason.

When Maddox turned around, he had a microphone in his hand. "I think we can all agree this girl's amazing," he said, and the crowd applauded, albeit in waves, as if they weren't sure what was going on. Normally, there weren't speeches after the events or even at the end of the rodeo.

What the French toast is he doing?

Brady rushed into the arena, and Harlow expected him to pry the mic from Maddox's hand and drag him away. Instead, he grabbed Bucky's reins from Maddox and stood at his side.

"Most of you don't know me," Maddox continued. "I live at Turn Around Ranch right now, which I realize might be a mark against me already, but I wanted to be completely honest and lay it all out there. That way, you know I'm telling the truth about everything."

Harlow's shallow breaths sawed in and out of her mouth, so fast it made her dizzy. She was beginning to suspect this entire day had been a dream, because none of this made any sense.

"I was lucky enough to meet Harlow when she came to the ranch to train us for this rodeo that—if I'm being honest—I couldn't care less about when I first heard it mentioned. But then…"

Maddox aimed a giant grin her way, one she felt down to her toes. "Harlow taught me how to rope and how to ride. She did a lot more than that, but if I rattled off the list of ways she's saved me, we'd be here all night. Long story short, she made me care about the rodeo because she cared about it, and I care about her." He ran a hand through his dark hair, mussing the strands. "Most of you are probably thinking that I'm not good enough for someone so pretty and sweet and smart and kind…"

He nodded slowly as his eyes scanned their stunned audience. "And you're right. I've thought that very same thing, but for some crazy reason, she cares about me. She's shown me what it's like to have a friend and for someone to accept me despite all the past sh—crap I've pulled."

Maddox flattened a hand to his forehead, shielding his eyes from the sun. "Mrs. Griffith, I know you wouldn't choose me for your daughter, and I don't blame you. But I want to assure you that I'd never do anything to hurt Harlow." He dropped his hand and turned from the crowd to look at Harlow. "I'm in love with her."

Harlow's heart stopped beating; she swore it did.

Maddox took a few steps in her direction, his amber eyes fixed on her. "That's right. I'm in love with you, Harlow Griffith."

Tears blurred his features, and Harlow brought her hands up to her mouth.

Maddox cleared his throat and lifted the microphone again. "And I'll do whatever it takes to show her mom and this entire town that I deserve her. I'm going to work like crazy to make sure I deserve her, too. I, uh, just thought I should make that clear while I had the chance."

He lowered the mic, and Harlow took three long strides and launched herself into his arms.

"You really love me?" she asked, needing to hear it one more time so it'd sink in.

He chuckled, and the happy sound echoed deep inside her. "I really, really do."

"Well, I love you, too."

Awe flooded his expression, as if he could hardly believe it, which was just silly. She lowered her mouth to his, and then they were kissing in the middle of the arena.

She couldn't tell if the audience was cheering more for the speech or the kiss or if they were yelling for them to move so they could finish the rodeo already, but she was enjoying having her lips against Maddox's far too much to care.

Brady tapped them both on the shoulder. "Okay, that's good. Much longer and you guys'll set a record."

They broke apart, and Maddox gave her a canary-eating grin. "I'm not opposed to setting records."

"Better kissing records than end up with a permanent record that lands you in jail, so let's remember that going forward." As hard-core as Brady pretended to be, pride radiated from him as he looked at Maddox.

"Yes, sir." Maddox grabbed Harlow's hand. Then he tensed, and right when Harlow was about to ask why, she saw her mama striding toward them.

"*Oh, shit,*" Harlow said and then slapped a hand over her mouth as Maddox sniggered.

He straightened his posture and lifted his chin as Mama approached. He was nervous. Anyone else might not have noticed, but Harlow could see the tic at the side of his mouth, along with that fluttering pulse point at the base of his neck. "Mrs. Griffith"—he extended his hand—"I'm Maddox Mikos."

Mama's gaze moved from him to Harlow, and Harlow tried not to flinch. Was she about to get grounded for life in front of the entire town? Totally worth it, but that didn't make it less embarrassing.

Finally, Mama took his extended hand. "There will be rules."

"Yes, ma'am."

"And I would like to sit down and have a dinner together where we discuss them in great detail."

Maddox glanced at Brady, who nodded. "Yes, ma'am."

"Now, I think we should get out of the center of the arena. The rodeo must go on."

Harlow giggled and threw her arms around her mama. "Thank you, thank you, thank you."

Their group led the horses out the gate, and as soon as they'd exited the arena, Harlow gave Maddox another kiss to make up for all the ones she'd missed.

And to show him that there were plenty more where that came from.

Chapter 27

FOR WHAT SEEMED LIKE THE HUNDREDTH TIME, BRADY surveyed the area where Tanya had been before the official rodeo started. Her team had taken a seat in the grandstands, but she wasn't among them. Partway through the amateur events, she'd disappeared, not even sticking around to see who won the competition.

A month of buildup and hard work, and she'd left early? What fun was that? Not to mention, it shot his plan to hell. Going over to gloat was going to be his excuse to talk to her and check in and just be where she was. He wouldn't have rubbed the loss in her face, not with her leaving and their predicament so heavy and sad. He could've consoled her, too, with his arms or his mouth or any damn body part she wanted him to use.

Then she'd missed her own event, something she'd *never* done before, and she still wasn't back. The antsy sensation that'd hounded him scraped at his nerves, rubbing them so raw there was hardly anything left.

Was this what it'd always be like? Searching for Tanya, only to remember she was gone? A sharp pain lanced the center of his chest, stabbing and slicing like he'd caught the wrong end of a bull's horn.

Brady glanced down, almost wishing there were blood and gore marking the aching spot. That could be seen and stitched up. If he lost Tanya…

The wound he couldn't see gushed.

Years of working with livestock and machinery and competing in rodeos had taught him that timing was a real bitch. One wrong move, a change in the weather, one second too early or too late, and you'd seal yourself into a different fate.

Fate. Another bullshit word. Brady thought that was what falling in love with his best friend had been, but it turned out to only be a cruel glimpse of everything they could be.

He wanted to kick himself for waiting so long to make a move, but as Ma always said, "No use dwelling in the past, or you'll wreck your present and your shot at a better future."

How could the future be better if it involved Tanya living somewhere he wasn't? The two of them had spent most of their lives together, yet that wasn't long enough. More than anything, Brady wanted a future with Tanya. But he also wanted her to have the best possible future, and he worried those two desires didn't go together.

Since staring at where she *used to be* wasn't doing much good, he turned to address Maddox. After the stunt the kid just pulled off, his outlook appeared much shinier than it had last week. "When you said you and Jess had cooked up a plan, I was worried."

"Her cooking is a bit hit or miss," Maddox joked, and Jess popped up out of nowhere.

"Hey! I heard that." Jess climbed the metal rungs of the fence and perched herself on the top.

"Thanks again, Miss Jess," Maddox said, raising his hand for a high five.

Harlow, who was still plastered to Maddox's side, added her thanks as well. Shortly before the team roping event, Maddox had told Brady he'd asked Jess what she'd like to hear as a mother with a daughter, and after chatting about his intentions and making sure they were genuine, they'd come up with the grand speech idea.

Brady had to give it to the kid. He went from pretending he didn't care about anything or anyone to pouring his heart out in front of the entire town. He clapped Maddox on the back. "I'm proud of you. It takes balls to take a chance like that. Just make sure you follow through."

"I will. And thank you." Maddox's expression turned solemn, and he rubbed the side of his neck. "For everything."

Suddenly, Brady's heart felt too big for his chest. This was the good stuff. These moments were what kept him going through the ups and downs of working with at-risk teens.

"Now," Maddox said, slapping him on the back, a bit harder than Brady had done to him. "You gonna stop being a pussy and go get your girl?"

Harlow gasped and jabbed his side with her elbow. "Maddox!"

"What?" Maddox shrugged. "There's no better word for it."

Brady dragged his hand along his jaw and sighed. "I'm afraid it's not that easy. Our issues are gonna be harder to overcome."

Harlow furrowed her forehead, her skepticism plain as day. "No offense, but considering adults were working to keep Maddox and me apart, I highly doubt that."

"Hey, I'm the one who put you together in the first place," Brady said.

"And I can never thank you enough for that." Maddox curled Harlow close and kissed her cheek before returning his gaze to Brady's. "Which is why I'm telling you to stop being an idiot and go get Tanya. Whatever it takes."

"Wait." Jess pushed off the fence, her bright-pink boots sending up a puff of dirt as she landed. "Are we telling Brady that he should go find Tanya and confess his love for her?"

Harlow and Maddox nodded.

"Kathy," Jess called, and Ma pushed into the circle they'd made. "Do you wanna add anything to our discussion about how your son should go find his best friend and confess he's in love with her and will do whatever it takes to make them work?"

Brady pinched the bridge of his nose. "Jeez, you guys. Not that it's any of your business, but Tanya's accepted a job offer in Palisade. She's going to move there and start her horse ranch, and it's not gonna do either one of us any good to ruin our friendship trying to make a long-distance relationship work."

"So what if she's moving?" Ma cocked her head at him like she must've dropped him on his head a few too many times when he was a baby. "Did you forget that you have legs and a truck? When you love someone that much, you go where she goes."

"But the ranch—"

"Can survive without you," Wade said, stepping up on his other side.

Brady glanced from one family member to the other. "How do you even know that we—?"

"Please," Ma said. "A mother knows. Plus, Jess saw Tanya sneaking into your place in the middle of the night. Then, a couple days later, while I was out tendin' to my garden, Tanya showed up and you two disappeared into the stables for long enough that I put two and two together. No one spends that much time in there unless they're muckin' stalls, and you haven't mucked in so long you probably forgot how. You and Tanya have been a long time coming, if you ask me, which unfortunately no one does around here."

Busted. On every side, apparently. "Okay, yes. She and I've moved past being just friends, and of course I love her—how could I not? But the timing's all off."

"Only a fool waits around for timing," Ma said.

"And if it's the ranch you're worried about, we can manage." Wade jerked his chin toward Jess. "I've been training her and, no offense, but she's a lot more fun to look at while we're feeding and fencing and doing the other chores."

Jess bounced on the balls of her feet, a scary amount of excitement on her face. "Am I finally going to get to drive a tractor?" she asked, and Wade paled.

"What we're saying is," Wade sidestepped, "do what you gotta do."

"I think this is where I repeat my earlier question," Maddox said, "but I'll edit it for the sweet girl at my side. Are you gonna cowboy up, or what?"

The encouragement and love of his family filled in the blanks Brady couldn't see earlier, leaving two paths before him.

The one without Tanya was dark and empty, full of shadows and regret.

The other path showed glimpses of curly red hair. Laughter and kisses and eventually kids who looked like both of them. Days and nights filled with his best friend and the woman he loved and adored, where he always had her back and she had his. The amount of need that washed over him nearly knocked him out of his boots, and he did feel like an idiot for being so close to letting her go without a proper fight.

"If you'll all excuse me, I've got somewhere to be." With that, Brady rushed toward his truck. Just before he pulled out of the rodeo grounds, he sent an SOS text to Tanya, requesting she meet him at their spot as soon as possible.

———

Tanya was seconds away from texting Brady to meet at their spot when he beat her to the punch.

Normally, she wasn't so nervous when she arrived at the place that would forever be theirs, but this was going to be an important, life-changing type of conversation. One that wouldn't be easy for her.

She parked her truck beside his, surprised he'd made it here first. He must've left the rodeo before the official end, because when she'd driven by, there were plenty of vehicles left in the lot. It'd made her worry she would have to wait another hour or so before Brady could meet her.

Better just to rip of the Band-Aid than to stew for hours.

Right?

Tanya found Brady seated at the shore of the pond, but his feet were still in his boots instead of dangling in the water. "Hey," she said, and her voice came out croaky after the countless phone calls she'd made, along with the fact that she'd talked to more people in the past couple hours than she normally did in an entire week.

"Hey." Brady patted the grass next to him, and she lowered herself to sit cross-legged at his side. Was it only a month and a half ago that Brady had told her his idea about the preshow and they'd had their archery competition where she'd tried—and failed—to flirt? It seemed like yesterday and a lifetime ago.

Since that'd been the start of the shift between them, it was only fitting they have this big talk here. "I—"

"You were right," he said.

Whoa. Did the cocky cowboy who never admitted defeat just tell her she was right? "About what?"

"I wasn't being fair to you. I was so caught up in what your leaving would mean to me and how much I'd miss you that I couldn't see what I was asking you to give up. I'm sorry for not being excited about your new job, for not supporting your horse-rescue dream the way you needed me to, and for not saying it's about time you get to steer your own ship."

She placed her hand on his and opened her mouth to tell him what she'd decided, but he kept on talking before she could get a word out.

"Tanya, I've loved you in one way or another as long as I can remember. I wouldn't dare tell you what to do, but I'm gonna tell you what *I'm* gonna do. I'm coming with you—that's *my* decision. Because we're a team, and a damn good one at that. A couple months back, I felt so restless, like I was missing something. But becoming an us changed all that. I don't need shiny belt buckles or fancy saddles. What I need is you by my side. I can't live without you, and I'm in love with you, and that means my dreams are your dreams."

Tears gathered in her eyes, and if this guy didn't have her whole heart already, she'd have handed it right over. "You'd be willing to move with me to Palisade? To leave your family ranch and your home to start over with me?"

Brady cupped her cheek, and the eyes she'd peered into at every single stage of both of their lives locked on to hers. "You're my home, Yaya. And a cowboy sticks to his home—*that's* the cowboy way."

Tanya curled her hand around his wrist. "You have no idea what that means to me. You're right. It is time for me to steer my own boat and live out my dreams." She sucked in a deep breath, one that might've been closer to a sniff. "I had this idea, and I spent the entire afternoon running around to see if I could pull it off."

Excitement sent her stomach somersaulting, even as an internal voice told her not to get too far ahead of herself. First things first, she needed to figure out where to even start. "I spoke with my parents about my plans and, after laying it all out there, Mom shocked the hell out of me and confessed to Pops that she'd asked me to come home from college. She stood up and told him I'd been doing most of the work on the ranch for the past couple years, and Pops agreed."

A strangled laugh came out. "Can you believe that? Because I couldn't. While it didn't magically fix everything, Pops did offer to allow me to build another set of stables on the back forty."

Hope shimmered in Brady's blue eyes, beautiful and bright. It buoyed her and left her soaring before her flawed nature took hold and yanked her back to earth.

"But then he started adding all these stipulations, and I realized that if I didn't break completely free, he and I would always butt heads. Work would become a battle, and he'd constantly be weighing my time with the rescue horses against the hours I put into the dude ranch. He's back on his feet well enough, and they can afford to hire help, but I can't afford to waste any more time not going after my dreams."

Brady's hope flickered out, although she could see how hard he was attempting to pretend it was still there.

"I also talked to the Thompsons, and the bank, and Eric…" This was the hard part, the moment she'd dreaded. But looking at this man she loved more than anything—the man who was her home as much as she was his—it didn't seem so hard after all.

The passion that'd fueled her frenzied afternoon surged, pushing her to let go and give this man everything. "I don't need you to save me—"

"I know," Brady said. "Like I said, I wasn't being fair, and you amaze me each and every day. You're the strongest women I've ever met, and I love that about you."

She pressed her fingertips to his lips. "If you'll just let me finish, I had a speech all prepared, and you're ruining my flow."

He grinned against her fingertips, and she lowered them so she could give him a quick peck on the mouth. "I don't need you to save me, but I do need you to help me save myself. The Thompsons are willing to split off a ten-acre lot. Unfortunately, the bank won't lend me the money to buy it and build a stable unless I have a cosigner. And I was hoping…"

If she left that hanging in the air, Tanya was confident Brady would fill in the blank, but it was important for her to take this step and cement the part of their relationship she'd been too stubborn to give on before. "My dream is you, Brady. Not just you but the two of us being able to do what we love—for me, that's running the rescue ranch, and I know you don't want to leave your family, land, or job. We can totally have it all, if…" She licked her lips, forcing out words that'd never been easy for her. "Will you cosign on the loan and help me?"

"Is that the end of the speech?" Brady asked.

"Guess it was shorter than I realized." Her heart beat double time, and she twisted a hair around her finger, around and around—and why was he taking so long to answer?

"Yes. I'd be honored to cosign the loan and help you build your rescue ranch. That thing you said about dreams…?" He plunged his fingers into her hair, cupping the back of her head and drawing her face toward his. "You're mine, too, and I can't wait to live out the rest of my days with you."

Brady sealed the words with a breath-robbing kiss, one that reached down and gripped hold of her very soul. "I just had a brilliant idea…"

Tanya pressed her lips together, but it wasn't enough to stifle her smile. "This is what I get for forgetting to schedule your narcissism intervention."

His deep laugh vibrated through her, and he nipped at her lower lip. "Oh, I'm about to show you that I think a lot about other people. For instance…" He moved his lips to the spot where her jaw met her neck and placed a hot, openmouthed kiss on her skin. "I've thought about your mouth and this neck." He tugged down the sleeve of her shirt, exposing her shoulder and drifting the tip of his tongue across her collarbone. "Thought about licking every inch of your body…"

"Okay, that is actually sounding rather brilliant," she breathed more than said.

"We could also throw in a bet about who can give who more orgasms."

"Ah, one of those 'participation trophy' challenges, where everyone wins."

Brady paused, his mouth hovering over the swell of her breast, two inches above where she needed his lips and scruffy chin. "Are you saying you don't want to play?"

Tanya slid her hands up the back of his shirt, running them over the muscles in his back. "Oh, I want to play."

"Good. I think we can do better than a participation trophy. Although come to think of it, I should be the one getting a prize. My team beat yours today after all."

"I can't believe you're going to bring that up right—" She moaned as the rasp of his whiskers hit her skin. "Then again, I'm sure I can think up a suitable reward."

She peeled off his shirt, and hers was quick to follow. Then they were exploring each other's bodies, adrift on a sea of euphoric sensations, as they claimed this place as theirs in every single way.

Read on for an excerpt of

a cowboy *never* quits

Available now from Sourcebooks Casablanca

Chapter 1

OF ALL THE PLACES JESSICA COOK HAD THOUGHT SHE'D SPEND the eve of her thirty-first birthday, a correctional ranch for teens wasn't one of them. Which was par for the course, really. None of her plans for life had gone the way she'd originally intended.

If she dwelled on that right now, she might lose the battle to hold back her tears, so she swallowed the lump in her throat and shoved that thought away to lament over later. The faces looking back at her were a range of ages, from the couple in their sixties to the three ridiculously handsome males in their late twenties to early thirties.

Don't think about the hot cowboys, either. She'd expected grizzled men with gray mustaches—which the eldest Dawson was sporting in the most Sam Elliott of ways. What she hadn't expected were the three dudes donning cowboy hats, some seriously sexy scruff, and jeans tight enough to display…well, something she hadn't noticed or thought about in quite some time, and she was totally going to stop thinking about it now.

While the five people on the other side of the wooden-walled office all wore kind expressions—save the furrow-browed one in the middle who'd hijacked the meeting about a minute in—Jessica's nerves stretched tighter, her panic ratcheting up a notch. She couldn't fail. Just couldn't.

She cleared her throat again since the last time didn't take. "Look, I packed a couple of bags, dragged my pissed-off teenage daughter here—thereby ruining her whole life, as she told me multiple times during the two-hour drive. There's gotta be something I can do. Some deal we can make."

The leather of her seat creaked as she shifted. "I'm not asking for charity. I…" To her dismay, her voice cracked. "Well, I guess I am asking for a pinch of it. Your place came so highly recommended and has so many amazing reviews. I especially like that it doesn't seem like a prison."

Gruff-and-Grumpy's brow furrowed more, making it clear she wasn't winning any points. She really should've paid attention to names. Their names had all blurred together as they'd introduced themselves, her anxiety making it impossible to focus on anything besides the fact they were western-sounding names.

"What I mean is, it's more open than I imagined," she continued. "Admittedly, I was afraid there for a bit that I was driving to some cabin-in-the-woods type thing. An elaborate setup to lure people out here so you could murder them and dump their body in the trees or something…"

Eyebrows raised all around, the offense transferring to the elder Dawsons, who'd been halfway on her side a moment or two ago. Dammit. Her mouth never knew when to stop. Where was her filter when she needed it? *Great job, Jess. Insult the people you're begging to help you. Excellent strategy.*

Maybe in this instance, in spite of things not going according to plan, she should've made a more solid plan.

"Shit, I'm doing this wrong," she said, dropping all pretense that she had any clue how to go about this. Her heart beat with a thready rhythm as she scooted forward. "I have a teenage daughter who needs help." She didn't want to end up as a case study about how rebellious teens who became moms too early had children who repeated the pattern. "It kills me that I don't know how to help her, but I've tried, and it didn't work, and now I need help." The squeeze in her chest made the next word come out rougher than the rest and about as desperate as she felt. "*Please.*"

Gruff-and-Grumpy opened his mouth, but his mom placed her hand on his arm and aimed a kind smile at Jess. "While we're real sympathetic to your cause, we have a large staff to support, the program isn't free to run, and even if you had the money, we're already runnin' at full capacity."

As Jess had packed in a wild rage, the scent of the jail cell she'd bailed her daughter out of still lingering, along with the image of her sitting there with that smug teenage boy who'd gotten his hooks into Chloe, she'd been so sure that all she needed to do was drive to Silver Springs. She thought if she could just meet the people who ran Turn Around Ranch, she could get them to take in Chloe. Usually she was pretty good at convincing people in person. The combo of friendly and refuses-to-take-no-for-an-answer was how she'd climbed her way to the top of every job she'd had. Not easy for a girl with nothing more than a GED.

The youngest and friendliest of the cowboys thrust a clipboard toward her. "You can fill out a form and put her on a wait list."

Gruff-and-Grumpy's flinty-gray eyes were still on her. The way he studied her left her gut churning in a not-altogether-unpleasant way, which made no sense. Every one of them had done a double take when she'd said her daughter was a few months shy of sixteen. It happened a lot. Comments about how she wasn't old enough to have a teenage daughter. People asking if Chloe was actually hers— most any time you put "actually" in a sentence, you should rethink it. Jess had been the age Chloe was now when she fell in love with a cute, rebellious boy with a tragic backstory. Her common sense had been left by the wayside, and she'd made bad decisions. Not so much sleeping with the guy, but not seeing through his lines until it was too late. Although, for the record, she was all for being a lot older than fifteen when it came to sex, especially in her daughter's case.

I want her to have a better life. If this is the only way to keep her from having to go through what I did, it'll be worth her hating me for a while. Even as she thought it, a raw spot opened up in her chest. She and Chloe used to be so close. Before the boy. Before the promotion that left Jess working extra-long hours, often late into the night.

It's my fault. Which is why I have to fix it.

Jess eyed the extended clipboard. The guy who offered it didn't seem to know if he should keep holding it out or not. "By then it might be too late." By the time the ranch made it through the wait-list, Chloe could be even more entangled in her boyfriend's web. Even if she didn't get pregnant—because heaven knew the lectures on birth control had been lengthy—she would end up heartbroken, with nothing to show for it but a criminal record. "I know way too much about regrets and too little, too late."

Chloe was too young to understand the way a stigma could follow you around your entire life. It hadn't ended. Jessica still got the looks. The comments. So much judging, which she should be above caring about—and was most days. But that had changed on the night her own now-estranged mother's words had come back to haunt her. *You keep that baby, and all you'll do is ruin both of your lives...*{~?~IQ: Editorial: Paragraph may be missing ending punctuation.}

Jess knew she should stand up, hold her head high, and go and collect her daughter from the porch swing where she was undoubtedly still sulking. But she'd done enough research to know that this was where she wanted her daughter. A friend of a friend had sent their teen here and claimed he came back a different person. Jess didn't want Chloe to be a different person. She wanted back the girl she'd lost about six months ago.

A hint of sympathy flickered through Gruff-and-Grumpy's eyes, but then the firmness crept back in. He reached up and readjusted his cowboy hat, which set off some kind of wave that made the other two brothers do the same.

Seriously, why do they have to look like they belong on the cover of Ride a Cowboy Weekly?

Wait. That sounded dirtier than she meant it. Not that she'd exactly take it back.

They practically dripped masculinity, their bodies speaking to hours of manual labor, and the effect kept hijacking her jumbled thoughts. It'd been so long since she'd more than half-heartedly checked out a guy that apparently now she couldn't even handle being in the presence of handsome men.

Back when she was in her early twenties—before guys discovered she came with baggage and a five-year-old—she used to be fairly decent at flirting her way into getting a guy to help her out with things like clearing that late fee or giving her a few more weeks on the rent. Once she'd even talked her disgruntled landlord into mowing the overgrown lawn he was harping on and on about. Clearly, she'd lost it, because the expressions aimed her way were immovable ones that conveyed disbelief in exceptions or wiggle room. Or the charity she'd shed her pride to ask for.

A spinster failure-of-a-mom at thirty-one. *Well, it took fifteen years, but Mom was right.* Just when she'd been so cocky about how much she'd accomplished. Now she wanted to Frisbee the employee-of-the month plaque she'd received from her boss last week, for all the good it did her.

"We're sorry you drove all the way here only to have to turn back," Mrs. Dawson said, tucking behind her ear the sandy-brown and gray strands of hair that'd fallen from her bun. The woman had a frail sense about her, her skinniness and the dark circles under her eyes speaking to a recent—or possibly even current—health issue. "I can give you some referrals, and I'll see if my contacts know of a good counselor in your area."

In a daze, Jess blinked at the woman, defeat weighing against her chest and tugging down her shoulders. She truly had failed. And curse her DNA for passing on traits she wished it would've held back. In a lot of ways, her daughter was too much like her: stubborn to a fault, blind when it came to guys, spurred on by the words *no* and *can't*, and turning the word *guideline* into *loose suggestion*.

If they simply returned home, it'd be harder and harder to keep Chloe from bad influences. This past year she'd struggled to fit in at school, and her solution had been to find the worst possible group of "friends." Friends who ditched and smoked pot and encouraged Chloe to sneak out at night so she could go meet a guy like Tyler. He was two years older and a whole mess of bad influences on his own. Rebellious, disrespectful, and mysterious—the same things Jessica had been attracted to at Chloe's age.

Not that her daughter was blameless. Chloe had made plenty of bad choices. She'd dived fully into the party lifestyle, snuck out yet again, and gone on the joyride in the stolen car while under the influence. It was a slippery slope, which was why Jess wanted her at the best place in the state.

Even the others were out of her price range. A counselor might be as well. Maybe they'd just move to a different state entirely. Leave it all behind and eat…ramen. Get a nice box hut under a bridge. Really live out the scenarios people had thrown at her when she'd refused to give her baby up for adoption.

Feeling both levels of failure, Jess shakily stood. "Thank you for your time."

"I'll walk you out," Gruff-and-Grumpy said, and she wanted to shout that she didn't want chivalry. She wanted her daughter enrolled in their program and a way to pay for it.

"It's fine. I've got it. Unless you're scared I'll just drive away without my kid, and then you'll *have* to take her."

"Well, I am now." An almost-smile crossed his face.

She almost returned it, but her lungs constricted more and more as she walked toward the door.

There in the corner, she caught sight of a wall of flyers on a corkboard. Along with a schedule that outlined class time, equine therapy time, and a few other events she couldn't quite make out, she saw a neon-yellow paper with the words HELP WANTED across the top. Even better, it was for a job here at Turn Around Ranch.

"You guys are looking for a cook?" It was as if she'd stepped out of her body and someone else had taken control—someone crazy and reckless, personality traits she'd tried very hard to suppress through the years. When you had a kid who depended on you, impulsiveness went out the window, and recklessness wasn't an option. Still, even as she told her mouth to hold up before it landed her in trouble, the next words were pushing from her lips. "You're in luck. I just so happen to be one."

Those dark eyebrows lowered again, only visible under the brim of his cowboy hat when he was giving the signature scowl he'd given her from the moment she'd stepped inside the office. "You're a cook?"

"Oh, we've been looking for a cook for forever and a day," Mrs. Dawson said, scooting to the edge of her chair.

Hope edged in desperation bobbed up inside Jess. She'd told her boss she needed some time off, and he'd been super understanding. He might not be as cool about her taking…a month? Two? Whatever. This was her daughter. Jobs came and went, but if she lost Chloe, she'd regret it forever. "Perhaps we could help each other out. If you let my daughter into your program, I'll stay and cook while she's here. The only other thing I need is a bed to sleep in. I'm not even picky as to where that bed is."

"Under the stars, then?" the looming cowboy next to her said.

"Okay, I'd prefer a roof over my head. Like a lean-to, at least."

That almost-smile quivered his lips, but he tamped it down. Why was he so determined to keep up the steely front? Or maybe it wasn't a front. Right now, she didn't care, and since she clearly wasn't going to get anywhere with him, she turned to Mrs. Dawson. "I can have a list of references to you within a matter of hours. My bosses all love me." At least that was true. At one point she hadn't known how to balance books or create databases, but she'd learned. Cooking had never been high on her priority list, but she could learn to do that as well. There were Google and the Food Network, and she could make a box of mac and cheese like nobody's business. How hard could it be?

"The job entails cooking rather large meals," Mrs. Dawson said. "We've got the ranch hands, the staff of the teen camp, and the teens. We're talking about thirty people, Monday through Sunday, morning and night."

Holy shit. "Great."

"Wade?" Mrs. Dawson glanced at the man standing next to Jess. Ah, yes—that was it. *Wade.* It fit him perfectly, too.

"Can you give us a moment?" he asked, cupping Jess's elbow and nudging her toward the door. Perfect. The first time a hot guy so much as touched her in over a year, and it was to kick her out.

"I can start tomorrow. Tonight, even," she added. "Just point me toward the kitchen." *So I can study it and figure out what everything is.* She hoped the assumption they kept food more on the basic side was correct. If these cowboys wanted quiches, well… well, she'd figure it out.

Note to self: Google quiche and find out what exactly that is.

Wade propelled her across the entryway, his long strides impossible to keep up with. He turned gentleman again as he waved a hand toward the chairs on the wooden porch. "Please have a seat. I'll be back shortly."

The door closed before she could add any more special skills: she could balance a ledger, fold clothes into perfect squares for display tables, and deliver food to people who were never happy and make them smile anyway.

Chloe sat on the suspended swing, her legs idly swaying the seat meant for two, and her jaw tightened as Jess sat in the rocking chair to the side. Other than the occasional comment about Jess ruining her life, the silent treatment had been in full force during the trip and was obviously here to stay. Her daughter even crossed her arms tighter. Sometimes it killed Jess how much Chloe was like her, save the blue eyes, which was the only thing her dad had left either of them with.

Jessica opened her mouth to start spouting her list of reasons this was the right call—from how she was only doing this for Chloe's good to how bad decisions had consequences. Then, of course, she'd add that she loved her no matter what. Since those type of remarks had gone unanswered during the drive here, she figured there wasn't much point. Either she'd get the job on the ranch and have more time to try to get Chloe to see the light, or they'd go back home, where she'd have to find another drastic measure to employ.

About the Author

Cindi Madsen is a *USA Today* bestselling author of contemporary romance and young adult novels. She sits at her computer every chance she gets, plotting, revising, and falling in love with her characters. She loves music and dancing and wishes summer lasted all year long. She lives in Colorado (where summer is most definitely *not* all year long) with her husband and three children. She and her family also take their Marvel addiction very seriously, as their one-eyed cat, Agent Fury, and their kitty named Valkyrie can attest.

You can visit Cindi at cindimadsen.com, where you can sign up for her newsletter to get all the up-to-date information on her books.

Follow her on Twitter @cindimadsen.

Find her on FB: facebook.com/CindiMadsenBooks

Acknowledgments

Huge thanks to Deb Werksman for saying yes to my new series, for giving it a home with Sourcebooks Casablanca, and for being so lovely to work with. Thanks to the entire team at Sourcebooks, from marketing to publicity to content and cover and anyone else who helps in the process of getting my books from my computer into the hands of readers.

I'm so grateful for my agent, Nicole Resciniti, for not only understanding the vision I had for my career but also pushing my goals to be even bigger and then helping me reach them. I adore you.

I can't thank Aaron Huey and the rest of the staff at Fire Mountain Residential Treatment Center enough for letting me come in and ask questions and check out the treatment center. They do such amazing things for struggling teens, and the Beyond Risk and Back podcasts were also great help and something I highly recommend to parents of tweens and teens. Thanks to the teens at Fire Mountain who let me have lunch with them while I asked a bunch of questions for my book.

My family, as usual, deserves tons of praise and gratitude for putting up with deadline brain, letting me talk plot points, and for all the times you send encouraging messages as I'm locked in my office for hours on end. Thanks to my real-life hero for his support and how hard he works to help me succeed. Plus he's superhot to boot.

Gina L. Maxwell and Rebecca Yarros, words cannot express my adoration for you both. Thank you for the plot calls and the catchup calls and for being my lifesavers in writing and in life.

Thanks, dear readers. Whether this is the first book of mine you've read or if you've read dozens, I appreciate every single one of you. You make dreams come true.

THE BEAUX' STRATAGEM
THE CONSCIOUS LOVERS
THE BEGGAR'S OPERA
THE LONDON MERCHANT
SCHOOL FOR SCANDAL
THE OCTOROON • RUDDIGORE
THE IMPORTANCE OF BEING EARNEST

The rise of the middle class in the eighteenth century had an important effect on the development of British drama. The bawdy amorality of Restoration comedy was gradually replaced by plays that offered a moral or social lesson. Sentimentality replaced cold intellectual repartee. And the changing values and interests of audiences were strongly reflected in the subjects playwrights dealt with and the characters they created.

This collection of eight milestones in British drama offers a rich theatrical perspective on two centuries in the artistic, cultural, political, and economic life of England.

KATHARINE ROGERS is Professor of English at the City University of New York Graduate Center and at Brooklyn College. She is the editor of the Signet Classic editions of Daniel Defoe's *Roxana* and *The Selected Writings of Samuel Johnson* (also available in a Signet Classic edition), she has also written *Feminism in Eighteenth Century England* (1982) and is currently working on an anthology of early women writers for a *Meridian* collection.

THE MERIDIAN CLASSIC BOOK OF 18TH- AND 19TH-CENTURY BRITISH DRAMA

Edited and with an Introduction by

KATHARINE ROGERS

David Girone

1994

A MERIDIAN CLASSIC

Published by the Penguin Group
Penguin Books USA Inc., 375 Hudson Street,
New York, New York 10014, U.S.A.
Penguin Books Ltd, 27 Wrights Lane,
London W8 5TZ, England
Penguin Books Australia Ltd, Ringwood,
Victoria, Australia
Penguin Books Canada Ltd, 2801 John Street,
Markham, Ontario, Canada L3R 1B4
Penguin Books (N.Z.) Ltd, 182-190 Wairau Road,
Auckland 10, New Zealand

Penguin Books Ltd, Registered Offices:
Harmondsworth, Middlesex, England

Library of Congress Catalog Card Number: 86-61376

Published by Meridian, an imprint of New American Library,
a division of Penguin Books USA Inc.

The Meridian Classic Book of 18th- and 19th-Century British Drama
previously appeared in a Signet Classic edition as *The Signet Classic
Book of 18th- and 19th-Century British Drama.*

REGISTERED TRADEMARK—MARCA REGISTRADA

First Meridian Classic Printing, July, 1986

2 3 4 5 6 7 8 9 10

PRINTED IN CANADA

CONTENTS

THE MERIDIAN CLASSIC BOOK OF 18TH- AND 19TH-CENTURY BRITISH DRAMA

GENERAL INTRODUCTION

WILLIAM CONGREVE'S BRILLIANT *The Way of the World*, which appeared in 1700, proved to be the last great example of its type of comedy. English theatrical audiences were ready for a new form. The old Restoration comedy of manners could be developed no further, and both taste in general and the composition of the theatrical audience were changing. The upper class ceased to flaunt its defiance of bourgeois morality, and at the same time the middle class returned to the theater in sufficient numbers to influence the drama offered. Jeremy Collier's *A Short View of the Immorality and Profaneness of the English Stage* (1698) was widely accepted as a proper reproof. The large mixed audiences which replaced the small sophisticated ones of the Restoration had less taste for wit, tough satire, and bold intellectual argument; they preferred conventional moral instruction and appeals to sympathy. Colley Cibber's *Love's Last Shift* (1696) showed a heroine reclaiming an erring husband through patient devotion rather than wit, and a rakish hero converted to loving constancy by his wife's virtue.

In *Love's Last Shift*, softening of the old standards of intellectualism and cynical honesty led to mere degeneration. But the same softening could humanize comedy and broaden its representation of life. George Farquhar's *The Beaux' Stratagem* (1707) makes the best of both worlds. Its pair of heroes share the cheerfully amoral hedonism of Restoration rakes, though only Archer retains this throughout, Aimwell reforming under the influence of true love. The play makes clear that the money at which both fortune hunters aim is necessary for the respect of society as well as for a comfortable life, but it also suggests that Aimwell has done well to sink his self-interest in idealistic love. Lacking the concentrated verbal brilliance of the Restora-

1

tion masterpieces, the play delights through increased comic bustle and humorous character contrasts. It shows a wider view of society than the modish parties of the Restoration. Not only has Farquhar set his comedy in provincial Lichfield rather than London, but his lower-class characters have a life of their own, rather than being mere extensions or tools of their employers.

What is more significant, Farquhar treats the problem of marital unhappiness with a depth and responsibility not possible in the artificial world of Restoration comedy. When William Wycherley shows an oppressed wife in *The Country Wife* (1675), he offers her relief only in the form of an adulterous fling with Mr. Horner—an expedient which satisfies the audience's sense of justice but would do nothing to solve the problem of real-life Margery Pinch-wifes. Farquhar, on the other hand, examines the sources of trouble in the Sullens' marriage, finds something less conventional and simplistic than the sexual failings of Restoration comedy, and develops a rationale for their final separation. He presents responsible arguments on the rights of a wife and the proper nature of marriage.

John Gay's *The Beggar's Opera* (1728) likewise combines the old and new values. Its characters—with the possible exception of the two heroines—are predatory and self-seeking, though they clothe their low motives in fine sentiments. The ludicrous discrepancy between actuality and rationalization, inescapable in the speeches of the thieves and prostitutes who populate the play, clearly extends to the reputable persons they resemble. The senior Peachums' business methods, which include reckoning their daughter's charms as a salable asset, mirror the selfish prudential morality of the middle class, in the same way that Macheath's unabashed self-indulgence does that of the dashing Restoration rake. Macheath and his gang of highwaymen justify their seizure and spending of money in terms recalling Archer and Aimwell (who were mistaken for highwaymen). Corruption rules all of society, from the government, which bribes Peachum to betray his employees, to the Beggar-poet, who cheerfully reverses the poetically just ending of his opera to suit public taste. This original ending itself serves to undermine complacency, as the Beggar's "most excellent moral" was that *poor* people are punished for their vices.

The Beggar's Opera, however, is not at all so grim as

this picture of human nature implies. Like Farquhar, Gay presents his rascals genially. They are raffishly charming human beings as well as symbols, and their criminal shop-talk regales us with authentic local color. And, of course, the delightful songs of this ballad opera soften and lighten its total effect.

More typical, unfortunately, was Richard Steele's *The Conscious Lovers* (1722), the first full-fledged sentimental comedy. "Sentimental" in the eighteenth century meant full of moral sentiments, in addition to its modern meaning of strongly appealing to sympathy. Steele's impeccable hero, Bevil, Junior, provides the first type of sentimentality with his never-failing stream of virtuous statements. Pathos is wrung from the misfortunes of the heroine, once "an infant captive" and now "an unhappy virgin." This ex-emplary pair, together with most of the other characters, confirm the sentimental assumption that human nature is basically good.

Bawdiness has been banished altogether, and laughter severely restricted, being practically limited to the servants Tom and Phillis, pale reductions of the Restoration rake and coquette. It must be remembered, however, that Steele's moral teaching, platitudinous as it seems to us, was relevant and interesting to his audience. At a time when the traditional class structure was crumbling, the breeding and worth of the business class, the evils of arranging marriage for social or economic reasons, and the honorable way to avoid a duel were live issues.

In the same way, George Lillo's bourgeois tragedy *The London Merchant* (1731) seemed fresh and realistic, and therefore moving, to its original audience. For some time, tragedy had turned toward sentimental treatment of domes-tic problems. Thomas Otway's *Venice Preserved* (1682) deals with the fate of a nation, but focuses emotionally on the devoted wife Belvidera. Nicholas Rowe's "she-tragedies" of the early eighteenth century carry this trend further. Although his characters are traditionally aristocratic, his concern is the personal problems of the heroine, developed with maximum pathos. But *The London Merchant* stands out as a thoroughly bourgeois play. Not only does Lillo militantly celebrate the merchant's contributions to society, but his Thorowgood is a far more convincing businessman than Steele's Sealand. Lillo's hero, George Barnwell, a virtuous apprentice seduced by an evil woman, induced by her to steal from his master, and finally hanged, could hardly be further from the classical tragic hero. The play also appealed through its emphatic moralizing and its sentimentality. Barnwell's repentance is drenched in tears—his own and those of the virtuous characters—and, in true sentimental fashion, the good feelings he expresses are accepted as evidence of a good heart, regardless of his vicious actions.

Lillo's aim is clearly more significant than his achievement; for, though he recognized the need for a form of tragedy which would speak to the middle class, he lacked the genius and technical resources to realize it. Seeking an appropriate language level, he wavered awkwardly between "high" and "low": he wrote in prose, but his inflated expressions often slipped into the rhythms of blank verse. Still, opening the way for serious treatment of the problems of ordinary people, *The London Merchant* had profound influence on continental drama and is the ancestor of modern works like Arthur Miller's *Death of a Salesman* (1949). Both plays are moving because they grapple with problems which seem real and relevant to a middle-class audience; they even preach similar moral lessons. Lillo's idealization of commercial values was as fresh in his day as Miller's condemnation was in 1949.

In the 1770s, two leading writers set themselves against the increasing sentimentality of the drama. Oliver Goldsmith's "Essay on the Theater; or, A Comparison Between Laughing and Sentimental Comedy" (1772) attacks both sentimental comedy and bourgeois tragedy on the grounds that they sacrifice the distinctive values of their respective genres. He demonstrated his theories in *She Stoops to Conquer* (1773), one of the jolliest comedies in the language. But only Richard Brinsley Sheridan was able to bring something like Restoration brilliance back to the stage. His *School for Scandal* (1777) sparkles with wit, though it does not satirize as caustically as the earlier comedies of manners. Sheridan's characters are as neatly, though not as blatantly, divided between good and evil as are Steele's; and there is nothing in his play to challenge convention or undermine complacency.

Joseph Surface, the hero of *The School for Scandal*, is a clever schemer who seems to have mastered the ways of a corrupt society, largely through mouthing moral sentiments of the sort that Bevil, Junior, preaches in all earnestness. The play's appeal is essentially intellectual, although the Teazle marriage is presented with more warmth and humanity than Congreve or Wycherley would have shown. The scandalmongers fill the play with a glittering appearance of sin, though no sexual lapses actually occur. The only evidence of sentimentality is the presentation of Charles Surface, who is justified not by his wit but by his good heart—a good heart which manifests itself not by useful actions, but by benevolent feelings.

English drama declined after Sheridan, to the point that critics thought literary art was unsuited to the theater. Charles Lamb not only declared that *King Lear* could not be acted, but actually called this evidence of the play's greatness.[1] Since intellectual and even respectable people tended to stay away from the theater in the early nineteenth century, writers were not stimulated to produce good acting plays. Moreover, playwrights were so poorly paid that they had to mass-produce potboilers to support themselves. In 1844 a successful author, Dion Boucicault, was offered only £100 for a play. When he protested, the manager asked why anyone should pay £300 or £500 for an original work which might not succeed when he could get a proven French comedy translated for £25. In 1860, however, Boucicault arranged to share the profits of a play and as a result made £10,000 from *The Colleen Bawn*. Once playwrights were able to earn more money, better works began to appear. At the same time, audiences became more discriminating. However, as they were far more straitlaced than people of Sheridan's time, and they went to the theater for light entertainment, they did not like plays to be unconventional or disturbing. These audience demands were probably more pervasively inhibiting than the rigid government censorship which dated from the Stage Licensing Act of 1737. Even when playwrights dealt with controversial issues, they did so in a frivolous or superficial manner, as did Thomas William Robertson in *Caste* (1867) and Arthur Wing Pinero in *The Second Mrs. Tanqueray* (1893).

Nevertheless, Dion Boucicault's *The Octoroon* (1859) presents the problem of slavery with enough honesty to be

[1] Charles Lamb, "On the Tragedies of Shakespeare" (1811), *The Complete Works and Letters of Charles Lamb* (New York: Modern Library, 1935), pp. 298–99.

genuinely moving. (Admittedly, Boucicault's northern American and British audiences already condemned slavery.) Zoe, the noble, ladylike heroine who is sold at auction because her mother was a quadroon slave, embodies the vicious unreason of the institution; and by opposing justice to law she clearly challenges the law which dooms her.

If the period lacked high dramatic art, *The Octoroon* proves that it could still produce extremely effective theater. The play shows the weaknesses of old-fashioned melodrama —a simplified moral scheme featuring impossible nobility in the good characters and focusing all evil in the villain, inflated speeches at emotional moments, a plot contrived to elicit the maximum possible pathos and thrills. At the same time it demonstrates how effective melodrama can be, as in the exciting sequences where Zoe is sold and M'Closky hunted. Boucicault's sense for topical interest is seen not only in his choice of theme, but in his use of the newly invented camera as a crucial element in his plot. He skillfully embellished his work with exotic local color —his Louisiana plantation is populated by an Indian savage as well as black slaves—lightened it with humor, and enlivened it with spectacular stage effects. *The Octoroon* was successfully revived in New York in 1961.

Both genuine tragedy and realistic comedy, however, were precluded by the inhibitions of the nineteenth-century stage. The most searching satire, as well as the finest comedy, comes disguised as nonsense in the work of William Schwenck Gilbert and Oscar Wilde. Both got comic effects by reversing the expected, and both sniped at convention, complacency, and sentimentality under cover of their absurd characters and purposefully contrived plots. Their characteristic method was, in Gilbert's words, "to treat a thoroughly farcical subject in a thoroughly serious manner."[2] Their characters draw impeccable logical conclusions from ridiculous premises and advance their absurd opinions with perfect gravity. This not only enhances the comic effect but, by connecting the fantasy with reality, points the satire. Gilbert reinforced this surface realism by his care for technical accuracy in manners, costumes, and sets.

---

[2] Quoted by Leslie Baily, *Gilbert and Sullivan: Their Lives and Times* (New York: Viking Press, 1974), p. 61.

Gilbert's *Ruddigore* (1887) burlesques melodrama and the sentimental assumptions that generally attend it. The plot is crowded with excitement—an abandoned maiden goes mad, ghosts emerge to terrorize their descendant, a wicked baronet abducts a maiden, and characters change from good to evil and back again. But everything is drolly turned upside down. The baronets commit crimes from family duty and defy convention by doing good deeds.

The disconnection between Sir Despard's respectable nature and his vile deeds is Gilbert's absurd exaggeration of the disconnection between character and action which writers like Lillo presented in all earnest. The characters' virtue springs from their good hearts, just as the sentimentalists would have it—except that in *Ruddigore* the heart is no fountain of natural virtue, but rather a convenient mask for self-interest. Richard has agreed to propose to Rose on Robin's behalf, but when he sees her, his heart tells him to propose for himself. Rose's heart, delighted with his bold compliments, tells her to accept him immediately regardless of propriety. Robin's heart prompts him to retaliate by pointing out that Richard is only a poor sailor. Rose's heart contrasts Robin's financial position with Richard's, and she returns to her original lover. Reference to the heart is particularly absurd in the case of Sweet Rose Maybud, who is invariably guided by narrow prudence. Rose's mindless worship of propriety and the unattractive results when Sir Despard and Margaret reform make a sly comment on Victorian respectability.

Oscar Wilde more openly flouted orthodox morality and sentimental illusions in *The Importance of Being Earnest* (1895), though he too used an absurd plot and characters speaking apparent nonsense to make his satire acceptable to the Victorian audience. His very title pokes fun at the Victorian tendency to equate earnestness with moral worth. As his characters reverse our conventional assumptions about what is serious, proper, or self-evident, we first laugh at the incongruity and then are roused to consider whether there is any truth in their outrageous statements.

Like the writers of Restoration comedy of manners, Wilde detached himself from conventional respectable society so as to criticize its assumptions, although their stance was aristocratic and his bohemian. His attitudes are similar to theirs, as when his Algy proves that even happily married people need the release of visiting Bunbury. But the absurdity of Wilde's characters causes his play to be more artificial and heartless than the Restoration masterpieces, which exaggerate but do not reverse real life. While Dorimant and Harriet (in George Etherege's *The Man of Mode*, 1676) court in an artful, formalized way, Wilde's couples care for nothing but form. Love and marriage are as meaningless to them as christening and business.

Their lack of solid values could be taken as grounds for indictment of the upper class or despair at the human condition, but such responses are belied by the gay tone of the play and the attractiveness of its characters. Moreover, the style these characters display was, for Wilde, as important a value as any and less easy to counterfeit. Perhaps the best way to deal with a society governed by empty conventions and false sentiments is to cultivate an elegant personal style.

The earlier plays in this collection were performed in theaters much like those which were opened in 1660 at the Restoration of King Charles II. Although scenery was often beautiful, it was not realistic; for it consisted of flats which slid in grooves across the stage to form scenes. Rooms, streets, landscapes, or battle scenes were simply painted on the flats. The forestage was deeper than in modern theaters (though not so deep as in Shakespeare's day); usually the actors entered through doors in the proscenium arch directly onto the forestage, where they performed most of the action. Lighting was inadequate, since nothing brighter than candles or oil lamps was available, and these could not be raised or lowered. The stage was lit by footlights and by chandeliers suspended overhead, which had to remain alight even in night scenes.

David Garrick, manager of Drury Lane Theatre from 1747 to 1776, introduced major improvements. He replaced the chandeliers over the stage with lamps concealed in the wings, which could be heightened by reflectors or dimmed by shields. During the eighteenth century the forestage was shortened, and actors withdrew behind the proscenium arch. Theaters became larger and larger, to accommodate a growing theatrical audience. In 1792, Drury Lane was rebuilt to seat 3,600 people. The oversized theaters, which forced actors to overplay in order to be seen and heard, help to account for the crudity of much nineteenth-century drama.

On the other hand, the later nineteenth century saw amazing improvements in stagecraft. For the first time, as the importance of details in ensemble playing and physical setting was recognized, productions were systematically organized by a stage manager or, as we would say now, a director. Very often this was the author: both Boucicault and Gilbert were known as exacting directors. Gilbert meticulously blocked out the placement of his principals and chorus on stage, dictated their every gesture and inflection, and designed sets and costumes. Concerned to achieve accuracy as well as picturesque effect, he dressed the *Ruddigore* chorus of Bucks and Blades in the early-nineteenth-century uniforms of twenty different regiments, which he had checked for accuracy by the Quartermaster of the Army. This concern for physical realism is characteristic of the period. The painted flats were replaced by the modern box set, an actual three-walled room with functioning doors and complete furnishings.

Spectacular stage effects, extensively developed during the eighteenth century, became ever more impressive. Boucicault included them in every play; in *The Octoroon*, a steamboat burns before the eyes of the audience and two characters swim onto the stage. Lighting was vastly improved with the introduction of gaslight in 1817 and electric light in 1881. The first theater to be lighted by electricity throughout was the Savoy, built by Richard D'Oyly Carte to house the light operas of Gilbert and Sullivan. Partly because the box set made scene changing more cumbersome, it became customary to drop the curtain after each act, instead of using it only at the end of the play. This led playwrights to contrive "strong curtains"—dramatic act endings with a tableau, such as we see in *The Octoroon* and *Ruddigore*. Generally speaking, the nineteenth century developed the resources and conventions of the stage as we understand them today.

The one generalization which can be made about the eight plays in this collection is that all enjoyed success ranging from good to spectacular. At least five of the comedies can still be appreciated as they were by their original audiences. The wit, humor, charm, and psychological insight of *The Beaux' Stratagem*, *The Beggar's Opera*, *The School for Scandal*, *Ruddigore*, and *The Importance of Being Earnest* have lost little over the generations. All are often and successfully revived; the Gilbert and Sullivan operas continue to be constantly performed in repertory. The three other plays have dated, for their particular forms of sentimentality, moralizing, and melodramatics now seem stiff and false. Undoubtedly, their modern equivalents, plays that succeed through the same timeless appeals, will look the same two hundred years hence.

THE BEAUX' STRATAGEM
⌒ 1707 ⌒

George Farquhar

INTRODUCTORY NOTE

IT IS HARD TO BELIEVE that this breezy comedy was written
by an author who knew he was dying. Yet George
Farquhar (1677?–1707) had to be roused from poverty-
stricken despondency to start it, recognized that his illness
was mortal as he completed it, and died shortly after its
opening night.

Farquhar was the son of a poor clergyman in Ireland.
He attended the university, but soon left to act at Smock-
Alley, the major theater in Dublin, where he met Robert
Wilks. Wilks, one of the leading actors of the age, was to
create the heroes of his comedies. Never successful as an
actor, Farquhar turned to playwriting after he accidentally
injured a man in a stage duel. Though his first play, *Love
and a Bottle* (1698), is crude, it was very successful.
Farquhar got a commission in the army, but his military
duties cannot have been onerous, since he quickly produced six more plays. The last and best of these, *The
Recruiting Officer* (1706), made use of his experience as
an officer recruiting men in Shrewsbury.

The Beaux' Stratagem (1707) marks a significant advance over Farquhar's earlier work, particularly in its
thoughtful social comment. How seriously he considered
the problem of incompatibility* in marriage is indicated
by his extensive use of the finest English work on the
subject, John Milton's *The Doctrine and Discipline of
Divorce* (1643). He drew from Milton his arguments that
divorce should be obtainable by mutual consent and that
mental compatibility is more important than physical
fidelity, and he sometimes made use of Milton's actual
words. The play skillfully pulls together this serious topic
with the witty sophistication of Archer, the agreeably con-

11

trasting sentiment of Aimwell and Dorinda, and the humorous vigor of the lower-class characters.

Farquhar's devoted friend Wilks, who is credited with giving him the necessary encouragement to write the play, created the role of Archer. Anne Oldfield, whose talents Farquhar had personally discovered when he heard her read at her aunt's tavern, was the original Mrs. Sullen; and the noted comedian Colley Cibber played Gibbet. The play was an immediate success and remained a stock piece into the nineteenth century.

BIBLIOGRAPHY

❧ ❧

Major Works:

Love and a Bottle, 1698 (comedy)
The Constant Couple, or A Trip to the Jubilee, 1699
    (comedy)
The Twin-Rivals, 1702 (comedy)
The Recruiting Officer, 1706 (comedy)
The Beaux' Stratagem, 1707 (comedy)

Edition:

The Complete Works of George Farquhar, ed. Charles
    Stonehill. London: Nonesuch Press, 1930. 2 vols.

Works About:

Rothstein, Eric. *George Farquhar*. New York: Twayne,
    1967.

THE BEAUX' STRATAGEM

Dramatis Personae

AIMWELL ⎱ *two gentlemen of broken fortunes, the first as*
ARCHER ⎰ *master, and the second as servant*

COUNT BELLAIR, *a French officer, prisoner at Lichfield*

SULLEN, *a country blockhead, brutal to his wife*

FREEMAN, *a gentleman from London*

FOIGARD, *a priest, chaplain to the French officers*

GIBBET, *a highwayman*

HOUNSLOW ⎱
BAGSHOT ⎰ *his companions*

BONIFACE, *landlord of the inn*

SCRUB, *servant to Mr. Sullen*

LADY BOUNTIFUL, *an old, civil, country gentlewoman, that cures all her neighbors of all distempers, and foolishly fond of her son Sullen*

DORINDA, *Lady Bountiful's daughter*

MRS. SULLEN, *her daughter-in-law*

GIPSY, *maid to the ladies*

CHERRY, *the landlord's daughter in the inn*

Scene: Lichfield

ADVERTISEMENT.—The reader may find some faults in this play, which my illness prevented the amending of, but there is great amends made in the representation, which cannot be matched, no more than the friendly and indefatigable care of Mr. Wilks, to whom I chiefly owe the success of the play.

GEORGE FARQUHAR

PROLOGUE
Spoken by Mr. Wilks

When strife disturbs, or sloth corrupts an age,
Keen satire is the business of the stage.
When the Plain Dealer[1] writ, he lashed those crimes
Which then infected most the modish times;
But now, when faction sleeps, and sloth is fled,
And all our youth in active fields are bred;[2]
When through Great Britain's fair extensive round,
The trumps of fame the notes of Union[3] sound;
When Anna's sceptre points the laws their course,
And her example gives her precepts force,
There scarce is room for satire; all our lays
Must be or songs of triumph or of praise.
But as in grounds best cultivated, tares
And poppies rise among the golden ears,
Our products so, fit for the field or school,
Must mix with Nature's favorite plant—a fool;
A weed that has to twenty summers ran,
Shoots up in stalk, and vegetates to man.
Simpling,[4] our author goes from field to field,
And culls such fools as may diversion yield;
And, thanks to Nature, there's no want of those,
For, rain or shine, the thriving coxcomb grows.
Follies tonight we show ne'er lashed before,
Yet such as Nature shows you every hour;
Nor can the pictures give a just offense,
For fools are made for jests to men of sense.

---

1 William Wycherley, author of the slashing satiric play *The Plain Dealer*.
2 Fighting in the War of the Spanish Succession (1701–13).
3 The union of England and Scotland, finally ratified two nights before the opening of *The Beaux' Stratagem*.
4 Collecting herbs, simples; with a pun on simpletons.

ACT I

(*Enter* BONIFACE *running.*)

BONIFACE. Chamberlain! maid! Cherry! daughter Cherry! all asleep? all dead?

(*Enter* CHERRY *running.*)

CHERRY. Here! here! Why d'ye bawl so, father? d'ye think we have no ears?

BONIFACE. You deserve to have none, you young minx! The company of the Warrington coach has stood in the hall this hour, and nobody to show them to their chambers.

CHERRY. And let 'em wait, father; there's neither redcoat in the coach, nor footman behind it.

BONIFACE. But they threaten to go to another inn to-night.

CHERRY. That they dare not, for fear the coachman should overturn them to-morrow.—Coming! coming!—Here's the London coach arrived.

(*Enter several People with trunks, bandboxes, and other luggage, and cross the stage.*)

BONIFACE. Welcome, ladies!

CHERRY. Very welcome, gentlemen!—Chamberlain, show the Lion and the Rose.[5] (*Exit with the company.*)

(*Enter* AIMWELL *in riding habit,* ARCHER *as Footman, carrying a portmantle.*[6])

---

[5] The chamberlain was the servant in charge of bedchambers; the Lion and the Rose were rooms, which were named, not numbered.
[6] Portmanteau, traveling bag.

BONIFACE. This way, this way, gentlemen!

AIMWELL (*To* ARCHER). Set down the things; go to the stable, and see my horses well rubbed.

ARCHER. I shall, sir. (*Exit.*)

AIMWELL. You're my landlord, I suppose?

BONIFACE. Yes, sir; I'm old Will Boniface, pretty well known upon this road, as the saying is.

AIMWELL. O Mr. Boniface, your servant!

BONIFACE. O sir!—What will your honor please to drink, as the saying is.

AIMWELL. I have heard your town of Lichfield much famed for ale; I think I'll taste that.

BONIFACE. Sir, I have now in my cellar ten tun of the best ale in Staffordshire; 'tis smooth as oil, sweet as milk, clear as amber, and strong as brandy; and will be just fourteen year old the fifth day of next March, old style.[7]

AIMWELL. You're very exact, I find, in the age of your ale.

BONIFACE. As punctual, sir, as I am in the age of my children. I'll show you such ale!—Here, tapster, broach number 1706, as the saying is.—Sir, you shall taste my *Anno Domini*.[8]—I have lived in Lichfield, man and boy, above eight-and-fifty years, and, I believe, have not consumed eight-and-fifty ounces of meat.

AIMWELL. At a meal, you mean, if one may guess your sense by your bulk.

BONIFACE. Not in my life, sir. I have fed purely upon ale. I have eat my ale, drank my ale, and I always sleep upon ale.

(*Enter* TAPSTER *with a bottle and glass[es, and exit]*.)

Now, sir, you shall see!—(*filling it out*) Your worship's health.—Ha! delicious, delicious! fancy it burgundy, only fancy it, and 'tis worth ten shillings a quart.

AIMWELL. (*Drinks*) 'Tis confounded strong!

BONIFACE. Strong! It must be so, or how should we be strong that drink it?

AIMWELL. And have you lived so long upon this ale, landlord?

---

[7] According to the Julian calendar, still used in England (until 1752), though replaced on the continent by the modern calendar.
[8] Simple code to the tapster to draw the ale brewed the previous autumn.

BONIFACE. Eight-and-fifty years, upon my credit, sir; but it killed my wife, poor woman, as the saying is.

AIMWELL. How came that to pass?

BONIFACE. I don't know how, sir; she would not let the ale take its natural course, sir; she was for qualifying it every now and then with a dram,[9] as the saying is; and an honest gentleman that came this way from Ireland made her a present of a dozen bottles of usquebaugh—but the poor woman was never well after. But, howe'er, I was obliged to the gentleman, you know.

AIMWELL. Why, was it the usquebaugh that killed her?

BONIFACE. My Lady Bountiful said so. She, good lady, did what could be done; she cured her of three tympanies, but the fourth carried her off. But she's happy, and I'm contented, as the saying is.

AIMWELL. Who's that Lady Bountiful you mentioned?

BONIFACE. Od's my life, sir, we'll drink her health.— (Drinks.) My Lady Bountiful is one of the best of women. Her last husband, Sir Charles Bountiful, left her worth a thousand pound a year; and, I believe, she lays out one-half on't in charitable uses for the good of her neighbors. She cures rheumatisms, ruptures, and broken shins in men; green sickness, obstructions, and fits of the mother, in women; the king's evil, chincough,[10] and chilblains, in children. In short, she has cured more people in and about Lichfield within ten years than the doctors have killed in twenty; and that's a bold word.

AIMWELL. Has the lady been any other way useful in her generation?

BONIFACE. Yes, sir; she has a daughter by Sir Charles, the finest woman in all our country, and the greatest fortune. She has a son too, by her first husband, Squire Sullen, who married a fine lady from London t'other day; if you please, sir, we'll drink his health.

AIMWELL. What sort of man is he?

BONIFACE. Why, sir, the man's well enough; says little, thinks less, and does—nothing at all, faith. But he's a man of great estate, and values nobody.

AIMWELL. A sportsman, I suppose?

[9] Of brandy or usquebaugh (whiskey).
[10] Anemia, constipation, hysterics, scrofula, whooping cough.

BONIFACE. Yes, sir, he's a man of pleasure; he plays at whisk[11] and smokes his pipe eight-and-forty hours together sometimes.

AIMWELL. And married, you say?

BONIFACE. Ay, and to a curious woman, sir. But he's a— he wants it; here, sir. (*pointing to his forehead*)

AIMWELL. He has it there, you mean?[12]

BONIFACE. That's none of my business; he's my landlord, and so a man, you know, would not—But—icod, he's no better than—Sir, my humble service to you.— (*Drinks.*) Though I value not a farthing what he can do to me; I pay him his rent at quarter-day, I have a good running trade, I have but one daughter, and I can give her—but no matter for that.

AIMWELL. You're very happy, Mr. Boniface. Pray, what other company have you in town?

BONIFACE. A power of fine ladies; and then we have the French officers.[13]

AIMWELL. Oh, that's right, you have a good many of those gentlemen. Pray, how do you like their company?

BONIFACE. So well, as the saying is, that I could wish we had as many more of 'em; they're full of money, and pay double for everything they have. They know, sir, that we paid good round taxes for the taking of 'em, and so they are willing to reimburse us a little. One of 'em lodges in my house.

(*Re-enter ARCHER.*)

ARCHER. Landlord, there are some French gentlemen below that ask for you.

BONIFACE. I'll wait on 'em.—(*aside to ARCHER*) Does your master stay long in town, as the saying is?

ARCHER. I can't tell, as the saying is.

BONIFACE. Come from London?

ARCHER. No.

BONIFACE. Going to London, mayhap?

ARCHER. No.

BONIFACE (*aside*). An odd fellow this.

---

[11] Whist, then a tavern card game.
[12] Boniface means that Sullen is stupid; Aimwell, that he has the horns of a cuckold.
[13] Captured in the War of the Spanish Succession and paroled in England.

(*To* AIMWELL): I beg your worship's pardon, I'll wait
on you in half a minute. (*Exit.*)

AIMWELL. The coast's clear, I see.—Now, my dear Archer,
welcome to Lichfield.

ARCHER. I thank thee, my dear brother in iniquity.

AIMWELL. Iniquity! prithee, leave canting; you need not
change your style with your dress.

ARCHER. Don't mistake me, Aimwell, for 'tis still my
maxim, that there is no scandal like rags, nor any
crime so shameful as poverty.

AIMWELL. The world confesses it every day in its practice, though men won't own it for their opinion. Who
did that worthy lord, my brother, single out of the
side-box[14] to sup with him t'other night?

ARCHER. Jack Handycraft, a handsome, well-dressed,
mannerly, sharping rogue, who keeps the best company in town.

AIMWELL. Right! And, pray, who married my Lady Manslaughter t'other day, the great fortune?

ARCHER. Why, Nick Marrabone,[15] a professed pickpocket,
and a good bowler; but he makes a handsome figure,
and rides in his coach, that he formerly used to ride
behind.

AIMWELL. But did you observe poor Jack Generous in the
Park last week?

ARCHER. Yes, with his autumnal periwig shading his melancholy face, his coat older than anything but its fashion,
with one hand idle in his pocket, and with the other
picking his useless teeth; and, though the Mall[16] was
crowded with company, yet was poor Jack as single
and solitary as a lion in a desert.

AIMWELL. And as much avoided, for no crime upon earth
but the want of money.

ARCHER. And that's enough. Men must not be poor; idleness is the root of all evil; the world's wide enough,
let 'em bustle. Fortune has taken the weak under her
protection, but men of sense are left to their industry.

AIMWELL. Upon which topic we proceed, and I think
luckily hitherto. Would not any man swear, now, that

---

[14] An expensive section of the theater.
[15] A corruption of "Marylebone," a district noted for gambling
on bowling and other games.
[16] The Mall was a fashionable walk in St. James's Park.

I am a man of quality, and you my servant; when if our intrinsic value were known—

ARCHER. Come, come, we are the men of intrinsic value, who can strike our fortunes out of ourselves, whose worth is independent of accidents in life, or revolutions in government; we have heads to get money and hearts to spend it.

AIMWELL. As to our hearts, I grant ye, they are as willing tits[17] as any within twenty degrees; but I can have no great opinion of our heads from the service they have done us hitherto, unless it be that they have brought us from London hither to Lichfield, made me a lord, and you my servant.

ARCHER. That's more than you could expect already. But what money have we left?

AIMWELL. But two hundred pound.

ARCHER. And our horses, clothes, rings, &c.—Why, we have very good fortunes now for moderate people; and, let me tell you besides, that this two hundred pound, with the experience that we are now masters of is a better estate than the ten thousand we have spent. Our friends, indeed, began to suspect that our pockets were low; but we came off with flying colors, showed no signs of want either in word or deed—

AIMWELL. Ay, and our going to Brussels was a good pretence enough for our sudden disappearing; and, I warrant you, our friends imagine that we are gone a-volunteering.

ARCHER. Why, faith, if this prospect fails, it must e'en come to that. I am for venturing one of the hundreds, if you will, upon this knight-errantry; but, in case it should fail, we'll reserve the t'other to carry us to some counterscarp,[18] where we may die, as we lived, in a blaze.

AIMWELL. With all my heart; and we have lived justly, Archer; we can't say that we have spent our fortunes, but that we have enjoyed 'em.

ARCHER. Right! So much pleasure for so much money, we have had our pennyworths; and, had I millions, I would go to the same market again.—Oh London! London!—Well, we have had our share, and let us be

17 Small, serviceable horses.
18 The outer wall of a fortification.

thankful; past pleasures, for aught I know, are best,
such as we are sure of; those to come may disappoint
us.

AIMWELL. It has often grieved the heart of me to see how
some inhuman wretches murder their kind fortunes;
those that, by sacrificing all to one appetite, shall
starve all the rest. You shall have some that live only
in their palates, and in their sense of tasting shall
drown the other four. Others are only epicures in
appearances, such who shall starve their nights to
make a figure a-days, and famish their own to feed
the eyes of others. A contrary sort confine their
pleasures to the dark, and contract their spacious
acres to the circuit of a muffstring.

ARCHER. Right; but they find the Indies in that spot where
they consume 'em. And I think your kind keepers[19]
have much the best on't; for they indulge the most
senses by one expense. There's the seeing, hearing, and
feeling, amply gratified; and some philosophers will
tell you that from such a commerce there arises a
sixth sense, that gives infinitely more pleasure than
the other five put together.

AIMWELL. And to pass to the other extremity, of all
keepers I think those the worst that keep their money.

ARCHER. Those are the most miserable wights in being:
they destroy the rights of nature, and disappoint the
blessings of Providence. Give me a man that keeps his
five senses keen and bright as his sword; that has 'em
always drawn out in their just order and strength, with
his reason as commander at the head of 'em; that de-
taches 'em by turns upon whatever party of pleasure
agreeably offers, and commands 'em to retreat upon
the least appearance of disadvantage or danger! For
my part, I can stick to my bottle while my wine, my
company, and my reason, holds good; I can be
charmed with Sappho's singing without falling in love
with her face; I love hunting, but would not, like
Actaeon, be eaten up by my own dogs; I love a fine
house, but let another keep it; and just so I love a
fine woman.

AIMWELL. In that last particular you have the better of me.

ARCHER. Ay, you're such an amorous puppy that I'm afraid

---

[19] Of mistresses.

you'll spoil our sport; you can't counterfeit the passion without feeling it.

AIMWELL. Though the whining part be out of doors[20] in town, 'tis still in force with the country ladies; and let me tell you, Frank, the fool in that passion shall outdo the knave at any time.

ARCHER. Well, I won't dispute it now; you command for the day, and so I submit. At Nottingham, you know, I am to be master.

AIMWELL. And at Lincoln, I again.

ARCHER. Then at Norwich I mount, which I think shall be our last stage; for, if we fail there, we'll embark for Holland, bid adieu to Venus, and welcome Mars.

AIMWELL. A match!—Mum!

(*Enter* BONIFACE.)

BONIFACE. What will your worship please to have for supper?

AIMWELL. What have you got?

BONIFACE. Sir, we have a delicate piece of beef in the pot, and a pig at the fire.

AIMWELL. Good supper-meat, I must confess. I can't eat beef, landlord.

ARCHER. And I hate pig.

AIMWELL. Hold your prating, sirrah! Do you know who you are?

BONIFACE. Please to bespeak something else; I have everything in the house.

AIMWELL. Have you any veal?

BONIFACE. Veal, sir! We had a delicate loin of veal on Wednesday last.

AIMWELL. Have you got any fish or wild-fowl?

BONIFACE. As for fish, truly, sir, we are an inland town and indifferently provided with fish, that's the truth on't; and then for wild-fowl—we have a delicate couple of rabbits.

AIMWELL. Get me the rabbits fricasseed.

BONIFACE. Fricasseed! Lard, sir, they'll eat much better smothered with onions.

ARCHER. Psha! damn your onions!

AIMWELL. Again, sirrah!— Well, landlord, what you please. But hold—I have a small charge of money, and your

20 Out of place.

house is so full of strangers, that I believe it may be safer in your custody than mine; for when this fellow of mine gets drunk he minds nothing.—Here, sirrah, reach me the strong-box.

ARCHER. Yes, sir.—(*aside*) This will give us a reputation. (*Brings the box.*)

AIMWELL. Here, landlord; the locks are sealed down both for your security and mine; it holds somewhat above two hundred pound; if you doubt it, I'll count it to you after supper. But be sure you lay it where I may have it at a minute's warning; for my affairs are a little dubious at present; perhaps I may be gone in half an hour, perhaps I may be your guest till the best part of that be spent; and pray order your ostler to keep my horses always saddled. But one thing above the rest I must beg, that you would let this fellow have none of your Anno Domini, as you call it; for he's the most insufferable sot.—Here, sirrah, light me to my chamber. (*Exit, lighted by* ARCHER.)

BONIFACE. Cherry! daughter Cherry!

(*Re-enter* CHERRY.)

CHERRY. D'ye call, father?

BONIFACE. Ay, child, you must lay by this box for the gentleman; 'tis full of money.

CHERRY. Money! all that money! why, sure, father, the gentleman comes to be chosen parliament-man. Who is he?

BONIFACE. I don't know what to make of him; he talks of keeping his horses ready saddled, and of going perhaps at a minute's warning, or staying perhaps till the best part of this be spent.

CHERRY. Ay, ten to one, father, he's a highwayman.

BONIFACE. A highwayman! upon my life, girl, you have hit it, and this box is some new-purchased booty. Now could we find him out, the money were ours.

CHERRY. He don't belong to our gang.

BONIFACE. What horses have they?

CHERRY. The master rides upon a black.

BONIFACE. A black! ten to one the man upon the black mare! And since he don't belong to our fraternity, we may betray him with a safe conscience; I don't think it lawful to harbor any rogues but my own. Look'ee, child, as the saying is, we must go cunningly to work: proofs we must have. The gentleman's servant loves drink, I'll ply him that way; and ten to one loves a wench—you must work him t'other way.

CHERRY. Father, would you have me give my secret for his?

BONIFACE. Consider, child, there's two hundred pound to boot.—(*ringing without*) Coming!—coming!—Child, mind your business. (*Exit.*)

CHERRY. What a rogue is my father! My father? I deny it. My mother was a good, generous, free-hearted woman, and I can't tell how far her good-nature might have extended for the good of her children. This landlord of mine, for I think I can call him no more, would betray his guest, and debauch his daughter into the bargain—by a footman, too!

(*Enter* ARCHER.)

ARCHER. What footman, pray, mistress, is so happy as to be the subject of your contemplation?

CHERRY. Whoever he is, friend, he'll be but little the better for't.

ARCHER. I hope so, for I'm sure you did not think of me.

CHERRY. Suppose I had?

ARCHER. Why then you're but even with me; for the minute I came in, I was a-considering in what manner I should make love to you.

CHERRY. Love to me, friend!

ARCHER. Yes, child.

CHERRY. Child! manners!—If you kept a little more distance, friend, it would become you much better.

ARCHER. Distance! Good-night, sauce-box. (*going*)

CHERRY (*aside*). A pretty fellow. I like his pride.—Sir, pray, sir, you see, sir,

(ARCHER *returns.*)

I have the credit to be entrusted with your master's fortune here, which sets me a degree above his footman; I hope, sir, you an't affronted?

ARCHER. Let me look you full in the face, and I'll tell you whether you can affront me or no.—'Sdeath, child, you have a pair of delicate eyes, and you don't know what to do with 'em!

CHERRY. Why sir, don't I see everybody?

ARCHER. Ay, but if some women had 'em, they would kill
   everybody. Prithee, instruct me, I would fain make
   love to you, but I don't know what to say.

CHERRY. Why, did you never make love to anybody before?

ARCHER. Never to a person of your figure, I can assure you,
   madam. My addresses have been always confined to
   people within my own sphere; I never aspired so
   high before.
   (*A song*)

> But you look so bright,
> And are dressed so tight,
> That a man would swear you're right,[21]
> As arm was e'er laid over.
> Such an air
> You freely wear
> To ensnare,
> As makes each guest a lover!

> Since then, my dear, I'm your guest,
> Prithee give me of the best
> Of what is ready dressed;
> Since then, my dear, etc.

CHERRY (*aside*). What can I think of this man?—Will you
   give me that song, sir?

ARCHER. Ay, my dear, take it while 'tis warm.—(*Kisses
   her.*) Death and fire! her lips are honeycombs.

CHERRY. And I wish there had been bees too, to have
   stung you for your impudence.

ARCHER. There's a swarm of Cupids, my little Venus, that
   has done the business much better.

CHERRY (*aside*). This fellow is misbegotten as well as I.—
   What's your name, sir?

ARCHER (*aside*). Name! igad, I have forgot it.—Oh!
   Martin.

CHERRY. Where were you born?

ARCHER. In St. Martin's parish.

CHERRY. What was your father?

ARCHER. St. Martin's parish.[22]

CHERRY. Then, friend, good night.

ARCHER. I hope not.

---

[21] Sexually willing or expert or both.
[22] Penniless orphans were raised by the parish.

CHERRY. You may depend upon't.

ARCHER. Upon what?

CHERRY. That you're very impudent.

ARCHER. That you're very handsome.

CHERRY. That you're a footman.

ARCHER. That you're an angel.

CHERRY. I shall be rude.

ARCHER. So shall I.

CHERRY. Let go my hand.

ARCHER. Give me a kiss. (*Kisses her.*)

 (*Call without*) Cherry! Cherry!

CHERRY. I'm—my father calls; you plaguy devil, how durst you stop my breath so? Offer to follow me one step, if you dare. (*Exit.*)

ARCHER. A fair challenge, by this light! This is a pretty fair opening of an adventure; but we are knight-errants, and so Fortune be our guide. (*Exit.*)

ACT II

[SCENE I.] *A Gallery in* LADY BOUNTIFUL'S *House*

(MRS. SULLEN *and* DORINDA, *meeting.*)

DORINDA. Morrow, my dear sister; are you for church this morning?

MRS. SULLEN. Anywhere to pray; for Heaven alone can help me. But I think, Dorinda, there's no form of prayer in the liturgy against bad husbands.

DORINDA. But there's a form of law in Doctors-Commons;[23] and I swear, sister Sullen, rather than see you thus continually discontented, I would advise you to apply to that; for besides the part that I bear in your vexatious broils, as being sister to the husband, and friend to the wife, your example gives me such an impression of matrimony, that I shall be apt to condemn my person to a long vacation all its life. But supposing, madam, that you brought it to a case of separation, what can you urge against your husband? My brother is, first, the most constant man alive.

---

23 The College of Doctors of Civil Law in London, entitled, among other things, to plead cases of separation in the ecclesiastical courts.

MRS. SULLEN. The most constant husband, I grant ye.

DORINDA. He never sleeps from you.

MRS. SULLEN. No; he always sleeps with me.

DORINDA. He allows you a maintenance suitable to your quality.

MRS. SULLEN. A maintenance! do you take me, madam, for an hospital child,[24] that I must sit down, and bless my benefactors for meat, drink, and clothes? As I take it, madam, I brought your brother ten thousand pounds, out of which I might expect some pretty things, called pleasures.

DORINDA. You share in all the pleasures that the country affords.

MRS. SULLEN. Country pleasures! racks and torments! Dost think, child, that my limbs were made for leaping of ditches, and clambering over stiles? or that my parents, wisely foreseeing my future happiness in country pleasures, had early instructed me in the rural accomplishments of drinking fat[25] ale, playing at whisk, and smoking tobacco with my husband? or of spreading of plasters, brewing of diet-drinks, and stilling rosemary-water, with the good old gentle-woman my mother-in-law?

DORINDA. I'm sorry, madam, that it is not more in our power to divert you; I could wish, indeed, that our entertainments were a little more polite, or your taste a little less refined. But, pray, madam, how came the poets and philosophers, that labored so much in hunting after pleasure, to place it at last in a country life?

MRS. SULLEN. Because they wanted money, child, to find out the pleasures of the town. Did you ever see a poet or philosopher worth ten thousand pound? If you can show me such a man, I'll lay you fifty pound you'll find him somewhere within the weekly bills.[26] Not that I disapprove rural pleasures, as the poets have painted them; in their landscape, every Phillis has her Corydon, every murmuring stream, and every

---

[24] Inmate of an orphan asylum.
[25] Full-bodied.
[26] Within the precincts of London, for which weekly bills of mortality (lists of deaths) were published.

flowery mead, gives fresh alarms to love. Besides, you'll find that their couples were never married.— But yonder I see my Corydon, and a sweet swain it is, Heaven knows! Come, Dorinda, don't be angry; he's my husband, and your brother; and between both, is he not a sad brute?

DORINDA. I have nothing to say to your part of him—you're the best judge.

MRS. SULLEN. O sister, sister! if ever you marry, beware of a sullen, silent sot, one that's always musing, but never thinks. There's some diversion in a talking blockhead; and since a woman must wear chains, I would have the pleasure of hearing 'em rattle a little. Now you shall see—but take this by the way: he came home this morning at his usual hour of four, wakened me out of a sweet dream of something else by tumbling over the tea-table, which he broke all to pieces; after his man and he had rolled about the room, like sick passengers in a storm, he comes flounce into bed, dead as a salmon into a fishmonger's basket; his feet cold as ice, his breath hot as a furnace, and his hands and his face as greasy as his flannel nightcap. O matrimony! He tosses up the clothes with a barbarous swing over his shoulders, disorders the whole economy of my bed, leaves me half naked, and my whole night's comfort is the tuneable serenade of that wakeful nightingale, his nose! Oh, the pleasure of counting the melancholy clock by a snoring husband! But now, sister, you shall see how handsomely, being a well-bred man, he will beg my pardon.

(*Enter* SULLEN.)

SQUIRE SULLEN. My head aches consumedly.

MRS. SULLEN. Will you be pleased, my dear, to drink tea with us this morning? It may do your head good.

SQUIRE SULLEN. No.

DORINDA. Coffee, brother?

SQUIRE SULLEN. Pshaw!

MRS. SULLEN. Will you please to dress, and go to church with me? The air may help you.

SQUIRE SULLEN. Scrub!

(*Enter* SCRUB.)

SCRUB. Sir!

SQUIRE SULLEN. What day o' th'week is this?

SCRUB. Sunday, an't please your worship.

SQUIRE SULLEN. Sunday! Bring me a dram; and d'ye hear, set out the venison-pasty, and a tankard of strong beer upon the hall-table; I'll go to breakfast. (*going*)

DORINDA. Stay, stay, brother, you shan't get off so; you were very naughty last night, and must make your wife reparation; come, come, brother, won't you ask pardon?

SQUIRE SULLEN. For what?

DORINDA. For being drunk last night.

SQUIRE SULLEN. I can afford it, can't I?

MRS. SULLEN. But I can't, sir.

SQUIRE SULLEN. Then you may let it alone.

MRS. SULLEN. But I must tell you, sir, that this is not to be borne.

SQUIRE SULLEN. I'm glad on't.

MRS. SULLEN. What is the reason, sir, that you use me thus inhumanly?

SQUIRE SULLEN. Scrub!

SCRUB. Sir!

SQUIRE SULLEN. Get things ready to shave my head. (*Exit [with* SCRUB].)

MRS. SULLEN. Have a care of coming near his temples, Scrub, for fear you meet something there that may turn the edge of your razor.—Inveterate stupidity! Did you ever know so hard, so obstinate a spleen as his? O sister, sister! I shall never ha' good of the beast till I get him to town; London, dear London, is the place for managing and breaking a husband.

DORINDA. And has not a husband the same opportunities there for humbling a wife?

MRS. SULLEN. No, no, child; 'tis a standing maxim in conjugal discipline, that when a man would enslave his wife, he hurries her into the country; and when a lady would be arbitrary with her husband she wheedles her booby up to town. A man dare not play the tyrant in London, because there are so many examples to encourage the subject to rebel. O Dorinda! Dorinda! a fine woman may do anything in London: o' my conscience, she may raise an army of forty thousand men.

DORINDA. I fancy, sister, you have a mind to be trying your power that way here in Lichfield; you have drawn the French count to your colors already.

MRS. SULLEN. The French are a people that can't live without their gallantries.

DORINDA. And some English that I know, sister, are not averse to such amusements.

MRS. SULLEN. Well, sister, since the truth must be out, it may do as well now as hereafter; I think one way to rouse my lethargic, sottish husband is to give him a rival. Security begets negligence in all people, and men must be alarmed to make 'em alert in their duty. Women are like pictures, of no value in the hands of a fool, till he hears men of sense bid high for the purchase.

DORINDA. This might do, sister, if my brother's understanding were to be convinced into a passion for you; but I fancy there's a natural aversion of his side; and I fancy, sister, that you don't come much behind him, if you dealt fairly.

MRS. SULLEN. I own it, we are united contradictions, fire and water: but I could be contented, with a great many other wives, to humor the censorious mob, and give the world an appearance of living well with my husband, could I bring him but to dissemble a little kindness to keep me in countenance.

DORINDA. But how do you know, sister, but that, instead of rousing your husband by this artifice to a counterfeit kindness, he should awake in a real fury?

MRS. SULLEN. Let him; if I can't entice him to the one, I would provoke him to the other.

DORINDA. But how must I behave myself between ye?

MRS. SULLEN. You must assist me.

DORINDA. What, against my own brother?

MRS. SULLEN. He's but half a brother, and I'm your entire friend. If I go a step beyond the bounds of honor, leave me; till then, I expect you should go along with me in everything; while I trust my honor in your hands, you must trust your brother's in mine. The count is to dine here to-day.

DORINDA. 'Tis a strange thing, sister, that I can't like that man.

MRS. SULLEN. You like nothing; your time is not come;

love and death have their fatalities, and strike home one time or other. You'll pay for all one day, I warrant ye. But come, my lady's tea is ready, and 'tis almost church time.

(*Exeunt.*)

[SCENE II.] *The Inn*

(*Enter* AIMWELL *dressed, and* ARCHER.)

AIMWELL. And was she the daughter of the house?

ARCHER. The landlord is so blind as to think so; but I dare swear she has better blood in her veins.

AIMWELL. Why dost think so?

ARCHER. Because the baggage has a pert *je ne sais quoi*;[27] she reads plays, keeps a monkey, and is troubled with vapors.[28]

AIMWELL. By which discoveries I guess that you know more of her.

ARCHER. Not yet, faith; the lady gives herself airs; forsooth, nothing under a gentleman!

AIMWELL. Let me take her in hand.

ARCHER. Say one word more o'that, and I'll declare myself, spoil your sport there and everywhere else; look ye, Aimwell, every man in his own sphere.

AIMWELL. Right; and therefore you must pimp for your master.

ARCHER. In the usual forms, good sir, after I have served myself.—But to our business. You are so well dressed, Tom, and make so handsome a figure, that I fancy you may do execution in a country church; the exterior part strikes first, and you're in the right to make that impression favorable.

AIMWELL. There's something in that which may turn to advantage. The appearance of a stranger in a country church draws as many gazers as a blazing star; no sooner he comes into the cathedral, but a train of whispers runs buzzing round the congregation in a moment: Who is he? Whence comes he? Do you know him? Then I, sir, tips me the verger with half-a-crown; he pockets the simony, and inducts me into the best

---

[27] Inexpressible something.
[28] Fashionable melancholy, similar to the spleen (see note 50).

pew in the church. I pull out my snuff-box, turn myself round, bow to the bishop or the dean, if he be the commanding officer; single out a beauty, rivet both my eyes to hers, set my nose a-bleeding by the strength of imagination, and show the whole church my concern by my endeavoring to hide it. After the sermon, the whole town gives me to her for a lover; and by persuading the lady that I am a-dying for her, the tables are turned, and she in good earnest falls in love with me.

ARCHER. There's nothing in this, Tom, without a precedent; but instead of riveting your eyes to a beauty, try and fix 'em upon a fortune; that's our business at present.

AIMWELL. Pshaw! no woman can be a beauty without a fortune. Let me alone, for I am a marksman.

ARCHER. Tom!

AIMWELL. Ay.

ARCHER. When were you at church before, pray?

AIMWELL. Um—I was there at the coronation.[29]

ARCHER. And how can you expect a blessing by going to church now?

AIMWELL. Blessing! nay, Frank, I ask but for a wife. (*Exit.*)

ARCHER. Truly, the man is not very unreasonable in his demands. (*Exit at the opposite door.*)

(*Enter* BONIFACE *and* CHERRY.)

BONIFACE. Well, daughter, as the saying is, have you brought Martin to confess?

CHERRY. Pray, father, don't put me upon getting anything out of a man; I'm but young, you know, father, and I don't understand wheedling.

BONIFACE. Young! why, you jade, as the saying is, can any woman wheedle that is not young? Your mother was useless at five-and-twenty. Not wheedle! would you make your mother a whore, and me a cuckold, as the saying is? I tell you, his silence confesses it; and his master spends his money so freely, and is so much a gentleman every manner of way, that he must be a highwayman.

(*Enter* GIBBET, *in a cloak.*)

29 Of Queen Anne in 1702.

GIBBET. Landlord, landlord, is the coast clear?

BONIFACE. O Mr. Gibbet, what's the news?

GIBBET. No matter, ask no questions, all fair and honorable.—Here, my dear Cherry.—(*Gives her a bag.*) Two hundred sterling pounds, as good as any that ever hanged or saved a rogue; lay 'em by with the rest; and here—three wedding or mourning rings, 'tis much the same, you know—here, two silver-hilted swords; I took those from fellows that never show any part of their swords but the hilts—here is a diamond necklace which the lady hid in the privatest place in the coach, but I found it out—this gold watch I took from a pawnbroker's wife; it was left in her hands by a person of quality, there's the arms upon the case.

CHERRY. But who had you the money from?

GIBBET. Ah! poor woman! I pitied her; from a poor lady just eloped from her husband. She had made up her cargo, and was bound for Ireland, as hard as she could drive; she told me of her husband's barbarous usage, and so I left her half a crown. But I had almost forgot, my dear Cherry, I have a present for you.

CHERRY. What is't?

GIBBET. A pot of ceruse, my child, that I took out of a lady's underpocket.

CHERRY. What, Mr. Gibbet, do you think that I paint?

GIBBET. Why, you jade, your betters do; I'm sure the lady that I took it from had a coronet upon her handkerchief. Here, take my cloak, and go, secure the premises.

CHERRY. I will secure 'em. (*Exit.*)

BONIFACE. But, heark'ee, where's Hounslow and Bagshot?[30]

GIBBET. They'll be here to-night.

BONIFACE. D'ye know of any other gentlemen o' the pad[31] on this road?

GIBBET. No.

BONIFACE. I fancy that I have two that lodge in the house just now.

GIBBET. The devil! How d'ye smoke[32] 'em?

---

[30] Named after two heaths in London famous as haunts of highwaymen.
[31] Highway robbers.
[32] Come to suspect.

BONIFACE. Why, the one is gone to church.

GIBBET. That's suspicious, I must confess.

BONIFACE. And the other is now in his master's chamber; he pretends to be servant to the other. We'll call him out and pump him a little.

GIBBET. With all my heart.

BONIFACE. Mr. Martin! Mr. Martin!

(*Enter* ARCHER, *combing a periwig and singing.*)

GIBBET. The roads are consumed deep, I'm as dirty as old Brentford[33] at Christmas.—A good pretty fellow that. Whose servant are you, friend?

ARCHER. My master's.

GIBBET. Really!

ARCHER. Really.

GIBBET. That's much. [*aside to* BONIFACE] The fellow has been at the bar, by his evasions.—But, pray, sir, what is your master's name?

ARCHER. Tall, all, dall!—(*Sings and combs the periwig.*) This is the most obstinate curl—

GIBBET. I ask you his name?

ARCHER. Name, sir—*tall, all, dall!*—I never asked him his name in my life.—*Tall, all, dall!*

BONIFACE (*aside to* GIBBET). What think you now?

GIBBET (*aside to* BONIFACE). Plain, plain; he talks now as if he were before a judge.—But, pray, friend, which way does your master travel?

ARCHER. A-horseback.

GIBBET (*aside*). Very well again, an old offender, right.— But, I mean, does he go upwards or downwards?

ARCHER. Downwards, I fear, sir.—*Tall, all!*

GIBBET. I'm afraid my fate will be a contrary way.

BONIFACE. Ha, ha, ha! Mr. Martin, you're very arch. This gentleman is only travelling towards Chester, and would be glad of your company, that's all.—Come, Captain, you'll stay to-night, I suppose? I'll show you a chamber—come, Captain.

GIBBET. Farewell, friend! (*Exit* [*with* BONIFACE].)

---

[33] Deep in mud; Brentford was proverbially muddy, especially in midwinter.

ARCHER. Captain, your servant.—Captain! a pretty fellow! 'Sdeath, I wonder that the officers of the army don't conspire to beat all scoundrels in red but their own.

(*Enter* CHERRY.)

CHERRY (*aside*). Gone! and Martin here! I hope he did not listen; I would have the merit of the discovery all my own, because I would oblige him to love me.—(*aloud*) Mr. Martin, who was that man with my father?

ARCHER. Some recruiting sergeant, or whipped-out trooper, I suppose.

CHERRY (*aside*). All's safe, I find.

ARCHER. Come, my dear, have you conned over the catechise I taught you last night?

CHERRY. Come, question me.

ARCHER. What is love?

CHERRY. Love is I know not what, it comes I know not how, and goes I know not when.

ARCHER. Very well, an apt scholar.—(*Chucks her under the chin.*) Where does love enter?

CHERRY. Into the eyes.

ARCHER. And where go out?

CHERRY. I won't tell ye.

ARCHER. What are the objects of that passion?

CHERRY. Youth, beauty, and clean linen.

ARCHER. The reason?

CHERRY. The two first are fashionable in nature, and the third at court.

ARCHER. That's my dear.—What are the signs and tokens of that passion?

CHERRY. A stealing look, a stammering tongue, words improbable, designs impossible, and actions impracticable.

ARCHER. That's my good child, kiss me.—What must a lover do to obtain his mistress?

CHERRY. He must adore the person that disdains him, he must bribe the chambermaid that betrays him, and court the footman that laughs at him. He must—he must—

ARCHER. Nay, child, I must whip you if you don't mind your lesson; he must treat his—

CHERRY. O ay!—he must treat his enemies with respect,

his friends with indifference, and all the world with contempt; he must suffer much, and fear more; he must desire much, and hope little; in short, he must embrace his ruin, and throw himself away.

ARCHER. Had ever man so hopeful a pupil as mine!—Come, my dear, why is Love called a riddle?

CHERRY. Because, being blind, he leads those that see, and, though a child, he governs a man.

ARCHER. Mighty well!—And why is Love pictured blind?

CHERRY. Because the painters out of the weakness or privilege of their art chose to hide those eyes that they could not draw.

ARCHER. That's my dear little scholar, kiss me again.—And why should Love, that's a child, govern a man?

CHERRY. Because that a child is the end of love.

ARCHER. And so ends Love's catechism.—And now, my dear, we'll go in and make my master's bed.

CHERRY. Hold, hold, Mr. Martin! You have taken a great deal of pains to instruct me, and what d'ye think I have learned by it?

ARCHER. What?

CHERRY. That your discourse and your habit are contradictions, and it would be nonsense in me to believe you a footman any longer.

ARCHER. 'Oons, what a witch it is!

CHERRY. Depend upon this, sir, nothing in this garb shall ever tempt me; for, though I was born to servitude, I hate it. Own your condition, swear you love me, and then—

ARCHER. And then we shall go make the bed?

CHERRY. Yes.

ARCHER. You must know then, that I am born a gentleman, my education was liberal; but I went to London, a younger brother, fell into the hands of sharpers, who stripped me of my money, my friends disowned me, and now my necessity brings me to what you see.

CHERRY. Then take my hand—promise to marry me before you sleep, and I'll make you master of two thousand pounds.

ARCHER. How!

CHERRY. Two thousand pounds that I have this minute in my own custody; so, throw off your livery this instant, and I'll go find a parson.

ARCHER. What said you? a parson!

CHERRY. What! do you scruple?

ARCHER. Scruple! no, no, but—Two thousand pound, you say?

CHERRY. And better.

ARCHER (*aside*). 'Sdeath, what shall I do?—But hark'ee, child, what need you make me master of yourself and money, when you may have the same pleasure out of me, and still keep your fortune in your hands.

CHERRY. Then you won't marry me?

ARCHER. I would marry you, but—

CHERRY. O, sweet sir, I'm your humble servant, you're fairly caught! Would you persuade me that any gentleman who could bear the scandal of wearing a livery would refuse two thousand pound, let the condition be what it would? No, no, sir. But I hope you'll pardon the freedom I have taken, since it was only to inform myself of the respect that I ought to pay you.

ARCHER (*aside*). Fairly hit, by Jupiter!—Hold! hold!—And have you actually two thousand pounds?

CHERRY. Sir, I have my secrets as well as you; when you please to be more open I shall be more free; and be assured that I have discoveries that will match yours, be what they will. In the meanwhile, be satisfied that no discovery I make shall ever hurt you; but beware of my father! (*Exit.*)

ARCHER. So! we're likely to have as many adventures in our inn as Don Quixote[34] had in his. Let me see—two thousand pounds!—If the wench would promise to die when the money were spent, igad, one would marry her; but the fortune may go off in a year or two, and the wife may live—Lord knows how long. Then an innkeeper's daughter; ay, that's the devil—there my pride brings me off.

For whatsoe'er the sages charge on pride,
The angels' fall, and twenty faults beside,
On earth, I'm sure, 'mong us of mortal calling,
Pride saves man oft, and woman too, from falling.
(Exit.)

---

[34] Cervantes' traveling knight, Don Quixote, had adventures at several inns, but the most relevant seems to be his fantasied love encounter described in Part I, Chapter 16 of *Don Quixote*.

ACT III

[SCENE I.] *The Gallery in* LADY BOUNTIFUL's *House*

(*Enter* MRS. SULLEN, DORINDA.)

MRS. SULLEN. Ha, ha, ha! my dear sister, let me embrace
thee! Now we are friends indeed; for I shall have a
secret of yours as a pledge for mine—now you'll be
good for something; I shall have you conversable in
the subjects of the sex.

DORINDA. But do you think that I am so weak as to fall in
love with a fellow at first sight?

MRS. SULLEN. Pshaw! now you spoil all; why should not
we be as free in our friendships as the men? I warrant
you the gentleman has got to his confidant already, has
avowed his passion, toasted your health, called you ten
thousand angels, has run over your lips, eyes, neck,
shape, air, and everything, in a description that warms
their mirth to a second enjoyment.

DORINDA. Your hand, sister, I an't well.

MRS. SULLEN. So—she's breeding already! Come, child, up
with it—hem a little—so—now tell me, don't you
like the gentleman that we saw at church just now?

DORINDA. The man's well enough.

MRS. SULLEN. Well enough! is he not a demigod, a
Narcissus, a star, the man i' the moon?

DORINDA. O sister, I'm extremely ill!

MRS. SULLEN. Shall I send to your mother, child, for a little
of her cephalic plaster[35] to put to the soles of your
feet, or shall I send to the gentleman for something
for you? Come, unlace your stays, unbosom yourself.
The man is perfectly a pretty fellow; I saw him when
he first came into church.

DORINDA. I saw him too, sister, and with an air that shone,
methought, like rays about his person.

MRS. SULLEN. Well said, up with it!

DORINDA. No forward coquet behavior, no airs to set him
off, no studied looks nor artful posture,—but nature
did it all—

[35] Supposed to cure by drawing "humours" from the head.

MRS. SULLEN. Better and better!—one touch more—come!

DORINDA. But then his looks—did you observe his eyes?

MRS. SULLEN. Yes, yes, I did—his eyes—well, what of his eyes?

DORINDA. Sprightly, but not wandering; they seemed to view, but never gazed on anything but me.—And then his looks so humble were, and yet so noble, that they aimed to tell me that he could with pride die at my feet, though he scorned slavery anywhere else.

MRS. SULLEN. The physic works purely![36]—How d'ye find yourself now, my dear?

DORINDA. Hem! much better, my dear.—Oh, here comes our Mercury!

(*Enter* SCRUB.)

—Well Scrub, what news of the gentleman?

SCRUB. Madam, I have brought you a packet of news.

DORINDA. Open it quickly, come.

SCRUB. In the first place I inquired who the gentleman was; they told me he was a stranger. Secondly, I asked what the gentleman was; they answered and said, that they never saw him before. Thirdly, I inquired what countryman he was; they replied, 'twas more than they knew. Fourthly, I demanded whence he came; their answer was, they could not tell. And fifthly, I asked whither he went; and they replied, they knew nothing of the matter,—and this is all I could learn.

MRS. SULLEN. But what do the people say? Can't they guess?

SCRUB. Why, some think he's a spy, some guess he's a mountebank, some say one thing, some another; but for my own part, I believe he's a Jesuit.

DORINDA. A Jesuit! Why a Jesuit?

SCRUB. Because he keeps his horses always ready saddled, and his footman talks French.

MRS. SULLEN. His footman!

SCRUB. Ay, he and the Count's footman were gabbering French like two intriguing ducks in a mill-pond; and I believe they talked of me, for they laughed consumedly.

DORINDA. What sort of livery has the footman?

SCRUB. Livery! Lord, madam, I took him for a captain, he's

[36] Finely.

so bedizened with lace! And then he has tops on his shoes up to his mid leg, a silver-headed cane dangling at his knuckles; he carries his hands in his pockets just so—(*Walks in the French air.*) and has a fine long periwig tied up in a bag. Lord, madam, he's clear another sort of man than I!

MRS. SULLEN. That may easily be.—But what shall we do now, sister?

DORINDA. I have it! This fellow has a world of simplicity, and some cunning; the first hides the latter by abundance.—Scrub!

SCRUB. Madam!

DORINDA. We have a great mind to know who this gentleman is, only for our satisfaction.

SCRUB. Yes, madam, it would be a satisfaction, no doubt.

DORINDA. You must go and get acquainted with his footman, and invite him hither to drink a bottle of your ale, because you're butler to-day.

SCRUB. Yes, madam, I am butler every Sunday.

MRS. SULLEN. O brave! Sister, o' my conscience, you understand the mathematics already. 'Tis the best plot in the world; your mother, you know, will be gone to church, my spouse will be got to the ale-house with his scoundrels, and the house will be our own—so we drop in by accident, and ask the fellow some questions ourselves. In the country, you know, any stranger is company, and we're glad to take up with the butler in a country dance, and happy if he'll do us the favor.

SCRUB. O madam, you wrong me! I never refused your ladyship the favor in my life.

(*Enter* GIPSY.)

GIPSY. Ladies, dinner's upon table.

DORINDA. Scrub, we'll excuse your waiting—go where we ordered you.

SCRUB. I shall.

(*Exeunt.*)

[SCENE II.] *Scene changes to the Inn.*

(*Enter* AIMWELL *and* ARCHER.)

ARCHER. Well, Tom, I find you're a marksman.

AIMWELL. A marksman! who so blind could be as not discern a swan among the ravens?

ARCHER. Well, but hark'ee, Aimwell—

AIMWELL. Aimwell! call me Oroondates, Cesario, Amadis,[37] all that romance can in a lover paint, and then I'll answer. O Archer! I read her thousands in her looks, she looked like Ceres in her harvest: corn, wine and oil, milk and honey, gardens, groves, and purling streams, played on her plenteous face.

ARCHER. Her face! her pocket, you mean; the corn, wine and oil, lies there. In short, she has ten thousand pound, that's the English on't.

AIMWELL. Her eyes—

ARCHER. Are demi-cannons, to be sure; so I won't stand their battery. (*going*)

AIMWELL. Pray excuse me, my passion must have vent.

ARCHER. Passion! what a plague, d'ye think these romantic airs will do our business? Were my temper as extravagant as yours, my adventures have something more romantic by half.

AIMWELL. Your adventures!

ARCHER. Yes.

The nymph that with her twice ten hundred pounds,
With brazen engine hot, and quoif[38] clear starched,
Can fire the guest in warming of the bed—

There's a touch of sublime Milton for you, and the subject but an inn-keeper's daughter! I can play with a girl as an angler does with his fish; he keeps it at the end of his line, runs it up the stream, and down the stream, till at last he brings it to hand, tickles the trout,[39] and so whips it into his basket.

(*Enter* BONIFACE.)

BONIFACE. Mr. Martin, as the saying is—yonder's an honest fellow below, my Lady Bountiful's butler, who begs the honor that you would go home with him and see his cellar.

ARCHER. Do my *baise-mains*[40] to the gentleman, and tell him I will do myself the honor to wait on him immediately.

[37] Well-known heroes of romance.
[38] Chambermaids wore caps (quoifs), and one of their duties was to warm guests' beds with a brass warming pan.
[39] Strokes it till it is quiet, so he can grasp it.
[40] Pay my respects.

(*Exit* BONIFACE.)

AIMWELL. What do I hear? Soft Orpheus play, and fair Toftida[41] sing!

ARCHER. Pshaw! damn your raptures; I tell you, here's a pump going to be put into the vessel, and the ship will get into harbor, my life on't. You say, there's another lady very handsome there?

AIMWELL. Yes, faith.

ARCHER. I'm in love with her already.

AIMWELL. Can't you give me a bill upon Cherry in the meantime?

ARCHER. No, no, friend, all her corn, wine and oil, is ingrossed to my market. And once more I warn you to keep your anchorage clear of mine; for if you fall foul of me, by this light you shall go to the bottom! What! make prize of my little frigate, while I am upon the cruise for you!——

AIMWELL. Well, well, I won't.

(*Exit* [ARCHER]. *Enter* BONIFACE.)

Landlord, have you any tolerable company in the house? I don't care for dining alone.

BONIFACE. Yes, sir, there's a captain below, as the saying is, that arrived about an hour ago.

AIMWELL. Gentlemen of his coat are welcome everywhere; will you make him a compliment from me, and tell him I should be glad of his company?

BONIFACE. Who shall I tell him, sir, would——

AIMWELL (*aside*). Ha! that stroke was well thrown in!—— [*aloud*] I'm only a traveller like himself, and would be glad of his company, that's all.

BONIFACE. I obey your commands, as the saying is. (*Exit.*)

(*Enter* ARCHER.)

ARCHER. 'Sdeath! I had forgot; what title will you give yourself?

AIMWELL. My brother's, to be sure; he would never give me anything else, so I'll make bold with his honor this bout!—You know the rest of your cue.

ARCHER. Ay, ay. (*Exit.*)

(*Enter* GIBBET.)

41 Katherine Tofts, a contemporary opera singer.

GIBBET. Sir, I'm yours.

AIMWELL. 'Tis more than I deserve, sir, for I don't know you.

GIBBET. I don't wonder at that, sir, for you never saw me before.—(*aside*) I hope.

AIMWELL. And pray, sir, how came I by the honor of seeing you now?

GIBBET. Sir, I scorn to intrude upon any gentleman—but my landlord—

AIMWELL. O sir, I ask your pardon; you're the captain he told me of?

GIBBET. At your service, sir.

AIMWELL. What regiment, may I be so bold?

GIBBET. A marching regiment, sir, an old corps.

AIMWELL (*aside*). Very old, if your coat be regimental.— You have served abroad, sir?

GIBBET. Yes, sir, in the plantations;[42] 'twas my lot to be sent into the worst service. I would have quitted it indeed, but a man of honor, you know—Besides, 'twas for the good of my country that I should be abroad. Anything for the good of one's country—I'm a Roman for that.

AIMWELL (*aside*). One of the first, I'll lay my life.[43]—You found the West Indies very hot, sir?

GIBBET. Ay, sir, too hot for me.

AIMWELL. Pray, sir, han't I seen your face at Will's coffeehouse?

GIBBET. Yes, sir, and at White's too.

AIMWELL. And where is your company now, Captain?

GIBBET. They an't come yet.

AIMWELL. Why, d'ye expect 'em here?

GIBBET. They'll be here to-night, sir.

AIMWELL. Which way do they march?

GIBBET. Across the country.—(*aside*) The devil's in't, if I han't said enough to encourage him to declare! But I'm afraid he's not right, I must tack about.

AIMWELL. Is your company to quarter in Lichfield?

GIBBET. In this house, sir.

AIMWELL. What! all?

---

[42] Colonies; convicted felons were often transported to the colonies for forced labor.
[43] Gibbet refers to the proverbial patriotism of the early Romans; Aimwell, to their lawless actions, such as raping the Sabine women.

GIBBET. My company's but thin, ha, ha, ha! we are but three, ha, ha, ha!

AIMWELL. You're merry, sir.

GIBBET. Ay, sir, you must excuse me, sir, I understand the world, especially the art of travelling: I don't care, sir, for answering questions directly upon the road—for I generally ride with a charge about me.

AIMWELL (*aside*). Three or four, I believe.[44]

GIBBET. I am credibly informed that there are highwaymen upon this quarter. Not, sir, that I could suspect a gentleman of your figure—but truly, sir, I have got such a way of evasion upon the road, that I don't care for speaking truth to any man.

AIMWELL. Your caution may be necessary.—Then I presume you're no captain?

GIBBET. Not I, sir. Captain is a good travelling name, and so I take it; it stops a great many foolish inquiries that are generally made about gentlemen that travel, it gives a man an air of something, and makes the drawers obedient; and thus far I am a captain, and no farther.

AIMWELL. And pray, sir, what is your true profession?

GIBBET. O sir, you must excuse me!—upon my word, sir, I don't think it safe to tell you.

AIMWELL. Ha, ha, ha! upon my word, I commend you.

(*Enter* BONIFACE.)

Well, Mr. Boniface, what's the news?

BONIFACE. There's another gentleman below, as the saying is, that hearing you were but two, would be glad to make the third man, if you would give him leave.

AIMWELL. What is he?

BONIFACE. A clergyman, as the saying is.

AIMWELL. A clergyman! Is he really a clergyman? or is it only his travelling name, as my friend the captain has it?

BONIFACE. O sir, he's a priest, and chaplain to the French officers in town.

AIMWELL. Is he a Frenchman?

BONIFACE. Yes, sir, born at Brussels.

---

[44] Gibbet means money; Aimwell puns upon *charge* as loads of powder and shot for a pistol.

GIBBET. A Frenchman, and a priest! I won't be seen in his company, sir; I have a value for my reputation, sir.

AIMWELL. Nay, but, captain, since we are by ourselves— Can he speak English, landlord?

BONIFACE. Very well, sir; you may know him, as the saying is, to be a foreigner by his accent, and that's all.

AIMWELL. Then he has been in England before?

BONIFACE. Never, sir; but he's a master of languages, as the saying is; he talks Latin—It does me good to hear him talk Latin.

AIMWELL. Then you understand Latin, Mr. Boniface?

BONIFACE. Not I, sir, as the saying is; but he talks it so very fast, that I'm sure it must be good.

AIMWELL. Pray, desire him to walk up.

BONIFACE. Here he is, as the saying is.

(*Enter* FOIGARD.)

FOIGARD. Save you, gentlemens, both.

AIMWELL (*aside*). A Frenchman!—[*To* FOIGARD] Sir, your most humble servant.

FOIGARD. Och, dear joy,[46] I am your most faithful shervant, and yours alsho.

GIBBET. Doctor,[45] you talk very good English, but you have a mighty twang of the foreigner.

FOIGARD. My English is very vell for the vords, but we foreigners, you know, cannot bring our tongues about the pronunciation so soon.

AIMWELL (*aside*). A foreigner! a downright Teague, by this light!—Were you born in France, doctor?

FOIGARD. I was educated in France, but I was borned at Brussels; I am a subject of the King of Spain, joy.

GIBBET. What King of Spain, sir? Speak![47]

FOIGARD. Upon my shoul, joy, I cannot tell you as yet.

AIMWELL. Nay, captain, that was too hard upon the doctor; he's a stranger.

FOIGARD. Oh, let him alone, dear joy, I am of a nation that is not easily put out of countenance.

---

[45] Courtesy title for a clergyman.
[46] A term of friendly address among the Irish, which Foigard's accent reveals him to be. *Teague* (in Aimwell's next speech) was a contemptuous term for an Irishman.
[47] The War of the Spanish Succession had not yet settled this question.

AIMWELL. Come, gentlemen, I'll end the dispute.—Here, landlord, is dinner ready?

BONIFACE. Upon the table, as the saying is.

AIMWELL. Gentlemen—pray—that door—

FOIGARD. No, no, fait, the captain must lead.

AIMWELL. No, doctor, the church is our guide.

GIBBET. Ay, ay, so it is—(*Exit foremost, they follow.*)

[SCENE III.] *Scene changes to a gallery in*
LADY BOUNTIFUL's *house.*

(*Enter* ARCHER *and* SCRUB *singing, and hugging one another,* SCRUB *with a tankard in his hand.* GIPSY *listening at a distance.*)

SCRUB. *Tall, all, dall!*—Come, my dear boy, let's have that song once more.

ARCHER. No, no, we shall disturb the family.—But will you be sure to keep the secret?

SCRUB. Pho! upon my honor, as I'm a gentleman.

ARCHER. 'Tis enough. You must know then, that my master is the Lord Viscount Aimwell; he fought a duel t'other day in London, wounded his man so dangerously that he thinks fit to withdraw till he hears whether the gentleman's wounds be mortal or not. He never was in this part of England before, so he chose to retire to this place—that's all.

GIPSY [*aside*]. And that's enough for me. (*Exit.*)

SCRUB. And where were you when your master fought?

ARCHER. We never know of our masters' quarrels.

SCRUB. No! If our masters in the country here receive a challenge, the first thing they do is to tell their wives; the wife tells the servants, the servants alarm the tenants, and in half an hour you shall have the whole country in arms.

ARCHER. To hinder two men from doing what they have no mind for.—But if you should chance to talk now of my business?

SCRUB. Talk! ay, sir, had I not learned the knack of holding my tongue, I had never lived so long in a great family.

ARCHER. Ay, ay, to be sure there are secrets in all families.

SCRUB. Secrets! ay;—but I'll say no more. Come, sit down, we'll make an end of our tankard; here—

ARCHER. With all my heart; who knows but you and I may come to be better acquainted, eh? Here's your ladies' healths; you have three, I think, and to be sure there must be secrets among 'em.

SCRUB. Secrets! ay, friend.—I wish I had a friend—

ARCHER. Am not I your friend? Come, you and I will be sworn brothers.

SCRUB. Shall we?

ARCHER. From this minute. Give me a kiss—and now, brother Scrub—

SCRUB. And now, brother Martin, I will tell you a secret that will make your hair stand on end. You must know that I am consumedly in love.

ARCHER. That's a terrible secret, that's the truth on't.

SCRUB. That jade, Gipsy, that was with us just now in the cellar, is the arrantest whore that ever wore a petticoat; and I'm dying for love of her.

ARCHER. Ha, ha, ha!—Are you in love with her person or her virtue, brother Scrub?

SCRUB. I should like virtue best, because it is more durable than beauty; for virtue holds good with some women long, and many a day after they have lost it.

ARCHER. In the country, I grant ye, where no woman's virtue is lost till a bastard be found.

SCRUB. Ay, could I bring her to a bastard, I should have her all to myself; but I dare not put it upon that lay, for fear of being sent for a soldier. Pray, brother, how do you gentlemen in London like that same Pressing Act?[48]

ARCHER. Very ill, brother Scrub; 'tis the worst that ever was made for us. Formerly I remember the good days, when we could dun our masters for our wages, and if they refused to pay us, we could have a warrant to carry 'em before a justice; but now if we talk of eating, they have a warrant for us, and carry us before three justices.

SCRUB. And to be sure we go, if we talk of eating; for the justices won't give their own servants a bad example. Now this is my misfortune—I dare not speak in the house, while that jade Gipsy dings about like a fury.— Once I had the better end of the staff.

---

[48] An act, occasioned by the War, empowering courts of three justices to draft unemployed able-bodied men into the army.

ARCHER. And how comes the change now?

SCRUB. Why, the mother of all this mischief is a priest!

ARCHER. A priest!

SCRUB. Ay, a damned son of a whore of Babylon, that came over hither to say grace to the French officers, and eat up our provisions. There's not a day goes over his head without a dinner or supper in this house.

ARCHER. How came he so familiar in the family?

SCRUB. Because he speaks English as if he had lived here all his life, and tells lies as if he had been a traveller from his cradle.

ARCHER. And this priest, I'm afraid, has converted the affections of your Gipsy.

SCRUB. Converted! ay, and perverted, my dear friend; for, I'm afraid, he has made her a whore and a papist! But this is not all; there's the French count and Mrs. Sullen, they're in the confederacy, and for some private ends of their own, to be sure.

ARCHER. A very hopeful family yours, brother Scrub! I suppose the maiden lady has her lover too?

SCRUB. Not that I know. She's the best on 'em, that's the truth on't. But they take care to prevent my curiosity by giving me so much business that I'm a perfect slave. What d'ye think is my place in this family?

ARCHER. Butler, I suppose.

SCRUB. Ah, Lord help you! I'll tell you. Of a Monday I drive the coach; of a Tuesday I drive the plough; on Wednesday I follow the hounds; a Thursday I dun the tenants; on Friday I go to market; on Saturday I draw warrants;[49] and a Sunday I draw beer.

ARCHER. Ha, ha, ha! if variety be a pleasure in life, you have enough on't, my dear brother. But what ladies are those?

SCRUB. Ours, ours; that upon the right hand is Mrs. Sullen, and the other is Mrs. Dorinda. Don't mind 'em, sit still, man.

(*Enter* MRS. SULLEN *and* DORINDA.)

MRS. SULLEN. I have heard my brother talk of my Lord Aimwell; but they say that his brother is the finer gentleman.

---

[49] Besides the usual menservants' duties, Scrub serves as law clerk to Squire Sullen, who is a Justice of the Peace.

DORINDA. That's impossible, sister.

MRS. SULLEN. He's vastly rich, but very close, they say.

DORINDA. No matter for that; if I can creep into his heart, I'll open his breast, I warrant him. I have heard say, that people may be guessed at by the behavior of their servants; I could wish we might talk to that fellow.

MRS. SULLEN. So do I; for I think he's a very pretty fellow. Come this way, I'll throw out a lure for him presently.

(*They walk towards the opposite side of the stage.*)

ARCHER (*aside*). Corn, wine, and oil indeed! But I think the wife has the greatest plenty of flesh and blood; she should be my choice.—Ah, a—say you so!—(MRS. SULLEN *drops her glove*, ARCHER *runs, takes it up, and gives to it her.*) Madam—your ladyship's glove.

MRS. SULLEN. O sir, I thank you!—(*To* DORINDA) What a handsome bow the fellow has!

DORINDA. Bow! why I have known several footmen come down from London set up here for dancing masters, and carry off the best fortunes in the country.

ARCHER (*aside*). That project, for aught I know, had been better than ours.—Brother Scrub, why don't you introduce me?

SCRUB. Ladies, this is the strange gentleman's servant that you see at church to-day; I understood he came from London, and so I invited him to the cellar, that he might show me the newest flourish in whetting my knives.

DORINDA. And I hope you have made much of him?

ARCHER. O yes, madam; but the strength of your ladyship's liquor is a little too potent for the constitution of your humble servant.

MRS. SULLEN. What! then you don't usually drink ale?

ARCHER. No, madam; my constant drink is tea, or a little wine and water. 'Tis prescribed me by the physician for a remedy against the spleen.

SCRUB. O la! O la! a footman have the spleen![50]

MRS. SULLEN. I thought that distemper had been only proper to people of quality?

ARCHER. Madam, like all other fashions it wears out, and so descends to their servants; though in a great many

---

[50] Melancholy or hypochondria, often affected by fashionable people.

of us. I believe, it proceeds from some melancholy
particles in the blood, occasioned by the stagnation
of wages.

DORINDA [*aside to* MRS. SULLEN]. How affectedly the fellow
talks!—How long, pray, have you served your present
master?

ARCHER. Not long; my life has been mostly spent in the
service of the ladies.

MRS. SULLEN. And pray, which service do you like best?

ARCHER. Madam, the ladies pay best; the honor of serving
them is sufficient wages; there is a charm in their looks
that delivers a pleasure with their commands, and gives
our duty the wings of inclination.

MRS. SULLEN [*aside*]. That flight was above the pitch of a
livery.—And, sir, would not you be satisfied to serve
a lady again?

ARCHER. As a groom of the chamber, madam, but not as
a footman.

MRS. SULLEN. I suppose you served as footman before?

ARCHER. For that reason I would not serve in that post
again; for my memory is too weak for the load of
messages that the ladies lay upon their servants in
London. My Lady Howd'ye,[51] the last mistress I
served, called me up one morning, and told me:
Martin, go to my Lady Allnight with my humble
service; tell her I was to wait on her ladyship yesterday, and left word with Mrs. Rebecca, that the pre-
liminaries of the affair she knows of are stopped till
we know the concurrence of the person that I know of,
for which there are circumstances wanting which we
shall accommodate at the old place; but that in the
meantime there is a person about her ladyship, that,
from several hints and surmises, was accessory at a
certain time to the disappointments that naturally
attend things, that to her knowledge are of more
importance—

MRS. SULLEN and DORINDA. Ha, ha, ha! where are you
going, sir?

ARCHER. Why, I han't half done!—The whole howd'ye was
about half an hour long; so I happened to misplace two
syllables, and was turned off, and rendered incapable.

DORINDA [*aside to* MRS. SULLEN]. The pleasantest fellow,

---

[51] A formal polite inquiry about someone's health or welfare.

sister, I ever saw!—But, friend, if your master be married, I presume you still serve a lady?

ARCHER. No, madam, I take care never to come into a married family; the commands of the master and the mistress are always so contrary, that 'tis impossible to please both.

DORINDA (*aside*). There's a main point gained: my lord is not married, I find.

MRS. SULLEN. But I wonder, friend, that in so many good services, you had not a better provision made for you.

ARCHER. I don't know how, madam. I had a lieutenancy offered me three or four times; but that is not bread, madam—I live much better as I do.

SCRUB. Madam, he sings rarely! I was thought to do pretty well here in the country till he came; but alack a day, I'm nothing to my brother Martin!

DORINDA. Does he?—Pray, sir, will you oblige us with a song?

ARCHER. Are you for passion or humor?

SCRUB. O la! he has the purest ballad about a trifle—

MRS. SULLEN. A trifle! pray, sir, let's have it.

ARCHER. I'm ashamed to offer you a trifle, madam; but since you command me—(*Sings to the tune of "Sir Simon the King."*)

> A trifling song you shall hear,
> Begun with a trifle and ended;
> All trifling people draw near,
> And I shall be nobly attended.
>
> Were it not for trifles a few,
> That lately have come into play,
> The men would want something to do,
> And the women want something to say.
>
> What makes men trifle in dressing?
> Because the ladies (they know)
> Admire, by often possessing,
> That eminent trifle, a beau.
>
> When the lover his moments has trifled,
> The trifle of trifles to gain,
> No sooner the virgin is rifled,
> But a trifle shall part 'em again.

What mortal man would be able
At White's half-an-hour to sit,
Or who could bear a tea-table,
Without talking of trifles for wit?

The Court is from trifles secure,
Gold keys are no trifles, we see!
White rods[52] are no trifles, I'm sure,
Whatever their bearers may be.

But if you will go to the place,
Where trifles abundantly breed,
The levee will show you his Grace
Makes promises trifles indeed.

A coach with six footmen behind,
I count neither trifle nor sin:
But, ye gods! how oft do we find
A scandalous trifle within.

A flask of champagne, people think it
A trifle, or something as bad:
But if you'll contrive how to drink it,
You'll find it no trifle, egad!

A parson's a trifle at sea,
A widow's a trifle in sorrow,
A peace is a trifle to-day,
Who knows what may happen to-morrow!

A black coat a trifle may cloak,
Or to hide it the red may endeavor:
But if once the army is broke,
We shall have more trifles than ever.

The stage is a trifle, they say,
The reason, pray carry along,
Because at every new play,
The house they with trifles so throng.

But with people's malice to trifle,
And to set us all on a foot:
The author of this is a trifle,
And his song is a trifle to boot.

[52] Insignia of office of the Lord Treasurer.

MRS. SULLEN. Very well, sir, we're obliged to you.—Something for a pair of gloves. (*offering him money*)

ARCHER. I humbly beg leave to be excused. My master, madam, pays me; nor dare I take money from any other hand, without injuring his honor, and disobeying his commands. (*Exit* [*with* SCRUB].)

DORINDA. This is surprising! Did you ever see so pretty a well-bred fellow?

MRS. SULLEN. The devil take him for wearing that livery!

DORINDA. I fancy, sister, he may be some gentleman, a friend of my lord's, that his lordship has pitched upon for his courage, fidelity, and discretion, to bear him company in this dress—and who, ten to one, was his second too.

MRS. SULLEN. It is so, it must be so, and it shall be so!—for I like him.

DORINDA. What! better than the count?

MRS. SULLEN. The count happened to be the most agreeable man upon the place; and so I chose him to serve me in my design upon my husband. But I should like this fellow better in a design upon myself.

DORINDA. But now, sister, for an interview with this lord and this gentleman; how shall we bring that about?

MRS. SULLEN. Patience! you country ladies give no quarter if once you be entered. Would you prevent[53] their desires, and give the fellows no wishing-time? Look'ee, Dorinda, if my Lord Aimwell loves you or deserves you, he'll find a way to see you, and there we must leave it.—My business comes now upon the tapis. Have you prepared your brother?

DORINDA. Yes, yes.

MRS. SULLEN. And how did he relish it?

DORINDA. He said little, mumbled something to himself, promised to be guided by me—but here he comes.

(*Enter* SULLEN.)

SQUIRE SULLEN. What singing was that I heard just now?

MRS. SULLEN. The singing in your head, my dear; you complained of it all day.

SQUIRE SULLEN. You're impertinent.

MRS. SULLEN. I was ever so, since I became one flesh with you.

[53] Anticipate.

SQUIRE SULLEN. One flesh! rather two carcasses joined unnaturally together.

MRS. SULLEN. Or rather a living soul coupled to a dead
body.[54]

DORINDA. So, this is fine encouragement for me!

SQUIRE SULLEN. Yes, my wife shows you what you must do.

MRS. SULLEN. And my husband shows you what you must
suffer.

SQUIRE SULLEN. 'Sdeath, why can't you be silent?

MRS. SULLEN. 'Sdeath, why can't you talk?

SQUIRE SULLEN. Do you talk to any purpose?

MRS. SULLEN. Do you think to any purpose?

SQUIRE SULLEN. Sister, heark'ye!—(*Whispers.*) [*aloud*] I
shan't be home till it be late. (*Exit.*)

MRS. SULLEN. What did he whisper to ye?

DORINDA. That he would go round the back way, come into
the closet, and listen as I directed him. But let me beg
you once more, dear sister, to drop this project; for
as I told you before, instead of awaking him to kindness, you may provoke him to a rage; and then who
knows how far his brutality may carry him?

MRS. SULLEN. I'm provided to receive him, I warrant you.
But here comes the Count, vanish!

(*Exit* DORINDA. *Enter* COUNT BELLAIR.)

Don't you wonder, Monsieur le Count, that I was not
at church this afternoon?

COUNT BELLAIR. I more wonder, madam, that you go dere
at all, or how you dare to lift those eyes to heaven that
are guilty of so much killing.

MRS. SULLEN. If Heaven, sir, has given to my eyes, with
the power of killing, the virtue of making a cure, I
hope the one may atone for the other.

COUNT BELLAIR. Oh, largely, madam, would your ladyship
be as ready to apply the remedy as to give the wound.
Consider, madam, I am doubly a prisoner; first to the
arms of your general, then to your more conquering
eyes. My first chains are easy, there a ransom may

---

[54] Cf. John Milton, *The Doctrine and Discipline of Divorce, Complete Prose Works*, ed. Don Wolfe *et al.* (New Haven: Yale University Press, 1959), p. 326: "Nay, instead of being one flesh, they
will be rather two carcasses chained unnaturally together; or, as it
may happen, a living soul bound to a dead corpse."

redeem me; but from your fetters I never shall get free.

MRS. SULLEN. Alas, sir! why should you complain to me of your captivity, who am in chains myself? You know, sir, that I am bound, nay, must be tied up in that particular that might give you ease. I am like you, a prisoner of war,—of war, indeed! I have given my parole of honor; would you break yours to gain your liberty?

COUNT BELLAIR. Most certainly I would, were I a prisoner among the Turks; dis is your case; you're a slave, madam, slave to the worst of Turks, a husband.

MRS. SULLEN. There lies my foible, I confess; no fortifications, no courage, conduct, nor vigilancy, can pretend to defend a place, where the cruelty of the governor forces the garrison to mutiny.

COUNT BELLAIR. And where de besieger is resolved to die before de place.—Here will I fix;—(*Kneels.*) with tears, vows, and prayers assault your heart, and never rise till you surrender; or if I must storm—Love and St. Michael!—And so I begin the attack—

MRS. SULLEN. Stand off!—(*aside*) Sure he hears me not!—And I could almost wish he—did not!—The fellow makes love very prettily.—But, sir, why should you put such a value upon my person, when you see it despised by one that knows it so much better?

COUNT BELLAIR. He knows it not, though he possesses it; if he but knew the value of the jewel he is master of, he would always wear it next his heart, and sleep with it in his arms.

MRS. SULLEN. But since he throws me unregarded from him—

COUNT BELLAIR. And one that knows your value well comes by and takes you up, is it not justice? (*Goes to lay hold on her.*)

(*Enter* SULLEN *with his sword drawn.*)

SQUIRE SULLEN. Hold, villain, hold!

MRS. SULLEN (*presenting a pistol*). Do you hold!

SQUIRE SULLEN. What! murther your husband, to defend your bully!

MRS. SULLEN. Bully! for shame, Mr. Sullen! Bullies wear long swords, the gentleman has none, he's a prisoner, you know. I was aware of your outrage, and prepared this to receive your violence; and, if occasion were, to preserve myself against the force of this other gentleman.

COUNT BELLAIR. O madam, your eyes be bettre firearms than your pistol; they nevre miss.

SQUIRE SULLEN. What! court my wife to my face!

MRS. SULLEN. Pray, Mr. Sullen, put up; suspend your fury for a minute.

SQUIRE SULLEN. To give you time to invent an excuse!

MRS. SULLEN. I need none.

SQUIRE SULLEN. No, for I heard every syllable of your discourse.

COUNT BELLAIR. Ay! and begar, I tink de dialogue was vera pretty.

MRS. SULLEN. Then I suppose, sir, you heard something of your own barbarity?

SQUIRE SULLEN. Barbarity! Oons, what does the woman call barbarity? Do I ever meddle with you?

MRS. SULLEN. No.

SQUIRE SULLEN. As for you, sir, I shall take another time.

COUNT BELLAIR. Ah, begar, and so must I.

SQUIRE SULLEN. Look'ee, madam, don't think that my anger proceeds from any concern I have for your honor, but for my own; and if you can contrive any way of being a whore without making me a cuckold, do it and welcome.

MRS. SULLEN. Sir, I thank you kindly; you would allow me the sin but rob me of the pleasure. No, no, I'm resolved never to venture upon the crime without the satisfaction of seeing you punished for't.

SQUIRE SULLEN. Then will you grant me this, my dear? Let anybody else do you the favor but that Frenchman, for I mortally hate his whole generation. (*Exit.*)

COUNT BELLAIR. Ah, sir, that be ungrateful, for begar, I love some of yours. Madam——(*approaching her*)

MRS. SULLEN. No, sir.

COUNT BELLAIR. No, sir! Garzoon, madam, I am not your husband.

MRS. SULLEN. 'Tis time to undeceive you, sir. I believed your addresses to me were no more than an amusement, and I hope you will think the same of my complaisance; and to convince you that you ought, you must know that I brought you hither only to make you instrumental in setting me right with my husband, for he was planted to listen by my appointment.

COUNT BELLAIR. By your appointment?

MRS. SULLEN. Certainly.

COUNT BELLAIR. And so, madam, while I was telling twenty stories to part you from your husband, begar, I was bringing you together all the while?

MRS. SULLEN. I ask your pardon, sir, but I hope this will give you a taste of the virtue of the English ladies.

COUNT BELLAIR. Begar, madam, your virtue be vera great, but garzoon, your honeste be vera little.

(*Enter* DORINDA.)

MRS. SULLEN. Nay, now, you're angry, sir.

COUNT BELLAIR. Angry!—Fair Dorinda (*Sings* DORINDA *the Opera Tune, and addresses to* DORINDA): Madam, when your ladyship want a fool, send for me. *Fair Dorinda, Revenge, &c.*[55] (*Exit.*)

MRS. SULLEN. There goes the true humor of his nation— resentment with good manners, and the height of anger in a song! Well, sister, you must be judge, for you have heard the trial.

DORINDA. And I bring in my brother guilty.

MRS. SULLEN. But I must bear the punishment. 'Tis hard, sister.

DORINDA. I own it; but you must have patience.

MRS. SULLEN. Patience! the cant of custom—Providence sends no evil without a remedy. Should I lie groaning under a yoke I can shake off, I were accessory to my ruin, and my patience were no better than self-murder.

DORINDA. But how can you shake off the yoke? Your divisions don't come within the reach of the law for a divorce.

MRS. SULLEN. Law! what law can search into the remote abyss of nature? What evidence can prove the unaccountable disaffections of wedlock? Can a jury sum up the endless aversions that are rooted in our souls, or can a bench give judgment upon antipathies?

---

[55] The Count sings snatches of two songs from Swiney's opera *Camilla*, "Fair Dorinda, happy, happy, happy may'st thou ever be," and a song about revenge sung by Dorinda.

DORINDA. They never pretended, sister; they never meddle, but in case of uncleanness.

MRS. SULLEN. Uncleanness! O sister! casual violation is a transient injury, and may possibly be repaired; but can radical hatreds be ever reconciled? No, no, sister; Nature is the first lawgiver; and when she has set tempers opposite, not all the golden links of wedlock nor iron manacles of law can keep 'em fast.[56]

Wedlock we own ordained by Heaven's decree,
But such as Heaven ordained it first to be—
Concurring tempers in the man and wife
As mutual helps to draw the load of life.
View all the works of Providence above:
The stars with harmony and concord move;
View all the works of Providence below:)
The fire, the water, earth and air, we know, }
All in one plant agree to make it grow.)
Must man, the chiefest work of art divine,
Be doomed in endless discord to repine?
No, we should injure Heaven by that surmise:
Omnipotence is just, were man but wise.

(*Exeunt.*)

---

56 Cf. Mrs. Sullen's speeches with Milton's *Doctrine and Discipline of Divorce*: "God sends remedies, as well as evils; under which he who lies and groans, that may lawfully acquit himself, is accessory to his own ruin: nor will it excuse him though he suffer, through a sluggish fearfulness to search thoroughly what is lawful, for fear of disquieting the secure falsity of an old opinion" (p. 341). God did not authorize "a judicial court to toss about and divulge the unaccountable and secret reasons of disaffection between man and wife" (p. 343). "Casual adultery . . . [is] but a transient injury, and soon amended," but "natural hatred" is "an unspeakable and unremitting sorrow and offence, whereof no amends can be made, no cure, no ceasing but by divorce" (pp. 332–33). "To couple hatred therefore, though wedlock try all her golden links, and borrow to her aid all the iron manacles and fetters of law, it does but seek to twist a rope of sand" (p. 345).

ACT IV

[SCENE I.] *Scene continues.*

(*Enter* MRS. SULLEN.)

MRS. SULLEN. Were I born an humble Turk, where women have no soul nor property, there I must sit contented. But in England, a country whose women are its glory, must women be abused? Where women rule, must women be enslaved? Nay, cheated into slavery, mocked by a promise of comfortable society into a wilderness of solitude! I dare not keep the thought about me. Oh, here comes something to divert me.

(*Enter a* COUNTRY WOMAN.)

WOMAN. I come, an't please your ladyship—you're my Lady Bountiful, an't ye?

MRS. SULLEN. Well, good woman, go on.

WOMAN. I come seventeen long mail[57] to have a cure for my husband's sore leg.

MRS. SULLEN. Your husband! what, woman, cure your husband!

WOMAN. Ay, poor man, for his sore leg won't let him stir from home.

MRS. SULLEN. There, I confess, you have given me a reason. Well, good woman, I'll tell you what you must do. You must lay your husband's leg upon a table, and with a chopping-knife you must lay it open as broad as you can; then you must take out the bone, and beat the flesh soundly with a rolling pin; then take salt, pepper, cloves, mace and ginger, some sweet herbs, and season it very well; then roll it up like brawn, and put it into the oven for two hours.

WOMAN. Heavens reward your ladyship! I have two little babies too that are piteous bad with the graips, an't please ye.

MRS. SULLEN. Put a little pepper and salt in their bellies, good woman.

---

[57] The woman's dialect for mile(s); cf. *graips* (gripes), a few speeches later.

(*Enter* LADY BOUNTIFUL.)

I beg your ladyship's pardon for taking your business out of your hands; I have been a-tampering here a little with one of your patients.

LADY BOUNTIFUL. Come, good woman, don't mind this mad creature; I am the person that you want, I suppose. What would you have, woman?

MRS. SULLEN. She wants something for her husband's sore leg.

LADY BOUNTIFUL. What's the matter with his leg, goody?

WOMAN. It comes first, as one might say, with a sort of dizziness in his foot, then he had a kind of laziness in his joints, and then his leg broke out, and then it swelled, and then it closed again, and then it broke out again, and then it festered, and then it grew better, and then it grew worse again.

MRS. SULLEN. Ha, ha, ha!

LADY BOUNTIFUL. How can you be merry with the misfortunes of other people?

MRS. SULLEN. Because my own make me sad, madam.

LADY BOUNTIFUL. The worst reason in the world, daughter; your own misfortunes should teach you to pity others.

MRS. SULLEN. But the woman's misfortunes and mine are nothing alike; her husband is sick, and mine, alas, is in health.

LADY BOUNTIFUL. What! would you wish your husband sick?

MRS. SULLEN. Not of a sore leg, of all things.

LADY BOUNTIFUL. Well, good woman, go to the pantry, get your bellyful of victuals, then I'll give you a receipt of diet-drink for your husband. But d'ye hear, goody, you must not let your husband move too much.

WOMAN. No, no, madam, the poor man's inclinable enough to lie still. (*Exit.*)

LADY BOUNTIFUL. Well, daughter Sullen, though you laugh, I have done miracles about the country here with my receipts.

MRS. SULLEN. Miracles indeed, if they have cured anybody; but I believe, madam, the patient's faith goes farther toward the miracle than your prescription.

LADY BOUNTIFUL. Fancy helps in some cases; but there's your husband, who has as little fancy as anybody, I brought him from death's door.

MRS. SULLEN. I suppose, madam, you made him drink plentifully of ass's milk.

(*Enter* DORINDA, *runs to* MRS. SULLEN.)

DORINDA. News, dear sister! news! news!

(*Enter* ARCHER, *running.*)

ARCHER. Where, where is my Lady Bountiful?—Pray, which is the old lady of you three?

LADY BOUNTIFUL. I am.

ARCHER. O madam, the fame of your ladyship's charity, goodness, benevolence, skill and ability, have drawn me hither to implore your ladyship's help in behalf of my unfortunate master, who is this moment breathing his last.

LADY BOUNTIFUL. Your master! where is he?

ARCHER. At your gate, madam. Drawn by the appearance of your handsome house to view it nearer, and walking up the avenue, within five paces of the courtyard, he was taken ill of a sudden with a sort of I know not what, but down he fell, and there he lies.

LADY BOUNTIFUL. Here, Scrub, Gipsy, all run, get my easy chair downstairs, put the gentleman in it, and bring him in quickly! quickly!

ARCHER. Heaven will reward your ladyship for this charitable act.

LADY BOUNTIFUL. Is your master used to these fits?

ARCHER. O yes, madam, frequently; I have known him have five or six of a night.

LADY BOUNTIFUL. What's his name?

ARCHER. Lord, madam, he's a-dying! a minute's care or neglect may save or destroy his life.

LADY BOUNTIFUL. Ah, poor gentleman!—Come, friend, show me the way; I'll see him brought in myself.
(*Exit with* ARCHER.)

DORINDA. O sister, my heart flutters about strangely! I can hardly forbear running to his assistance.

MRS. SULLEN. And I'll lay my life he deserves your assistance more than he wants[58] it. Did not I tell you that my lord would find a way to come at you? Love's his distemper, and you must be the physician; put on all your charms, summon all your fire into your eyes,

[58] Needs.

plant the whole artillery of your looks against his
breast, and down with him.

DORINDA. O sister! I'm but a young gunner; I shall be afraid
to shoot, for fear the piece should recoil, and hurt
myself.

MRS. SULLEN. Never fear! You shall see me shoot before
you, if you will.

DORINDA. No, no, dear sister; you have missed your mark
so unfortunately, that I shan't care for being instructed
by you.

(*Enter* AIMWELL, *in a chair, carried by* ARCHER *and*
SCRUB; LADY BOUNTIFUL [*and*] GIPSY; AIMWELL *counter-
feiting a swoon.*)

LADY BOUNTIFUL. Here, here, let's see the hartshorn drops.
—Gipsy, a glass of fair water! His fit's very strong.—
Bless me, how his hands are clenched!

ARCHER. For shame, ladies, what d'ye do? why don't you
help us?—(*To* DORINDA): Pray, madam, take his hand
and open it, if you can, whilst I hold his head.
(DORINDA *takes his hand.*)

DORINDA. Poor gentleman!—Oh!—he has got my hand
within his, and he squeezes it unmercifully—

LADY BOUNTIFUL. 'Tis the violence of his convulsion, child.

ARCHER. Oh, madam, he's perfectly possessed in these
cases—he'll bite you if you don't have a care.

DORINDA. Oh, my hand! my hand!

LADY BOUNTIFUL. What's the matter with the foolish girl?
I have got this hand open you see with a great deal
of ease.

ARCHER. Ay, but, madam, your daughter's hand is somewhat warmer than your ladyship's, and the heat of it
draws the force of the spirits that way.

MRS. SULLEN. I find, friend, you're very learned in these
sorts of fits.

ARCHER. 'Tis no wonder, madam, for I'm often troubled
with them myself; I find myself extremely ill at this
minute. (*looking hard at* MRS. SULLEN)

MRS. SULLEN (*aside*). I fancy I could find a way to cure
you.

LADY BOUNTIFUL. His fit holds him very long.

ARCHER. Longer than usual, madam.—Pray, young lady,
open his breast, and give him air.

LADY BOUNTIFUL. Where did his illness take him first, pray?

ARCHER. To-day, at church, madam.

LADY BOUNTIFUL. In what manner was he taken?

ARCHER. Very strangely, my lady. He was of a sudden touched with something in his eyes, which, at the first, he only felt, but could not tell whether 'twas pain or pleasure.

LADY BOUNTIFUL. Wind, nothing but wind!

ARCHER. By soft degrees it grew and mounted to his brain; there his fancy caught it, there formed it so beautiful, and dressed it up in such gay, pleasing colors, that his transported appetite seized the fair idea, and straight conveyed it to his heart. That hospitable seat of life sent all its sanguine spirits forth to meet, and opened all its sluicy gates to take the stranger in.

LADY BOUNTIFUL. Your master should never go without a bottle to smell to.—Oh,—he recovers!—The lavender water—some feathers to burn under his nose— Hungary water to rub his temples.—Oh, he comes to himself!—Hem a little, sir, hem.—Gipsy! bring the cordial-water.

(AIMWELL *seems to awake in amaze.*)

DORINDA. How d'ye, sir?

AIMWELL. Where am I? (*rising*)

> Sure I have pass'd the gulf of silent death,
> And now I land on the Elysian shore!—
> Behold the goddess of those happy plains,
> Fair Proserpine—Let me adore thy bright divinity.

(*Kneels to* DORINDA, *and kisses her hand.*)

MRS. SULLEN. So, so, so! I knew where the fit would end!

AIMWELL. Eurydice perhaps—

> How could thy Orpheus keep his word,
> And not look back upon thee?
> No treasure but thyself could sure have bribed him
> To look one minute off thee.

LADY BOUNTIFUL. Delirious, poor gentleman!

ARCHER. Very delirious, madam, very delirious.

AIMWELL. Martin's voice, I think.

ARCHER. Yes, my lord.—How does your lordship?

LADY BOUNTIFUL. Lord! did you mind that, girls?

AIMWELL. Where am I?

ARCHER. In very good hands, sir. You were taken just now with one of your old fits, under the trees, just by this good lady's house; her ladyship had you taken in, and has miraculously brought you to yourself, as you see—

AIMWELL. I am so confounded with shame, madam, that I can now only beg pardon, and refer my acknowledgments for your ladyship's care till an opportunity offers of making some amends. I dare be no longer troublesome.—Martin, give two guineas to the servants. (*going*)

DORINDA. Sir, you may catch cold by going so soon into the air; you don't look, sir, as if you were perfectly recovered.

(*Here* ARCHER *talks to* LADY BOUNTIFUL *in dumb show.*)

AIMWELL. That I shall never be, madam; my present illness is so rooted that I must expect to carry it to my grave.

MRS. SULLEN. Don't despair, sir; I have known several in your distemper shake it off with a fortnight's physic.

LADY BOUNTIFUL. Come, sir, your servant has been telling me that you're apt to relapse if you go into the air. Your good manners sha'n't get the better of ours— you shall sit down again, sir. Come, sir, we don't mind ceremonies in the country. Here, sir, my service t'ye.—You shall taste my water; 'tis a cordial I can assure you, and of my own making—drink it off, sir. —(AIMWELL *drinks.*) And how d'ye find yourself now, sir?

AIMWELL. Somewhat better—though very faint still.

LADY BOUNTIFUL. Ay, ay, people are always faint after these fits.—Come, girls, you shall show the gentleman the house.—'Tis but an old family building, sir; but you had better walk about, and cool by degrees, than venture immediately into the air. You'll find some tolerable pictures.—Dorinda, show the gentleman the way, I must go to the poor woman below. (*Exit.*)

DORINDA. This way, sir.

AIMWELL. Ladies, shall I beg leave for my servant to wait on you, for he understands pictures very well?

MRS. SULLEN. Sir, we understand originals[59] as well as he does pictures, so he may come along.

(*Exeunt* DORINDA, MRS. SULLEN, AIMWELL, ARCHER. AIMWELL *leads* DORINDA. *Enter* FOIGARD *and* SCRUB, *meeting.*)

FOIGARD. Save you, Master Scrub!

SCRUB. Sir, I won't be saved your way—I hate a priest, I abhor the French, and I defy the devil. Sir, I'm a bold Briton, and will spill the last drop of my blood to keep out popery and slavery.

FOIGARD. Master Scrub, you would put me down in politics, and so I would be speaking with Mrs. Gipsy.

SCRUB. Good Mr. Priest, you can't speak with her; she's sick, sir, she's gone abroad, sir, she's—dead two months ago, sir.

(*Enter* GIPSY.)

GIPSY. How now, impudence! how dare you talk so saucily to the doctor?—Pray, sir, don't take it ill; for the common people of England are not so civil to strangers, as—

SCRUB. You lie! you lie! 'tis the common people that are civilest to strangers.

GIPSY. Sirrah, I have a good mind to—get you out, I say!

SCRUB. I won't.

GIPSY. You won't, sauce-box!—Pray, doctor, what is the captain's name that came to your inn last night?

SCRUB (*aside*). The captain! ah, the devil, there she hampers me again; the captain has me on one side, and the priest on t'other: so between the gown and the sword, I have a fine time on't.—But, *Cedunt arma togae.*[60] (*going*)

GIPSY. What, sirrah, won't you march?

SCRUB. No my dear, I won't march—but I'll walk.— [*aside*] And I'll make bold to listen a little too. (*Goes behind the side-scene, and listens.*)

GIPSY. Indeed, doctor, the count has been barbarously treated, that's the truth on't.

[59] Mrs. Sullen puns on *originals* as (1) what a picture portrays, (2) odd people.
[60] A phrase adapted from Cicero: Arms yield to the gown.

FOIGARD. Ah, Mrs. Gipsy, upon my shoul, now, gra,[61] his complainings would mollify the marrow in your bones, and move the bowels of your commiseration! He veeps, and he dances, and he fistles, and he swears, and he laughs, and he stamps, and he sings: in conclusion, joy, he's afflicted *à la française* and a stranger would not know whider to cry or to laugh with him.

GIPSY. What would you have me do, doctor?

FOIGARD. Noting, joy, but only hide the count in Mrs. Sullen's closet when it is dark.

GIPSY. Nothing! is that nothing? It would be both a sin and a shame, doctor.

FOIGARD. Here is twenty louis d'ors, joy, for your shame; and I will give you an absolution for the shin.

GIPSY. But won't that money look like a bribe?

FOIGARD. Dat is according as you shall tauk it. If you receive the money beforehand, 'twill be, *logicè*,[62] a bribe; but if you stay till afterwards, 'twill be only a gratification.

GIPSY. Well, doctor, I'll take it *logicè*. But what must I do with my conscience, sir?

FOIGARD. Leave dat wid me, joy; I am your priest, gra; and your conscience is under my hands.

GIPSY. But should I put the count into the closet—

FOIGARD. Vel, is dere any shin for a man's being in a closhet? One may go to prayers in a closhet.

GIPSY. But if the lady should come into her chamber, and go to bed?

FOIGARD. Vel, and is dere any shin in going to bed, joy?

GIPSY. Ay, but if the parties should meet, doctor?

FOIGARD. Vel den—the parties must be responsible. Do you be after putting the count in the closhet, and leave the shins wid themselves. I will come with the count to instruct you in your chamber.

GIPSY. Well, doctor, your religion is so pure! Methinks I'm so easy after an absolution, and can sin afresh with so much security, that I'm resolved to die a martyr to't. Here's the key of the garden door, come in the back way when 'tis late. I'll be ready to receive you; but don't so much as whisper, only take hold of my

61 Dear.
62 Logically.

hand; I'll lead you, and do you lead the count and follow me.

(*Exeunt. Enter* SCRUB.)

SCRUB. What witchcraft now have these two imps of the devil been a-hatching here? There's twenty louis d'ors; I heard that, and saw the purse.—But I must give room to my betters. (*Exit.*)

(*Enter* AIMWELL, *leading* DORINDA, *and making love in dumb show;* MRS. SULLEN *and* ARCHER.)

MRS. SULLEN (*To* ARCHER). Pray, sir, how d'ye like that piece?

ARCHER. Oh, 'tis Leda! You find, madam, how Jupiter comes disguised to make love—

MRS. SULLEN. But what think you there of Alexander's battles?

ARCHER. We want only a Le Brun, madam, to draw greater battles, and a greater general of our own. The Danube, madam, would make a greater figure in a picture than the Granicus; and we have our Ramilies to match their Arbela.[63]

MRS. SULLEN. Pray, sir, what head is that in the corner there?

ARCHER. O madam, 'tis poor Ovid in his exile.

MRS. SULLEN. What was he banished for?

ARCHER. His ambitious love, madam.—(*bowing*) His misfortune touches me.

MRS. SULLEN. Was he successful in his amours?

ARCHER. There he has left us in the dark.—He was too much a gentleman to tell.

MRS. SULLEN. If he were secret, I pity him.

ARCHER. And if he were successful, I envy him.

MRS. SULLEN. How d'ye like that Venus over the chimney?

ARCHER. Venus! I protest, madam, I took it for your picture; but now I look again, 'tis not handsome enough.

MRS. SULLEN. Oh, what a charm is flattery! If you would see my picture, there it is, over that cabinet. How d'ye like it?

---

[63] Charles Le Brun, Court painter to Louis XIV, painted murals depicting the exploits of Alexander the Great. The "greater general" is John Churchill, Duke of Marlborough, whose victories at Blenheim (on the Danube) and at Ramilies matched those of Alexander on the Granicus and at Arbela.

ARCHER. I must admire anything, madam, that has the least resemblance of you. But, methinks, madam— (*He looks at the picture and* MRS. SULLEN *three or four times, by turns.*) Pray, madam, who drew it?

MRS. SULLEN. A famous hand, sir.

(*Here* AIMWELL *and* DORINDA *go off.*)

ARCHER. A famous hand, madam!—Your eyes, indeed, are featured there; but where's the sparkling moisture, shining fluid, in which they swim? The picture, indeed, has your dimples; but where's the swarm of killing Cupids that should ambush there? The lips too are figured out; but where's the carnation dew, the pouting ripeness, that tempts the taste in the original?

MRS. SULLEN [*aside*]. Had it been my lot to have matched with such a man!

ARCHER. Your breasts too—presumptuous man! what, paint Heaven!—*À propos*, madam, in the very next picture is Salmoneus, that was struck dead with lightning for offering to imitate Jove's thunder; I hope you served the painter so, madam?

MRS. SULLEN. Had my eyes the power of thunder, they should employ their lightning better.

ARCHER. There's the finest bed in that room, madam! I suppose 'tis your ladyship's bed-chamber.

MRS. SULLEN. And what then, sir?

ARCHER. I think the quilt is the richest that ever I saw. I can't at this distance, madam, distinguish the figures of the embroidery; will you give me leave, madam—? [*Goes toward the door.*]

MRS. SULLEN. The devil take his impudence!—Sure, if I gave him an opportunity, he durst not offer it?—I have a great mind to try.—(*Going; returns.*) S'death, what am I doing?—And alone, too!—Sister! sister! (*Runs out.*)

ARCHER. I'll follow her close—
For where a Frenchman durst attempt to storm,
A Briton sure may well the work perform. (*going*)

(*Enter* SCRUB.)

SCRUB. Martin! brother Martin!

ARCHER. O brother Scrub, I beg your pardon, I was not a-going; here's a guinea my master ordered you.

SCRUB. A guinea! hi! hi! hi! a guinea! eh—by this light, it

is a guinea! But I suppose you expect one and twenty shillings in change?

ARCHER. Not at all; I have another for Gipsy.

SCRUB. A guinea for her! Faggot and fire for the witch! Sir, give me that guinea, and I'll discover[64] a plot.

ARCHER. A plot!

SCRUB. Ay, sir, a plot, horrid plot! First, it must be a plot, because there's a woman in't; secondly, it must be a plot, because there's a priest in't; thirdly, it must be a plot, because there's French gold in't; and fourthly, it must be a plot, because I don't know what to make on't.

ARCHER. Nor anybody else, I'm afraid, brother Scrub.

SCRUB. Truly, I'm afraid so too; for where there's a priest and a woman, there's always a mystery and a riddle. This I know, that here has been the doctor with a temptation in one hand and an absolution in the other, and Gipsy has sold herself to the devil; I saw the price paid down, my eyes shall take their oath on't.

ARCHER. And is all this bustle about Gipsy?

SCRUB. That's not all; I could hear but a word here and there; but I remember they mentioned a count, a closet, a back-door, and a key.

ARCHER. The count!—Did you hear nothing of Mrs. Sullen?

SCRUB. I did hear some word that sounded that way; but whether it was Sullen or Dorinda, I could not distinguish.

ARCHER. You have told this matter to nobody, brother?

SCRUB. Told! no, sir, I thank you for that; I'm resolved never to speak one word, pro nor con, till we have a peace.

ARCHER. You're i'the right, brother Scrub. Here's a treaty afoot between the count and the lady; the priest and the chambermaid are the plenipotentiaries. It shall go hard but I find a way to be included in the treaty.— Where's the doctor now?

SCRUB. He and Gipsy are this moment devouring my lady's marmalade in the closet.

AIMWELL (from without). Martin! Martin!

ARCHER. I come, sir, I come.

SCRUB. But you forgot the other guinea, brother Martin.

64 Reveal.

ARCHER. Here, I give it with all my heart.

SCRUB. And I take it with all my soul.—

[*Exit* ARCHER.]

Ecod, I'll spoil your plotting, Mrs. Gipsy! and if you should set the captain upon me, these two guineas will buy me off. (*Exit.*)

(*Enter* MRS. SULLEN *and* DORINDA, *meeting.*)

MRS. SULLEN. Well, sister!

DORINDA. And well, sister!

MRS. SULLEN. What's become of my lord?

DORINDA. What's become of his servant?

MRS. SULLEN. Servant! he's a prettier fellow, and a finer gentleman by fifty degrees, than his master.

DORINDA. O' my conscience, I fancy you could beg that fellow at the gallows-foot![65]

MRS. SULLEN. O' my conscience I could, provided I could put a friend of yours in his room.

DORINDA. You desired me, sister, to leave you when you transgressed the bounds of honor.

MRS. SULLEN. Thou dear censorious country girl! what dost mean? You can't think of the man without the bed-fellow, I find.

DORINDA. I don't find anything unnatural in that thought: while the mind is conversant with flesh and blood, it must conform to the humors of the company.

MRS. SULLEN. How a little love and good company improves a woman! Why, child, you begin to live—you never spoke before.

DORINDA. Because I was never spoke to.—My lord has told me that I have more wit and beauty than any of my sex; and truly I begin to think the man is sincere.

MRS. SULLEN. You're in the right, Dorinda; pride is the life of a woman, and flattery is our daily bread; and she's a fool that won't believe a man there, as much as she that believes him in anything else. But I'll lay you a guinea that I had finer things said to me than you had.

DORINDA. Done! What did your fellow say to ye?

---

[65] Occasionally a condemned criminal was reprieved if a respectable woman offered to marry him.

MRS. SULLEN. My fellow took the picture of Venus for mine.

DORINDA. But my lover took me for Venus herself.

MRS. SULLEN. Common cant! Had my spark called me a Venus directly, I should have believed him a footman in good earnest.

DORINDA. But my lover was upon his knees to me.

MRS. SULLEN. And mine was upon his tip-toes[66] to me.

DORINDA. Mine vowed to die for me.

MRS. SULLEN. Mine swore to die with[67] me.

DORINDA. Mine spoke the softest moving things.

MRS. SULLEN. Mine had his moving things too.

DORINDA. Mine kissed my hand ten thousand times.

MRS. SULLEN. Mine has all that pleasure to come.

DORINDA. Mine offered marriage.

MRS. SULLEN. O Lard! d'ye call that a moving thing?

DORINDA. The sharpest arrow in his quiver, my dear sister! Why, my ten thousand pounds may lie brooding here this seven years, and hatch nothing at last but some ill-natured clown like yours! Whereas, if I marry my Lord Aimwell, there will be title, place, and precedence, the Park, the play, and the drawing-room, splendor, equipage, noise, and flambeaux.—Hey, my Lady Aimwell's servants there!—Lights, lights to the stairs!—My Lady Aimwell's coach put forward!—Stand by, make room for her ladyship!—Are not these things moving?—What! melancholy of a sudden?

MRS. SULLEN. Happy, happy sister! your angel has been watchful for your happiness, whilst mine has slept, regardless of his charge. Long smiling years of circling joys for you, but not one hour for me! (*Weeps.*)

DORINDA. Come, my dear, we'll talk of something else.

MRS. SULLEN. O Dorinda! I own myself a woman, full of my sex; a gentle, generous soul, easy and yielding to soft desires; a spacious heart, where love and all his train might lodge. And must the fair apartment of my breast be made a stable for a brute to lie in?

DORINDA. Meaning your husband, I suppose?

MRS. SULLEN. Husband! no; even husband is too soft a name for him.—But, come, I expect my brother here

---

66 Eagerly expectant.
67 *Die* had a slang meaning of copulate.

to-night or to-morrow; he was abroad when my father married me; perhaps he'll find a way to make me easy.

DORINDA. Will you promise not to make yourself easy in the meantime with my lord's friend?

MRS. SULLEN. You mistake me, sister. It happens with us as among the men, the greatest talkers are the greatest cowards; and there's a reason for it; those spirits evaporate in prattle, which might do more mischief if they took another course.—Though, to confess the truth, I do love that fellow;—and if I met him dressed as he should be, and I undressed as I should be— look'ye, sister, I have no supernatural gifts—I can't swear I could resist the temptation; though I can safely promise to avoid it; and that's as much as the best of us can do.

(*Exeunt.*)

[SCENE II.] *The Inn*

(*Enter* AIMWELL *and* ARCHER, *laughing.*)

ARCHER. And the awkward kindness of the good motherly old gentlewoman—

AIMWELL. And the coming easiness of the young one— 'Sdeath, 'tis pity to deceive her!

ARCHER. Nay, if you adhere to those principles, stop where you are.

AIMWELL. I can't stop, for I love her to distraction.

ARCHER. 'Sdeath, if you love her a hair's breadth beyond discretion, you must go no farther.

AIMWELL. Well, well, anything to deliver us from saunter- ing away our idle evenings at White's, Tom's or Will's,[68] and be stinted to bare looking at our old acquaintance, the cards, because our impotent pockets can't afford us a guinea for the mercenary drabs.

ARCHER. Or be obliged to some purse-proud coxcomb for a scandalous bottle, where we must not pretend to our share of the discourse, because we can't pay our club o'th' reckoning.—Damn it, I had rather sponge upon Morris, and sup upon a dish of bohea scored behind the door![69]

[68] Coffee houses in London.
[69] Live on credit at Morris's Coffee House in the Strand, supping on black tea.

AIMWELL. And there expose our want of sense by talking criticisms, as we should our want of money by railing at the government.

ARCHER. Or be obliged to sneak into the side-box, and between both houses steal two acts of a play, and because we han't money to see the other three, we come away discontented, and damn the whole five.[70]

AIMWELL. And ten thousand such rascally tricks—had we outlived our fortunes among our acquaintance.—But now—

ARCHER. Ay, now is the time to prevent all this. Strike while the iron is hot.—This priest is the luckiest part of our adventure; he shall marry you, and pimp for me.

AIMWELL. But I should not like a woman that can be so fond of a Frenchman.

ARCHER. Alas, sir, necessity has no law. The lady may be in distress; perhaps she has a confounded husband, and her revenge may carry her farther than her love. Igad, I have so good an opinion of her, and of myself, that I begin to fancy strange things; and we must say this for the honor of our women, and indeed of ourselves, that they do stick to their men as they do to their *Magna Charta*. If the plot lies as I suspect, I must put on the gentleman.—But here comes the doctor—I shall be ready. (*Exit.*)

(*Enter* FOIGARD.)

FOIGARD. Sauve you, noble friend.

AIMWELL. O sir, your servant! Pray, doctor, may I crave your name?

FOIGARD. Fat naam is upon me! My naam is Foigard, joy.

AIMWELL. Foigard! A very good name for a clergyman.[71] Pray, Doctor Foigard, were you ever in Ireland?

FOIGARD. Ireland! No joy. Fat sort of plaace is date saam Ireland? Dey say de people are catched dere when dey are young.

AIMWELL. And some of 'em when they're old—as for example.—(*Takes* FOIGARD *by the shoulder.*) Sir, I arrest you as a traitor against the government; you're a subject of England, and this morning showed me a

---

[70] People who left the theater after the first act did not have to pay.
[71] *Foigard* means keeper of the faith.

commission, by which you served as chaplain in the French army. This is death by our law, and your reverence must hang for't.[72]

FOIGARD. Upon my shoul, noble friend, dis is strange news you tell me! Fader Foigard a subject of England! de son of a burgomaster of Brussels a subject of England! Ubooboo—

AIMWELL. The son of a bog-trotter in Ireland! Sir, your tongue will condemn you before any bench in the kingdom.

FOIGARD. And is my tongue all your evidensh, joy?

AIMWELL. That's enough.

FOIGARD. No, no, joy, for I vil never spake English no more.

AIMWELL. Sir, I have other evidence.—Here, Martin!

(*Enter* ARCHER.)

You know this fellow?

ARCHER (*in a brogue*). Saave you, my dear cussen, how does your health?

FOIGARD (*aside*). Ah! upon my shoul dere is my countryman, and his brogue will hang mine.—*Mynhr, Ick wet neat watt hey zacht, Ick universton ewe neat, sacramant!*[73]

AIMWELL. Altering your language won't do, sir; this fellow knows your person, and will swear to your face.

FOIGARD. Faash! fey, is dere a brogue upon my faash too?

ARCHER. Upon my soulvation, dere ish, joy!—But cussen Mackshane, vil you not put a remembrance upon me?

FOIGARD (*aside*). Mackshane! by St. Patrick, dat ish naame sure enough.

AIMWELL [*aside to* ARCHER]. I fancy, Archer, you have it.

FOIGARD. The devil hang you, joy! by fat acquaintance are you my cussen?

ARCHER. Oh, de devil hang yourshelf, joy! you know we were little boys togeder upon de school, and your fostermoder's son was married upon my nurse's chister, joy, and so we are Irish cussens.

---

[72] Foigard is in serious trouble because, though a British subject, he (1) holds a commission in the enemy's army; (2) is functioning as a priest.
[73] Defective Flemish: "Sir, I do not know what he says; I do not understand you, on my word."

FOIGARD. De devil taak de relation! Vel, joy, and fat school was it?

ARCHER. I tinks it vas—aay,—'twas Tipperary.

FOIGARD. No, no, joy; it vas Kilkenny.

AIMWELL. That's enough for us—self-confession. Come, sir, we must deliver you into the hands of the next magistrate.

ARCHER. He sends you to jail, you're tried next assizes, and away you go swing into purgatory.

FOIGARD. And is it so wid you, cussen?

ARCHER. It vil be sho wid you, cussen, if you don't immediately confess the secret between you and Mrs. Gipsy. Look'ee, sir, the gallows or the secret, take your choice.

FOIGARD. The gallows! upon my shoul I hate that saame gallow, for it is a diseash dat is fatal to our family. Vel den, dere is nothing, shentlemens, but Mrs. Shullen would spaak wid the count in her chamber at midnight, and dere is no harm, joy, for I am to conduct the count to the plash myshelf.

ARCHER. As I guessed.—Have you communicated the matter to the count?

FOIGARD. I have not sheen him since.

ARCHER. Right again! Why then, doctor—you shall conduct me to the lady instead of the count.

FOIGARD. Fat, my cussen to the lady! upon my shoul, gra, dat is too much upon the brogue.

ARCHER. Come, come, doctor; consider we have got a rope about your neck, and if you offer to squeak, we'll stop your windpipe, most certainly. We shall have another job for you in a day or two, I hope.

AIMWELL. Here's company, coming this way; let's into my chamber, and there concert our affair farther.

ARCHER. Come, my dear cussen, come along.

(*Exeunt. Enter* BONIFACE, HOUNSLOW *and* BAGSHOT *at one door,* GIBBET *at the opposite.*)

GIBBET. Well, gentlemen, 'tis a fine night for our enterprise.

HOUNSLOW. Dark as hell.

BAGSHOT. And blows like the devil; our landlord here has showed us the window where we must break in, and tells us the plate stands in the wainscot cupboard in the parlor.

BONIFACE. Ay, ay, Mr. Bagshot, as the saying is, knives and forks, and cups and cans, and tumblers and tankards. There's one tankard, as the saying is, that's near upon as big as me; it was a present to the squire from his godmother, and smells of nutmeg and toast like an East-India ship.

HOUNSLOW. Then you say we must divide at the stair-head?

BONIFACE. Yes, Mr. Hounslow, as the saying is. At one end of that gallery lies my Lady Bountiful and her daughter, and at the other Mrs. Sullen. As for the squire—

GIBBET. He's safe enough, I have fairly entered him, and he's more than half seas over already. But such a parcel of scoundrels are got about him now, that, egad, I was ashamed to be seen in their company.

BONIFACE. 'Tis now twelve, as the saying is—gentlemen, you must set out at one.

GIBBET. Hounslow, do you and Bagshot see our arms fixed and I'll come to you presently.

HOUNSLOW *and* BAGSHOT. We will. (*Exeunt.*)

GIBBET. Well, my dear Bonny, you assure me that Scrub is a coward?

BONIFACE. A chicken, as the saying is. You'll have no creature to deal with but the ladies.

GIBBET. And I can assure you, friend, there's a great deal of address and good manners in robbing a lady; I am the most a gentleman that way that ever travelled the road.—But, my dear Bonny, this prize will be a galleon, a Vigo business.[74]—I warrant you we shall bring off three or four thousand pound.

BONIFACE. In plate, jewels, and money, as the saying is, you may.

GIBBET. Why then, Tyburn, I defy thee! I'll get up to town, sell off my horse and arms, buy myself some pretty employment in the household,[75] and be as snug and as honest as any courtier of 'em all.

BONIFACE. And what think you then of my daughter Cherry for a wife?

GIBBET. Look'ee, my dear Bonny—Cherry "is the Goddess I adore," as the song goes; but it is a maxim that man

---

[74] The reference is to the capture of Spanish treasure ships by the English and Dutch in 1702.
[75] The royal household, the Court.

and wife should never have it in their power to hang one another; for if they should, the Lord have mercy on 'um both!

(*Exeunt.*)

ACT V

[SCENE I.] *Scene continues*

(*Knocking without, enter* BONIFACE.)

BONIFACE. Coming! coming!—A coach and six foaming horses at this time o'night! Some great man, as the saying is, for he scorns to travel with other people.

(*Enter* SIR CHARLES FREEMAN.)

SIR CHARLES. What, fellow! a public house, and abed when other people sleep!

BONIFACE. Sir, I an't abed, as the saying is.

SIR CHARLES. Is Mr. Sullen's family abed, think'ee?

BONIFACE. All but the squire himself, sir, as the saying is —he's in the house.

SIR CHARLES. What company has he?

BONIFACE. Why, sir, there's the constable, Mr. Gage, the exciseman, the hunchbacked barber, and two or three other gentlemen.

SIR CHARLES [*aside*]. I find my sister's letters gave me the true picture of her spouse.

(*Enter* SULLEN, *drunk.*)

BONIFACE. Sir, here's the squire.

SQUIRE SULEN. The puppies left me asleep—Sir!

SIR CHARLES. Well, sir.

SQUIRE SULLEN. Sir, I'm an unfortunate man—I have three thousand pound a year, and I can't get a man to drink a cup of ale with me.

SIR CHARLES. That's very hard.

SQUIRE SULLEN. Ay, sir; and unless you have pity upon me, and smoke one pipe with me, I must e'en go home to my wife, and I had rather go to the devil by half.

SIR CHARLES. But, I presume, sir, you won't see your wife tonight; she'll be gone to bed. You don't use to lie with your wife in that pickle?

SQUIRE SULLEN. What! not lie with my wife! Why sir, do you take me for an atheist or a rake?

SIR CHARLES. If you hate her, sir, I think you had better lie from her.

SQUIRE SULLEN. I think so too, friend. But I'm a justice of peace, and must do nothing against the law.

SIR CHARLES. Law! As I take it, Mr. Justice, nobody observes law for law's sake, only for the good of those for whom it was made.

SQUIRE SULLEN. But, if the law orders me to send you to jail, you must lie there, my friend.

SIR CHARLES. Not unless I commit a crime to deserve it.

SQUIRE SULLEN. A crime! oons, an't I married?

SIR CHARLES. Nay, sir, if you call marriage a crime, you must disown it for a law.

SQUIRE SULLEN. Eh! I must be acquainted with you, sir.— But, sir, I should be very glad to know the truth of this matter.

SIR CHARLES. Truth, sir, is a profound sea, and few there be that dare wade deep enough to find out the bottom on't. Besides, sir, I'm afraid the line of your understanding mayn't be long enough.

SQUIRE SULLEN. Look'ee, sir, I have nothing to say to your sea of truth, but if a good parcel of land can entitle a man to a little truth, I have as much as any he in the country.

BONIFACE. I never heard your worship, as the saying is, talk so much before.

SQUIRE SULLEN. Because I never met with a man that I liked before.

BONIFACE. Pray, sir, as the saying is, let me ask you one question: art not man and wife one flesh?

SIR CHARLES. You and your wife, Mr. Guts, may be one flesh, because ye are nothing else; but rational creatures have minds that must be united.

SQUIRE SULLEN. Minds!

SIR CHARLES. Ay, minds, sir: don't you think that the mind takes place of[76] the body?

SQUIRE SULLEN. In some people.

SIR CHARLES. Then the interest of the master must be consulted before that of his servant.

[76] Takes precedence over.

SQUIRE SULLEN. Sir, you shall dine with me to-morrow!—
Oons, I always thought that we were naturally one.

SIR CHARLES. Sir, I know that my two hands are naturally
one, because they love one another, kiss one another,
help one another in all the actions of life; but I could
not say so much if they were always at cuffs.

SQUIRE SULLEN. Then 'tis plain that we are two.

SIR CHARLES. Why don't you part with her, sir?

SQUIRE SULLEN. Will you take her, sir?

SIR CHARLES. With all my heart.

SQUIRE SULLEN. You shall have her to-morrow morning,
and a venison-pasty into the bargain.

SIR CHARLES. You'll let me have her fortune too?

SQUIRE SULLEN. Fortune! why sir, I have no quarrel at her
fortune; I only hate the woman, sir, and none but the
woman shall go.

SIR CHARLES. But her fortune, sir—

SQUIRE SULLEN. Can you play at whisk, sir?

SIR CHARLES. No, truly, sir.

SQUIRE SULLEN. Not at all-fours?

SIR CHARLES. Neither.

SQUIRE SULLEN (*aside*). Oons! where was this man bred?—
Burn me, sir! I can't go home, 'tis but two a clock.

SIR CHARLES. For half an hour, sir, if you please; but you
must consider, 'tis late.

SQUIRE SULLEN. Late! that's the reason I can't go to bed—
Come, sir!

(*Exeunt. Enter* CHERRY, *runs across the stage, and knocks
at* AIMWELL's *chamber-door. Enter* AIMWELL *in his
nightcap and gown.*)

AIMWELL. What's the matter? You tremble, child, you're
frighted.

CHERRY. No wonder, sir.—But, in short, sir, this very
minute a gang of rogues are gone to rob my Lady
Bountiful's house.

AIMWELL. How!

CHERRY. I dogged 'em to the very door, and left 'em breaking in.

AIMWELL. Have you alarmed anybody else with the news?

CHERRY. No, no, sir, I wanted to have discovered the whole
plot, and twenty other things, to your man Martin; but
I have searched the whole house, and can't find him!
Where is he?

AIMWELL. No matter, child; will you guide me immediately to the house?

CHERRY. With all my heart, sir; my Lady Bountiful is my godmother, and I love Mrs. Dorinda so well—

AIMWELL. Dorinda! the name inspires me! The glory and the danger shall be all my own.—Come, my life, let me but get my sword.

(*Exeunt.*)

[SCENE II.] *Scene changes to a bedchamber in* LADY BOUNTIFUL'S *house.*

(*Enter* MRS. SULLEN *and* DORINDA *undressed.*[77] *A table and lights.*)

DORINDA. 'Tis very late, sister—no news of your spouse yet?

MRS. SULLEN. No, I'm condemned to be alone till towards four, and then perhaps I may be executed with his company.

DORINDA. Well, my dear, I'll leave you to your rest. You'll go directly to bed, I suppose?

MRS. SULLEN. I don't know what to do.—Heigh-ho!

DORINDA. That's a desiring sigh, sister.

MRS. SULLEN. This is a languishing hour, sister.

DORINDA. And might prove a critical minute, if the pretty fellow were here.

MRS. SULLEN. Here! what, in my bed-chamber at two o'clock o'th' morning, I undressed, the family asleep, my hated husband abroad, and my lovely fellow at my feet!—O 'gad sister!

DORINDA. Thoughts are free, sister, and them I allow you.— So, my dear, good night.

MRS. SULLEN. A good rest to my dear Dorinda!—

[*Exit* DORINDA.]

Thoughts free! are they so? Why, then, suppose him here, dressed like a youthful, gay, and burning bridegroom (*Here* ARCHER *steals out of the closet.*) with tongue enchanting, eyes bewitching, knees imploring.—(*Turns a little one side and sees* ARCHER *in the posture she describes.*)—Ah!—(*Shrieks and runs to the other side of the stage.*) Have my thoughts raised a spirit?—What are you, sir?—a man or a devil?

77 That is, in dressing gowns.

ARCHER. A man, a man, madam. (*rising*)

MRS. SULLEN. How shall I be sure of it?

ARCHER. Madam, I'll give you demonstration this minute. (*Takes her hand.*)

MRS. SULLEN. What, sir! do you intend to be rude?

ARCHER. Yes, madam, if you please.

MRS. SULLEN. In the name of wonder, whence came ye?

ARCHER. From the skies, madam—I'm a Jupiter in love, and you shall be my Alcmena.

MRS. SULLEN. How came you in?

ARCHER. I flew in at the window, madam; your cousin Cupid lent me his wings, and your sister Venus opened the casement.

MRS. SULLEN. I'm struck dumb with admiration!

ARCHER. And I—with wonder. (*Looks passionately at her.*)

MRS. SULLEN. What will become of me?

ARCHER. How beautiful she looks!—The teeming jolly Spring smiles in her blooming face, and, when she was conceived, her mother smelt to roses, looked on lilies—

Lilies unfold their white, their fragrant charms,
When the warm sun thus darts into their arms.

(*Runs to her.*)

MRS. SULLEN. Ah! (*Shrieks.*)

ARCHER. Oons, madam, what d'ye mean? You'll raise the house.

MRS. SULLEN. Sir, I'll wake the dead before I bear this!— What! approach me with the freedoms of a keeper! I'm glad on't, your impudence has cured me.

ARCHER. If this be impudence,—(*Kneels.*) I leave to your partial self; no panting pilgrim, after a tedious, painful voyage, e'er bowed before his saint with more devotion.

MRS. SULLEN (*aside*). Now, now, I'm ruined if he kneels! —Rise, thou prostrate engineer,[78] not all thy undermining skill shall reach my heart.—Rise, and know, I am a woman without my sex; I can love to all the tenderness of wishes, sighs, and tears—but go no farther. Still to convince you that I'm more than woman, I can speak my frailty, confess my weakness even for you—but—

[78] A builder of military engines to undermine fortifications.

ARCHER. For me! (*going to lay hold on her*)

MRS. SULLEN. Hold, sir! build not upon that; for my most mortal hatred follows if you disobey what I command you now.—Leave me this minute.—(*aside*) If he denies I'm lost.

ARCHER. Then you'll promise—

MRS. SULLEN. Anything another time.

ARCHER. When shall I come?

MRS. SULLEN. To-morrow when you will.

ARCHER. Your lips must seal the promise.

MRS. SULLEN. Pshaw!

ARCHER. They must! they must!—(*Kisses her.*) Raptures and paradise!—And why not now, my angel? the time, the place, silence, and secrecy, all conspire—And the now conscious stars have preordained this moment for my happiness. (*Takes her in his arms.*)

MRS. SULLEN. You will not! cannot, sure!

ARCHER. If the sun rides fast, and disappoints not mortals of to-morrow's dawn, this night shall crown my joys.

MRS. SULLEN. My sex's pride assist me!

ARCHER. My sex's strength help me!

MRS. SULLEN. You shall kill me first!

ARCHER. I'll die with you. (*carrying her off*)

MRS. SULLEN. Thieves! thieves! murther!—

(*Enter* SCRUB *in his breeches and one shoe.*)

Thieves! thieves! murther!—

SCRUB. Thieves! thieves! murther! popery!

ARCHER. Ha! the very timorous stag will kill in rutting time. (*Draws and offers to stab* SCRUB.)

SCRUB (*kneeling*). O pray, sir, spare all I have, and take my life!

MRS. SULLEN (*holding* ARCHER's *hand*). What does the fellow mean?

SCRUB. O madam, down upon your knees, your marrow-bones!—he's one of 'em.

ARCHER. Of whom?

SCRUB. One of the rogues—I beg your pardon, sir, one of the honest gentlemen that just now are broke into the house.

ARCHER. How!

MRS. SULLEN. I hope you did not come to rob me?

ARCHER. Indeed I did, madam, but I would have taken nothing but what you might ha' spared; but your crying "Thieves" has waked this dreaming fool, and so he takes 'em for granted.

SCRUB. Granted! 'tis granted, sir, take all we have.

MRS. SULLEN. The fellow looks as if he were broke out of Bedlam.

SCRUB. Oons, madam, they're broke into the house with fire and sword! I saw them, heard them, they'll be here this minute.

ARCHER. What, thieves?

SCRUB. Under favor, sir, I think so.

MRS. SULLEN. What shall we do, sir?

ARCHER. Madam, I wish your ladyship a good night.

MRS. SULLEN. Will you leave me?

ARCHER. Leave you! Lord, madam, did not you command me to be gone just now, upon pain of your immortal hatred?

MRS. SULLEN. Nay, but pray, sir——(*Takes hold of him.*)

ARCHER. Ha, ha, ha! now comes my turn to be ravished.—— You see now, madam, you must use men one way or other; but take this by the way, good madam, that none but a fool will give you the benefit of his courage, unless you'll take his love along with it.——How are they armed, friend?

SCRUB. With sword and pistol, sir.

ARCHER. Hush!——I see a dark lantern coming through the gallery.——Madam, be assured I will protect you, or lose my life.

MRS. SULLEN. Your life! no sir, they can rob me of nothing that I value half so much; therefore, now, sir, let me entreat you to be gone.

ARCHER. No, madam, I'll consult my own safety for the sake of yours; I'll work by stratagem. Have you courage enough to stand the appearance of 'em!

MRS. SULLEN. Yes, yes, since I have 'scaped your hands, I can face anything.

ARCHER. Come hither, brother Scrub! don't you know me?

SCRUB. Eh, my dear brother, let me kiss thee. (*Kisses* ARCHER.)

ARCHER. This way——here——

(ARCHER *and* SCRUB *hide behind the bed. Enter* GIBBET, *with a dark lantern in one hand, and a pistol in t'other.*)

GIBBET. Ay, ay, this is the chamber, and the lady alone.

MRS. SULLEN. Who are you, sir? what would you have? d'ye come to rob me?

GIBBET. Rob you! alack a day, madam, I'm only a younger brother, madam; and so, madam, if you make a noise, I'll shoot you through the head; but don't be afraid, madam,—(*laying his lantern and pistol upon the table*) These rings, madam—don't be concerned, madam, I have a profound respect for you, madam! Your keys, madam—don't be frighted, madam, I'm the most of a gentleman.—(*searching her pockets*) This necklace, madam—I never was rude to any lady. —I have a veneration—for this necklace—

(*Here* ARCHER *having come round and seized the pistol, takes* GIBBET *by the collar, trips up his heels, and claps the pistol to his breast.*)

ARCHER. Hold, profane villain, and take the reward of thy sacrilege!

GIBBET. Oh! pray, sir, don't kill me; I an't prepared.

ARCHER. How many is there of 'em, Scrub?

SCRUB. Five-and-forty, sir.

ARCHER. Then I must kill the villain, to have him out of the way.

GIBBET. Hold, hold, sir; we are but three, upon my honor.

ARCHER. Scrub, will you undertake to secure him?

SCRUB. Not I, sir; kill him, kill him!

ARCHER. Run to Gipsy's chamber, there you'll find the doctor; bring him hither presently.—

(*Exit* SCRUB, *running.*)

Come, rogue, if you have a short prayer, say it.

GIBBET. Sir, I have no prayer at all; the government has provided a chaplain to say prayers for us on these occasions.

MRS. SULLEN. Pray, sir, don't kill him; you fright me as much as him.

ARCHER. The dog shall die, madam, for being the occasion of my disappointment.—Sirrah, this moment is your last.

GIBBET. Sir, I'll give you two hundred pound to spare my life.

ARCHER. Have you no more, rascal?

GIBBET. Yes, sir, I can command four hundred, but I must reserve two of 'em to save my life at the sessions.[79]

(*Enter* SCRUB *and* FOIGARD.)

ARCHER. Here, doctor—I suppose Scrub and you between you may manage him. Lay hold of him, doctor.

(FOIGARD *lays hold of* GIBBET.)

GIBBET. What! turned over to the priest already!—Look'ye, doctor, you come before your time; I an't condemned yet, I thank ye.

FOIGARD. Come, my dear joy, I vill secure your body and your shoul too; I will make you a good Catholic, and give you an absolution.

GIBBET. Absolution! Can you procure me a pardon, doctor?

FOIGARD. No, joy.

GIBBET. Then you and your absolution may go to the devil!

ARCHER. Convey him into the cellar, there bind him—take the pistol, and if he offers to resist, shoot him through the head—and come back to us with all the speed you can.

SCRUB. Ay, ay; come, doctor—do you hold him fast, and I'll guard him.

[*Exit* FOIGARD *with* GIBBET, SCRUB *following*.]

MRS. SULLEN. But how came the doctor?

ARCHER. In short, madam—(*shrieking without*) 'Sdeath! the rogues are at work with the other ladies—I'm vexed I parted with the pistol; but I must fly to their assistance.—Will you stay here, madam, or venture yourself with me?

MRS. SULLEN. Oh, with you, dear sir, with you.

(*Takes him by the arm, and exeunt.*)

[SCENE III.] *Scene changes to another apartment in the same house.*

(*Enter* HOUNSLOW *dragging in* LADY BOUNTIFUL, *and* BAGSHOT *hauling in* DORINDA; *the rogues with swords drawn.*)

HOUNSLOW. Come, come, your jewels, mistress!

BAGSHOT. Your keys, your keys, old gentlewoman!

[79] To save himself by bribery when he is tried.

(*Enter* AIMWELL *and* CHERRY.)

AIMWELL. Turn this way, villains! I durst engage an army in such a cause. (*He engages 'em both.*)

DORINDA. O madam, had I but a sword to help the brave man!

LADY BOUNTIFUL. There's three or four hanging up in the hall; but they won't draw. I'll go fetch one, however. (*Exit.*)

(*Enter* ARCHER *and* MRS. SULLEN.)

ARCHER. Hold, hold, my lord! every man his bird, pray.

(*They engage man to man, the rogues are thrown and disarmed.*)

CHERRY [*aside*]. What! the rogues taken! then they'll impeach my father; I must give him timely notice. (*Runs out.*)

ARCHER. Shall we kill the rogues?

AIMWELL. No, no, we'll bind them.

ARCHER. Ay, ay.—(*To* MRS. SULLEN *who stands by him*): Here, madam, lend me your garter.

MRS. SULLEN [*aside*]. The devil's in this fellow! he fights, loves, and banters, all in a breath.—Here's a cord that the rogues brought with 'em, I suppose.

ARCHER. Right, right, the rogue's destiny, a rope to hang himself.—Come, my lord—this is but a scandalous sort of an office, (*binding the rogues together*) if our adventures should end in this sort of hangman-work; but I hope there is something in prospect, that—

(*Enter* SCRUB.)

Well, Scrub, have you secured your Tartar?

SCRUB. Yes, sir, I left the priest and him disputing about religion.

AIMWELL. And pray carry these gentlemen to reap the benefit of the controversy.

(*Delivers the prisoners to* SCRUB, *who leads 'em out.*)

MRS. SULLEN. Pray, sister, how came my lord here?

DORINDA. And pray how came the gentleman here?

MRS. SULLEN. I'll tell you the greatest piece of villainy—

(*They talk in dumb show.*)

AIMWELL. I fancy, Archer, you have been more successful in your adventures than the housebreakers.

ARCHER. No matter for my adventure, yours is the principal. Press her this minute to marry you—now while she's hurried between the palpitation of her fear and the joy of her deliverance, now, while the tide of her spirits are at high-flood—throw yourself at her feet, speak some romantic nonsense or other—address her like Alexander in the height of his victory,[80] confound her senses, bear down her reason, and away with her. The priest is now in the cellar, and dare not refuse to do the work.

(*Enter* LADY BOUNTIFUL.)

AIMWELL. But how shall I get off without being observed?

ARCHER. You a lover, and not find a way to get off!—Let me see—

AIMWELL. You bleed, Archer.

ARCHER. 'Sdeath, I'm glad on't; this wound will do the business. I'll amuse the old lady and Mrs. Sullen about dressing my wound, while you carry off Dorinda.

LADY BOUNTIFUL. Gentlemen, could we understand how you would be gratified for the services—

ARCHER. Come, come, my lady, this is no time for compliments; I'm wounded, madam.

LADY BOUNTIFUL *and* MRS. SULLEN. How! Wounded!

DORINDA [*To* AIMWELL]. I hope, sir, you have received no hurt.

AIMWELL. None but what you may cure—(*Makes love in dumb show.*)

LADY BOUNTIFUL. Let me see your arm, sir—I must have some powder-sugar to stop the blood.—O me! an ugly gash, upon my word, sir! You must go into bed.

ARCHER. Ay, my lady, a bed would do very well.—
(*To* MRS. SULLEN): Madam, will you do me the favor to conduct me to a chamber?

LADY BOUNTIFUL. Do, do, daughter—while I get the lint and the probe and the plaster ready.

(*Runs out one way,* AIMWELL *carries off* DORINDA *another.*)

---

80 As Alexander the Great persuades Statira in Nathaniel Lee's heroic tragedy *The Rival Queens* (1677).

ARCHER. Come, madam, why don't you obey your mother's commands?

MRS. SULLEN. How can you, after what is passed, have the confidence to ask me?

ARCHER. And if you go to that, how can you, after what is passed, have the confidence to deny me? Was not this blood shed in your defence, and my life exposed for your protection? Look'ye, madam, I'm none of your romantic fools, that fight giants and monsters for nothing; my valor is downright Swiss;[81] I'm a soldier of fortune, and must be paid.

MRS. SULLEN. 'Tis ungenerous in you, sir, to upbraid me with your services!

ARCHER. 'Tis ungenerous in you, madam, not to reward 'em.

MRS. SULLEN. How! at the expense of my honor?

ARCHER. Honor! can honor consist with ingratitude? If you would deal like a woman of honor, do like a man of honor. D'ye think I would deny you in such a case?

(*Enter a* SERVANT.)

SERVANT. Madam, my lady ordered me to tell you that your brother is below at the gate. [*Exit.*]

MRS. SULLEN. My brother! Heavens be praised!—Sir, he shall thank you for your services, he has it in his power.

ARCHER. Who is your brother, madam?

MRS. SULLEN. Sir Charles Freeman.—You'll excuse me, sir; I must go and receive him. [*Exit.*]

ARCHER. Sir Charles Freeman! 'Sdeath and hell! my old acquaintance! Now unless Aimwell has made good use of his time, all our fair machine goes souse into the sea like the Eddystone.[82]

[SCENE IV.] *Scene changes to the gallery in the same house.*

(*Enter* AIMWELL *and* DORINDA.)

DORINDA. Well, well, my lord, you have conquered; your late generous action will, I hope, plead for my easy yielding; though I must own your lordship had a friend in the fort before.

81 The Swiss were known as mercenary soldiers.
82 The Eddystone Lighthouse was destroyed by a storm in 1703.

AIMWELL. The sweets of Hybla dwell upon her tongue!—
Here, doctor—

(*Enter* FOIGARD, *with a book.*)

FOIGARD. Are you prepared boat?

DORINDA. I'm ready. But first, my lord, one word—I have
a frightful example of a hasty marriage in my own
family; when I reflect upon't, it shocks me. Pray, my
lord, consider a little—

AIMWELL. Consider! do you doubt my honor or my love?

DORINDA. Neither; I do believe you equally just as brave,
and were your whole sex drawn out for me to choose,
I should not cast a look upon the multitude if you
were absent. But, my lord, I'm a woman; colors, con-
cealments may hide a thousand faults in me—therefore
know me better first. I hardly dare affirm I know
myself, in anything except my love.

AIMWELL (*aside*). Such goodness who could injure! I find
myself unequal to the task of villain; she has gained
my soul, and made it honest like her own—I cannot,
cannot hurt her.—Doctor, retire.—

(*Exit* FOIGARD.)

Madam, behold your lover and your proselyte, and
judge of my passion by my conversion!—I'm all a lie,
nor dare I give a fiction to your arms; I'm all counterfeit, except my passion.

DORINDA. Forbid it, Heaven! a counterfeit!

AIMWELL. I am no lord, but a poor needy man, come with
a mean, a scandalous design to prey upon your
fortune; but the beauties of your mind and person
have so won me from myself that, like a trusty servant,
I prefer the interest of my mistress to my own.

DORINDA. Sure I have had the dream of some poor mariner,
a sleepy image of a welcome port, and wake involved
in storms!—Pray, sir, who are you?

AIMWELL. Brother to the man whose title I usurped, but
stranger to his honor or his fortune.

DORINDA. Matchless honesty!—Once I was proud, sir, of
your wealth and title, but now am prouder that you
want it; now I can show my love was justly levelled,
and had no aim but love.—Doctor, come in.

(*Enter* FOIGARD *at one door,* GIPSY *at another, who whispers* DORINDA.)

[*To* FOIGARD]. Your pardon, sir, we sha'not want you now.—
[*To* AIMWELL]: Sir, you must excuse me—I'll wait on you presently. (*Exit with* GIPSY.)

FOIGARD. Upon my shoul, now, dis is foolish. (*Exit.*)

AIMWELL. Gone! and bid the priest depart!—It has an ominous look.

(*Enter* ARCHER.)

ARCHER. Courage, Tom!—Shall I wish you joy?

AIMWELL. No.

ARCHER. Oons, man, what ha' you been doing?

AIMWELL. O Archer! my honesty, I fear, has ruined me.

ARCHER. How!

AIMWELL. I have discovered myself.

ARCHER. Discovered! and without my consent? What! have I embarked my small remains in the same bottom with yours, and you dispose of all without my partnership?

AIMWELL. O Archer! I own my fault.

ARCHER. After conviction—'tis then too late for pardon. You may remember, Mr. Aimwell, that you proposed this folly; as you begun, so end it. Henceforth I'll hunt my fortune single—so farewell!

AIMWELL. Stay, my dear Archer, but a minute.

ARCHER. Stay! what, to be despised, exposed, and laughed at! No, I would sooner change conditions with the worst of the rogues we just now bound, than bear one scornful smile from the proud knight that once I treated as my equal.

AIMWELL. What knight?

ARCHER. Sir Charles Freeman, brother to the lady that I had almost—but no matter for that, 'tis a cursed night's work, and so I leave you to make the best on't. (*going*)

AIMWELL. Freeman!—One word, Archer. Still I have hopes; methought she received my confession with pleasure.

ARCHER. 'Sdeath, who doubts it?

AIMWELL. She consented after to the match; and still I dare believe she will be just.

ARCHER. To herself, I warrant her, as you should have been.

AIMWELL. By all my hopes, she comes, and smiling comes!

(*Enter* DORINDA *mighty gay.*)

DORINDA. Come, my dear lord—I fly with impatience to your arms—the minutes of my absence was a tedious year. Where's this tedious priest?

(*Enter* FOIGARD.)

ARCHER. Oons, a brave girl!

DORINDA. I suppose, my lord, this gentleman is privy to our affairs?

ARCHER. Yes, yes, madam; I'm to be your father.

DORINDA. Come, priest, do your office.

ARCHER. Make haste, make haste, couple 'em any way.— (*Takes* AIMWELL's *hand.*) Come, madam, I'm to give you—

DORINDA. My mind's altered; I won't.

ARCHER. Eh!—

AIMWELL. I'm confounded!

FOIGARD. Upon my shoul, and sho is myshelf.

ARCHER. What's the matter now, madam?

DORINDA. Look'ye, sir, one generous action deserves another.—This gentleman's honor obliged him to hide nothing from me; my justice engages me to conceal nothing from him. In short, sir, you are the person that you thought you counterfeited; you are the true Lord Viscount Aimwell, and I wish your lordship joy.—Now, priest, you may be gone; if my lord is pleased now with the match, let his lordship marry me in the face of the world.

AIMWELL *and* ARCHER. What does she mean?

DORINDA. Here's a witness for my truth.

(*Enter* SIR CHARLES FREEMAN *and* MRS. SULLEN.)

SIR CHARLES. My dear Lord Aimwell, I wish you joy.

AIMWELL. Of what?

SIR CHARLES. Of your honor and estate. Your brother died the day before I left London; and all your friends have writ after you to Brussels; among the rest I did myself the honor.

ARCHER. Hark'ye, sir knight, don't you banter now?

SIR CHARLES. 'Tis truth, upon my honor.

AIMWELL. Thanks to the pregnant stars that formed this accident!

ARCHER. Thanks to the womb of time that brought it forth! —away with it!

AIMWELL. Thanks to my guardian angel that led me to the prize. (*taking* DORINDA's *hand*)

ARCHER. And double thanks to the noble Sir Charles Freeman.—My lord, I wish you joy.—My lady, I wish you joy.—Egad, Sir Freeman, you're the honestest fellow living!—'Sdeath, I'm grown strange airy upon this matter.—My lord, how d'ye?—A word, my lord; don't you remember something of a previous agreement, that entitles me to the moiety of this lady's fortune, which I think will amount to five thousand pound?

AIMWELL. Not a penny, Archer; you would ha' cut my throat just now, because I would not deceive this lady.

ARCHER. Ay, and I'll cut your throat again, if you should deceive her now.

AIMWELL. That's what I expected; and to end the dispute, the lady's fortune is ten thousand pounds, we'll divide stakes: take the ten thousand pounds or the lady.

DORINDA. How! is your lordship so indifferent?

ARCHER. No, no, no, madam! his lordship knows very well that I'll take the money; I leave you to his lordship, and so we're both provided for.

(*Enter* COUNT BELLAIR.)

COUNT BELLAIR. Mesdames et Messieurs, I am your servant trice humble! I hear you be rob here.

AIMWELL. The ladies have been in some danger, sir.

COUNT BELLAIR. And, begar, our inn be rob too!

AIMWELL. Our inn! by whom?

COUNT BELLAIR. By the landlord, begar!—Garzoon, he has rob himself, and run away!

ARCHER. Robbed himself?

COUNT BELLAIR. Ay, begar, and me too of a hundre pound.

ARCHER. A hundred pound?

COUNT BELLAIR. Yes, that I owed him.

AIMWELL. Our money's gone, Frank.

ARCHER. Rot the money! my wench is gone.—

(*To* COUNT BELLAIR): *Savez-vous quelque chose de Mademoiselle Cherry?*[83]

(*Enter a* FELLOW *with a strong box and a letter.*)

FELLOW. Is there one Martin here?

ARCHER. Ay, ay—who wants him?

FELLOW. I have a box here, and letter for him. [*Gives the box and letter to* ARCHER *and exit.*]

ARCHER. Ha, ha, ha! what's here? Legerdemain!—By this light, my lord, our money again!—But this unfolds the riddle.—(*Opening the letter, reads.*) Hum, hum, hum!—Oh, 'tis for the public good, and must be communicated to the company.

[*Reads*]:

Mr. Martin,

My father being afraid of an impeachment by the rogues that are taken to-night, is gone off; but if you can procure him a pardon, he will make great discoveries that may be useful to the country. Could I have met you instead of your master to-night, I would have delivered myself into your hands, with a sum that much exceeds that in your strong-box, which I have sent you, with an assurance to my dear Martin that I shall ever be his most faithful friend till death.

Cherry Boniface

There's a billet-doux for you! As for the father, I think he ought to be encouraged; and for the daughter —pray, my lord, persuade your bride to take her into her service instead of Gipsy.

AIMWELL. I can assure you, madam, your deliverance was owing to her discovery.

DORINDA. Your command, my lord, will do without the obligation. I'll take care of her.

SIR CHARLES. This good company meets opportunely in favor of a design I have in behalf of my unfortunate sister. I intend to part her from her husband—gentlemen, will you assist me?

ARCHER. Assist you! 'sdeath, who would not?

COUNT BELLAIR. Assist! garzoon, we all assist!

---

[83] Do you know anything about Miss Cherry?

(*Enter* SULLEN.)

SQUIRE SULLEN. What's all this? They tell me, spouse, that you had like to have been robbed.

MRS. SULLEN. Truly, spouse, I was pretty near it—had not these two gentlemen interposed.

SQUIRE SULLEN. How came these gentlemen here?

MRS. SULLEN. That's his way of returning thanks, you must know.

COUNT BELLAIR. Garzoon, the question be *àpropos* for all dat.

SIR CHARLES. You promised last night, sir, that you would deliver your lady to me this morning.

SQUIRE SULLEN. Humph!

ARCHER. Humph! what do you mean by humph? Sir, you shall deliver her! In short, sir, we have saved you and your family; and if you are not civil, we'll unbind the rogues, join with 'em, and set fire to your house. What does the man mean? not part with hs wife!

COUNT BELLAIR. Ay, garzoon, de man no understan common justice.

MRS. SULLEN. Hold, gentlemen! All things here must move by consent; compulsion would spoil us. Let my dear and I talk the matter over, and you shall judge it between us.

SQUIRE SULLEN. Let me know first who are to be our judges. Pray, sir, who are you?

SIR CHARLES. I am Sir Charles Freeman, come to take away your wife.

SQUIRE SULLEN. And you, good sir?

AIMWELL. [Thomas], Viscount Aimwell, come to take away your sister.

SQUIRE SULLEN. And you, pray, sir?

ARCHER. Francis Archer, esquire, come—

SQUIRE SULLEN. To take away my mother, I hope. Gentlemen, you're heartily welcome; I never met with three more obliging people since I was born!—And now, my dear, if you please, you shall have the first word.

ARCHER. And the last, for five pound!

MRS. SULLEN. Spouse!

SQUIRE SULLEN. Rib!

MRS. SULLEN. How long have we been married?

SQUIRE SULLEN. By the almanac, fourteen months, but by my account, fourteen years.

MRS. SULLEN. 'Tis thereabout by my reckoning.

COUNT BELLAIR. Garzoon, their account will agree.

MRS. SULLEN. Pray, spouse, what did you marry for?

SQUIRE SULLEN. To get an heir to my estate.

SIR CHARLES. And have you succeeded?

SQUIRE SULLEN. No.

ARCHER. The condition fails of his side.—Pray, madam, what did you marry for?

MRS. SULLEN. To support the weakness of my sex by the strength of his, and to enjoy the pleasures of an agreeable society.

SIR CHARLES. Are your expectations answered?

MRS. SULLEN. No.

COUNT BELLAIR. A clear case! a clear case!

SIR CHARLES. What are the bars to your mutual contentment?

MRS. SULLEN. In the first place, I can't drink ale with him.

SQUIRE SULLEN. Nor can I drink tea with her.

MRS. SULLEN. I can't hunt with you.

SQUIRE SULLEN. Nor can I dance with you.

MRS. SULLEN. I hate cocking and racing.

SQUIRE SULLEN. And I abhor ombre and piquet.

MRS. SULLEN. Your silence is intolerable.

SQUIRE SULLEN. Your prating is worse.

MRS. SULLEN. Have we not been a perpetual offence to each other? a gnawing vulture at the heart?

SQUIRE SULLEN. A frightful goblin to the sight?

MRS. SULLEN. A porcupine to the feeling?

SQUIRE SULLEN. Perpetual wormwood to the taste?

MRS. SULLEN. Is there on earth a thing we could agree in?

SQUIRE SULLEN. Yes—to part.

MRS. SULLEN. With all my heart.

SQUIRE SULLEN. Your hand.

MRS. SULLEN. Here.

SQUIRE SULLEN. These hands joined us, these shall part us. —Away!

MRS. SULLEN. North.

SQUIRE SULLEN. South.

MRS. SULLEN. East.

SQUIRE SULLEN. West—far as the poles asunder.

COUNT BELLAIR. Begar, the ceremony be very pretty.

SIR CHARLES. Now, Mr. Sullen, there wants only my sister's fortune to make us easy.

SQUIRE SULLEN. Sir Charles, you love your sister, and I love her fortune; every one to his fancy.

ARCHER. Then you won't refund?

SQUIRE SULLEN. Not a stiver.

ARCHER. Then I find, madam, you must e'en go to your prison again.

COUNT BELLAIR. What is the portion?[84]

SIR CHARLES. Ten thousand pound, sir.

COUNT BELLAIR. Garzoon, I'll pay it, and she shall go home wid me.

ARCHER. Ha, ha, ha! French all over.—Do you know, sir, what ten thousand pound English is?

COUNT BELLAIR. No, begar, not *justement*.[85]

ARCHER. Why, sir, 'tis a hundred thousand livres.

COUNT BELLAIR. A hundre tousand livres! A garzoon, me canno' do't! Your beauties and their fortunes are both too much for me.

ARCHER. Then I will. This night's adventure has proved strangely lucky to us all—for Captain Gibbet in his walk had made bold, Mr. Sullen, with your study and escritoire, and had taken out all the writings of your estate, all the articles of marriage with your lady, bills, bonds, leases, receipts to an infinite value; I took 'em from him, and I deliver 'em to Sir Charles. (*Gives him a parcel of papers and parchments.*)

SQUIRE SULLEN. How, my writings!—my head aches consumedly.—Well, gentlemen, you shall have her fortune, but I can't talk. If you have a mind, Sir Charles, to be merry, and celebrate my sister's wedding and my divorce,[86] you may command my house—but my head aches consumedly.—Scrub, bring me a dram.

ARCHER (*To* MRS. SULLEN). Madam, there's a country dance to the trifle that I sung to-day; your hand, and we'll lead it up.

(*Here a Dance*)

---

84 The money that a woman would bring into her marriage; like all family property, it then belonged to the husband.
85 Exactly.
86 Since divorces were unobtainable at this time except by act of Parliament, Sullen means a formal separation.

ARCHER. 'Twould be hard to guess which of these parties
is the better pleased, the couple joined, or the couple
parted; the one rejoicing in hopes of an untasted
happiness, and the other in their deliverance from an
experienced misery.

Both happy in their several states we find,
Those parted by consent, and those conjoined.
Consent, if mutual, saves the lawyer's fee—
Consent is law enough to set you free.

EPILOGUE

Designed to be spoke in "The Beaux' Stratagem"

If to our play your judgment can't be kind,
Let its expiring author pity find;
Survey his mournful case with melting eyes,
Nor let the bard be damned before he dies.
Forbear, you fair, on his last scene to frown,
But his true exit with a plaudit crown;
Then shall the dying poet cease to fear
The dreadful knell, while your applause he hears.
At Leuctra so the conquering Theban died,[87]
Claimed his friends' praises, but their tears denied;
Pleased in the pangs of death, he greatly thought
Conquest with loss of life but cheaply bought.
The difference this—the Greek was one would fight,
As brave, though not so gay, as Serjeant Kite.[88]
Ye sons of Will's,[89] what's that to those who write?
To Thebes alone the Grecian owed his bays;
You may the bard above the hero raise,
Since yours is greater than Athenian praise.

[87] Epaminondas actually died at the battle of Mantinea, nine years after his victory at Leuctra.
[88] In Farquhar's *The Recruiting Officer*.
[89] Men of letters met at Will's Coffee House.

THE CONSCIOUS LOVERS
∽ 1722 ∼

Richard Steele

INTRODUCTORY NOTE

RICHARD STEELE (1672–1729) is best known as an essayist who collaborated with Joseph Addison on *The Tatler* (1709–11) and *The Spectator* (1711–12). An important purpose of these periodicals was to unite wit and good breeding with the new middle-class respectability, and thus to refine manners and reform morals.

Steele believed the theater should promote these ends, and accordingly condemned Restoration comedies such as George Etherege's *The Man of Mode* (in *The Spectator*, Number 65). His own plays are sexually clean, though the earlier ones, notably *The Funeral* (1701) and *The Tender Husband* (1705), have the humor and gentle social satire of his periodical essays. When he wrote *The Conscious Lovers* (1722), however, he had come to believe that the purpose of a play was to instruct, that instruction was best achieved directly through precept and good example, and that the appeal to tears was more amiable and refined than the appeal to laughter. Steele's Preface shows how consciously he had developed his reformed type of comedy.

The Conscious Lovers was modeled on the *Andria* of Terence, a Roman playwright noted for "worthy sentiments" and "sober and polite mirth" (*Spectator*, Number 502). Steele added the female characters, moved comedy from the main to the subplots, developed the two fathers to contrast a landed gentleman with a merchant, and changed the leading female figure from a unwed mother to an unfortunate virgin.

Robert Wilks played Myrtle in the original production; Anne Oldfield, Indiana; and Colley Cibber, Tom. The play was immediately successful and remained so until the late eighteenth century, when audiences began to be bored by its sententiousness.

BIBLIOGRAPHY

Major Works:

The Funeral, 1701 (comedy)
The Lying Lover, 1704 (comedy)
The Tender Husband, 1705 (comedy)
The Tatler, 1709–11 (periodical essays)
The Spectator, 1711–12 (periodical essays)
The Guardian, 1713 (periodical essays)
The Theatre, 1720 (periodical essays)
The Conscious Lovers, 1722 (comedy)

Works About:

Loftis, John. *Steele at Drury Lane*. Berkeley: University of California Press, 1952.
Parnell, Paul E. "The Sentimental Mask," *PMLA*, LXXVIII (1963), 529–35.

THE CONSCIOUS LOVERS

The Preface

This comedy has been received with universal acceptance, for it was in every part excellently performed; and
there needs no other applause of the actors, but that they
excelled according to the dignity and difficulty of the
character they represented. But this great favor done to
the work in acting, renders the expectation still the greater
from the author, to keep up the spirit in the representation
of the closet,[1] or any other circumstance of the reader,
whether alone or in company; to which I can only say, that
it must be remembered a play is to be seen and is made to
be represented with the advantage of action, nor can appear
but with half the spirit, without it; for the greatest effect of
a play in reading is to excite the reader to go see it; and
when he does so, it is then a play has the effect of example
and precept.

The chief design of this was to be an innocent perfor-
mance, and the audience have abundantly showed how ready
they are to support what is visibly intended that way; nor
do I make any difficulty to acknowledge, that the whole
was writ for the sake of the scene of the fourth act, wherein
Mr. Bevil evades the quarrel with his friend, and hope it
may have some effect upon the Goths and Vandals that
frequent the theaters, or a more polite audience may supply
their absence.

But this incident, and the case of the father and
daughter, are esteemed by some people no subjects of
comedy; but I cannot be of their mind; for any thing that
has its foundation in happiness and success, must be
allowed to be the object of comedy, and sure it must be
improvement of it, to introduce a joy too exquisite for

[1] Small private room or study.

laughter, that can have no spring but in delight, which is the case of this young lady. I must, therefore, contend, that the tears which were shed on that occasion flowed from reason and good sense, and that men ought not to be laughed at for weeping, till we are come to a more clear notion of what is to be imputed to the hardness of the head, and the softness of the heart; and I think it was very politely said of Mr. Wilks to one who told him there was a general weeping for Indiana, "I'll warrant he'll fight never the worse for that." To be apt to give way to the impressions of humanity is the excellence of a right disposition and the natural working of a well-turned spirit. But as I have suffered by critics who are got no farther than to inquire whether they ought to be pleased or not, I would willingly find them properer matter for their employment, and revive here a song which was omitted for want of a performer, and designed for the entertainment of Indiana; Signor Carbonelli instead of it played on the fiddle, and it is for want of a singer that such advantageous things are said of an instrument which were designed for a voice. The song is the distress of a love-sick maid and may be a fit entertainment for some small critics to examine whether the passion is just, or the distress male or female.

I

From place to place forlorn I go,
    With downcast eyes a silent shade;
Forbidden to declare my woe;
    To speak, till spoken to, afraid.

II

My inward pangs, my secret grief,
    My soft consenting looks betray.
He loves, but gives me no relief.
    Why speaks not he who may?

It remains to say a word concerning Terence, and I am extremely surprised to find what Mr. Cibber told me prove a truth, that what I value myself so much upon, the translation of him, should be imputed to me as a reproach. Mr. Cibber's zeal for the work, his care and application in instructing the actors, and altering the disposition of the scenes, when I was through sickness unable to cultivate such things myself, has been a very obliging favor and friendship to me. For this reason, I was very hardly persuaded to throw away Terence's celebrated funeral,[2] and take only the bare authority of the young man's character, and how I have worked it into an Englishman, and made use of the same circumstances of discovering a daughter when we least hoped for one, is humbly submitted to the learned reader.

___

[2] Terence's hero revealed his affection for the heroine at a funeral, which Steele changed to a masquerade (see page 111).

Dramatis Personae

MEN

SIR JOHN BEVIL
MR. SEALAND
BEVIL, JUNIOR, *in love with Indiana*
MYRTLE, *in love with Lucinda*
CIMBERTON, *a coxcomb*
HUMPHREY, *an old servant to Sir John*
TOM, *servant to Bevil, junior*
DANIEL, *a country boy, servant to Indiana*

WOMEN

MRS. SEALAND, *second wife to Sealand*
ISABELLA, *sister to Sealand*
INDIANA, *Sealand's daughter by his first wife*
LUCINDA, *Sealand's daughter by his second wife*
PHILLIS, *maid to Lucinda*

Scene: London

PROLOGUE
By Mr. Welsted
Spoken by Mr. Wilks

To win your hearts, and to secure your praise,
The comic writers strive by various ways;
By subtle stratagems they act their game,
And leave untried no avenue to fame.
One writes the spouse a beating from his wife;
And says each stroke was copied from the life.
Some fix all wit and humor in grimace,
And make a livelihood of Pinkey's face.
Here one gay show and costly habits[3] tries,
Confiding to the judgment of your eyes;
Another smuts his scene (a cunning shaver)
Sure of the rakes' and of the wenches' favor.
Oft have these arts prevailed; and one may guess,
If practised o'er again, would find success.
But the bold sage, the poet of to-night,
By new and desp'rate rules resolved to write;
Fain would he give more just applauses rise,
And please by wit that scorns the aids of vice;
The praise he seeks, from worthier motives springs,
Such praise, as praise to those that give, it brings.
 Your aid, most humbly sought, then, Britons lend,
And liberal mirth, like liberal men, defend.
No more let ribaldry, with licence writ,
Usurp the name of eloquence or wit;
No more let lawless farce uncensured go,
The lewd dull gleanings of a Smithfield show.
'Tis yours, with breeding to refine the age,

---

[3] Examples of less edifying theatrical entertainment: the mugging of the low comedian William Pinkethman, expensive costumes, and, below, a licentious farce performed at Bartholomew Fair in Smithfield.

To chasten wit, and moralize the stage.
　　Ye modest, wise and good, ye fair, ye brave,
To-night the champion of your virtues save,
Redeem from long contempt the comic name,
And judge politely for your country's fame.

ACT I

[SCENE I.] *Sir John Bevil's House*

(*Enter* SIR JOHN BEVIL *and* HUMPHREY.)

SIR JOHN. Have you ordered that I should not be interrupted while I am dressing?

HUMPHREY. Yes, sir. I believed you had something of
moment to say to me.

SIR JOHN. Let me see, Humphrey; I think it is now full
forty years since I first took thee to be about myself.

HUMPHREY. I thank you, sir, it has been an easy forty
years; and I have passed 'em without much sickness,
care, or labor.

SIR JOHN. Thou hast a brave constitution; you are a year
or two older than I am, sirrah.

HUMPHREY. You have ever been of that mind, sir.

SIR JOHN. You knave, you know it; I took thee for thy
gravity and sobriety in my wild years.

HUMPHREY. Ah, sir! our manners were formed from our
different fortunes, not our different age. Wealth gave
a loose to your youth, and poverty put a restraint upon
mine.

SIR JOHN. Well, Humphrey, you know I have been a kind
master to you. I have used you, for the ingenuous
nature I observed in you from the beginning, more
like an humble friend than a servant.

HUMPHREY. I humbly beg you'll be so tender of me as to
explain your commands, sir, without any farther
preparation.

SIR JOHN. I'll tell thee then. In the first place, this wedding
of my son's, in all probability—shut the door—will
never be at all.

109

HUMPHREY. How, sir! not be at all? For what reason is it carried on in appearance?

SIR JOHN. Honest Humphrey, have patience; and I'll tell thee all in order. I have myself, in some part of my life, lived, indeed, with freedom, but, I hope without reproach. Now, I thought liberty would be as little injurious to my son, therefore, as soon as he grew towards man, I indulged him in living after his own manner. I knew not how, otherwise, to judge of his inclination; for what can be concluded from a behavior under restraint and fear? But what charms me above all expression is that my son has never in the least action, the most distant hint or word, valued himself upon that great estate of his mother's, which, according to our marriage settlement, he has had ever since he came to age.

HUMPHREY. No, sir; on the contrary, he seems afraid of appearing to enjoy it, before you or any belonging to you. He is as dependent and resigned to your will, as if he had not a farthing but what must come from your immediate bounty. You have ever acted like a good and generous father, and he like an obedient and grateful son.

SIR JOHN. Nay, his carriage is so easy to all with whom he converses, that he is never assuming, never prefers himself to others, nor ever is guilty of that rough sincerity which a man is not called to, and certainly disobliges most of his acquaintance; to be short, Humphrey, his reputation was so fair in the world, that old Sealand, the great India merchant, has offered his only daughter, and sole heiress to that vast estate of his, as a wife for him. You may be sure I made no difficulties, the match was agreed on, and this very day named for the wedding.

HUMPHREY. What hinders the proceeding?

SIR JOHN. Don't interrupt me. You know, I was last Thursday at the masquerade. My son, you may remember, soon found us out. He knew his grandfather's habit, which I then wore, and though it was the mode in the last age, yet the maskers, you know, followed us as if we had been the most monstrous figures in that whole assembly.

HUMPHREY. I remember indeed a young man of quality in the habit of a clown that was particularly troublesome.

SIR JOHN. Right. He was too much what he seemed to be. You remember how impertinently he followed and teased us and would know who we were.

HUMPHREY (*aside*). I know he has a mind to come into that particular.

SIR JOHN. Ay, he followed us, till the gentleman who led the lady in the Indian mantle presented that gay creature to the rustic and bid him, like Cymon in the fable,[4] grow polite by falling in love and let that worthy old gentleman alone, meaning me. The clown was not reformed, but rudely persisted, and offered to force off my mask. With that the gentleman throwing off his own, appeared to be my son, and in his concern for me, tore off that of the nobleman. At this, they seized each other; the company called the guards; and in the surprise, the lady swooned away, upon which my son quitted his adversary and had now no care but of the lady. When raising her in his arms, "Art thou gone," cried he, "forever? Forbid it, heaven!" She revives at his known voice, and with the most familiar though modest gesture hangs in safety over his shoulder weeping, but wept as in the arms of one before whom she could give herself a loose, were she not under observation. While she hides her face in his neck, he carefully conveys her from the company.

HUMPHREY. I have observed this accident has dwelt upon you very strongly.

SIR JOHN. Her uncommon air, her noble modesty, the dignity of her person, and the occasion itself, drew the whole assembly together, and I soon heard it buzzed about, she was the adopted daughter of a famous sea officer, who had served in France. Now this unexpected and public discovery of my son's so deep concern for her—

HUMPHREY. Was what I suppose alarmed Mr. Sealand in behalf of his daughter to break off the match.

SIR JOHN. You are right. He came to me yesterday, and said he thought himself disengaged from the bargain, being credibly informed my son was already married, or worse, to the lady at the masquerade. I palliated

---

4 Cymon, in John Dryden's *Fables* (1700), was a lout who learned refinement as a result of falling in love.

matters and insisted on our agreement; but we parted with little less than a direct breach between us.

HUMPHREY. Well, sir, and what notice have you taken of all this to my young master?

SIR JOHN. That's what I wanted to debate with you. I have said nothing to him yet; but look you, Humphrey: if there is so much in this amour of his that he denies my summons to marry, I have cause enough to be offended; and then by my insisting upon his marrying today, I shall know how far he is engaged to this lady in masquerade, and from thence only shall be able to take my measures. In the meantime, I would have you find out how far that rogue his man is let into his secret. He, I know, will play tricks as much to cross me as to serve his master.

HUMPHREY. Why do you think so of him, sir? I believe he is no worse than I was for you at your son's age.

SIR JOHN. I see it in the rascal's looks. But I have dwelt on these things too long. I'll go to my son immediately, and while I'm gone, your part is to convince his rogue Tom that I am in earnest. I'll leave him to you. (*Exit.*)

HUMPHREY. Well, though this father and son live as well together as possible, yet their fear of giving each other pain is attended with constant mutual uneasiness. I'm sure I have enough to do to be honest and yet keep well with them both. But they know I love 'em, and that makes the task less painful, however.—Oh, here's the prince of poor coxcombs, the representative of all the better fed than taught.—Ho! ho! Tom, whither so gay and so airy this morning?

(*Enter* TOM, *singing.*)

TOM. Sir, we servants of single gentlemen are another kind of people than you domestic ordinary drudges that do business. We are raised above you. The pleasures of board wages, tavern dinners, and many a clear gain. Vails,[5] alas! you never heard or dreamed of.

HUMPHREY. Thou hast follies and vices enough for a man of ten thousand a year, though 'tis but as t'other day that I sent for you to town, to put you into Mr.

---

[5] Extra perquisites enjoyed by fashionable London servants: board wages, extra wages allowed for servants' food; vails, tips.

Sealand's family that you might learn a little before I put you to my young master, who is too gentle for training such a rude thing as you were into proper obedience. You then pulled off your hat to every one you met in the street like a bashful great awkward cub as you were. But your great oaken cudgel when you were a booby became you much better than that dangling stick at your button, now you are a fop. That's fit for nothing, except it hangs there to be ready for your master's hand when you are impertinent.

TOM. Uncle Humphrey, you know my master scorns to strike his servants. You talk as if the world was now just as it was when my old master and you were in your youth, when you went to dinner because it was so much o'clock, when the great blow[6] was given in the hall at the pantry door, and all the family came out of their holes in such strange dresses and formal faces as you see in the pictures in our long gallery in the country.

HUMPHREY. Why, you wild rogue!

TOM. You could not fall to your dinner till a formal fellow in a black gown said something over the meat, as if the cook had not made it ready enough.

HUMPHREY. Sirrah, who do you prate after? Despising men of sacred characters! I hope you never heard my good young master talk so like a profligate?

TOM. Sir, I say you put upon me, when I first came to town, about being orderly, and the doctrine of wearing shams to make linen last clean a fortnight, keeping my clothes fresh, and wearing a frock[7] within doors.

HUMPHREY. Sirrah, I gave you those lessons because I supposed at that time your master and you might have dined at home every day and cost you nothing. Then you might have made a good family servant, but the gang you have frequented since at chocolate houses and taverns, in a continual round of noise and extravagance—

TOM. I don't know what you heavy inmates call noise and extravagance, but we gentlemen, who are well fed, and cut a figure, sir, think it a fine life, and that we must

---

[6] Upon the dinner gong.
[7] Devices for economy: shams, false shirt-fronts; frock, a loose coat worn to keep one's clothes clean.

be very pretty fellows who are kept only to be
looked at.

HUMPHREY. Very well, sir, I hope the fashion of being lewd
and extravagant, despising of decency and order, is
almost at an end, since it is arrived at persons of your
quality.

TOM. Master Humphrey, ha! ha! you were an unhappy lad
to be sent up to town in such queer days as you were.
Why, now, sir, the lackeys are the men of pleasure of
the age, the top gamesters; and many a laced coat
about town have had their education in our party-
colored regiment. We are false lovers; have a taste
of music, poetry, *billet-doux*, dress, politics; ruin
damsels; and when we are weary of this lewd town,
and have a mind to take up,[8] whip into our masters'
wigs and linen, and marry fortunes.

HUMPHREY. Hey-day!

TOM. Nay, sir, our order is carried up to the highest digni-
ties and distinctions; step but into the Painted
Chamber, and by our titles you'd take us all for men
of quality. Then again, come down to the Court of
Requests,[9] and you see us all laying our broken
heads together for the good of the nation; and though
we never carry a question *nemine contradicente*,[10] yet
this I can say with a safe conscience (and I wish every
gentleman of our cloth could lay his hand upon his
heart and say the same) that I never took so much as
a single mug of beer for my vote in all my life.

HUMPHREY. Sirrah, there is no enduring your extravagance.
I'll hear you prate no longer. I wanted to see you,
to enquire how things go with your master, as far
as you understand them. I suppose he knows he is to
be married today.

TOM. Ay, sir, he knows it, and is dressed as gay as the
sun; but, between you and I, my dear, he has a very
heavy heart under all that gaiety. As soon as he was
dressed I retired, but overheard him sigh in the most
heavy manner. He walked thoughtfully to and fro in
the room, then went into his closet; when he came

8 Mend our ways.
9 Rooms in or near Parliament, where servants, waiting for their
masters, assumed their masters' titles and aped the parliamentary
debates.
10 Unanimously.

out, he gave me this for his mistress, whose maid you know——

HUMPHREY. Is passionately fond of your fine person.

TOM. The poor fool is so tender and loves to hear me talk of the world, and the plays, operas and *ridottos* for the winter; the parks and Belsize[11] for our summer diversions; and, "Lard!" says she, "you are so wild—— But you have a world of humor——"

HUMPHREY. Coxcomb! Well, but why don't you run with your master's letter to Mrs. Lucinda,[12] as he ordered you?

TOM. Because Mrs. Lucinda is not so easily come at as you think for.

HUMPHREY. Not easily come at. Why, sirrah, are not her father and my old master agreed that she and Mr. Bevil are to be one flesh before tomorrow morning?

TOM. It's no matter for that; her mother, it seems, Mrs. Sealand, has not agreed to it; and you must know, Mr. Humphrey, that in that family the grey mare is the better horse.

HUMPHREY. What dost thou mean?

TOM. In one word, Mrs. Sealand pretends to have a will of her own and has provided a relation of hers, a stiff, starched philosopher and a wise fool, for her daughter; for which reason for these ten days past she has suffered no message nor letter from my master to come near her.

HUMPHREY. And where had you this intelligence?

TOM. From a foolish, fond soul, that can keep nothing from me,—one that will deliver this letter, too, if she is rightly managed.

HUMPHREY. What! Her pretty handmaid, Mrs. Phillis?

TOM. Even she, sir; this is the very hour, you know, she usually comes hither, under pretense of a visit to your housekeeper, forsooth, but in reality to have a glance at——

HUMPHREY. Your sweet face, I warrant you.

TOM. Nothing else in nature. You must know I love to fret and play with the little wanton——

---

11 *Ridottos* were a new kind of musical entertainment; Belsize, a pleasure garden.
12 At this period, *Mrs.* was a courtesy title for unmarried as well as married ladies.

HUMPHREY. Play with the little wanton! What will this world come to!

TOM. I met her this morning in a new manteau and petticoat, not a bit the worse for her lady's wearing; and she has always new thoughts and new airs with new clothes;—then she never fails to steal some glance or gesture from every visitant at their house, and is, indeed, the whole town of coquettes at second hand. But here she comes. In one motion she speaks and describes herself better than all the words in the world can.

HUMPHREY. Then I hope, dear sir, when your own affair is over, you will be so good as to mind your master's with her.

TOM. Dear Humphrey, you know my master is my friend and those are people I never forget—

HUMPHREY. Sauciness itself! But I'll leave you to do your best for him. (*Exit.*)

(*Enter* PHILLIS.)

PHILLIS. Oh, Mr. Thomas, is Mrs. Sugarkey at home?— Lard, one is almost ashamed to pass along the streets. The town is quite empty, and nobody of fashion left in it; and the ordinary people do so stare to see anything dressed like a woman of condition, as it were on the same floor with them, pass by. Alas! Alas! it is a sad thing to walk. Oh, Fortune! Fortune!

TOM. What! a sad thing to walk? Why, Madam Phillis, do you wish yourself lame?

PHILLIS. No, Mr. Tom, but I wish I were generally carried in a coach or chair and of a fortune neither to stand nor go, but to totter, or slide, to be shortsighted, or to stare, to fleer in the face, to look distant, to observe, to overlook, yet all become me; and, if I was rich, I could twire[13] and loll as well as the best of them. Oh, Tom! Tom! is it not a pity that you should be so great a coxcomb and I so great a coquette, and yet be such poor devils as we are?

TOM. Mrs. Phillis, I am your humble servant for that—

PHILLIS. Yes, Mr. Thomas, I know how much you are my humble servant, and know what you said to Mrs. Judy upon seeing her in one of her lady's cast manteaus—

[13] Fleer, laugh scornfully; twire, ogle.

that anyone would have thought her the lady and that
she had ordered the other to wear it till it sat easy, for
now only it was becoming—to my lady it was only
a covering, to Mrs. Judy it was a habit. This you said
after somebody or other. Oh, Tom! Tom! thou art as
false and as base as the best gentleman of them all; but,
you wretch, talk to me no more on the old odious
subject. Don't I say.

TOM. I know not how to resist your commands, madam.
(*in a submissive tone, retiring*)

PHILLIS. Commands about parting are grown mighty easy
to you of late.

TOM (*aside*). Oh, I have her; I have nettled and put her
into the right temper to be wrought upon and set a-
prating.—Why truly, to be plain with you, Mrs.
Phillis, I can take little comfort of late in frequenting
your house.

PHILLIS. Pray, Mr. Thomas, what is it all of a sudden
offends your nicety at our house?

TOM. I don't care to speak particulars, but I dislike the
whole.

PHILLIS. I thank you, sir, I am a part of that whole.

TOM. Mistake me not, good Phillis.

PHILLIS. Good Phillis! Saucy enough. But however—

TOM. I say, it is that thou art a part, which gives me pain
for the disposition of the whole. You must know,
madam, to be serious, I am a man at the bottom of
prodigious nice honor. You are too much exposed to
company at your house. To be plain, I don't like so
many that would be your mistress's lovers whispering
to you.

PHILLIS. Don't think to put that upon me. You say this
because I wrung you to the heart when I touched your
guilty conscience about Judy.

TOM. Ah, Phillis! Phillis! If you but knew my heart!

PHILLIS. I know too much on't.

TOM. Nay then, poor Crispo's fate and mine are one.
Therefore give me leave to say, or sing at least, as he
does upon the same occasion—

Se vedete, &c. (Sings.)[14]

[14] Crispo, hero of an Italian opera, is falsely accused of deceit and
sings "Se vedete": "If you see/ My thoughts/ Ye just Gods, defend/
The innocence of my heart." Cf. Note 23.

PHILLIS. What, do you think I'm to be fobbed off with a song? I don't question but you have sung the same to Mrs. Judy, too.

TOM. Don't disparage your charms, good Phillis, with jealousy of so worthless an object; besides she is a poor hussy, and if you doubt the sincerity of my love, you will allow me true to my interest. You are a fortune, Phillis—

PHILLIS. What would the fop be at now? In good time indeed, you shall be setting up for a fortune!

TOM. Dear Mrs. Phillis, you have such a spirit that we shall never be dull in marriage, when we come together. But I tell you, you are a fortune; you have an estate in my hands.

(*He pulls out a purse. She eyes it.*)

PHILLIS. What pretense have I to what is in your hands, Mr. Tom?

TOM. As thus: there are hours, you know, when a lady is neither pleased or displeased, neither sick or well, when she lolls and loiters, when she's without desires, from having more of everything than she knows what to do with.

PHILLIS. Well, what then?

TOM. When she has not life enough to keep her bright eyes quite open, to look at her own dear image in the glass.

PHILLIS. Explain thyself, and don't be so fond of thy own prating.

TOM. There are also prosperous and good-natured moments, as when a knot or a patch is happily fixed, when the complexion particularly flourishes.

PHILLIS. Well, what then? I have not patience!

TOM. Why then—or on the like occasions—we servants who have skill to know how to time business, see when such a pretty folded thing as this (*Shows a letter.*) may be presented, laid, or dropped, as best suits the present humor. And, madam, because it is a long wearisome journey to run through all the several stages of a lady's temper, my master, who is the most reasonable man in the world, presents you this to bear your charges on the road. (*Gives her the purse.*)

PHILLIS. Now you think me a corrupt hussy.

TOM. Oh, fie, I only think you'll take the letter.

PHILLIS. Nay, I know you do, but I know my own innocence. I take it for my mistress's sake.

TOM. I know it, my pretty one, I know it.

PHILLIS. Yes, I say I do it, because I would not have my
mistress deluded by one who gives no proof of his
passion; but I'll talk more of this, as you see me on
my way home. No, Tom, I assure thee, I take this
trash of thy master's, not for the value of the thing,
but as it convinces me he has a true respect for my
mistress. I remember a verse to the purpose,

They may be false who languish and complain,
But they who part with money never feign.

(*Exeunt.*)

[SCENE II.] BEVIL, JUNIOR's *Lodgings*

(BEVIL, JUNIOR. *Reading.*)

BEVIL. These moral writers practise virtue after death. This
charming *Vision of Mirzai!*[15] Such an author consulted in a morning sets the spirit for the vicissitudes
of the day better than the glass does a man's person.
But what a day have I to go through! To put on an
easy look with an aching heart!—If this lady my
father urges me to marry should not refuse me, my
dilemma is insupportable. But why should I fear it?
Is not she in equal distress with me? Has not the
letter I have sent her this morning confessed my inclination to another? Nay, have I not moral assurances
of her engagements, too, to my friend Myrtle? It's
impossible but she must give in to it; for sure to be
denied is a favor any man may pretend to. It must be
so. Well then, with the assurance of being rejected,
I think I may confidently say to my father I am
ready to marry her. Then let me resolve upon (what
I am not very good at, though it is) an honest
dissimulation.

(*Enter* TOM.)

TOM. Sir John Bevil, sir, is in the next room.

BEVIL. Dunce! Why did you not bring him in?

---

15 A moral tale in *The Spectator*, written by Addison, who had died
in 1719.

TOM. I told him, sir, you were in your closet.

BEVIL. I thought you had known, sir, it was my duty to see my father anywhere. (*going himself to the door*)

TOM (*aside*). The devil's in my master! He has always more wit than I have.

BEVIL (*introducing* SIR JOHN). Sir, you are the most gallant, the most complaisant of all parents. Sure 'tis not a compliment to say these lodgings are yours. Why would you not walk in, sir?

SIR JOHN. I was loth to interrupt you unseasonably on your wedding-day.

BEVIL. One to whom I am beholden for my birthday might have used less ceremony.

SIR JOHN. Well, son, I have intelligence you have writ your mistress this morning. It would please my curiosity to know the contents of a wedding-day letter, for courtship must then be over.

BEVIL. I assure you, sir, there was no insolence in it, upon the prospect of such a vast fortune's being added to our family, but much acknowledgment of the lady's greater desert.

SIR JOHN. But, dear Jack, are you in earnest in all this? And will you really marry her?

BEVIL. Did I ever disobey any command of yours, sir? Nay, any inclination that I saw you bent upon?

SIR JOHN. Why, I can't say you have, son; but methinks in this whole business you have not been so warm as I could have wished you. You have visited her, it's true, but you have not been particular.[16] Every one knows you can say and do as handsome things as any man; but you have done nothing but lived in the general; been complaisant only.

BEVIL. As I am ever prepared to marry if you bid me, so I am ready to let it alone if you will have me.

(HUMPHREY *enters unobserved.*)

SIR JOHN. Look you there now! Why, what am I to think of this so absolute and indifferent a resignation?

BEVIL. Think? That I am still your son, sir. Sir, you have been married, and I have not. And you have, sir, found the inconvenience there is when a man weds with too much love in his head. I have been told,

---

[16] Especially attentive.

sir, that at the time you married, you made a mighty
bustle on the occasion. There was challenging and
fighting, scaling walls—locking up the lady—and the
gallant under arrest for fear of killing all his rivals.
Now, sir, I suppose you having found the ill consequences of these strong passions and prejudices in
preference of one woman to another in case of a man's
becoming a widower—

SIR JOHN. How is this!

BEVIL. I say, sir, experience has made you wiser in your
care of me; for, sir, since you lost my dear mother,
your time has been so heavy, so lonely, and so taste-
less that you are so good as to guard me against the
like unhappiness by marrying me prudentially by way
of bargain and sale. For, as you well judge, a woman
that is espoused for a fortune is yet a better bargain
if she dies; for then a man still enjoys what he did
marry, the money, and is disencumbered of what he
did not marry, the woman.

SIR JOHN. But pray, sir, do you think Lucinda, then, a
woman of such little merit?

BEVIL. Pardon me, sir, I don't carry it so far neither; I am
rather afraid I shall like her too well. She has for one
of her fortune a great many needless and superfluous
good qualities.

SIR JOHN. I am afraid, son, there's something I don't see
yet, something that's smothered under all this raillery.

BEVIL. Not in the least, sir. If the lady is dressed and ready,
you see I am. I suppose the lawyers are ready, too.

HUMPHREY (*aside*). This may grow warm if I don't inter-
pose.—Sir, Mr. Sealand is at the coffee-house and has
sent to speak with you.

SIR JOHN. Oh! that's well! Then I warrant the lawyers are
ready. Son, you'll be in the way,[17] you say—

BEVIL. If you please, sir, I'll take a chair and go to Mr.
Sealand's, where the young lady and I will await your
leisure.

SIR JOHN. By no means. The old fellow will be so vain if
he sees—

BEVIL. Ay, but the young lady, sir, will think me so
indifferent—

HUMPHREY (*aside to* BEVIL, JUN.). Ay, there you are right.

[17] Available.

Press your readiness to go to the bride. He won't let you.

BEVIL (*aside to* HUMPHREY). Are you sure of that?

HUMPHREY (*aside*). How he likes being prevented!

SIR JOHN. No, no. You are an hour or two too early. (*looking at his watch*)

BEVIL. You'll allow me, sir, to think it too late to visit a beautiful, virtuous young woman in the pride and bloom of life, ready to give herself to my arms; and to place her happiness or misery for the future in being agreeable or displeasing to me, is a—Call a chair.

SIR JOHN. No, no, no, dear Jack; this Sealand is a moody old fellow. There's no dealing with some people but by managing with indifference. We must leave to him the conduct of this day. It is the last of his commanding his daughter.

BEVIL. Sir, he can't take it ill that I am impatient to be hers.

SIR JOHN. Pray let me govern in this matter. You can't tell how humorsome old fellows are. There's no offering reason to some of 'em, especially when they are rich. (*aside*) If my son should see him before I've brought old Sealand into better temper, the match would be impracticable.

HUMPHREY. Pray, sir, let me beg you to let Mr. Bevil go.— (*aside to* SIR JOHN): See whether he will or not. (*Then to* BEVIL): Pray, sir, command yourself; since you see my master is positive, it is better you should not go.

BEVIL. My father commands me as to the object of my affections, but I hope he will not as to the warmth and height of them.

SIR JOHN [*aside*]. So! I must even leave things as I found them. And in the meantime, at least, keep old Sealand out of his sight.—Well, son, I'll go myself and take orders in your affair. You'll be in the way, I suppose, if I send to you. I'll leave your old friend with you.— Humphrey, don't let him stir, d'ye hear.—Your servant, your servant. (*Exit.*)

HUMPHREY. I have had a sad time on't, sir, between you and my master. I see you are unwilling, and I know his violent inclinations for the match. I must betray neither and yet deceive you both for your common good. Heaven grant a good end of this matter. But there is a lady, sir, that gives your father much trouble and sorrow. You'll pardon me.

BEVIL. Humphrey, I know thou art a friend to both and in that confidence I dare tell thee—that lady is a woman of honor and virtue. You may assure yourself I never will marry without my father's consent. But give me leave to say, too, this declaration does not come up to a promise that I will take whomever he pleases.

HUMPHREY. Come, sir, I wholly understand you. You would engage my services to free you from this woman whom my master intends you, to make way in time for the woman you have really a mind to.

BEVIL. Honest Humphrey, you have always been an useful friend to my father and myself; I beg you continue your good offices and don't let us come to the necessity of a dispute; for, if we should dispute, I must either part with more than life or lose the best of fathers.

HUMPHREY. My dear master, were I but worthy to know this secret that so near concerns you, my life, my all, should be engaged to serve you. This, sir, I dare promise, that I am sure I will and can be secret. Your trust, at worst, but leaves you where you were; and if I cannot serve you, I will at once be plain and tell you so.

BEVIL. That's all I ask. Thou hast made it now my interest to trust thee. Be patient, then, and hear the story of my heart.

HUMPHREY. I am all attention, sir.

BEVIL. You may remember, Humphrey, that in my last travels my father grew uneasy at my making so long a stay at Toulon.

HUMPHREY. I remember it; he was apprehensive some woman had laid hold of you.

BEVIL. His fears were just; for there I first saw this lady. She is of English birth. Her father's name was Danvers, a younger brother of an ancient family and originally an eminent merchant of Bristol, who upon repeated misfortunes was reduced to go privately to the Indies. In this retreat Providence again grew favorable to his industry and in six years' time, restored him to his former fortunes. On this he sent directions over that his wife and little family should follow him to the Indies. His wife, impatient to obey such welcome orders, would not wait the leisure of a convoy but took the first occasion of a single ship, and with her husband's sister only and this daughter, then scarce seven years old, undertook the fatal voyage. For here, poor creature, she lost her liberty and life. She and her family with all they had were unfortunately taken by a privateer from Toulon. Being thus made a prisoner, though as such not ill treated, yet the fright, the shock, and cruel disappointment seized with such violence upon her unhealthy frame she sickened, pined, and died at sea.

HUMPHREY. Poor soul! O the helpless infant!

BEVIL. Her sister yet survived and had the care of her. The captain too proved to have humanity and became a father to her; for having himself married an English woman and being childless, he brought home into Toulon this her little country-woman, presenting her, with all her dead mother's moveables of value, to his wife to be educated as his own adopted daughter.

HUMPHREY. Fortune here seemed again to smile on her.

BEVIL. Only to make her frowns more terrible; for in his height of fortune this captain, too, her benefactor, unfortunately was killed at sea and, dying intestate, his estate fell wholly to an advocate, his brother, who coming soon to take possession, there found among his other riches this blooming virgin at his mercy.

HUMPHREY. He durst not, sure, abuse his power!

BEVIL. No wonder if his pampered blood was fired at the sight of her. In short, he loved. But when all arts and gentle means had failed to move, he offered, too, his menaces in vain, denouncing vengeance on her cruelty, demanding her to account for all her maintenance from her childhood, seized on her little fortune as his own inheritance and was dragging her by violence to prison when Providence at the instant interposed and sent me, by miracle, to relieve her.

HUMPHREY. 'Twas Providence indeed; but pray, sir, after all this trouble, how came this lady at last to England?

BEVIL. The disappointed advocate, finding she had so unexpected a support, on cooler thoughts descended to a composition;[18] which I without her knowledge secretly discharged.

---

[18] Compromise settlement.

HUMPHREY. That generous concealment made the obligation double.

BEVIL. Having thus obtained her liberty, I prevailed not without some difficulty, to see her safe to England, where no sooner arrived, but my father, jealous of my being imprudently engaged, immediately proposed this other fatal match that hangs upon my quiet.

HUMPHREY. I find, sir, you are irrecoverably fixed upon this lady.

BEVIL. As my vital life dwells in my heart. And yet, you see—what I do to please my father: walk in this pageantry of dress, this splendid covering of sorrow. But, Humphrey, you have your lesson.

HUMPHREY. Now, sir, I have but one material question—

BEVIL. Ask it freely.

HUMPHREY. Is it, then, your own passion for this secret lady, or hers for you, that gives you this aversion to the match your father has proposed?

BEVIL. I shall appear, Humphrey, more romantic in my answer than in all the rest of my story; for though I dote on her to death and have no little reason to believe she has the same thoughts for me; yet in all my acquaintance and utmost privacies with her I never once directly told her that I loved.

HUMPHREY. How was it possible to avoid it?

BEVIL. My tender obligations to my father have laid so inviolable a restraint upon my conduct that till I have his consent to speak, I am determined on that subject to be dumb forever.

HUMPHREY. Well, sir, to your praise be it spoken, you are certainly the most unfashionable lover in Great Britain.

(*Enter* TOM.)

TOM. Sir, Mr. Myrtle's at the next door and if you are at leisure will be glad to wait on you.

BEVIL. Whenever he pleases—Hold, Tom! Did you receive no answer to my letter?

TOM. Sir, I was desired to call again, for I was told her mother would not let her be out of her sight; but about an hour hence, Mrs. Lettice said I should certainly have one.

BEVIL. Very well.

(*Exit* TOM.)

HUMPHREY. Sir, I will take another opportunity. In the meantime, I think it only proper to tell you that, from a secret I know, you may appear to your father as forward as you please to marry Lucinda without the least hazard of its coming to a conclusion. Sir, your most obedient servant.

BEVIL. Honest Humphrey, continue but my friend in this exigence and you shall always find me yours.

(*Exit* HUMPHREY.)

I long to hear how my letter has succeeded with Lucinda; but I think it cannot fail, for at worst were it possible she could take it ill, her resentment of my indifference may as probably occasion a delay as her taking it right. Poor Myrtle! What terrors must he be in all this while? Since he knows she is offered to me and refused to him, there is no conversing or taking any measures with him for his own service. But I ought to bear with my friend and use him as one in adversity.

All his disquiets by my own I prove
The greatest grief's perplexity in love.

(*Exit.*)

ACT II

[SCENE I.] *Scene continues.*

(*Enter* BEVIL, JUNIOR, *and* TOM.)

TOM. Sir, Mr. Myrtle.
BEVIL. Very well. Do you stop again and wait for an answer to my letter.

(*Exit* TOM. *Enter* MYRTLE.)

BEVIL. Well, Charles, why so much care in thy countenance? Is there any thing in this world deserves it? You, who used to be so gay, so open, so vacant![19]

19 Carefree.

MYRTLE. I think we have of late changed complexions. You, who used to be much the graver man, are now all air in your behavior. But the cause of my concern may, for ought I know, be the same object that gives you all this satisfaction. In a word, I am told that you are this day (and your dress confirms me in it) to be married to Lucinda.

BEVIL. You are not misinformed. Nay, put not on the terrors of a rival till you hear me out. I shall disoblige the best of fathers if I don't seem ready to marry Lucinda; and you know I have ever told you you might make use of my secret resolution never to marry her for your own service as you please. But I am now driven to the extremity of immediately refusing or complying unless you help me to escape the match.

MYRTLE. Escape? Sir, neither her merit or her fortune are below your acceptance. Escaping do you call it!

BEVIL. Dear sir, do you wish I should desire the match?

MYRTLE. No, but such is my humorous[20] and sickly state of mind since it has been able to relish nothing but Lucinda, that though I must owe my happiness to your aversion to this marriage I can't bear to hear her spoken of with levity or unconcern.

BEVIL. Pardon me, sir; I shall transgress that way no more. She has understanding, beauty, shape, complexion, wit—

MYRTLE. Nay, my dear Bevil, don't speak of her as if you loved her, neither.

BEVIL. Why then, to give you ease at once, though I allow Lucinda to have good sense, wit, beauty, and virtue, I know another in whom these qualities appear to me more amiable than in her.

MYRTLE. There you spoke like a reasonable and good-natured friend. When you acknowledge her merit and own your prepossession for another, at once you gratify my fondness and cure my jealousy.

BEVIL. But all this while you take no notice, you have no apprehension of another man that has twice the fortune of either of us.

MYRTLE. Cimberton! Hang him! A formal, philosophical, pedantic coxcomb—For the sot, with all these crude notions of divers things, under the direction of great

vanity and very little judgment, shows his strongest
bias is avarice, which is so predominant in him that
he will examine the limbs of his mistress with the
caution of a jockey and pays no more compliment to
her personal charms than if she were a mere breeding animal.

BEVIL. Are you sure that is not affected? I have known
some women sooner set on fire by that sort of negligence than by—

MYRTLE. No, no! Hang him, the rogue has no art, it is
pure simple insolence and stupidity.

BEVIL. Yet, with all this, I don't take him for a fool.

MYRTLE. I own the man is not a natural;[21] he has a very
quick sense though very slow understanding. He says
indeed many things that want only the circumstances
of time and place to be very just and agreeable.

BEVIL. Well, you may be sure of me, if you can disappoint
him; but my intelligence says the mother has actually
sent for the conveyancer to draw articles for his
marriage with Lucinda, though those for mine are, by
her father's orders, ready for signing. But it seems
she has not thought fit to consult either him or his
daughter in the matter.

MYRTLE. Pshaw! A poor troublesome woman. Neither
Lucinda nor her father will ever be brought to comply
with it. Besides, I am sure Cimberton can make no
settlement upon her without the concurrence of his
great uncle, Sir Geoffry, in the West.

BEVIL. Well, sir, and I can tell you that's the very point
that is now laid before her counsel, to know whether a
firm settlement can be made without this uncle's
actually joining in it. Now pray consider, sir, when
my affair with Lucinda comes, as it soon must, to
an open rupture, how are you sure that Cimberton's
fortune may not then tempt her father too to hear
his proposals?

MYRTLE. There you are right indeed. That must be provided against. Do you know who are her council?

BEVIL. Yes. For your service I have found out that too.
They are Sergeant Bramble and old Target—by the
way, they are neither of 'em known in the family. Now
I was thinking why you might not put a couple of

false counsel upon her to delay and confound matters
a little. Besides, it may probably let you into the
bottom of her whole design against you.

MYRTLE. As how, pray?

BEVIL. Why can't you slip on a black wig and a gown and
be old Bramble yourself?

MYRTLE. Ha! I don't dislike it! But what shall I do for a
brother in the case?

BEVIL. What do you think of my fellow, Tom? The rogue's
intelligent and is a good mimic. All his part will be
but to stutter heartily, for that's old Target's case.
Nay, it would be an immoral thing to mock him were
it not that his impertinence is the occasion of its breaking out to that degree. The conduct of the scene will
chiefly lie upon you.

MYRTLE. I like it of all things. If you'll send Tom to my
chambers, I will give him full instructions. This will
certainly give me occasion to raise difficulties, to
puzzle or confound her project for a while at least.

BEVIL. I'll warrant you success. So far we are right, then.
And now, Charles, your apprehension of my marrying
her is all you have to get over.

MYRTLE. Dear Bevil, though I know you are my friend, yet
when I abstract myself from my own interest in the
thing, I know no objection she can make to you, or
you to her, and therefore hope—

BEVIL. Dear Myrtle, I am as much obliged to you for the
cause of your suspicion as I am offended at the effect;
but be assured I am taking measures for your certain
security and that all things with regard to me will end
in your entire satisfaction.

MYRTLE. Well, I'll promise you to be as easy and as
confident as I can, though I cannot but remember that
I have more than life at stake on your fidelity. (*going*)

BEVIL. Then depend upon it, you have no chance against
you.

MYRTLE. Nay, no ceremony. You know I must be going.
(*Exit.*)

BEVIL. Well, this is another instance of the perplexities
which arise too in faithful friendship. We must often
in this life go on in our good offices even under the
displeasure of those to whom we do them in compassion to their weaknesses and mistakes. But all this
while poor Indiana is tortured with the doubt of me.

She has no support or comfort but in my fidelity, yet sees me daily pressed to marriage with another. How painful in such a crisis must be every hour she thinks on me! I'll let her see, at least, my conduct to her is not changed. I'll take this opportunity to visit her; for, though the religious vow I have made to my father restrains me from ever marrying without his approbation, yet that confines me not from seeing a virtuous woman that is the pure delight of my eyes and the guiltless joy of my heart. But the best condition of human life is but a gentler misery.

> To hope for perfect happiness is vain,
> And love has ever its allays of pain.

(*Exit.*)

[SCENE II.]

(*Enter* ISABELLA *and* INDIANA *in her own lodgings.*)

ISABELLA. Yes, I say 'tis artifice, dear child. I say to thee again and again, 'tis all skill and management.

INDIANA. Will you persuade me there can be an ill design in supporting me in the condition of a woman of quality! attended, dressed, and lodged like one, in my appearance abroad and my furniture at home, every way in the most sumptuous manner, and he that does it has an artifice, a design in it?

ISABELLA. Yes, yes.

INDIANA. And all this without so much as explaining to me that all about me comes from him!

ISABELLA. Aye, aye. The more for that, that keeps the title to all you have the more in him.

INDIANA. The more in him! He scorns the thought.

ISABELLA. Then he—he—he—

INDIANA. Well, be not so eager. If he is an ill man, let us look into his stratagems. Here is another of them. (*showing a letter*) Here's two hundred and fifty pound in bank notes, with these words, "To pay for the set of dressing plate which will be brought home tomorrow." Why, dear aunt, now here's another piece of skill for you, which I own I cannot comprehend, —and it is with a bleeding heart I hear you say anything to the disadvantage of Mr. Bevil. When he is present, I look upon him as one to whom I owe my life and the support of it; then again, as the man who loves me with sincerity and honor. When his eyes are cast another way and I dare survey him, my heart is painfully divided between shame and love. Oh! could I tell you!

ISABELLA. Ah! You need not. I imagine all this for you.

INDIANA. This is my state of mind in his presence; and when he is absent, you are ever dinning my ears with notions of the arts of men—that his hidden bounty, his respectful conduct, his careful provision for me, after his preserving me from the utmost misery, are certain signs he means nothing but to make I know not what of me.

ISABELLA. Oh! You have a sweet opinion of him, truly.

INDIANA. I have, when I am with him, ten thousand things besides my sex's natural decency and shame to suppress my heart that yearns to thank him, to praise, to say it loves him. I say thus it is with me while I see him; and in his absence I am entertained with nothing but your endeavors to tear this amiable image from my heart and in its stead to place a base dissembler, an artful invader of my happiness, my innocence, my honor.

ISABELLA. Ah poor soul! Has not his plot taken? Don't you die for him? Has not the way he has taken been the most proper with you? Oh, ho! He has sense and has judged the thing right.

INDIANA. Go on then, since nothing can answer you. Say what you will of him. Heigh ho!

ISABELLA. Heigh ho, indeed! It is better to say so, as you are now, than as many others are. There are among the destroyers of women, the gentle, the generous, the mild, the affable, the humble who all soon after their success in their designs turn to the contrary of those characters. I will own to you, Mr. Bevil carries his hypocrisy the best of any man living, but still he is a man and therefore a hypocrite. They have usurped an exemption from shame for any baseness, any cruelty, towards us. They embrace without love; they make vows without conscience of obligation; they are partners, nay, seducers to the crime wherein they pretend to be less guilty.

INDIANA (*aside*). That's truly observed.—But what's all this to Bevil?

ISABELLA. This it is to Bevil and all mankind. Trust not those who will think the worse of you for your confidence in them—serpents who lie in wait for doves. Won't you be on your guard against those who would betray you? Won't you doubt those who would condemn you for believing 'em? Take it from me, fair and natural dealing is to invite injuries; 'tis bleating to escape wolves who would devour you! Such is the world—(*aside*) and such (since the behavior of one man to myself) have I believed all the rest of the sex.

INDIANA. I will not doubt the truth of Bevil, I will not doubt it. He has not spoken it by an organ that is given to lying. His eyes are all that have ever told me that he was mine. I know his virtue, I know his filial piety and ought to trust his management with a father to whom he has uncommon obligations. What have I to be concerned for? My lesson is very short. If he takes me forever, my purpose of life is only to please him. If he leaves me (which Heaven avert) I know he'll do it nobly, and I shall have nothing to do but to learn to die, after worse than death has happened to me.

ISABELLA. Ay, do; persist in your credulity! Flatter yourself that a man of his figure and fortune will make himself the jest of the town and marry a handsome beggar for love.

INDIANA. The town! I must tell you, madam, the fools that laugh at Mr. Bevil will but make themselves more ridiculous. His actions are the result of thinking, and he has sense enough to make even virtue fashionable.

ISABELLA. O' my conscience, he has turned her head!— Come, come! If he were the honest fool you take him for, why has he kept you here these three weeks without sending you to Bristol in search of your father, your family, and your relations?

INDIANA. I am convinced he still designs it and that nothing keeps him here but the necessity of not coming to a breach with his father in regard to the match he has proposed him. Beside, has he not writ to Bristol, and has not he advice that my father has not been heard of there almost these twenty years?

ISABELLA. All sham, mere evasion. He is afraid if he should carry you thither your honest relations may take you out of his hands and so blow up all his wicked hopes at once.

INDIANA. Wicked hopes! Did I ever give him any such?

ISABELLA. Has he ever given you any honest ones? Can you say in your conscience he has ever once offered to marry you?

INDIANA. No: but by his behavior I am convinced he will offer it the moment 'tis in his power or consistent with his honor to make such a promise good to me.

ISABELLA. His honor!

INDIANA. I will rely upon it; therefore desire you will not make my life uneasy by these ungrateful jealousies of one to whom I am, and wish to be, obliged, for from his integrity alone I have resolved to hope for happiness.

ISABELLA. Nay! I have done my duty. If you won't see, at your peril be it—

INDIANA. Let it be! This is his hour of visiting me.

ISABELLA (*apart*). Oh, to be sure, keep up your form! Don't see him in a bed chamber. This is pure[22] prudence, when she is liable whenever he meets her to be conveyed where'er he pleases.

INDIANA. All the rest of my life is but waiting till he comes. I only live when I'm with him. (*Exit.*)

ISABELLA. Well, go thy ways, thou willful innocent! I once had almost as much love for a man who poorly left me to marry an estate. And I am now, against my will, what they call an old maid; but I will not let the peevishness of that condition grow upon me, only keep up the suspicion of it to prevent this creature's being any other than a virgin except upon proper terms. (*Exit.*)

(*Re-enter* INDIANA *speaking to a servant.*)

INDIANA. Desire Mr. Bevil to walk in.—Design! Impossible! A base, designing mind could never think of what he hourly puts in practice. And yet, since the late rumor of his marriage, he seems more reserved than formerly. He sends in, too, before he sees me, to know

22 Admirable.

if I am at leisure. Such new respect may cover coldness in the heart. It certainly makes me thoughtful. I'll know the worst at once; I'll lay such fair occasions in his way that it shall be impossible to avoid an explanation, for these doubts are insupportable. But see! He comes and clears them all!

(*Enter* BEVIL, JUNIOR.)

BEVIL. Madam, your most obedient! I am afraid I broke in upon your rest last night. 'Twas very late before we parted, but 'twas your own fault. I never saw you in such agreeable humor.

INDIANA. I am extremely glad we were both pleased, for I thought I never saw you better company.

BEVIL. Me, madam! You rally. I said very little.

INDIANA. But I am afraid you heard me say a great deal, and when a woman is in the talking vein the most agreeable thing a man can do, you know, is to have patience to hear her.

BEVIL. Then it's pity, madam, you should ever be silent, that we might be always agreeable to one another.

INDIANA. If I had your talent or power to make my actions speak for me, I might indeed be silent and yet pretend to something more than the agreeable.

BEVIL. If I might be vain of anything in my power, madam, 'tis that my understanding, from all your sex, has marked you out as the most deserving object of my esteem.

INDIANA. Should I think I deserve this, 'twere enough to make my vanity forfeit the very esteem you offer me.

BEVIL. How so, madam?

INDIANA. Because esteem is the result of reason; and to deserve it from good sense the height of human glory. Nay, I had rather a man of honor should pay me that than all the homage of a sincere and humble love.

BEVIL. You certainly distinguish right, madam. Love often kindles from external merit only—

INDIANA. But esteem arises from a higher source, the merit of the soul.

BEVIL. True. And great souls only can deserve it. (*bowing respectfully*)

INDIANA. Now I think they are greater still that can so charitably part with it.

BEVIL. Now, madam, you make me vain, since the utmost pride and pleasure of my life is that I esteem you—as I ought.

INDIANA (*aside*). As he ought! Still more perplexing! He neither saves nor kills my hope.

BEVIL. But, madam, we grow grave, methinks. Let's find some other subject. Pray how did you like the opera last night?

INDIANA. First, give me leave to thank you for my tickets.

BEVIL. Oh, your servant, madam! But pray tell me—you, now, who are never partial to the fashion, I fancy, must be the properest judge of a mighty dispute among the ladies, that is, whether *Crispo* or *Griselda* is the more agreeable entertainment.

INDIANA. With submission now, I cannot be a proper judge of this question.

BEVIL. How so, madam?

INDIANA. Because I find I have a partiality for one of them.

BEVIL. Pray which is that?

INDIANA. I do not know—There's something in that rural cottage of Griselda, her forlorn condition, her poverty, her solitude, her resignation, her innocent slumbers, and that lulling *dolce sogno*[23] that's sung over her. It had an effect upon me, that—in short I never was so well deceived at any of them.

BEVIL. Oh! Now then I can account for the dispute. *Griselda*, it seems, is the distress of an injured, innocent woman; *Crispo*, that only of a man in the same condition; therefore the men are mostly concerned for Crispo, and, by a natural indulgence, both sexes for Griselda.

INDIANA. So that judgment, you think, ought to be for one though fancy and complaisance have got ground for the other. Well! I believe you will never give me leave to dispute with you on any subject, for I own *Crispo* has its charms for me too, though in the main all the pleasure the best opera gives us is but mere sensation. Methinks it's pity the mind can't have a little more share in the entertainment. The music's certainly fine;

---

[23] *Crispo* and *Griselda* were popular operas by Giovanni Battista Bononcini, performed in London in 1722. Griselda, persecuted by enemies, has to hide in a rural cottage, where her husband finds her sleeping and sings the song "Dolce Sogno," "Sweet Dream."

but, in my thoughts, there's none of your composers come up to old Shakespeare and Otway.

BEVIL. How, madam! Why, if a woman of your sense were to say this in a drawing-room——

(*Enter a* SERVANT.)

SERVANT. Sir, here's Signor Carbonelli says he waits your commands in the next room.

BEVIL. *À propos!* You were saying yesterday, madam, you had a mind to hear him. Will you give him leave to entertain you now?

INDIANA. By all means! Desire the gentleman to walk in.

(*Exit* SERVANT.)

BEVIL. I fancy you will find something in this hand that is uncommon.

INDIANA. You are always finding ways, Mr. Bevil, to make life seem less tedious to me.

(*Enter* MUSIC MASTER.)

When the gentleman pleases.

(*After a sonata is played,* BEVIL *waits on the master to the door, &c.*)

BEVIL. You smile, madam, to see me so complaisant to one whom I pay for his visit. Now I own I think it is not enough barely to pay those whose talents are superior to our own. (I mean such talents as would become our condition if we had them.) Methinks we ought to do something more than barely gratify them for what they do at our command only because their fortune is below us.

INDIANA. You say I smile. I assure you it was a smile of approbation, for indeed I cannot but think it the distinguishing part of a gentleman to make his superiority of fortune as easy to his inferiors as he can.—(*aside*) Now, once more to try him.—I was saying just now I believed you would never let me dispute with you and I dare say it will always be so. However I must have your opinion upon a subject which created a debate between my aunt and me just before you came hither. She would needs have it that no man ever does any extraordinary kindness or service for a woman but for his own sake.

BEVIL. Well, madam! Indeed I can't but be of her mind.

INDIANA. What, though he should maintain and support her without demanding anything of her on her part?

BEVIL. Why, madam, is making an expense in the service of a valuable woman (for such I must suppose her) though she should never do him any favor—nay, though she should never know who did her such service—such a mighty heroic business?

INDIANA. Certainly! I should think he must be a man of an uncommon mold.

BEVIL. Dear madam, why so? 'Tis but at best a better taste in expense. To bestow upon one whom he may think one of the ornaments of the whole creation; to be conscious that from his superfluity an innocent, a virtuous spirit is supported above the temptations and sorrows of life; that he sees satisfaction, health, and gladness in her countenance while he enjoys the happiness of seeing her—as that I will suppose too, or he must be too abstracted, too insensible—I say, if he is allowed to delight in that prospect—Alas, what mighty matter is there in all this?

INDIANA. No mighty matter in so disinterested a friendship!

BEVIL. Disinterested! I can't think him so. Your hero, madam, is no more than what every gentleman ought to be and I believe very many are. He is only one who takes more delight in reflections than in sensations. He is more pleased with thinking than eating; that's the utmost you can say of him. Why, madam, a greater expense than all this men lay out upon an unnecessary stable of horses.

INDIANA. Can you be sincere in what you say?

BEVIL. You may depend upon it, if you know any such man, he does not love dogs inordinately.

INDIANA. No, that he does not.

BEVIL. Nor cards, nor dice.

INDIANA. No.

BEVIL. Nor bottle companions.

INDIANA. No.

BEVIL. Nor loose women.

INDIANA. No, I'm sure he does not.

BEVIL. Take my word, then, if your admired hero is not liable to any of these kinds of demands there's no such preëminence in this as you imagine. Nay, this way of expense you speak of is what exalts and raises him that has a taste for it; and, at the same time, his delight is incapable of satiety, disgust, or penitence.

INDIANA. But still I insist his having no private interest in the action makes it prodigious, almost incredible.

BEVIL. Dear madam, I never knew you more mstaken. Why, who can be more an usurer than he who lays out his money in such valuable purchases? If pleasure be worth purchasing, how great a pleasure is it to him who has a true taste of life to ease an aching heart, to see the human countenance lighted up into smiles of joy on the receipt of a bit of ore which is superfluous and otherwise useless in a man's own pocket? What could a man do better with his cash? This is the effect of an humane disposition, where there is only a general type of nature and common necessity. What then must it be when we serve an object of merit, of admiration!

INDIANA. Well! The more you argue against it, the more I shall admire the generosity.

BEVIL. Nay, nay! Then, madam, 'tis time to fly after a declaration that my opinion strengthens my adversary's argument. I had best hasten to my appointment with Mr. Myrtle and be gone while we are friends and— before things are brought to an extremity.—(*Exit carelessly.*)

(*Enter* ISABELLA.)

ISABELLA. Well, madam, what think you of him now, pray?

INDIANA. I protest, I begin to fear he is wholly disinterested in what he does for me. On my heart, he has no other view but the mere pleasure of doing it and has neither good or bad designs upon me.

ISABELLA. Ah, dear niece, don't be in fear of both! I'll warrant you, you will know time enough that he is not indifferent.

INDIANA. You please me when you tell me so, for if he has any wishes towards me I know he will not pursue them but with honor.

ISABELLA. I wish I were as confident of one as t'other. I saw the respectful downcast of his eye when you catched him gazing at you during the music. He, I warrant, was surprised as if he had been taken stealing your watch. Oh, the dissembled guilty look!

INDIANA. But did you observe any such thing, really? I thought he looked most charmingly graceful! How engaging is modesty in a man when one knows there is a great mind within. So tender a confusion, and yet in other respects so much himself, so collected, so dauntless, so determined!

ISABELLA. Ah, niece! There is a sort of bashfulness which is the best engine to carry on a shameless purpose. Some men's modesty serves their wickedness as hypocrisy gains the respect due to piety. But I will own to you there is one hopeful symptom, if there could be such a thing as a disinterested lover. But it's all a perplexity, till—till—till—

INDIANA. Till what?

ISABELLA. Till I know whether Mr. Myrtle and Mr. Bevil are really friends or foes. And that I will be convinced of before I sleep. For you shall not be deceived.

INDIANA. I'm sure I never shall if your fears can guard me. In the meantime, I'll wrap myself up in the integrity of my own heart, nor dare to doubt of his.

> As conscious honor all his actions steers,
> So conscious innocence dispels my fears.

(*Exeunt.*)

ACT III

[SCENE I.] *Sealand's House*

(*Enter* TOM *meeting* PHILLIS.)

TOM. Well, Phillis!—What, with a face as if you had never seen me before—(*aside*) What a work have I to do now? She has seen some new visitant at their house whose airs she has catched and is resolved to practise them upon me. Numberless are the changes she'll dance through before she'll answer this plain question, *videlicet*, "Have you delivered my master's letter to your lady?" Nay, I know her too well to ask an account of it in an ordinary way. I'll be in my airs as well as she.—Well, madam, as unhappy as you are at present pleased to make me, I would not

in the general be any other than what I am. I would
not be a bit wiser, a bit richer, a bit taller, a bit
shorter than I am at this instant. (*looking steadfastly
at her*)

PHILLIS. Did ever anybody doubt, Master Thomas, but
that you were extremely satisfied with your sweet self?

TOM. I am indeed. The thing I have least reason to be
satisfied with is my fortune and I am glad of my
poverty. Perhaps if I were rich I should overlook the
finest woman in the world, that wants nothing but
riches to be thought so.

PHILLIS (*aside*). How prettily was that said! But I'll have
a great deal more before I'll say one word.

TOM. I should perhaps have been stupidly above her had I
not been her equal, and by not being her equal never
had an opportunity of being her slave. I am my
master's servant for hire; I am my mistress's, from
choice, would she but approve my passion.

PHILLIS. I think it's the first time I ever heard you speak
of it with any sense of anguish, if you really do
suffer any.

TOM. Ah, Phillis, can you doubt after what you have seen?

PHILLIS. I know not what I have seen, nor what I have
heard; but since I'm at leisure, you may tell me when
you fell in love with me, how you fell in love with me,
and what you have suffered or are ready to suffer
for me.

TOM (*aside*). Oh, the unmerciful jade! When I'm in haste
about my master's letter. But I must go through it.—
Ah, too well I remember when and how, and on what
occasion I was first surprised. It was on the first of
April, one thousand, seven hundred and fifteen, I came
into Mr. Sealand's service. I was then a hobble-de-hoy
and you a pretty little tight girl, a favorite handmaid
of the housekeeper. At that time we neither of us knew
what was in us. I remember I was ordered to get out
of the window, one pair of stairs, to rub the sashes
clean. The person employed on the inner side was
your charming self, whom I had never seen before.

PHILLIS. I think I remember the silly accident. What made
ye, you oaf, ready to fall down into the street?

TOM. You know not, I warrant you. You could not guess
what surprised me. You took no delight when you

immediately grew wanton in your conquest and put your lips close and breathed upon the glass, and when my lips approached, a dirty cloth you rubbed against my face and hid your beauteous form. When I again drew near, you spit and rubbed and smiled at my undoing.

PHILLIS. What silly thoughts you men have!

TOM. We were Pyramus and Thisbe—but ten times harder was my fate. Pyramus could peep only through a wall; I saw her, saw my Thisbe in all her beauty, but as much kept from her as if a hundred walls between, for there was more, there was her will against me. Would she but yet relent! Oh, Phillis, Phillis, shorten my torment and declare you pity me.

PHILLIS. I believe it's very sufferable. The pain is not so exquisite but that you may bear it a little longer.

TOM. Oh, my charming Phillis, if all depended on my fair one's will I could with glory suffer. But, dearest creature, consider our miserable state.

PHILLIS. How! Miserable!

TOM. We are miserable to be in love and under the command of others than those we love—with that generous passion in the heart, to be sent to and fro on errands, called, checked and rated for the meanest trifles. Oh, Phillis, you don't know how many china cups and glasses my passion for you has made me break. You have broke my fortune as well as my heart.

PHILLIS. Well, Mr. Thomas, I cannot but own to you that I believe your master writes and you speak the best of any men in the world. Never was woman so well pleased with a letter as my young lady was with his, and this is an answer to it. (*Gives him a letter.*)

TOM. This was well done, my dearest. Consider, we must strike out some livelihood for ourselves by closing their affairs. It will be nothing for them to give us a little being of our own, some small tenement out of their large possessions. Whatever they give us, 'twill be more than what they keep for themselves. One acre with Phillis would be worth a whole county without her.

PHILLIS. Oh, could I but believe you!

TOM. If not the utterance, believe the touch of my lips. (*Kisses her.*)

PHILLIS. There's no contradicting you; how closely you argue, Tom!

TOM. And will closer in due time. But I must hasten with this letter, to hasten towards the possession of you.— Then, Phillis, consider how I must be revenged—look to it!—of all your skittishness, shy looks, and at best but coy compliances.

PHILLIS. Oh, Tom! You grow wanton and sensual, as my lady calls it. I must not endure it. Oh! Foh! You are a man, an odious, filthy male creature; you should behave, if you had a right sense or were a man of sense like Mr. Cimberton, with distance and indifference; or—let me see—some other becoming hard word—with seeming in—in—inadvertency, and not rush on one as if you were seizing a prey. But hush! The ladies are coming. Good Tom, don't kiss me above once, and be gone. Lard, we have been fooling and toying and not considered the main business of our masters and mistresses.

TOM. Why, their business is to be fooling and toying as soon as the parchments are ready.

PHILLIS. Well remembered! Parchments! My lady, to my knowledge, is preparing writings between her coxcomb cousin Cimberton and my mistress, though master has an eye to the parchments already prepared between your master, Mr. Bevil, and my mistress; and I believe my mistress herself has signed and sealed in her heart to Mr. Myrtle.—Did I not bid you kiss me but once and be gone? But I know you won't be satisfied.

TOM. No, you smooth creature, how should I! (*kissing her hand*)

PHILLIS. Well, since you are so humble, or so cool, as to ravish my hand only, I'll take my leave of you like a great lady and you a man of quality. (*They salute*[24] *formally.*)

TOM. Pox of all this state. (*Offers to kiss her more closely.*)

PHILLIS. No, prithee, Tom, mind your business. We must follow that interest which will take, but endeavor at that which will be most for us and we like most.— Oh, here's my young mistress! (TOM *taps her neck*

[24] Kiss.

behind and kisses his fingers.) Go, ye liquorish[25] fool! (*Exit.*)

(*Enter* LUCINDA.)

LUCINDA. Who was that you was hurrying away?

PHILLIS. One that I had no mind to part with.

LUCINDA. Why did you turn him away then?

PHILLIS. For your ladyship's service, to carry your ladyship's letter to his master. I could hardly get the rogue away.

LUCINDA. Why, has he so little love for his master?

PHILLIS. No; but he has so much love for his mistress.

LUCINDA. But I thought I heard him kiss you. Why do you suffer that?

PHILLIS. Why, madam, we vulgar take it to be a sign of love; we servants, we poor people that have nothing but our persons to bestow or treat for are forced to deal and bargain by way of sample; and therefore, as we have no parchments or wax necessary in our agreements, we squeeze with our hands and seal with our lips to ratify vows and promises.

LUCINDA. But can't you trust one another without such earnest down?

PHILLIS. We don't think it safe any more than you gentry to come together without deeds executed.

LUCINDA. Thou art a pert, merry hussy.

PHILLIS. I wish, madam, your lover and you were as happy as Tom and your servant are.

LUCINDA. You grow impertinent.

PHILLIS. I have done, madam; and I won't ask you what you intend to do with Mr. Myrtle, what your father will do with Mr. Bevil, nor what you all, especially my lady, mean by admitting Mr. Cimberton as particularly here as if he were married to you already. Nay, you are married actually as far as people of quality are.

LUCINDA. How's that?

PHILLIS. You have different beds in the same house.

LUCINDA. Pshaw! I have a very great value for Mr. Bevil, but I have absolutely put an end to his pretensions in the letter I gave you for him. But my father, in his heart, still has a mind to him, were it not for this woman they talk of; and I am apt to imagine he is married to her or never designs to marry at all.

PHILLIS. Then Mr. Myrtle—

LUCINDA. He had my parents' leave to apply to me and by that has won me and my affections. Who is to have this body of mine without 'em, it seems is nothing to me. My mother says it's indecent for me to let my thoughts stray about the person of my husband. Nay, she says a maid rigidly virtuous, though she may have been where her lover was a thousand times, should not have made observations enough to know him from another man when she sees him in a third place.

PHILLIS. That is more than the severity of a nun, for not to see when one may is impossible; not to see when one can't is very easy. At this rate, madam, there are a great many whom you have not seen who—

LUCINDA. Mamma says the first time you see your husband should be at that instant he is made so, when your father with the help of the minister gives you to him; then you are to observe and take notice of him because then you are to obey him.

PHILLIS. But does not my lady remember you are to love as well as obey?

LUCINDA. To love is a passion, 'tis a desire, and we must have no desires. Oh! I cannot endure the reflection. With what insensibility on my part, with what more than patience, have I been exposed and offered to some awkward booby or other in every county of Great Britain.

PHILLIS. Indeed, madam, I wonder I never heard you speak of it before with this indignation.

LUCINDA. Every corner of the land has presented me with a wealthy coxcomb. As fast as one treaty has gone off, another has come on till my name and person have been the tittle tattle of the whole town. What is this world come to? No shame left! To be bartered for like the beasts of the fields, and that in such an instance as coming together to an entire familiarity and union of soul and body. Oh! and this without being so much as well-wishers to each other, but for the increase of fortune.

PHILLIS. But, madam, all these vexations will end very soon in one for all. Mr. Cimberton is your mother's kinsman and three hundred years an older gentleman than any lover you ever had, for which reason, with that of his prodigious large estate, she is resolved on him and has sent to consult the lawyers accordingly—nay, has (whether you know it or no) been in treaty with Sir Geoffry, who to join in the settlement has accepted of a sum to do it and is every moment expected in town for that purpose.

LUCINDA. How did you get all this intelligence?

PHILLIS. By an art I have, I thank my stars, beyond all the waiting-maids in Great Britain, the art of listening, madam, for your ladyship's service.

LUCINDA. I shall soon know as much as you do. Leave me, leave me, Phillis, begone. Here, here, I'll turn you out. My mother says I must not converse with my servants, though I must converse with no one else.

(*Exit* PHILLIS.)

How unhappy are we who are born to great fortunes! No one looks at us with indifference or acts towards us on the foot of plain dealing; yet by all I have been heretofore offered to or treated for I have been used with the most agreeable of all abuses, flattery; but now by this phlegmatic fool I am used as nothing, or a mere thing. He, forsooth, is too wise, too learned, to have any regard to desires; and I know not what the learned oaf calls sentiments of love and passion.— Here he comes with my mother. It's much if he looks at me, or if he does, takes no more notice of me than of any other movable in the room.

(*Enter* MRS. SEALAND *and* MR. CIMBERTON.)

MRS. SEALAND. How do I admire this noble, this learned taste of yours, and the worthy regard you have to our own ancient and honorable house, in consulting a means to keep the blood as pure and as regularly descended as may be.

CIMBERTON. Why, really, madam, the young women of this age are treated with discourses of such a tendency, and their imaginations so bewildered in flesh and blood, that a man of reason can't talk to be understood. They have no ideas of happiness but what are more gross than the gratification of hunger and thirst.

LUCINDA (*aside*). With how much reflection he is a coxcomb!

CIMBERTON. And in truth, madam, I have considered it as a most brutal custom that persons of the first character in the world should go as ordinarily and with as little shame to bed as to dinner with one another. They proceed to the propagation of the species as openly as to the preservation of the individual.

LUCINDA (*aside*). She that willingly goes to bed to thee must have no shame, I'm sure.

MRS. SEALAND. Oh, cousin Cimberton! Cousin Cimberton! How abstracted, how refined, is your sense of things! But, indeed it is too true, there is nothing so ordinary as to say in the best governed families, "My master and lady are gone to bed." One does not know but it might have been said of one's self. (*hiding her face with her fan*)

CIMBERTON. Lycurgus, madam, instituted otherwise; among the Lacedemonians the whole female world was pregnant, but none but the mothers themselves knew by whom. Their meetings were secret, and the amorous congress always by stealth, and no such professed doings between the sexes as are tolerated among us under the audacious word, *marriage*.

MRS. SEALAND. Oh, had I lived in those days and been a matron of Sparta, one might with less indecency have had ten children according to that modest institution than one under the confusion of our modern, barefaced manner.

LUCINDA (*aside*). And yet, poor woman, she has gone through the whole ceremony and here I stand a melancholy proof of it.

MRS. SEALAND. We will talk then of business. That girl walking about the room there is to be your wife. She has, I confess, no ideas, no sentiments, that speak her born of a thinking mother.

CIMBERTON. I have observed her. Her lively look, free air, and disengaged countenance speak her very—

LUCINDA. Very what?

CIMBERTON. If you please, madam, to set her a little that way.

MRS. SEALAND. Lucinda, say nothing to him; you are not a match for him. When you are married, you may speak to such a husband when you're spoken to. But I am disposing of you above yourself every way.

CIMBERTON. Madam, you cannot but observe the inconveniences I expose myself to in hopes that your ladyship will be the consort of my better part. As for the young woman, she is rather an impediment than a help to a man of letters and speculation. Madam, there is no reflection, no philosophy, can at all times subdue the sensitive life, but the animal shall sometimes carry away the man. Ha! Ay, the vermilion of her lips!

LUCINDA. Pray, don't talk of me thus.

CIMBERTON. The pretty enough—pant of her bosom.

LUCINDA. Sir! Madam, don't you hear him?

CIMBERTON. Her forward chest—

LUCINDA. Intolerable!

CIMBERTON. High health—

LUCINDA. The grave, easy impudence of him!

CIMBERTON. Proud heart—

LUCINDA. Stupid coxcomb!

CIMBERTON. I say, madam, her impatience while we are looking at her throws out all attractions—her arms, her neck—what a spring in her step!

LUCINDA. Don't you run me over thus, you strange unaccountable!

CIMBERTON. What an elasticity in her veins and arteries!

LUCINDA. I have no veins, no arteries!

MRS. SEALAND. Oh, child, hear him, he talks finely. He's a scholar, he knows what you have.

CIMBERTON. The speaking invitation of her shape, the gathering of herself up, and the indignation you see in the pretty little thing—Now, I am considering her, on this occasion, but as one that is to be pregnant.

LUCINDA (aside). The familiar, learned, unseasonable puppy!

CIMBERTON. And pregnant undoubtedly she will be yearly. I fear I shan't for many years have discretion enough to give her one fallow season.

LUCINDA. Monster! There's no bearing it. The hideous sot! There's no enduring it, to be thus surveyed like a steed at sale.

CIMBERTON. At sale! She's very illiterate. But she's very well limbed too. Turn her in; I see what she is.

(*Exit* LUCINDA *in a rage.*)

MRS. SEALAND. Go, you creature, I am ashamed of you.

CIMBERTON. No harm done. You know, madam, the better sort of people, as I observed to you, treat by their lawyers of weddings (*adjusting himself at the glass*), and the woman in the bargain, like her mansion-house in the sale of the estate, is thrown in, and what that is, whether good or bad, is not at all considered.

MRS. SEALAND. I grant it and therefore make no demand for her youth and beauty and every other accomplishment, as the common world think 'em, because she is not polite.

CIMBERTON. Madam, I know your exalted understanding, abstracted as it is from vulgar prejudices, will not be offended when I declare to you I marry to have an heir to my estate and not to beget a colony or a plantation. This young woman's beauty and constitution will demand provision for a tenth child at least.

MRS. SEALAND (*aside*). With all that wit and learning, how considerate! What an economist!—Sir, I cannot make her other than she is, or say she is much better than the other young women of this age or fit for much besides being a mother; but I have given directions for the marriage settlements, and Sir Geoffry Cimberton's counsel is to meet ours here at this hour, concerning his joining in the deed, which, when executed, makes you capable of settling what is due to Lucinda's fortune. Herself, as I told you, I say nothing of.

CIMBERTON. No, no, no, indeed, madam, it is not usual; and I must depend upon my own reflection and philosophy not to overstock my family.

MRS. SEALAND. I cannot help her, cousin Cimberton; but she is, for aught I see, as well as the daughter of anybody else.

CIMBERTON. That is very true, madam.

(*Enter a Servant who whispers [to]* MRS. SEALAND.)

MRS. SEALAND. The lawyers are come, and now we are to hear what they have resolved as to the point whether it's necessary that Sir Geoffry should join in the settlement, as being what they call in the remainder. But, good cousin, you must have patience with 'em. These lawyers, I am told, are of a different kind; one is what they call a chamber-counsel, the other a pleader. The conveyancer is slow from an imperfection in his speech, and therefore shunned the bar, but extremely passionate and impatient of contradiction. The other is as warm as he but has a tongue so voluble and a head so conceited he will suffer nobody to speak but himself.

CIMBERTON. You mean old Sergeant Target and Counsellor Bramble? I have heard of 'em.

MRS. SEALAND. The same. Show in the gentlemen.

(*Exit Servant. Re-enter Servant introducing* MYRTLE *and* TOM *disguised as* BRAMBLE *and* TARGET.)

MRS. SEALAND. Gentlemen, this is the party concerned, Mr. Cimberton; and I hope you have considered of the matter.

TARGET. Yes, madam, we have agreed that it must be by indent—dent—dent—dent—

BRAMBLE. Yes, madam, Mr. Sergeant and myself have agreed, as he is pleased to inform you, that it must be by an indenture tripartite, and tripartite let it be, for Sir Geoffry must needs be a party. Old Cimberton in the year 1619 says, in that ancient roll in Mr. Sergeant's hands, as recourse being thereto had, will more at large appear—

TARGET. Yes, and by the deeds in your hands it appears that—

BRAMBLE. Mr. Sergeant, I beg of you to make no inferences upon what is in our custody, but to speak to the titles in your own deeds. I shall not show that deed till my client is in town.

CIMBERTON. You know best your own methods.

MRS. SEALAND. The single question is whether the entail is such that my cousin, Sir Geoffry, is necessary in this affair?

BRAMBLE. Yes, as to the lordship of Tretriplet but not as to the message of Grimgribber.

TARGET. I say that Gr—Gr—that Gr—Gr—Grimgribber, Grimgribber is in us. That is to say, the remainder thereof as well as that of Tr—Tr—Triplet.

BRAMBLE. You go upon the deed of Sir Ralph, made in the middle of the last century, precedent to that in which old Cimberton made over the remainder and made it pass to the heirs general, by which your client comes in; and I question whether the remainder even of Tretriplet is in him. But we are willing to waive that and give him a valuable consideration. But we shall not purchase what is in us forever, as Grimgribber is, at the rate as we guard against the contingent of Mr. Cimberton having no son. Then we know Sir Geoffry is the first of the collateral male line in this family; yet—

TARGET. Sir, Gr—Gr—ber is—

BRAMBLE. I apprehend you very well, and your argument might be of force, and we would be inclined to hear that in all parts. But, sir, I see very plainly what you are going into. I tell you it is as probable a contingent that Sir Geoffry may die before Mr. Cimberton as that he may outlive him.

TARGET. Sir, we are not ripe for that yet, but I must say—

BRAMBLE. Sir, I allow you the whole extent of that argument; but that will go no farther than as to the claimants under old Cimberton. I am of opinion that according to the instruction of Sir Ralph he could not dock the entail and then create a new estate for the heirs general.

TARGET. Sir, I have not patience to be told that, when Gr—Gr—ber—

BRAMBLE. I will allow it to you, Mr. Sergeant; but there must be the word "heirs forever" to make such an estate as you pretend.

CIMBERTON. I must be impartial, though you are counsel for my side of the question. Were it not that you are so good as to allow him what he has not said, I should think it very hard you should answer him without hearing him. But, gentlemen, I believe you have both considered this matter and are firm in your different opinions. 'Twere better, therefore, you proceeded according to the particular sense of each of you and gave your thoughts distinctly in writing. And do you see, sirs, pray let me have a copy of what you say in English.

BRAMBLE. Why, what is all we have been saying? In English!—Oh, but I forgot myself, you're a wit. But however, to please you, sir, you shall have it in as plain terms as the law will admit of.

CIMBERTON. But I would have it, sir, without delay.

BRAMBLE. That, sir, the law will not admit of. The courts are sitting at Westminster, and I am this moment obliged to be at every one of them, and 'twould be wrong if I should not be in the Hall to attend one of 'em at least;[26] the rest would take it ill else. Therefore, I must leave what I have said to Mr. Sergeant's consideration, and I will digest his arguments on my part, and you shall hear from me again, sir. (*Exit.*)

TARGET. Agreed, agreed.

CIMBERTON. Mr. Bramble is very quick. He parted a little abruptly.

TARGET. He could not bear my argument, I pinched him to the quick about that Gr—Gr—ber.

MRS. SEALAND. I saw that, for he durst not so much as hear you. I shall send to you, Mr. Sergeant, as soon as Sir Geoffry comes to town, and then I hope all may be adjusted.

TARGET. I shall be at my chambers at my usual hours. (*Exit.*)

CIMBERTON. Madam, if you please, I'll now attend you to the tea table, where I shall hear from your ladyship reason and good sense after all this law and gibberish.

MRS. SEALAND. 'Tis a wonderful thing, sir, that men of professions do not study to talk the substance of what they have to say in the language of the rest of the world. Sure they'd find their account[27] in it.

CIMBERTON. They might, perhaps, madam, with people of your good sense; but with the generality 'twould never do. The vulgar would have no respect for truth and knowledge if they were exposed to naked view.

Truth is too simple, of all art bereaved.
Since the world will—why, let it be deceived.

(*Exeunt.*)

---

[26] Trials were held in Westminster Hall.
[27] Profit.

ACT IV

[SCENE I.] BEVIL, JUNIOR'S *Lodgings*

(BEVIL, JUNIOR, *with a letter in his hand, followed by* TOM.)

TOM. Upon my life, sir, I know nothing of the matter. I never opened my lips to Mr. Myrtle about anything of your honor's letter to Madam Lucinda.

BEVIL. What's the fool in such a fright for? I don't suppose you did. What I would know is whether Mr. Myrtle showed any suspicion, or asked you any questions, to lead you to say casually that you had carried any such letter for me this morning.

TOM. Why, sir, if he did ask me any questions, how could I help it?

BEVIL. I don't say you could, oaf! I am not questioning you, but him. What did he say to you?

TOM. Why, sir, when I came to his chambers to be dressed for the lawyer's part your honor was pleased to put me upon, he asked me if I had been at Mr. Sealand's this morning. So I told him, sir, I often went thither—because, sir, if I had not said that he might have thought there was something more in my going now than at another time.

BEVIL. Very well!—(*aside*) The fellow's caution, I find, has given him this jealousy.—Did he ask you no other questions?

TOM. Yes, sir, now I remember, as we came away in the hackney coach from Mr. Sealand's, "Tom," says he, "as I came in to your master this morning, he bade you go for an answer to a letter he had sent. Pray did you bring him any?" says he. "Ah," says I, "sir, your honor is pleased to joke with me; you have a mind to know whether I can keep a secret or no!"

BEVIL. And so, by showing him you could, you told him you had one.

TOM (*confused*). Sir—

BEVIL. What mean actions does jealousy make a man stoop to! How poorly has he used art[28] with a servant to

---

[28] Trickery.

make him betray his master! Well, and when did he give you this letter for me?

TOM. Sir, he writ it before he pulled off his lawyer's gown at his own chambers.

BEVIL. Very well; and what did he say when you brought him my answer to it?

TOM. He looked a little out of humor, sir, and said it was very well.

BEVIL. I knew he would be grave upon't. Wait without.

TOM. Humh! 'Gad, I don't like this. I am afraid we are all in the wrong box here. (*Exit.*)

BEVIL. I put on a serenity while my fellow was present, but I have never been more thoroughly disturbed. This hot man! To write me a challenge on supposed artificial dealing when I professed myself his friend! I can live contented without glory, but I cannot suffer shame. What's to be done? But first let me consider Lucinda's letter again.

(*Reads*):

> Sir:
>
> I hope it is consistent with the laws a woman ought to impose upon herself to acknowledge that your manner of declining a treaty of marriage in our family, and desiring the refusal may come from me, has something more engaging in it than the courtship of him who, I fear, will fall to my lot, except your friend exerts himself for our common safety and happiness. I have reasons for desiring Mr. Myrtle may not know of this letter till hereafter, and am your most obliged, humble servant,
>
> Lucinda Sealand

Well, but the postscript.

(*Reads*):

> I won't, upon second thoughts, hide anything from you. But my reason for concealing this is that Mr. Myrtle has a jealousy in his temper which gives me some terrors; but my esteem for him inclines me to hope that only an ill effect which sometimes accompanies a tender love, and what may be cured by a careful and unblameable conduct.

Thus has this lady made me her friend and confidant and put herself, in a kind, under my protection. I cannot tell him immediately the purport of her letter except I could cure him of the violent and untractable passion of jealousy and so serve him and her by disobliging her in the article of secrecy more than I should by complying with her directions. But then this dueling, which custom has imposed upon every man who would live with reputation and honor in the world! How must I preserve myself from imputations there? He'll, forsooth, call it or think it fear, if I explain without fighting. But his letter—I'll read it again:

Sir:

You have used me basely in corresponding and carrying on a treaty where you told me you were indifferent. I have changed my sword since I saw you, which advertisement I thought proper to send you against the next meeting between you and the injured
                                          Charles Myrtle.

(*Enter* TOM.)

TOM. Mr. Myrtle, sir. Would your honor please to see him?
BEVIL. Why, you stupid creature! Let Mr. Myrtle wait at my lodgings! Show him up.

(*Exit* TOM.)

Well, I am resolved upon my carriage to him. He is in love and in every circumstance of life a little distrustful, which I must allow for—but here he is.

(*Enter* TOM *introducing* MYRTLE.)

BEVIL. Sir, I am extremely obliged to you for this honor. [*To* TOM]: But, sir, you, with your very discerning face, leave the room.

(*Exit* TOM.)

Well, Mr. Myrtle, your commands with me?
MYRTLE. The time, the place, our long acquaintance and many other circumstances which affect me on this occasion oblige me without farther ceremony or conference to desire you would not only, as you already have, acknowledge the receipt of my letter but also

comply with the request in it. I must have farther notice taken of my message than these half lines: "I have yours. I shall be at home."

BEVIL. Sir, I own I have received a letter from you in a very unusual style; but, as I design everything in this matter shall be your own action, your own seeking, I shall understand nothing but what you are pleased to confirm face to face, and I have already forgot the contents of your epistle.

MYRTLE. This cool manner is very agreeable to the abuse you have already made of my simplicity and frankness; and I see your moderation tends to your own advantage and not mine, to your own safety, not consideration of your friend.

BEVIL. My own safety, Mr. Myrtle!

MYRTLE. Your own safety, Mr. Bevil.

BEVIL. Look you, Mr. Myrtle, there's no disguising that I understand what you would be at. But, sir, you know I have often dared to disapprove of the decisions a tyrant custom has introduced, to the breach of all laws, both divine and human.

MYRTLE. Mr. Bevil, Mr. Bevil, it would be a good first principle in those who have so tender a conscience that way to have as much abhorrence of doing injuries as—

BEVIL. As what?

MYRTLE. As fear of answering for 'em.

BEVIL. As fear of answering for 'em! But that apprehension is just or blameable according to the object of that fear. I have often told you in confidence of heart, I abhorred the daring to offend the Author of Life and rushing into His presence—I say, by the very same act, to commit the crime against Him and immediately to urge on to His tribunal.

MYRTLE. Mr. Bevil, I must tell you, this coolness, this gravity, this show of confidence shall never cheat me of my mistress. You have, indeed, the best excuse for life, the hopes of possessing Lucinda. But consider, sir, I have as much reason to be weary of it, if I am to lose her; and my first attempt to recover her shall be to let her see the dauntless man who is to be her guardian and protector.

BEVIL. Sir, show me but the least glimpse of argument that I am authorized by my own hand to vindicate any

lawless insult of this nature and I will show thee—
to chastise thee hardly deserves the name of courage
—slight, inconsiderate man! There is, Mr. Myrtle, no
such terror in quick anger; and you shall, you know
not why, be cool, as you have, you know not why,
been warm.

MYRTLE. Is the woman one loves so little an occasion of
anger? You, perhaps, who know not what it is to
love, who have your ready, your commodious, your
foreign trinket for your loose hours; and from your
fortune, your specious outward carriage, and other
lucky circumstances as easy a way to the possession
of a woman of honor, you know nothing of what it is
to be alarmed, to be distracted with anxiety and
terror of losing more than life. Your marriage, happy
man, goes on like common business; and in the interim
you have your rambling captive, your Indian princess,
for your soft moments of dalliance—your convenient,
your ready Indiana.

BEVIL. You have touched me beyond the patience of a man;
and I'm excusable, in the guard of innocence (or from
the infirmity of human nature, which will bear no
more) to accept your invitation and observe your
letter. Sir, I'll attend you!

(*Enter* TOM.)

TOM. Did you call, sir? I thought you did. I heard you
speak aloud.

BEVIL. Yes, go call a coach.

TOM. Sir—master—Mr. Myrtle—friends—gentlemen—
what d'ye mean? I am but a servant, or—

BEVIL. Call a coach.

(*Exit* TOM. *A long pause, walking sullenly by each
other*.)

(*aside*): Shall I, though provoked to the uttermost,
recover myself at the entrance of a third person and
that my servant, too, and not have respect enough to
all I have ever been receiving from infancy, the
obligation to the best of fathers, to an unhappy virgin
too, whose life depends on mine? (*shutting the door*).
(*To* MYRTLE): I have, thank heaven, had time to
recollect myself and shall not, for fear of what such
a rash man as you think of me, keep longer unex-

plained the false appearances under which your infirmity of temper makes you suffer, when perhaps too much regard to a false point of honor makes me prolong that suffering.

MYRTLE. I am sure Mr. Bevil cannot doubt but I had rather have satisfaction from his innocence than his sword.

BEVIL. Why, then, would you ask it first that way?

MYRTLE. Consider, you kept your temper yourself no longer than till I spoke to the disadvantage of her you loved.

BEVIL. True. But let me tell you I have saved you from the most exquisite distress even though you had succeeded in the dispute. I know you so well that I am sure to have found this letter about a man you had killed would have been worse than death to yourself. Read it. [aside] When he is thoroughly mortified and shame has got the better of jealousy, when he has seen himself thoroughly, he will deserve to be assisted towards obtaining Lucinda.

MYRTLE [aside]. With what a superiority has he turned the injury on me as the aggressor! I begin to fear I have been too far transported.—"A treaty in our family—" Is not that saying too much? I shall relapse—But I find on the postscript, "—something like jealousy—" With what face can I see my benefactor, my advocate, whom I have treated like a betrayer?—Oh, Bevil, with what words shall I—

BEVIL. There needs none; to convince is much more than to conquer.

MYRTLE. But can you—

BEVIL. You have o'erpaid the inquietude you gave me in the change I see in you towards me. Alas, what machines are we! Thy face is altered to that of another man, to that of my companion, my friend.

MYRTLE. That I could be such a precipitant wretch!

BEVIL. Pray, no more.

MYRTLE. Let me reflect how many friends have died by the hands of friends for the want of temper; and you must give me leave to say again and again how much I am beholden to that superior spirit you have subdued me with. What had become of one of us, or perhaps both, had you been as weak as I was and as incapable of reason?

BEVIL. I congratulate to us both the escape from ourselves
and hope the memory of it will make us dearer friends
than ever.

MYRTLE. Dear Bevil, your friendly conduct has convinced
me there is nothing manly but what is conducted by
reason and agreeable to the practice of virtue and
justice. And yet how many have been sacrificed to that
idol, the unreasonable opinion of men! Nay, they
are so ridiculous in it that they often use their swords
against each other with dissembled anger and real fear.

> Betrayed by honor and compelled by shame,
> They hazard being to preserve a name,
> Nor dare enquire into the dread mistake,
> Till plunged in sad eternity they wake.

(*Exeunt.*)

[SCENE II.] *St. James's Park*

(*Enter* SIR JOHN BEVIL *and* MR. SEALAND.)

SIR JOHN. Give me leave, however, Mr. Sealand, as we are
upon a treaty for uniting our families, to mention only
the business of an ancient house. Genealogy and
descent are to be of some consideration in an affair
of this sort.

MR. SEALAND. Genealogy and descent! Sir, there has been
in our family a very large one. There was Galfrid, the
father of Edward, the father of Ptolemy, the father
of Crassus, the father of Earl Richard, the father of
Henry the marquis, the father of Duke John—

SIR JOHN. What, do you rave, Mr. Sealand? All these great
names in your family?

MR. SEALAND. These? Yes, sir. I have heard my father name
'em all, and more.

SIR JOHN. Ay, sir, and did he say they were all in your
family?

MR. SEALAND. Yes, sir, he kept 'em all. He was the greatest
cocker[29] in all England. He said Duke John won him
many battles and never lost one.

SIR JOHN. Oh, sir, your servant. You are laughing at my
laying any stress upon descent; but I must tell you,
sir, I never knew anyone but he that wanted that
advantage turn it into ridicule.

---

[29] Breeder of fighting cocks.

MR. SEALAND. And I never knew anyone who had many better advantages put that into his account. But, Sir John, value yourself as you please upon your ancient house; I am to talk freely of everything you are pleased to put into your bill of rates on this occasion. Yet, sir, I have made no objections to your son's family. 'Tis his morals that I doubt.

SIR JOHN. Sir, I can't help saying that what might injure a citizen's credit may be no stain to a gentleman's honor.

MR. SEALAND. Sir John, the honor of a gentleman is liable to be tainted by as small a matter as the credit of a trader; we are talking of a marriage, and in such a case the father of a young woman will not think it an addition to the honor or credit of her lover that he is a keeper—

SIR JOHN. Mr. Sealand, don't take upon you to spoil my son's marriage with any woman else.

MR. SEALAND. Sir John, let him apply to any woman else and have as many mistresses as he pleases—

SIR JOHN. My son, sir, is a discreet and sober gentleman—

MR. SEALAND. Sir, I never saw a man that wenched soberly and discreetly that ever left it off. The decency observed in the practice hides even from the sinner the iniquity of it. They pursue it, not that their appetites hurry them away, but, I warrant you, because 'tis their opinion they may do it.

SIR JOHN. Were what you suspect a truth—do you design to keep your daughter a virgin till you find a man unblemished that way?

MR. SEALAND. Sir, as much a cit[30] as you take me for, I know the town and the world; and give me leave to say that we merchants are a species of gentry that have grown into the world this last century and are as honorable and almost as useful as you landed folks that have always thought yourselves so much above us; for your trading, forsooth, is extended no farther than a load of hay or a fat ox. You are pleasant people, indeed, because you are bred up to be lazy; therefore, I warrant you, industry is dishonorable.

SIR JOHN. Be not offended, sir. Let us go back to our point.

MR. SEALAND. Oh, not at all offended! But I don't love to

---

30 Contemptuous term for a citizen; i.e., a merchant.

leave any part of the account unclosed. Look you, Sir John, comparisons are odious and more particularly so on occasions of this kind when we are projecting races that are to be made out of both sides of the comparisons.

SIR JOHN. But my son, sir, is, in the eye of the world, a gentleman of merit.

MR. SEALAND. I own to you I think him so. But, Sir John, I am a man exercised and experienced in chances and disasters. I lost in my earlier years a very fine wife and with her a poor little infant; this makes me, perhaps, overcautious to preserve the second bounty of providence to me and be as careful as I can of this child. You'll pardon me; my poor girl, sir, is as valuable to me as your boasted son to you.

SIR JOHN. Why, that's one very good reason, Mr. Sealand, why I wish my son had her.

MR. SEALAND. There is nothing but this strange lady here, this *incognita*, that can be objected to him. Here and there a man falls in love with an artful creature and gives up all the motives of life to that one passion.

SIR JOHN. A man of my son's understanding cannot be supposed to be one of them.

MR. SEALAND. Very wise men have been so enslaved; and when a man marries with one of them upon his hands, whether moved from the demand of the world or slighter reasons, such a husband soils[31] with his wife for a month perhaps; then, "Good b'w'y', madam!" The show's over. Ah! John Dryden points out such a husband to a hair where he says,

"And while abroad so prodigal the dolt is,
   Poor spouse at home as ragged as a colt is."[32]

Now, in plain terms, sir, I shall not care to have my poor girl turned a-grazing, and that must be the case when——

SIR JOHN. But pray consider, sir, my son——

MR. SEALAND. Look you, sir, I'll make the matter short. This unknown lady, as I told you, is all the objection I have to him. But one way or other, he is, or has

---

[31] Cohabits.
[32] From Dryden's epilogue to John Vanbrugh's *The Pilgrim*, slightly misquoted.

been, certainly engaged to her. I am therefore resolved this very afternoon to visit her. Now from her behavior or appearance I shall soon be let into what I may fear or hope for.

SIR JOHN. Sir, I am very confident there can be nothing enquired into relating to my son that will not upon being understood turn to his advantage.

MR. SEALAND. I hope that as sincerely as you believe it. Sir John Bevil, when I am satisfied in this great point, if your son's conduct answers the character you give of him, I shall wish your alliance more than that of any gentleman in Great Britain, and so your servant. (*Exit.*)

SIR JOHN. He is gone in a way but barely civil; but his great wealth and the merit of his only child, the heiress of it, are not to be lost for a little peevishness—

(*Enter* HUMPHREY.)

Oh, Humphrey, you are come in a seasonable minute. I want to talk to thee, and to tell thee that my head and heart are on the rack about my son.

HUMPHREY. Sir, you may trust his discretion; I am sure you may.

SIR JOHN. Why, I do believe I may, and yet I am in a thousand fears when I lay this vast wealth before me. When I consider his prepossessions, either generous to a folly in an honorable love or abandoned past redemption in a vicious one, and from the one or the other his insensibility to the fairest prospect towards doubling our estate—a father who knows how useful wealth is and how necessary even to those who despise it, I say a father, Humphrey, a father cannot bear it.

HUMPHREY. Be not transported, sir. You will grow incapable of taking any resolution in your perplexity.

SIR JOHN. Yet, as angry as I am with him, I would not have him surprised in anything. This mercantile rough man may go grossly into the examination of this matter and talk to the gentlewoman so as to—

HUMPHREY. No, I hope not in an abrupt manner.

SIR JOHN. No, I hope not! Why, dost thou know anything of her, or of him, or of anything of it, or of all of it?

HUMPHREY. My dear master, I know so much that I told him this very day you had reason to be secretly out of humor about her.

SIR JOHN. Did you go so far? Well, what said he to that?

HUMPHREY. His words were, looking upon me steadfastly, "Humphrey," says he, "that woman is a woman of honor."

SIR JOHN. How! Do you think he is married to her or designs to marry her?

HUMPHREY. I can say nothing to the latter; but he says he can marry no one without your consent while you are living.

SIR JOHN. If he said so much, I know he scorns to break his word with me.

HUMPHREY. I am sure of that.

SIR JOHN. You are sure of that? Well, that's some comfort. Then I have nothing to do but to see the bottom of this matter during this present ruffle[33]—Oh, Humphrey!

HUMPHREY. You are not ill, I hope, sir.

SIR JOHN. Yes, a man is very ill that's in a very ill humor. To be a father is to be in care for one whom you oftener disoblige than please by that very care. Oh, that sons could know the duty to a father before they themselves are fathers! But perhaps you'll say now that I am one of the happiest fathers in the world; but, I assure you, that of the very happiest is not a condition to be envied.

HUMPHREY. Sir, your pain arises not from the thing itself but your particular sense of it. You are overfond, nay, give me leave to say you are unjustly apprehensive from your fondness. My master Bevil never disobliged you and he will, I know he will, do everything you ought to expect.

SIR JOHN. He won't take all this money with this girl. For aught I know he will, forsooth, have so much moderation as to think he ought not to force his liking for any consideration.

HUMPHREY. He is to marry her, not you; he is to live with her, not you, sir.

SIR JOHN. I know not what to think. But I know nothing can be more miserable than to be in this doubt. Follow me; I must come to some resolution.

(*Exeunt.*)

[33] Commotion.

[SCENE III.] BEVIL, JUNIOR's *Lodgings*

(*Enter* TOM *and* PHILLIS.)

TOM. Well, madam, if you must speak with Mr. Myrtle, you shall. He is now with my master in the library.

PHILLIS. But you must leave me alone with him, for he can't make me a present nor I so handsomely take anything from him before you. It would not be decent.

TOM. It will be very decent, indeed, for me to retire and leave my mistress with another man.

PHILLIS. He is a gentleman and will treat one properly—

TOM. I believe so, but, however, I won't be far off and therefore will venture to trust you. I'll call him to you. (*Exit.*)

PHILLIS. What a deal of pother and sputter here is between my mistress and Mr. Myrtle from mere punctilio! I could any hour of the day get her to her lover and would do it. But she, forsooth, will allow no plot to get [to] him; but if he can come to her, I know she will be glad of it. I must, therefore, do her an acceptable violence and surprise her into his arms. I am sure I go by the best ruse imaginable. If she were my maid, I should think her the best servant in the world for doing so by me.

(*Enter* MYRTLE *and* TOM.)

Oh, sir! You and Mr. Bevil are fine gentlemen to let a lady remain under such difficulties as my poor mistress, and not attempt to set her at liberty or release her from the danger of being instantly married to Cimberton.

MYRTLE. Tom has been telling—but what is to be done?

PHILLIS. What is to be done! When a man can't come at his mistress! Why, can't you fire our house or the next house to us to make us run out and you take us?

MYRTLE. How, Mrs. Phillis—

PHILLIS. Ay! Let me see that rogue deny to fire a house, make a riot, or any other little thing when there were no other way to come at me.

TOM. I'm obliged to you, madam.

PHILLIS. Why, don't we hear every day of people's hanging themselves for love, and won't they venture the hazard of being hanged for love? Oh, were I a man—

MYRTLE. What manly thing would you have me undertake, according to your ladyship's notion of a man?

PHILLIS. Only be at once what one time or other you may be and wish to be or must be.

MYRTLE. Dear girl, talk plainly to me and consider, I in my condition can't be in very good humor. You say to be at once what I must be.

PHILLIS. Ay, ay! I mean no more than to be an old man. I saw you do it very well at the masquerade. In a word, old Sir Geoffry Cimberton is every hour expected in town to join the deeds and settlements for marrying Mr. Cimberton. He is half blind, half lame, half dumb; though as to his passions and desires, he is as warm and ridiculous as when in the heat of youth.

TOM. Come to business and don't keep the gentleman in suspense for the pleasure of being courted as you serve me.

PHILLIS. I saw you at the masquerade act such a one to perfection. Go and put on that very habit and come to our house as Sir Geoffry. There is not one there but myself knows his person. I was born in the parish where he is lord of the manor. I have seen him often and often at church in the country. Do not hesitate, but come hither. They will think you bring a certain security against Mr. Myrtle, and you bring Mr. Myrtle. Leave the rest to me. I leave this with you and expect —they don't, I told you, know you; they think you out of town, which you had as good be forever, if you lose this opportunity. I must be gone; I know I am wanted at home.

MYRTLE. My dear Phillis! (*Catches and kisses her and gives her money.*)

PHILLIS. O fie! My kisses are not my own; you have committed violence; but I'll carry 'em to the right owner. (*Tom kisses her.*) Come, see me down stairs (*To* TOM) and leave the lover to think of his last game for the prize.

(*Exeunt* TOM *and* PHILLIS.)

MYRTLE. I think I will instantly attempt this wild expedient. The extravagance of it will make me less suspected and it will give me opportunity to assert my own right to Lucinda, without whom I cannot live. But I am so mortified at this conduct of mine towards poor

Bevil. He must think meanly of me. I know not how to reassume myself and be in spirit enough for such an adventure as this. Yet I must attempt it if it be only to be near Lucinda under her perplexities; and sure

> The next delight to transport with the fair,
> Is to relieve her in her hours of care.

(*Exit.*)

ACT V

[SCENE I.] SEALAND's *House*

(*Enter* PHILLIS *with lights, before* MYRTLE *disguised like old* SIR GEOFFRY, *supported by* MRS. SEALAND, LUCINDA, *and* CIMBERTON.)

MRS. SEALAND. Now I have seen you thus far, Sir Geoffry, will you excuse me a moment while I give my necessary orders for your accommodation? (*Exit.*)

MYRTLE. I have not seen you, Cousin Cimberton, since you were ten years old; and as it is incumbent on you to keep up our name and family, I shall, upon very reasonable terms, join with you in a settlement to that purpose. Though I must tell you, cousin, this is the first merchant that has married into our house.

LUCINDA (*aside*). Deuce on 'em! Am I a merchant because my father is?

MYRTLE. But is he directly a trader at this time?

CIMBERTON. There's no hiding the disgrace, sir; he trades to all parts of the world.

MYRTLE. We never had one of our family before who descended from persons that did anything.

CIMBERTON. Sir, since it is a girl that they have, I am, for the honor of the family, willing to take it in again and to sink her into our name, and no harm done.

MYRTLE. 'Tis prudently and generously resolved. Is this the young thing?

CIMBERTON. Yes, sir.

PHILLIS [*aside*]. Good madam, don't be out of humor, but let them run to the utmost of their extravagance. Hear them out.

MYRTLE. Can't I see her nearer? My eyes are but weak.

PHILLIS. Beside, I am sure the uncle has something worth your notice. I'll take care to get off the young one and leave you to observe what may be wrought out of the old one for your good. (*Exit.*)

CIMBERTON. Madam, this old gentleman, your great uncle, desires to be introduced to you and to see you nearer. —Approach, sir!

MYRTLE. By your leave, young lady—(*Puts on spectacles.*) Cousin Cimberton, she has exactly that sort of neck and bosom for which my sister Gertrude was so much admired in the year sixty one, before the French dresses first discovered anything in women below the chin.

LUCINDA (*aside*). What a very odd situation am I in! Though I cannot but be diverted at the extravagance of their humors equally unsuitable to their age. Chin, quotha! I don't believe my passionate lover there knows whether I have one or not. Ha! Ha!

MYRTLE. Madam, I would not willingly offend, but I have a better glass—(*Pulls out a large one.*)

(*Enter* PHILLIS *to* CIMBERTON.)

PHILLIS. Sir, my lady desires to show the apartment to you that she intends for Geoffry.

CIMBERTON. Well, sir, by that time you have sufficiently gazed and sunned yourself in the beauties of my spouse there, I will wait on you again.

([*Exeunt*] CIMBERTON *and* PHILLIS.)

MYRTLE. Were it not, madam, that I might be troublesome, there is something of importance, though we are alone, which I would say more safe from being heard.

LUCINDA. There is something in this old fellow, methinks, that raises my curiosity.

MYRTLE. To be free, madam, I as heartily contemn this kinsman of mine as you do and am sorry to see so much beauty and merit devoted by your parents to so insensible a possessor.

LUCINDA. Surprising! I hope then, sir, you will not contribute to the wrong you are so generous as to pity, whatever may be the interest of your family.

MYRTLE. This hand of mine shall never be employed to sign anything against your good and happiness.

LUCINDA. I am sorry, sir, it is not in my power to make you proper acknowledgments; but there is a gentleman in the world whose gratitude will, I am sure, be worthy of the favor.

MYRTLE. All the thanks I desire, madam, are in your power to give.

LUCINDA. Name them and command them.

MYRTLE. Only, madam, that the first time you are alone with your lover you will with open arms receive him.

LUCINDA. As willingly as his heart could wish it.

MYRTLE. Thus then he claims your promise! Oh, Lucinda!

LUCINDA. Oh! A cheat! a cheat! a cheat!

MYRTLE. Hush! 'Tis I, 'tis I, your lover, Myrtle himself, madam.

LUCINDA. Oh, bless me, what a rashness and folly to surprise me so! But hush—My mother—

(*Enter* MRS. SEALAND, CIMBERTON, *and* PHILLIS.)

MRS. SEALAND. How now! What's the matter?

LUCINDA. Oh, madam, as soon as you left the room, my uncle fell into a sudden fit, and—and—so I cried out for help to support him and conduct him to his chamber.

MRS. SEALAND. That was kindly done!—Alas, sir, how do you find yourself?

MYRTLE. Never was so taken in so odd a way in my life. Pray lead me. Oh, I was talking here—pray carry me —to my cousin Cimberton's young lady—

MRS. SEALAND (*aside*). My Cousin Cimberton's young lady! How zealous he is even in his extremity for the match! A right Cimberton!

(CIMBERTON *and* LUCINDA *lead him as one in pain, &c.*)

CIMBERTON. Pox, Uncle! You will pull my ear off.

LUCINDA. Pray, uncle! You will squeeze me to death.

MRS. SEALAND. No matter, no matter! He knows not what he does.—Come, sir, shall I help you out?

MYRTLE. By no means; I'll trouble nobody but my young cousins here.

(*They lead him off.*)

PHILLIS. But pray, madam, does your ladyship intend that
Mr. Cimberton shall really marry my young mistress
at last? I don't think he likes her.

MRS. SEALAND. That's not material! Men of his speculation are above desires, but be it as it may. Now I
have given old Sir Geoffry the trouble of coming up
to sign and seal, with what countenance can I be off?

PHILLIS. As well as with twenty others, madam. It is the
glory and honor of a great fortune to live in continual
treaties and still to break off. It looks great, madam.

MRS. SEALAND. True, Phillis. Yet to return our blood again
into the Cimbertons' is an honor not to be rejected.
But were you not saying that Sir John Bevil's creature,
Humphrey, has been with Mr. Sealand?

PHILLIS. Yes, madam. I overheard them agree that Mr.
Sealand should go himself and visit the unknown lady
that Mr. Bevil is so great with; and if he found nothing
there to fright him, that Mr. Bevil should still marry
my young mistress.

MRS. SEALAND. How! Nay, then, he shall find she is my
daughter as well as his. I'll follow him this instant and
take the whole family along with me. The disputed
power of disposing of my own daughter shall be at an
end this very night. I'll live no longer in anxiety for a
little hussy that hurts my appearance wherever I
carry her and for whose sake I seem to be not at all
regarded, and that in the best of my days.

PHILLIS. Indeed, madam, if she were married, your ladyship might very well be taken for Mr. Sealand's
daughter.

MRS. SEALAND. Nay, when the chit has not been with me,
I have heard the men say as much. I'll no longer cut
off the greatest pleasure of a woman's life—the shining
in assemblies—by her forward anticipation of the
respect that's due to her superior. She shall down to
Cimberton Hall. She shall, she shall!

PHILLIS. I hope, madam, I shall stay with your ladyship.

MRS. SEALAND. Thou shalt, Phillis, and I'll place thee then
more about me. But order chairs immediately. I'll be
gone this minute.

(*Exeunt.*)

[SCENE II.] *Charing Cross*

(*Enter* MR. SEALAND *and* HUMPHREY.)

MR. SEALAND. I am very glad, Mr. Humphrey, that you
agree with me that it is for our common good I should
look into this matter.

HUMPHREY. I am indeed of that opinion, for there is no
artifice, nothing concealed, in our family which ought
in justice to be known. I need not desire you, sir,
to treat the lady with care and respect.

MR. SEALAND. Master Humphrey, I shall not be rude,
though I design to be a little abrupt and come into
the matter at once to see how she will bear upon a
surprise.

HUMPHREY. That's the door, sir. I wish you success.
(*While* HUMPHREY *speaks* [*aside*], SEALAND *consults his
table-book*)[34] I am less concerned what happens there
because I hear Mr. Myrtle is well lodged as old Sir
Geoffry; so I am willing to let this gentleman employ
himself here to give them time at home, for I am
sure 'tis necessary for the quiet of our family Lucinda
were well disposed of out of it, since Mr. Bevil's
inclination is so much otherwise engaged. (*Exit.*)

MR. SEALAND. I think this is the door. (*Knocks.*) I'll carry
this matter with an air of authority to enquire, though
I make an errand to begin discourse.

(*Knocks again, and enter a* FOOT-BOY.)

So, young man! Is your lady within?

BOY. Alack, sir, I am but a country boy. I don't know
whether she is or noa; but an you'll stay a bit, I'll goa
and ask the gentlewoman that's with her.

MR. SEALAND. Why, sirrah, though you are a country boy,
you can see, can't you? You know whether she is at
home when you see her, don't you?

BOY. Nay, nay, I'm not such a country lad neither, master,
to think she's at home because I see her. I have been
in town but a month and I lost one place already for
believing my own eyes.

MR. SEALAND. Why, sirrah, have you learnt to lie already?

BOY. Ah, master, things that are lies in the country are not

34 Memorandum book.

lies at London. I begin to know my business a little better than so. But an you please to walk in, I'll call a gentlewoman to you that can tell you for certain. She can make bold to ask my lady herself.

MR. SEALAND. Oh, then, she is within, I find, though you dare not say so.

BOY. Nay, nay! That's neither here nor there. What matter whether she is within or no, if she has not a mind to see anybody.

MR. SEALAND. I can't tell, sirrah, whether you are arch or simple, but however, get me a direct answer, and here's a shilling for you.

BOY. Will you please to walk in? I'll see what I can do for you.

MR. SEALAND. I see you will be fit for your business in time, child. But I expect to meet with nothing but extraordinaries in such a house.

BOY. Such a house! Sir, you han't seen it yet. Pray walk in.

MR. SEALAND. Sir, I'll wait upon you.

(*Exeunt.*)

[SCENE III.] *Indiana's House*

(*Enter* ISABELLA.)

ISABELLA. What anxiety do I feel for this poor creature! What will be the end of her? Such a languishing unreserved passion for a man that at last must certainly leave or ruin her! And perhaps both! Then the aggravation of the distress is that she does not believe he will—not but I must own if they are both what they would seem they are made for one another as much as Adam and Eve were, for there is no other of their kind but themselves.

(*Enter* BOY.)

So, Daniel! What news with you?

BOY. Madam, there's a gentleman below would speak with my lady.

ISABELLA. Sirrah, don't you know Mr. Bevil yet?

BOY. Madam, 'tis not the gentleman who comes every day and asks for you and won't go in till he knows whether you are with her or no.

ISABELLA. Ha! That's a particular I did not know before.—
Well, be it who it will, let him come up to me.

(*Exit* BOY, *and re-enters with* MR. SEALAND. ISABELLA
looks amazed.)

MR. SEALAND. Madam, I can't blame your being a little
surprised to see a perfect stranger make a visit and—

ISABELLA. I am indeed surprised!—[*aside*] I see he does not
know me.

MR. SEALAND. You are very prettily lodged here, madam;
in troth, you seem to have everything in plenty.—
(*aside and looking about*) A thousand a year, I
warrant you, upon this pretty nest of rooms and the
dainty one within them.

ISABELLA (*apart*). Twenty years, it seems, have less effect
in the alteration of a man of thirty than a girl of fourteen. He's almost still the same; but, alas, I find by
other men as well as himself I am not what I was.
As soon as he spoke I was convinced 'twas he. How
shall I contain my surprise and satisfaction? He must
not know me yet.

MR. SEALAND. Madam, I hope I don't give you any disturbance, but there's a young lady here with whom
I have a particular business to discourse, and I hope
she will admit me to that favor.

ISABELLA. Why, sir, have you had any notice concerning
her? I wonder who could give it you.

MR. SEALAND. That, madam, is fit only to be communicated to herself.

ISABELLA. Well, sir, you shall see her.—[*aside*] I find he
knows nothing as yet, nor shall he from me. I am
resolved I will observe this interlude, this sport of
nature and of fortune.—You shall see her presently,
sir, for now I am as a mother and will trust her with
you. (*Exit.*)

MR. SEALAND. As a mother! Right. That's the old phrase
for one of those commode[35] ladies, who lend out
beauty for hire to young gentlemen that have pressing
occasions. But here comes the precious lady herself.
In troth, a very fine sightly woman—

(*Enter* INDIANA.)

[35] Accommodating.

INDIANA. I am told, sir, you have some affair that requires your speaking with me.

MR. SEALAND. Yes, madam. There came into my hands a bill drawn by Mr. Bevil, which is payable tomorrow; and he in the intercourse of business sent it to me, who have cash of his, and desired me to send a servant with it; but I have made bold to bring you the money myself.

INDIANA. Sir! Was that necessary?

MR. SEALAND. No, madam; but, to be free with you, the fame of your beauty and the regard which Mr. Bevil is a little too well known to have for you excited my curiosity.

INDIANA. Too well known to have for me! Your sober appearance, sir, which my friend described, made me expect no rudeness, or absurdity at least.—Who's there?—Sir, if you pay the money to a servant 'twill be as well.

MR. SEALAND. Pray, madam, be not offended. I came hither on an innocent, nay a virtuous, design; and if you will have patience to hear me it may be as useful to you, as you are in friendship with Mr. Bevil, as to my only daughter, whom I was this day disposing of.

INDIANA. You make me hope, sir, I have mistaken you. I am composed again. Be free, say on—(*aside*) what I am afraid to hear.

MR. SEALAND. I feared, indeed, an unwarranted passion here, but I did not think it was in abuse of so worthy an object, so accomplished a lady as your sense and mine bespeak. But the youth of our age care not what merit and virtue they bring to shame so they gratify—

INDIANA. Sir! You are going into very great errors; but as you are pleased to say you see something in me that has changed at least the color of your suspicions, so has your appearance altered mine; and made me earnestly attentive to what has any way concerned you to enquire into my affairs and character.

MR. SEALAND [*aside*]. How sensibly, with what an air she talks!

INDIANA. Good sir, be seated and tell me tenderly. Keep all your suspicions concerning me alive, that you may in a proper and prepared way acquaint me why the care of your daughter obliges a person of your seeming worth and fortune to be thus inquisitive about a

wretched, helpless, friendless—(*weeping*) But I beg
your pardon. Though I am an orphan, your child is
not; and your concern for her, it seems, has brought
you hither. I'll be composed. Pray go on, sir.

MR. SEALAND. How could Mr. Bevil be such a monster to
injure such a woman?

INDIANA. Sir, you wrong him. He has not injured me. My
support is from his bounty.

MR. SEALAND. Bounty! When gluttons give high prices for
delicates, they are prodigious bountiful!

INDIANA. Still, still you will persist in that error. But my
own fears tell me all. You are the gentleman, I suppose, for whose happy daughter he is designed a
husband by his good father; and he has perhaps
consented to the overture. He was here this morning
dressed beyond his usual plainness, nay, most sump-
tuously, and he is to be, perhaps, this night a
bridegroom.

MR. SEALAND. I own he was intended such. But, madam,
on your account, I have determined to defer my
daughter's marriage till I am satisfied from your own
mouth of what nature are the obligations you are
under to him.

INDIANA. His actions, sir, his eyes, have only made me
think he designed to make me the partner of his heart.
The goodness and gentleness of his demeanor made
me misinterpret all. 'Twas my own hope, my own
passion, that deluded me. He never made one amorous
advance to me. His large heart and bestowing hand
have only helped the miserable. Nor know I why, but
from his mere delight in virtue, that I have been his
care, the object on which to indulge and please himself with pouring favors.

MR. SEALAND. Madam, I know not why it is, but I, as well
as you, am, methinks, afraid of entering into the
matter I came about; but 'tis the same thing as if we
had talked never so distinctly. He ne'er shall have a
daughter of mine.

INDIANA. If you say this from what you think of me, you
wrong yourself and him. Let not me, miserable though
I may be, do injury to my benefactor. No, sir, my
treatment ought rather to reconcile you to his virtues.
If to bestow without a prospect of return, if to delight
in supporting what might perhaps be thought an object

of desire with no other view than to be her guard against those who would not be so disinterested—if these actions, sir, can in a careful parent's eye commend him to a daughter, give yours, sir, give her to my honest, generous Bevil. What have I to do but sigh and weep, to rave, run wild, a lunatic in chains or hid in darkness, mutter in distracted starts and broken accents my strange, strange story!

MR. SEALAND. Take comfort, madam.

INDIANA. All my comfort must be to expostulate in madness, to relieve with frenzy my despair, and shrieking to demand of fate why—why was I born to such variety of sorrows!

MR. SEALAND. If I have been the least occasion—

INDIANA. No! 'Twas heaven's high will I should be such. To be plundered in my cradle! Tossed on the seas and even there an infant captive! To lose my mother, hear but of my father! To be adopted, lose my adopter; then plunged again in worse calamities!

MR. SEALAND. An infant captive!

INDIANA. Yet then, to find the most charming of mankind, once more to set me free from what I thought the last distress, to load me with his services, his bounties, and his favors, to support my very life in a way that stole at the same time my soul itself from me.

MR. SEALAND. And has young Bevil been this worthy man?

INDIANA. Yet then again, this very man to take another. Without leaving me the right, the pretense of easing my fond heart with tears! For, oh, I can't reproach him, though the same hand that raised me to this height, now throws me down the precipice.

MR. SEALAND. Dear lady! Oh, yet one moment's patience. My heart grows full with your affliction. But yet there's something in your story that—

INDIANA. My portion here is bitterness and sorrow.

MR. SEALAND. Do not think so. Pray answer me. Does Bevil know your name and family?

INDIANA. Alas, too well! Oh, could I be any other thing than what I am! I'll tear away all traces of my former self, my little ornaments, the remains of my first state, the hints of what I ought to have been—

(*In her disorder she throws away a bracelet, which* SEALAND *takes up and looks earnestly on it.*)

MR. SEALAND. Ha! What's this? My eyes are not deceived.
It is, it is the same. The very bracelet which I be-
queathed my wife at our last mournful parting.

INDIANA. What said you, sir! Your wife! Whither does my
fancy carry me? What means this unfelt motion at my
heart? And yet again my fortune but deludes me, for
if I err not, sir, your name is Sealand but my lost
father's name was—

MR. SEALAND. Danvers, was it not?

INDIANA. What new amazement! That is indeed my family.

MR. SEALAND. Know then, when my misfortunes drove me
to the Indies, for reasons too tedious now to mention,
I changed my name of Danvers into Sealand.

(*Enter* ISABELLA.)

ISABELLA. If yet there wants an explanation of your
wonder, examine well this face. Yours, sir, I well
remember. Gaze on and read in me your sister
Isabella.

MR. SEALAND. My sister!

ISABELLA. But here's a claim more tender yet—your
Indiana, sir, your long lost daughter.

MR. SEALAND. Oh, my child, my child!

INDIANA. All-gracious heaven! Is it possible? Do I embrace
my father!

MR. SEALAND. And do I hold thee—These passions are too
strong for utterance. Rise, rise, my child, and give
my tears their way.—Oh, my sister! (*embracing her*)

ISABELLA. Now, dearest niece, my groundless fears, my
painful cares no more shall vex thee. If I have wronged
thy noble lover with too hard suspicions, my just
concern for thee I hope will plead my pardon.

MR. SEALAND. Oh, make him then the full amends and be
yourself the messenger of joy. Fly this instant! Tell
him all these wondrous turns of providence in his
favor. Tell him I have now a daughter to bestow
which he no longer will decline, that this day he still
shall be a bridegroom; nor shall a fortune, the merit
which his father seeks, be wanting. Tell him the
reward for all his virtues waits on his acceptance.

(*Exit* ISABELLA.)

My dearest Indiana! (*Turns and embraces her.*)

INDIANA. Have I then at last a father's sanction on my

love! His bounteous hand to give and make my heart
a present worthy of Bevil's generosity.

MR. SEALAND. Oh, my child, how are our sorrows past
o'erpaid by such a meeting! Though I have lost so
many years of soft paternal dalliance with thee, yet,
in one day, to find thee thus and thus bestow thee in
such perfect happiness is ample, ample reparation!
And yet again the merit of thy lover!

INDIANA. Oh, had I spirit left to tell you of his actions!
How strongly filial duty has suppressed his love, and
how concealment still has doubled all his obligations!
The pride, the joy of this alliance, sir, would warm
your heart as he has conquered mine.

MR. SEALAND. How laudable is love when born of virtue!
I burn to embrace him—

INDIANA. See, sir, my aunt already has succeeded and
brought him to your wishes.

(*Enter* ISABELLA *with* SIR JOHN BEVIL, BEVIL, JUNIOR,
MRS. SEALAND, CIMBERTON, MYRTLE, *and* LUCINDA.)

SIR JOHN (*entering*). Where, where's this scene of wonder?
—Mr. Sealand, I congratulate, on this occasion, our
mutual happiness. Your good sister, sir, has with the
story of your daughter's fortune filled us with surprise
and joy! Now all exceptions are removed; my son has
now avowed his love and turned all former jealousies
and doubts to approbation; and, I am told, your goodness has consented to reward him.

MR. SEALAND. If, sir, a fortune equal to his father's hopes
can make this object worthy his acceptance.

BEVIL. I hear your mention, sir, of fortune with pleasure
only as it may prove the means to reconcile the best
of fathers to my love. Let him be provident, but let me
be happy! My ever-destined, my acknowledged wife!
(*embracing* INDIANA)

INDIANA. Wife! Oh, my ever loved! My lord, my master!

SIR JOHN. I congratulate myself as well as you that I had
a son who could under such disadvantages discover
your great merit.

MR. SEALAND. Oh, Sir John, how vain, how weak is human
prudence! What care, what foresight, what imagination could contrive such blest events to make our
children happy as Providence in one short hour has
laid before us!

CIMBERTON (*To* MRS. SEALAND). I am afraid, madam, Mr. Sealand is a little too busy for our affair. If you please, we'll take another opportunity.

MRS. SEALAND. Let us have patience, sir.

CIMBERTON. But we make Sir Geoffry wait, madam.

MYRTLE. Oh, sir, I am not in haste.

(*During this,* BEVIL *presents* LUCINDA *to* INDIANA)

MR. SEALAND. But here, here's our general benefactor! Excellent young man that could be at once a lover to her beauty and a parent to her virtue!

BEVIL. If you think that an obligation, sir, give me leave to overpay myself in the only instance that can now add to my felicity by begging you to bestow this lady on Mr. Myrtle.

MR. SEALAND. She is his without reserve. I beg he may be sent for. Mr. Cimberton, notwithstanding you never had my consent, yet there is since I last saw you another objection to your marriage with my daughter.

CIMBERTON. I hope, sir, your lady has concealed nothing from me?

MR. SEALAND. Troth, sir, nothing but what was concealed from myself, another daughter who has an undoubted title to half my estate.

CIMBERTON. How, Mr. Sealand! Why then, if half Mrs. Lucinda's fortune is gone, you can't say that any of my estate is settled upon her. I was in treaty for the whole, but if that is not to be come at, to be sure there can be no bargain. Sir, I have nothing to do but to take my leave of your good lady, my cousin, and beg pardon for the trouble I have given this old gentleman.

MYRTLE. That you have, Mr. Cimberton, with all my heart. (*Discovers himself.*)

OMNES. Mr. Myrtle!

MYRTLE. And I beg pardon of the whole company that I assumed the person of Sir Geoffry only to be present at the danger of this lady's being disposed of, and in her utmost exigence to assert my right to her, which if her parents will ratify, as they once favored my pretensions, no abatement of fortune shall lessen her value to me.

LUCINDA. Generous man!

MR. SEALAND. If, sir, you can overlook the injury of being

in treaty with one who as meanly left her as you have
generously asserted your right in her, she is yours.

LUCINDA. Mr. Myrtle, though you have ever had my heart,
yet now I find I love you more because I bring you
less.

MYRTLE. We have much more than we want, and I am glad
any event has contributed to the discovery of our real
inclinations to each other.

MRS. SEALAND (*aside*). Well! However, I'm glad the girl's
disposed of any way.

BEVIL. Myrtle, no longer rivals now but brothers!

MYRTLE. Dear Bevil, you are born to triumph over me!
But now our competition ceases. I rejoice in the preëminence of your virtue, and your alliance adds
charms to Lucinda.

SIR JOHN. Now ladies and gentlemen, you have set the
world a fair example. Your happiness is owing to
your constancy and merit, and the several difficulties
you have struggled with evidently show,

> Whate'er the generous mind itself denies,
> The secret care of Providence supplies.

(*Exeunt.*)

EPILOGUE
By Mr. Welsted
Intended to be spoken by Indiana

Our author, whom entreaties cannot move,
Spite of the dear coquetry that you love,
Swears he'll not frustrate (so he plainly means)
By a loose epilogue, his decent scenes.
Is it not, sirs, hard fate I meet to-day
To keep me rigid still beyond the play?
And yet I'm saved a world of pains that way.
I now can look, I now can move at ease,
Nor need I torture these poor limbs to please,
Nor with the hand or foot attempt surprise,
Nor wrest my features, nor fatigue my eyes.
Bless me! What freakish gambols have I played!
What motions tried and wanton looks betrayed,
Out of pure kindness all to overrule
The threatened hiss, and screen some scribbling fool!
With more respect I'm entertained tonight.
Our author thinks I can with ease delight;
My artless looks while modest graces arm,
He says I need but to appear and charm.
A wife so formed, by these examples bred,
Pours joy and gladness round the marriage bed.
Soft source of comfort, kind relief from care,
And 'tis her least perfection to be fair.
The nymph with Indiana's worth who vies
A nation will behold with Bevil's eyes.

THE BEGGAR'S OPERA
⟡ 1728 ⟡

John Gay

INTRODUCTORY NOTE

JOHN GAY (1685–1732), born in Devonshire, went to London as a mercer's apprentice, but soon became a writer of poems and plays and a friend of the great Tory wits Alexander Pope and Jonathan Swift. A charming, child-like man, he always found someone to look after him— first his writer friends and in later life the Duke and Duchess of Queensberry.

Though he may have derived the germinal idea for *The Beggar's Opera* (1728) from Swift, the work is alto-gether characteristic of Gay in its blend of burlesque and poetic beauty, of ridicule and affection for its subject. In *The Shepherd's Week* (1714) he exposed the absurdity of applying elegant pastoral conventions to realistic yokels, yet at the same time conveyed the appeal of country life. In his mock georgic *Trivia* (1716) he contrasted the squalid reality of London with the idealized country life of Virgil's *Georgics*, yet at the same time showed the vitality and excitement·of the city. Similarly, although the ruffians and whores of *The Beggar's Opera* are realistically drawn, they are not destroyed by the debased heroism of their presenta-tion. Macheath is genuinely dashing, and Polly charming.

Of course, Gay's satire is directed not primarily against these lower-class characters, but against the supposedly more respectable groups they resemble. Peachum and Lockit are not only methodical businessmen who exploit the labor and risk of their employees, but political leaders who thrive in a corrupt society which has lost its traditional values. As such, they represent Sir Robert Walpole, the able but dishonest Whig Prime Minister, and Charles, Vis-count Townshend, his associate and brother-in-law.

Artistically, Gay's play satirizes the Italian opera, a highly artificial form which seemed to be displacing native English drama. The early operas featured noble heroes spouting high-flown sentiments, absurd melodramatic plots, trite imagery, and a general sacrifice of sense to sound. At the same time, Gay satirizes English sentimental drama in his improbable happy ending and his two romantic heroines, so absurdly oblivious to the sordid self-interest of the world around them.

Needing a musical form in order to satirize opera, Gay devised the ballad opera, in which he fitted new words to familiar tunes. He used folk and popular songs and even a march from George Frederick Handel's opera *Rinaldo*, taking two thirds of his songs from Thomas D'Urfey's collection, *Pills to Purge Melancholy* (final edition, 1719–1720). Thus the original audience could compare Gay's new words with the traditional ones, getting a variety of comic and ironic effects. For example, Macheath's sentimental "When the heart of a man is depressed with cares" is set to the tune of the bawdy popular song "Would ye have a young virgin of fifteen years?"

Gay's play was so original that the manager of Drury Lane refused it, and even John Rich of Lincoln's Inn Fields hesitated about producing it. But once Polly had sung "O ponder well!" the audience was enraptured. The play went on to unprecedented success, with sixty-two performances in five months. According to a contemporary *bon mot*, it "made Gay rich, and Rich gay."

BIBLIOGRAPHY

~ ❧ ~

Major Works:

The Mohocks, 1712 (farce)
The Shepherd's Week, 1714 (mock pastoral)
The What d'ye Call It, 1715 (farce)
Trivia, 1716 (mock georgic)
Three Hours After Marriage, 1717 (farce, with Pope and John Arbuthnot)
Poems on Several Occasions, 1720
The Captives, 1724 (tragedy)
Fables, 1727
The Beggar's Opera, 1728 (ballad opera)
Polly, 1729 (inferior sequel to *The Beggar's Opera*)
Acis and Galatea, 1732 (pastoral opera, with music by Handel)
Achilles, 1733 (ballad opera)
Fables, Volume II, 1738

Edition:

Poetry and Prose. Ed. V. A. Dearing and C. E. Beckwith. Oxford: Clarendon, 1974. 2 volumes.

Works About:

Armens, Sven M. *John Gay, Social Critic*. New York: King's Crown Press, 1954.
Bronson, Bertrand H. "The Beggar's Opera," *Studies in the Comic: University of California Publications in English, VIII*, 2 (1941), 197–231.
Donaldson, Ian. " 'A Double Capacity': *The Beggar's Opera*," *The World Upside Down: Comedy from*

Jonson to Fielding. Oxford: Clarendon, 1970, pp. 159–82.

Empson, William. "*The Beggar's Opera*: Mock-Pastoral as the Cult of Independence," *Some Versions of Pastoral*. Norfolk, Conn.: New Directions, 1960, pp. 185–240.

Irving, William Henry. *John Gay, Favorite of the Wits*. Durham, N. C.: Duke University Press, 1940.

Spacks, Patricia Meyer. *John Gay*. New York: Twayne, 1965.

THE BEGGAR'S OPERA

Dramatis Personae[1]

MEN

PEACHUM
LOCKIT
MACHEATH
FILCH
JEREMY TWITCHER
CROOK-FINGERED JACK
WAT DREARY
ROBIN OF BAGSHOT
NIMMING NED
HARRY PADINGTON
MATT OF THE MINT
BEN BUDGE
BEGGAR
PLAYER

Macheath's gang

WOMEN

MRS. PEACHUM
POLLY PEACHUM
LUCY LOCKIT
DIANA TRAPES

[1] Almost all the names are symbolic, many coming from contemporary thieves' slang. *Peach* meant to inform against, and *nim* to steal; Macheath is "son of the heath" because the open heaths surrounding London were favorite haunts of highwaymen; a *twitcher* was a pickpocket, and a *budge* a sneak thief; Bagshot was a heath near London, Paddington the location of the gallows at Tyburn, and the Mint a sanctuary for debtors and criminals. *Trapes* and *slammekin* mean slattern; *trull* and *doxy*, prostitute; and *diver*, pickpocket.

MRS. COAXER
DOLLY TRULL
MRS. VIXEN
BETTY DOXY
JENNY DIVER
MRS. SLAMMEKIN
SUKY TAWDRY
MOLLY BRAZEN
} *Women of
the town*

Constables, drawers, turnkey, etc.

INTRODUCTION
Beggar, Player

BEGGAR. If poverty be a title to poetry, I am sure nobody
can dispute mine. I own myself of the company of
beggars, and I make one at their weekly festivals at
St. Giles's.[2] I have a small yearly salary for my
catches[3] and am welcome to a dinner there whenever
I please, which is more than most poets can say.

PLAYER. As we live by the Muses, 'tis but gratitude in us
to encourage poetical merit wherever we find it. The
Muses, contrary to all other ladies, pay no distinction
to dress, and never partially mistake the pertness of
embroidery for wit, nor the modesty of want for dulness. Be the author who he will, we push his play as
far as it will go. So (though you are in want) I wish
you success heartily.

BEGGAR. This piece, I own, was originally writ for the celebrating the marriage of James Chanter and Moll Lay,
two most excellent ballad-singers. I have introduced
the similes that are in your celebrated operas: the
Swallow, the Moth, the Bee, the Ship, the Flower,
etc. Besides, I have a prison-scene, which the ladies
always reckon charmingly pathetic. As to the parts,
I have observed such a nice impartiality to our two
ladies, that it is impossible for either of them to take
offence.[4] I hope I may be forgiven, that I have not
made my opera throughout unnatural, like those in

2 A notorious haunt of thieves and beggars.
3 Songs.
4 Gay alludes to the public feud between the two leading prima
donnas, Faustina Bordoni and Francesca Cuzzoni, whose rivalry
mounted to hair pulling on stage during Bononcini's *Astyanax*
(1727). Handel's *Alessandro* (1726) was actually written with a
view to provide the two with arias equal in number and showiness.

vogue; for I have no recitative; excepting this, as I have consented to have neither prologue nor epilogue, it must be allowed an opera in all its forms. The piece indeed hath been heretofore frequently represented by ourselves in our great room at St. Giles's, so that I cannot too often acknowledge your charity in bringing it now on the stage.

PLAYER. But I see 'tis time for us to withdraw; the actors are preparing to begin. Play away the overture.

(*Exeunt.*)

ACT I

[SCENE I.] PEACHUM's *house*

(PEACHUM *sitting at a table with a large book of accounts before him.*)

AIR I—*An old woman clothed in gray, etc.*

Through all the employments of life,
　Each neighbor abuses his brother;
Whore and rogue they call husband and wife:
　All professions be-rogue one another.
The priest calls the lawyer a cheat,
　The lawyer be-knaves the divine;
And the statesman, because he's so great,
　Thinks his trade as honest as mine.

A lawyer is an honest employment; so is mine. Like me, too, he acts in a double capacity, both against rogues and for 'em; for 'tis but fitting that we should protect and encourage cheats, since we live by them.

[SCENE II.]

(PEACHUM, FILCH.)

FILCH. Sir, Black Moll hath sent word her trial comes on in the afternoon, and she hopes you will order matters so as to bring her off.

PEACHUM. Why, she may plead her belly at worst;[5] to my knowledge she hath taken care of that security. But as the wench is very active and industrious, you may satisfy her that I'll soften the evidence.

---

[5] Pregnant women were not hanged.

FILCH. Tom Gagg, sir, is found guilty.

PEACHUM. A lazy dog! When I took him the time before, I told him what he would come to if he did not mend his hand. This is death without reprieve. I may venture to book him. (*Writes*) For Tom Gagg, forty pounds.[6] Let Betty Sly know that I'll save her from transportation,[7] for I can get more by her staying in England.

FILCH. Betty hath brought more goods into our lock[8] to-year, than any five of the gang; and in truth, 'tis a pity to lose so good a customer.

PEACHUM. If none of the gang take her off,[9] she may, in the common course of business, live a twelve-month longer. I love to let women 'scape. A good sportsman always lets the hen partridges fly, because the breed of the game depends upon them. Besides, here the law allows us no reward; there is nothing to be got by the death of women—except our wives.

FILCH. Without dispute, she is a fine woman! 'Twas to her I was obliged for my education, and (to say a bold word) she hath trained up more young fellows to the business than the gaming-table.

PEACHUM. Truly, Filch, thy observation is right. We and the surgeons are more beholden to women than all the professions besides.

FILCH.

AIR II—*The bonny gray-eyed morn, etc.*

'Tis woman that seduces all mankind,
  By her we first were taught the wheedling arts;
Her very eyes can cheat; when most she's kind,
  She tricks us of our money with our hearts.
For her, like wolves by night we roam for prey,
  And practise ev'ry fraud to bribe her charms;
For suits of love, like law, are won by pay,
  And beauty must be fee'd into our arms.

---

[6] People who turned in criminals received a reward. Cf. II, x.
[7] Convicted criminals were often sent to forced labor in the colonies or "plantations" (p. 214). This is the fate that Polly envisions in her duet with Macheath "Over the hills and far away."
[8] Warehouse for stolen goods.
[9] Betray her to the authorities.

PEACHUM. But make haste to Newgate,[10] boy, and let my
friends know what I intend; for I love to make them
easy one way or other.

FILCH. When a gentleman is long kept in suspense, penitence may break his spirit ever after. Besides, certainty
gives a man a good air upon his trial, and makes him
risk another without fear or scruple. But I'll away, for
'tis a pleasure to be the messenger of comfort to
friends in affliction. (*Exit*.)

[SCENE III.]

(PEACHUM.)

PEACHUM. But 'tis now high time to look about me for a
decent execution against next sessions.[11] I hate a
lazy rogue, by whom one can get nothing till he is
hanged. A register of the gang: (*Reading*) "Crook-
fingered Jack. A year and a half in the service." Let
me see how much the stock owes to his industry; one,
two, three, four, five gold watches, and seven silver
ones.—A mighty clean-handed fellow!—Sixteen snuff-
boxes, five of them of true gold. Six dozen of handkerchiefs, four silver-hilted swords, half a dozen of
shirts, three tie-periwigs, and a piece of broadcloth.—
Considering these are only the fruits of his leisure
hours, I don't know a prettier fellow, for no man alive
hath a more engaging presence of mind upon the road.
"Wat Dreary, alias Brown Will"—an irregular dog,
who hath an underhand way of disposing of his goods.
I'll try him only for a sessions or two longer upon his
good behavior. "Harry Padington"—a poor petty-
larceny rascal, without the least genius; that fellow,
though he were to live these six months, will never
come to the gallows with any credit. "Slippery Sam"—
he goes off the next sessions, for the villain hath the
impudence to have views of following his trade as a
tailor, which he calls an honest employment. "Matt
of the Mint"—listed[12] not above a month ago, a

10 The chief prison of London, adjacent to the Old Bailey, the main
criminal court.
11 The next session of the criminal court, held eight times each year
at the Old Bailey.
12 Enlisted in the gang.

promising sturdy fellow, and diligent in his way: somewhat too bold and hasty, and may raise good contributions on the public, if he does not cut himself short by murder. "Tom Tipple"—a guzzling, soaking sot, who is always too drunk to stand himself, or to make others stand. A cart is absolutely necessary for him. "Robin of Bagshot, alias Gorgon, alias Bob Bluff, alias Carbuncle, alias Bob Booty!—"[13]

[SCENE IV.]

(PEACHUM, MRS. PEACHUM.)

MRS. PEACHUM. What of Bob Booty, husband? I hope nothing bad hath betided him. You know, my dear, he's a favorite customer of mine. 'Twas he made me a present of this ring.

PEACHUM. I have set his name down in the black list, that's all, my dear; he spends his life among women, and as soon as his money is gone, one or other of the ladies will hang him for the reward, and there's forty pound lost to us forever.

MRS. PEACHUM. You know, my dear, I never meddle in matters of death; I always leave those affairs to you. Women indeed are bitter bad judges in these cases, for they are so partial to the brave that they think every man handsome who is going to the camp or the gallows.

AIR III—*Cold and raw, etc.*

If any wench Venus's girdle wear,
    Though she be never so ugly;
Lilies and roses will quickly appear,
    And her face look wond'rous smugly.
Beneath the left ear so fit but a cord,
    (A rope so charming a zone is!)
The youth in his cart hath the air of a lord,
    And we cry, There dies an Adonis!

But really, husband, you should not be too hard-hearted, for you never had a finer, braver set of men than at present. We have not had a murder among

---

[13] The highwayman Robin of Bagshot is used to satirize Walpole, as are Peachum and Macheath. The aliases hit at Walpole's rough manners, drinking, and alleged plundering of the public.

them all, these seven months. And truly, my dear, that
is a great blessing.

PEACHUM. What a dickens is the woman always a-
whimp'ring about murder for? No gentleman is ever
looked upon the worse for killing a man in his own
defence; and if business cannot be carried on without
it, what would you have a gentleman do?

MRS. PEACHUM. If I am in the wrong, my dear, you must
excuse me, for nobody can help the frailty of an over-
scrupulous conscience.

PEACHUM. Murder is as fashionable a crime as a man can
be guilty of. How many fine gentlemen have we in
Newgate every year, purely upon that article! If they
have wherewithal to persuade the jury to bring it in
manslaughter, what are they the worse for it? So,
my dear, have done upon this subject. Was Captain
Macheath here this morning, for the bank-notes[14] he
left with you last week?

MRS. PEACHUM. Yes, my dear; and though the bank hath
stopped payment, he was so cheerful and so agreeable!
Sure there is not a finer gentleman upon the road than
the captain! If he comes from Bagshot at any reasonable hour he hath promised to make one with Polly
and me, and Bob Booty, at a party of quadrille. Pray,
my dear, is the captain rich?

PEACHUM. The captain keeps too good company ever to
grow rich. Marybone and the chocolate houses[15] are
his undoing. The man that proposes to get money by
play should have the education of a fine gentleman,
and be trained up to it from his youth.

MRS. PEACHUM. Really, I am sorry upon Polly's account
the captain hath not more discretion. What business
hath he to keep company with lords and gentlemen?
he should leave them to prey upon one another.

PEACHUM. Upon Polly's account! What, a plague, does the
woman mean?—Upon Polly's account!

MRS. PEACHUM. Captain Macheath is very fond of the girl.

PEACHUM. And what then?

---

14 Bank notes, or bank bills, similar to cashier's checks today, were
made payable to the bearer; and therefore thieves could cash them
if they got to the bank before stop-payment notice was sent.
15 Marylebone was the center for gambling on the game of bowling;
the chocolate houses, for gambling with cards and dice.

MRS. PEACHUM. If I have any skill in the ways of women, I am sure Polly thinks him a very pretty man.

PEACHUM. And what then? You would not be so mad to have the wench marry him! Gamesters and highwaymen are generally very good to their whores, but they are very devils to their wives.

MRS. PEACHUM. But if Polly should be in love, how should we help her, or how can she help herself? Poor girl, I am in the utmost concern about her.

AIR IV—*Why is your faithful slave disdained? etc.*

If love the virgin's heart invade,
How, like a moth, the simple maid
  Still plays about the flame!
If soon she be not made a wife,
Her honor's singed, and then, for life,
She's—what I dare not name.

PEACHUM. Look ye, wife. A handsome wench in our way of business is as profitable as at the bar of a Temple coffee-house, who looks upon it as her livelihood to grant every liberty but one. You see I would indulge the girl as far as prudently we can—in anything but marriage! After that, my dear, how shall we be safe? Are we not then in her husband's power? For a husband hath the absolute power over all a wife's secrets but her own. If the girl had the discretion of a court lady, who can have a dozen young fellows at her ear without complying with one, I should not matter it; but Polly is tinder, and a spark will at once set her on a flame. Married! If the wench does not know her own profit, sure she knows her own pleasure better than to make herself a property! My daughter to me should be, like a court lady to a minister of state, a key to the whole gang. Married! if the affair is not already done, I'll terrify her from it by the example of our neighbors.

MRS. PEACHUM. Mayhap, my dear, you may injure the girl. She loves to imitate the fine ladies, and she may only allow the captain liberties in the view of interest.

PEACHUM. But 'tis your duty, my dear, to warn the girl against her ruin, and to instruct her how to make the most of her beauty. I'll go to her this moment, and

sift her.[16] In the meantime, wife, rip out the coronets
and marks of these dozen of cambric handkerchiefs,
for I can dispose of them this afternoon to a chap[17]
in the city. (*Exit.*)

[SCENE V.]

(MRS. PEACHUM.)

MRS. PEACHUM. Never was a man more out of the way in
an argument than my husband! Why must our Polly,
forsooth, differ from her sex, and love only her
husband? And why must Polly's marriage, contrary
to all observation, make her the less followed by other
men? All men are thieves in love, and like a woman
the better for being another's property.

AIR V—*Of all the simple things we do, etc.*

A maid is like the golden ore,
    Which hath guineas intrinsical in't;
Whose worth is never known, before
    It is tried and impressed in the mint.
A wife's like a guinea in gold,
    Stamped with the name of her spouse;
Now here, now there; is bought, or is sold;
    And is current in every house.

[SCENE VI.]

(MRS. PEACHUM, FILCH.)

MRS. PEACHUM. Come hither, Filch. [*aside*] I am as fond
of this child as though my mind misgave me he were
my own. He hath as fine a hand at picking a pocket
as a woman, and is as nimble-fingered as a juggler—
If an unlucky session does not cut the rope of thy
life, I pronounce, boy, thou wilt be a great man in
history. Where was your post last night, my boy?

FILCH. I plied at the opera, madam; and considering 'twas
neither dark nor rainy, so that there was no great
hurry in getting chairs and coaches, made a tolerable
hand on't. These seven handkerchiefs, madam.

[16] Question her closely.
[17] Chapman, dealer.

MRS. PEACHUM. Colored ones, I see. They are of sure sale from our warehouse at Redriff[18] among the seamen.

FILCH. And this snuff-box.

MRS. PEACHUM. Set in gold! A pretty encouragement this to a young beginner.

FILCH. I had a fair tug at a charming gold watch. Pox take the tailors for making the fobs so deep and narrow. It stuck by the way, and I was forced to make my escape under a coach. Really, madam, I fear, I shall be cut off in the flower of my youth, so that every now and then (since I was pumped)[19] I have thoughts of taking up and going to sea.

MRS. PEACHUM. You should go to Hockley-in-the-Hole[20] and to Marybone, child, to learn valor. These are the schools that have bred so many brave men. I thought, boy, by this time, thou hadst lost fear as well as shame.—Poor lad! how little does he know as yet of the Old Bailey! For the first fact I'll insure thee from being hanged; and going to sea, Filch, will come time enough upon a sentence of transportation. But now, since you have nothing better to do, ev'n go to your book, and learn your catechism; for really a man makes but an ill figure in the ordinary's paper,[21] who cannot give a satisfactory answer to his questions. But, hark you, my lad. Don't tell me a lie; for you know I hate a liar. Do you know of anything that hath passed between Captain Macheath and our Polly?

FILCH. I beg you, madam, don't ask me; for I must either tell a lie to you or to Miss Polly—for I promised her I would not tell.

MRS. PEACHUM. But when the honor of our family is concerned—

FILCH. I shall lead a sad life with Miss Polly if ever she come to know that I told you. Besides, I would not willingly forfeit my own honor by betraying anybody.

MRS. PEACHUM. Yonder comes my husband and Polly. Come, Filch, you shall go with me into my own room,

---

[18] Rotherhithe, near the docks.
[19] Young pickpockets were often held under a pump as punishment.
[20] A tough district famous for bear gardens and cockfights.
[21] The report of the prison chaplain.

and tell me the whole story. I'll give thee a glass of a most delicious cordial that I keep for my own drinking.

(*Exeunt.*)

[SCENE VII.]

(PEACHUM, POLLY.)

POLLY. I know as well as any of the fine ladies how to make the most of myself and of my man too. A woman knows how to be mercenary, though she hath never been in a court or at an assembly. We have it in our natures, papa. If I allow Captain Macheath some trifling liberties, I have this watch and other visible marks of his favor to show for it. A girl who cannot grant some things, and refuse what is most material, will make but a poor hand of her beauty, and soon be thrown upon the common.

AIR VI—*What shall I do to show how much I love her, etc.*

Virgins are like the fair flower in its luster,
    Which in the garden enamels the ground;
Near it the bees in play flutter and cluster,
    And gaudy butterflies frolic around.
But, when once plucked, 'tis no longer alluring;
    To Covent-garden[22] 'tis sent (as yet sweet),
There fades, and shrinks, and grows past all enduring,
    Rots, stinks, and dies, and is trod under feet.

PEACHUM. You know, Polly, I am not against your toying and trifling with a customer in the way of business, or to get out a secret or so. But if I find out that you have played the fool and are married, you jade you, I'll cut your throat, hussy! Now you know my mind.

[SCENE VIII.]

(PEACHUM, POLLY, MRS. PEACHUM.)

MRS. PEACHUM (*in a very great passion*).

AIR VII—*Oh London is a fine town*

Our Polly is a sad slut! nor heeds what we taught her.
I wonder any man alive will ever rear a daughter!

22 London's flower and vegetable market and also a haunt of prostitutes.

For she must have both hoods and gowns, and hoops to
    swell her pride,
With scarfs and stays, and gloves and lace; and she will
    have men beside;
And when she's dressed with care and cost, all-tempting
    fine and gay,
As men should serve a cowcumber, she flings herself away.

You baggage, you hussy! you inconsiderate jade! Had
you been hanged, it would not have vexed me, for that
might have been your misfortune; but to do such a
mad thing by choice! The wench is married, husband.

PEACHUM. Married! The captain is a bold man, and will
risk anything for money; to be sure, he believes her a
fortune!—Do you think your mother and I should
have lived comfortably so long together, if ever we
had been married? Baggage!

MRS. PEACHUM. I knew she was always a proud slut; and
now the wench has played the fool and married because, forsooth, she would do like the gentry. Can you
support the expense of a husband, hussy, in gaming,
drinking, and whoring? Have you money enough to
carry on the daily quarrels of man and wife about
who shall squander most? There are not many husbands and wives who can bear the charges of plaguing
one another in a handsome way. If you must be married, could you introduce nobody into our family but
a highwayman? Why, thou foolish jade, thou wilt be
as ill used, and as much neglected, as if thou hadst
married a lord!

PEACHUM. Let not your anger, my dear, break through the
rules of decency, for the captain looks upon himself
in the military capacity, as a gentleman by his profession. Besides what he hath already, I know he is in
a fair way of getting, or of dying; and both these ways,
let me tell you, are most excellent chances for a wife.
—Tell me, hussy, are you ruined or no?

MRS. PEACHUM. With Polly's fortune, she might very well
have gone off to a person of distinction. Yes, that you
might, you pouting slut!

PEACHUM. What, is the wench dumb? Speak, or I'll make
you plead by squeezing out an answer from you. Are
you really bound wife to him, or are you only upon
liking? (*Pinches her.*)

POLLY (*screaming*). Oh!

MRS. PEACHUM. How the mother is to be pitied who hath handsome daughters! Locks, bolts, bars, and lectures of morality are nothing to them; they break through them all. They have as much pleasure in cheating a father and mother as in cheating at cards.

PEACHUM. Why, Polly, I shall soon know if you are married, by Macheath's keeping from our house.

POLLY.

AIR VIII—*Grim king of the ghosts, etc.*

Can love be controlled by advice?
    Will Cupid our mothers obey?
Though my heart were as frozen as ice,
    At his flame 'twould have melted away.
When he kissed me, so closely he pressed,
    'Twas so sweet that I must have complied,
So I thought it both safest and best
    To marry, for fear you should chide.

MRS. PEACHUM. Then all the hopes of our family are gone for ever and ever!

PEACHUM. And Macheath may hang his father- and mother-in-law, in hope to get into their daughter's fortune!

POLLY. I did not marry him (as 'tis the fashion) coolly and deliberately for honor or money—but I love him.

MRS. PEACHUM. Love him! Worse and worse! I thought the girl had been better bred. Oh, husband, husband! her folly makes me mad! my head swims! I'm distracted! I can't support myself—Oh! (*Faints.*)

PEACHUM. See, wench, to what a condition you have reduced your poor mother! a glass of cordial, this instant. How the poor woman takes it to heart!

(POLLY *goes out and returns with it.*)

Ah, hussy, now this is the only comfort your mother has left!

POLLY. Give her another glass, sir; my mama drinks double the quantity whenever she is out of order.— This, you see, fetches her.

MRS. PEACHUM. The girl shows such a readiness, and so much concern, that I could almost find in my heart to forgive her.

AIR IX—*O Jenny, O Jenny, where hast thou been*

> O Polly, you might have toyed and kissed;
> By keeping men off, you keep them on.

POLLY.

> But he so teased me,
> And he so pleased me,
> What I did, you must have done—

MRS. PEACHUM. Not with a highwayman. You sorry slut!

PEACHUM. A word with you, wife. 'Tis no new thing for a wench to take a man without consent of parents. You know 'tis the frailty of woman, my dear.

MRS. PEACHUM. Yes, indeed, the sex is frail. But the first time a woman is frail, she should be somewhat nice, methinks, for then or never is the time to make her fortune. After that, she hath nothing to do but to guard herself from being found out, and she may do what she pleases.

PEACHUM. Make yourself a little easy; I have a thought shall soon set all matters again to rights. Why so melancholy, Polly? Since what is done cannot be undone, we must all endeavor to make the best of it.

MRS. PEACHUM. Well, Polly, as far as one woman can forgive another, I forgive thee.—Your father is too fond of you, hussy.

POLLY. Then all my sorrows are at an end.

MRS. PEACHUM. A mighty likely speech in troth, for a wench who is just married.

POLLY.

AIR X—*Thomas, I cannot, etc.*

> I, like a ship in storms, was tossed,
>   Yet afraid to put into land;
> For seized in the port, the vessel's lost,
>   Whose treasure is contraband.
>   The waves are laid,
>   My duty's paid,
>   Oh, joy beyond expression!
>   Thus, safe ashore,
>   I ask no more,
>   My all is in my possession.

PEACHUM. I hear customers in t'other room. Go, talk with 'em, Polly; but come to us again as soon as they are gone.—But, hark ye, child, if 'tis the gentleman who was here yesterday about the repeating watch, say you believe we can't get intelligence of it till tomorrow —for I lent it to Suky Straddle, to make a figure with it to-night at a tavern in Drury Lane. If t'other gentleman calls for the silver-hilted sword, you know beetle-browed Jemmy hath it on; and he doth not come from Tunbridge till Tuesday night; so that it cannot be had till then.

(*Exit* POLLY.)

[SCENE IX.]

(PEACHUM, MRS. PEACHUM.)

PEACHUM. Dear wife, be a little pacified. Don't let your passion run away with your senses. Polly, I grant you, hath done a rash thing.

MRS. PEACHUM. If she had had only an intrigue with the fellow, why, the very best families have excused and huddled up a frailty of that sort. 'Tis marriage, hus-band, that makes it a blemish.

PEACHUM. But money, wife, is the true fuller's earth for reputations; there is not a spot or a stain but what it can take out. A rich rogue nowadays is fit company for any gentleman, and the world, my dear, hath not such a contempt for roguery as you imagine. I tell you, wife, I can make this match turn to our advantage.

MRS. PEACHUM. I am very sensible, husband, that Captain Macheath is worth money, but I am in doubt whether he hath not two or three wives already, and then if he should die in a sessions or two, Polly's dower would come into dispute.

PEACHUM. That, indeed, is a point which ought to be considered.

AIR XI—*A soldier and a sailor*

A fox may steal your hens, sir,
A whore your health and pence, sir,
Your daughter rob your chest, sir,
Your wife may steal your rest, sir,
    A thief your goods and plate.

But this is all but picking;
With rest, pence, chest, and chicken;
It ever was decreed, sir,
If lawyer's hand is fee'd, sir,
    He steals your whole estate.

The lawyers are bitter enemies to those in our way.
They don't care that anybody should get a clandestine
livelihood but themselves.

[SCENE X.]

(MRS. PEACHUM, PEACHUM, POLLY.)

POLLY. 'Twas only Nimming Ned. He brought in a damask
window-curtain, a hoop petticoat, a pair of silver
candlesticks, a periwig, and one silk stocking, from
the fire that happened last night.

PEACHUM. There is not a fellow that is cleverer in his way
and saves more goods out of the fire, than Ned. But
now, Polly, to your affairs; for matters must not be left
as they are. You are married then, it seems?

POLLY. Yes, sir.

PEACHUM. And how do you propose to live, child?

POLLY. Like other women, sir,—upon the industry of my
husband.

MRS. PEACHUM. What, is the wench turned fool? A highwayman's wife, like a soldier's, hath as little of his
pay as of his company.

PEACHUM. And had not you the common views of a gentlewoman in your marriage, Polly?

POLLY. I don't know what you mean, sir.

PEACHUM. Of a jointure, and of being a widow.

POLLY. But I love him, sir; how then could I have thoughts
of parting with him?

PEACHUM. Parting with him! Why, that is the whole
scheme and intention of all marriage articles.[23] The
comfortable estate of widowhood is the only hope that
keeps up a wife's spirits. Where is the woman who
would scruple to be a wife, if she had it in her power
to be a widow whenever she pleased? If you have any
views of this sort, Polly, I shall think the match not
so very unreasonable.

[23] The legal contract drawn up before an upper-class marriage,
where much attention was given to the disposition of the property
if the husband died.

POLLY. How I dread to hear your advice! Yet I must beg
you to explain yourself.

PEACHUM. Secure what he hath got, have him peached
the next sessions, and then at once you are made a
rich widow.

POLLY. What, murder the man I love! The blood runs cold
at my heart with the very thought of it.

PEACHUM. Fie, Polly! What hath murder to do in the affair?
Since the thing sooner or later must happen, I dare
say the captain himself would like that we should get
the reward for his death sooner than a stranger. Why,
Polly, the captain knows that as 'tis his employment to
rob, so 'tis ours to take robbers; every man in his
business. So that there is no malice in the case.

MRS. PEACHUM. Ay, husband, now you have nicked the
matter. To have him peached is the only thing could
ever make me forgive her.

POLLY.

AIR XII—*Now ponder well, ye parents dear*

> Oh, ponder well! be not severe;
>   So save a wretched wife!
> For on the rope that hangs my dear
>   Depends poor Polly's life.

MRS. PEACHUM. But your duty to your parents, hussy,
obliges you to hang him. What would many a wife
give for such an opportunity!

POLLY. What is a jointure, what is a widowhood to me? I
know my heart. I cannot survive him.

AIR XIII—*Le printemps rappelle aux armes*

> The turtle[24] thus with plaintive crying,
>   Her lover dying,
> The turtle thus with plaintive crying,
>   Laments her dove.
> Down she drops, quite spent with sighing;
>   Pair'd in death, as pair'd in love.

Thus, sir, it will happen to your poor Polly.

MRS. PEACHUM. What, is the fool in love in earnest then?

---

[24] Turtledove.

I hate thee for being particular. Why, wench, thou art a shame to thy very sex.

POLLY. But hear me, mother,—if you ever loved—

MRS. PEACHUM. Those cursed play-books she reads have been her ruin. One word more, hussy, and I shall knock your brains out, if you have any.

PEACHUM. Keep out of the way, Polly, for fear of mischief, and consider of what is proposed to you.

MRS. PEACHUM. Away, hussy! Hang your husband, and be dutiful.

[SCENE XI.]

(MRS. PEACHUM, PEACHUM, POLLY *listening*.)

MRS. PEACHUM. The thing, husband, must and shall be done. For the sake of intelligence, we must take other measures and have him peached the next sessions without her consent. If she will not know her duty, we know ours.

PEACHUM. But really, my dear, it grieves one's heart to take off a great man. When I consider his personal bravery, his fine stratagem, how much we have already got by him, and how much more we may get, methinks I can't find in my heart to have a hand in his death. I wish you could have made Polly undertake it.

MRS. PEACHUM. But in a case of necessity—our own lives are in danger.

PEACHUM. Then indeed, we must comply with the customs of the world, and make gratitude give way to interest. He shall be taken off.

MRS. PEACHUM. I'll undertake to manage Polly.

PEACHUM. And I'll prepare matters for the Old Bailey.

(*Exeunt.*)

[SCENE XII.]

(POLLY.)

POLLY. Now I'm a wretch, indeed—methinks I see him already in the cart, sweeter and more lovely than the nosegay in his hand!—I hear the crowd extolling his resolution and intrepidity!—What volleys of sighs are sent from the windows of Holborn, that so comely a youth should be brought to disgrace!—I see him at

the tree! The whole circle are in tears!—even butchers
weep!—Jack Ketch[25] himself hesitates to perform his
duty, and would be glad to lose his fee, by a reprieve.
What then will become of Polly? As yet I may inform
him of their design, and aid him in his escape. It shall
be so!—But then he flies, absents himself, and I bar
myself from his dear, dear conversation! That too
will distract me. If he keep out of the way, my papa
and mama may in time relent, and we may be happy.
If he stays, he is hanged, and then he is lost forever!
He intended to lie concealed in my room till the dusk
of the evening. If they are abroad, I'll this instant let
him out, lest some accident should prevent him. (*Exit,
and returns.*)

[SCENE XIII.]

(POLLY, MACHEATH.)

MACHEATH.

AIR XIV—*Pretty Parrot, say*

Pretty Polly, say,
When I was away,
Did your fancy never stray
To some newer lover?

POLLY.

Without disguise,
Heaving sighs,
Doating eyes,
My constant heart discover.
Fondly let me loll!

MACHEATH.

O pretty, pretty Poll.

POLLY. And are *you* as fond as ever, my dear?
MACHEATH. Suspect my honor, my courage—suspect anything but my love. May my pistols miss fire, and my

---

[25] Condemned criminals, carrying a nosegay, were brought to the
gallows ("the tree") in a cart. If young and handsome, they were
pitied and admired by the numerous spectators. Jack Ketch was a
generic name for executioners.

mare slip her shoulder while I am pursued, if I ever
forsake thee!

POLLY. Nay, my dear, I have no reason to doubt you, for
I find in the romance you lent me, none of the great
heroes were ever false in love.

MACHEATH.

AIR XV—*Pray, fair one, be kind*

My heart was so free,
It roved like the bee,
Till Polly my passion requited;
I sipped each flower,
I changed ev'ry hour,
But here ev'ry flower is united.

POLLY. Were you sentenced to transportation, sure, my
dear, you could not leave me behind you,—could you?

MACHEATH. Is there any power, any force that could tear
me from thee? You might sooner tear a pension out of
the hands of a courtier, a fee from a lawyer, a pretty
woman from a looking glass, or any woman from
quadrille. But to tear me from thee is impossible!

AIR XVI—*Over the hills and far away*

Were I laid on Greenland's coast,
And in my arms embraced my lass;
Warm amidst eternal frost,
Too soon the half year's night would pass.

POLLY.

Were I sold on Indian soil,
Soon as the burning day was closed,
I could mock the sultry toil,
When on my charmer's breast reposed.

MACHEATH. And I would love you all the day,
POLLY. Every night would kiss and play,
MACHEATH. If with me you'd fondly stray
POLLY. Over the hills and far away.

POLLY. Yes, I would go with thee. But oh!—how shall I
speak it? I must be torn from thee. We must part.

MACHEATH. How! Part!

POLLY. We must, we must. My papa and mama are set
against thy life. They now, even now are in search
after thee. They are preparing evidence against thee.
Thy life depends upon a moment.

AIR XVII—*'Gin thou wert mine awn thing*

Oh, what pain it is to part!
Can I leave thee, can I leave thee?
Oh, what pain it is to part!
Can thy Polly ever leave thee?
But lest death my love should thwart
And bring thee to the fatal cart,
Thus I tear thee from my bleeding heart!
Fly hence, and let me leave thee.

One kiss and then—one kiss. Begone—farewell.

MACHEATH. My hand, my heart, my dear, is so riveted to
thine, that I cannot unloose my hold.

POLLY. But my papa may intercept thee, and then I should
lose the very glimmering of hope. A few weeks,
perhaps, may reconcile us all. Shall thy Polly hear
from thee?

MACHEATH. Must I then go?

POLLY. And will not absence change your love?

MACHEATH. If you doubt it, let me stay—and be hanged.

POLLY. Oh, how I fear! how I tremble!—Go—but when
safety will give you leave, you will be sure to see me
again; for till then Polly is wretched.

(*Parting, and looking back at each other with fondness;
he at one door, she at the other*)

MACHEATH.

AIR XVIII—*Oh the broom, etc.*

The miser thus a shilling sees,
    Which he's obliged to pay,
With sighs resigns it by degrees,
    And fears 'tis gone for aye.

POLLY.

The boy, thus, when his sparrow's flown,
    The bird in silence eyes;
But soon as out of sight 'tis gone,
    Whines, whimpers, sobs, and cries.

ACT II

[SCENE I.] *A tavern near Newgate*

(JEREMY TWITCHER, CROOK-FINGERED JACK, WAT DREARY, ROBIN OF BAGSHOT, NIMMING NED, HARRY PADINGTON, MATT OF THE MINT, BEN BUDGE, *and the rest of the gang, at the table, with wine, brandy, and tobacco.*)

BEN. But prithee, Matt, what is become of thy brother Tom? I have not seen him since my return from transportation.

MATT. Poor brother Tom had an accident this time twelve-month, and so clever a made fellow he was, that I could not save him from those flaying rascals the surgeons; and now, poor man, he is among the anatomies at Surgeons' Hall.[26]

BEN. So, it seems, his time was come.

JEREMY. But the present time is ours, and nobody alive hath more. Why are the laws levelled at us? Are we more dishonest than the rest of mankind? What we win, gentlemen, is our own by the law of arms and the right of conquest.

JACK. Where shall we find such another set of practical philosophers, who to a man are above the fear of death?

WAT. Sound men, and true!

ROBIN. Of tried courage, and indefatigable industry!

NED. Who is there here that would not die for his friend?

HARRY. Who is there here that would betray him for his interest?

MATT. Show me a gang of courtiers that can say as much.

BEN. We are for a just partition of the world, for every man hath a right to enjoy life.

MATT. We retrench the superfluities of mankind. The world is avaricious, and I hate avarice. A covetous fellow, like a jackdaw, steals what he was never made to enjoy, for the sake of hiding it. These are the robbers of mankind, for money was made for the free-

---

[26] The bodies of hanged felons were sent to Surgeons' Hall for dissection, if their relatives were unable to claim them.

hearted and generous; and where is the injury of taking from another, what he hath not the heart to make use of?

JEREMY. Our several stations for the day are fixed. Good luck attend us! Fill the glasses.

AIR I—*Fill ev'ry glass, etc.*

Fill ev'ry glass, for wine inspires us,
    And fires us
With courage, love, and joy.
Women and wine should life employ.
Is there aught else on earth desirous?

CHORUS.

      Fill ev'ry glass, etc.

[SCENE II.]

(*To them enter* MACHEATH.)

MACHEATH. Gentlemen, well met. My heart hath been with you this hour, but an unexpected affair hath detained me. No ceremony, I beg you.

MATT. We were just breaking up to go upon duty. Am I to have the honor of taking the air with you, sir, this evening upon the heath? I drink a dram now and then with the stage-coachmen in the way of friendship and intelligence, and I know that about this time there will be passengers upon the Western Road who are worth speaking with.

MACHEATH. I was to have been of that party—but—

MATT. But what, sir?

MACHEATH. Is there any man who suspects my courage?—

MATT. We have all been witnesses of it.—

MACHEATH. My honor and truth to the gang?

MATT. I'll be answerable for it.

MACHEATH. In the division of our booty, have I ever shown the least marks of avarice or injustice?

MATT. By these questions something seems to have ruffled you. Are any of us suspected?

MACHEATH. I have a fixed confidence, gentlemen, in you all, as men of honor, and as such I value and respect you. Peachum is a man that is useful to us.

MATT. Is he about to play us any foul play? I'll shoot him through the head.

MACHEATH. I beg you, gentlemen, act with conduct and discretion. A pistol is your last resort.

MATT. He knows nothing of this meeting.

MACHEATH. Business cannot go on without him. He is a man who knows the world, and is a necessary agent to us. We have had a slight difference, and till it is accommodated I shall be obliged to keep out of his way. Any private dispute of mine shall be of no ill consequence to my friends. You must continue to act under his direction, for the moment we break loose from him, our gang is ruined.

MATT. As a bawd to a whore, I grant you, he is to us of great convenience.

MACHEATH. Make him believe I have quitted the gang, which I can never do but with life. At our private quarters I will continue to meet you. A week or so will probably reconcile us.

MATT. Your instructions shall be observed. 'Tis now high time for us to repair to our several duties; so till the evening at our quarters in Moorfields we bid you farewell.

MACHEATH. I shall wish myself with you. Success attend you. (*Sits down melancholy at the table.*)

MATT.

AIR II—*March in Rinaldo, with drums and trumpets*

> Let us take the road.
>   Hark! I hear the sound of coaches!
>   The hour of attack approaches,
> To your arms, brave boys, and load.
>
>   See the ball I hold!
> Let the chymists[27] toil like asses,
> Our fire their fire surpasses,
>   And turns all our lead to gold.

(*The gang, ranged in the front of the stage, load their pistols, and stick them under their girdles, then go off singing the first part in chorus.*)

[27] Alchemists.

[SCENE III.]

(MACHEATH, DRAWER.)

MACHEATH. What a fool is a fond wench! Polly is most
confoundedly bit—I love the sex. And a man who
loves money might be as well contented with one
guinea, as I with one woman. The town perhaps hath
been as much obliged to me, for recruiting it with
freehearted ladies, as to any recruiting officer in the
army. If it were not for us, and the other gentlemen
of the sword, Drury Lane[28] would be uninhabited.

AIR III—*Would you have a young virgin, etc.*

If the heart of a man is depressed with cares,
The mist is dispelled when a woman appears;
Like the notes of a fiddle, she sweetly, sweetly
Raises the spirits, and charms our ears.
   Roses and lilies her cheeks disclose,
   But her ripe lips are more sweet than those.
         Press her,
         Caress her
         With blisses,
         Her kisses
Dissolve us in pleasure and soft repose.

I must have women. There is nothing unbends the
mind like them. Money is not so strong a cordial for
the time. Drawer!

(*Enter* DRAWER.)

Is the porter gone for all the ladies, according to my
directions?

DRAWER. I expect him back every minute. But you know,
sir, you sent him as far as Hockley-in-the-Hole for
three of the ladies, for one in Vinegar Yard, and for
the rest of them somewhere about Lewkner's Lane.
Sure some of them are below, for I hear the bar bell.
As they come I will show them up. Coming! coming!
(*Exit.*)

[28] Inhabited mainly by prostitutes.

[SCENE IV.]

(MACHEATH, MRS. COAXER, DOLLY TRULL, MRS. VIXEN, BETTY DOXY, JENNY DIVER, MRS. SLAMMEKIN, SUKY TAWDRY, *and* MOLLY BRAZEN.)

MACHEATH. Dear Mrs. Coaxer, you are welcome. You look charmingly to-day. I hope you don't want the repairs of quality, and lay on paint.—Dolly Trull! kiss me, you slut; are you as amorous as ever, hussy? You are always so taken up with stealing hearts, that you don't allow yourself time to steal anything else. Ah Dolly, thou wilt ever be a coquette.—Mrs. Vixen, I'm yours! I always loved a woman of wit and spirit; they make charming mistresses, but plaguy wives.—Betty Doxy! come hither, hussy. Do you drink as hard as ever? You had better stick to good, wholesome beer; for in troth, Betty, strong waters will, in time, ruin your constitution. You should leave those to your betters. —What! and my pretty Jenny Diver too! As prim and demure as ever! There is not any prude, though ever so high bred, hath a more sanctified look, with a more mischievous heart. Ah! thou art a dear artful hypocrite!—Mrs. Slammekin! as careless and genteel as ever! all you fine ladies, who know your own beauty, affect an undress.—But see, here's Suky Tawdry come to contradict what I was saying. Everything she gets one way, she lays out upon her back. Why, Suky, you must keep at least a dozen tally-men.[29]—Molly Brazen! (*She kisses him*) That's well done. I love a free-hearted wench. Thou hast a most agreeable assurance, girl, and art as willing as a turtle.—But hark! I hear music. The harper is at the door. "If music be the food of love, play on." Ere you seat yourselves, ladies, what think you of a dance? Come in.

(*Enter* HARPER.)

Play the French tune that Mrs. Slammekin was so fond of.

---

[29] Dealers who sell on credit. Cf. tally-woman, p. 233.

(*A dance à la ronde in the French manner; near the end of it this song and chorus*):

AIR IV—*Cotillion*

Youth's the season made for joys,
  Love is then our duty;
She alone who that employs,
  Well deserves her beauty.
    Let's be gay,
    While we may,
Beauty's a flower despised in decay.

Youth's the season, etc.

Let us drink and sport to-day,
  Ours is not to-morrow.
Love with youth flies swift away,
  Age is nought but sorrow.
    Dance and sing,
    Time's on the wing,
Life never knows the return of spring.

CHORUS.

  Let us drink, etc.

MACHEATH. Now pray, ladies, take your places. Here, fellow. (Pays the HARPER.) Bid the drawer bring us more wine.

(*Exit* HARPER.)

If any of the ladies choose gin, I hope they will be so free to call for it.

JENNY. You look as if you meant me. Wine is strong enough for me. Indeed, sir, I never drink strong waters but when I have the colic.

MACHEATH. Just the excuse of the fine ladies! Why, a lady of quality is never without the colic. I hope, Mrs. Coaxer, you have had good success of late in your visits among the mercers.

MRS. COAXER. We have so many interlopers. Yet, with industry, one may still have a little picking. I carried a silver-flowered lute-string and a piece of black padesoy[30] to Mr. Peachum's lock but last week.

---

[30] Expensive fabrics.

MRS. VIXEN. There's Molly Brazen hath the ogle of a rattle-snake. She riveted a linen-draper's eye so fast upon her, that he was nicked[31] of three pieces of cambric before he could look off.

MOLLY BRAZEN. Oh, dear madam! But sure nothing can come up to your handling of laces! And then you have such a sweet deluding tongue! To cheat a man is nothing; but the woman must have fine parts indeed who cheats a woman!

MRS. VIXEN. Lace, madam, lies in a small compass, and is of easy conveyance. But you are apt, madam, to think too well of your friends.

MRS. COAXER. If any woman hath more art than another, to be sure, 'tis Jenny Diver. Though her fellow be never so agreeable, she can pick his pocket as coolly as if money were her only pleasure. Now, that is a command of the passions uncommon in a woman!

JENNY. I never go to the tavern with a man but in the view of business. I have other hours, and other sort of men for my pleasure. But had I your address, madam—

MACHEATH. Have done with your compliments, ladies, and drink about. You are not so fond of me, Jenny, as you use to be.

JENNY. 'Tis not convenient, sir, to show my kindness among so many rivals. 'Tis your own choice, and not the warmth of my inclination, that will determine you.

AIR V—*All in a misty morning, etc.*

Before the barn-door crowing,
    The cock by hens attended,
His eyes around him throwing,
    Stands for a while suspended.

Then one he singles from the crew,
    And cheers the happy hen;
With "How do you do," and "How do you do,"
    And "How do you do" again.

MACHEATH. Ah Jenny! thou art a dear slut.

TRULL. Pray, madam, were you ever in keeping?

TAWDRY. I hope, madam, I han't been so long upon the

---

31 Tricked or cheated.

town but I have met with some good fortune as well as my neighbors.

TRULL. Pardon me, madam, I meant no harm by the question; 'twas only in the way of conversation.

TAWDRY. Indeed, madam, if I had not been a fool, I might have lived very handsomely with my last friend. But upon his missing five guineas, he turned me off. Now, I never suspected he had counted them.

SLAMMEKIN. Who do you look upon, madam, as your best sort of keepers?

TRULL. That, madam, is thereafter as they be.

SLAMMEKIN. I, madam, was once kept by a Jew; and bating their religion, to women they are a good sort of people.

TAWDRY. Now for my part, I own I like an old fellow; for we always make them pay for what they can't do.

VIXEN. A spruce prentice, let me tell you, ladies, is no ill thing; they bleed freely. I have sent at least two or three dozen of them in my time to the plantations.

JENNY. But to be sure, sir, with so much good fortune as you have had upon the road, you must be grown immensely rich.

MACHEATH. The road, indeed, hath done me justice, but the gaming-table hath been my ruin.

JENNY.

AIR VI—*When once I lay with another man's wife, etc.*

The gamesters and lawyers are jugglers alike,
  If they meddle, your all is in danger:
Like gypsies, if once they can finger a souse,[32]
  Your pockets they pick, and they pilfer your house,
And give your estate to a stranger.

A man of courage should never put anything to the risk but his life.

(*She takes up his pistol.* TAWDRY *takes up the other.*)

These are the tools of men of honor. Cards and dice are only fit for cowardly cheats, who prey upon their friends.

[32] Sou, a small coin.

TAWDRY. This, sir, is fitter for your hand. Besides your loss of money, 'tis a loss to the ladies. Gaming takes you off from women. How fond could I be of you!—but before company, 'tis ill-bred.

MACHEATH. Wanton hussies!

JENNY. I must and will have a kiss, to give my wine a zest.

(*They take him about the neck, and make signs to* PEACHUM *and* CONSTABLES, *who rush in upon him.*)

[SCENE V.]

(*To them* PEACHUM *and* CONSTABLES.)

PEACHUM. I seize you, sir, as my prisoner.

MACHEATH. Was this well done, Jenny? Women are decoy ducks: who can trust them? Beasts, jades, jilts, harpies, furies, whores!

PEACHUM. Your case, Mr. Macheath, is not particular. The greatest heroes have been ruined by women. But, to do them justice, I must own they are a pretty sort of creatures, if we could trust them. You must now, sir, take your leave of the ladies, and if they have a mind to make you a visit, they will be sure to find you at home. This gentleman, ladies, lodges in Newgate. Constables, wait upon the captain to his lodgings.

MACHEATH.

AIR VII—*When first I laid siege to my Chloris, etc.*

> At the tree I shall suffer with pleasure,
> At the tree I shall suffer with pleasure;
> Let me go where I will,
> In all kinds of ill,
> I shall find no such furies as these are.

PEACHUM. Ladies, I'll take care the reckoning shall be discharged.

(*Exit* MACHEATH, *guarded, with* PEACHUM *and* CONSTABLES.)

[SCENE VI.]

(*The* WOMEN *remain.*)

VIXEN. Look ye, Mrs. Jenny; though Mr. Peachum may
have made a private bargain with you and Suky
Tawdry for betraying the captain, as we were all assisting, we ought all to share alike.

COAXER. I think Mr. Peachum, after so long an acquaintance, might have trusted me as well as Jenny Diver.

SLAMMEKIN. I am sure at least three men of his hanging,
and in a year's time too (if he did me justice), should
be set down to my account.

TRULL. Mrs. Slammekin, that is not fair. For you know
one of them was taken in bed with me.

JENNY. As far as a bowl of punch or a treat, I believe
Mrs. Suky will join with me. As for anything else,
ladies, you cannot in conscience expect it.

SLAMMEKIN. Dear madam—

TRULL. I would not for the world—

SLAMMEKIN. 'Tis impossible for me—

TRULL. As I hope to be saved, madam—

SLAMMEKIN. Nay, then I must stay here all night.—

TRULL. Since you command me.

(*Exeunt with great ceremony.*)

[SCENE VII.] *Newgate*

(LOCKIT, TURNKEYS, MACHEATH, CONSTABLES.)

LOCKIT. Noble captain, you are welcome. You have not
been a lodger of mine this year and half. You know
the custom, sir. Garnish,[33] captain, garnish! Hand me
down those fetters there.

MACHEATH. Those, Mr. Lockit, seem to be the heaviest of
the whole set! With your leave, I should like the
further pair better.

LOCKIT. Look ye, captain, we know what is fittest for our
prisoners. When a gentleman uses me with civility, I
always do the best I can to please him.—Hand them

---

[33] Fee extorted from a new prisoner. Since jailors received little or
no salary, they were legally entitled to exact fees for light chains
and other amenities.

down, I say.—We have them of all prices, from one guinea to ten, and 'tis fitting every gentleman should please himself.

MACHEATH. I understand you, sir. (*Gives money.*) The fees here are so many, and so exorbitant, that few fortunes can bear the expense of getting off handsomely, or of dying like a gentleman.

LOCKIT. Those, I see, will fit the captain better. Take down the further pair. Do but examine them, sir,—never was better work. How genteelly they are made! They will fit as easy as a glove, and the nicest man in England might not be ashamed to wear them. (*He puts on the chains.*) If I had the best gentleman in the land in my custody, I could not equip him more handsomely. And so, sir—I now leave you to your private meditations.

[SCENE VIII.]

(MACHEATH.)

AIR VIII—*Courtiers, courtiers, think it no harm, etc.*

> Man may escape from rope and gun;
> Nay, some have outlived the doctor's pill;
> Who takes a woman must be undone,
>   That basilisk is sure to kill.
>
> The fly that sips treacle is lost in the sweets,
> So he that tastes woman, woman, woman,
>   He that tastes woman, ruin meets.

To what a woeful plight have I brought myself! Here must I (all day long, till I am hanged) be confined to hear the reproaches of a wench who lays her ruin at my door. I am in the custody of her father, and to be sure if he knows of the matter, I shall have a fine time on't betwixt this and my execution. But I promised the wench marriage. What signifies a promise to a woman? Does not a man in marriage itself promise a hundred things that he never means to perform? Do all we can, women will believe us; for they look upon a promise as an excuse for following their own inclinations.—But here comes Lucy, and I cannot get from her. Would I were deaf!

[SCENE IX.]

(MACHEATH, LUCY.)

LUCY. You base man, you, how can you look me in the face after what hath passed between us?—See here, perfidious wretch, how I am forced to bear about the load of infamy you have laid upon me—Oh, Macheath! thou hast robbed me of my quiet—to see thee tortured would give me pleasure.

AIR IX—*A lovely lass to a friar came, etc.*

Thus when a good housewife sees a rat
In her trap in the morning taken,
With pleasure her heart goes pit-a-pat
In revenge for her loss of bacon.
Then she throws him
To the dog or cat,
To be worried, crushed, and shaken.

MACHEATH. Have you no bowels, no tenderness, my dear Lucy, to see a husband in these circumstances?

LUCY. A husband!

MACHEATH. In every respect but the form, and that, my dear, may be said over us at any time. Friends should not insist upon ceremonies. From a man of honor, his word is as good as his bond.

LUCY. 'Tis the pleasure of all you fine men to insult the women you have ruined.

AIR X—*'Twas when the sea was roaring, etc.*

How cruel are the traitors
Who lie and swear in jest,
To cheat unguarded creatures
Of virtue, fame, and rest!

Whoever steals a shilling
Through shame the guilt conceals;
In love, the perjured villain
With boasts the theft reveals.

MACHEATH. The very first opportunity, my dear (have but patience), you shall be my wife in whatever manner you please.

LUCY. Insinuating monster! And so you think I know nothing of the affair of Miss Polly Peachum. I could tear thy eyes out!

MACHEATH. Sure, Lucy, you can't be such a fool as to be jealous of Polly!

LUCY. Are you not married to her, you brute, you?

MACHEATH. Married! Very good. The wench gives it out only to vex thee, and to ruin me in thy good opinion. 'Tis true I go to the house; chat with the girl, I kiss her, I say a thousand things to her (as all gentlemen do) that mean nothing, to divert myself; and now the silly jade hath set it about that I am married to her, to let me know what she would be at. Indeed, my dear Lucy, these violent passions may be of ill consequence to a woman in your condition.

LUCY. Come, come, captain, for all your assurance, you know that Miss Polly hath put it out of your power to do me the justice you promised me.

MACHEATH. A jealous woman believes everything her passion suggests. To convince you of my sincerity, if we can find the ordinary, I shall have no scruples of making you my wife—and I know the consequence of having two at a time.

LUCY. That you are only to be hanged, and so get rid of them both.

MACHEATH. I am ready, my dear Lucy, to give you satisfaction—if you think there is any in marriage. What can a man of honor say more?

LUCY. So then it seems—you are not married to Miss Polly.

MACHEATH. You know, Lucy, the girl is prodigiously conceited. No man can say a civil thing to her, but (like other fine ladies) her vanity makes her think he's her own for ever and ever.

AIR XI—*The sun had loosed his weary teams, etc.*

> The first time at the looking-glass
>   The mother sets her daughter,
> The image strikes the smiling lass
>   With self-love ever after.
> Each time she looks, she, fonder grown,
>   Thinks ev'ry charm grows stronger.
> But alas, vain maid, all eyes but your own
>   Can see you are not younger.

When women consider their own beauties, they are all
alike unreasonable in their demands; for they expect
their lovers should like them as long as they like
themselves.

LUCY. Yonder is my father. Perhaps this way we may light
upon the ordinary, who shall try if you will be as good
as your word; for I long to be made an honest woman.

(*Exeunt.*)

[SCENE X.]

(PEACHUM, LOCKIT *with an account-book.*)

LOCKIT. In this last affair, brother Peachum, we are agreed.
You have consented to go halves in Macheath.

PEACHUM. We shall never fall out about an execution. But
as to that article, pray how stands our last year's
account?

LOCKIT. If you will run your eye over it, you'll find 'tis
fair and clearly stated.

PEACHUM. This long arrear of the government is very hard
upon us! Can it be expected that we should hang our
acquaintance for nothing, when our betters will hardly
save theirs without being paid for it? Unless the
people in employment pay better, I promise them
for the future, I shall let other rogues live besides their
own.

LOCKIT. Perhaps, brother, they are afraid these matters
may be carried too far. We are treated, too, by them
with contempt, as if our profession were not reputable.

PEACHUM. In one respect, indeed, our employment may
be reckoned dishonest, because, like great statesmen,
we encourage those who betray their friends.

LOCKIT. Such language, brother, anywhere else might turn
to your prejudice. Learn to be more guarded, I beg
you.

AIR XII—*How happy are we, etc.*

When you censure the age,
Be cautious and sage,
Lest the courtiers offended should be.
If you mention vice or bribe,
'Tis so pat to all the tribe
Each cries—That was levelled at me.

PEACHUM. Here's poor Ned Clincher's[34] name, I see. Sure, brother Lockit, there was a little unfair proceeding in Ned's case; for he told me in the condemned hold, that for value received, you had promised him a sessions or two longer without molestation.

LOCKIT. Mr. Peachum, this is the first time my honor was ever called in question.

PEACHUM. Business is at an end, if once we act dishonorably.

LOCKIT. Who accuses me?

PEACHUM. You are warm, brother.

LOCKIT. He that attacks my honor, attacks my livelihood. And this usage, sir, is not to be borne.

PEACHUM. Since you provoke me to speak, I must tell you too, that Mrs. Coaxer charges you with defrauding her of her information-money, for the apprehending of curl-pated Hugh. Indeed, indeed, brother, we must punctually pay our spies, or we shall have no information.

LOCKIT. Is this language to me, sirrah? Who have saved you from the gallows, sirrah!

(*Collaring each other*)

PEACHUM. If I am hanged, it shall be for ridding the world of an arrant rascal.

LOCKIT. This hand shall do the office of the halter you deserve, and throttle you, you dog!

PEACHUM. Brother, brother, we are both in the wrong. We shall be both losers in the dispute—for you know we have it in our power to hang each other. You should not be so passionate.

LOCKIT. Nor you so provoking.

PEACHUM. 'Tis our mutual interest; 'tis for the interest of the world we should agree. If I said anything, brother, to the prejudice of your character, I ask pardon.

LOCKIT. Brother Peachum, I can forgive as well as resent. Give me your hand. Suspicion does not become a friend.

PEACHUM. I only meant to give you occasion to justify yourself. But I must now step home, for I expect the gentleman about this snuff-box that Filch nimmed

---

34 "Clinch" was slang for the condemned hold.

two nights ago in the park. I appointed him at this hour. (*Exit.*)

[SCENE XI.]

(LOCKIT, LUCY.)

LOCKIT. Whence come you, hussy?

LUCY. My tears might answer that question.

LOCKIT. You have then been whimpering and fondling, like a spaniel, over the fellow that hath abused you.

LUCY. One can't help love; one can't cure it. 'Tis not in my power to obey you, and hate him.

LOCKIT. Learn to bear your husband's death like a reasonable woman. 'Tis not the fashion, nowadays, so much as to affect sorrow upon these occasions. No woman would ever marry if she had not the chance of mortality for a release. Act like a woman of spirit, hussy, and thank your father for what he is doing.

LUCY.

AIR XIII—*Of a noble race was Shenkin*

Is then his fate decreed, sir?
    Such a man can I think of quitting?
When first we met, so moves me yet,
    Oh, see how my heart is splitting!

LOCKIT. Look ye, Lucy—there is no saving him—so, I think, you must ev'n do like other widows, buy yourself weeds, and be cheerful.

AIR XIV

You'll think, ere many days ensue,
    This sentence not severe;
I hang your husband, child, 'tis true,
    But with him hang your care.
        Twang dang dillo dee.

Like a good wife, go moan over your dying husband; that, child, is your duty.—Consider, girl, you can't have the man and the money too—so make yourself as easy as you can by getting all you can from him.

(*Exeunt.*)

[SCENE XII.]

(LUCY, MACHEATH.)

LUCY. Though the ordinary was out of the way to-day, I hope, my dear, you will, upon the first opportunity, quiet my scruples.—Oh, sir!—my father's hard heart is not to be softened, and I am in the utmost despair.

MACHEATH. But if I could raise a small sum—would not twenty guineas, think you, move him? Of all the arguments in the way of business, the perquisite is the most prevailing. Your father's perquisites for the escape of prisoners must amount to a considerable sum in the year. Money well timed and properly applied, will do anything.

AIR XV—*London ladies*

If you at an office solicit your due,
 And would not have matters neglected;
You must quicken the clerk with the perquisite too,
 To do what his duty directed.
Or would you the frowns of a lady prevent,
 She too has this palpable failing,
The perquisite softens her into consent;
 That reason with all is prevailing.

LUCY. What love or money can do shall be done, for all my comfort depends upon your safety.

[SCENE XIII.]

(LUCY, MACHEATH, POLLY.)

POLLY. Where is my dear husband?—Was a rope ever intended for this neck? Oh, let me throw my arms about it, and throttle thee with love! Why dost thou turn away from me? 'Tis thy Polly—'tis thy wife.

MACHEATH. Was there ever such an unfortunate rascal as I am!

LUCY. Was there ever such another villain!

POLLY. Oh, Macheath! was it for this we parted? Taken! imprisoned! tried! hanged!—cruel reflection! I'll stay with thee till death—no force shall tear thy dear wife from thee now. What means my love?—not one kind word—not one kind look! Think what thy Polly suffers to see thee in this condition.

Air XVI—*All in the downs, etc.*

Thus when the swallow, seeking prey,
    Within the sash is closely pent,
His consort, with bemoaning lay,
    Without, sits pining for th'event.
Her chattering lovers all around her skim;
She heeds them not (poor bird!)—her soul's with him.

MACHEATH (*aside*). I must disown her.—The wench is distracted.

LUCY. Am I then bilked of my virtue? Can I have no reparation? Sure, men were born to lie, and women to believe them. Oh, villain! villain!

POLLY. Am I not thy wife? Thy neglect of me, thy aversion to me, too severely proves it.—Look on me. Tell me; am I not thy wife?

LUCY. Perfidious wretch!

POLLY. Barbarous husband!

LUCY. Hadst thou been hanged five months ago, I had been happy.

POLLY. And I too. If you had been kind to me till death, it would not have vexed me—and that's no very unreasonable request (though from a wife) to a man who hath not above seven or eight days to live.

LUCY. Art thou then married to another? Hast thou two wives, monster?

MACHEATH. If women's tongues can cease for an answer— hear me.

LUCY. I won't! Flesh and blood can't bear my usage.

POLLY. Shall I not claim my own? Justice bids me speak.

MACHEATH.

Air XVII—*Have you heard of a frolicsome ditty, etc.*

How happy I could be with either,
    Were t'other dear charmer away!
But while you thus tease me together,
    To neither a word will I say;
      But tol de rol, etc.

POLLY. Sure, my dear, there ought to be some preference shown to a wife! At least she may claim the appearance of it.—He must be distracted with his misfortunes, or he could not use me thus!

LUCY. Oh, villain, villain! thou hast deceived me—I could even inform against thee with pleasure. Not a prude wishes more heartily to have facts against her intimate acquaintance, than I now wish to face facts against thee. I would have her satisfaction, and they should all out.

AIR XVIII—*Irish Trot*

POLLY. I'm bubbled.

LUCY.   —I'm bubbled!

POLLY. Oh how I am troubled!

LUCY. Bamboozled, and bit![35]

POLLY.   —My distresses are doubled.

LUCY.

When you come to the tree, should the hangman refuse,
These fingers, with pleasure, could fasten the noose.

POLLY. I'm bubbled, etc.

MACHEATH. Be pacified, my dear Lucy!—This is all a fetch[36] of Polly's to make me desperate with you in case I get off. If I am hanged, she would fain have the credit of being thought my widow.—Really, Polly, this is no time for a dispute of this sort; for whenever you are talking of marriage, I am thinking of hanging.

POLLY. And hast thou the heart to persist in disowning me?

MACHEATH. And hast thou the heart to persist in persuading me that I am married? Why, Polly, dost thou seek to aggravate my misfortunes?

LUCY. Really, Miss Peachum, you but expose yourself. Besides, 'tis barbarous in you to worry a gentleman in his circumstances.

POLLY.

AIR XIX

Cease your funning,
    Force or cunning
Never shall my heart trepan.
    All these sallies
    Are but malice
To seduce my constant man.

---

[35] Bubbled, bamboozled, and bit all meant cheated.
[36] Trick.

> 'Tis most certain,
>   By their flirting,
> Women oft have envy shown;
>   Pleased to ruin
>   Others' wooing
> Never happy in their own!

LUCY. Decency, madam, methinks, might teach you to behave yourself with some reserve with the husband while his wife is present.

MACHEATH. But, seriously, Polly, this is carrying the joke a little too far.

LUCY. If you are determined, madam, to raise a disturbance in the prison, I shall be obliged to send for the turnkey to show you the door. I am sorry, madam, you force me to be so ill-bred.

POLLY. Give me leave to tell you, madam, these forward airs don't become you in the least, madam. And my duty, madam, obliges me to stay with my husband, madam.

LUCY.

AIR XX—*Good morrow, gossip Joan*

> Why, how now, Madam Flirt?
>   If you thus must chatter;
> And are for flinging dirt,
>   Let's try who best can spatter!
>   Madam Flirt!

POLLY.

> Why, how now, saucy jade;
>   Sure the wench is tipsy!
> How can you see me made (*To him*)
>   The scoff of such a gipsy?
>   Saucy jade! (*To her*)

[SCENE XIV.]

(LUCY, MACHEATH, POLLY, PEACHUM.)

PEACHUM. Where's my wench? Ah hussy! hussy!—Come you home, you slut; and when your fellow is hanged, hang yourself, to make your family some amends.

POLLY. Dear, dear father, do not tear me from him; I must speak; I have more to say to him.

[*To* MACHEATH]:Oh! twist thy fetters about me, that he
may not haul me from thee!

PEACHUM. Sure, all women are alike! If ever they commit
the folly, they are sure to commit another by exposing themselves.—Away—not a word more—you are
my prisoner now, hussy!

POLLY (*holding* MACHEATH, PEACHUM *pulling her*).

Air XXI—*Irish howl*

No power on earth can e'er divide
The knot that sacred love hath tied.
When parents draw against our mind,
The true-love's knot they faster bind.
    Oh, oh ray, oh amborah—Oh, oh, etc.

(*Exeunt* POLLY *and* PEACHUM.)

[SCENE XV.]

(LUCY, MACHEATH.)

MACHEATH. I am naturally compassionate, wife, so that I
could not use the wench as she deserved, which made
you at first suspect there was something in what she
said.

LUCY. Indeed, my dear, I was strangely puzzled.

MACHEATH. If that had been the case, her father would
never have brought me into this circumstance. No,
Lucy, I had rather die than be false to thee.

LUCY. How happy am I if you say this from your heart!
For I love thee so, that I could sooner bear to see
thee hanged than in the arms of another.

MACHEATH. But couldst thou bear to see me hanged?

LUCY. Oh, Macheath, I can never live to see that day.

MACHEATH. You see, Lucy; in the account of love you are
in my debt, and you must now be convinced that I
rather choose to die than to be another's. Make me,
if possible, love thee more, and let me owe my life
to thee. If you refuse to assist me, Peachum and your
father will immediately put me beyond all means of
escape.

LUCY. My father, I know, hath been drinking hard with
the prisoners, and I fancy he is now taking his nap
in his own room. If I can procure the keys, shall I
go off with thee, my dear?

MACHEATH. If we are together, 'twill be impossible to lie
    concealed. As soon as the search begins to be a little
    cool, I will send to thee—till then, my heart is thy
    prisoner.

LUCY. Come then, my dear husband—owe thy life to me
    —and though you love me not—be grateful. But that
    Polly runs in my head strangely.

MACHEATH. A moment of time may make us unhappy
    forever.

LUCY.

AIR XXII—*The lass of Patie's mill, etc.*

> I like the fox shall grieve,
>   Whose mate hath left her side,
> Whom hounds, from morn till eve,
>   Chase o'er the country wide,
> Where can my lover hide?
>   Where cheat the weary pack?
> If love be not his guide,
>   He never will come back!

ACT III

[SCENE I.] *Newgate*

(LOCKIT, LUCY.)

LOCKIT. To be sure, wench, you must have been aiding and
    abetting to help him to this escape.

LUCY. Sir, here hath been Peachum and his daughter Polly,
    and to be sure they know the ways of Newgate as well
    as if they had been born and bred in the place all
    their lives. Why must all your suspicion light upon
    me?

LOCKIT. Lucy, Lucy, I will have none of these shuffling
    answers.

LUCY. Well then—if I know anything of him, I wish I
    may be burnt!

LOCKIT. Keep your temper, Lucy, or I shall pronounce you
    guilty.

LUCY. Keep yours, sir. I do wish I may be burnt, I do.
    And what can I say more to convince you?

LOCKIT. Did he tip handsomely? How much did he come down with? Come, hussy, don't cheat your father, and I shall not be angry with you. Perhaps you have made a better bargain with him than I could have done. How much, my good girl?

LUCY. You know, sir, I am fond of him, and would have given money to have kept him with me.

LOCKIT. Ah, Lucy! thy education might have put thee more upon thy guard; for a girl in the bar of an ale-house is always besieged.

LUCY. Dear sir, mention not my education—for 'twas to that I owe my ruin.

AIR I—*If love's a sweet passion, etc.*

When young, at the bar you first taught me to score,
And bid me be free of my lips, and no more.
I was kissed by the parson, the squire, and the sot;
When the guest was departed, the kiss was forgot.
But his kiss was so sweet, and so closely he pressed,
That I languished and pined till I granted the rest.

If you can forgive me, sir, I will make a fair confession, for to be sure he hath been a most barbarous villain to me.

LOCKIT. And so you have let him escape, hussy, have you?

LUCY. When a woman loves, a kind look, a tender word can persuade her to anything, and I could ask no other bribe.

LOCKIT. Thou wilt always be a vulgar slut, Lucy. If you would not be looked upon as a fool, you should never do anything but upon the foot of interest. Those that act otherwise are their own bubbles.

LUCY. But love, sir, is a misfortune that may happen to the most discreet woman, and in love we are all fools alike. Notwithstanding all he swore, I am now fully convinced that Polly Peachum is actually his wife. Did I let him escape (fool that I was!) to go to her? Polly will wheedle herself into his money, and then Peachum will hang him, and cheat us both.

LOCKIT. So I am to be ruined, because, forsooth, you must be in love!—a very pretty excuse!

LUCY. I could murder that impudent happy strumpet! I gave him his life, and that creature enjoys the sweets of it. Ungrateful Macheath!

AIR II—*South-sea Ballad*

My love is all madness and folly,
    Alone I lie,
    Toss, tumble, and cry
What a happy creature is Polly!
Was e'er such a wretch as I!
With rage I redden like scarlet,
That my dear, inconstant varlet,
    Stark blind to my charms,
    Is lost in the arms
Of that jilt, that inveigling harlot!
This, this my resentment alarms.

LOCKIT. And so, after all this mischief, I must stay here
to be entertained with your caterwauling, mistress
Puss! Out of my sight, wanton strumpet! You shall
fast and mortify yourself into reason, with now and
then a little handsome discipline to bring you to your
senses. Go!

(*Exit* LUCY.)

[SCENE II.]

(LOCKIT.)

LOCKIT. Peachum then intends to outwit me in this affair,
but I'll be even with him. The dog is leaky in his
liquor; so I'll ply him that way, get the secret from
him, and turn this affair to my own advantage. Lions,
wolves, and vultures don't live together in herds,
droves, or flocks. Of all animals of prey, man is the
only sociable one. Every one of us preys upon his
neighbor, and yet we herd together. Peachum is my
companion, my friend. According to the custom of
the world, indeed, he may quote thousands of prece-
dents for cheating me. And shall not I make use of
the privilege of friendship to make him a return?

AIR III—*Packington's Pound*

Thus gamesters united in friendship are found,
Though they know that their industry all is a cheat;
They flock to their prey at the dice-box's sound,
And join to promote one another's deceit.
    But if by mishap
    They fail of a chap,

To keep in their hands, they each other entrap.
Like pikes, lank with hunger, who miss of their ends,
They bite their companions, and prey on their friends.

Now, Peachum, you and I, like honest tradesmen, are to have a fair trial which of us two can over-reach the other. Lucy!

(*Enter* LUCY.)

Are there any of Peachum's people now in the house?
LUCY. Filch, sir, is drinking a quartern of strong waters in the next room with Black Moll.
LOCKIT. Bid him come to me.

(*Exit* LUCY.)

[SCENE III.]

(LOCKIT, FILCH.)

LOCKIT. Why, boy, thou lookest as if thou wert half starved—like a shotten[37] herring.
FILCH. One had need have the constitution of a horse to go through the business. Since the favorite child-getter was disabled by a mishap, I have picked up a little money by helping the ladies to a pregnancy against their being called down to sentence. But if a man cannot get an honest livelihood any easier way, I am sure 'tis what I can't undertake for another sessions.
LOCKIT. Truly, if that great man should tip off, 'twould be an irreparable loss. The vigor and prowess of a knight-errant never saved half of the ladies in distress that he hath done.—But, boy, canst thou tell me where thy master is to be found?
FILCH. At his lock, sir, at the Crooked Billet.
LOCKIT. Very well. I have nothing more with you.

(*Exit* FILCH.)

I'll go to him there, for I have many important affairs to settle with him; and in the way of those trans-actions, I'll artfully get into his secret, so that Mac-heath shall not remain a day longer out o' my clutches.

---

[37] Shotten meant thin after spawning, appropriate because Filch has been wearing himself out impregnating condemned women so they will not be hanged.

[SCENE IV.] *A gaming-house*

(MACHEATH *in a fine tarnished coat,* BEN BUDGE, MATT *of the* MINT.)

MACHEATH. I am sorry, gentlemen, the road was so barren of money. When my friends are in difficulties, I am always glad that my fortune can be serviceable to them. (*Gives them money.*) You see, gentlemen, I am not a mere court friend, who professes everything and will do nothing.

AIR IV—*Lillibullero*

The modes of the court so common are grown,
    That a true friend can hardly be met;
Friendship for interest is but a loan,
    Which they let out for what they can get.
        'Tis true, you find
        Some friends so kind,
Who will give you good counsel themselves to defend.
        In sorrowful ditty,
        They promise, they pity,
But shift you, for money, from friend to friend.

But we, gentlemen, have still honor enough to break through the corruptions of the world. And while I can serve you, you may command me.

BEN. It grieves my heart that so generous a man should be involved in such difficulties as oblige him to live with such ill company, and herd with gamesters.

MATT. See the partiality of mankind! One man may steal a horse, better than another look over a hedge. Of all mechanics, of all servile handicrafts-men, a gamester is the vilest. But yet, as many of the quality are of the profession, he is admitted amongst the politest company. I wonder we are not more respected.

MACHEATH. There will be deep play tonight at Marybone and consequently money may be picked up upon the road. Meet me there, and I'll give you the hint who is worth setting.

MATT. The fellow with a brown coat with narrow gold binding, I am told, is never without money.

MACHEATH. What do you mean, Matt? Sure you will not think of meddling with him! He's a good honest kind of a fellow, and one of us.

BEN. To be sure, sir, we will put ourselves under your direction.

MACHEATH. Have an eye upon the money-lenders. A rouleau or two would prove a pretty sort of an expedition. I hate extortion.

MATT. These rouleaus are very pretty things. I hate your bank bills. There is such a hazard in putting them off.[38]

MACHEATH. There is a certain man of distinction who in his time hath nicked me out of a great deal of the ready. He is in my cash,[39] Ben. I'll point him out to you this evening, and you shall draw upon him for the debt.—The company are met; I hear the dice-box in the other room. So, gentlemen, your servant! You'll meet me at Marybone.

(*Exeunt.*)

[SCENE V.] PEACHUM'S *lock. A table with wine, brandy, pipes and tobacco*

(PEACHUM, LOCKIT.)

LOCKIT. The Coronation account,[40] brother Peachum, is of so intricate a nature, that I believe it will never be settled.

PEACHUM. It consists, indeed, of a great variety of articles. It was worth to our people, in fees of different kinds, above ten installments. This is part of the account, brother, that lies open before us.

LOCKIT. A lady's tail[41] of rich brocade—that, I see, is disposed of—

PEACHUM. To Mrs. Diana Trapes, the tally-woman, and she will make a good hand on't in shoes and slippers, to trick out young ladies upon their going into keeping.

LOCKIT. But I don't see any article of the jewels.

PEACHUM. Those are so well known that they must be sent abroad. You'll find them entered under the article

---

[38] Matt prefers a rouleau, a roll of gold coins, to a bank bill, which would have to be cashed at the risk of being identified as an illegal possessor.

[39] The ready, money; in my cash, indebted to me.

[40] Account of articles stolen at the coronation of George II, in 1727. More was got there than at ten installments; i.e., annual installations of the Lord Mayor (Peachum's next speech).

[41] Train.

of exportation. As for the snuff-boxes, watches, swords, etc., I thought it best to enter them under their several heads.

LOCKIT. Seven and twenty women's pockets[42] complete, with the several things therein contained—all sealed, numbered, and entered.

PEACHUM. But, brother, it is impossible for us now to enter upon this affair. We should have the whole day before us. Besides, the account of the last half-year's plate is in a book by itself, which lies at the other office.

LOCKIT. Bring us then more liquor.—Today shall be for pleasure—tomorrow for business.—Ah, brother, those daughters of ours are two slippery hussies. Keep a watchful eye upon Polly, and Macheath in a day or two shall be our own again.

LOCKIT.

AIR V—*Down in the North Country, etc.*

What gudgeons are we men!
   Ev'ry woman's easy prey,
Though we have felt the hook, again
   We bite and they betray.
The bird that hath been trapped,
   When he hears his calling mate,
To her he flies, again he's clapped
   Within the wiry grate.

PEACHUM. But what signifies catching the bird if your daughter Lucy will set open the door of the cage?

LOCKIT. If men were answerable for the follies and frailties of their wives and daughters, no friends could keep a good correspondence together for two days. This is unkind of you, brother; for among good friends, what they say or do goes for nothing.

(*Enter a* SERVANT.)

SERVANT. Sir, here's Mrs. Diana Trapes wants to speak with you.

PEACHUM. Shall we admit her, brother Lockit?

---

[42] Small bags, coin purses.

LOCKIT. By all means—she's a good customer, and a fine-spoken woman—and a woman who drinks and talks so freely, will enliven the conversation.

PEACHUM. Desire her to walk in.

(*Exit* SERVANT.)

[SCENE VI.]

(PEACHUM, LOCKIT, MRS. TRAPES.)

PEACHUM. Dear Mrs. Dye, your servant—one may know by your kiss, that your gin is excellent.

TRAPES. I was always very curious[43] in my liquors.

LOCKIT. There is no perfumed breath like it. I have been long acquainted with the flavor of those lips—han't I, Mrs. Dye?

TRAPES. Fill it up. I take as large draughts of liquor as I did of love. I hate a flincher in either.

AIR VI—*A shepherd kept sheep, etc.*

In the days of my youth I could bill like a dove,
    fa, la, la, etc.
Like a sparrow at all times was ready for love,
    fa, la, la, etc.
The life of all mortals in kissing should pass,
Lip to lip while we're young—then the lip to the
    glass, fa, etc.

But now, Mr. Peachum, to our business.—If you have blacks of any kind, brought in of late; manteaus—velvet scarfs—petticoats—let it be what it will, I am your chap—for all my ladies are very fond of mourning.

PEACHUM. Why, look ye, Mrs. Dye—you deal so hard with us, that we can afford to give the gentlemen who venture their lives for the goods, little or nothing.

TRAPES. The hard times oblige me to go very near in my dealing. To be sure, of late years I have been a great sufferer by the parliament. Three thousand pounds would hardly make me amends. The act for destroying the Mint was a severe cut upon our business—till then, if a customer stepped out of the way—we knew

43Fastidious.

where to have her. No doubt you know Mrs. Coaxer—
there's a wench now (till to-day) with a good suit of
clothes of mine upon her back, and I could never set
eyes upon her for three months together. Since the
act, too, against imprisonment for small sums, my loss
there too hath been very considerable; and it must be
so, when a lady can borrow a handsome petticoat, or
a clean gown, and I not have the least hank upon
her! And, o' my conscience, nowadays most ladies
take a delight in cheating, when they can do it with
safety!

PEACHUM. Madam, you had a handsome gold watch of us
t'other day for seven guineas. Considering we must
have our profit—to a gentleman upon the road, a gold
watch will be scarce worth the taking.

TRAPES. Consider, Mr. Peachum, that watch was remark-
able and not of very safe sale. If you have any black
velvet scarfs—they are handsome winter wear, and
take with most gentlemen who deal with my customers. 'Tis I that put the ladies upon a good foot.
'Tis not youth or beauty that fixes their price. The
gentlemen always pay according to their dress, from
half a crown to two guineas; and yet those hussies
make nothing of bilking me. Then, too, allowing for
accidents—I have eleven fine customers now down
under the surgeon's hands; what with fees and other
expenses, there are great goings-out, and no comings-
in, and not a farthing to pay for at least a month's
clothing. We run great risks—great risks, indeed.

PEACHUM. As I remember, you said something just now
of Mrs. Coaxer.

TRAPES. Yes, sir. To be sure, I stripped her of a suit of my
own clothes about two hours ago, and have left her
as she should be, in her shift, with a lover of hers, at
my house. She called him upstairs as he was going to
Marybone in a hackney coach. And I hope, for her
sake and mine, she will persuade the captain to redeem her, for the captain is very generous to the
ladies.

LOCKIT. What captain?

TRAPES. He thought I did not know him—an intimate acquaintance of yours, Mr. Peachum—only Captain
Macheath—as fine as a lord.

PEACHUM. To-morrow, dear Mrs. Dye, you shall set your own price upon any of the goods you like. We have at least half a dozen velvet scarfs, and all at your service. Will you give me leave to make you a present of this suit of nightclothes for your own wearing? But are you sure it is Captain Macheath?

TRAPES. Though he thinks I have forgot him, nobody knows him better. I have taken a great deal of the captain's money in my time at second-hand, for he always loved to have his ladies well dressed.

PEACHUM. Mr. Lockit and I have a little business with the captain—you understand me—and we will satisfy you for Mrs. Coaxer's debt.

LOCKIT. Depend upon it—we will deal like men of honor.

TRAPES. I don't enquire after your affairs—so whatever happens, I wash my hands on't. It hath always been my maxim, that one friend should assist another. But if you please, I'll take one of the scarfs home with me. 'Tis always good to have something in hand.

[SCENE VII.] *Newgate*

(LUCY.)

LUCY. Jealousy, rage, love, and fear are at once tearing me to pieces. How I am weather-beaten and shattered with distresses!

AIR VII—*One evening, having lost my way, etc.*

I'm like a skiff on the ocean tossed,
   Now high, now low, with each billow borne;
With her rudder broke, and her anchor lost,
      Deserted and all forlorn.

While thus I lie rolling and tossing all night,
That Polly lies sporting on seas of delight!
      Revenge, revenge, revenge,
Shall appease my restless sprite.

I have the ratsbane ready. I run no risk; for I can lay her death upon the gin, and so many die of that naturally that I shall never be called in question. But say I were to be hanged—I never could be hanged for anything that would give me greater comfort than the poisoning that slut.

(*Enter* FILCH.)

FILCH. Madam, here's our Miss Polly come to wait upon
    you.

LUCY. Show her in.

[SCENE VIII.]

(LUCY, POLLY.)

LUCY. Dear madam, your servant. I hope you will pardon
    my passion when I was so happy to see you last. I was
    so overrun with the spleen,[44] that I was perfectly out
    of myself. And really when one hath the spleen, every-
    thing is to be excused by a friend.

> AIR VIII—*Now Roger, I'll tell thee, because
>   thou'rt my son, etc.*

> When a wife's in her pout,
> (As she's sometimes, no doubt);
> The good husband, as meek as a lamb,
>   Her vapors to still,
>   First grants her her will,
> And the quieting draught is a dram.
> Poor man! And the quieting draught is a dram.

I wish all our quarrels might have so comfortable a
    reconciliation.

POLLY. I have no excuse for my own behavior, madam,
    but my misfortunes. And really, madam, I suffer too
    upon your account.

LUCY. But, Miss Polly—in the way of friendship, will you
    give me leave, to propose a glass of cordial to you?

POLLY. Strong waters are apt to give me the headache; I
    hope, madam, you will excuse me.

LUCY. Not the greatest lady in the land could have better
    in her closet, for her own private drinking. You seem
    mighty low in spirits, my dear.

POLLY. I am sorry, madam, my health will not allow me to
    accept of your offer. I should not have left you in the
    rude manner I did when we met last, madam, had
    not my papa hauled me away so unexpectedly. I was

---

44 The spleen or the vapors (in the song which follows) was melancholy, often the fashionable excuse for low spirits or ill temper.

indeed somewhat provoked, and perhaps might use some expressions that were disrespectful. But really, madam, the captain treated me with so much contempt and cruelty, that I deserved your pity, rather than your resentment.

LUCY. But since his escape, no doubt, all matters are made up again. Ah Polly! Polly! 'tis I am the unhappy wife, and he loves you as if you were only his mistress.

POLLY. Sure, madam, you cannot think me so happy as to be the object of your jealousy! A man is always afraid of a woman who loves him too well—so that I must expect to be neglected and avoided.

LUCY. Then our cases, my dear Polly, are exactly alike. Both of us, indeed, have been too fond.

AIR IX—*O Bessy Bell*

> POLLY. A curse attends that woman's love,
>> Who always would be pleasing.
> LUCY. The pertness of the billing dove,
>> Like tickling, is but teasing.
> POLLY. What then in love can woman do?
> LUCY. If we grow fond they shun us.
> POLLY. And when we fly them, they pursue.
> LUCY. But leave us when they've won us.

LUCY. Love is so very whimsical in both sexes, that it is impossible to be lasting. But my heart is particular,[45] and contradicts my own observation.

POLLY. But really, Mistress Lucy, by his last behavior, I think I ought to envy you. When I was forced from him, he did not shew the least tenderness. But perhaps he hath a heart not capable of it.

AIR X—*Would fate to me Belinda give*

> Among the men, coquets we find,
> Who court by turns all womankind;
> And we grant all their hearts desired,
> When they are flattered and admired.

The coquets of both sexes are self-lovers, and that is a love no other whatever can dispossess. I fear, my dear Lucy, our husband is one of those.

---

[45] Special or unique, and partial to only one man.

LUCY. Away with these melancholy reflections!—indeed,
   my dear Polly, we are both of us a cup too low. Let
   me prevail upon you to accept of my offer.

AIR XI—*Come, sweet lass, etc.*

Come, sweet lass,
Let's banish sorrow
'Till to-morrow;
Come, sweet lass,
Let's take a chirping[46] glass.
Wine can clear
The vapors of despair;
And make us light as air;
Then drink, and banish care.

I can't bear, child, to see you in such low spirits. And
I must persuade you to what I know will do you good.
(*aside*) I shall now soon be even with the hypocritical
strumpet. (*Exit* LUCY.)

[SCENE IX.]

(POLLY.)

POLLY. All this wheedling of Lucy cannot be for nothing
   —at this time too, when I know she hates me! The
   dissembling of a woman is always the forerunner of
   mischief. By pouring strong waters down my throat,
   she thinks to pump some secrets out of me. I'll be
   upon my guard and won't taste a drop of her liquor,
   I'm resolved.

[SCENE X.]

(LUCY, *with strong waters;* POLLY.)

LUCY. Come, Miss Polly.
POLLY. Indeed, child, you have given yourself trouble to
   no purpose. You must, my dear, excuse me.
LUCY. Really, Miss Polly, you are as squeamishly affected
   about taking a cup of strong waters as a lady before
   company. I vow, Polly, I shall take it monstrously ill
   if you refuse me. Brandy and men (though women
   love them never so well) are always taken by us with
   some reluctance—unless 'tis in private.

46 Cheering.

POLLY. I protest, madam, it goes against me. What do I see! Macheath again in custody! Now every glimmering of happiness is lost. (*Drops the glass of liquor on the ground.*)

LUCY (*aside*). Since things are thus, I am glad the wench hath escaped: for by this event, 'tis plain, she was not happy enough to deserve to be poisoned.

[SCENE XI.]

(LOCKIT, MACHEATH, PEACHUM, LUCY, POLLY.)

LOCKIT. Set your heart to rest, captain. You have neither the chance of love or money for another escape; for you are ordered to be called down upon your trial immediately.

PEACHUM. Away, hussies! This is not a time for a man to be hampered with his wives. You see, the gentleman is in chains already.

LUCY. Oh, husband, husband, my heart longed to see thee; but to see thee thus distracts me!

POLLY. Will not my dear husband look upon his Polly? Why hadst thou not flown to me for protection? With me thou hadst been safe.

AIR XII—*The last time I went o'er the moor*

POLLY. Hither, dear husband, turn your eyes.
LUCY. Bestow one glance to cheer me.
POLLY. Think, with that look, thy Polly dies.
LUCY. Oh shun me not—but hear me.
POLLY. 'Tis Polly sues.
LUCY.   —'Tis Lucy speaks.
POLLY. Is thus true love requited?
LUCY. My heart is bursting.
POLLY.   —Mine too breaks.
LUCY. Must I?
POLLY.   —Must I be slighted?

MACHEATH. What would you have me say, ladies? You see, this affair will soon be at an end without my disobliging either of you.

PEACHUM. But the settling this point, captain, might prevent a lawsuit between your two widows.

MACHEATH.

AIR XIII—*Tom Tinker's my true love*

Which way shall I turn me? How can I decide?
Wives, the day of our death, are as fond as a bride.
One wife is too much for most husbands to hear,
But two at a time there's no mortal can bear.
This way, and that way, and which way I will,
What would comfort the one, t'other wife would take ill.

POLLY (*aside*). But if his own misfortunes have made him
insensible to mine—a father sure will be more compassionate.—[*To* PEACHUM] Dear, dear sir, sink the
material evidence, and bring him off at his trial! Polly
upon her knees begs it of you.

AIR XIV—*I am a poor shepherd undone*

When my hero in court appears,
    And stands arraigned for his life;
Then think of poor Polly's tears;
    For ah! poor Polly's his wife.
Like the sailor he holds up his hand,
    Distressed on the dashing wave.
To die a dry death at land,
    Is as bad as a wat'ry grave.
        And alas, poor Polly;
        Alack, and well-a-day!
        Before I was in love,
        Oh, every month was May!

LUCY [*To* LOCKIT]. If Peachum's heart is hardened, sure
you, sir, will have more compassion on a daughter.
I know the evidence is in your power. How can you
be a tyrant to me? (*kneeling*)

AIR XV—*Ianthe the lovely, etc.*

When he holds up his hand arraigned for his life,
Oh, think of your daughter, and think I'm his wife!
What are cannons, or bombs, or clashing of swords?
For death is more certain by witnesses' words.
Then nail up their lips; that dread thunder allay;
And each month of my life will hereafter be May.

LOCKIT. Macheath's time is come, Lucy. We know our own
affairs; therefore let us have no more whimpering or
whining.

AIR—*A cobbler there was, etc.*

Ourselves, like the great, to secure a retreat,
When matters require it, must give up our gang.
   And good reason why,
   Or instead of the fry,
   Ev'n Peachum and I,
Like poor petty rascals, might hang, hang;
Like poor petty rascals might hang.

PEACHUM. Set your heart at rest, Polly. Your husband is to die to-day! therefore, if you are not already provided, 'tis high time to look about for another. There's comfort for you, you slut.

LOCKIT. We are ready, sir, to conduct you to the Old Bailey.

MACHEATH.

AIR XVI—*Bonny Dundee*

The charge is prepared; the lawyers are met,
The judges all ranged (a terrible show!).
I go, undismayed—for death is a debt,
A debt on demand. So, take what I owe.
Then farewell, my love—dear charmers, adieu.
Contented I die—'tis the better for you.
Here ends all dispute the rest of our lives,
  For this way at once I please all my wives.

Now, gentlemen, I am ready to attend you.

(*Exeunt* MACHEATH, LOCKIT *and* PEACHUM.)

[SCENE XII.]

(LUCY, POLLY, FILCH.)

POLLY. Follow them, Filch, to the court; and when the trial is over, bring me a particular account of his behavior, and of everything that happened. You'll find me here with Miss Lucy.

(*Exit* FILCH.)

But why is all this music?

LUCY. The prisoners whose trials are put off till next sessions are diverting themselves.

POLLY. Sure there is nothing so charming as music! I'm fond of it to distraction! But alas! now, all mirth seems an insult upon my affliction.—Let us retire, my dear Lucy, and indulge our sorrows. The noisy crew, you see, are coming upon us.

(*Exeunt.*)

(*A dance of prisoners in chains, etc.*)

[SCENE XIII.] *The condemned hold*

(MACHEATH *in a melancholy posture.*)

AIR XVII—*Happy groves*

O cruel, cruel, cruel case!
Must I suffer this disgrace?

AIR XVIII—*Of all the girls that are so smart*

Of all the friends in time of grief,
When threat'ning death looks grimmer,
Not one so sure can bring relief,
As this best friend, a brimmer. (*Drinks.*)

AIR XIX—*Britons, strike home*

Since I must swing, I scorn, I scorn to wince or whine.
(*Rises.*)

AIR XX—*Chevy Chase*

But now again my spirits sink;
I'll raise them high with wine. (*Drinks a glass of wine.*)

AIR XXI—*To old Sir Simon the king*

But valor the stronger grows,
The stronger liquor we're drinking.
And how can we feel our woes,
When we've lost the trouble of thinking? (*Drinks.*)

AIR XXII—*Joy to great Caesar*

If thus—a man can die,
Much bolder with brandy. (*Pour out a bumper of brandy.*)

AIR XXIII—*There was an old woman*

So I drink off this bumper.—And now I can stand the test,
And my comrades shall see that I die as brave as the best.
(*Drinks.*)

AIR XXIV—*Did you ever hear of a gallant sailor*

> But can I leave my pretty hussies,
> Without one tear, or tender sigh?

AIR XXV—*Why are mine eyes still flowing*

> Their eyes, their lips, their busses,
> Recall my love. Ah, must I die?

AIR XXVI—*Greensleeves*

Since laws were made for ev'ry degree,
To curb vice in others, as well as me,
I wonder we han't better company,
> Upon Tyburn tree!
But gold from law can take out the sting;
And if rich men like us were to swing,
'Twould thin the land, such numbers to string
> Upon Tyburn tree!

(*Enter a* JAILOR.)

JAILOR. Some friends of yours, captain, desire to be admitted. I leave you together. (*Exit.*)

[SCENE XIV.]

(MACHEATH, BEN BUDGE, MATT OF THE MINT.)

MACHEATH. For my having broke prison, you see, gentlemen, I am ordered immediate execution. The sheriff's officers, I believe, are now at the door. That Jemmy Twitcher should peach me, I own, surprised me! 'Tis a plain proof that the world is all alike, and that even our gang can no more trust one another than other people. Therefore, I beg you, gentlemen, look well to yourselves, for in all probability you may live some months longer.

MATT. We are heartily sorry, captain, for your misfortune. But 'tis what we must all come to.

MACHEATH. Peachum and Lockit, you know, are infamous scoundrels. Their lives are as much in your power, as yours are in theirs. Remember your dying friend!— 'Tis my last request. Bring those villains to the gallows before you, and I am satisfied.

MATT. We'll do't.

[*Re-enter* JAILOR.]

JAILOR. Miss Polly and Miss Lucy entreat a word with you.
MACHEATH. Gentlemen, adieu.

(*Exeunt* BEN, MATT, *and* JAILOR.)

[SCENE XV.]

MACHEATH. My dear Lucy—my dear Polly! Whatsoever
hath passed between us is now at an end. If you are
fond of marrying again, the best advice I can give you
is to ship yourselves off for the West Indies, where
you'll have a fair chance of getting a husband apiece
—or by good luck, two or three, as you like best.

POLLY. How can I support this sight!

LUCY. There is nothing moves one so much as a great
man in distress.

AIR XXVII—*All you that must take a leap, etc.*

LUCY. Would I might be hanged!
POLLY.   —And I would so too!
LUCY. To be hanged with you.
POLLY.   —My dear, with you.
MACHEATH. Oh, leave me to thought! I fear! I doubt!
I tremble! I droop! See, my courage is out.
                              (*Turns up the empty bottle.*)
POLLY. No token of love?
MACHEATH.   See, my courage is out.
                              (*Turns up the empty pot.*)
LUCY. No token of love?
POLLY.   Adieu.
LUCY.   Farewell!
MACHEATH. But hark! I hear the toll of the bell!
CHORUS. Tol de rol lol, etc.

[*Enter* JAILOR.]

JAILOR. Four women more, captain, with a child apiece!
See, here they come.

(*Enter* WOMEN *and* CHILDREN.)

MACHEATH. What—four wives more! This is too much.—
Here, tell the Sheriff's officers I am ready.

(*Exit* MACHEATH *guarded.*)

[SCENE XVI.]

(*To them enter* PLAYER *and* BEGGAR.)

PLAYER. But, honest friend, I hope you don't intend that Macheath shall be really executed.

BEGGAR. Most certainly, sir. To make the piece perfect, I was for doing strict poetical justice. Macheath is to be hanged; and for the other personages of the drama, the audience must have supposed they were all either hanged or transported.

PLAYER. Why then, friend, this is a downright deep tragedy. The catastrophe is manifestly wrong, for an opera must end happily.

BEGGAR. Your objection, sir, is very just, and is easily removed; for you must allow that in this kind of drama, 'tis no matter how absurdly things are brought about. So—you rabble there! run and cry a reprieve!—let the prisoner be brought back to his wives in triumph.

PLAYER. All this we must do, to comply with the taste of the town.

BEGGAR. Through the whole piece you may observe such a similitude of manners in high and low life, that it is difficult to determine whether (in the fashionable vices) the fine gentlemen imitate the gentlemen of the road, or the gentlemen of the road the fine gentlemen. Had the play remained as I at first intended, it would have carried a most excellent moral. 'Twould have shown that the lower sort of people have their vices in a degree as well as the rich, and that they are punished for them.

[SCENE XVII.]

(*To them* MACHEATH, *with rabble, etc.*)

MACHEATH. So it seems I am not left to my choice, but must have a wife at last.—Look ye, my dears, we will have no controversy now. Let us give this day to mirth, and I am sure she who thinks herself my wife will testify her joy by a dance.

ALL. Come, a dance—a dance!

MACHEATH. Ladies, I hope you will give me leave to present a partner to each of you. And (if I may without offence) for this time, I take Polly for mine. [*To*

POLLY] And for life, you slut, for we were really married. As for the rest—but at present keep your own secret.

A Dance

AIR XXVIII—*Lumps of pudding, etc.*

Thus I stand like the Turk, with his doxies around;
From all sides their glances his passion confound:
For black, brown, and fair, his inconstancy burns,
And the different beauties subdue him by turns.
Each calls forth her charms, to provoke his desires;
Though willing to all, with but one he retires.
But think of this maxim, and put off your sorrow,
The wretch of today may be happy to-morrow.
    CHORUS. But think of this maxim, etc.

THE LONDON MERCHANT

OR,

THE HISTORY OF GEORGE BARNWELL

1731

George Lillo

INTRODUCTORY NOTE

GEORGE LILLO (1695–1739) was a dissenting Protestant who carried on his father's business as a jeweler. He wrote eight plays, of which the only notable ones are the bourgeois tragedies *The London Merchant* (1731) and *Fatal Curiosity* (1736). He was known for good nature as well as strict morals, and Henry Fielding eulogized him as "one of the best of men" (*The Champion*, February 26, 1740).

The London Merchant is based on the seventeenth-century "Ballad of George Barnwell," which supposedly told the tale of an actual murder. Lillo humanized Barnwell by giving him the devotion of Maria and Trueman and having Millwood instigate the murder of his uncle. When Lillo publicized his play by circulating copies of the ballad, people came to jeer because of the low theme; but, it is reported, they soon took out their handkerchiefs to weep over Barnwell's progressive ruin. The play became very successful and was admired by such sophisticated judges as Pope and Fielding. For a century thereafter it was regularly produced on holidays as a solemn warning to London apprentices, a practice which inspired Charles Dickens' hilarious ridicule in *Great Expectations*.

Despite his heavy moralizing, Lillo allowed his villain, Millwood, both sympathy and stature. Her defiance of the society which has debased her has genuine power.

BIBLIOGRAPHY

❧ ❧

Major Works:

*The London Merchant; or, The History of George Barn-
    well*, 1731 (tragedy)
Guilt Its Own Punishment; or, Fatal Curiosity, 1736
    (tragedy)

THE LONDON MERCHANT

DEDICATION
TO

SIR JOHN EYLES, Bart., Member of Parliament for, and Alderman of, the city of *London*, and Sub-Governor of the *South-Sea* Company

Sir,

If tragic poetry be, as Mr. Dryden has some where said, the most excellent and most useful kind of writing, the more extensively useful the moral of any tragedy is, the more excellent that piece must be of its kind.

I hope I shall not be thought to insinuate that this, to which I have presumed to prefix your name, is such; that depends on its fitness to answer the end of tragedy, the exciting of the passions in order to the correcting such of them as are criminal, either in their nature, or through their excess. Whether the following scenes do this in any tolerable degree, is, with the deference that becomes one who would not be thought vain, submitted to your candid and impartial judgment.

What I would infer is this, I think, evident truth: that tragedy is so far from losing its dignity by being accommodated to the circumstances of the generality of mankind that it is more truly august in proportion to the extent of its influence, and the numbers that are properly affected by it. As it is more truly great to be the instrument of good to many, who stand in need of our assistance, than to a very small part of that number.

If princes, &c., were alone liable to misfortunes arising from vice or weakness in themselves or others, there would be good reason for confining the characters in tragedy to those of superior rank; but, since the contrary is evident, nothing can be more reasonable than to proportion the remedy to the disease.

I am far from denying that tragedies founded on any instructive and extraordinary events in history, or a well-invented fable where the persons introduced are of the highest rank, are without their use, even to the bulk of the audience. The strong contrast between a *Tamerlane* and a *Bajazet*,[1] may have its weight with an unsteady people and contribute to the fixing of them in the interest of a prince of the character of the former, when, thro' their own levity or the arts of designing men, they are rendered factious and uneasy though they have the highest reason to be satisfied. The sentiments and example of a *Cato*,[2] may inspire his spectators with a just sense of the value of liberty when they see that honest patriot prefer death to an obligation from a tyrant who would sacrifice the constitution of his country and the liberties of mankind to his ambition or revenge. I have attempted, indeed, to enlarge the province of the graver kind of poetry, and should be glad to see it carried on by some abler hand. Plays founded on moral tales in private life may be of admirable use by carrying conviction to the mind with such irresistible force as to engage all the faculties and powers of the soul in the cause of virtue by stifling vice in its first principles. They who imagine this to be too much to be attributed to tragedy must be strangers to the energy of that noble species of poetry. Shakespeare, who has given such amazing proofs of his genius in that as well as in comedy, in his *Hamlet*, has the following lines:

> Had he the motive and the cause for passion
> That I have, he would drown the stage with tears
> And cleave the general ear with horrid speech;
> Make mad the guilty, and appall the free,
> Confound the ignorant, and amaze indeed
> The very faculty of eyes and ears.

And farther, in the same speech,

> I've heard that guilty creatures at a play,
> Have, by the very cunning of the scene,
> Been so struck to the soul that presently
> They have proclaim'd their malefactions.

---

[1] Tamerlane is a benevolent monarch and Bajazet a tyrant in Nicholas Rowe's heroic play *Tamerlane* (1702).
[2] The noble hero of Joseph Addison's *Cato* (1713).

Prodigious! yet strictly just. But I shan't take up your valuable time with my remarks; only give me leave just to observe that he seems so firmly persuaded of the power of a well wrote piece to produce the effect here ascribed to it, as to make Hamlet venture his soul on the event, and rather trust that, than a messenger from the other world, though it assumed, as he expresses it, his noble father's form, and assured him that it was his spirit. I'll have, says Hamlet, grounds more relative.

> . . . The Play's the thing
> Wherein I'll catch the conscience of the king.

Such plays are the best answer to them who deny the lawfulness of the stage.

Considering the novelty of this attempt, I thought it would be expected from me to say something in its excuse; and I was unwilling to lose the opportunity of saying something of the usefulness of tragedy in general, and what may be reasonably expected from the farther improvement of this excellent kind of poetry.

Sir, I hope you will not think I have said too much of an art, a mean specimen of which I am ambitious enough to recommend to your favor and protection. A mind conscious of superior worth as much despises flattery as it is above it. Had I found in myself an inclination to so contemptible a vice, I should not have chose Sir John Eyles for my patron. And indeed the best writ panegyric, though strictly true, must place you in a light, much inferior to that in which you have long been fixed by the love and esteem of your fellow citizens, whose choice of you for one of their representatives in Parliament has sufficiently declared their sense of your merit. Nor hath the knowledge of your worth been confined to the City. The proprietors in the South-Sea Company, in which are included numbers of persons as considerable for their rank, fortune, and understanding as any in the kingdom, gave the greatest proof of their confidence in your capacity and probity when they chose you Sub-Governor of their company, at a time when their affairs were in the utmost confusion, and their properties in the greatest danger. Nor is the court insensible of your importance. I shall not therefore attempt your character, nor pretend to add any thing to a reputation so well established.

Whatever others may think of a dedication, wherein
there is so much said of other things and so little of the
person to whom it is addressed, I have reason to believe
that you will the more easily pardon it on that very account.

I am, sir,

Your most obedient
humble servant,
George Lillo

Dramatis Personae

MEN

THOROWGOOD
BARNWELL, *uncle to George*
GEORGE BARNWELL
TRUEMAN
BLUNT

WOMEN

MARIA
MILLWOOD
LUCY

Officers with their attendants, Keeper, and Footmen
Scene: London and an adjacent village

PROLOGUE
Spoke by Mr. Cibber, Jun.

The tragic muse, sublime, delights to show
Princes distressed, and scenes of royal woe;
In awful pomp, majestic, to relate
The fall of nations or some hero's fate,
That sceptered chiefs may by example know
The strange vicissitude of things below;
What dangers on security attend;
How pride and cruelty in ruin end;
Hence Providence supreme to know, and own
Humanity adds glory to a throne.
   In ev'ry former age, and foreign tongue,
With native grandeur thus the goddess sung.
Upon our stage indeed with wished success
You've sometimes seen her in a humbler dress,
Great only in distress. When she complains
In Southerne's, Rowe's, or Otway's moving strains
The brilliant drops that fall from each bright eye,
The absent pomp with brighter gems supply.
Forgive us then, if we attempt to show
In artless strains a tale of private woe.
A London 'prentice ruined is our theme,
Drawn from the famed old song that bears his name.
We hope your taste is not so high to scorn
A moral tale esteemed e'er you were born,
Which for a century of rolling years
Has filled a thousand-thousand eyes with tears.
If thoughtless youth to warn and shame the age
From vice destructive well becomes the stage,
If this example innocence insure,
Prevent our guilt, or by reflection cure,

If Millwood's dreadful guilt, and sad despair,
Commend the virtue of the good and fair,
Though art be wanting, and our numbers fail,
Indulge th' attempt, in justice to the tale.

ACT I

[SCENE I.] *A Room in* THOROWGOOD's *House*

([*Enter*] THOROWGOOD *and* TRUEMAN.)

TRUEMAN. Sir, the packet from Genoa is arrived. (*Gives letters.*)

THOROWGOOD. Heaven be praised, the storm that threatened our royal mistress, pure religion, liberty, and laws is for a time diverted; the haughty and revengeful Spaniard, disappointed of the loan on which he depended from Genoa, must now attend the slow return of wealth from his new world to supply his empty coffers, e'er he can execute his purposed invasion of our happy island;[3] by which means time is gained to make such preparations on our part as may, Heaven concurring, prevent his malice or turn the meditated mischief on himself.

TRUEMAN. He must be insensible indeed who is not affected when the safety of his country is concerned. Sir, may I know by what means—if I am too bold—

THOROWGOOD. Your curiosity is laudable; and I gratify it with the greater pleasure because from thence you may learn how honest merchants, as such, may sometimes contribute to the safety of their country as they do at all times to its happiness; that if hereafter you should be tempted to any action that has the appearance of vice or meanness in it, upon reflecting on the dignity of our profession, you may with honest scorn reject whatever is unworthy of it.

---

[3] The time of the play is about 1587, when the Spaniards were preparing the Armada to invade England.

TRUEMAN. Should Barnwell or I, who have the benefit of your example, by our ill conduct bring any imputation on that honorable name, we must be left without excuse.

THOROWGOOD. You compliment, young man. (TRUEMAN *bows respectfully*) Nay, I'm not offended. As the name of merchant never degrades the gentleman, so by no means does it exclude him; only take heed not to purchase the character of complaisant at the expense of your sincerity. But to answer your question —the bank of Genoa had agreed, at excessive interest and on good security, to advance the King of Spain a sum of money sufficient to equip his vast armada, of which our peerless Elizabeth (more than in name the mother of her people), being well informed, sent Walsingham, her wise and faithful secretary, to consult the merchants of this loyal city, who all agreed to direct their several agents to influence, if possible, the Genoese to break their contract with the Spanish court. 'Tis done; the state and bank of Genoa, having maturely weighed and rightly judged of their true interest, prefer the friendship of the merchants of London to that of a monarch who proudly styles himself King of both Indies.

TRUEMAN. Happy success of prudent councils. What an expense of blood and treasure is here saved! Excellent queen! O how unlike to former princes, who made the danger of foreign enemies a pretense to oppress their subjects by taxes great and grievous to be borne.

THOROWGOOD. Not so our gracious queen, whose richest exchequer is her people's love, as their happiness her greatest glory.

TRUEMAN. On these terms to defend us is to make our protection a benefit worthy her who confers it, and well worth our acceptance. Sir, have you any commands for me at this time?

THOROWGOOD. Only to look carefully over the files to see whether there are any tradesmen's bills unpaid; and if there are, to send and discharge 'em. We must not let artificers lose their time, so useful to the public and their families, in unnecessary attendance.

([*Exit* TRUEMAN. *Enter*] MARIA.)

THOROWGOOD. Well, Maria, have you given orders for the
  entertainment? I would have it in some measure
  worthy the guests. Let there be plenty, and of the
  best, that the courtiers, though they should deny us
  citizens politeness, may at least commend our
  hospitality.

MARIA. Sir, I have endeavored not to wrong your well-
  known generosity by an ill-timed parsimony.

THOROWGOOD. Nay, 'twas a needless caution; I have no
  cause to doubt your prudence.

MARIA. Sir, I find myself unfit for conversation at present.
  I should but increase the number of the company,
  without adding to their satisfaction.

THOROWGOOD. Nay, my child, this melancholy must not
  be indulged.

MARIA. Company will but increase it. I wish you would
  dispense with[4] my absence; solitude best suits my
  present temper.

THOROWGOOD. You are not insensible that it is chiefly on
  your account these noble lords do me the honor so
  frequently to grace my board; should you be absent,
  the disappointment may make them repent their
  condescension and think their labor lost.

MARIA. He that shall think his time or honor lost in visiting you, can set no real value on your daughter's
  company, whose only merit is that she is yours. The
  man of quality, who chooses to converse with a gentleman and merchant of your worth and character, may
  confer honor by so doing, but he loses none.

THOROWGOOD. Come, come, Maria, I need not tell you
  that a young gentleman may prefer your conversation
  to mine, yet intend me no disrespect at all; for though
  he may lose no honor in my company, 'tis very
  natural for him to expect more pleasure in yours. I
  remember the time when the company of the greatest
  and wisest man in the kingdom would have been
  insipid and tiresome to me, if it had deprived me of
  an opportunity of enjoying your mother's.

MARIA. Yours no doubt was as agreeable to her; for
  generous minds know no pleasure in society but where
  'tis mutual.

---

[4] Excuse.

THOROWGOOD. Thou know'st I have no heir, no child, but thee; the fruits of many years' successful industry must all be thine. Now it would give me pleasure great as my love, to see on whom you would bestow it. I am daily solicited by men of the greatest rank and merit for leave to address you, but I have hitherto declined it, in hopes that by observation I should learn which way your inclination tends; for as I know love to be essential to happiness in the marriage state, I had rather my approbation should confirm your choice than direct it.

MARIA. What can I say? How shall I answer as I ought this tenderness, so uncommon even in the best of parents; but you are without example; yet had you been less indulgent, I had been most wretched. That I look on the crowd of courtiers that visit here with equal esteem but equal indifference you have observed, and I must needs confess; yet had you asserted your authority, and insisted on a parent's right to be obeyed, I had submitted, and to my duty sacrificed my peace.

THOROWGOOD. From your perfect obedience in every other instance, I feared as much; and therefore would leave you without a bias in an affair wherein your happiness is so immediately concerned.

MARIA. Whether from a want of that just ambition that would become your daughter or from some other cause I know not; but I find high birth and titles don't recommend the man who owns them, to my affections.

THOROWGOOD. I would not that they should, unless his merit recommends him more. A noble birth and fortune, though they make not a bad man good, yet they are a real advantage to a worthy one, and place his virtues in the fairest light.

MARIA. I cannot answer for my inclinations, but they shall ever be submitted to your wisdom and authority; and as you will not compel me to marry where I cannot love, so love shall never make me act contrary to my duty. Sir, have I your permission to retire?

THOROWGOOD. I'll see you to your chamber.

[*Exeunt.*]

[SCENE II.] *A Room in* MILLWOOD's *house*

(MILLWOOD [*at her toilet*]. LUCY *waiting*.)

MILLWOOD. How do I look to-day, Lucy?

LUCY. Oh, killingly, madam! A little more red, and you'll
be irresistible! But why this more than ordinary care
of your dress and complexion? What new conquest
are you aiming at?

MILLWOOD. A conquest would be new indeed!

LUCY. Not to you, who make 'em every day, but to me—
well! 'tis what I'm never to expect, unfortunate as I
am. But your wit and beauty—

MILLWOOD. First made me a wretch, and still continue me
so. Men, however generous or sincere to one another,
are all selfish hypocrites in their affairs with us. We
are no otherwise esteemed or regarded by them, but
as we contribute to their satisfaction.

LUCY. You are certainly, madam, on the wrong side in this
argument. Is not the expense all theirs? And I am
sure it is our own fault if we haven't our share of the
pleasure.

MILLWOOD. We are but slaves to men.

LUCY. Nay, 'tis they that are slaves most certainly; for we
lay them under contribution.

MILLWOOD. Slaves have no property; no, not even in themselves. All is the victor's.

LUCY. You are strangely arbitrary in your principles,
madam.

MILLWOOD. I would have my conquests complete, like those
of the Spaniards in the New World, who first
plundered the natives of all the wealth they had, and
then condemned the wretches to the mines for life to
work for more.

LUCY. Well, I shall never approve of your scheme of government. I should think it much more politic, as well
as just, to find my subjects an easier employment.

MILLWOOD. It's a general maxim among the knowing part
of mankind that a woman without virtue, like a man
without honor or honesty, is capable of any action,
though never so vile; and yet what pains will they not
take, what arts not use, to seduce us from our innocence and make us contemptible and wicked even in
their own opinions? Then is it not just, the villains, to

their cost, should find us so? But guilt makes them suspicious, and keeps them on their guard; therefore we can take advantage only of the young and innocent part of the sex, who, having never injured women, apprehend no injury from them.

LUCY. Ay, they must be young indeed.

MILLWOOD. Such a one, I think, I have found. As I've passed through the City, I have often observed him receiving and paying considerable sums of money; from thence I conclude he is employed in affairs of consequence.

LUCY. Is he handsome?

MILLWOOD. Ay, ay, the stripling is well made.

LUCY. About—

MILLWOOD. Eighteen.

LUCY. Innocent, handsome, and about eighteen. You'll be vastly happy. Why, if you manage well, you may keep him to your self these two or three years.

MILLWOOD. If I manage well, I shall have done with him much sooner. Having long had a design on him, and meeting him yesterday, I made a full stop and gazing wistfully on his face, asked him his name. He blushed, and bowing very low, answered, George Barnwell. I begged his pardon for the freedom I had taken, and told him that he was the person I had long wished to see, and to whom I had an affair of importance to communicate at a proper time and place. He named a tavern; I talked of honor and reputation, and invited him to my house. He swallowed the bait, promised to come, and this is the time I expect him. (*knocking at the door*) Somebody knocks—d'ye hear? I am at home to nobody to-day, but him.—

[*Exit* LUCY.]

Less affairs must give way to those of more consequence; and I am strangely mistaken if this does not prove of great importance to me and him, too, before I have done with him. Now, after what manner shall I receive him? Let me consider. What manner of person am I to receive? He is young, innocent, and bashful; therefore I must take care not to shock him at first. But then, if I have any skill in physiognomy, he is amorous, and, with a little assistance, will soon get the better of his modesty. I'll trust to nature, who does wonders in these matters. If to seem what one is not, in order to be the better liked for what one really is; if to speak one thing, and mean the direct contrary, be art in a woman, I know nothing of nature.

([*Enter*] BARNWELL *bowing very low.* LUCY *at a distance.*)

MILLWOOD. Sir, the surprise and joy!—

BARNWELL. Madam—

MILLWOOD. This is such a favor—(*advancing*)

BARNWELL. Pardon me, madam—

MILLWOOD. So unhoped for—

(*Still advances.* BARNWELL *salutes her, and retires in confusion.*)

To see you here—Excuse the confusion—

BARNWELL. I fear I am too bold.

MILLWOOD. Alas, sir! All my apprehensions proceed from my fears of your thinking me so. Please, sir, to sit. I am as much at a loss how to receive this honor as I ought, as I am surprised at your goodness in conferring it.

BARNWELL. I thought you had expected me. I promised to come.

MILLWOOD. That is the more surprising; few men are such religious observers of their word.

BARNWELL. All who are honest are.

MILLWOOD. To one another. But we silly women are seldom thought of consequence enough to gain a place in your remembrance. (*laying her hand on his, as by accident*)

BARNWELL (*aside*). Her discomfort is so great, she don't perceive she has laid her hand on mine. Heaven! how she trembles! What can this mean!

MILLWOOD. The interest I have in all that relates to you (the reason of which you shall know hereafter) excites my curiosity; and, were I sure you would pardon my presumption, I should desire to know your real sentiments on a very particular subject.

BARNWELL. Madam, you may command my poor thoughts on any subject; I have none that I would conceal.

MILLWOOD. You'll think me bold.

BARNWELL. No, indeed.

MILLWOOD. What then are your thoughts of love?

BARNWELL. If you mean the love of women, I have not
thought of it at all. My youth and circumstances make
such thoughts improper in me yet. But if you mean the
general love we owe to mankind, I think no one has
more of it in his temper than myself. I don't know
that person in the world whose happiness I don't wish,
and wouldn't promote, were it in my power. In an
especial manner I love my uncle and my master, but
above all my friend.

MILLWOOD. You have a friend then whom you love?

BARNWELL. As he does me, sincerely.

MILLWOOD. He is, no doubt, often blessed with your company and conversation.

BARNWELL. We live in one house together, and both serve
the same worthy merchant.

MILLWOOD. Happy, happy youth!—Who e'er thou art, I
envy thee, and so must all who see and know this
youth.—What I have lost, by being formed a woman!
I hate my sex, myself. Had I been a man, I might,
perhaps, have been as happy in your friendship as he
who now enjoys it. But as it is—oh!

BARNWELL (*aside*). I never observed women before, or this
is sure the most beautiful of her sex.—You seem dis-
ordered, madam! May I know the cause?

MILLWOOD. Do not ask me. I can never speak it, whatever is the cause. I wish for things impossible. I would
be a servant, bound to the same master as you are, to
live in one house with you.

BARNWELL (*aside*). How strange, and yet how kind, her
words and actions are! And the effect they have on
me is as strange. I feel desires I never knew before. I
must be gone, while I have power to go. Madam, I
humbly take my leave.

MILLWOOD. You will not sure leave me so soon!

BARNWELL. Indeed I must.

MILLWOOD. You cannot be so cruel! I have prepared a
poor supper, at which I promised myself your
company.

BARNWELL. I am sorry I must refuse the honor that you
designed me, but my duty to my master calls me
hence. I never yet neglected his service. He is so
gentle and so good a master that should I wrong him,

though he might forgive me, I never should forgive
myself.

MILLWOOD. Am I refused, by the first man, the second
favor I ever stooped to ask? Go then, thou proud, hard-
hearted youth. But know, you are the only man that
could be found who would let me sue twice for
greater favors.

BARNWELL (*aside*). What shall I do! How shall I go or
stay!

MILLWOOD. Yet do not, do not, leave me. I wish my sex's
pride would meet your scorn; but when I look upon
you, when I behold those eyes—oh! spare my tongue,
and let my blushes—this flood of tears, too, that will
force its way—declare what woman's modesty should
hide.

BARNWELL [*aside*]. Oh, heavens! she loves me, worthless
as I am; her looks, her words, her flowing tears confess
it. And can I leave her then? Oh, never, never!—
Madam, dry up your tears. You shall command me
always; I will stay here for ever, if you'd have me.

LUCY (*aside*). So! she has wheedled him out of his virtue
of obedience already and will strip him of all the rest,
one after another, till she has left him as few as her
ladyship or myself.

MILLWOOD. Now you are kind, indeed; but I mean not to
detain you always. I would have you shake off all
slavish obedience to your master, but you may serve
him still.

LUCY [*aside*]. Serve him still! Aye, or he'll have no opportunity of fingering his cash, and then he'll not serve
your end, I'll be sworn.

([*Enter*] BLUNT.)

BLUNT. Madam, supper's on the table.

MILLWOOD. Come, sir, you'll excuse all defects. My
thoughts were too much employed on my guest to
observe the entertainment.

[*Exeunt* MILLWOOD *and* BARNWELL.]

BLUNT. What! is all this preparation, this elegant supper,
variety of wines and music, for the entertainment of
that young fellow!

LUCY. So it seems.

BLUNT. What! is our mistress turned fool at last! She's in love with him, I suppose.

LUCY. I suppose not, but she designs to make him in love with her if she can.

BLUNT. What will she get by that? He seems under age, and can't be supposed to have much money.

LUCY. But his master has; and that's the same thing, as she'll manage it.

BLUNT. I don't like this fooling with a handsome young fellow; while she's endeavoring to ensnare him, she may be caught herself.

LUCY. Nay, were she like me, that would certainly be the consequence; for, I confess, there is something in youth and innocence that moves me mightily.

BLUNT. Yes, so does the smoothness and plumpness of a partridge move a mighty desire in the hawk to be the destruction of it.

LUCY. Why, birds are their prey, as men are ours; though, as you observed, we are sometimes caught ourselves. But that, I dare say, will never be the case with our mistress.

BLUNT. I wish it may prove so; for you know we all depend upon her. Should she trifle away her time with a young fellow that there's nothing to be got by, we must all starve.

LUCY. There's no danger of that, for I am sure she has no view in this affair but interest.

BLUNT. Well, and what hopes are there of success in that?

LUCY. The most promising that can be. 'Tis true, the youth has his scruples; but she'll soon teach him to answer them by stifling his conscience. Oh, the lad is in a hopeful way, depend upon't.

[*Exeunt.*]

[SCENE III.] *Draws and discovers* BARNWELL *and* MILLWOOD *at supper. An entertainment of music and singing. After which they come forward.*

BARNWELL. What can I answer! All that I know is, that you are fair and I am miserable.

MILLWOOD. We are both so, and yet the fault is in ourselves.

BARNWELL. To ease our present anguish by plunging into guilt is to buy a moment's pleasure with an age of pain.

MILLWOOD. I should have thought the joys of love as lasting as they are great. If ours prove otherwise, 'tis your inconstancy must make them so.

BARNWELL. The law of heaven will not be reversed, and that requires us to govern our passions.

MILLWOOD. To give us sense of beauty and desires, and yet forbid us to taste and be happy, is cruelty to nature. Have we passions only to torment us!

BARNWELL. To hear you talk, though in the cause of vice, to gaze upon your beauty, press your hand, and see your snow-white bosom heave and fall, enflames my wishes; my pulse beats high, my senses all are in a hurry, and I am on the rack of wild desire; yet for a moment's guilty pleasure, shall I lose my innocence, my peace of mind, and hopes of solid happiness?

MILLWOOD. Chimeras all! Come on with me and prove, No joy's like woman-kind, nor heaven like love.

BARNWELL. I would not, yet must on.—

Reluctant thus, the merchant quits his ease
And trusts to rocks, and sands, and stormy seas;
In hopes some unknown golden coast to find,
Commits himself, though doubtful, to the wind,
Longs much for joys to come, yet mourns those left behind.

[*Exeunt.*]

ACT II

[SCENE I.] *A Room in* THOROWGOOD's *House*

([*Enter*] BARNWELL.)

BARNWELL. How strange are all things round me! Like some thief, who treads forbidden ground, fearful I enter each apartment of this well-known house. To guilty love, as if that were too little, already have I added breach of trust. A thief! Can I know myself that wretched thing, and look my honest friend and injured master in the face? Though hypocrisy may a while conceal my guilt, at length it will be known, and public shame and ruin must ensue. In the meantime, what must be my life? Ever to speak a language foreign to my heart; hourly to add to the number of my crimes in order to conceal 'em. Sure, such was the condition of the grand apostate,[5] when first he lost his purity; like me disconsolate he wandered, and, while yet in heaven, bore all his future hell about him.

([*Enter*] TRUEMAN.)

TRUEMAN. Barnwell! Oh, how I rejoice to see you safe! So will our master and his gentle daughter, who during your absence often inquired after you.

BARNWELL (*aside*). Would he were gone! his officious love will pry into the secrets of my soul.

TRUEMAN. Unless you knew the pain the whole family has felt on your account, you can't conceive how much you are beloved. But why thus cold and silent? When my heart is full of joy for your return, why do you turn away? Why thus avoid me? What have I done? How am I altered since you saw me last? Or rather what have you done, and why are you thus changed, for I am still the same?

BARNWELL (*aside*). What have I done, indeed?

TRUEMAN. Not speak nor look upon me!

BARNWELL (*aside*). By my face he will discover all I would conceal; methinks already I begin to hate him.

TRUEMAN. I cannot bear this usage from a friend, one whom till now I ever found so loving, whom yet I love, though this unkindness strikes at the root of friendship, and might destroy it in any breast but mine.

BARNWELL. I am not well. (*turning to him*) Sleep has been a stranger to these eyes since you beheld them last.

TRUEMAN. Heavy they look indeed, and swollen with tears; now they o'erflow; rightly did my sympathizing heart forebode last night, when thou wast absent, something fatal to our peace.

BARNWELL. Your friendship engages you too far. My troubles, whate'er they are, are mine alone; you have no interest in them, nor ought your concern for me give you a moment's pain.

[5] Lucifer.

TRUEMAN. You speak as if you knew of friendship nothing but the name. Before I saw your grief I felt it. Since we parted last I have slept no more than you, but, pensive in my chamber, sat alone and spent the tedious night in wishes for your safety and return; e'en now, though ignorant of the cause, your sorrow wounds me to the heart.

BARNWELL. 'Twill not be always thus. Friendship and all engagements cease, as circumstances and occasions vary; and, since you once may hate me, perhaps it might be better for us both that now you loved me less.

TRUEMAN. Sure I but dream! Without a cause would Barnwell use me thus? Ungenerous and ungrateful youth, farewell. (*going*) I shall endeavor to follow your advice. [*Aside*] Yet stay, perhaps I am too rash, and angry when the cause demands compassion. Some unforeseen calamity may have befallen him, too great to bear.

BARNWELL [*aside*.] What part am I reduced to act! 'Tis vile and base to move his temper thus, the best of friends and men.

TRUEMAN. I am to blame; prithee forgive me, Barnwell. Try to compose your ruffled mind, and let me know the cause that thus transports you from yourself. My friendly counsel may restore your peace.

BARNWELL. All that is possible for man to do for man, your generous friendship may effect; but here even that's in vain.

TRUEMAN. Something dreadful is laboring in your breast. Oh, give it vent and let me share your grief! 'Twill ease your pain should it admit no cure and make it lighter by the part I bear.

BARNWELL. Vain supposition! My woes increase by being observed; should the cause be known, they would exceed all bounds.

TRUEMAN. So well I know thy honest heart, guilt cannot harbor there.

BARNWELL (*aside*). Oh, torture insupportable!

TRUEMAN. Then why am I excluded? Have I a thought I would conceal from you?

BARNWELL. If still you urge me on this hated subject, I'll never enter more beneath this roof, nor see your face again.

TRUEMAN. 'Tis strange. But I have done; say but you hate me not.

BARNWELL. Hate you! I am not that monster yet.

TRUEMAN. Shall our friendship still continue?

BARNWELL. It's a blessing I never was worthy of, yet now must stand on terms, and but upon conditions can confirm it.

TRUEMAN. What are they?

BARNWELL. Never hereafter, though you should wonder at my conduct, desire to know more than I am willing to reveal.

TRUEMAN. 'Tis hard, but upon any conditions I must be your friend.

BARNWELL. Then, as much as one lost to himself can be another's, I am yours. (*embracing*)

TRUEMAN. Be ever so, and may heaven restore your peace.

BARNWELL. Will yesterday return? We have heard the glorious sun, that till then incessant rolled, once stopped his rapid course, and once went back. The dead have risen; and parched rocks poured forth a liquid stream to quench a people's thirst. The sea divided and formed walls of water while a whole nation passed in safety through its sandy bosom. Hungry lions have refused their prey; and men unhurt have walked amidst consuming flames;[6] but never yet did time, once past, return.

TRUEMAN. Though the continued chain of time has never once been broke, nor ever will, but uninterrupted must keep on its course till, lost in eternity, it ends there where it first begun; yet as heaven can repair whatever evils time can bring upon us, we ought never to despair. But business requires our attendance, business the youth's best preservative from ill, as idleness his worst of snares. Will you go with me?

BARNWELL. I'll take a little time to reflect on what has past, and follow you.—

[*Exit* TRUEMAN.]

---

[6] Barnwell refers to the Old Testament miracles of Joshua's stopping the sun (Joshua 10:12–13), Elijah's raising a boy from the dead (I Kings 17:17–24), Moses's drawing water from rock (Numbers 20:8–11), the parting of the Red Sea (Exodus 14:21–31), the preservation of Daniel in the lions' den (Daniel 6:22) and of the three Jews in the fiery furnace (Daniel 3:19–27).

I might have trusted Trueman and engaged him to apply to my uncle to repair the wrong I have done my master; but what of Millwood? Must I expose her too? Ungenerous and base! Then heaven requires it not. But heaven requires that I forsake her. What! Never see her more! Does heaven require that! I hope I may see her, and heaven not be offended. Presumptuous hope! Dearly already have I proved my frailty; should I once more tempt heaven, I may be left to fall never to rise again. Yet shall I leave her, forever leave her, and not let her know the cause? She who loves me with such a boundless passion? Can cruelty be duty? I judge of what she then must feel, by what I now endure. The love of life and fear of shame, opposed by inclination strong as death or shame, like wind and tide in raging conflict met, when neither can prevail, keep me in doubt. How then can I determine?

(*[Enter]* THOROWGOOD.)

THOROWGOOD. Without a cause assigned, or notice given, to absent yourself last night was a fault, young man, and I came to chide you for it, but hope I am prevented.[7] That modest blush, the confusion so visible in your face, speak grief and shame. When we have offended heaven, it requires no more; and shall man, who needs himself to be forgiven, be harder to appease? If my pardon or love be of moment to your peace, look up, secure of both.

BARNWELL (*aside*). This goodness has o'er-come me.—Oh, sir! you know not the nature and extent of my offence; and I should abuse your mistaken bounty to receive it. Though I had rather die than speak my shame; though racks could not have forced the guilty secret from my breast, your kindness has.

THOROWGOOD. Enough, enough! Whate'er it be, this concern shows you're convinced, and I am satisfied. [*aside*] How painful is the sense of guilt to an ingenuous mind!—some youthful folly, which it were prudent not to enquire into. When we consider the frail condition of humanity, it may raise our pity, not our

---

7 Anticipated.

wonder, that youth should go astray; when reason, weak at the best when opposed to inclination, scarce formed, and wholly unassisted by experience, faintly contends, or willingly becomes the slave of sense. The state of youth is much to be deplored, and the more so because they see it not; being then to danger most exposèd when they are least prepared for their defence.

BARNWELL. It will be known, and you recall your pardon and abhor me.

THOROWGOOD. I never will; so heaven confirm to me the pardon of my offences. Yet be upon your guard in this gay, thoughtless season of your life; now, when the sense of pleasure's quick, and passion high, the voluptuous appetites, raging and fierce, demand the strongest curb; take heed of a relapse. When vice becomes habitual, the very power of leaving it is lost.

BARNWELL. Hear me, on my knees confess.

THOROWGOOD. I will not hear a syllable more upon this subject; it were not mercy, but cruelty, to hear what must give you such torment to reveal.

BARNWELL. This generosity amazes and distracts me.

THOROWGOOD. This remorse makes thee dearer to me than if thou hadst never offended; whatever is your fault, of this I'm certain, 'twas harder for you to offend than me to pardon. [*Exit* THOROWGOOD.]

BARNWELL. Villain, villain, villain! basely to wrong so excellent a man. Should I again return to folly?— detested thought!—But what of Millwood then? Why, I renounce her! I give her up; the struggle's over, and virtue has prevailed. Reason may convince, but gratitude compels. This unlooked for generosity has saved me from destruction. (*going*)

([*Enter*] *a* FOOTMAN.)

FOOTMAN. Sir, two ladies, from your uncle in the country, desire to see you.

BARNWELL (*aside*). Who should they be?—Tell them I'll wait upon 'em.—

[*Exit* FOOTMAN.]

Methinks I dread to see 'em. Guilt, what a coward hast thou made me! Now everything alarms me. [*Exit.*]

[SCENE II.] *Another room in* THOROWGOOD's *house*

([*Enter*] MILLWOOD *and* LUCY, *and to them a* FOOTMAN.)

FOOTMAN. Ladies, he'll wait upon you immediately.
MILLWOOD. 'Tis very well. I thank you.

[*Exit* FOOTMAN. *Enter* BARNWELL.]

BARNWELL [*aside*]. Confusion! Millwood!
MILLWOOD. That angry look tells me that here I'm an un-
    welcome guest; I feared as much—the unhappy are
    so everywhere.
BARNWELL. Will nothing but my utter ruin content you?
MILLWOOD. Unkind and cruel! Lost myself, your happi-
    ness is now my only care.
BARNWELL. How did you gain admission?
MILLWOOD. Saying we were desired by your uncle to visit
    and deliver a message to you, we were received by the
    family without suspicion, and with much respect con-
    ducted here.
BARNWELL. Why did you come at all?
MILLWOOD. I never shall trouble you more; I'm come to
    take my leave forever. Such is the malice of my fate,
    I go hopeless, despairing ever to return. This hour is
    all I have left. One short hour is all I have to bestow
    on love and you, for whom I thought the longest
    life too short.
BARNWELL. Then we are met to part forever?
MILLWOOD. It must be so; yet think not that time or
    absence shall ever put a period to my grief or make
    me love you less; though I must leave you, yet con-
    demn me not.
BARNWELL. Condemn you? No, I approve your resolution,
    and rejoice to hear it; 'tis just, 'tis necessary. I have
    well weighed, and found it so.
LUCY (*aside*). I'm afraid the young man has more sense
    than she thought he had.
BARNWELL. Before you came I had determined never to
    see you more.
MILLWOOD (*aside*). Confusion!
LUCY (*aside*). Ay! we are all out; this is a turn so un-
    expected that I shall make nothing of my part; they
    must e'en play the scene betwixt themselves.

MILLWOOD. 'Twas some relief to think, though absent, you would love me still; but to find, though fortune had been indulgent, that you, more cruel and inconstant, had resolved to cast me off—this, as I never could expect, I have not learnt to bear.

BARNWELL. I am sorry to hear you blame in me a resolution that so well becomes us both.

MILLWOOD. I have reason for what I do, but you have none.

BARNWELL. Can we want a reason for parting, who have so many to wish we never had met?

MILLWOOD. Look on me, Barnwell; am I deformed or old, that satiety so soon succeeds enjoyment? Nay, look again; am I not she whom yesterday you thought the fairest and the kindest of her sex, whose hand, trembling with ecstasy, you pressed and molded thus, while on my eyes you gazed with such delight, as if desire increased by being fed?

BARNWELL. No more! Let me repeat my former follies, if possible, without remembering what they were.

MILLWOOD. Why?

BARNWELL. Such is my frailty that 'tis dangerous.

MILLWOOD. Where is the danger, since we are to part?

BARNWELL. The thought of that already is too painful.

MILLWOOD. If it be painful to part, then I may hope at least you do not hate me?

BARNWELL. No—no—I never said I did!—Oh, my heart!

MILLWOOD. Perhaps you pity me?

BARNWELL. I do, I do, indeed, I do.

MILLWOOD. You'll think upon me?

BARNWELL. Doubt it not while I can think at all.

MILLWOOD. You may judge an embrace at parting too great a favor, though it would be the last? (*He draws back*) A look shall then suffice—farewell forever.

[*Exeunt* MILLWOOD *and* LUCY.]

BARNWELL. If to resolve to suffer be to conquer, I have conquered. Painful victory!

([*Re-enter*] MILLWOOD *and* LUCY.)

MILLWOOD. One thing I had forgot. I never must return to my own house again. This I thought proper to let you know, lest your mind should change, and you should seek in vain to find me there. Forgive me this second intrusion; I only came to give you this caution, and that, perhaps, was needless.

BARNWELL. I hope it was, yet it is kind, and I must thank you for it.

MILLWOOD (*To* LUCY). My friend, your arm. Now I am gone forever. (*going*)

BARNWELL. One thing more. Sure, there's no danger in my knowing where you go? If you think otherwise—

MILLWOOD. Alas! (*weeping*)

LUCY (*aside*). We are right I find, that's my cue.—Ah, dear sir, she's going she knows not whither, but go she must.

BARNWELL. Humanity obliges me to wish you well. Why will you thus expose yourself to needless troubles?

LUCY. Nay, there's no help for it. She must quit the town immediately, and the kingdom as soon as possible; it was no small matter, you may be sure, that could make her resolve to leave you.

MILLWOOD. No more, my friend; since he for whose dear sake alone I suffer, and am content to suffer, is kind and pities me. Where'er I wander through wilds and deserts, benighted and forlorn, that thought shall give me comfort.

BARNWELL. For my sake! Oh, tell me how; which way am I so cursed as to bring such ruin on thee?

MILLWOOD. No matter, I am contented with my lot.

BARNWELL. Leave me not in this uncertainty.

MILLWOOD. I have said too much.

BARNWELL. How, how am I the cause of your undoing?

MILLWOOD. To know it will but increase your troubles.

BARNWELL. My troubles can't be greater than they are.

LUCY. Well, well, sir, if she won't satisfy you, I will.

BARNWELL. I am bound to you beyond expression.

MILLWOOD. Remember, sir, that I desired you not to hear it.

BARNWELL. Begin, and ease my racking expectation.

LUCY. Why you must know, my lady here was an only child; but her parents dying while she was young, left her and her fortune, (no inconsiderable one, I assure you) to the care of a gentleman who has a good estate of his own.

MILLWOOD. Ay, ay, the barbarous man is rich enough—but what are riches when compared to love?

LUCY. For a while he performed the office of a faithful guardian, settled her in a house, hired her servants—but you have seen in what manner she lived, so I need say no more of that.

MILLWOOD. How shall I live hereafter, heaven knows.

LUCY. All things went on as one could wish, till, some time ago, his wife dying, he fell violently in love with his charge, and would fain have married her. Now the man is neither old nor ugly, but a good, personable sort of a man, but I don't know how it was, she could never endure him. In short, her ill usage so provoked him that he brought in an account of his executorship, wherein he makes her debtor to him.

MILLWOOD. A trifle in itself, but more than enough to ruin me, whom, by his unjust account, he had stripped of all before.

LUCY. Now she having neither money nor friend, except me, who am as unfortunate as herself, he compelled her to pass his account, and give bond for the sum he demanded; but still provided handsomely for her and continued his courtship, till, being informed by his spies (truly I suspect some in her own family) that you were entertained at her house and stayed with her all night, he came this morning raving and storming like a madman, talks no more of marriage (so there's no hopes of making up matters that way) but vows her ruin, unless she'll allow him the same favor that he supposes she granted you.

BARNWELL. Must she be ruined, or find her refuge in another's arms?

MILLWOOD. He gave me but an hour to resolve in, that's happily spent with you—and now I go.

BARNWELL. To be exposed to all the rigors of the various seasons; the summer's parching heat, and winter's cold; unhoused to wander friendless through the unhospitable world, in misery and want; attended with fear and danger, and pursued by malice and revenge—wouldst thou endure all this for me, and can I do nothing, nothing to prevent it?

LUCY. 'Tis really a pity, there can be no way found out.

BARNWELL. Oh, where are all my resolutions now? Like early vapors, or the morning dew, chased by the sun's warm beams they're vanished and lost, as though they had never been.

LUCY. Now I advised her, sir, to comply with the gentleman; that would not only put an end to her troubles, but make her fortune at once.

BARNWELL. Tormenting fiend, away! I had rather perish, nay, see her perish, than have her saved by him; I will myself prevent her ruin, though with my own. A moment's patience, I'll return immediately. [*Exit.*]

LUCY. 'Twas well you came, or, by what I can perceive, you had lost him.

MILLWOOD. That, I must confess, was a danger I did not foresee; I was only afraid he should have come without money. You know a house of entertainment like mine is not kept without expense.

LUCY. That's very true; but then you should be reasonable in your demands; 'tis pity to discourage a young man.

([*Re-enter*] BARNWELL [*with a bag of money*].)

BARNWELL (*aside*). What am I about to do! Now you, who boast your reason all sufficient, suppose yourselves in my condition, and determine for me whether it's right to let her suffer for my faults, or, by this small addition to my guilt, prevent the ill effects of what is past.

LUCY (*aside*). These young sinners think everything in the ways of wickedness so strange,—but I could tell him that this is nothing but what's very common; for one vice as naturally begets another, as a father a son. But he'll find out that himself, if he lives long enough.

BARNWELL. Here, take this, and with it purchase your deliverance; return to your house, and live in peace and safety.

MILLWOOD. So I may hope to see you there again.

BARNWELL. Answer me not, but fly—lest, in the agonies of my remorse, I take again what is not mine to give, and abandon thee to want and misery.

MILLWOOD. Say but you'll come!

BARNWELL. You are my fate, my heaven, or my hell. Only leave me now, dispose of me hereafter as you please.—

[*Exeunt* MILLWOOD *and* LUCY.]

What have I done? Were my resolutions founded on reason, and sincerely made? why then has heaven suffered me to fall? I sought not the occasion; and, if my heart deceives me not, compassion and generosity were my motives. Is virtue inconsistent with itself, or are vice and virtue only empty names? Or do they depend on accidents beyond our power to produce, or to prevent, wherein we have no part, and yet must be determined by the event? But why should I attempt to reason? All is confusion, horror, and remorse. I find I am lost, cast down from all my late erected hopes and plunged again in guilt, yet scarce know how or why—

Such undistinguished horrors make my brain,
Like hell, the seat of darkness, and of pain. [*Exit.*]

ACT III

[SCENE I.] [*A room in* THOROWGOOD's *house*]

(THOROWGOOD *and* TRUEMAN [*discovered sitting at a table*].)

THOROWGOOD. Methinks I would not have you only learn the method of merchandise and practise it hereafter merely as a means of getting wealth. 'Twill be well worth your pains to study it as a science, to see how it is founded in reason and the nature of things, how it has promoted humanity, as it has opened and yet keeps up an intercourse between nations far remote from one another in situation, customs, and religion; promoting arts, industry, peace and plenty, by mutual benefits diffusing mutual love from pole to pole.

TRUEMAN. Something of this I have considered, and hope, by your assistance, to extend my thoughts much farther. I have observed those countries where trade is promoted and encouraged do not make discoveries to destroy, but to improve mankind by love and friendship, to tame the fierce, and polish the most savage, to teach them the advantages of honest traffic by taking from them with their own consent their useless superfluities, and giving them in return what, from their ignorance in manual arts, their situation, or some other accident, they stand in need of.

THOROWGOOD. 'Tis justly observed. The populous east, luxuriant, abounds with glittering gems, bright pearls, aromatic spices, and health-restoring drugs. The late found western world glows with unnumbered veins of gold and silver ore. On every climate, and on every country, heaven has bestowed some good peculiar to itself. It is the industrious merchant's business to collect the various blessings of each soil and climate, and, with the product of the whole, to enrich his native country.

Well! I have examined your accounts. They are not only just, as I have always found them, but regularly kept, and fairly entered. I commend your diligence. Method in business is the surest guide. He who neglects it frequently stumbles, and always wanders perplexed, uncertain, and in danger. Are Barnwell's accounts ready for my inspection? He does not use to be the last on these occasions.

TRUEMAN. Upon receiving your orders he retired, I thought in some confusion. If you please, I'll go and hasten him. I hope he hasn't been guilty of any neglect.

THOROWGOOD. I'm now going to the Exchange; let him know, at my return I expect to find him ready.

(*[Exeunt. Enter]* MARIA *with a book; sits and reads.*)

MARIA. How forcible is truth! The weakest mind, inspired with love of that, fixed and collected in itself, with indifference beholds the united force of earth and hell opposing. Such souls are raised above the sense of pain, or so supported that they regard it not. The martyr cheaply purchases his heaven. Small are his sufferings, great is his reward. Not so the wretch who combats love with duty, when the mind, weakened and dissolved by the soft passion, feeble and hopeless, opposes its own desire. What is an hour, a day, a year of pain, to a whole life of tortures such as these?

[*Enter* TRUEMAN.]

TRUEMAN. Oh, Barnwell! Oh, my friend, how art thou fallen!

MARIA. Ha! Barnwell! What of him? Speak, say what of Barnwell?

TRUEMAN. 'Tis not to be concealed. I've news to tell of him that will afflict your generous father, yourself, and all who knew him.

MARIA. Defend us, Heaven!

TRUEMAN. I cannot speak it. See there. (*Gives a letter,* MARIA *reads.*)

MARIA.

> Trueman,
> I know my absence will surprise my honored master and yourself; and the more, when you shall understand that the reason of my withdrawing, is my having embezzled part of the cash with which I was entrusted. After this, 'tis needless to inform you that I intend never to return again. Though this might have been known by examining my accounts; yet, to prevent that unnecessary trouble, and to cut off all fruitless expectations of my return, I have left this from the lost
> George Barnwell.

TRUEMAN. Lost indeed! Yet how he should be guilty of what he there charges himself withal, raises my wonder equal to my grief. Never had youth a higher sense of virtue. Justly he thought, and as he thought he practised; never was life more regular than his; an understanding uncommon at his years; an open, generous, manliness of temper; his manners easy, unaffected and engaging.

MARIA. This and much more you might have said with truth. He was the delight of every eye, and joy of every heart that knew him.

TRUEMAN. Since such he was, and was my friend, can I support his loss? See, the fairest and happiest maid this wealthy city boasts, kindly condescends to weep for thy unhappy fate, poor, ruined Barnwell!

MARIA. Trueman, do you think a soul so delicate as his, so sensible of shame, can e'er submit to live a slave to vice?

TRUEMAN. Never, never! So well I know him, I'm sure this act of his, so contrary to his nature, must have been caused by some unavoidable necessity.

MARIA. Is there no means yet to preserve him?

TRUEMAN. Oh, that there were! But few men recover
reputation lost, a merchant never. Nor would he, I
fear, though I should find him, ever be brought to
look his injured master in the face.

MARIA. I fear as much—and therefore would never have
my father know it.

TRUEMAN. That's impossible.

MARIA. What's the sum?

TRUEMAN. 'Tis considerable. I've marked it here, to show
it, with the letter, to your father, at his return.

MARIA. If I should supply the money, could you so dispose
of that, and the account, as to conceal this unhappy
mismanagement from my father?

TRUEMAN. Nothing more easy. But can you intend it? Will
you save a helpless wretch from ruin? Oh! 'twere an
act worthy such exalted virtue as Maria's. Sure, heaven
in mercy to my friend inspired the generous thought!

MARIA. Doubt not but I would purchase so great a happiness at a much dearer price. But how shall he be
found?

TRUEMAN. Trust to my diligence for that. In the meantime,
I'll conceal his absence from your father, or find such
excuses for it that the real cause shall never be
suspected.

MARIA. In attempting to save from shame one whom we
hope may yet return to virtue, to heaven and you, the
judges of this action, I appeal, whether I have done
anything misbecoming my sex and character.

TRUEMAN. Earth must approve the deed, and heaven, I
doubt not, will reward it.

MARIA. If heaven succeeds it, I am well rewarded. A
virgin's fame is sullied by suspicion's slightest breath;
and therefore as this must be a secret from my father
and the world, for Barnwell's sake, for mine, let it be
so to him.

[SCENE II.] MILLWOOD'S *House*

([*Enter*] LUCY *and* BLUNT.)

LUCY. Well! what do you think of Millwood's conduct
now?

BLUNT. I own it is surprising. I don't know which to admire
most, her feigned, or his real passion, though I have

sometimes been afraid that her avarice would discover[8] her. But his youth and want of experience make it the easier to impose on him.

LUCY. No, it is his love. To do him justice, notwithstanding his youth, he don't want understanding; but you men are much easier imposed on in these affairs than your vanity will allow you to believe. Let me see the wisest of you all as much in love with me as Barnwell is with Millwood, and I'll engage to make as great a fool of him.

BLUNT. And all circumstances considered, to make as much money of him, too?

LUCY. I can't answer for that. Her artifice in making him rob his master at first, and the various stratagems, by which she has obliged him to continue in that course, astound even me, who know her so well.

BLUNT. But then you are to consider that the money was his master's.

LUCY. There was the difficulty of it. Had it been his own, it had been nothing. Were the world his, she might have it for a smile. But those golden days are done; he's ruined, and Millwood's hopes of farther profits there are at an end.

BLUNT. That's no more than we all expected.

LUCY. Being called by his master to make up his accounts, he was forced to quit his house and service, and wisely flies to Millwood for relief and entertainment.

BLUNT. I have not heard of this before! How did she receive him?

LUCY. As you would expect. She wondered what he meant, was astonished at his impudence, and, with an air of modesty peculiar to herself, swore so heartily that she never saw him before that she put me out of countenance.

BLUNT. That's much indeed! But how did Barnwell behave?

LUCY. He grieved, and at length, enraged at this barbarous treatment, was preparing to be gone; and, making toward the door, showed a sum of money, which he had brought from his master's—the last he's ever like to have from thence.

BLUNT. But then Millwood?

---

8 Reveal.

LUCY. Aye, she, with her usual address, returned to her old arts of lying, swearing, and dissembling, hung on his neck, and wept, and swore 'twas meant in jest. The amorous youth melted into tears, threw the money into her lap, and swore he had rather die than think her false.

BLUNT. Strange infatuation!

LUCY. But what followed was stranger still. As doubts and fears followed by reconcilement ever increase love where the passion is sincere, so in him it caused so wild a transport of excessive fondness, such joy, such grief, such pleasure, and such anguish, that nature in him seemed sinking with the weight, and the charmed soul disposed to quit his breast for hers. Just then, when every passion with lawless anarchy prevailed, and reason was in the raging tempest lost, the cruel, artful Millwood prevailed upon the wretched youth to promise what I tremble but to think on.

BLUNT. I am amazed! What can it be?

LUCY. You will be more so to hear it is to attempt the life of his nearest relation, and best benefactor.

BLUNT. His uncle, whom we have often heard him speak of as a gentleman of a large estate and fair character in the country where he lives?

LUCY. The same. She was no sooner possessed of the last dear purchase of his ruin, but her avarice, insatiate as the grave, demanded this horrid sacrifice. Barnwell's near relation and unsuspected virtue must give too easy means to seize the good man's treasure, whose blood must seal the dreadful secret, and prevent the terrors of her guilty fears.

BLUNT. Is it possible she could persuade him to do an act like that! He is, by nature, honest, grateful, compassionate, and generous. And though his love and her artful persuasions have wrought him to practise what he most abhors; yet we all can witness for him with what reluctance he has still complied! So many tears he shed o'er each offence, as might, if possible, sanctify theft, and make a merit of a crime.

LUCY. 'Tis true, at the naming the murder of his uncle, he started into rage; and, breaking from her arms, where she till then had held him with well dissembled love and false endearments, called her cruel, monster,

devil; and told her she was born for his destruction.
She thought it not for her purpose to meet his rage
with rage, but affected a most passionate fit of grief,
railed at her fate, and cursed her wayward stars, that
still her wants should force her to press him to act
such deeds as she must needs abhor as well as he; but
told him necessity had no law and love no bounds;
that therefore he never truly loved, but meant in her
necessity to forsake her. Then kneeled and swore, that
since by his refusal he had given her cause to doubt
his love, she never would see him more, unless, to
prove it true, he robbed his uncle to supply her wants,
and murdered him to keep it from discovery.

BLUNT. I am astonished! What said he?

LUCY. Speechless he stood; but in his face you might have
read that various passions tore his very soul. Oft he
in anguish threw his eyes towards heaven, and then
as often bent their beams on her; then wept and
groaned and beat his troubled breast; at length, with
horror not to be expressed, he cried, "Thou cursed
fair! have I not given dreadful proofs of love? What
drew me from my youthful innocence to stain my then
unspotted soul but love? What caused me to rob my
worthy, gentle master but cursed love? What makes
me now a fugitive from his service, loathed by myself,
and scorned by all the world, but love? What fills my
eyes with tears, my soul with torture never felt on this
side death before? Why love, love, love! And why,
above all, do I resolve (for, tearing his hair, he cried,
I do resolve!) to kill my uncle?"

BLUNT. Was she not moved? It makes me weep to hear
the sad relation.

LUCY. Yes, with joy that she had gained her point. She
gave him no time to cool, but urged him to attempt it
instantly. He's now gone; if he performs it and
escapes, there's more money for her; if not, he'll ne'er
return, and then she's fairly rid of him.

BLUNT. 'Tis time the world was rid of such a monster.

LUCY. If we don't do our endeavors to prevent this murder,
we are as bad as she.

BLUNT. I'm afraid it is too late.

LUCY. Perhaps not. Her barbarity to Barnwell makes me
hate her. We have run too great a length with her

already. I did not think her or myself so wicked, as I find upon reflection we are.

BLUNT. 'Tis true, we have all been too much so. But there is something so horrid in murder that all other crimes seem nothing when compared to that. I would not be involved in the guilt of that for all the world.

LUCY. Nor I, heaven knows; therefore let us clear ourselves by doing all that is in our power to prevent it. I have just thought of a way that, to me, seems probable. Will you join with me to detect this cursed design?

BLUNT. With all my heart. He who knows of a murder intended to be committed and does not discover it, in the eye of the law and reason is a murderer.

LUCY. Let us lose no time; I'll acquaint you with the particulars as we go.

[SCENE III.] *A walk at some distance from a country seat.*

([*Enter*] BARNWELL.)

BARNWELL. A dismal gloom obscures the face of day; either the sun has slipped behind a cloud, or journeys down the west of heaven with more than common speed to avoid the sight of what I'm doomed to act. Since I set forth on this accursed design, where'er I tread, methinks, the solid earth trembles beneath my feet. Yonder limpid stream, whose hoary fall has made a natural cascade, as I passed by, in doleful accents seemed to murmur, "Murder." The earth, the air, the water, seem concerned; but that's not strange, the world is punished, and nature feels the shock when Providence permits a good man's fall! Just heaven! Then what should I be! for him that was my father's only brother, and since his death has been to me a father, who took me up an infant, and an orphan, reared me with tenderest care, and still indulged me with most paternal fondness; yet here I stand avowed his destined murderer! I stiffen with horror at my own impiety; 'tis yet unperformed. What if I quit my bloody purpose and fly the place! (*Going, then stops*) But whither, oh, whither, shall I fly? My master's once friendly doors are ever shut against me; and without money Millwood will never see me more, and life is not to be endured without her! She's got such firm possession of my heart, and governs there with such despotic sway! Aye, there's the cause of all my sin and sorrow. 'Tis more than love; 'tis the fever of the soul and madness of desire. In vain does nature, reason, conscience, all oppose it; the impetuous passion bears down all before it, and drives me on to lust, to theft, and murder.—Oh conscience! feeble guide to virtue, who only shows us when we go astray, but wants the power to stop us in our course.—Ha! in yonder shady walk I see my uncle. He's alone. Now for my disguise. (*Plucks out a visor*) This is his hour of private meditation. Thus daily he prepares his soul for heaven, whilst I—but what have I to do with heaven!—Ha! No struggles, conscience.—

Hence! Hence remorse, and ev'ry thought that's good;
The storm that lust began must end in blood.

(*Puts on the visor, draws a pistol, and exit.*)

[SCENE IV.] *A close walk in a wood*

(*[Enter]* UNCLE.)

UNCLE. If I were superstitious, I should fear some danger lurked unseen, or death were nigh. A heavy melancholy clouds my spirits; my imagination is filled with gashly forms of dreary graves, and bodies changed by death, when the pale lengthened visage attracts each weeping eye, and fills the musing soul at once with grief and horror, pity and aversion. I will indulge the thought. The wise man prepares himself for death by making it familiar to his mind. When strong reflections hold the mirror near, and the living in the dead behold their future selves, how does each inordinate passion and desire cease or sicken at the view. The mind scarce moves; the blood, curdling and chilled, creeps slowly through the veins. Fixed, still, and motionless we stand, so like the solemn object of our thoughts, we are almost at present what we must be hereafter—till curiosity awakes the soul and sets it on enquiry.

(*[Enter]* GEORGE BARNWELL *at a distance.*)

—O death, thou strange mysterious power, seen every day, yet never understood but by the incommunicative dead, what art thou? The extensive mind of man, that with a thought circles the earth's vast globe, sinks to the center, or ascends above the stars; that worlds exotic finds, or thinks it finds, thy thick clouds attempts to pass in vain; lost and bewildered in the horrid gloom, defeated she returns more doubtful than before; of nothing certain, but of labor lost.

(*During this speech,* BARNWELL *sometimes presents the pistol, and draws it back again; at last he drops it, at which his* UNCLE *starts, and draws his sword.*)

BARNWELL. Oh, 'tis impossible!

UNCLE. A man so near me, armed and masked!

BARNWELL. Nay, then there's no retreat. (*Plucks a poniard from his bosom, and stabs him.*)

UNCLE. Oh! I am slain! All-gracious heaven, regard the prayer of thy dying servant! Bless with thy choicest blessings my dearest nephew, forgive my murderer, and take my fleeting soul to endless mercy!

(BARNWELL *throws off his mask, runs to him, and, kneeling by him, raises and chafes him.*)

BARNWELL. Expiring saint! Oh, murdered, martyred uncle! Lift up your dying eyes, and view your nephew in your murderer. Oh, do not look so tenderly upon me! Let indignation lighten from your eyes, and blast me ere you die. By heaven, he weeps in pity of my woes. Tears, tears, for blood! The murdered, in the agonies of death, weeps for his murderer! Oh, speak your pious purpose, pronounce my pardon then, and take me with you!—He would, but cannot.—Oh, why, with such fond affection do you press my murdering hand! What! will you kiss me! (*Kisses him.*—UNCLE *groans and dies.*) Life, that hovered on his lips but till he had sealed my pardon, in that sigh expired. He's gone forever, and oh! I follow.—(*Swoons away upon his uncle's dead body.*) Do I still live to press the suffering bosom of the earth? Do I still breathe, and taint with my infectious breath the wholesome air? Let heaven, from its high throne, in justice or in mercy, now look down on that dear murdered saint, and me the murderer. And, if his vengeance spares, let pity strike and end my wretched being. Murder the worst of crimes, and parricide the worst of murders, and this the worst of parricides! Cain, who stands on record from the birth of time, and must to its last final period, as accursed, slew a brother favored above him. Detested Nero, by another's hand, dispatched a mother, that he feared and hated. But I, with my own hand, have murdered a brother, mother, father, and a friend; most loving and beloved. This execrable act of mine's without a parallel! Oh, may it ever stand alone!—the last of murders, as it is the worst!

The rich man thus, in torment and despair,
Preferred his vain, but charitable prayer.[9]
The fool, his own soul lost, would fain be wise
For others' good; but heaven his suit denies.
By laws and means well known we stand or fall,
And one eternal rule remains for all.

ACT IV

[SCENE I.] *A Room in* THOROWGOOD's *house*

([*Enter*] MARIA.)

MARIA. How falsely do they judge who censure or applaud, as we're afflicted or rewarded here! I know I am unhappy, yet cannot charge myself with any crime more than the common frailties of our kind that should provoke just heaven to mark me out for sufferings so uncommon and severe. Falsely to accuse ourselves, heaven must abhor; then it is just and right that innocence should suffer, for heaven must be just in all its ways. Perhaps by that we are kept from moral evils much worse than penal, or more improved in virtue; or may not the lesser ills that we sustain, be the means of greater good to others? Might all the joyless days and sleepless nights that I have passed, but purchase peace for thee—

9 See Luke 16:19–31.

Thou dear, dear cause of all my grief and pain,
Small were the loss, and infinite the gain;
Though to the grave in secret love I pine,
So life, and fame, and happiness were thine.

([*Enter*] TRUEMAN.)

What news of Barnwell?

TRUEMAN. None. I have sought him with the greatest diligence, but all in vain.

MARIA. Does my father yet suspect the cause of his absenting himself?

TRUEMAN. All appeared so just and fair to him, it is not possible he ever should; but his absence will no longer be concealed. Your father's wise; and though he seems to harken to the friendly excuses I would make for Barnwell, yet I am afraid he regards 'em only as such, without suffering them to influence his judgment.

MARIA. How does the unhappy youth defeat all our designs to serve him. Yet I can never repent what we have done. Should he return, 'twill make his reconciliation with my father easier, and preserve him from future reproach from a malicious, unforgiving world.

([*Enter*] THOROWGOOD *and* LUCY.)

THOROWGOOD. This woman here has given me a sad, and (bating some circumstances) too probable account of Barnwell's defection.

LUCY. I am sorry, sir, that my frank confession of my former unhappy course of life should cause you to suspect my truth on this occasion.

THOROWGOOD. It is not that; your confession has in it all the appearance of truth.

(*To them*): Among many other particulars, she informs me that Barnwell has been influenced to break his trust, and wrong me, at several times, of considerable sums of money; now, as I know this to be false, I would fain doubt the whole of her relation, too dreadful to be willingly believed.

MARIA. Sir, your pardon; I find myself on a sudden so indisposed, that I must retire. (*aside*) Providence opposes all attempts to save him. Poor ruined Barnwell! Wretched lost Maria! [*Exit* MARIA.]

THOROWGOOD. How am I distressed on every side! Pity for that unhappy youth, fear for the life of a much valued friend—and then my child—the only joy and hope of my declining life. Her melancholy increases hourly and gives me painful apprehensions of her loss.—Oh, Trueman! this person informs me that your friend, at the instigation of an impious woman, is gone to rob and murder his venerable uncle.

TRUEMAN. Oh, execrable deed! I am blasted with the horror of the thought.

LUCY. This delay may ruin all.

THOROWGOOD. What to do or think I know not; that he ever wronged me, I know is false; the rest may be so too—there's all my hope.

TRUEMAN. Trust not to that, rather suppose all true than lose a moment's time; even now the horrid deed may be a-doing—dreadful imagination! or it may be done, and we be vainly debating on the means to prevent what is already past.

THOROWGOOD [*aside*]. This earnestness convinces me that he knows more than he has yet discovered—What ho! Without there! who waits?

([*Enter*] a SERVANT.)

Order the groom to saddle the swiftest horse, and prepare himself to set out with speed. An affair of life and death demands his diligence.—

[*Exit* SERVANT.]

[*To* LUCY]: For you, whose behavior on this occasion I have no time to commend as it deserves, I must engage your farther assistance. Return and observe this Millwood till I come. I have your directions, and will follow you as soon as possible.—

[*Exit* LUCY.]

Trueman, you, I am sure, would not be idle on this occasion. [*Exit* THOROWGOOD.]

TRUEMAN. He only who is a friend can judge of my distress. [*Exit*.]

[SCENE II.] MILLWOOD'S *house*

([*Enter*] MILLWOOD.)

MILLWOOD. I wish I knew the event[10] of his design; the attempt without success would ruin him. Well! what have I to apprehend from that? I fear too much. The mischief being only intended, his friends, in pity of his youth, turn all their rage on me. I should have thought of that before. Suppose the deed done; then, and then only, I shall be secure. Or what if he returns without attempting it at all?

([*Enter*] BARNWELL, *bloody*.)

But he is here, and I have done him wrong; his bloody hands show he has done the deed; but show he wants the prudence to conceal it.

BARNWELL. Where shall I hide me? Whither shall I fly to avoid the swift unerring hand of justice?

MILLWOOD. Dismiss those fears; though thousands had pursued you to the door, yet being entered here, you are safe as innocence. I have such a cavern, by art so cunningly contrived, that the piercing eyes of jealousy and revenge may search in vain, nor find the entrance to the safe retreat. There will I hide you if any danger's near.

BARNWELL. Oh, hide me from myself if it be possible, for while I bear my conscience in my bosom, though I were hid where man's eye never saw, nor light e'er dawned, 'twere all in vain. For oh! that inmate, that impartial judge, will try, convict, and sentence me for murder, and execute me with never-ending torments. Behold these hands all crimsoned o'er with my dear uncle's blood! Here's a sight to make a statue start with horror or turn a living man into a statue.

MILLWOOD. Ridiculous! Then it seems you are afraid of your own shadow; or what's less than a shadow, your conscience.

BARNWELL. Though to man unknown I did the accursed act, what can we hide from heaven's all-seeing eye?

MILLWOOD. No more of this stuff. What advantage have you made of his death, or what advantage may yet be made of it? Did you secure the keys of his treasure?

---

10 Outcome.

Those no doubt were about him? What gold, what jewels, or what else of value have you brought me?

BARNWELL. Think you I added sacrilege to murder? Oh! had you seen him as his life flowed from him in a crimson flood, and heard him praying for me by the double name of nephew and murderer—alas, alas! he knew not then that his nephew was his murderer—how would you have wished as I did, though you had a thousand years of life to come, to have given them all to have lengthened his one hour. But, being dead, I fled the sight of what my hands had done, nor could I, to have gained the empire of the world, have violated by theft his sacred corpse.

MILLWOOD. Whining, preposterous, canting villain! to murder your uncle, rob him of life, nature's first, last, dear prerogative, after which there's no injury—then fear to take what he no longer wanted! and bring to me your penury and guilt. Do you think I'll hazard my reputation, nay, my life, to entertain you?

BARNWELL. Oh! Millwood! This from thee? But I have done; if you hate me, if you wish me dead, then are you happy—for oh! 'tis sure my grief will quickly end me.

MILLWOOD [aside]. In his madness he will discover all, and involve me in his ruin; we are on a precipice from whence there's no retreat for both. Then to preserve myself—(Pauses.) There is no other way—'tis dreadful, but reflection comes too late when danger's pressing, and there's no room for choice. It must be done. (Rings a bell.)

([Enter] a SERVANT.)

MILLWOOD. Fetch me an officer and seize this villain; he has confessed himself a murderer. Should I let him escape, I justly might be thought as bad as he.

[Exit SERVANT.]

BARNWELL. Oh, Millwood! sure you do not, cannot mean it. Stop the messenger; upon my knees I beg you would call him back. 'Tis fit I die indeed, but not by you. I will this instant deliver myself into the hands of justice; indeed I will, for death is all I wish. But thy ingratitude so tears my wounded soul, 'tis worse ten thousand times than death with torture!

MILLWOOD. Call it what you will, I am willing to live; and live secure; which nothing but your death can warrant.

BARNWELL. If there be a pitch of wickedness that seats the author beyond the reach of vengeance, you must be secure. But what remains for me but a dismal dungeon, hard-galling fetters, an awful trial, and an ignominious death, justly to fall unpitied and abhorred?—after death to be suspended between heaven and earth, a dreadful spectacle, the warning and horror of a gaping crowd. This I could bear, nay, wish not to avoid, had it but come from any hand but thine.

([*Enter*] BLUNT, OFFICER *and* ATTENDANTS.)

MILLWOOD. Heaven defend me! Conceal a murderer! Here, sir, take this youth into your custody; I accuse him of murder and will appear to make good my charge.

(*They seize him.*)

BARNWELL. To whom, of what, or how shall I complain? I'll not accuse her; the hand of heaven is in it, and this the punishment of lust and parricide! Yet heaven, that justly cuts me off, still suffers her to live, perhaps to punish others. Tremendous mercy! So fiends are cursed with immortality to be the executioners of heaven—

Be warned, ye youths, who see my sad despair,
Avoid lewd women, false as they are fair,
By reason guided, honest joys pursue.
The fair, to honor, and to virtue true,
Just to herself, will ne'er be false to you.
By my example learn to shun my fate,
(How wretched is the man who's wise too late!)
Ere innocence, and fame, and life be lost,
Here purchase wisdom cheaply, at my cost.

[*Exeunt* BARNWELL, OFFICER, *and* ATTENDANTS.]

MILLWOOD. Where's Lucy? Why is she absent at such a time?

BLUNT. Would I had been so too! Lucy will soon be here; and I hope to thy confusion, thou devil!

MILLWOOD. Insolent! This to me?

BLUNT. The worst that we know of the devil is that he first seduces to sin and then betrays to punishment. [*Exit* BLUNT.]

MILLWOOD. They disapprove of my conduct then, and mean to take this opportunity to set up for themselves. My ruin is resolved; I see my danger, but scorn both it and them. I was not born to fall by such weak instruments. [*going*]

[*Enter* THOROWGOOD.]

THOROWGOOD. Where is the scandal of her own sex, and curse of ours?

MILLWOOD. What means this insolence? Who do you seek?

THOROWGOOD. Millwood.

MILLWOOD. Well, you have found her then. I am Millwood.

THOROWGOOD. Then you are the most impious wretch that e'er the sun beheld.

MILLWOOD. From your appearance I should have expected wisdom and moderation, but your manners belie your aspect. What is your business here? I know you not.

THOROWGOOD. Hereafter you may know me better; I am Barnwell's master.

MILLWOOD. Then you are master to a villain, which, I think, is not much to your credit.

THOROWGOOD. Had he been as much above thy arts as my credit[11] is superior to thy malice, I need not have blushed to own him.

MILLWOOD. My arts? I don't understand you, sir! If he has done amiss, what's that to me? Was he my servant, or yours? You should have taught him better.

THOROWGOOD. Why should I wonder to find such uncommon impudence in one arrived to such a height of wickedness! When innocence is banished, modesty soon follows. Know, sorceress, I'm not ignorant of any of the arts by which you first deceived the unwary youth. I know how, step by step, you've led him on, reluctant and unwilling, from crime to crime to this last horrid act, which you contrived and by your cursed wiles even forced him to commit.

MILLWOOD (*aside*). Ha! Lucy has got the advantage, and

---

[11] Reputation.

accused me first; unless I can turn the accusation, and fix it upon her and Blunt, I am lost.

THOROWGOOD. Had I known your cruel design sooner, it had been prevented. To see you punished as the law directs is all that now remains. Poor satisfaction, for he, innocent as he is compared to you, must suffer too. But heaven, who knows our frame, and graciously distinguishes between frailty and presumption, will make a difference, though man cannot, who sees not the heart, but only judges by the outward action.

MILLWOOD. I find, sir, we are both unhappy in our servants. I was surprised at such ill treatment, without cause, from a gentleman of your appearance, and therefore too hastily returned it, for which I ask your pardon. I now perceive you have been so far imposed on as to think me engaged in a former correspondence with your servant, and, some way or other, accessory to his undoing.

THOROWGOOD. I charge you as the cause, the sole cause of all his guilt, and all his suffering, of all he now endures, and must endure, till a violent and shameful death shall put a dreadful period to his life and miseries together.

MILLWOOD. 'Tis very strange; but who's secure from scandal and detraction? So far from contributing to his ruin, I never spoke to him till since that fatal accident, which I lament as much as you. 'Tis true, I have a servant, on whose account he has of late frequented my house; if she has abused my good opinion of her, am I to blame? Hasn't Barnwell done the same by you?

THOROWGOOD. I hear you; pray go on.

MILLWOOD. I have been informed he had a violent passion for her, and she for him; but till now I always thought it innocent; I know her poor and given to expensive pleasures. Now who can tell but she may have influenced the amorous youth to commit this murder, to supply her extravagancies? It must be so. I now recollect a thousand circumstances that confirm it. I'll have her and a man servant that I suspect as an accomplice, secured immediately. I hope, sir, you will lay aside your ill-grounded suspicions of me, and join to punish the real contrivers of this bloody deed. (*Offers to go.*)

THOROWGOOD. Madam, you pass not this way. I see your design, but shall protect them from your malice.

MILLWOOD. I hope you will not use your influence and the credit of your name to screen such guilty wretches. Consider, sir, the wickedness of persuading a thoughtless youth to such a crime.

THOROWGOOD. I do, and of betraying him when it was done.

MILLWOOD. That which you call betraying him, may convince you of my innocence. She who loves him, though she contrived the murder, would never have delivered him into the hands of justice, as I, struck with the horror of his crimes, have done.

THOROWGOOD [*aside*]. How should an unexperienced youth escape her snares? The powerful magic of her wit and form might betray the wisest to simple dotage and fire the blood that age had froze long since. Even I, that with just prejudice came prepared, had, by her artful story, been deceived, but that my strong conviction of her guilt makes even a doubt impossible.—Those whom subtly you would accuse, you know are your accusers; and—what proves unanswerably their innocence and your guilt—they accused you before the deed was done, and did all that was in their power to prevent it.

MILLWOOD. Sir, you are very hard to be convinced; but I have such a proof, which, when produced, will silence all objections. [*Exit.*]

([*Enter*] LUCY, TRUEMAN, BLUNT, OFFICERS, &c.)

LUCY. Gentlemen, pray place yourselves, some on one side of that door, and some on the other; watch her entrance, and act as your prudence shall direct you.— This way—

(*To* THOROWGOOD): and note her behavior; I have observed her, she's driven to the last extremity, and is forming some desperate resolution. I guess at her design.

([*Enter*] MILLWOOD *with a Pistol.* TRUEMAN *secures her.*)

TRUEMAN. Here thy power of doing mischief ends, deceitful, cruel, bloody woman!

MILLWOOD. Fool, hypocrite, villain!—man! thou can'st not call me that.

TRUEMAN. To call thee woman were to wrong the sex, thou devil!

MILLWOOD. That imaginary being is an emblem of thy cursed sex collected. A mirror, wherein each particular man may see his own likeness and that of all mankind!

TRUEMAN. Think not, by aggravating the fault of others, to extenuate thy own, of which the abuse of such uncommon perfections of mind and body is not the least.

MILLWOOD. If such I had, well may I curse your barbarous sex, who robbed me of 'em ere I knew their worth, then left me, too late, to count their value by their loss! Another and another spoiler came, and all my gain was poverty and reproach. My soul disdained, and yet disdains, dependence and contempt. Riches, no matter by what means obtained, I saw, secured the worst of men from both; I found it therefore necessary to be rich; and, to that end, I summoned all my arts. You call 'em wicked; be it so! They were such as my conversation with your sex had furnished me withal.

THOROWGOOD. Sure, none but the worst of men conversed with thee.

MILLWOOD. Men of all degrees and all professions I have known, yet found no difference but in their several capacities; all were alike wicked to the utmost of their power. In pride, contention, avarice, cruelty, and revenge, the reverend priesthood were my unerring guides. From suburb-magistrates, who live by ruined reputations, as the unhospitable natives of Cornwall do by shipwrecks,[12] I learned that to charge my innocent neighbors with my crimes was to merit their protection; for to screen the guilty is the less scandalous when many are suspected, and detraction, like darkness and death, blackens all objects and levels all distinction. Such are your venal magistrates, who favor none but such as, by their office, they are sworn to punish. With them, not to be guilty is the worst of crimes; and large fees privately paid are every needful virtue.

---

[12] As the natives of Cornwall often plundered shipwrecked vessels, magistrates in the environs of London, who received no regular salaries, plundered wrecked reputations, encouraging vice in order to increase their profits from bribes.

THOROWGOOD. Your practice has sufficiently discovered your contempt of laws, both human and divine; no wonder then that you should hate the officers of both.

MILLWOOD. I know you, and I hate you all; I expect no mercy, and I ask for none. I followed my own inclinations, and that the best of you do every day. All actions seem alike natural and indifferent to man and beast, who devour, or are devoured, as they meet with others weaker or stronger than themselves.

THOROWGOOD. What pity it is, a mind so comprehensive, daring, and inquisitive, should be a stranger to religion's sweet and powerful charms.

MILLWOOD. I am not fool enough to be an atheist, though I have known enough of men's hypocrisy to make a thousand simple women so. Whatever religion is in itself, as practised by mankind it has caused the evils you say it was designed to cure. War, plague, and famine have not destroyed so many of the human race as this pretended piety has done, and with such barbarous cruelty, as if the only way to honor heaven were to turn the present world into hell.

THOROWGOOD. Truth is truth, though from an enemy and spoke in malice. You bloody, blind, and superstitious bigots, how will you answer this?

MILLWOOD. What are your laws, of which you make your boast, but the fool's wisdom and the coward's valor—the instrument and screen of all your villainies, by which you punish in others what you act yourselves, or would have acted had you been in their circumstances? The judge who condemns the poor man for being a thief had been a thief himself had he been poor. Thus you go on deceiving and being deceived, harassing, plaguing, and destroying one another; but women are your universal prey.

Women, by whom you are, the source of joy,
With cruel arts you labor to destroy.
A thousand ways our ruin you pursue,
Yet blame in us those arts, first taught by you.
Oh, may, from hence, each violated maid,
By flattering, faithless, barb'rous man betrayed,
When robbed of innocence and virgin fame,

From your destruction raise a nobler name;
To right their sex's wrongs devote their mind,
And future Millwoods prove, to plague mankind.

ACT V

[SCENE I.] *A room in a prison*

([*Enter*] THOROWGOOD, BLUNT *and* LUCY.)

THOROWGOOD. I have recommended to Barnwell a reverend divine whose judgment and integrity I am well acquainted with; nor has Millwood been neglected, but she, unhappy woman, still obstinate, refuses his assistance.

LUCY. This pious charity to the afflicted well becomes your character; yet pardon me, sir, if I wonder you were not at their trial.

THOROWGOOD. I knew it was impossible to save him, and I and my family bear so great a part in his distress, that to have been present would have aggravated our sorrows without relieving his.

BLUNT. It was mournful, indeed. Barnwell's youth and modest deportment as he passed drew tears from every eye. When placed at the bar and arraigned before the reverend judges, with many tears and interrupting sobs he confessed and aggravated his offences, without accusing, or once reflecting on, Millwood, the shameless author of his ruin, who, dauntless and unconcerned, stood by his side, viewing with visible pride and contempt the vast assembly, who all with sympathizing sorrow wept for the wretched youth. Millwood, when called upon to answer, loudly insisted upon her innocence, and made an artful and a bold defence; but finding all in vain, the impartial jury and the learned bench concurring to find her guilty, how did she curse herself, poor Barnwell, us, her judges, all mankind! But what could that avail? She was condemned, and is this day to suffer with him.

THOROWGOOD. The time draws on; I am going to visit Barnwell, as you are Millwood.

LUCY. We have not wronged her, yet I dread this interview. She's proud, impatient, wrathful, and unforgiving. To be the branded instruments of vengeance, to suffer in her shame, and sympathize with her in all she suffers, is the tribute we must pay for our former ill-spent lives, and long confederacy with her in wickedness.

THOROWGOOD. Happy for you it ended when it did. What you have done against Millwood, I know, proceeded from a just abhorrence of her crimes, free from interest, malice, or revenge. Proselytes to virtue should be encouraged. Pursue your proposed reformation, and know me hereafter for your friend.

LUCY. This is a blessing as unhoped for as unmerited, but heaven, that snatched us from impending ruin, sure intends you as its instrument to secure us from apostasy.

THOROWGOOD. With gratitude to impute your deliverance to heaven is just. Many, less virtuously disposed than Barnwell was, have never fallen in the manner he has done; may not such owe their safety rather to Providence than to themselves? With pity and compassion let us judge him. Great were his faults, but strong was the temptation. Let his ruin learn[13] us diffidence, humanity and circumspection; for we, who wonder at his fate—perhaps had we like him, been tried, like him, we had fallen, too.

[SCENE II.] *A dungeon, a table and lamp*

(BARNWELL *reading.* [*Enter*] THOROWGOOD.)

THOROWGOOD. See there the bitter fruits of passion's detested reign and sensual appetite indulged—severe reflections, penitence, and tears!

BARNWELL [*rising*]. My honored, injured master, whose goodness has covered me a thousand times with shame, forgive this last unwilling disrespect. Indeed I saw you not.

THOROWGOOD. 'Tis well. I hope you were better employed in viewing of yourself; your journey's long, your time

13 Teach.

for preparation almost spent. I sent a reverend divine to teach you to improve it and should be glad to hear of his success.

BARNWELL. The word of truth, which he recommended for my constant companion in this my sad retirement, has at length removed the doubts I labored under. From thence I've learned the infinite extent of heavenly mercy; that my offences, though great, are not unpardonable; and that 'tis not my interest only, but my duty, to believe and to rejoice in that hope. So shall heaven receive the glory, and future penitents the profit of my example.

THOROWGOOD. Proceed!

BARNWELL. 'Tis wonderful that words should charm despair, speak peace and pardon to a murderer's conscience; but truth and mercy flow in every sentence, attended with force and energy divine. How shall I describe my present state of mind? I hope in doubt, and trembling I rejoice. I feel my grief increase, even as my fears give way. Joy and gratitude now supply more tears than the horror and anguish of despair before.

THOROWGOOD. These are the genuine signs of true receptance, the only preparatory, the certain way to everlasting peace. Oh, the joy it gives to see a soul formed and prepared for heaven! For this the faithful minister devotes himself to meditation, abstinence, and prayer, shunning the vain delights of sensual joys, and daily dies that others may live forever. For this he turns the sacred volumes o'er, and spends his life in painful search of truth. The love of riches and the lust of power, he looks upon with just contempt and detestation, who only counts for wealth the souls he wins, and whose highest ambition is to serve mankind. If the reward of all his pains be to preserve one soul from wandering or turn one from the error of his ways, how does he then rejoice and own his little labors over-paid!

BARNWELL. What do I owe for all your generous kindness! But though I cannot, heaven can, and will, reward you.

THOROWGOOD. To see thee thus is joy too great for words. Farewell! Heaven strengthen thee! Farewell!

BARNWELL. Oh, sir, there's something I could say, if my sad swelling heart would give me leave.

THOROWGOOD. Give it vent a while and try.

BARNWELL. I had a friend ('tis true I am unworthy), yet methinks your generous example might persuade—could I not see him once before I go from whence there's no return?

THOROWGOOD. He's coming, and as much thy friend as ever; but I'll not anticipate his sorrow. (*aside*) Too soon he'll see the sad effect of this contagious ruin. This torrent of domestic misery bears too hard upon me; I must retire to indulge a weakness I find impossible to overcome.—Much loved and much lamented youth, farewell! Heaven strengthen thee! Eternally farewell!

BARNWELL. The best of masters and of men, farewell! While I live, let me not want your prayers!

THOROWGOOD. Thou shalt not. Thy peace being made with heaven, death's already vanquished; bear a little longer the pains that attend this transitory life, and cease from pain forever. [*Exit.*]

BARNWELL. I find a power within that bears my soul above the fears of death, and, spite of conscious shame and guilt, gives me a taste of pleasure more than mortal.

([*Enter*] TRUEMAN *and* KEEPER.)

KEEPER. Sir, there's the prisoner. [*Exit.*]

BARNWELL. Trueman! My friend, whom I so wished to see, yet now he's here I dare not look upon him.

TRUEMAN. Oh, Barnwell! Barnwell!

BARNWELL. Mercy! Mercy! gracious heaven! For death, but not for this, was I prepared!

TRUEMAN. What have I suffered since I saw you last! What pain has absence given me! But oh, to see thee thus!

BARNWELL. I know it is dreadful! I feel the anguish of thy generous soul—but I was born to murder all who love me.

(*Both weep.*)

TRUEMAN. I came not to reproach you; I thought to bring you comfort. But I'm deceived, for I have none to give. I came to share thy sorrow, but cannot bear my own.

BARNWELL. My sense of guilt, indeed, you cannot know; 'tis what the good and innocent like you can ne'er conceive; but other griefs at present I have none but what I feel for you. In your sorrow I read you love me still, but yet methinks 'tis strange, when I consider what I am.

TRUEMAN. No more of that. I can remember nothing but thy virtues, thy honest, tender friendship, our former happy state and present misery. Oh, had you trusted me when first the fair seducer tempted you, all might have been prevented!

BARNWELL. Alas, thou know'st not what a wretch I've been! Breach of friendship was my first and least offence. So far was I lost to goodness, so devoted to the author of my ruin, that had she insisted on my murdering thee, I think I should have done it.

TRUEMAN. Prithee, aggravate thy faults no more.

BARNWELL. I think I should! Thus good and generous as you are, I should have murdered you!

TRUEMAN. We have not yet embraced, and may be interrupted. Come to my arms.

BARNWELL. Never, never will I taste such joys on earth; never will I so soothe my just remorse. Are those honest arms and faithful bosom fit to embrace and to support a murderer? These iron fetters only shall clasp and flinty pavement bear me. (*throwing himself on the ground*) Even these too good for such a bloody monster!

TRUEMAN. Shall fortune sever those whom friendship joined! Thy miseries cannot lay thee so low, but love will find thee. (*Lies down by him*) Upon this rugged couch then let us lie, for well it suits our most deplorable condition. Here will we offer to stern calamity, this earth the altar, and ourselves the sacrifice. Our mutual groans shall echo to each other through the dreary vault. Our sighs shall number the moments as they pass, and mingling tears communicate such anguish as words were never made to express.

BARNWELL. Then be it so. [*rising*] Since you propose an intercourse of woe, pour all your griefs into my breast, and in exchange take mine. (*embracing*) Where's now the anguish that you promised? You've taken mine, and make me no return. Sure peace and comfort dwell within these arms, and sorrow can't approach me while I'm here! This, too, is the work of heaven, who, having before spoke peace and pardon to me, now sends thee to confirm it. Oh, take, take some of the joy that overflows my breast!

TRUEMAN. I do, I do. Almighty Power, how have you made us capable to bear, at once, the extremes of pleasure and of pain?

([*Enter*] KEEPER.)

KEEPER. Sir.
TRUEMAN. I come.

[*Exit* KEEPER.]

BARNWELL. Must you leave me? Death would soon have parted us forever.

TRUEMAN. Oh, my Barnwell, there's yet another task behind. Again your heart must bleed for others' woes.

BARNWELL. To meet and part with you, I thought was all I had to do on earth! What is there more for me to do or suffer?

TRUEMAN. I dread to tell thee, yet it must be known. Maria—

BARNWELL. Our master's fair and virtuous daughter!

TRUEMAN. The same.

BARNWELL. No misfortune, I hope, has reached that lovely maid! Preserve her, heaven, from every ill, to show mankind that goodness is your care.

TRUEMAN. Thy, thy misfortunes, my unhappy friend, have reached her. Whatever you and I have felt, and more, if more be possible, she feels for you.

BARNWELL (*aside*). I know he doth abhor a lie, and would not trifle with his dying friend. This is, indeed, the bitterness of death!

TRUEMAN. You must remember, for we all observed it, for some time past a heavy melancholy weighed her down. Disconsolate she seemed, and pined and languished from a cause unknown; till hearing of your dreadful fate, the long stifled flame blazed out. She wept, she wrung her hands, and tore her hair, and in the transport of her grief discovered her own lost state, whilst she lamented yours.

BARNWELL. Will all the pain I feel restore thy case, lovely, unhappy maid? (*weeping*) Why didn't you let me die and never know it?

TRUEMAN. It was impossible; she makes no secret of her passion for you, and is determined to see you ere you die. She waits for me to introduce her. [*Exit.*]

BARNWELL. Vain busy thoughts be still! What avails it to think on what I might have been. I now am what I've made myself.

([*Enter*] TRUEMAN *and* MARIA.)

TRUEMAN. Madam, reluctant I lead you to this dismal scene. This is the seat of misery and guilt. Here awful justice reserves her public victims. This is the entrance to shameful death.

MARIA. To this sad place, then, no improper guest, the abandoned, lost Maria brings despair; and see the subject and the cause of all this world of woe! Silent and motionless he stands, as if his soul had quitted her abode, and the lifeless form alone was left behind; yet that so perfect that beauty and death, ever at enmity, now seem united there.

BARNWELL. I groan, but murmur not. Just Heaven, I am your own; do with me what you please.

MARIA. Why are your streaming eyes still fixed below as though thou'dst give the greedy earth thy sorrows, and rob me of my due? Were happiness within your power, you should bestow it where you please; but in your misery I must and will partake.

BARNWELL. Oh! say not so, but fly, abhor, and leave me to my fate. Consider what you are! How vast your fortune, and how bright your fame! Have pity on your youth, your beauty, and unequalled virtue, for which so many noble peers have sighed in vain. Bless with your charms some honorable lord. Adorn with your beauty and, by your example, improve the English court, that justly claims such merit; so shall I quickly be to you as though I had never been.

MARIA. When I forget you, I must be so, indeed. Reason, choice, virtue, all forbid it. Let women like Millwood, if there be more such women, smile in prosperity and in adversity forsake. Be it the pride of virtue to repair or to partake the ruin such have made.

TRUEMAN. Lovely, ill-fated maid! Was there ever such generous distress before? How must this pierce his grateful heart and aggravate his woes!

BARNWELL. Ere I knew guilt or shame, when fortune smiled, and when my youthful hopes were at the highest—if then to have raised my thoughts to you had been presumption in me, never to have been pardoned, think how much beneath yourself you condescend to regard me now.

MARIA. Let her blush, who, professing love, invades the freedom of your sex's choice and meanly sues in hopes of a return. Your inevitable fate hath rendered hope impossible as vain. Then why should I fear to avow a passion so just and so disinterested?

TRUEMAN. If any should take occasion from Millwood's crimes to libel the best and fairest part of the creation, here let them see their error. The most distant hopes of such a tender passion from so bright a maid might add to the happiness of the most happy and make the greatest proud. Yet here 'tis lavished in vain. Though by the rich present the generous donor is undone, he on whom it is bestowed receives no benefit.

BARNWELL. So the aromatic spices of the East, which all the living covet and esteem, are with unavailing kindness wasted on the dead.

MARIA. Yes, fruitless is my love, and unavailing all my sighs and tears. Can they save thee from approaching death, from such a death? Oh, terrible idea! What is her misery and distress, who sees the first, last object of her love, for whom alone she'd live, for whom she'd die a thousand, thousand deaths if it were possible, expiring in her arms? Yet she is happy, when compared to me. Were millions of words mine, I'd gladly give them in exchange for her condition. The most consummate woe is light to mine. The last of curses to other miserable maids is all I ask; and that's denied me.

TRUEMAN. Time and reflection cure all ills.

MARIA. All but this; his dreadful catastrophe virtue herself abhors. To give a holiday to suburb slaves, and, passing, entertain the savage herd who, elbowing each other for a sight, pursue and press upon him like his

fate.[14] A mind with piety and resolution armed may
smile on death. But public ignominy! everlasting
shame! shame the death of souls! to die a thousand
times and yet survive even death itself in never-dying
infamy, is this to be endured? Can I, who live in him,
and must each hour of my devoted[15] life feel these
woes renewed—can I endure this!

TRUEMAN. Grief has impaired her spirits; she pants as in
the agonies of death.

BARNWELL. Preserve her, heaven, and restore her peace,
nor let her death be added to my crimes! (*Bell tolls.*)
I am summoned to my fate.

([*Enter*] KEEPER.)

KEEPER. The officers attend you, sir. Mrs. Millwood is
already summoned.

BARNWELL. Tell 'em I'm ready.—And now, my friend,
farewell. (*embracing*) Support and comfort the best
you can this mourning fair. No more! Forget not to
pray for me—(*turning to* MARIA) Would you, bright
excellence, permit me the honor of a chaste embrace,
the last happiness this world could give were mine.
(*She inclines towards him; they embrace.*) Exalted
goodness! Oh, turn your eyes from earth and me to
heaven, where virtue like yours is ever heard. Pray
for the peace of my departing soul.—Early my race
of wickedness began and soon has reached the summit.
Ere nature has finished her work, and stamped me
man, just at the time that others begin to stray, my
course is finished! Though short my span of life, and
few my days, yet count my crimes for years, and I
have lived whole ages. Justice and mercy are in heaven
the same. Its utmost severity is mercy to the whole,
thereby to cure man's folly and presumption, which
else would render even infinite mercy vain and in-
effectual. Thus justice in compassion to mankind cuts
off a wretch like me, by one such example to secure
thousands from future ruin.

[14] Barnwell's passage on his way to execution will entertain the
lowest class of people, those who (in Elizabethan times) lived in
the suburbs.
[15] Doomed.

If any youth, like you, in future times,
Shall mourn my fate, though he abhors my crimes;
Or tender maid, like you, my tale shall hear,
And to my sorrows give a pitying tear:
To each such melting eye, and throbbing heart,
Would gracious heaven this benefit impart,
Never to know my guilt, nor feel my pain;
Then must you own, you ought not to complain;
Since you nor weep, nor shall I die, in vain.

([*Exeunt* KEEPER *and* BARNWELL.[16] *Enter*] BLUNT *and*
LUCY.)

LUCY. Heart-breaking sight! O wretched, wretched Millwood!

TRUEMAN. You came from her then—how is she disposed
to meet her fate?

BLUNT. Who can describe unalterable woe?

LUCY. She goes to death encompassed with horror, loath-
ing life, and yet afraid to die; no tongue can tell her
anguish and despair.

TRUEMAN. Heaven be better to her than her fears; may
she prove a warning to others, a monument of mercy
in herself.

LUCY. O sorrow insupportable! Break, break, my heart!

TRUEMAN. In vain

With bleeding hearts and weeping eyes we show
A human gen'rous sense of others' woe;
Unless we mark what drew their ruin on,
And by avoiding that, prevent our own.

---

16 Lillo had originally included at this point a ninety-line scene at
the gallows; he was persuaded to suppress it for stage production,
but reinstated it in the fifth edition of his play. This scene brings
Barnwell and Millwood together immediately before their execution
in order to contrast his thorough repentance with her defiant despair.

EPILOGUE
Written by Colley Cibber, Esq. and Spoke by Mrs. Cibber[17]

Since Fate has robbed me of the hopeless youth,
For whom my heart had hoarded up its truth;
By all the laws of love and honor, now,
I'm free again to choose—and one of you.

But soft! With caution first I'll round me peep;
Maids, in my case, should look before they leap.
Here's choice enough, of various sorts and hue,
The cit, the wit, the rake cocked up in cue,
The fair, spruce mercer, and the tawny Jew.

Suppose I search the sober gallery. No,
There's none but prentices, and cuckolds all a row;
And these, I doubt, are those that make 'em so.
                              (*Points to the boxes*)

'Tis very well, enjoy the jest. But you,
Fine powdered sparks, nay, I'm told 'tis true,
Your happy spouses—can make cuckolds too.
'Twixt you and them, the diff'rence this perhaps,
The cit's ashamed whene'er his duck he traps;
But you, when madam's tripping, let her fall,
Cock up your hats, and take no shame at all.

What if some favored poet I could meet,
Whose love would lay his laurels at my feet?
No,—painted passion real love abhors,—
His flame would prove the suit of creditors.

Not to detain you then with longer pause,
In short; my heart to this conclusion draws,
I yield it to the hand, that's loudest in applause.

17 Mrs. Cibber played Maria; her husband, Theophilus, son of
Colley Cibber, played Barnwell.

THE SCHOOL FOR SCANDAL
〜 1777 〜

Richard Brinsley Sheridan

INTRODUCTORY NOTE

RICHARD BRINSLEY SHERIDAN (1751–1816), his father the
manager of the Smock-Alley Theatre in Dublin and his
mother an author, early turned to playwriting to support
himself and his wife, a beautiful and sensationally popular
singer, whom he insisted retire from the stage after marriage. His first play, *The Rivals* (1775), almost failed; but
after he revised it, it became a perennial favorite. He took
over the management of Drury Lane Theatre when David
Garrick retired, and wrote for it *The School for Scandal*
(1777). Two years later, at the age of twenty-eight, he produced his last original play, a brilliant dramatic burlesque
called *The Critic*. Though he continued as manager of
Drury Lane for thirty years, the main interest of Sheridan's
later life was liberal politics. He was one of the greatest
orators ever heard in Parliament, capable of holding an
audience spellbound for five hours.

The School for Scandal, the first work of Sheridan's
maturity, is as brilliantly constructed as it is witty. Consider, for example, how the screen scene (IV, iii) succeeds
both symbolically and realistically, as the screen at first
serves to conceal Joseph's vicious intrigues, then enables
his dupes to hear precisely what he wants to conceal from
them, and finally falls to expose him. Without any appearance of contrivance, the characters he has been deceiving
come to his room and say the very things that will demolish
his plans. Moreover, Sheridan builds up to this climax by
the preceding parallel scene in which Charles's essentially
good nature and minor follies are exposed to his uncle;
and capitalizes on it by showing us how ludicrously the
scandalmongers elaborate upon the events we have just
seen.

One reason this play was a brilliant success was its acting: Sheridan knew his Drury Lane company and used its strength. John Palmer, the original Joseph, was known as "Plausible Jack"; he was very attractive, with an insinuating manner well calculated to lend conviction to hypocritical sentiments. Frances Abington, who created Lady Teazle, was able to combine "artificial refinement and natural vivacity" and excelled in tart repartee with Thomas King, the original Sir Peter.

BIBLIOGRAPHY

Major Works:

The Rivals, 1775 (comedy)
The Duenna, 1775 (comic opera)
The School for Scandal, 1777 (comedy)
The Critic; or, A Tragedy Rehearsed, 1779 (burlesque)
Pizarro, 1799 (tragedy, adapted from the German of
　　August von Kotzebue)

Editions:

Dramatic Works of Richard Brinsley Sheridan. Ed. Cecil
　　Price. Oxford: Clarendon, 1973. 2 vols.
Letters of Richard Brinsley Sheridan. Ed. Cecil Price.
　　Oxford: Clarendon, 1966.

Works About:

Deelman, Christian. "The Original Cast of *The School for
　　Scandal*," *Review of English Studies*, New Series XIII
　　(1962), 257–66.
Durant, Jack D. *Richard Brinsley Sheridan*. Boston:
　　Twayne, 1975.
Loftis, John. *Sheridan and the Drama of Georgian
　　England*. Oxford: Basil Blackwell, 1976.

THE SCHOOL FOR SCANDAL

Dramatis Personae

MEN

SIR PETER TEAZLE
SIR OLIVER SURFACE
JOSEPH SURFACE
CHARLES SURFACE
CRABTREE
SIR BENJAMIN BACKBITE
ROWLEY
MOSES
TRIP
SNAKE
CARELESS
SIR TOBY BUMPER
    and other companions to Charles, servants, etc.

WOMEN

LADY TEAZLE
MARIA
LADY SNEERWELL
MRS. CANDOUR

[Scene: London]

PROLOGUE

Written by Mr. Garrick
Spoken by Mr. King

A school for scandal! tell me, I beseech you,
Needs there a school this modish art to teach you?
No need of lessons now, the knowing think;
We might as well be taught to eat and drink.
Caused by a dearth of scandal, should the vapors
Distress our fair ones, let 'em read the papers;
Their powerful mixtures such disorders hit,
Crave what you will, there's *quantum sufficit.*
"Lord!" cries my Lady Wormwood (who loves tattle,
And puts much salt and pepper in her prattle),
Just risen at noon, all night at cards when threshing
Strong tea and scandal, "Bless me, how refreshing!
Give me the papers, Lisp,—how bold and free! (*Sips.*)
Last night Lord L. (Sips) was caught with Lady D.
For aching heads what charming sal volatile! (*Sips.*)
If Mrs. B. will still continue flirting,
We hope she'll draw, or we'll undraw the curtain.
Fine satire, poz! In public all abuse it,
But by ourselves (*Sips*) our praise we can't refuse it.
Now, Lisp, read you—there at that dash and star."
"Yes, ma'am. *A certain lord had best beware,*
Who lives not twenty miles from Grosvenor Square,
For, should he Lady W. find willing,
Wormwood is bitter—" "Oh! that's me! the villain!
Throw it behind the fire and never more
Let that vile paper come within my door."
Thus at our friends we laugh, who feel the dart;
To reach our feelings, we ourselves must smart.
Is our young bard so young to think that he
Can stop the full spring-tide of calumny?
Knows he the world so little, and its trade?
Alas! the devil's sooner raised than laid.

So strong, so swift, the monster there's no gagging;
Cut Scandal's head off, still the tongue is wagging.
Proud of your smiles once lavishly bestowed,
Again our young Don Quixote takes the road;
To show his gratitude he draws his pen
And seeks this hydra, Scandal, in his den.
For your applause all perils he would through—
He'll fight (that's write) a cavalliero true,
Till every drop of blood (that's ink) is spilt for you.

ACT I

[SCENE I.] LADY SNEERWELL's *House*

(*Discovered,* LADY SNEERWELL *at the dressing table;* SNAKE *drinking chocolate.*)

LADY SNEERWELL. The paragraphs, you say, Mr. Snake, were all inserted?

SNAKE. They were, madam; and as I copied them myself in a feigned hand, there can be no suspicion whence they came.

LADY SNEERWELL. Did you circulate the report of Lady Brittle's intrigue with Captain Boastall?

SNAKE. That's in as fine a train as your ladyship could wish. In the common course of things, I think it must reach Mrs. Clackitt's ears within four-and-twenty hours; and then, you know, the business is as good as done.

LADY SNEERWELL. Why, truly, Mrs. Clackitt has a very pretty talent and a great deal of industry.

SNAKE. True, madam, and has been tolerably successful in her day. To my knowledge, she has been the cause of six matches being broken off and three sons being disinherited; of four forced elopements and as many close confinements; nine separate maintenances and two divorces. Nay, I have more than once traced her causing a *tête-à-tête* in the *Town and Country Magazine*[1] when the parties, perhaps, had never seen each other's faces before in the course of their lives.

LADY SNEERWELL. She certainly has talents, but her manner is gross.

[1] The scandal column in this magazine was entitled "Tête-à-Tête."

SNAKE. 'Tis very true. She generally designs well, has a free tongue and a bold invention; but her coloring is too dark and her outline often extravagant. She wants that delicacy of hint and mellowness of sneer which distinguish your ladyship's scandal.

LADY SNEERWELL. You are partial, Snake.

SNAKE. Not in the least; everybody allows that Lady Sneerwell can do more with a word or look than many can with the most labored detail, even when they happen to have a little truth on their side to support it.

LADY SNEERWELL. Yes, my dear Snake; and I am no hypocrite to deny the satisfaction I reap from the success of my efforts. Wounded myself in the early part of my life by the envenomed tongue of slander, I confess I have since known no pleasure equal to the reducing others to the level of my own reputation.

SNAKE. Nothing can be more natural. But, Lady Sneerwell, there is one affair in which you have lately employed me, wherein, I confess, I am at a loss to guess your motives.

LADY SNEERWELL. I conceive you mean with respect to my neighbor, Sir Peter Teazle, and his family?

SNAKE. I do. Here are two young men to whom Sir Peter has acted as a kind of guardian since their father's death, the eldest possessing the most amiable character and universally well spoken of, the youngest, the most dissipated and extravagant young fellow in the kingdom, without friends or character; the former an avowed admirer of your ladyship and apparently your favorite; the latter attached to Maria, Sir Peter's ward, and confessedly beloved by her. Now, on the face of these circumstances, it is utterly unaccountable to me why you, the widow of a city knight, with a good jointure, should not close with the passion of a man of such character and expectations as Mr. Surface; and more so, why you should be so uncommonly earnest to destroy the mutual attachment subsisting between his brother Charles and Maria.

LADY SNEERWELL. Then at once to unravel this mystery, I must inform you that love has no share whatever in the intercourse between Mr. Surface and me.

SNAKE. No!

LADY SNEERWELL. His real attachment is to Maria, or her fortune; but finding in his brother a favored rival, he has been obliged to mask his pretensions and profit by my assistance.

SNAKE. Yet still I am more puzzled why you should interest yourself in his success.

LADY SNEERWELL. Heavens! how dull you are! Cannot you surmise the weakness which I hitherto, through shame, have concealed even from you? Must I confess that Charles, that libertine, that extravagant, that bankrupt in fortune and reputation—that he it is for whom I am thus anxious and malicious, and to gain whom I would sacrifice everything?

SNAKE. Now, indeed, your conduct appears consistent; but how came you and Mr. Surface so confidential?

LADY SNEERWELL. For our mutual interest. I have found him out a long time since. I know him to be artful, selfish, and malicious—in short, a sentimental knave.

SNAKE. Yet Sir Peter vows he has not his equal in England; and, above all, he praises him as a man of sentiment.

LADY SNEERWELL. True; and with the assistance of his sentiment and hypocrisy he has brought Sir Peter entirely into his interest with regard to Maria.

(*Enter* SERVANT.)

SERVANT. Mr. Surface.

LADY SNEERWELL. Show him up.

(*Exit* SERVANT.)

He generally calls about this time. I don't wonder at people's giving him to me for a lover.

(*Enter* JOSEPH SURFACE.)

JOSEPH SURFACE. My dear Lady Sneerwell, how do you do today? Mr. Snake, your most obedient.

LADY SNEERWELL. Snake has just been arraigning me on our mutual attachment; but I have informed him of our real views. You know how useful he has been to us, and, believe me, the confidence is not ill placed.

JOSEPH SURFACE. Madam, it is impossible for me to suspect a man of Mr. Snake's sensibility and discernment.

LADY SNEERWELL. Well, well, no compliments now; but tell me when you saw your mistress, Maria—or what is more material to me, your brother.

JOSEPH SURFACE. I have not seen either since I left you; but I can inform you that they never meet. Some of your stories have taken a good effect on Maria.

LADY SNEERWELL. Ah, my dear Snake, the merit of this belongs to you. But do your brother's distresses increase?

JOSEPH SURFACE. Every hour. I am told he has had another execution[2] in the house yesterday. In short, his dissipation and extravagance exceed anything I ever heard of.

LADY SNEERWELL. Poor Charles!

JOSEPH SURFACE. True, madam, notwithstanding his vices, one can't help feeling for him. Ay, poor Charles! I'm sure I wish it were in my power to be of any essential service to him, for the man who does not share in the distresses of a brother, even though merited by his own misconduct, deserves—

LADY SNEERWELL. Oh, lud! you are going to be moral and forget that you are among friends.

JOSEPH SURFACE. Egad, that's true! I'll keep that sentiment till I see Sir Peter. However, it is certainly a charity to rescue Maria from such a libertine, who, if he is to be reclaimed, can be so only by a person of your ladyship's superior accomplishments and understanding.

SNAKE. I believe, Lady Sneerwell, here's company coming. I'll go and copy the letter I mentioned to you.—Mr. Surface, your most obedient.

JOSEPH SURFACE. Sir, your very devoted.—

(*Exit* SNAKE.)

Lady Sneerwell, I am very sorry you have put any further confidence in that fellow.

LADY SNEERWELL. Why so?

JOSEPH SURFACE. I have lately detected him in frequent conference with old Rowley, who was formerly my father's steward and has never, you know, been a friend of mine.

---

[2] Legal seizure of a debtor's goods in default of payment.

LADY SNEERWELL. And do you think he would betray us?

JOSEPH SURFACE. Nothing more likely. Take my word for't, Lady Sneerwell, that fellow hasn't virtue enough to be faithful even to his own villainy.—Hah! Maria!

(*Enter* MARIA.)

LADY SNEERWELL. Maria, my dear, how do you do? What's the matter?

MARIA. Oh! there's that disagreeable lover of mine, Sir Benjamin Backbite, has just called at my guardian's with his odious uncle, Crabtree; so I slipped out and ran hither to avoid them.

LADY SNEERWELL. Is that all?

JOSEPH SURFACE. If my brother Charles had been of the party, madam, perhaps you would not have been so much alarmed.

LADY SNEERWELL. Nay, now you are too severe, for I dare swear the truth of the matter is, Maria heard you were here.—But, my dear, what has Sir Benjamin done that you should avoid him so?

MARIA. Oh, he has done nothing; but 'tis for what he has said. His conversation is a perpetual libel on all his acquaintance.

JOSEPH SURFACE. Ay, and the worst of it is, there is no advantage in not knowing him, for he'll abuse a stranger just as soon as his best friend—and his uncle's as bad.

LADY SNEERWELL. Nay, but we should make allowance; Sir Benjamin is a wit and a poet.

MARIA. For my part, I own, madam, wit loses its respect with me when I see it in company with malice.—What do you think, Mr. Surface?

JOSEPH SURFACE. Certainly, madam. To smile at the jest which plants a thorn in another's breast is to become a principal in the mischief.

LADY SNEERWELL. Psha, there's no possibility of being witty without a little ill nature. The malice of a good thing is the barb that makes it stick. What's your opinion, Mr. Surface?

JOSEPH SURFACE. To be sure, madam, that conversation where the spirit of raillery is suppressed will ever appear tedious and insipid.

MARIA. Well, I'll not debate how far scandal may be allowable; but in a man, I am sure, it is always contemptible. We have pride, envy, rivalship, and a thousand motives to depreciate each other; but the male slanderer must have the cowardice of a woman before he can traduce one.

(Enter SERVANT.)

SERVANT. Madam, Mrs. Candour is below and, if your ladyship's at leisure, will leave her carriage.

LADY SNEERWELL. Beg her to walk in.

(*Exit* SERVANT.)

Now, Maria, here is a character to your taste, for though Mrs. Candour is a little talkative, everybody allows her to be the best natured and best sort of woman.

MARIA. Yes, with a very gross affectation of good-nature and benevolence, she does more mischief than the direct malice of old Crabtree.

JOSEPH SURFACE. I' faith 'tis very true, Lady Sneerwell. Whenever I hear the current running against the characters of my friends, I never think them in such danger as when Candour undertakes their defence.

LADY SNEERWELL. Hush!—Here she is.

(*Enter* MRS. CANDOUR.)

MRS. CANDOUR. My dear Lady Sneerwell, how have you been this century?—Mr. Surface, what news do you hear—though indeed it is no matter, for I think one hears nothing else but scandal.

JOSEPH SURFACE. Just so, indeed, ma'am.

MRS. CANDOUR. Oh, Maria, child! What, is the whole affair off between you and Charles? His extravagance, I presume—the town talks of nothing else.

MARIA. I am very sorry, ma'am, the town has so little to do.

MRS. CANDOUR. True, true, child; but there's no stopping people's tongues. I own I was hurt to hear it, as I indeed was to learn from the same quarter that your guardian, Sir Peter, and Lady Teazle have not agreed lately so well as could be wished.

MARIA. 'Tis strangely impertinent for people to busy themselves so.

MRS. CANDOUR. Very true, child, but what's to be done? People will talk; there's no preventing it. Why, it was but yesterday I was told that Miss Gadabout had eloped with Sir Filigree Flirt. But, Lord, there's no minding what one hears, though, to be sure, I had this from very good authority.

MARIA. Such reports are highly scandalous.

MRS. CANDOUR. So they are, child—shameful, shameful! But the world is so censorious, no character escapes. Lord, now who would have suspected your friend, Miss Prim, of an indiscretion? Yet such is the ill nature of people that they say her uncle stopped her last week just as she was stepping into the York diligence with her dancing master.[3]

MARIA. I'll answer for 't there are no grounds for that report.

MRS. CANDOUR. Oh, no foundation in the world, I dare swear; no more probably than for the story circulated last month of Mrs. Festino's affair with Colonel Cassino—though, to be sure, that matter was never rightly cleared up.

JOSEPH SURFACE. The license of invention some people take is monstrous indeed.

MARIA. 'Tis so; but in my opinion those who report such things are equally culpable.

MRS. CANDOUR. To be sure they are; tale bearers are as bad as the tale makers. 'Tis an old observation and a very true one; but what's to be done, as I said before? How wil you prevent people from talking? Today, Mrs. Clackitt assured me Mr. and Mrs. Honeymoon were at last become mere man and wife like the rest of their acquaintance. She likewise hinted that a certain widow in the next street had got rid of her dropsy and recovered her shape in a most surprising manner. And at the same time Miss Tattle, who was by, affirmed that Lord Buffalo had discovered his lady at a house of no extraordinary fame; and that Sir Harry Bouquet and Tom Saunter were to measure swords on a similar provocation. But, Lord, do you

---

[3] They were purportedly taking the stagecoach northward to Scotland, where minors could be married without consent of parents or guardians.

think I would report these things! No, no! Tale
bearers, as I said before, are just as bad as tale makers.

JOSEPH SURFACE. Ah! Mrs. Candour, if everybody had
your forbearance and good nature!

MRS. CANDOUR. I confess, Mr. Surface, I cannot bear to
hear people attacked behind their backs; and when ugly
circumstances come out against one's acquaintance,
I own I always love to think the best. By the by, I
hope 'tis not true that your brother is absolutely
ruined.

JOSEPH SURFACE. I am afraid his circumstances are very
bad indeed, ma'am.

MRS. CANDOUR. Ah, I heard so; but you must tell him to
keep up his spirits. Everybody almost is in the same
way. Lord Spindle, Sir Thomas Splint, Captain Quinze,
and Mr. Nickit—all up,[4] I hear, within this week; so,
if Charles is undone, he'll find half his acquaintance
ruined too; and that, you know, is a consolation.

JOSEPH SURFACE. Doubtless, ma'am, a very great one.

(*Enter* SERVANT.)

SERVANT. Mr. Crabtree and Sir Benjamin Backbite. (*Exit.*)

LADY SNEERWELL. So, Maria, you see your lover pursues
you. Positively you shan't escape.

(*Enter* CRABTREE *and* SIR BENJAMIN BACKBITE.)

CRABTREE. Lady Sneerwell, I kiss your hands.—Mrs.
Candour, I don't believe you are acquainted with my
nephew, Sir Benjamin Backbite? Egad, ma'am, he has
a pretty wit and is a pretty poet too; isn't he, Lady
Sneerwell?

SIR BENJAMIN. Oh, fie, uncle!

CRABTREE. Nay, egad, it's true; I'll back him at a rebus or
a charade against the best rhymer in the kingdom.
Has your ladyship heard the epigram he wrote last
week on Lady Frizzle's feather catching fire?—Do,
Benjamin, repeat it, or the charade you made last
night extempore at Mrs. Drowzie's *conversazione*.
Come, now, your first is the name of a fish, your
second a great naval commander, and—

---

[4] Arrested for debt or "sold up."

SIR BENJAMIN. Uncle, now, prithee—

CRABTREE. I' faith, ma'am, 'twould surprise you to hear how ready he is at these things.

LADY SNEERWELL. I wonder, Sir Benjamin, you never publish anything.

SIR BENJAMIN. To say truth, ma'am, 'tis very vulgar to print; and, as my little productions are mostly satires and lampoons on particular people, I find they circulate more by giving copies in confidence to the friends of the parties. However, I have some love elegies, which, when favored with this lady's smiles, I mean to give the public. (*pointing to* MARIA)

CRABTREE. 'Fore heaven, ma'am, they'll immortalize you! —You'll be handed down to posterity like Petrarch's Laura or Waller's Sacharissa.[5]

SIR BENJAMIN. Yes, madam, I think you will like them when you shall see them on a beautiful quarto page, where a neat rivulet of text shall meander through a meadow of margin. 'Fore gad they will be the most elegant things of their kind!

CRABTREE. But, ladies, that's true—Have you heard the news?

MRS. CANDOUR. What, sir, do you mean the report of—

CRABTREE. No, ma'am, that's not it. Miss Nicely is going to be married to her own footman.

MRS. CANDOUR. Impossible!

CRABTREE. Ask Sir Benjamin.

SIR BENJAMIN. 'Tis very true, ma'am. Everything is fixed, and the wedding liveries bespoke.

CRABTREE. Yes; and they do say there were pressing reasons for it.

LADY SNEERWELL. Why, I have heard something of this before.

MRS. CANDOUR. It can't be! And I wonder anyone should believe such a story of so prudent a lady as Miss Nicely.

SIR BENJAMIN. Oh, lud! ma'am, that's the very reason 'twas believed at once. She has always been so cautious and so reserved that everybody was sure there was some reason for it at bottom.

---

[5] Edmund Waller wrote love poems to "Sacharissa" (Lady Dorothy Sidney) as Petrarch did to Laura.

MRS. CANDOUR. Why, to be sure, a tale of scandal is as fatal to the credit of a prudent lady of her stamp as a fever is generally to those of the strongest constitutions. But there is a sort of puny, sickly reputation that is always ailing, yet will outlive the robuster characters of a hundred prudes.

SIR BENJAMIN. True, madam, there are valetudinarians in reputation as well as in constitution, who, being conscious of their weak part, avoid the least breath of air and supply their want of stamina by care and circumspection.

MRS. CANDOUR. Well, but this may be all a mistake. You know, Sir Benjamin, very trifling circumstances often give rise to the most injurious tales.

CRABTREE. That they do, I'll be sworn, ma'am. Did you ever hear how Miss Piper came to lose her lover and her character last summer at Tunbridge?—Sir Benjamin, you remember it?

SIR BENJAMIN. Oh, to be sure—the most whimsical circumstance.

LADY SNEERWELL. How was it, pray?

CRABTREE. Why, one evening at Mrs. Ponto's assembly the conversation happened to turn on the difficulty of breeding Nova Scotia sheep in this country. Says a young lady in company, "I have known instances of it, for Miss Letitia Piper, a first cousin of mine, had a Nova Scotia sheep that produced her twins." "What," cries the old Dowager Lady Dundizzy, who, you know, is as deaf as a post, "has Miss Piper had twins?" This mistake, as you may imagine, threw the whole company into a fit of laughter. However, 'twas next morning everywhere reported, and in a few days believed by the whole town, that Miss Letitia Piper had actually been brought to bed of a fine boy and a girl; and in less than a week there were people who could name the father and the farm-house where the babies were put to nurse.

LADY SNEERWELL. Strange, indeed!

CRABTREE. Matter of fact, I assure you.—Oh, lud, Mr. Surface, pray is it true that your uncle, Sir Oliver, is coming home?

JOSEPH SURFACE. Not that I know of, indeed, sir.

CRABTREE. He has been in the East Indies a long time. You can scarcely remember him, I believe? Sad comfort, whenever he returns, to hear how your brother has gone on.

JOSEPH SURFACE. Charles has been imprudent, sir, to be sure; but I hope no busy people have already prejudiced Sir Oliver against him. He may reform.

SIR BENJAMIN. To be sure, he may. For my part, I never believed him to be so utterly void of principle as people say; and, though he has lost all his friends, I am told nobody is better spoken of by the Jews.

CRABTREE. That's true, egad, nephew. If the Old Jewry were a ward, I believe Charles would be an alderman. No man is more popular there, 'fore gad! I hear he pays as many annuities as the Irish tontine;[6] and that whenever he is sick, they have prayers for the recovery of his health in the synagogue.

SIR BENJAMIN. Yet no man lives in greater splendor. They tell me that when he entertains his friends he can sit down to dinner with a dozen of his own securities, have a score of tradesmen waiting in the antechamber, and an officer behind every guest's chair.

JOSEPH SURFACE. This may be entertaining to you, gentlemen, but you pay very little regard to the feelings of a brother.

MARIA (*aside*). Their malice is intolerable!—Lady Sneerwell, I must wish you a good morning; I'm not very well. (*Exit.*)

MRS. CANDOUR. Oh, dear, she changes color very much!

LADY SNEERWELL. Do, Mrs. Candour, follow her. She may want assistance.

MRS. CANDOUR. That I will, with all my soul, ma'am. Poor dear girl, who knows what her situation may be! (*Exit.*)

---

6 Loans could be negotiated by agreeing to make periodical payments to the creditor, called annuities. A tontine, a special variant of this type of loan, had been set up by the Irish government; Crabtree facetiously compares Charles's personal debts to this national debt. The securities of Sir Benjamin's following speech are people who have agreed to be responsible should Charles not pay his debts, the tradesmen are waiting to be paid, and the officers are sheriff's officers on duty to watch the property.

LADY SNEERWELL. 'Twas nothing but that she could not bear to hear Charles reflected on, notwithstanding their difference.

SIR BENJAMIN. The young lady's *penchant* is obvious.

CRABTREE. But, Benjamin, you mustn't give up the pursuit for that. Follow her and put her into good humor. Repeat her some of your own verses. Come, I'll assist you.

SIR BENJAMIN. Mr. Surface, I did not mean to hurt you; but depend on 't your brother is utterly undone. (*going*)

CRABTREE. Oh, lud, ay! Undone as ever man was! Can't raise a guinea! (*going*)

SIR BENJAMIN. And everything sold, I'm told, that was moveable. (*going*)

CRABTREE. I have seen one that was at his house. Not a thing left but some empty bottles that were overlooked and the family pictures, which I believe are framed in the wainscot. (*going*)

SIR BENJAMIN. And I'm very sorry also to hear some bad stories against him. (*going*)

CRABTREE. Oh, he has done many mean things, that's certain. (*going*)

SIR BENJAMIN. But, however, as he's your brother— (*going*)

CRABTREE. We'll tell you all another opportunity.

(*Exeunt* CRABTREE *and* SIR BENJAMIN.)

LADY SNEERWELL. Ha! ha! 'tis very hard for them to leave a subject they have not quite run down.

JOSEPH SURFACE. And I believe the abuse was no more acceptable to your ladyship than to Maria.

LADY SNEERWELL. I doubt her affections are farther engaged than we imagined. But the family are to be here this evening, so you may as well dine where you are and we shall have an opportunity of observing farther. In the meantime, I'll go and plot mischief and you shall study sentiments.

(*Exeunt.*)

[SCENE II.] SIR PETER TEAZLE's *House*

(*Enter* SIR PETER.)

SIR PETER. When an old bachelor takes a young wife, what is he to expect? 'Tis now six months since Lady Teazle made me the happiest of men—and I have been the miserablest dog ever since that ever committed wedlock! We tiffed a little going to church, and came to a quarrel before the bells were done ringing. I was more than once nearly choked with gall during the honeymoon and had lost all comfort in life before my friends had done wishing me joy. Yet I chose with caution—a girl bred wholly in the country, who never knew luxury beyond one silk gown nor dissipation above the annual gala of a race ball. Yet she now plays her part in all the extravagant fopperies of the fashion and the town with as ready a grace as if she never had seen a bush or a grass-plot out of Grosvenor Square. I am sneered at by my old acquaintance and paragraphed in the newspapers. She dissipates my fortune and contradicts all my humors; yet the worst of it is, I doubt[7] I love her, or I should never bear all this. However, I'll never be weak enough to own it.

(*Enter* ROWLEY.)

ROWLEY. Oh, Sir Peter, your servant! How is it with you, sir?

SIR PETER. Very bad, Master Rowley, very bad. I meet with nothing but crosses and vexations.

ROWLEY. What can have happened to trouble you since yesterday?

SIR PETER. A good question to a married man!

ROWLEY. Nay, I'm sure your lady, Sir Peter, can't be the cause of your uneasiness.

SIR PETER. Why, has anybody told you she was dead?

ROWLEY. Come, come, Sir Peter, you love her, notwithstanding your tempers don't exactly agree.

SIR PETER. But the fault is entirely hers, Master Rowley. I am myself the sweetest tempered man alive and hate a teasing temper; and so I tell her a hundred times a day.

---

[7] Suspect.

ROWLEY. Indeed!

SIR PETER. Ay; and what is very extraordinary, in all our
disputes she is always in the wrong. But Lady Sneerwell and the set she meets at her house encourage the
perverseness of her disposition. Then, to complete my
vexation, Maria, my ward, whom I ought to have the
power of a father over, is determined to turn rebel too
and absolutely refuses the man whom I have long
resolved on for her husband, meaning, I suppose, to
bestow herself on his profligate brother.

ROWLEY. You know, Sir Peter, I have always taken the
liberty to differ with you on the subject of these two
young gentlemen. I only wish you may not be deceived in your opinion of the elder. For Charles, my
life on 't, he will retrieve his errors yet. Their worthy
father, once my honored master, was at his years
nearly as wild a spark; yet when he died, he did not
leave a more benevolent heart to lament his loss.

SIR PETER. You are wrong, Master Rowley. On their
father's death, you know, I acted as a kind of guardian
to them both, till their uncle Sir Oliver's Eastern
liberality gave them an early independence. Of course,
no person could have more opportunities of judging
of their hearts, and I was never mistaken in my life.
Joseph is indeed a model for the young men of the
age. He is a man of sentiment and acts up to the
sentiments he professes; but for the other, take my
word for 't, if he had any grain of virtue by descent,
he has dissipated it with the rest of his inheritance.
Ah! my old friend Sir Oliver will be deeply mortified
when he finds how part of his bounty has been
misapplied.

ROWLEY. I am sorry to find you so violent against the
young man, because this may be the most critical
period of his fortune. I came hither with news that
will surprise you.

SIR PETER. What? Let me hear!

ROWLEY. Sir Oliver is arrived and at this moment in town.

SIR PETER. How! You astonish me! I thought you did not
expect him this month.

ROWLEY. I did not; but his passage has been remarkably
quick.

SIR PETER. Egad, I shall rejoice to see my old friend. 'Tis

sixteen years since we met. We have had many a day
together. But does he still enjoin us not to inform
his nephews of his arrival?

ROWLEY. Most strictly. He means, before it is known, to
make some trial of their dispositions.

SIR PETER. Ah! There needs no art to discover their merits.
However, he shall have his way; but, pray, does he
know I am married?

ROWLEY. Yes, and will soon wish you joy.

SIR PETER. What, as we drink health to a friend in a con-
sumption? Ah! Oliver will laugh at me. We used to rail
at matrimony together, but he has been steady to his
text. Well, he must be at my house, though—I'll
instantly give orders for his reception. But, Master
Rowley, don't drop a word that Lady Teazle and I
ever disagree.

ROWLEY. By no means.

SIR PETER. For I should never be able to stand Noll's
jokes; so I'll have him think, Lord forgive me! that
we are a very happy couple.

ROWLEY. I understand you; but then you must be very
careful not to differ while he is in the house with you.

SIR PETER. Egad, and so we must—and that's impossible.
Ah! Master Rowley, when an old bachelor marries a
young wife, he deserves—no, the crime carries its
punishment along with it.

(*Exeunt*.)

ACT II

[SCENE I.] SIR PETER TEAZLE's *House*

(Enter SIR PETER *and* LADY TEAZLE.)

SIR PETER. Lady Teazle, Lady Teazle, I'll not bear it!

LADY TEAZLE. Sir Peter, Sir Peter, you may bear it or not
as you please; but I ought to have my own way in
everything, and, what's more, I will, too. What! though
I was educated in the country, I know very well that
women of fashion in London are accountable to nobody after they are married.

SIR PETER. Very well, ma'am, very well; so a husband is to have no influence, no authority?

LADY TEAZLE. Authority! No, to be sure! If you wanted authority over me, you should have adopted me and not married me. I am sure you were old enough.

SIR PETER. Old enough! Ay, there it is! Well, well, Lady Teazle, though my life may be made unhappy by your temper, I'll not be ruined by your extravagance.

LADY TEAZLE. My extravagance! I'm sure I'm not more extravagant than a woman of fashion ought to be.

SIR PETER. No, no, madam, you shall throw away no more sums on such unmeaning luxury. 'Slife! to spend as much to furnish your dressing-room with flowers in winter as would suffice to turn the Pantheon into a greenhouse and give a *fête champêtre*[8] at Christmas.

LADY TEAZLE. Lord! Sir Peter, am I to blame, because flowers are dear in cold weather? You should find fault with the climate, and not with me. For my part, I'm sure I wish it was spring all the year round and that roses grew under one's feet!

SIR PETER. Oons, madam! If you had been born to this, I shouldn't wonder at your talking thus; but you forget what your situation was when I married you.

LADY TEAZLE. No, no, I don't. 'Twas a very disagreeable one, or I should never have married you.

SIR PETER. Yes, yes, madam, you were then in somewhat a humbler style—the daughter of a plain country squire. Recollect, Lady Teazle, when I saw you first, sitting at your tambour in a pretty figured linen gown, with a bunch of keys at your side, your hair combed smooth over a roll, and your apartment hung round with fruits in worsted of your own working.

LADY TEAZLE. Oh, yes! I remember it very well, and a curious life I led. My daily occupation to inspect the dairy, superintend the poultry, make extracts from the family receipt-book, and comb my Aunt Deborah's lap-dog.

SIR PETER. Yes, yes, ma'am, 'twas so indeed.

LADY TEAZLE. And then you know, my evening amusements! To draw patterns for ruffles, which I had not

---

8 The Pantheon was a large concert hall; a *fête champêtre*, an outdoor entertainment.

the materials to make up; to play Pope Joan[9] with the curate; to read a sermon to my aunt; or to be stuck down to an old spinet to strum my father to sleep after a fox-chase.

SIR PETER. I am glad you have so good a memory. Yes, madam, these were the recreations I took you from; but now you must have your coach,—*vis-à-vis*,—and three powdered footmen before your chair, and in the summer a pair of white cats[10] to draw you to Kensington Gardens. No recollection, I suppose, when you were content to ride double behind the butler on a docked coach-horse.

LADY TEAZLE. No—I swear I never did that. I deny the butler and the coach-horse.

SIR PETER. This, madam, was your situation; and what have I not done for you? I have made you a woman of fashion, of fortune, of rank—in short, I have made you my wife.

LADY TEAZLE. Well, then, and there is but one thing more you can make me to add to the obligation—and that is—

SIR PETER. My widow, I suppose?

LADY TEAZLE. Hem! hem!

SIR PETER. I thank you, madam; but don't flatter yourself; for, though your ill conduct may disturb my peace, it shall never break my heart, I promise you. However, I am equally obliged to you for the hint.

LADY TEAZLE. Then why will you endeavor to make yourself so disagreeable to me and thwart me in every little elegant expense?

SIR PETER. 'Slife, madam, I say, had you any of these little elegant expenses when you married me?

LADY TEAZLE. Lud, Sir Peter, would you have me be out of the fashion?

SIR PETER. The fashion, indeed! What had you to do with the fashion before you married me?

LADY TEAZLE. For my part, I should think you would like to have your wife thought a woman of taste.

SIR PETER. Ay! There again! Taste! Zounds, madam, you had no taste when you married me!

---

9 An old-fashioned card game.
10 Her *vis-à-vis*, an elegant coach, was drawn by ponies ("cats").

LADY TEAZLE. That's very true, indeed, Sir Peter; and, after having married you, I am sure I should never pretend to taste again. But now, Sir Peter, if we have finished our daily jangle, I presume I may go to my engagement at Lady Sneerwell's?

SIR PETER. Ay, there's another precious circumstance! A charming set of acquaintance you have made there!

LADY TEAZLE. Nay, Sir Peter, they are people of rank and fortune and remarkably tenacious of reputation.

SIR PETER. Yes, egad, they are tenacious of reputation with a vengeance, for they don't choose anybody should have a character but themselves! Such a crew! Ah, many a wretch has rid on a hurdle[11] who has done less mischief than those utterers of forged tales, coiners of scandal, and clippers of reputation.

LADY TEAZLE. What, would you restrain the freedom of speech!

SIR PETER. Ah! they have made you just as bad as any one of the society.

LADY TEAZLE. Why, I believe I do bear a part with a tolerable grace. But I vow I have no malice against the people I abuse. When I say an ill-natured thing, 'tis out of pure good humor; and I take it for granted they deal exactly in the same manner with me. But, Sir Peter, you know you promised to come to Lady Sneerwell's too.

SIR PETER. Well, well, I'll call in just to look after my own character.

LADY TEAZLE. Then, indeed, you must make haste after me, or you'll be too late. So good by to ye! (Exit.)

SIR PETER. So, I have gained much by my intended expostulations! Yet with what a charming air she contradicts everything I say, and how pleasingly she shows her contempt for my authority! Well, though I can't make her love me, there is a great satisfaction in quarreling with her; and I think she never appears to such advantage as when she is doing everything in her power to plague me. (Exit.)

---

[11] Rough cart on which criminals, including counterfeiters, were taken to execution.

[SCENE II.] *At* LADY SNEERWELL'S

(*Enter* LADY SNEERWELL, MRS. CANDOUR, CRABTREE, SIR BENJAMIN BACKBITE, *and* JOSEPH SURFACE.)

LADY SNEERWELL. Nay, positively, we will hear it.

JOSEPH SURFACE. Yes, yes, the epigram, by all means.

SIR BENJAMIN. Plague on it, uncle! 'Tis mere nonsense.

CRABTREE. No, no! 'Fore gad, very clever for an extempore!

SIR BENJAMIN. But, ladies, you should be acquainted with the circumstance. You must know that one day last week as Lady Betty Curricle was taking the dust in Hyde Park in a sort of duodecimo phaëton,[12] she desired me to write some verses on her ponies; upon which I took out my pocketbook and in one moment produced the following:

Sure never were seen two such beautiful ponies;
Other horses are clowns, but these macaronies.[13]
To give them this title I'm sure can't be wrong,
Their legs are so slim, and their tails are so long.

CRABTREE. There, ladies, done in the smack of a whip and on horseback too!

JOSEPH SURFACE. A very Phœbus mounted! Indeed, Sir Benjamin!

SIR BENJAMIN. Oh, dear sir! Trifles, trifles.

(*Enter* LADY TEAZLE *and* MARIA.)

MRS. CANDOUR. I must have a copy.

LADY SNEERWELL. Lady Teazle, I hope we shall see Sir Peter?

LADY TEAZLE. I believe he'll wait on your ladyship presently.

LADY SNEERWELL. Maria, my love, you look grave. Come, you shall sit down to cards with Mr. Surface.

MARIA. I take very little pleasure in cards; however I'll do as your ladyship pleases.

---

[12] Curricles and phaëtons were both fashionable light carriages. Duodecimo, a small book, indicates small size.
[13] Macaroni was the contemporary word for a fop, whose legs would presumably lack muscle and whose wig would be adorned with a long tail of hair.

LADY TEAZLE (*aside*). I am surprised Mr. Surface should sit down with her; I thought he would have embraced this opportunity of speaking to me before Sir Peter came.

MRS. CANDOUR. Now, I'll die; but you are so scandalous I'll forswear your society.

LADY TEAZLE. What's the matter, Mrs. Candour?

MRS. CANDOUR. They'll not allow our friend Miss Vermilion to be handsome.

LADY SNEERWELL. Oh, surely she is a pretty woman.

CRABTREE. I am very glad you think so, ma'am.

MRS. CANDOUR. She has a charming, fresh color.

LADY TEAZLE. Yes, when it is fresh put on.

MRS. CANDOUR. Oh, fie! I'll swear her color is natural. I have seen it come and go.

LADY TEAZLE. I dare swear you have, ma'am; it goes of a night and comes again in the morning.

SIR BENJAMIN. True, ma'am, it not only comes and goes; but what's more, egad, her maid can fetch and carry it!

MRS. CANDOUR. Ha, ha, ha! How I hate to hear you talk so! But surely, now, her sister is, or was, very handsome.

CRABTREE. Who? Mrs. Evergreen? Oh, Lord! She's six-and-fifty if she's an hour!

MRS. CANDOUR. Now positively you wrong her; fifty-two or fifty-three in the utmost,—and I don't think she looks more.

SIR BENJAMIN. Ah! There's no judging by her looks unless one could see her face.

LADY SNEERWELL. Well, well, if Mrs. Evergreen does take some pains to repair the ravages of time, you must allow she effects it with great ingenuity; and surely that's better than the careless manner in which the widow Ochre chalks her wrinkles.

SIR BENJAMIN. Nay, now, Lady Sneerwell, you are severe upon the widow. Come, come, 'tis not that she paints so ill; but, when she has finished her face, she joins it on so badly to her neck that she looks like a mended statue in which the connoisseur may see at once that the head's modern though the trunk's antique.

CRABTREE. Ha! ha! ha! Well said, nephew!

MRS. CANDOUR. Ha! ha! ha! Well, you make me laugh; but I vow I hate you for it. What do you think of Miss Simper?

SIR BENJAMIN. Why, she has very pretty teeth.

LADY TEAZLE. Yes; and on that account, when she is neither speaking nor laughing, which very seldom happens, she never absolutely shuts her mouth, but leaves it always on a-jar, as it were.

MRS. CANDOUR. How can you be so ill natured?

LADY TEAZLE. Nay, I allow even that's better than the pains Mrs. Prim takes to conceal her losses in front. She draws her mouth till it positively resembles the aperture of a poor's box,[14] and all her words appear to slide out edgewise.

LADY SNEERWELL. Very well, Lady Teazle. I see you can be a little severe.

LADY TEAZLE. In defence of a friend it is but justice. But here comes Sir Peter to spoil our pleasantry.

(*Enter* SIR PETER.)

SIR PETER. Ladies, your most obedient.—(*aside*) Mercy on me, here is the whole set! A character dead at every word, I suppose.

MRS. CANDOUR. I am rejoiced you are come, Sir Peter. They have been so censorious, and Lady Teazle as bad as any one.

SIR PETER. That must be very distressing to you, Mrs. Candour, I dare swear.

MRS. CANDOUR. Oh, they will allow good qualities to nobody, not even good nature to our friend Mrs. Pursy.

LADY TEAZLE. What, the fat dowager who was at Mrs. Quadrille's last night?

MRS. CANDOUR. Nay, her bulk is her misfortune; and, when she takes so much pains to get rid of it, you ought not to reflect on her.

LADY SNEERWELL. That's very true, indeed.

LADY TEAZLE. Yes, I know she almost lives on acids and small whey; laces herself by pulleys; and often in the hottest noon of summer you may see her on a little squat pony, with her hair plaited up behind like a drummer's and puffing round the Ring[15] on a full trot.

MRS. CANDOUR. I thank you, Lady Teazle, for defending her.

---

[14] The poor box in a church had a narrow slit in the top for contributions.

[15] The fashionable circular drive in Hyde Park.

SIR PETER. Yes, a good defence, truly.

MRS. CANDOUR. But Sir Benjamin is as censorious as Miss Sallow.

CRABTREE. Yes, and she is a curious being to pretend to be censorious, an awkward gawky without any one good point under heaven.

MRS. CANDOUR. Positively you shall not be so very severe. Miss Sallow is a relation of mine by marriage, and, as for her person, great allowance is to be made; for, let me tell you, a woman labors under many disadvantages who tries to pass for a girl at six-and-thirty.

LADY SNEERWELL. Though, surely, she is handsome still; and for the weakness in her eyes, considering how much she reads by candlelight, it is not to be wondered at.

MRS. CANDOUR. True, and then as to her manner; upon my word, I think it is particularly graceful, considering she never had the least education; for you know her mother was a Welsh milliner and her father a sugar-baker at Bristol.

SIR BENJAMIN. Ah! you are both of you too good natured!

SIR PETER (*aside*). Yes, damned good natured! This their own relation! Mercy on me!

MRS. CANDOUR. For my part, I own I cannot bear to hear a friend ill spoken of.

SIR PETER. No, to be sure!

SIR BENJAMIN. Oh, you are of a moral turn, Mrs. Candour, and can sit for an hour and hear Lady Stucco talk sentiment.

LADY TEAZLE. Nay, I vow Lady Stucco is very well with the dessert after dinner, for she's just like the French fruit one cracks for mottoes, made up of paint and proverb.

MRS. CANDOUR. Well, I never will join in ridiculing a friend; and so I constantly tell my cousin Ogle, and you all know what pretensions she has to be critical on beauty.

CRABTREE. Oh, to be sure, she has herself the oddest countenance that ever was seen; 'tis a collection of features from all the different countries of the globe.

SIR BENJAMIN. So she has, indeed! An Irish front—

CRABTREE. Caledonian locks—

SIR BENJAMIN. Dutch nose—

CRABTREE. Austrian lips—

SIR BENJAMIN. Complexion of a Spaniard—

CRABTREE. And teeth *à la Chinoise*—

SIR BENJAMIN. In short, her face resembles a *table d'hôte* at Spa—where no two guests are of a nation—

CRABTREE. Or a congress at the close of a general war—wherein all the members, even to her eyes, appear to have a different interest, and her nose and chin are the only parties likely to join issue.

MRS. CANDOUR. Ha! ha! ha!

SIR PETER (*aside*). Mercy on my life! A person they dine with twice a week!

LADY SNEERWELL. Go, go! You are a couple of provoking toads.

MRS. CANDOUR. Nay, but I vow you shall not carry the laugh off so, for give me leave to say that Mrs. Ogle—

SIR PETER. Madam, madam, I beg your pardon. There's no stopping these good gentlemen's tongues. But when I tell you, Mrs. Candour, that the lady they are abusing is a particular friend of mine, I hope you'll not take her part.

LADY SNEERWELL. Ha! ha! ha! Well said, Sir Peter! But you are a cruel creature—too phlegmatic yourself for a jest, and too peevish to allow wit in others.

SIR PETER. Ah, madam, true wit is more nearly allied to good nature than your ladyship is aware of.

LADY TEAZLE. True, Sir Peter. I believe they are so near akin that they can never be united.

SIR BENJAMIN. Or rather, madam, suppose them to be man and wife because one seldom sees them together.

LADY TEAZLE. But Sir Peter is such an enemy to scandal I believe he would have it put down by parliament.

SIR PETER. 'Fore heaven, madam, if they were to consider the sporting with reputation of as much importance as poaching on manors and pass an act for the preservation of fame, I believe many would thank them for the bill.

LADY SNEERWELL. Oh, lud, Sir Peter, would you deprive us of our privileges?

SIR PETER. Ay, madam; and then no person should be permitted to kill characters and run down reputations but qualified old maids and disappointed widows.

LADY SNEERWELL. Go, you monster!

MRS. CANDOUR. But, surely, you would not be quite so severe on those who only report what they hear!

SIR PETER. Yes, madam, I would have law merchant for
them, too; and in all cases of slander currency, whenever the drawer of the lie was not to be found, the
injured parties should have a right to come on any of
the indorsers.[16]

CRABTREE. Well, for my part, I believe there never was a
scandalous tale without some foundation.

LADY SNEERWELL. Come, ladies, shall we sit down to cards
in the next room?

(*Enter* SERVANT, *who whispers to* SIR PETER.)

SIR PETER (*To* SERVANT). I'll be with them directly.

(*Exit* SERVANT.)

(*Aside.*) I'll get away unperceived.

LADY SNEERWELL. Sir Peter, you are not leaving us?

SIR PETER. Your ladyship must excuse me; I'm called away
by particular business. But I leave my character
behind me. (*Exit.*)

SIR BENJAMIN. Well—certainly, Lady Teazle, that lord of
yours is a strange being. I could tell you some stories
of him would make you laugh heartily if he were not
your husband.

LADY TEAZLE. Oh, pray don't mind that; come, do let's hear
them.

(*They join the rest of the company, all talking as they
are going into the next room.*)

JOSEPH SURFACE (*rising with* MARIA). Maria, I see you
have no satisfaction in this society.

MARIA. How is it possible I should? If to raise malicious
smiles at the infirmities or misfortunes of those who
have never injured us be the province of wit or humor,
Heaven grant me a double portion of dulness!

JOSEPH SURFACE. Yet they appear more ill-natured than
they are; they have no malice at heart.

---

[16] Drawing his metaphor from commercial law ("law merchant"),
Sir Peter says that those who circulate scandalous tales should be
held responsible like those who endorse bad checks or bank notes,
if the original offender cannot be found.

MARIA. Then is their conduct still more contemptible; for, in my opinion, nothing could excuse the intemperance of their tongues but a natural and uncontrollable bitterness of mind.

JOSEPH SURFACE. But can you, Maria, feel thus for others and be unkind to me alone? Is hope to be denied the tenderest passion?

MARIA. Why will you distress me by renewing this subject?

JOSEPH SURFACE. Ah, Maria, you would not treat me thus and oppose your guardian, Sir Peter's will, but that I see that profligate Charles is still a favored rival.

MARIA. Ungenerously urged! But whatever my sentiments are for that unfortunate young man, be assured I shall not feel more bound to give him up because his distresses have lost him the regard even of a brother.

JOSEPH SURFACE. Nay, but Maria, do not leave me with a frown. (*Kneels.*) By all that's honest I swear—

(*Enter* LADY TEAZLE.)

(*Aside*) Gad's life, here's Lady Teazle!—You must not—no, you shall not—for though I have the greatest regard for Lady Teazle—

MARIA. Lady Teazle!

JOSEPH SURFACE. Yet were Sir Peter to suspect—

(LADY TEAZLE *comes forward.*)

LADY TEAZLE [*aside*]. What is this, pray? Does he take her for me?—Child, you are wanted in the next room.

(*Exit* MARIA.)

What is all this, pray?

JOSEPH SURFACE. Oh, the most unlucky circumstance in nature! Maria has somehow suspected the tender concern I have for your happiness and threatened to acquaint Sir Peter with her suspicions, and I was just endeavoring to reason with her when you came in.

LADY TEAZLE. Indeed! but you seemed to adopt a very tender mode of reasoning. Do you usually argue on your knees?

JOSEPH SURFACE. Oh, she's a child and I thought a little bombast—But, Lady Teazle, when are you to give me your judgment on my library, as you promised?

LADY TEAZLE. No, no; I begin to think it would be imprudent, and you know I admit you as a lover no
farther than fashion requires.

JOSEPH SURFACE. True—a mere Platonic *cicisbeo*[17]—what
every London wife is entitled to.

LADY TEAZLE. Certainly, one must not be out of the fashion.
However, I have so many of my country prejudices
left that, though Sir Peter's ill humor may vex me ever
so, it shall never provoke me to—

JOSEPH SURFACE. The only revenge in your power. Well, I
applaud your moderation.

LADY TEAZLE. Go! You are an insinuating wretch! But we
shall be missed. Let us join the company.

JOSEPH SURFACE. But we had best not return together.

LADY TEAZLE. Well, don't stay, for Maria shan't come to
hear any more of your reasoning, I promise you.
(*Exit*).

JOSEPH SURFACE. A curious dilemma, truly, my politics
have run me into! I wanted at first only to ingratiate
myself with Lady Teazle that she might not be my
enemy with Maria; and I have, I don't know how,
become her serious lover. Sincerely I begin to wish I
had never made such a point of gaining so very good
a character, for it has led me into so many cursed
rogueries that I doubt I shall be exposed at last.
(*Exit*.)

[SCENE III.] SIR PETER TEAZLE's *house*

(*Enter* ROWLEY *and* SIR OLIVER SURFACE.)

SIR OLIVER. Ha! ha! ha! and so my old friend is married,
hey? A young wife out of the country! Ha! ha! ha!
that he should have stood bluff[18] to old bachelor so
long and sink into a husband at last!

ROWLEY. But you must not rally him on the subject, Sir
Oliver; 'tis a tender point, I assure you, though he has
been married only seven months.

SIR OLIVER. Then he has been just half a year on the stool
of repentance! Poor Peter! But you say he has entirely given up Charles—never sees him, hey?

---

17 The recognized lover of a married woman.
18 Steadfast.

ROWLEY. His prejudice against him is astonishing, and I am sure greatly increased by a jealousy of him with Lady Teazle, which he has industriously been led into by a scandalous society in the neighborhood who have contributed not a little to Charles's ill name. Whereas the truth is, I believe, if the lady is partial to either of them, his brother is the favorite.

SIR OLIVER. Ay, I know there are a set of malicious, prating, prudent gossips, both male and female, who murder characters to kill time and will rob a young fellow of his good name before he has years to know the value of it. But I am not to be prejudiced against my nephew by such, I promise you. No, no; if Charles has done nothing false or mean, I shall compound for his extravagance.

ROWLEY. Then, my life on 't, you will reclaim him. Ah, sir, it gives me new life to find that your heart is not turned against him and that the son of my good old master has one friend, however, left.

SIR OLIVER. What! Shall I forget, Master Rowley, when I was at his years myself? Egad, my brother and I were neither of us very prudent youths; and yet I believe you have not seen many better men than your old master was?

ROWLEY. Sir, 'tis this reflection gives me assurance that Charles may yet be a credit to his family. But here comes Sir Peter.

SIR OLIVER. Egad, so he does. Mercy on me, he's greatly altered and seems to have a settled, married look! One may read *husband* in his face at this distance.

(*Enter* SIR PETER.)

SIR PETER. Ha! Sir Oliver, my old friend! Welcome to England a thousand times!

SIR OLIVER. Thank you, thank you, Sir Peter! And i' faith I am glad to find you well, believe me!

SIR PETER. Oh, 'tis a long time since we met—sixteen years, I doubt, Sir Oliver, and many a cross accident in the time.

SIR OLIVER. Ay, I have had my share. But, what! I find you are married, hey, my old boy? Well, well, it can't be helped; and so—I wish you joy with all my heart!

SIR PETER. Thank you, thank you, Sir Oliver. Yes, I have

entered into—the happy state; but we'll not talk of that now.

SIR OLIVER. True, true, Sir Peter. Old friends should not begin on grievances at first meeting. No, no, no.

ROWLEY [*aside to* SIR OLIVER]. Take care, pray, sir.

SIR OLIVER. Well, so one of my nephews is a wild rogue, hey?

SIR PETER. Wild! Ah, my old friend, I grieve for your disappointment there. He's a lost young man, indeed. However, his brother will make you amends; Joseph is, indeed, what a youth should be—everybody in the world speaks well of him.

SIR OLIVER. I am sorry to hear it; he has too good a character to be an honest fellow. "Everybody speaks well of him!" Psha! then he has bowed as low to knaves and fools as to the honest dignity of genius or virtue.

SIR PETER. What, Sir Oliver! Do you blame him for not making enemies?

SIR OLIVER. Yes, if he has merit enough to deserve them.

SIR PETER. Well, well, you'll be convinced when you know him. 'Tis edification to hear him converse; he professes the noblest sentiments.

SIR OLIVER. Oh, plague of his sentiments! If he salutes me with a scrap of morality in his mouth, I shall be sick directly. But, however, don't mistake me, Sir Peter; I don't mean to defend Charles's errors; but before I form my judgment of either of them, I intend to make a trial of their hearts; and my old friend Rowley and I have planned something for the purpose.

ROWLEY. And Sir Peter shall own for once he has been mistaken.

SIR PETER. Oh, my life on Joseph's honor!

SIR OLIVER. Well, come, give us a bottle of good wine, and we'll drink the lads' health and tell you our scheme.

SIR PETER. *Allons*, then!

SIR OLIVER. And don't, Sir Peter, be so severe against your old friend's son. Odds, my life! I am not sorry that he has run out of the course a little. For my part, I hate to see prudence clinging to the green suckers of youth; 'tis like ivy round a sapling and spoils the growth of the tree.

(*Exeunt.*)

ACT III

[SCENE I.] SIR PETER TEAZLE'S *house*

(*Enter* SIR PETER TEAZLE, SIR OLIVER SURFACE, *and* ROWLEY.)

SIR PETER. Well, then, we will see this fellow first and have our wine afterwards. But how is this, Master Rowley? I don't see the jet[19] of your scheme.

ROWLEY. Why, sir, this Mr. Stanley, whom I was speaking of, is nearly related to them by their mother. He was once a merchant in Dublin but has been ruined by a series of undeserved misfortunes. He has applied by letter, since his confinement,[20] to both Mr. Surface and Charles. From the former he has received nothing but evasive promises of future service, while Charles has done all that his extravagance has left him power to do; and he is at this time endeavoring to raise a sum of money, part of which, in the midst of his own distresses, I know he intends for the service of poor Stanley.

SIR OLIVER. Ah! he is my brother's son.

SIR PETER. Well, but how is Sir Oliver personally to—

ROWLEY. Why, sir, I will inform Charles and his brother that Stanley has obtained permission to apply personally to his friends; and, as they have neither of them ever seen him, let Sir Oliver assume his character and he will have a fair opportunity of judging at least of the benevolence of their dispositions. And, believe me, sir, you will find in the youngest brother one who, in the midst of folly and dissipation, has still, as our immortal bard expresses it,

> a tear for pity and a hand,
> Open as day for melting charity.[21]

SIR PETER. Psha! What signifies his having an open hand or purse either when he has nothing left to give?

---

19 Point.
20 In debtors' prison.
21 *II Henry IV*, IV, iv, 31–32.

Well, well, make the trial, if you please. But where is the fellow whom you brought for Sir Oliver to examine relative to Charles's affairs?

ROWLEY. Below, waiting his commands, and no one can give him better intelligence. This, Sir Oliver, is a friendly Jew, who, to do him justice, has done everything in his power to bring your nephew to a proper sense of his extravagance.

SIR PETER. Pray, let us have him in.

ROWLEY (calls to SERVANT). Desire Mr. Moses to walk upstairs.

SIR PETER. But why should you suppose he will speak the truth?

ROWLEY. Oh, I have convinced him that he has no chance of recovering certain sums advanced to Charles but through the bounty of Sir Oliver, who, he knows, has arrived, so that you may depend on his fidelity to his own interests. I have also another evidence in my power, one Snake, whom I have detected in a matter little short of forgery and shall speedily produce him to remove some of your prejudices, Sir Peter, relative to Charles and Lady Teazle.

SIR PETER. I have heard too much on that subject.

ROWLEY. Here comes the honest Israelite.

(Enter MOSES.)

—This is Sir Oliver.

SIR OLIVER. Sir, I understand you have lately had great dealings with my nephew Charles.

MOSES. Yes, Sir Oliver, I have done all I could for him; but he was ruined before he came to me for assistance.

SIR OLIVER. That was unlucky, truly, for you have had no opportunity of showing your talents.

MOSES. None at all. I hadn't the pleasure of knowing his distresses till he was some thousands worse than nothing.

SIR OLIVER. Unfortunate, indeed! But I suppose you have done all in your power for him, honest Moses?

MOSES. Yes, he knows that. This very evening I was to have brought him a gentleman from the city, who does not know him and will, I believe, advance him some money.

SIR PETER. What, one Charles has never had money from before!

MOSES. Yes. Mr. Premium, of Crutched Friars, formerly a broker.

SIR PETER. Egad, Sir Oliver, a thought strikes me!—Charles, you say, does not know Mr. Premium?

MOSES. Not at all.

SIR PETER. Now then, Sir Oliver, you may have a better opportunity of satisfying yourself than by an old, romancing tale of a poor relation. Go with my friend Moses and represent Mr. Premium, and then, I'll answer for it, you'll see your nephew in all his glory.

SIR OLIVER. Egad, I like this idea better than the other, and I may visit Joseph afterwards as old Stanley.

SIR PETER. True—so you may.

ROWLEY. Well, this is taking Charles rather at a disadvantage, to be sure. However, Moses, you understand Sir Peter and will be faithful?

MOSES. You may depend upon me. This is near the time I was to have gone.

SIR OLIVER. I'll accompany you as soon as you please, Moses. But hold! I have forgot one thing—how the plague shall I be able to pass for a Jew?

MOSES. There's no need. The principal is Christian.

SIR OLIVER. Is he? I'm sorry to hear it; but then, again, an't I rather too smartly dressed to look like a money-lender?

SIR PETER. Not at all; 'twould not be out of character, if you went in your own carriage, would it, Moses?

MOSES. Not in the least.

SIR OLIVER. Well, but how must I talk? There's certainly some cant of usury and mode of treating that I ought to know.

SIR PETER. Oh, there's not much to learn. The great point, as I take it, is to be exorbitant enough in your demands. Hey, Moses?

MOSES. Yes, that's a very great point.

SIR OLIVER. I'll answer for 't I'll not be wanting in that. I'll ask him eight or ten per cent. on the loan at least.

MOSES. If you ask him no more than that, you'll be discovered immediately.

SIR OLIVER. Hey! what the plague! how much then?

MOSES. That depends upon the circumstances. If he appears not very anxious for the supply, you should require only forty or fifty per cent.; but if you find him in great distress and want the moneys very bad, you may ask double.

SIR PETER. A good honest trade you're learning, Sir Oliver!

SIR OLIVER. Truly, I think so—and not unprofitable.

MOSES. Then you know, you haven't the moneys yourself but are forced to borrow them for him of an old friend.

SIR OLIVER. Oh! I borrow it of a friend, do I?

MOSES. Yes, and your friend is an unconscionable dog; but you can't help that.

SIR OLIVER. My friend is an unconscionable dog, is he?

MOSES. Yes, and he himself has not the moneys by him but is forced to sell stock at a great loss.

SIR OLIVER. He is forced to sell stock at a great loss, is he? Well, that's very kind of him.

SIR PETER. I'faith, Sir Oliver—Mr. Premium, I mean— you'll soon be master of the trade. But, Moses, wouldn't you have him run out a little against the annuity bill?[22] That would be in character, I should think.

MOSES. Very much.

ROWLEY. And lament that a young man now must be at years of discretion before he is suffered to ruin himself?

MOSES. Ay, great pity!

SIR PETER. And abuse the public for allowing merit to an act whose only object is to snatch misfortune and imprudence from the rapacious gripe of usury and give the minor a chance of inheriting his estate without being undone by coming into possession.

SIR OLIVER. So, so—Moses shall give me further particulars as we go together.

SIR PETER. You will not have much time, for your nephew lives hard by.

SIR OLIVER. Oh, never fear! My tutor appears so able that though Charles lived in the next street, it must be my

---

[22] The main purpose of the Annuity Bill, then before Parliament and passed shortly after the opening of *The School for Scandal*, was to protect minors by preventing them from borrowing from unscrupulous moneylenders on annuity.

own fault if I am not a complete rogue before I turn the corner. (*Exit with* MOSES.)

SIR PETER. So, now, I think Sir Oliver will be convinced. You are partial, Rowley, and would have prepared Charles for the other plot.

ROWLEY. No, upon my word, Sir Peter.

SIR PETER. Well, go bring me this Snake, and I'll hear what he has to say presently. I see Maria and want to speak with her.

(*Exit* ROWLEY.)

I should be glad to be convinced my suspicions of Lady Teazle and Charles were unjust. I have never yet opened my mind on this subject to my friend Joseph. I am determined I will do it; he will give me his opinion sincerely.

(*Enter* MARIA.)

So, child, has Mr. Surface returned with you?

MARIA. No, sir. He was engaged.

SIR PETER. Well, Maria, do you not reflect, the more you converse with that amiable young man, what return his partiality for you deserves?

MARIA. Indeed, Sir Peter, your frequent importunity on this subject distresses me extremely. You compel me to declare that I know no man who has ever paid me a particular attention whom I would not prefer to Mr. Surface.

SIR PETER. So—here's perverseness! No, no, Maria, 'tis Charles only whom you would prefer. 'Tis evident his vices and follies have won your heart.

MARIA. This is unkind, sir. You know I have obeyed you in neither seeing nor corresponding with him. I have heard enough to convince me that he is unworthy my regard. Yet I cannot think it culpable, if, while my understanding severely condemns his vices, my heart suggests some pity for his distresses.

SIR PETER. Well, well, pity him as much as you please, but give your heart and hand to a worthier object.

MARIA. Never to his brother!

SIR PETER. Go, perverse and obstinate! But take care, madam; you have never yet known what the authority of a guardian is. Don't compel me to inform you of it.

MARIA. I can only say, you shall not have just reason. 'Tis
true, by my father's will I am for a short period
bound to regard you as his substitute, but must cease
to think you so when you would compel me to be
miserable. (*Exit.*)

SIR PETER. Was ever man so crossed as I am, everything
conspiring to fret me! I had not been involved in
matrimony a fortnight before her father, a hale and
hearty man, died—on purpose, I believe, for the
pleasure of plaguing me with the care of his daughter.
But here comes my helpmate! She appears in great
good humor. How happy I should be if I could tease
her into loving me, though but a little!

(*Enter* LADY TEAZLE.)

LADY TEAZLE. Lud, Sir Peter, I hope you haven't been
quarreling with Maria? It isn't using me well to be
ill-humored when I am not by.

SIR PETER. Ah, Lady Teazle, you might have the power to
make me good humored at all times.

LADY TEAZLE. I am sure I wish I had, for I want you to
be in a charming, sweet temper at this moment. Do
be good humored now and let me have two hundred
pounds, will you?

SIR PETER. Two hundred pounds! What, ain't I to be in a
good humor without paying for it? But speak to me
thus and, i' faith, there's nothing I could refuse you.
You shall have it, but seal me a bond for the re-
payment.

LADY TEAZLE. Oh, no! There—my note of hand will do as
well. (*offering her hand*)

SIR PETER (*kissing her hand*). And you shall no longer reproach me with not giving you an independent settlement.[23] I mean shortly to surprise you. But shall we
always live thus, hey?

LADY TEAZLE. If you please. I'm sure I don't care how soon
we leave off quarreling, provided you'll own you were
tired first.

SIR PETER. Well, then let our future contest be who shall
be most obliging.

---

[23] Legally settling an allowance on her, so she would not have to
keep asking him for money.

LADY TEAZLE. I assure you, Sir Peter, good nature becomes you. You look now as you did before we were married, when you used to walk with me under the elms and tell me stories of what a gallant you were in your youth and chuck me under the chin, you would, and ask me if I thought I could love an old fellow who would deny me nothing—didn't you?

SIR PETER. Yes, yes, and you were as kind and attentive—

LADY TEAZLE. Ay, so I was, and would always take your part when my acquaintance used to abuse you and turn you into ridicule.

SIR PETER. Indeed!

LADY TEAZLE. Ay, and when my cousin Sophy has called you a stiff, peevish old bachelor and laughed at me for thinking of marrying one who might be my father, I have always defended you and said I didn't think you so ugly by any means; and that I dared say you'd make a very good sort of husband.

SIR PETER. And you prophesied right; and we shall certainly now be the happiest couple—

LADY TEAZLE. And never differ again?

SIR PETER. No, never. Though at the same time, indeed, my dear Lady Teazle, you must watch your temper very narrowly, for in all our quarrels, my dear, if you recollect, my love, you always began first.

LADY TEAZLE. I beg your pardon, my dear Sir Peter. Indeed you always gave the provocation.

SIR PETER. Now see, my angel! Take care! Contradicting isn't the way to keep friends.

LADY TEAZLE. Then don't you begin it, my love.

SIR PETER. There, now, you—you—are going on. You don't perceive, my life, that you are just doing the very thing which you know always makes me angry.

LADY TEAZLE. Nay, you know if you will be angry without any reason, my dear—

SIR PETER. There, now you want to quarrel again.

LADY TEAZLE. No, I'm sure I don't; but if you will be so peevish—

SIR PETER. There now! Who begins first?

LADY TEAZLE. Why, you to be sure. I said nothing; but there's no bearing your temper.

SIR PETER. No, no, madam! The fault's in your own temper.

LADY TEAZLE. Ay, you are just what my cousin Sophy said you would be.

SIR PETER. Your cousin Sophy is a forward, impertinent gipsy.

LADY TEAZLE. You are a great bear, I'm sure, to abuse my relations.

SIR PETER. Now may all the plagues of marriage be doubled on me if ever I try to be friends with you any more!

LADY TEAZLE. So much the better.

SIR PETER. No, no, madam. 'Tis evident you never cared a pin for me, and I was a madman to marry you—a pert, rural coquette that had refused half the honest squires in the neighborhood.

LADY TEAZLE. And I am sure I was a fool to marry you— an old dangling bachelor, who was single at fifty only because he never could meet with anyone who would have him.

SIR PETER. Ay, ay, madam; but you were pleased enough to listen to me. You never had such an offer before.

LADY TEAZLE. No? Didn't I refuse Sir Tivy Terrier, who everybody said would have been a better match, for his estate is just as good as yours, and he has broke his neck since we have been married?

SIR PETER. I have done with you, madam! You are an unfeeling, ungrateful—but there's an end of everything. I believe you capable of anything that is bad. Yes, madam, I now believe the reports relative to you and Charles, madam. Yes, madam, you and Charles are— not without grounds—

LADY TEAZLE. Take care, Sir Peter! You had better not insinuate any such thing! I'll not be suspected without cause, I promise you.

SIR PETER. Very well, madam, very well! A separate maintenance as soon as you please. Yes, madam, or a divorce![24] I'll make an example of myself for the benefit of all old bachelors. Let us separate, madam.

LADY TEAZLE. Agreed, agreed! And now, my dear Sir Peter, we are of a mind once more, we may be the happiest couple and never differ again, you know.

---

[24] A separate maintenance was an allowance for support to a wife not living under her husband's roof; a divorce was a former legal separation.

Ha, ha, ha! Well, you are going to be in a passion, I see, and I shall only interrupt you; so bye, bye! (*Exit.*)

SIR PETER. Plagues and tortures! Can't I make her angry neither? Oh, I am the most miserable fellow! But I'll not bear her presuming to keep her temper. No! She may break my heart, but she shan't keep her temper. (*Exit.*)

[SCENE II.] CHARLES SURFACE's *House*

(*Enter* TRIP, MOSES, *and* SIR OLIVER SURFACE.)

TRIP. Here, Master Moses! If you'll stay a moment, I'll try whether—what's the gentleman's name?

SIR OLIVER (*aside*). Mr. Moses, what is my name?

MOSES. Mr. Premium.

TRIP. Premium. Very well. (*Exit, taking snuff.*)

SIR OLIVER. To judge by the servants, one wouldn't believe the master was ruined. But what! Sure, this was my brother's house?

MOSES. Yes, sir; Mr. Charles bought it of Mr. Joseph, with the furniture, pictures, &c., just as the old gentleman left it. Sir Peter thought it a great piece of extravagance in him.

SIR OLIVER. In my mind, the other's economy in selling it to him was more reprehensible by half.

(*Enter* TRIP.)

TRIP. My master says you must wait, gentlemen. He has company and can't speak with you yet.

SIR OLIVER. If he knew who it was wanted to see him, perhaps he wouldn't have sent such a message?

TRIP. Yes, yes, sir; he knows you are here. I didn't forget little Premium. No, no, no.

SIR OLIVER. Very well; and I pray, sir, what may be your name?

TRIP. Trip, sir; my name is Trip, at your service.

SIR OLIVER. Well, then, Mr. Trip, you have a pleasant sort of place here, I guess.

TRIP. Why, yes. Here are three or four of us pass our time agreeably enough; but then our wages are sometimes a little in arrear, and not very great either, but fifty pounds a year and find our own bags and bouquets.[25]

---

[25] Bag wigs (with the back hair tied up in a bag) and shoulder bouquets were worn by fashionable footmen.

SIR OLIVER (*aside*). Bags and bouquets! Halters and bastinadoes!

TRIP. But *à propos*, Moses, have you been able to get me that little bill discounted?

SIR OLIVER (*aside*). Wants to raise money too! Mercy on me! has his distresses, I warrant, like a lord and affects creditors and duns.

MOSES. 'Twas not to be done, indeed, Mr. Trip.

TRIP. Good lack, you surprise me! My friend Brush has indorsed it, and I thought when he put his name at the back of a bill 'twas the same as cash.

MOSES. No, 'twouldn't do.

TRIP. A small sum—but twenty pounds. Harkee, Moses, do you think you couldn't get it me by way of annuity?

SIR OLIVER (*aside*). An annuity! Ha, ha! A footman raise money by way of annuity! Well done, luxury, egad!

MOSES. But you must insure your place.

TRIP. Oh, with all my heart! I'll insure my place and my life too, if you please.

SIR OLIVER (*aside*). It's more than I would your neck.

MOSES. But is there nothing you could deposit?

TRIP. Why, nothing capital of my master's wardrobe has dropped lately; but I could give you a mortgage on some of his winter clothes with equity of redemption before November; or you shall have the reversion of the French velvet or a post-obit on the blue and silver.[26] These I should think, Moses, with a few pairs of point ruffles as collateral security—hey, my little fellow?

MOSES. Well, well. (*Bell rings.*)

TRIP. Egad, I heard the bell! I believe, gentlemen, I can now introduce you. Don't forget the annuity, little

---

[26] Trip, aping the ways of a man of fashion, wants to get a bank bill discounted, i.e., cashed (less a service charge). When he finds that his friend's endorsement will not serve as guarantee for payment, he tries to borrow money on annuity. Moses will not agree unless Trip assures regular payment by taking out insurance in case he should lose his job. Trip offers as security the reversion (future possession) of his master's clothes, which will ultimately come to him. A post-obit was a bond pledging to pay a debt upon the death of a person from whom the borrower expected to inherit money. Cf. the more conventional "post-obit on Sir Oliver's life," p. 359.

MOSES. This way, gentlemen; insure my place, you know.

SIR OLIVER (*aside*). If the man be a shadow of the master, this is the temple of dissipation indeed.

(*Exeunt.*)

[SCENE III.] *Another room*

(CHARLES SURFACE, CARELESS, &c., &c., *at a table with wine, &c.*)

CHARLES. 'Fore heaven, 'tis true! There's the great degeneracy of the age. Many of our acquaintance have taste, spirit, and politeness; but, plague on't, they won't drink.

CARELESS. It is so, indeed, Charles. They give in to all the substantial luxuries of the table and abstain from nothing but wine and wit.

CHARLES. Oh, certainly society suffers by it intolerably, for now instead of the social spirit of raillery that used to mantle over a glass of bright Burgundy, their conversation is become just like the Spa-water they drink, which has all the pertness and flatulency of champagne without its spirit or flavor.

1ST GENTLEMAN. But what are they to do who love play better than wine?

CARELESS. True! There's Harry diets himself for gaming and is now under a hazard regimen.

CHARLES. Then he'll have the worst of it. What! you wouldn't train a horse for the course by keeping him from corn? For my part, egad, I am never so successful as when I am a little merry. Let me throw on a bottle of champagne and I never lose.—At least I never feel my losses, which is exactly the same thing.

2D GENTLEMAN. Ay, that I believe.

CHARLES. And then, what man can pretend to be a believer in love who is an abjurer of wine? 'Tis the test by which the lover knows his own heart. Fill a dozen bumpers to a dozen beauties, and she that floats atop is the maid that has bewitched you.

CARELESS. Now, then, Charles, be honest and give us your real favorite.

CHARLES. Why, I have withheld her only in compassion to
you. If I toast her, you must give a round of her peers,
which is impossible—on earth.

CARELESS. Oh, then, we'll find some canonized vestals or
heathen goddesses that will do, I warrant!

CHARLES. Here, then, bumpers, you rogues! Bumpers!
Maria! Maria! (*Drinks.*)

1ST GENTLEMAN. Maria who?

CHARLES. Oh, damn the surname! 'Tis too formal to be
registered in love's calendar. But now, Sir Toby
Bumper, beware! We must have beauty superlative.

CARELESS. Nay, never study, Sir Toby. We'll stand to the
toast though your mistress should want an eye; and
you know you have a song will excuse you.

SIR TOBY. Egad, so I have, and I'll give him the song
instead of the lady. (*Sings*):

> Here's to the maiden of bashful fifteen;
> Here's to the widow of fifty;
> Here's to the flaunting, extravagant quean,
> And here's to the housewife that's thrifty.
> CHORUS.   Let the toast pass,
> Drink to the lass—
> I'll warrant she'll prove an excuse for the glass!
>
> Here's to the charmer whose dimples we prize;
> Now to the maid who has none, sir!
> Here's to the girl with a pair of blue eyes,
> And here's to the nymph with but one, sir!
> CHORUS.   Let the toast pass, &c.
>
> Here's to the maid with a bosom of snow!
> Now to her that's as brown as a berry!
> Here's to the wife with a face full of woe,
> And now to the damsel that's merry!
> CHORUS.   Let the toast pass, &c.
>
> For let 'em be clumsy, or let 'em be slim,
> Young or ancient, I care not a feather:
> So fill a pint bumper quite up to the brim,
> And let us e'en toast them together!
> CHORUS.   Let the toast pass, &c.

ALL. Bravo! Bravo!

(*Enter* TRIP *and whispers* CHARLES SURFACE.)

CHARLES. Gentlemen, you must excuse me a little. Careless, take the chair, will you?

CARELESS. Nay, pr'ythee, Charles, what now? This is one of your peerless beauties, I suppose, has dropped in by chance?

CHARLES. No, faith! To tell you the truth, 'tis a Jew and a broker, who are come by appointment.

CARELESS. Oh, damn it, let's have the Jew in.

1ST GENTLEMAN. Ay, and the broker too, by all means.

2D GENTLEMAN. Yes, yes, the Jew and the broker!

CHARLES. Egad, with all my heart! Trip, bid the gentlemen walk in.—

(*Exit* TRIP.)

Though there's one of them a stranger, I can tell you.

CARELESS. Charles, let us give them some generous Burgundy, and perhaps they'll grow conscientious.

CHARLES. Oh, hang 'em, no! Wine does but draw forth a man's natural qualities; and to make them drink would only be to whet their knavery.

(*Enter* TRIP, SIR OLIVER, *and* MOSES.)

CHARLES. So, honest Moses!—Walk in, pray, Mr. Premium. —That's the gentleman's name, isn't it, Moses?

MOSES. Yes, sir.

CHARLES. Set chairs, Trip.—Sit down, Mr. Premium.— Glasses, Trip.—Sit down, Moses.—Come, Mr. Premium, I'll give you a sentiment: here's *Success to usury!*—Moses, fill the gentleman a bumper.

MOSES. Success to usury! (*Drinks.*)

CARELESS. Right, Moses! Usury is prudence and industry, and deserves to succeed.

SIR OLIVER. Then here's—all the success it deserves! (*Drinks.*)

CARELESS. No, no, that won't do! Mr. Premium, you have demurred to the toast and must drink it in a pint bumper.

1ST GENTLEMAN. A pint bumper at least!

MOSES. Oh, pray sir, consider! Mr. Premium's a gentleman.

CARELESS. And therefore loves good wine.

2ND GENTLEMAN. Give Moses a quart glass. This is mutiny and a high contempt of the chair.

CARELESS. Here, now for 't! I'll see justice done, to the last drop of my bottle.

SIR OLIVER. Nay, pray, gentlemen! I did not expect this usage.

CHARLES. No, hang it, Careless, you shan't. Mr. Premium's a stranger.

SIR OLIVER (aside). Odd! I wish I was well out of their company.

CARELESS. Plague on 'em then! If they won't drink, we'll not sit down with them. Come, Harry, the dice are in the next room.—Charles, you'll join us when you have finished your business with these gentlemen?

CHARLES. I will! I will!

(Exeunt [GENTLEMEN].)

Careless!

CARELESS (returning). Well?

CHARLES. Perhaps I may want you.

CARELESS. Oh, you know I am always ready. Word, note, or bond, 'tis all the same to me![27] (Exit.)

MOSES. Sir, this is Mr. Premium, a gentleman of the strictest honor and secrey, and always performs what he undertakes. Mr. Premium, this is—

CHARLES. Psha! Have done! Sir, my friend Moses is a very honest fellow but a little slow at expression. He'll be an hour giving us our titles. Mr. Premium, the plain state of the matter is this: I am an extravagant young fellow who wants to borrow money; you I take to be a prudent old fellow who have got money to lend. I am blockhead enough to give fifty per cent. sooner than not have it; and you, I presume, are rogue enough to take a hundred if you can get it. Now, sir, you see we are acquainted at once and may proceed to business without farther ceremony.

SIR OLIVER. Exceeding frank, upon my word. I see, sir, you are not a man of many compliments.

CHARLES. Oh, no, sir! Plain dealing in business I always think best.

[27] Careless would be happy to act as security for the loan Charles is about to negotiate.

SIR OLIVER. Sir, I like you better for it. However, you are mistaken in one thing. I have no money to lend, but I believe I could procure some of a friend; but then he's an unconscionable dog, isn't he, Moses? And must sell stock to accommodate you, mustn't he, Moses?

MOSES. Yes, indeed! You know I always speak the truth and scorn to tell a lie.

CHARLES. Right! People that speak truth generally do. But these are trifles, Mr. Premium. What, I know money isn't to be bought without paying for 't!

SIR OLIVER. Well, but what security could you give? You have no land, I suppose?

CHARLES. Not a mole-hill, nor a twig, but what's in the beau-pots[28] at the window!

SIR OLIVER. Nor any stock, I presume?

CHARLES. Nothing but live stock—and that's only a few pointers and ponies. But, pray, Mr. Premium, are you acquainted at all with any of my connections?

SIR OLIVER. Why, to say truth, I am.

CHARLES. Then you must know that I have a devilish rich uncle in the East Indies, Sir Oliver Surface, from whom I have the greatest expectations.

SIR OLIVER. That you have a wealthy uncle, I have heard; but how your expectations will turn out is more, I believe, than you can tell.

CHARLES. Oh, no! There can be no doubt! They tell me I'm a prodigious favorite and that he talks of leaving me everything.

SIR OLIVER. Indeed! This is the first I've heard of it.

CHARLES. Yes, yes, 'tis just so. Moses knows 'tis true, don't you, Moses?

MOSES. Oh, yes! I'll swear to 't.

SIR OLIVER (aside). Egad, they'll persuade me presently I'm at Bengal.

CHARLES. Now I propose, Mr. Premium, if it's agreeable to you, a post-obit on Sir Oliver's life, though at the same time the old fellow has been so liberal to me that I give you my word I should be very sorry to hear anything had happened to him.

SIR OLIVER. Not more than I should, I assure you. But the bond you mention happens to be just the worst security

---

[28] Flower pots.

you could offer me—for I might live to a hundred and never recover the principal.

CHARLES. Oh, yes, you would! The moment Sir Oliver dies, you know, you would come on me for the money.

SIR OLIVER. Then I believe I should be the most unwelcome dun you ever had in your life.

CHARLES. What! I suppose you're afraid that Sir Oliver is too good a life?

SIR OLIVER. No, indeed I am not, though I have heard he is as hale and hearty as any man of his years in Christendom.

CHARLES. There, again, now you are misinformed. No, no, the climate has hurt him considerably, poor uncle Oliver. Yes, yes, he breaks apace, I'm told, and is so much altered lately that his nearest relations don't know him.

SIR OLIVER. No! Ha, ha, ha! So much altered lately that his nearest relations don't know him! Ha, ha, ha! Egad! Ha, ha, ha!

CHARLES. Ha, ha! You're glad to hear that, little Premium?

SIR OLIVER. No, no, I'm not.

CHARLES. Yes, yes, you are! Ha, ha, ha! You know that mends your chance.

SIR OLIVER. But I'm told Sir Oliver is coming over. Nay, some say he is actually arrived.

CHARLES. Psha! sure I must know better than you whether he's come or not. No, no, rely on't, he's at this moment at Calcutta, isn't he, Moses?

MOSES. Oh, yes, certainly.

SIR OLIVER. Very true, as you say, you must know better than I, though I have it from pretty good authority— haven't I, Moses?

MOSES. Yes, most undoubted!

SIR OLIVER. But, sir, as I understand you want a few hundreds immediately, is there nothing you would dispose of?

CHARLES. How do you mean?

SIR OLIVER. For instance, now, I have heard that your father left behind him a great quantity of massy old plate.

CHARLES. Oh, Lud! that's gone long ago. Moses can tell you how better than I can.

SIR OLIVER (*aside*). Good lack, all the family race-cups and corporation bowls![29]—Then it was also supposed that his library was one of the most valuable and complete.

CHARLES. Yes, yes, so it was—vastly too much so for a private gentleman. For my part, I was always of a communicative disposition; so I thought it a shame to keep so much knowledge to myself.

SIR OLIVER (*aside*). Mercy upon me! Learning that had run in the family like an heirloom!—Pray what are become of the books?

CHARLES. You must inquire of the auctioneer, Master Premium, for I don't believe even Moses can direct you.

MOSES. I never meddle with books.

SIR OLIVER. So, so, nothing of the family property left, I suppose?

CHARLES. Not much, indeed, unless you have a mind to the family pictures. I have got a room full of ancestors above; and if you have a taste for painting, egad, you shall have 'em for a bargain.

SIR OLIVER. Hey! What the devil? Sure, you wouldn't sell your forefathers, would you?

CHARLES. Every man of them to the best bidder.

SIR OLIVER. What! Your great-uncles and aunts?

CHARLES. Ay, and my great-grandfathers and grandmothers too.

SIR OLIVER (*aside*). Now I give him up!—What the plague, have you no bowels for your own kindred? Odd's life, do you take me for Shylock in the play that you would raise money of me on your own flesh and blood?

CHARLES. Nay, my little broker, don't be angry. What need you care if you have your money's worth?

SIR OLIVER. Well, I'll be the purchaser. I think I can dispose of the family. (*aside*) Oh, I'll never forgive him this, never!

(*Enter* CARELESS.)

CARELESS. Come, Charles; what keeps you?

CHARLES. I can't come yet. I' faith, we are going to have a sale above stairs. Here's little Premium will buy all my ancestors.

[29] Trophies and testimonial bowls.

CARELESS. Oh, burn your ancestors!

CHARLES. No, he may do that afterwards, if he pleases.
Stay, Careless, we want you. Egad, you shall be
auctioneer; so come along with us.

CARELESS. Oh, have with you, if that's the case. I can
handle a hammer as well as a dice-box!

SIR OLIVER (aside). Oh, the profligates!

CHARLES. Come, Moses, you shall be appraiser if we want
one.—Gad's life, little Premium, you don't seem to
like the business.

SIR OLIVER. Oh, yes, I do, vastly! Ha, ha, ha! Yes, yes,
I think it a rare joke to sell one's family by auction.
Ha, ha! (aside) Oh, the prodigal!

CHARLES. To be sure! When a man wants money, where
the plague should he get assistance, if he can't make
free with his own relations?

(Exeunt.)

ACT IV

[SCENE I.] *Picture room at* CHARLES's

(*Enter* CHARLES SURFACE, SIR OLIVER SURFACE, MOSES,
and CARELESS.)

CHARLES. Walk in, gentlemen, pray walk in. Here they are,
the family of the Surfaces up to the Conquest.

SIR OLIVER. And, in my opinion, a goodly collection.

CHARLES. Ay, ay, these are done in the true spirit of
portrait-painting; no volunteer grace or expression.
Not like the works of your modern Raphaels,[30] who
give you the strongest resemblance, yet contrive to
make your portrait independent of you, so that you
may sink the original and not hurt the picture. No, no;
the merit of these is the inveterate likeness,—all stiff
and awkward as the originals, and like nothing in
human nature besides.

SIR OLIVER. Ah! We shall never see such figures of men
again.

---

[30] Sir Joshua Reynolds, the leading English portrait painter of the
time, was referred to as the modern Raphael.

CHARLES. I hope not! Well, you see, Master Premium, what a domestic character I am; here I sit of an evening surrounded by my family. But come, get to your pulpit, Mr. Auctioneer; here's an old, gouty chair of my grandfather's will answer the purpose.

CARELESS. Ay, ay, this will do. But, Charles, I have ne'er a hammer; and what's an auctioneer without his hammer!

CHARLES. Egad, that's true! What parchment have we here? *Richard, heir to Thomas.* Oh, our genealogy in full. Here, Careless, you shall have no common bit of mahogany; here's the family tree for you, you rogue! This shall be your hammer, and now you may knock down my ancestors with their own pedigree.

SIR OLIVER (*aside*). What an unnatural rogue! An *ex post facto* parricide!

CARELESS. Yes, yes, here's a list of your generation, indeed. Faith, Charles, this is the most convenient thing you could have found for the business, for 'twill serve not only as a hammer but a catalogue into the bargain. Come, begin! A-going, a-going, a-going!

CHARLES. Bravo, Careless! Well, here's my great-uncle, Sir Richard Raveline, a marvellous good general in his day, I assure you. He served in all the Duke of Marlborough's wars and got that cut over his eye at the battle of Malplaquet. What say you, Mr. Premium? Look at him. There's a hero for you! Not cut out of his feathers as your modern clipped captains are, but enveloped in wig and regimentals as a general should be. What do you bid?

MOSES. Mr. Premium would have you speak.

CHARLES. Why, then, he shall have him for ten pounds, and I'm sure that's not dear for a staff officer.

SIR OLIVER (*aside*). Heaven deliver me! His famous uncle Richard for ten pounds!—Very well, sir, I take him at that.

CHARLES. Careless, knock down my uncle Richard.—Here, now, is a maiden sister of his, my great-aunt Deborah, done by Kneller, thought to be in his best manner, and a very formidable likeness. There she is, you see, a shepherdess feeding her flock. You shall have her for five pounds ten—the sheep are worth the money.

SIR OLIVER (*aside*). Ah, poor Deborah, a woman who set

such a value on herself!—Five pounds ten—She's
mine.

CHARLES. Knock down my aunt Deborah! Here, now, are
two that were a sort of cousins of theirs. You see,
Moses, these pictures were done some time ago when
beaux wore wigs and the ladies their own hair.

SIR OLIVER. Yes, truly, head-dresses appear to have been a
little lower in those days.

CHARLES. Well, take that couple for the same.

MOSES. 'Tis a good bargain.

CHARLES. Careless!—This now, is a grandfather of my
mother's, a learned judge, well known on the western
circuit. What do you rate him at, Moses?

MOSES. Four guineas.

CHARLES. Four guineas! Gad's life, you don't bid me the
price of his wig. Mr. Premium, you have more respect
for the woolsack.[31] Do let us knock his lordship down
at fifteen.

SIR OLIVER. By all means.

CARELESS. Gone!

CHARLES. And these are two brothers of his, William and
Walter Blunt, Esquires, both members of parliament
and noted speakers; and what's very extraordinary, I
believe this is the first time they were ever bought
or sold.

SIR OLIVER. That is very extraordinary, indeed! I'll take
them at your own price for the honor of Parliament.

CARELESS. Well said, little Premium! I'll knock them down
at forty.

CHARLES. Here's a jolly fellow! I don't know what relation,
but he was mayor of Manchester; take him at eight
pounds.

SIR OLIVER. No, no; six will do for the mayor.

CHARLES. Come, make it guineas,[32] and I'll throw you the
two aldermen there into the bargain.

SIR OLIVER. They're mine.

CHARLES. Careless, knock down the mayor and aldermen.
But, plague on 't, we shall be all day retailing in this
manner. Do let us deal wholesale—what say you,

---

[31] Symbol of the legal profession, since the Lord Chancellor sits on
the Woolsack in the House of Lords.
[32] A pound is worth twenty shillings, a guinea, twenty-one.

little Premium? Give me three hundred pounds for the rest of the family in the lump.

CARELESS. Ay, ay, that will be the best way.

SIR OLIVER. Well, well, anything to accommodate you. They are mine. But there is one portrait which you have always passed over.

CARELESS. What, that ill-looking little fellow over the settee?

SIR OLIVER. Yes, sir, I mean that, though I don't think him so ill-looking a little fellow by any means.

CHARLES. What, that? Oh, that's my uncle Oliver. 'Twas done before he went to India.

CARELESS. Your uncle Oliver! Gad, then you'll never be friends, Charles. That, now, is as stern a looking rogue as ever I saw, an unforgiving eye and a damned disinheriting countenance! An inveterate knave, depend on't, don't you think so, little Premium?

SIR OLIVER. Upon my soul, sir, I do not. I think it is as honest a looking face as any in the room, dead or alive. But I suppose Uncle Oliver goes with the rest of the lumber?

CHARLES. No, hang it! I'll not part with poor Noll. The old fellow has been very good to me, and, egad, I'll keep his picture while I've a room to put it in.

SIR OLIVER (*aside*). The rogue's my nephew after all!— But, sir, I have somehow taken a fancy to that picture.

CHARLES. I'm sorry for't, for you certainly will not have it. Oons, haven't you got enough of them?

SIR OLIVER (*aside*). I forgive him for everything!—But, sir, when I take a whim in my head, I don't value money. I'll give you as much for that as for all the rest.

CHARLES. Don't tease me, master broker. I tell you I'll not part with it, and there's an end of it.

SIR OLIVER (*aside*). How like his father the dog is!—Well, well, I have done. (*aside*) I did not perceive it before, but I think I never saw such a striking resemblance. —Here's a draft for your sum.

CHARLES. Why, 'tis for eight hundred pounds!

SIR OLIVER. You will not let Sir Oliver go?

CHARLES. Zounds, no! I tell you once more.

SIR OLIVER. Then never mind the difference, we'll balance that another time. But give me your hand on the bargain. You are an honest fellow, Charles—I beg pardon, sir, for being so free.—Come, Moses.

CHARLES. Egad, this is a whimsical old fellow!—But hark'ee, Premium, you'll prepare lodgings for these gentlemen.

SIR OLIVER. Yes, yes, I'll send for them in a day or two.

CHARLES. But hold! Do, now, send a genteel conveyance for them, for, I assure you, they were most of them used to ride in their own carriages.

SIR OLIVER. I will, I will—for all but little Oliver.

CHARLES. Ay, all but the little nabob.

SIR OLIVER. You're fixed on that?

CHARLES. Peremptorily.

SIR OLIVER (*aside*). A dear extravagant rogue!—Good day! —Come, Moses. (*aside*) Let me hear now who dares call him profligate!

(*Exeunt* SIR OLIVER *and* MOSES.)

CARELESS. Why, this is the oddest genius of the sort I ever met with.

CHARLES. Egad, he's the prince of brokers, I think. I wonder how the devil Moses got acquainted with so honest a fellow. Ha! here's Rowley.—Do, Careless, say I'll join the company in a moment.

CARELESS. I will, but don't let that old blockhead persuade you to squander any of that money on old, musty debts or any such nonsense; for tradesmen, Charles, are the most exorbitant fellows.

CHARLES. Very true, and paying them is only encouraging them.

CARELESS. Nothing else.

CHARLES. Ay, ay, never fear.

(*Exit* CARELESS.)

So, this was an odd old fellow, indeed. Let me see, two-thirds of this is mine by right, five hundred and thirty odd pounds. 'Fore heaven, I find one's ancestors are more valuable relations than I took them for! [*bowing to the pictures*] Ladies and gentlemen, your most obedient and very grateful servant.

(*Enter* ROWLEY.)

Hah, old Rowley! Egad, you are just come in time to take leave of your old acquaintance.

ROWLEY. Yes, I heard they were a-going. But I wonder you can have such spirits under so many distresses.

CHARLES. Why, there's the point, my distresses are so many that I can't afford to part with my spirits; but I shall be rich and splenetic, all in good time. However, I suppose you are surprised that I am not more sorrowful at parting with so many near relations. To be sure, 'tis very affecting; but you see they never move a muscle; so why should I?

ROWLEY. There's no making you serious a moment.

CHARLES. Yes, faith, I am so now. Here, my honest Rowley, here get me this changed directly and take a hundred pounds of it immediately to old Stanley.

ROWLEY. A hundred pounds! Consider only—

CHARLES. Gad's life, don't talk about it! Poor Stanley's wants are pressing and, if you don't make haste, we shall have someone call that has a better right to the money.

ROWLEY. Ah, there's the point! I never will cease dunning you with the old proverb—

CHARLES. "Be just before you're generous."—Why, so I would if I could; but Justice is an old, lame, hobbling beldame, and I can't get her to keep pace with Generosity, for the soul of me.

ROWLEY. Yet, Charles, believe me, one hour's reflection—

CHARLES. Ay, ay, it's all very true; but hark'ee, Rowley, while I have, by heaven I'll give; so damn your economy. And now for hazard!

(*Exeunt.*)

[SCENE II.] *The parlor*

(*Enter* SIR OLIVER SURFACE *and* MOSES.)

MOSES. Well, sir, I think, as Sir Peter said, you have seen Mr. Charles in high glory; 'tis great pity he's so extravagant.

SIR OLIVER. True, but he would not sell my picture.

MOSES. And loves wine and women so much.

SIR OLIVER. But he would not sell my picture.

MOSES. And games so deep.

SIR OLIVER. But he would not sell my picture. Oh, here's Rowley!

(*Enter* ROWLEY.)

ROWLEY. So, Sir Oliver, I find you have made a purchase—

SIR OLIVER. Yes, yes, our young rake has parted with his
    ancestors like old tapestry.

ROWLEY. And here he has commissioned me to re-deliver
    you part of the purchase money. I mean, though, in
    your necessitous character of old Stanley.

MOSES. Ah, there's the pity of all; he is so damned
    charitable.

ROWLEY. And left a hosier and two tailors in the hall, who,
    I'm sure, won't be paid; and this hundred would
    satisfy them.

SIR OLIVER. Well, well, I'll pay his debts—and his benevo-
    lence, too. But now I am no more a broker, and you
    shall introduce me to the elder brother as old Stanley.

ROWLEY. Not yet awhile. Sir Peter, I know, means to call
    there about this time.

(*Enter* TRIP.)

TRIP. Oh, gentlemen, I beg pardon for not showing you
    out. This way.—Moses, a word. (*Exit with* MOSES.)

SIR OLIVER. There's a fellow for you! Would you believe
    it, that puppy intercepted the Jew on our coming and
    wanted to raise money before he got to his master!

ROWLEY. Indeed!

SIR OLIVER. Yes, they are now planning an annuity busi-
    ness. Ah, Master Rowley, in my days servants were
    content with the follies of their masters when they
    were worn a little threadbare, but now they have their
    vices, like their birthday clothes,[33] with the gloss on.

(*Exeunt.*)

[SCENE III.] *A library* [*in* JOSEPH SURFACE's *house*]

(*Enter* JOSEPH SURFACE *and* SERVANT.)

JOSEPH SURFACE. No letter from Lady Teazle?

SERVANT. No, sir.

JOSEPH SURFACE (*aside*). I am surprised she has not sent
    if she is prevented from coming. Sir Peter certainly
    does not suspect me. Yet I wish I may not lose the

[33] Especially elegant clothes worn to celebrate the King's birthday.

heiress through the scrape I have drawn myself into with the wife. However, Charles's imprudence and bad character are great points in my favor. (*knocking without*)

SERVANT. Sir, I believe that must be Lady Teazle.

JOSEPH SURFACE. Hold! See whether it is or not before you go to the door. I have a particular message for you if it should be my brother.

SERVANT. 'Tis her ladyship, sir. She always leaves her chair at the milliner's in the next street.

JOSEPH SURFACE. Stay, stay! Draw that screen before the window. That will do. My opposite neighbor is a maiden lady of so curious a temper.

(SERVANT *draws the screen and exit.*)

I have a difficult hand to play in this affair. Lady Teazle has lately suspected my views on Maria, but she must by no means be let into that secret—at least, till I have her more in my power.

(*Enter* LADY TEAZLE.)

LADY TEAZLE. What, sentiment in soliloquy now? Have you been very impatient? Oh, lud! don't pretend to look grave. I vow I couldn't come before.

JOSEPH SURFACE. Oh, madam, punctuality is a species of constancy, a very unfashionable quality in a lady.

LADY TEAZLE. Upon my word, you ought to pity me. Do you know Sir Peter is grown so ill-natured to me of late, and so jealous of Charles too! That's the best of the story, isn't it?

JOSEPH SURFACE (*aside*). I am glad my scandalous friends keep that up.

LADY TEAZLE. I am sure I wish he would let Maria marry him and then, perhaps, he would be convinced, don't you, Mr. Surface?

JOSEPH SURFACE (*aside*). Indeed I do not.—Oh, certainly I do! for then my dear Lady Teazle would also be convinced how wrong her suspicions were of my having any design on the silly girl.

LADY TEAZLE. Well, well, I'm inclined to believe you. But isn't it provoking to have the most ill-natured things said of one? And there's my friend Lady Sneerwell has circulated I don't know how many scandalous tales of me, and all without any foundation too. That's what vexes me.

JOSEPH SURFACE. Ay, madam, to be sure, that is the provoking circumstance—without foundation. Yes, yes, there's the mortification, indeed; for, when a scandalous story is believed against one, there certainly is no comfort like the consciousness of having deserved it.

LADY TEAZLE. No, to be sure, then I'd forgive their malice. But to attack me, who am really so innocent and who never say an ill-natured thing of anybody—that is, of any friend—and then Sir Peter, too, to have him so peevish and so suspicious, when I know the integrity of my own heart—indeed, 'tis monstrous!

JOSEPH SURFACE. But, my dear Lady Teazle, 'tis your own fault if you suffer it. When a husband entertains a groundless suspicion of his wife and withdraws his confidence from her, the original compact is broken; and she owes it to the honor of her sex to endeavor to outwit him.

LADY TEAZLE. Indeed! So that, if he suspects me without cause, it follows that the best way of curing his jealousy is to give him reason for it?

JOSEPH SURFACE. Undoubtedly—for your husband should never be deceived in you; and in that case it becomes you to be frail in compliment to his discernment.

LADY TEAZLE. To be sure, what you say is very reasonable, and when the consciousness of my innocence—

JOSEPH SURFACE. Ah, my dear madam, there is the great mistake! 'Tis this very conscious innocence that is of the greatest prejudice to you. What is it makes you negligent of forms and careless of the world's opinion? Why, the consciousness of your own innocence. What makes you thoughtless in your conduct and apt to run into a thousand little imprudences? Why, the consciousness of your own innocence. What makes you impatient of Sir Peter's temper and outrageous at his suspicions? Why, the consciousness of your own innocence.

LADY TEAZLE. 'Tis very true.

JOSEPH SURFACE. Now, my dear Lady Teazle, if you would but once make a trifling *faux pas*, you can't conceive how cautious you would grow—and how ready to humor and agree with your husband.

LADY TEAZLE. Do you think so?

JOSEPH SURFACE. Oh, I am sure on't! And then you would find all scandal would cease at once, for, in short, your character at present is like a person in a plethora, absolutely dying from too much health.

LADY TEAZLE. So, so; then I perceive your prescription is that I must sin in my own defense and part with my virtue to preserve my reputation?

JOSEPH SURFACE. Exactly so, upon my credit, ma'am.

LADY TEAZLE. Well, certainly this is the oddest doctrine and the newest receipt for avoiding calumny!

JOSEPH SURFACE. An infallible one, believe me. Prudence, like experience, must be paid for.

LADY TEAZLE. Why, if my understanding were once convinced—

JOSEPH SURFACE. Oh, certainly, madam, your understanding should be convinced. Yes, yes—heaven forbid I should persuade you to do anything you thought wrong. No, no, I have too much honor to desire it.

LADY TEAZLE. Don't you think we may as well leave honor out of the question?

JOSEPH SURFACE. Ah, the ill effects of your country education, I see, still remain with you.

LADY TEAZLE. I doubt they do, indeed; and I will fairly own to you that if I could be persuaded to do wrong, it would be by Sir Peter's ill usage sooner than your honorable logic after all.

JOSEPH SURFACE. Then, by this hand, which he is unworthy of—(*taking her hand*)

(*Enter* SERVANT.)

'Sdeath, you blockhead, what do you want?

SERVANT. I beg your pardon, sir, but I thought you would not choose Sir Peter to come up without announcing him.

JOSEPH SURFACE. Sir Peter! Oons—the devil!

LADY TEAZLE. Sir Peter! Oh, lud! I'm ruined! I'm ruined!

SERVANT. Sir, 'twasn't I let him in.

LADY TEAZLE. Oh, I'm quite undone! What will become of me now, Mr. Logic? Oh, mercy, he's on the stairs— I'll get behind here, and if ever I'm so imprudent again—(*Goes behind the screen.*)

JOSEPH SURFACE. Give me that book. (*Sits down.* SERVANT *pretends to adjust his chair.*)

(*Enter* SIR PETER TEAZLE.)

SIR PETER. Ay, ever improving himself! Mr. Surface, Mr. Surface—

JOSEPH SURFACE. Oh, my dear Sir Peter, I beg your pardon. (*Gaping, throws away the book.*) I have been dozing over a stupid book. Well, I am much obliged to you for this call. You haven't been here, I believe, since I fitted up this room. Books, you know, are the only things I am a coxcomb in.

SIR PETER. 'Tis very neat indeed. Well, well, that's proper; and you can make even your screen a source of knowledge—hung, I perceive, with maps.

JOSEPH SURFACE. Oh, yes, I find great use in that screen.

SIR PETER. I dare say you must, certainly, when you want to find anything in a hurry.

JOSEPH SURFACE (*aside*). Ay, or to hide anything in a hurry either.

SIR PETER. Well, I have a little private business—

JOSEPH (*To* SERVANT). You need not stay.

SERVANT. No, sir. (*Exit.*)

JOSEPH SURFACE. Here's a chair, Sir Peter, I beg—

SIR PETER. Well, now we are alone, there's a subject, my dear friend, on which I wish to unburden my mind to you, a point of the greatest moment to my peace; in short, my good friend, Lady Teazle's conduct of late has made me extremely unhappy.

JOSEPH SURFACE. Indeed! I am very sorry to hear it.

SIR PETER. Ay, 'tis but too plain she has not the least regard for me; but, what's worse, I have pretty good authority to suspect she has formed an attachment to another.

JOSEPH SURFACE. You astonish me!

SIR PETER. Yes, and, between ourselves, I think I've discovered the person.

JOSEPH SURFACE. How! You alarm me exceedingly.

SIR PETER. Ay, my dear friend, I knew you would sympathize with me!

JOSEPH SURFACE. Yes, believe me, Sir Peter, such a discovery would hurt me just as much as it would you.

SIR PETER. I am convinced of it. Ah, it is a happiness to have a friend whom one can trust even with one's family secrets. But have you no guess who I mean?

JOSEPH SURFACE. I haven't the most distant idea. It can't be Sir Benjamin Backbite!

SIR PETER. Oh, no! What say you to Charles?

JOSEPH SURFACE. My brother? Impossible!

SIR PETER. Ah, my dear friend, the goodness of your own heart misleads you. You judge of others by yourself.

JOSEPH SURFACE. Certainly, Sir Peter, the heart that is conscious of its own integrity is ever slow to credit another's treachery.

SIR PETER. True, but your brother has no sentiment. You never hear him talk so.

JOSEPH SURFACE. Yet I can't but think Lady Teazle herself has too much principle—

SIR PETER. Ay, but what is principle against the flattery of a handsome, lively young fellow?

JOSEPH SURFACE. That's very true.

SIR PETER. And then, you know, the difference of our ages makes it very improbable that she should have any great affection for me; and, if she were to be frail, and I were to make it public, why, the town would only laugh at me, the foolish old bachelor who had married a girl.

JOSEPH SURFACE. That's true, to be sure. They would laugh.

SIR PETER. Laugh, ay! And make ballads and paragraphs and the devil knows what of me.

JOSEPH SURFACE. No, you must never make it public.

SIR PETER. But then, again, that the nephew of my old friend, Sir Oliver, should be the person to attempt such a wrong, hurts me more nearly.

JOSEPH SURFACE. Ay, there's the point. When ingratitude barbs the dart of injury, the wound has double danger in it.

SIR PETER. Ay! I that was, in a manner, left his guardian, in whose house he had been so often entertained, who never in my life denied him—my advice!

JOSEPH SURFACE. Oh, 'tis not to be credited! There may be a man capable of such baseness, to be sure; but, for my part, till you can give me positive proofs, I cannot but doubt it. However, if it should be proved on him, he is no longer a brother of mine; I disclaim kindred with him; for the man who can break through the laws of hospitality and attempt the wife of his friend deserves to be branded as the pest of society.

SIR PETER. What a difference there is between you! What noble sentiments!

JOSEPH SURFACE. Yet I cannot suspect Lady Teazle's honor.

SIR PETER. I am sure I wish to think well of her and to remove all ground of quarrel between us. She has lately reproached me more than once with having made no settlement on her, and, in our last quarrel, she almost hinted that she should not break her heart if I was dead. Now, as we seem to differ in our ideas of expenses, I have resolved she shall be her own mistress in that respect for the future; and, if I were to die, she will find I have not been inattentive to her interest while living. Here, my friend, are the drafts of two deeds, which I wish to have your opinion on. By one, she will enjoy eight hundred a year independent while I live; and, by the other, the bulk of my fortune at my death.

JOSEPH SURFACE. This conduct, Sir Peter, is indeed truly generous. (*aside*) I wish it may not corrupt my pupil.

SIR PETER. Yes, I am determined she shall have no cause to complain, though I would not have her acquainted with the latter instance of my affection yet awhile.

JOSEPH SURFACE (*aside*). Nor I, if I could help it.

SIR PETER. And now, my dear friend, if you please, we will talk over the situation of your hopes with Maria.

JOSEPH SURFACE (*softly*). Oh, no, Sir Peter! Another time, if you please.

SIR PETER. I am sensibly chagrined at the little progress you seem to make in her affections.

JOSEPH SURFACE (*softly*). I beg you will not mention it. What are my disappointments when your happiness is in debate! (*aside*) 'Sdeath, I shall be ruined every way!

SIR PETER. And though you are so averse to my acquainting Lady Teazle with your passion, I'm sure she's not your enemy in the affair.

JOSEPH SURFACE. Pray, Sir Peter, now oblige me. I am really too much affected by the subject we have been speaking of to bestow a thought on my own concerns. The man who is entrusted with his friend's distresses can never——

(*Enter* SERVANT.)

Well, sir?

SERVANT. Your brother, sir, is speaking to a gentleman in the street and says he knows you are within.

JOSEPH SURFACE. 'Sdeath, blockhead! I'm not within. I'm out for the day.

SIR PETER. Stay—hold—a thought has struck me. You shall be at home.

JOSEPH SURFACE. Well, well, let him up.

(*Exit* SERVANT.)

(*Aside*) He'll interrupt Sir Peter, however.

SIR PETER. Now, my good friend, oblige me, I entreat you. Before Charles comes, let me conceal myself somewhere; then do you tax him on the point we have been talking on, and his answers may satisfy me at once.

JOSEPH SURFACE. Oh, fie, Sir Peter! Would you have me join in so mean a trick? To trepan my brother too!

SIR PETER. Nay, you tell me you are sure he is innocent. If so, you do him the greatest service by giving him an opportunity to clear himself, and you will set my heart at rest. Come, you shall not refuse me. Here, behind the screen will be—(*Goes to the screen.*) Hey! What the devil! There seems to be one listener here already! I'll swear I saw a petticoat!

JOSEPH SURFACE. Ha! ha! ha! Well, this is ridiculous enough. I'll tell you, Sir Peter, though I hold a man of intrigue to be a most despicable character, yet, you know, it does not follow that one is to be an absolute Joseph either. Hark'ee, 'tis a little French milliner—a silly rogue that plagues me—and having some character to lose, on your coming, sir, she ran behind the screen.

SIR PETER. Ah, you rogue!—But, egad, she has overheard all I have been saying of my wife.

JOSEPH SURFACE. Oh, 'twill never go any farther, you may depend upon it!

SIR PETER. No? Then, faith, let her hear it out.—Here's a closet will do as well.

JOSEPH SURFACE. Well, go in there.

SIR PETER. Sly rogue! Sly rogue! (*going into the closet*)

JOSEPH SURFACE. A narrow escape, indeed! And a curious situation I'm in, to part man and wife in this manner.

LADY TEAZLE (*peeping*). Couldn't I steal off?

JOSEPH SURFACE. Keep close, my angel!

SIR PETER (*peeping*). Joseph, tax him home!

JOSEPH SURFACE. Back, my dear friend!

LADY TEAZLE (*peeping*). Couldn't you lock Sir Peter in?

JOSEPH SURFACE. Be still, my life!

SIR PETER (*peeping*). You're sure the little milliner won't blab?

JOSEPH SURFACE. In, in, my dear Sir Peter!—'Fore gad, I wish I had a key to the door!

(*Enter* CHARLES SURFACE.)

CHARLES. Holla, brother, what has been the matter? Your fellow would not let me up at first. What, have you had a Jew or a wench with you?

JOSEPH SURFACE. Neither, brother, I assure you.

CHARLES. But what has made Sir Peter steal off? I thought he had been with you.

JOSEPH SURFACE. He was, brother; but, hearing you were coming, he did not choose to stay.

CHARLES. What, was the old gentleman afraid I wanted to borrow money of him?

JOSEPH SURFACE. No, sir; but I am sorry to find, Charles, you have lately given that worthy man grounds for great uneasiness.

CHARLES. Yes, they tell me I do that to a great many worthy men. But how so, pray?

JOSEPH SURFACE. To be plain with you, brother, he thinks you are endeavoring to gain Lady Teazle's affections from him.

CHARLES. Who, I? Oh, lud, not I, upon my word. Ha! ha! ha! ha! so the old fellow has found out that he has got a young wife, has he?—or, what's worse, has her ladyship discovered she has an old husband?

JOSEPH SURFACE. This is no subject to jest on, brother. He who can laugh—

CHARLES. True, true, as you were going to say—Then, seriously, I never had the least idea of what you charge me with, upon my honor.

JOSEPH SURFACE (*aloud*). Well, it will give Sir Peter great satisfaction to hear this.

CHARLES. To be sure, I once thought the lady seemed to have taken a fancy to me; but, upon my soul, I never gave her the least encouragement. Besides, you know my attachment to Maria.

JOSEPH SURFACE. But, sure, brother, even if Lady Teazle had betrayed the fondest partiality for you—

CHARLES. Why, look'ee, Joseph, I hope I shall never deliberately do a dishonorable action; but if a pretty woman was purposely to throw herself in my way—and that pretty woman married to a man old enough to be her father—

JOSEPH SURFACE. Well?

CHARLES. Why, I believe I should be obliged to borrow a little of your morality, that's all. But, brother, do you know now that you surprise me exceedingly by naming me with Lady Teazle; for, i' faith, I always understood you were her favorite.

JOSEPH SURFACE. Oh, for shame, Charles! This retort is foolish.

CHARLES. Nay, I swear I have seen you exchange such significant glances—

JOSEPH SURFACE. Nay, nay, sir, this is no jest.

CHARLES. Egad, I'm serious! Don't you remember one day when I called here—

JOSEPH SURFACE. Nay, pr'ythee, Charles—

CHARLES. And found you together—

JOSEPH SURFACE. Zounds, sir, I insist—

CHARLES. And another time when your servant—

JOSEPH SURFACE. Brother, brother, a word with you! (*aside*) Gad, I must stop him.

CHARLES. Informed me, I say, that—

JOSEPH SURFACE. Hush! I beg your pardon, but Sir Peter has overheard all we have been saying. I knew you would clear yourself, or I should not have consented.

CHARLES. How, Sir Peter! Where is he?

JOSEPH SURFACE. Softly! There! (*Points to the closet.*)

CHARLES. Oh, 'fore heaven, I'll have him out.—Sir Peter, come forth!

JOSEPH SURFACE. No, no—

CHARLES. I say, Sir Peter, come into court! (*Pulls in* SIR PETER.) What! My old guardian! What, turn inquisitor and take evidence *incog.?*

SIR PETER. Give me your hand, Charles. I believe I have suspected you wrongfully; but you mustn't be angry with Joseph. 'Twas my plan.

CHARLES. Indeed!

SIR PETER. But I acquit you. I promise you I don't think near so ill of you as I did. What I have heard has given me great satisfaction.

CHARLES. Egad, then, 'twas lucky you didn't hear any more. (*Apart to* JOSEPH): Wasn't it, Joseph?

SIR PETER. Ah, you would have retorted on him.

CHARLES. Ah, ay, that was a joke.

SIR PETER. Yes, yes, I know his honor too well.

CHARLES. But you might as well have suspected him as me in this matter, for all that. (*Apart to* JOSEPH): Mightn't he, Joseph?

SIR PETER. Well, well, I believe you.

JOSEPH SURFACE (*aside*). Would they were both out of the room!

SIR PETER. And in future, perhaps, we may not be such strangers.

(*Enter* SERVANT *who whispers* JOSEPH SURFACE.)

JOSEPH SURFACE. Lady Sneerwell! Stop her by all means.

(*Exit* SERVANT.)

Gentlemen—I beg pardon—I must wait on you downstairs—here's a person come on particular business.

CHARLES. Well, you can see him in another room. Sir Peter and I have not met a long time, and I have something to say to him.

JOSEPH SURFACE (*aside*). They must not be left together. I'll send Lady Sneerwell away and return directly. (*Apart to* SIR PETER): Sir Peter, not a word of the French milliner.

SIR PETER (*apart to* JOSEPH). Oh! Not for the world.

(*Exit* JOSEPH SURFACE.)

—Ah, Charles, if you associated more with your brother, one might indeed hope for your reformation. He is a man of sentiment. Well, there is nothing in the world so noble as a man of sentiment.

CHARLES. Psha, he is too moral by half, and so apprehensive of his good name, as he calls it, that I suppose he would as soon let a priest into his house as a girl.

SIR PETER. No, no! Come, come! You wrong him. No, no, Joseph is no rake, but he is no such saint either, in that respect. (*aside*) I have a great mind to tell him. We should have such a laugh!

CHARLES. Oh, hang him, he's a very anchorite, a young hermit.

SIR PETER. Hark'ee, you must not abuse him. He may chance to hear of it again, I promise you.

CHARLES. Why, you won't tell him?

SIR PETER. No, but—this way. (*aside*) Egad, I'll tell him. —Hark'ee, have you a mind to have a good laugh at Joseph?

CHARLES. I should like it, of all things.

SIR PETER. Then, i' faith, we will! I'll be quit with him for discovering me. He had a girl with him when I called.

CHARLES. What! Joseph? You jest.

SIR PETER. Hush! A little French milliner, and the best of the jest is—she's in the room now.

CHARLES. The devil she is!

SIR PETER. Hush, I tell you! (*Points.*)

CHARLES. Behind the screen? 'Slife, let's unveil her!

SIR PETER. No, no, he's coming. You shan't, indeed!

CHARLES. Oh, egad, we'll have a peep at the little milliner!

SIR PETER. Not for the world! Joseph will never forgive me.

CHARLES. I'll stand by you—

SIR PETER. Odds, here he is!

(JOSEPH SURFACE *enters just as* CHARLES SURFACE *throws down the screen.*)

CHARLES. Lady Teazle, by all that's wonderful!

SIR PETER. Lady Teazle, by all that's horrible!

CHARLES. Sir Peter, this is one of the smartest French milliners I ever saw. Egad, you seem all to have been diverting yourselves here at hide and seek, and I don't see who is out of the secret. Shall I beg your ladyship to inform me? Not a word!—Brother, will you be pleased to explain this matter? What! Is morality dumb too?—Sir Peter, though I found you in the dark, perhaps you are not so now! All mute! Well, though I can make nothing of the affair, I suppose you perfectly understand one another; so I'll leave you to yourselves. (*going*) Brother, I'm sorry to find you have given that worthy man grounds for so much uneasiness.—Sir Peter, there's nothing in the world so noble as a man of sentiment!

(*Exit* CHARLES. *They stand for some time looking at each other.*)

JOSEPH SURFACE. Sir Peter, notwithstanding—I confess—that appearances are against me—if you will afford me your patience, I make no doubt—but I shall explain everything to your satisfaction.

SIR PETER. If you please, sir.

JOSEPH SURFACE. The fact is, sir, that Lady Teazle, knowing my pretensions to your ward Maria—I say, sir, Lady Teazle, being apprehensive of the jealousy of your temper—and knowing my friendship to the family—she, sir, I say—called here—in order that—I might explain these pretensions; but on your coming—being apprehensive—as I said,—of your jealousy, she withdrew; and this, you may depend on it, is the whole truth of the matter.

SIR PETER. A very clear account, upon my word, and I dare swear the lady will vouch for every article of it.

LADY TEAZLE (*coming forward*). For not one word of it, Sir Peter.

SIR PETER. How! Don't you think it worth while to agree in the lie?

LADY TEAZLE. There is not one syllable of truth in what that gentleman has told you.

SIR PETER. I believe you, upon my soul, ma'am.

JOSEPH SURFACE (*aside*). 'Sdeath, madam, will you betray me?

LADY TEAZLE. Good Mr. Hypocrite, by your leave, I'll speak for myself.

SIR PETER. Ay, let her alone, sir; you'll find she'll make out a better story than you, without prompting.

LADY TEAZLE. Hear me, Sir Peter! I came here on no matter relating to your ward and even ignorant of this gentleman's pretensions to her. But I came, seduced by his insidious arguments, at least to listen to his pretended passion, if not to sacrifice your honor to his baseness.

SIR PETER. Now, I believe the truth is coming, indeed.

JOSEPH SURFACE. The woman's mad!

LADY TEAZLE. No, sir; she has recovered her senses, and your own arts have furnished her with the means.—Sir Peter, I do not expect you to credit me, but the tenderness you expressed for me when I am sure you could not think I was a witness to it has so penetrated to my heart that, had I left this place without the shame of this discovery, my future life should have spoken the sincerity of my gratitude. As for that smooth-tongued hypocrite, who would have seduced the wife of his too credulous friend while he affected honorable addresses to his ward, I behold him now in a light so truly despicable that I shall never again respect myself for having listened to him. (*Exit.*)

JOSEPH SURFACE. Notwithstanding all this, Sir Peter, heaven knows—

SIR PETER. That you are a villain!—and so I leave you to your conscience.

JOSEPH SURFACE (*following* SIR PETER). You are too rash, Sir Peter. You shall hear me. The man who shuts out conviction by refusing to—

SIR PETER. Oh!

(*Exeunt,* JOSEPH SURFACE *following and speaking.*)

ACT V

[SCENE I.] *The library*

(*Enter* JOSEPH SURFACE *and* SERVANT.)

JOSEPH SURFACE. Mr. Stanley! And why should you think I would see him? You must know he comes to ask something.

SERVANT. Sir, I would not have let him in, but that Mr. Rowley came to the door with him.

JOSEPH SURFACE. Psha, blockhead! To suppose that I should now be in a temper to receive visits from poor relations! Well, why don't you show the fellow up?

SERVANT. I will, sir. Why, sir, it was not my fault that Sir Peter discovered my lady—

JOSEPH SURFACE. Go, fool!

(*Exit* SERVANT.)

Sure, Fortune never played a man of my policy such a trick before. My character with Sir Peter, my hopes with Maria, destroyed in a moment! I'm in a rare humor to listen to other people's distresses. I shan't be able to bestow even a benevolent sentiment on Stanley.—So! here he comes and Rowley with him. I must try to recover myself and put a little charity into my face, however. (*Exit.*)

(*Enter* SIR OLIVER SURFACE *and* ROWLEY.)

SIR OLIVER. What, does he avoid us? That was he, was it not?

ROWLEY. It was, sir. But I doubt you are come a little too abruptly. His nerves are so weak that the sight of a poor relation may be too much for him. I should have gone first to break you to him.

SIR OLIVER. Oh, plague of his nerves! Yet this is he whom Sir Peter extols as a man of the most benevolent way of thinking.

ROWLEY. As to his way of thinking, I cannot pretend to decide; for, to do him justice, he appears to have as much speculative benevolence as any private gentleman in the kingdom, though he is seldom so sensual as to indulge himself in the exercise of it.

SIR OLIVER. Yet he has a string of charitable sentiments, I suppose, at his fingers' ends.

ROWLEY. Or, rather, at his tongue's end, Sir Oliver, for I believe there is no sentiment he has more faith in than that "Charity begins at home."

SIR OLIVER. And his, I presume, is of that domestic sort which never stirs abroad at all.

ROWLEY. I doubt you'll find it so. But he's coming. I mustn't seem to interrupt you; and you know immediately as you leave him, I come in to announce your arrival in your real character.

SIR OLIVER. True, and afterwards you'll meet me at Sir Peter's.

ROWLEY. Without losing a moment. (*Exit.*)

SIR OLIVER. So! I don't like the complaisance of his features.

(*Enter* JOSEPH SURFACE.)

JOSEPH SURFACE. Sir, I beg you ten thousand pardons for keeping you a moment waiting. Mr. Stanley, I presume.

SIR OLIVER. At your service.

JOSEPH SURFACE. Sir, I beg you will do me the honor to sit down. I entreat you, sir.

SIR OLIVER. Dear sir—there's no occasion. (*aside*) Too civil by half.

JOSEPH SURFACE. I have not the pleasure of knowing you, Mr. Stanley, but I am extremely happy to see you look so well. You were nearly related to my mother, I think, Mr. Stanley?

SIR OLIVER. I was, sir; so nearly that my present poverty, I fear, may do discredit to her wealthy children, else I should not have presumed to trouble you.

JOSEPH SURFACE. Dear sir, there needs no apology! He that is in distress, though a stranger, has a right to claim kindred with the wealthy. I am sure I wish I was of that class and had it in my power to offer you even a small relief.

SIR OLIVER. If your uncle, Sir Oliver, were here, I should have a friend.

JOSEPH SURFACE. I wish he was, sir, with all my heart. You should not want an advocate with him, believe me, sir.

SIR OLIVER. I should not need one; my distresses would recommend me. But I imagined his bounty had enabled you to become the agent of his charity.

JOSEPH SURFACE. My dear sir, you were strangely misinformed. Sir Oliver is a worthy man, a very worthy man; but avarice, Mr. Stanley, is the vice of age. I will tell you, my good sir, in confidence, what he has done for me has been a mere nothing, though people, I know, have thought otherwise; and, for my part, I never chose to contradict the report.

SIR OLIVER. What! Has he never transmitted you bullion, rupees, pagodas?[34]

JOSEPH SURFACE. Oh, dear sir, nothing of the kind! No, no, a few presents now and then—china, shawls, congou tea, avadavats, and Indian crackers[35]—little more, believe me.

SIR OLIVER (*aside*). Here's gratitude for twelve thousand pounds! Avadavats and Indian crackers!

---

[34] Indian silver and gold coins.
[35] Black tea, colorful songbirds, and small firecrackers.

JOSEPH SURFACE. Then, my dear sir, you have heard, I doubt not, of the extravagance of my brother. There are very few would credit what I have done for that unfortunate young man.

SIR OLIVER (*aside*). Not, I, for one!

JOSEPH SURFACE. The sums I have lent him! Indeed I have been exceedingly to blame; it was an amiable weakness; however, I don't pretend to defend it; and now I feel it doubly culpable since it has deprived me of the pleasure of serving you, Mr. Stanley, as my heart dictates.

SIR OLIVER (*aside*). Dissembler!—Then, sir, you can't assist me?

JOSEPH SURFACE. At present, it grieves me to say, I cannot; but whenever I have the ability, you may depend upon hearing from me.

SIR OLIVER. I am extremely sorry—

JOSEPH SURFACE. Not more than I, believe me. To pity without the power to relieve is still more painful than to ask and be denied.

SIR OLIVER. Kind sir, your most obedient, humble servant!

JOSEPH SURFACE. You leave me deeply affected, Mr. Stanley.—William, be ready to open the door.

SIR OLIVER. Oh, dear sir, no ceremony.

JOSEPH SURFACE. Your very obedient!

SIR OLIVER. Sir, your most obsequious!

JOSEPH SURFACE. You may depend upon hearing from me whenever I can be of service.

SIR OLIVER. Sweet sir, you are too good!

JOSEPH SURFACE. In the meantime I wish you health and spirits.

SIR OLIVER. Your ever grateful and perpetual humble servant!

JOSEPH SURFACE. Sir, yours as sincerely!

SIR OLIVER (*aside*). Charles, you are my heir! (*Exit.*)

JOSEPH SURFACE. This is one bad effect of a good character; it invites applications from the unfortunate, and there needs no small degree of address to gain the reputation of benevolence without incurring the expense. The silver ore of pure charity is an expensive article in the catalogue of a man's good qualities, whereas the sentimental French plate I use instead of it, makes just as good a show and pays no tax.

(*Enter* ROWLEY.)

ROWLEY. Mr. Surface, your servant! I was apprehensive of interrupting you, though my business demands immediate attention, as this note will inform you.

JOSEPH SURFACE. Always happy to see Mr. Rowley. (*Reads the letter.*) How! Oliver—Surface! My uncle arrived!

ROWLEY. He is, indeed; we have just parted. Quite well after a speedy voyage and impatient to embrace his worthy nephew.

JOSEPH SURFACE. I am astonished!—William, stop Mr. Stanley, if he's not gone!

ROWLEY. Oh, he's out of reach, I believe.

JOSEPH SURFACE. Why did you not let me know this when you came in together?

ROWLEY. I thought you had particular business. But I must be gone to inform your brother and appoint him here to meet your uncle. He will be with you in a quarter of an hour.

JOSEPH SURFACE. So he says. Well, I am strangely overjoyed at his coming. (*aside*) Never, to be sure, was anything so damned unlucky!

ROWLEY. You will be delighted to see how well he looks.

JOSEPH SURFACE. Ah, I'm rejoiced to hear it.—(*aside*) Just at this time!

ROWLEY. I'll tell him how impatiently you expect him.

JOSEPH SURFACE. Do, do! Pray give him my best duty and affection. Indeed, I cannot express the sensations I feel at the thought of seeing him.

(*Exit* ROWLEY.)

Certainly his coming just at this time is the cruellest piece of ill fortune. (*Exit.*)

[SCENE II.] SIR PETER TEAZLE's

(*Enter* MRS. CANDOUR *and* MAID.)

MAID. Indeed, ma'am, my lady will see nobody at present.

MRS. CANDOUR. Did you tell her it was her friend Mrs. Candour?

MAID. Yes, ma'am; but she begs you will excuse her.

MRS. CANDOUR. Do go again. I shall be glad to see her if it be only for a moment, for I am sure she must be in great distress.

(*Exit* MAID.)

Dear heart, how provoking! I'm not mistress of half the circumstances! We shall have the whole affair in the newspapers, with the names of the parties at length before I have dropped the story at a dozen houses.

(*Enter* SIR BENJAMIN BACKBITE.)

—Oh, Sir Benjamin, you have heard, I suppose—

SIR BENJAMIN. Of Lady Teazle and Mr. Surface—

MRS. CANDOUR. And Sir Peter's discovery—

SIR BENJAMIN. Oh, the strangest piece of business, to be sure!

MRS. CANDOUR. Well, I never was so surprised in my life. I am sorry for all parties, indeed.

SIR BENJAMIN. Now, I don't pity Sir Peter at all; he was so extravagantly partial to Mr. Surface.

MRS. CANDOUR. Mr. Surface! Why, 'twas with Charles Lady Teazle was detected.

SIR BENJAMIN. No such thing—Mr. Surface is the gallant.

MRS. CANDOUR. No, no—Charles is the man. 'Twas Mr. Surface brought Sir Peter to discover[36] them.

SIR BENJAMIN. I tell you I have it from one—

MRS. CANDOUR. And I have it from one—

SIR BENJAMIN. Who had it from one, who had it—

MRS. CANDOUR. From one immediately—But here comes Lady Sneerwell; perhaps she knows the whole affair.

(*Enter* LADY SNEERWELL.)

LADY SNEERWELL. So, my dear Mrs. Candour, here's a sad affair of our friend Lady Teazle.

MRS. CANDOUR. Ay, my dear friend, who could have thought it—

LADY SNEERWELL. Well, there is no trusting appearances, though, indeed, she was always too lively for me.

MRS. CANDOUR. To be sure, her manners were a little too free; but she was very young!

LADY SNEERWELL. And had, indeed, some good qualities.

MRS. CANDOUR. So she had, indeed. But have you heard the particulars?

LADY SNEERWELL. No; but everybody says that Mr. Surface—

[36] Expose.

SIR BENJAMIN. Ay, there, I told you Mr. Surface was the man.

MRS. CANDOUR. No, no, indeed—the assignation was with Charles.

LADY SNEERWELL. With Charles? You alarm me, Mrs. Candour!

MRS. CANDOUR. Yes, yes; he was the lover. Mr. Surface—do him justice—was only the informer.

SIR BENJAMIN. Well, I'll not dispute with you, Mrs. Candour; but, be it which it may, I hope that Sir Peter's wound will not—

MRS. CANDOUR. Sir Peter's wound! Oh, mercy! I didn't hear a word of their fighting.

LADY SNEERWELL. Nor I, not a syllable.

SIR BENJAMIN. No? What, no mention of the duel?

MRS. CANDOUR. Not a word.

SIR BENJAMIN. Oh, Lord, yes. They fought before they left the room.

LADY SNEERWELL. Pray let us hear.

MRS. CANDOUR. Ay, do oblige us with the duel.

SIR BENJAMIN. "Sir," says Sir Peter, immediately after the discovery, "you are a most ungrateful fellow."

MRS. CANDOUR. Ay, to Charles—

SIR BENJAMIN. No, no, to Mr. Surface. "A most ungrateful fellow; and old as I am, sir," says he, "I insist on immediate satisfaction."

MRS. CANDOUR. Ay, that must have been to Charles, for 'tis very unlikely Mr. Surface should go to fight in his own house.

SIR BENJAMIN. Gad's life, ma'am, not at all—"giving me immediate satisfaction!" On this, ma'am, Lady Teazle, seeing Sir Peter in such danger, ran out of the room in strong hysterics and Charles after her calling out for hartshorn and water. Then, madam, they began to fight with swords—

(*Enter* CRABTREE.)

CRABTREE. With pistols, nephew, pistols! I have it from undoubted authority.

MRS. CANDOUR. Oh, Mr. Crabtree, then it is all true?

CRABTREE. Too true, indeed, madam, and Sir Peter is dangerously wounded—

SIR BENJAMIN. By a thrust in *seconde* quite through his left side—

CRABTREE. By a bullet lodged in the thorax.

MRS. CANDOUR. Mercy on me! Poor Sir Peter!

CRABTREE. Yes, madam, though Charles would have avoided the matter if he could.

MRS. CANDOUR. I knew Charles was the person.

SIR BENJAMIN. My uncle, I see, knows nothing of the matter.

CRABTREE. But Sir Peter taxed him with the basest ingratitude—

SIR BENJAMIN. That I told you, you know—

CRABTREE. Do, nephew, let me speak!—And insisted on immediate—

SIR BENJAMIN. Just as I said—

CRABTREE. Odd's life, nephew, allow others to know something too! A pair of pistols lay on the bureau (for Mr. Surface, it seems, had come home the night before late from Salthill, where he had been to see the Montem with a friend who has a son at Eton)[37] so, unluckily, the pistols were left charged.

SIR BENJAMIN. I heard nothing of this.

CRABTREE. Sir Peter forced Charles to take one, and they fired, it seems, pretty nearly together. Charles's shot took place, as I told you, and Sir Peter's missed; but what is very extraordinary, the ball struck a little bronze Pliny that stood over the fireplace, grazed out of the window at a right angle and wounded the postman, who was just coming to the door with a double letter from Northamptonshire.

SIR BENJAMIN. My uncle's account is more circumstantial, I must confess; but I believe mine is the true one, for all that.

LADY SNEERWELL (aside). I am more interested in this affair than they imagine and must have better information. (Exit.)

SIR BENJAMIN (after a pause, looking at each other). Ah, Lady Sneerwell's alarm is very easily accounted for.

CRABTREE. Yes, yes, they certainly do say—but that's neither here nor there.

MRS. CANDOUR. But, pray, where is Sir Peter at present?

CRABTREE. Oh, they brought him home, and he is now

---

[37] On Whit-Tuesday of every third year, Eton schoolboys went to Salt-Hill (processus ad montem) for a ceremony.

in the house, though the servants are ordered to deny
him.

MRS. CANDOUR. I believe so, and Lady Teazle, I suppose,
attending him.

CRABTREE. Yes, yes; and I saw one of the faculty[38] enter
just before me.

SIR BENJAMIN. Hey! Who comes here?

CRABTREE. Oh, this is he, the physician, depend on't.

MRS. CANDOUR. Oh, certainly, it must be the physician; and
now we shall know.

(*Enter* SIR OLIVER SURFACE.)

CRABTREE. Well, doctor, what hopes?

MRS. CANDOUR. Ay, doctor, how's your patient?

SIR BENJAMIN. Now, doctor, isn't it a wound with a smallsword?

CRABTREE. A bullet lodged in the thorax, for a hundred!

SIR OLIVER. Doctor? A wound with a smallsword? And a
bullet in the thorax?—Oons, are you mad, good
people?

SIR BENJAMIN. Perhaps, sir, you are not a doctor?

SIR OLIVER. Truly, I am to thank you for my degree, if
I am.

CRABTREE. Only a friend of Sir Peter's, then, I presume.
But, sir, you must have heard of his accident.

SIR OLIVER. Not a word.

CRABTREE. Not of his being dangerously wounded?

SIR OLIVER. The devil he is!

SIR BENJAMIN. Run through the body—

CRABTREE. Shot in the breast—

SIR BENJAMIN. By one Mr. Surface—

CRABTREE. Ay, the younger—

SIR OLIVER. Hey, what the plague! You seem to differ
strangely in your accounts; however you agree that
Sir Peter is dangerously wounded.

SIR BENJAMIN. Oh, yes, we agree there.

CRABTREE. Yes, yes, I believe there can be no doubt of
that.

SIR OLIVER. Then, upon my word, for a person in that
situation he is the most imprudent man alive, for here
he comes, walking as if nothing at all was the matter.

---

[38] A physician.

(*Enter* SIR PETER TEAZLE.)

—Odd's heart, Sir Peter, you are come in good time,
I promise you, for we had just given you over.

SIR BENJAMIN. Egad, uncle, this is the most sudden recovery!

SIR OLIVER. Why, man, what do you out of bed with a
smallsword through your body and a bullet lodged in
your thorax?

SIR PETER. A smallsword and a bullet!

SIR OLIVER. *Ay!* These gentlemen would have killed you
without law or physic, and wanted to dub me a doctor
to make me an accomplice.

SIR PETER. Why, what is all this?

SIR BENJAMIN. We rejoice, Sir Peter, that the story of the
duel is not true, and are sincerely sorry for your other
misfortune.

SIR PETER (*aside*). So, so! All over the town already.

CRABTREE. Though, Sir Peter, you were certainly vastly to
blame to marry at all, at your years.

SIR PETER. Sir, what business is that of yours?

MRS. CANDOUR. Though, indeed, as Sir Peter made so good
a husband, he's very much to be pitied.

SIR PETER. Plague on your pity, ma'am! I desire none of it.

SIR BENJAMIN. However, Sir Peter, you must not mind the
laughing and jests you will meet with on this occasion.

SIR PETER. Sir, sir, I desire to be master in my own house.

CRABTREE. 'Tis no uncommon case, that's one comfort.

SIR PETER. I insist on being left to myself. Without ceremony, I insist on your leaving my house directly.

MRS. CANDOUR. Well, well, we are going; and depend on't,
we'll make the best report of you we can. (*Exit.*)

CRABTREE. And tell how hardly you've been treated. (*Exit.*)

SIR PETER. Leave my house!

SIR BENJAMIN. And how patiently you bear it. (*Exit.*)

SIR PETER. Fiends! Vipers! Furies! Oh, that their own
venom would choke them!

SIR OLIVER. They are very provoking indeed, Sir Peter.

(*Enter* ROWLEY.)

ROWLEY. I heard high words. What has ruffled you, Sir
Peter?

SIR PETER. Psha, what signifies asking? Do I ever pass a
day without my vexations?

SIR OLIVER. Well, I'm not inquisitive. I come only to tell you that I have seen both my nephews in the manner we proposed.

SIR PETER. A precious couple they are!

ROWLEY. Yes, and Sir Oliver is convinced that your judgment was right, Sir Peter.

SIR OLIVER. Yes, I find Joseph is indeed the man, after all.

ROWLEY. Ay, as Sir Peter says, he is a man of sentiment.

SIR OLIVER. And acts up to the sentiments he professes.

ROWLEY. It certainly is edification to hear him talk.

SIR OLIVER. Oh, he's a model for the young men of the age! But how's this, Sir Peter, you don't join us in your friend Joseph's praise, as I expected?

SIR PETER. Sir Oliver, we live in a damned wicked world, and the fewer we praise the better.

ROWLEY. What, do you say so, Sir Peter, who were never mistaken in your life?

SIR PETER. Psha! Plague on you both! I see by your sneering you have heard the whole affair. I shall go mad among you!

ROWLEY. Then, to fret you no longer, Sir Peter, we are indeed acquainted with it all. I met Lady Teazle coming from Mr. Surface's, so humbled that she deigned to request me to be her advocate with you.

SIR PETER. And does Sir Oliver know all too?

SIR OLIVER. Every circumstance.

SIR PETER. What? Of the closet and the screen, hey?

SIR OLIVER. Yes, yes, and the little French milliner. Oh, I have been vastly diverted with the story! Ha! ha! ha!

SIR PETER. 'Twas very pleasant.

SIR OLIVER. I never laughed more in my life, I assure you. Ha! ha! ha!

SIR PETER. Oh, vastly diverting, Ha! ha! ha!

ROWLEY. To be sure, Joseph with his sentiments! Ha! ha! ha!

SIR PETER. Yes, yes, his sentiments! Ha! ha! ha! A hypocritical villain!

SIR OLIVER. Ay, and that rogue Charles to pull Sir Peter out of the closet! Ha! ha! ha!

SIR PETER. Ha! ha! 'Twas devilish entertaining, to be sure!

SIR OLIVER. Ha! ha! ha! Egad, Sir Peter, I should like to have seen your face when the screen was thrown down! Ha! ha!

SIR PETER. Yes, yes, my face when the screen was thrown
down! Ha! ha! ha! Oh, I must never show my head
again!

SIR OLIVER. But come, come, it isn't fair to laugh at you
neither, my old friend, though, upon my soul, I can't
help it.

SIR PETER. Oh, pray don't restrain your mirth on my
account. It does not hurt me at all. I laugh at the
whole affair myself. Yes, yes, I think being a standing
jest for all one's acquaintance a very happy situation.
Oh, yes, and then of a morning to read the paragraphs about Mr. S——, Lady T——, and Sir P—— will
be so entertaining.

ROWLEY. Without affectation, Sir Peter, you may despise
the ridicule of fools. But I see Lady Teazle going
towards the next room. I am sure you must desire a
reconciliation as earnestly as she does.

SIR OLIVER. Perhaps my being here prevents her coming
to you. Well, I'll leave honest Rowley to mediate
between you; but he must bring you all presently to
Mr. Surface's, where I am now returning, if not to
reclaim a libertine, at least to expose hypocrisy.

SIR PETER. Ah, I'll be present at your discovering yourself
there with all my heart, though 'tis a vile unlucky
place for discoveries.

ROWLEY. We'll follow.

(*Exit* SIR OLIVER.)

SIR PETER. She is not coming here, you see, Rowley.

ROWLEY. No, but she has left the door of that room open,
you perceive. See, she is in tears.

SIR PETER. Certainly a little mortification appears very
becoming in a wife. Don't you think it will do her
good to let her pine a little?

ROWLEY. Oh, this is ungenerous in you!

SIR PETER. Well, I know not what to think. You remember
the letter I found of hers, evidently intended for
Charles?

ROWLEY. A mere forgery, Sir Peter, laid in your way on
purpose. This is one of the points which I intend
Snake shall give you conviction on.

SIR PETER. I wish I were once satisfied of that. She looks
this way. What a remarkably elegant turn of the head
she has! Rowley, I'll go to her.

ROWLEY. Certainly.

SIR PETER. Though, when it is known that we are reconciled, people will laugh at me ten times more.

ROWLEY. Let them laugh and retort their malice only by showing them you are happy in spite of it.

SIR PETER. I' faith, so I will! And, if I'm not mistaken, we may yet be the happiest couple in the country.

ROWLEY. Nay, Sir Peter, he who once lays aside suspicion—

SIR PETER. Hold, Master Rowley! If you have any regard for me, never let me hear you utter anything like a sentiment. I have had enough of them to serve me the rest of my life.

(*Exeunt.*)

[SCENE III.] *The library* [*in* JOSEPH SURFACE'*s house*]

(*Enter* JOSEPH SURFACE *and* LADY SNEERWELL.)

LADY SNEERWELL. Impossible! Will not Sir Peter immediately be reconciled to Charles and, of consequence, no longer oppose his union with Maria? The thought is distraction to me!

JOSEPH SURFACE. Can passion furnish a remedy?

LADY SNEERWELL. No, nor cunning neither. Oh, I was a fool, an idiot, to league with such a blunderer!

JOSEPH SURFACE. Sure, Lady Sneerwell, I am the greatest sufferer; yet you see I bear the accident with calmness.

LADY SNEERWELL. Because the disappointment doesn't reach your heart; your interest only attached you to Maria. Had you felt for her what I have for that ungrateful libertine, neither your temper nor hypocrisy could prevent your showing the sharpness of your vexation.

JOSEPH SURFACE. But why should your reproaches fall on me for this disappointment?

LADY SNEERWELL. Are you not the cause of it? What had you to do to bate in your pursuit of Maria to pervert Lady Teazle by the way? Had you not a sufficient field for your roguery in blinding Sir Peter and supplanting your brother? I hate such an avarice of crimes. 'Tis an unfair monopoly and never prospers.

JOSEPH SURFACE. Well, I admit I have been to blame. I

confess I deviated from the direct road of wrong, but I don't think we're so totally defeated neither.

LADY SNEERWELL. No?

JOSEPH SURFACE. You tell me you have made a trial of Snake since we met, and that you still believe him faithful to us?

LADY SNEERWELL. I do believe so.

JOSEPH SURFACE. And that he has undertaken, should it be necessary, to swear and prove that Charles is at this time contracted by vows and honor to your ladyship, which some of his former letters to you will serve to support?

LADY SNEERWELL. This, indeed, might have assisted.

JOSEPH SURFACE. Come, come; it is not too late yet. (*Knocking at the door*) But hark! This is probably my uncle, Sir Oliver. Retire to that room; we'll consult farther when he is gone.

LADY SNEERWELL. Well, but if he should find you out, too?

JOSEPH SURFACE. Oh, I have no fear of that. Sir Peter will hold his tongue for his own credit's sake. And you may depend on it I shall soon discover Sir Oliver's weak side.

LADY SNEERWELL. I have no diffidence[39] of your abilities; only be constant to one roguery at a time. (*Exit.*)

JOSEPH SURFACE. I will, I will!—So! 'Tis confounded hard, after such bad fortune, to be baited by one's confederate in evil. Well, at all events, my character is so much better than Charles's that I certainly—hey! what! this is not Sir Oliver but old Stanley again—! Plague on't that he should return to tease me just now! I shall have Sir Oliver come and find him here —and—

(*Enter* SIR OLIVER SURFACE.)

Gad's life, Mr. Stanley! why have you come back to plague me at this time? You must not stay now, upon my word.

SIR OLIVER. Sir, I hear your uncle Oliver is expected here and, though he has been so penurious to you, I'll try what he'll do for me.

---

[39] Doubt.

JOSEPH SURFACE. Sir, 'tis impossible for you to stay now; so I must beg—Come any other time and I promise you, you shall be assisted.

SIR OLIVER. No. Sir Oliver and I must be acquainted.

JOSEPH SURFACE. Zounds, sir! Then I insist on your quitting the room directly.

SIR OLIVER. Nay, sir—

JOSEPH SURFACE. Sir, I insist on 't!—Here William, show this gentleman out.—Since you compel me, sir, not one moment—this is such insolence! (*going to push him out*)

(*Enter* CHARLES SURFACE.)

CHARLES. Heyday! What's the matter now? What the devil? Have you got hold of my little broker here! Zounds, brother, don't hurt little Premium. What's the matter, my little fellow?

JOSEPH SURFACE. So, he has been with you too, has he?

CHARLES. To be sure, he has. Why, he's as honest a little— But sure, Joseph, you have not been borrowing money too, have you?

JOSEPH SURFACE. Borrowing? No! But, brother, you know we expect Sir Oliver here every—

CHARLES. Oh, Gad, that's true! Noll mustn't find the little broker here, to be sure!

JOSEPH SURFACE. Yet Mr. Stanley insists—

CHARLES. Stanley! Why, his name's Premium.

JOSEPH SURFACE. No, sir, Stanley.

CHARLES. No, no, Premium!

JOSEPH SURFACE. Well, no matter which, but—

CHARLES. Ay, ay, Stanley or Premium, 'tis the same thing, as you say; for I suppose he goes by half a hundred names besides A. B. at the coffee-houses.[40]

(*Knocking*)

JOSEPH SURFACE. 'Sdeath, here's Sir Oliver at the door! Now, I beg, Mr. Stanley—

CHARLES. Ay, ay, and I beg, Mr. Premium—

[40] Unscrupulous moneylenders would trade under several names, so that their victims, thinking they were borrowing from a new creditor to liquidate an old debt, would in fact be becoming more and more deeply entangled with the same person.

SIR OLIVER. Gentlemen—

JOSEPH SURFACE. Sir, by heaven, you shall go!

CHARLES. Ay, out with him, certainly!

SIR OLIVER. This violence—

JOSEPH SURFACE. Sir, 'tis your own fault.

CHARLES. Out with him, to be sure! (*both forcing Sir Oliver out*)

(*Enter* SIR PETER *and* LADY TEAZLE, MARIA, *and* ROWLEY.)

SIR PETER. My old friend, Sir Oliver—Hey! What in the name of wonder? Here are two dutiful nephews! Assault their uncle at a first visit!

LADY TEAZLE. Indeed, Sir Oliver, 'twas well we came in to rescue you.

ROWLEY. Truly it was, for I perceive, Sir Oliver, the character of old Stanley was no protection to you.

SIR OLIVER. Nor of Premium either. The necessities of the former could not extort a shilling from that benevolent gentleman; and now, egad, I stood a chance of faring worse than my ancestors and being knocked down without being bid for.

JOSEPH SURFACE. Charles!

CHARLES. Joseph!

JOSEPH SURFACE. 'Tis now complete!

CHARLES. Very!

SIR OLIVER. Sir Peter, my friend, and Rowley, too, look on that elder nephew of mine. You know what he has already received from my bounty; and you know also how gladly I would have regarded half my fortune as held in trust for him. Judge then my disappointment in discovering him to be destitute of truth, charity, and gratitude!

SIR PETER. Sir Oliver, I should be more surprised at this declaration if I had not myself found him to be selfish, treacherous, and hypocritical.

LADY TEAZLE. And if the gentleman pleads not guilty to these, pray let him call me to his character.

SIR PETER. Then, I believe, we need add no more. If he knows himself, he will consider it as the most perfect punishment that he is known to the world.

CHARLES (*aside*). If they talk this way to honesty, what will they say to me, by and by?

SIR OLIVER. As for that prodigal, his brother there—

CHARLES (*aside*). Ay, now comes my turn. The damned
family pictures will ruin me!

JOSEPH SURFACE. Sir Oliver—uncle!—will you honor me
with a hearing?

CHARLES (*aside*). Now, if Joseph would make one of his
long speeches, I might recollect myself a little.

SIR OLIVER (*To* JOSEPH). I suppose you would undertake
to justify yourself entirely?

JOSEPH SURFACE. I trust I could.

SIR OLIVER. Psha!—
(*To* CHARLES): Well, sir, and you could justify yourself,
too, I suppose?

CHARLES. Not that I know of, Sir Oliver.

SIR OLIVER. What? Little Premium has been let too much
into the secret, I suppose?

CHARLES. True, sir; but they were family secrets and should
not be mentioned again, you know.

ROWLEY. Come, Sir Oliver, I know you cannot speak of
Charles's follies with anger.

SIR OLIVER. Odd's heart, no more I can, nor with gravity
either. Sir Peter, do you know the rogue bargained
with me for all his ancestors, sold me judges and
generals by the foot, and maiden aunts as cheap as
broken china?

CHARLES. To be sure, Sir Oliver, I did make a little free
with the family canvas, that's the truth on 't. My
ancestors may certainly rise in judgment against me,
there's no denying it; but believe me sincere when I
tell you—and upon my soul I would not say so if
I was not—that if I do not appear mortified at the
exposure of my follies, it is because I feel at this
moment the warmest satisfaction in seeing you, my
liberal benefactor.

SIR OLIVER. Charles, I believe you. Give me your hand
again. The ill-looking little fellow over the settee has
made your peace.

CHARLES. Then, sir, my gratitude to the original is still
increased.

LADY TEAZLE (*pointing to* MARIA). Yet I believe, Sir Oliver,
here is one whom Charles is still more anxious to be
reconciled to.

SIR OLIVER. Oh, I have heard of his attachment there; and, with the young lady's pardon, if I construe right, that blush—

SIR PETER. Well, child, speak your sentiments!

MARIA. Sir, I have little to say, but that I shall rejoice to hear that he is happy. For me, whatever claim I had to his attention, I willingly resign to one who has a better title.

CHARLES. How, Maria!

SIR PETER. Heyday! What's the mystery now? While he appeared an incorrigible rake, you would give your hand to no one else; and now that he is likely to reform, I'll warrant you won't have him!

MARIA. His own heart and Lady Sneerwell know the cause.

CHARLES. Lady Sneerwell!

JOSEPH SURFACE. Brother, it is with great concern I am obliged to speak on this point, but my regard for justice compels me, and Lady Sneerwell's injuries can no longer be concealed. (*Goes to the door.*)

(*Enter* LADY SNEERWELL.)

SIR PETER. So! Another French milliner! Egad, he has one in every room in the house, I suppose!

LADY SNEERWELL. Ungrateful Charles! Well may you be surprised and feel for the indelicate situation your perfidy has forced me into.

CHARLES. Pray, uncle, is this another plot of yours? For, as I have life, I don't understand it.

JOSEPH SURFACE. I believe, sir, there is but the evidence of one person more necessary to make it extremely clear.

SIR PETER. And that person, I imagine, is Mr. Snake.— Rowley, you were perfectly right to bring him with us, and pray let him appear.

ROWLEY. Walk in, Mr. Snake.

(*Enter* SNAKE.)

—I thought his testimony might be wanted; however, it happens unluckily that he comes to confront Lady Sneerwell, not to support her.

LADY SNEERWELL (*aside*). A villain! Treacherous to me at last!—Speak, fellow, have you, too, conspired against me?

SNAKE. I beg your ladyship ten thousand pardons. You paid me extremely liberally for the lie in question, but I unfortunately have been offered double to speak the truth.

SIR PETER. Plot and counterplot, egad! I wish your ladyship joy of the success of your negotiations.

LADY SNEERWELL. The torments of shame and disappointment on you all!

LADY TEAZLE. Hold, Lady Sneerwell! Before you go, let me thank you for the trouble you and that gentleman have taken in writing letters to me from Charles and answering them yourself; and let me also request you to make my respects to the scandalous college, of which you are president, and inform them that Lady Teazle, licentiate, begs leave to return the diploma they granted her, as she leaves off practice and kills characters no longer.

LADY SNEERWELL. You too, madam! Provoking! Insolent! May your husband live these fifty years! (*Exit.*)

SIR PETER. Oons, what a fury!

LADY TEAZLE. A malicious creature, indeed!

SIR PETER. Hey! Not for her last wish?

LADY TEAZLE. Oh, no!

SIR OLIVER. Well, sir, and what have you to say now?

JOSEPH SURFACE. Sir, I am so confounded to find that Lady Sneerwell could be guilty of suborning Mr. Snake in this manner to impose on us all that I know not what to say. However, lest her revengeful spirit should prompt her to injure my brother, I had certainly better follow her directly. (*Exit.*)

SIR PETER. Moral to the last drop!

SIR OLIVER. Ay, and marry her, Joseph, if you can. Oil and vinegar! Egad, you'll do very well together.

ROWLEY. I believe we have no more occasion for Mr. Snake at present?

SNAKE. Before I go, I beg pardon once for all, for whatever uneasiness I have been the humble instrument of causing to the parties present.

SIR PETER. Well, well, you have made atonement by a good deed at last.

SNAKE. But I must request of the company that it shall never be known.

SIR PETER. Hey! What the plague! Are you ashamed of having done a right thing once in your life?

SNAKE. Ah, sir, consider. I live by the badness of my character. I have nothing but my infamy to depend on; and, if it were once known that I had been betrayed into an honest action, I should lose every friend I have in the world.

SIR OLIVER. Well, well, we'll not traduce you by saying anything in your praise, never fear.

(*Exit* SNAKE.)

SIR PETER. There's a precious rogue!

LADY TEAZLE. See, Sir Oliver, there needs no persuasion now to reconcile your nephew and Maria.

(CHARLES *and* MARIA *apart*)

SIR OLIVER. Ay, ay, that's as it should be; and, egad, we'll have the wedding tomorrow morning.

CHARLES. Thank you, dear uncle.

SIR PETER. What, you rogue! Don't you ask the girl's consent first?

CHARLES. Oh, I have done that a long time—above a minute ago—and she has looked *yes*.

MARIA. For shame, Charles!—I protest, Sir Peter, there has not been a word—

SIR OLIVER. Well then, the fewer the better. May your love for each other never know abatement!

SIR PETER. And may you live as happily together as Lady Teazle and I—intend to do!

CHARLES. Rowley, my old friend, I am sure you congratulate me; and I suspect that I owe you much.

SIR OLIVER. You do, indeed, Charles.

ROWLEY. If my efforts to serve you had not succeeded, you would have been in my debt for the attempt; but deserve to be happy and you overpay me!

SIR PETER. Ay, honest Rowley always said you would reform.

CHARLES. Why, as to reforming, Sir Peter, I'll make no promises, and that I take to be a proof that I intend to set about it.—But here shall be my monitor, my gentle guide. Ah, can I leave the virtuous path those eyes illumine?

Though thou, dear maid, shouldst waive thy beauty's sway,
Thou still must rule, because I will obey.
An humble fugitive from Folly view,
No sanctuary near but love and you.
(*To the audience*): You can, indeed, each anxious
    fear remove,
For even Scandal dies, if you approve!

EPILOGUE

By Mr. Colman
Spoken by Lady Teazle

I, who was late so volatile and gay,
Like a trade-wind must now blow all one way,
Bend all my cares, my studies, and my vows,
To one dull, rusty weathercock—my spouse!
So wills our virtuous bard—the motley Bayes
Of crying epilogues and laughing plays!
Old bachelors who marry smart young wives
Learn from our play to regulate your lives;
Each bring his dear to town, all faults upon her—
London will prove the very source of honor.
Plunged fairly in, like a cold bath it serves,
When principles relax, to brace the nerves.
Such is my case; and yet I must deplore
That the gay dream of dissipation's o'er,
And say, ye fair, was ever lively wife,
Born with a genius for the highest life,
Like me untimely blasted in her bloom,
Like me condemned to such a dismal doom?
Save money, when I just knew how to waste it!
Leave London, just as I began to taste it!
　　Must I then watch the early-crowing cock,
The melancholy ticking of a clock;
In a lone rustic hall forever pounded,
With dogs, cats, rats, and squalling brats surrounded?
With humble curate can I now retire,
(While good Sir Peter boozes with the squire)
And at backgammon mortify my soul,
That pants for loo or flutters at a vole?
Seven's the main! Dear sound!—that must expire,

Lost at hot cockles[41] round a Christmas fire.
The transient hour of fashion too soon spent,
Farewell the tranquil mind, farewell content![42]
Farewell the plumèd head, the cushioned *tête*,
That takes the cushion from its proper seat!
That spirit-stirring drum! Card drums, I mean,
Spadille, odd trick, pam, basto, king and queen!
And you, ye knockers that with brazen throat
The welcome visitors' approach denote,
Farewell! all quality of high renown,
Pride, pomp, and circumstance of glorious town!
Farewell! Your revels I partake no more,
And Lady Teazle's occupation's o'er!
All this I told our bard; he smiled and said 'twas clear,
I ought to play deep tragedy next year.
Meanwhile he drew wise morals from his play,
And in these solemn periods stalked away:—
"Blessed were the fair like you, her faults who stopped,
And closed her follies when the curtain dropped!
No more in vice or error to engage
Or play the fool at large on life's great stage."

---

[41] Backgammon and hot cockles were old-fashioned countrified games; she regrets giving up the fashionable games of loo (a vole was equivalent to a grand slam in bridge) and hazard ("Seven's the main").

[42] This and the following ten lines are a clever travesty of *Othello* III, iii, 349–58, in which the glories of fashionable life replace those of warlike ambition, and the card drum, a party, replaces the drum of war.

THE OCTOROON

OR,

LIFE IN LOUISIANA

⁓ *1859* ⁓

Dion Boucicault

INTRODUCTORY NOTE

DION BOUCICAULT (1820?–90), born in Dublin, was apprenticed to an engineer, but ran away in his teens to become an actor and soon started to write plays. His first success, a great one, was *London Assurance* (1841), a pale imitation of eighteenth-century comedy of manners. For the remaining fifty years of his life, he was a prominent figure in the theatrical world—as actor, author, director, and manager. He wrote, adapted, or translated at least 134 plays.

A skilled character actor, he took important roles in his own plays, along with his second wife, Agnes Robertson. He created Wahnotee when *The Octoroon* opened in New York in 1859, and she starred as Zoe. The Boucicaults played in England, Ireland, North America, and even Australia. They toured widely in America, and for three months in 1855 Boucicault managed a theater in New Orleans, where he doubtless picked up local color for *The Octoroon*. One of the earliest stage directors, Boucicault carefully supervised all aspects of the production of his plays. Actors dreaded his severity, but respected his competence.

Boucicault is best remembered for plays such as *The Colleen Bawn* (1860), *Arrah-na-Pogue* (1864), and *The Shaughraun* (1874), in which he drew on his Irish inheritance. (He retained a brogue all his life.) These highly romantic works were filled with authentic local color, though they made no attempt to deal with the serious problems of Ireland. Boucicault's Irish characters stand midway between the burlesque stage Irishmen of the eighteenth century and the full characterizations of Sean O'Casey.

A similar equivocation can be seen in Boucicault's presentation of slavery in America. While he makes us feel the horror of selling Zoe, he softens the presentation of slavery in general and represents the Peyton slaves as suspiciously devoted. The Southerners are all kindly, untainted by the vicious institution they uphold; and villainy is conveniently restricted to the Yankee overseer. Boucicault really gave away his lack of artistic conscience by providing an alternative ending: the tragic ending required for American audiences was replaced for the less racist London audience by a more comfortable resolution, in which Zoe lives to marry George.

BIBLIOGRAPHY

Major Works:

London Assurance, 1841 (comedy)
The Octoroon; or, Life in Louisiana, 1859 (melodrama)
The Colleen Bawn; or, The Brides of Garryowen, 1860 (melodrama)
Arrah-na-Pogue; or, The Wicklow Wedding, 1864 (melodrama)
The Shaughraun, 1874 (melodrama)

Works About:

Hogan, Robert. *Dion Boucicault*. New York: Twayne, 1969.

THE OCTOROON

Dramatis Personae

GEORGE PEYTON
SALEM SCUDDER
MR. SUNNYSIDE
JACOB M'CLOSKY
WAHNOTEE
CAPTAIN RATTS
COLONEL POINTDEXTER
JULES THIBODEAUX
JUDGE CAILLOU
LAFOUCHE
JACKSON
OLD PETE
PAUL (*a boy slave*)
SOLON

MRS. PEYTON
ZOE
DORA SUNNYSIDE
GRACE
MINNIE
DIDO

ACT I

[SCENE I.] *A view of the Plantation Terrebonne, in Louisiana.—A branch of the Mississippi is seen winding through the Estate.—A low built, but extensive Planter's Dwelling, surrounded with a veranda, and raised a few feet from the ground, occupies the left side.—A table and chairs, right center.*

(GRACE *discovered sitting at breakfast-table with* CHILDREN. *Enter* SOLON, *from house.*)

SOLON. Yah! you bomn'ble fry—git out—a gen'leman can't
    pass for you.
GRACE (*seizing a fly whisk*). Hee! Ha—git out!

(*Drives* CHILDREN *away: in escaping they tumble against and trip up* SOLON, *who falls with tray; the* CHILDREN *steal the bananas and rolls that fall about.*)

(*Enter* PETE; *he is lame; he carries a mop and pail.*)

PETE. Hey! laws a massey! why, clar out! drop dat
    banana! I'll murder this yer crowd.

(*He chases* CHILDREN *about; they leap over railing at back. Exit* SOLON.)

    Dem little niggers is a judgment upon dis generation.

(*Enter* GEORGE, *from house.*)

GEORGE. What's the matter, Pete?
PETE. It's dem black trash, Mas'r George; dis 'ere property
    wants claring; dem's getting too numerous round:
    when I gets time I'll kill some on 'em, sure!
GEORGE. They don't seem to be scared by the threat.

PETE. 'Top, you varmin! 'top till I get enough of you in one place!

GEORGE. Were they all born on this estate?

PETE. Guess they nebber was born—dem tings! what, dem? —get away! Born here—dem darkies? What, on Terrebonne? Don't b'lieve it, Mas'r George; dem black tings never was born at all; dey swarmed one mornin' on a sassafras tree in the swamp: I cotched 'em; dey ain't no 'count. Don't b'lieve dey'll turn out niggers when dey're growed; dey'll come out sunthin else.

GRACE. Yes, Mas'r George, dey was born here; and old Pete is fonder on 'em dan he is of his fiddle on a Sunday.

PETE. What? dem tings—dem?—get away (*Makes blow at the* CHILDREN.) Born here! dem darkies! What, on Terrebonne? Don't b'lieve it, Mas'r George,—no. One morning dey swarmed on a sassafras tree in de swamp, and I cotched 'em all in a sieve—dat's how dey come on top of dis yearth—git out, you,—ya, ya! (*Laughs.*)

(*Exit* GRACE. *Enter* MRS. PEYTON, *from house.*)

MRS. PEYTON. So, Pete, you are spoiling those children as usual!

PETE. Dat's right, missus! gib it to ole Pete! he's allers in for it. Git away dere! Ya! if dey ain't all lighted, like coons, on dat snake fence, just out of shot. Look dar! Ya! ya! Dem debils. Ya!

MRS. PEYTON. Pete, do you hear?

PETE. Git down dar! I'm arter you! (*Hobbles off.*)

MRS. PEYTON. You are out early this morning, George.

GEORGE. I was up before daylight. We got the horses saddled, and galloped down the shell road over the Piney Patch; then coasting the Bayou Lake, we crossed the long swamps, by Paul's Path, and so came home again.

MRS. PEYTON (*laughing*). You seem already familiar with the names of every spot on the estate.

(*Enter* PETE.—*Arranges breakfast, &c.*)

GEORGE. Just one month ago I quitted Paris. I left that siren city as I would have left a beloved woman.

MRS. PEYTON. No wonder! I dare say you left at least a dozen beloved women there, at the same time.

GEORGE. I feel that I departed amid universal and sincere regret. I left my loves and my creditors equally inconsolable.

MRS. PEYTON. George, you are incorrigible. Ah! You remind me so much of your uncle, the judge.

GEORGE. Bless his dear old handwriting, it's all I ever saw of him. For ten years his letters came every quarter-day, with a remittance and a word of advice in his formal cavalier style; and then a joke in the postscript, that upset the dignity of the foregoing. Aunt, when he died, two years ago, I read over those letters of his, and if I didn't cry like a baby—

MRS. PEYTON. No, George; say you wept like a man. And so you really kept those foolish letters?

GEORGE. Yes; I kept the letters, and squandered the money.

MRS. PEYTON (*embracing him*). Ah! why were you not my son—you are so like my dear husband.

(*Enter* SALEM SCUDDER.)

SCUDDER. Ain't he! Yes—when I saw him and Miss Zoe galloping through the green sugar crop, and doing ten dollars' worth of damage at every stride, says I, how like his old uncle he do make the dirt fly.

GEORGE. O, Aunt! what a bright, gay creature she is!

SCUDDER. What, Zoe! Guess that you didn't leave anything female in Europe that can lift an eyelash beside that gal. When she goes along, she just leaves a streak of love behind her. It's a good drink to see her come into the cotton fields—the niggers get fresh on the sight of her. If she ain't worth her weight in sunshine you may take one of my fingers off, and choose which you like.

MRS. PEYTON. She need not keep us waiting breakfast, though. Pete, tell Miss Zoe that we are waiting.

PETE. Yes, missus. Why, Minnie, why don't you run when you hear, you lazy crittur?

(MINNIE *runs off.*)

Dat's de laziest nigger on dis yere property. (*Sits down.*) Don't do nuffin.

MRS. PEYTON. My dear George, you are left in your uncle's will heir to this estate.

GEORGE. Subject to your life interest and an annuity to Zoe, is it not so?

MRS. PEYTON. I fear that the property is so involved that the strictest economy will scarcely recover it. My dear husband never kept any accounts, and we scarcely know in what condition the estate really is.

SCUDDER. Yes, we do, ma'am; it's in a darned bad condition. Ten years ago the judge took as overseer a bit of Connecticut hardware called M'Closky. The judge didn't understand accounts—the overseer did. For a year or two all went fine. The judge drew money like Bourbon whiskey from a barrel, and never turned off the tap. But out it flew, free for everybody or anybody to beg, borrow, or steal. So it went, till one day the judge found the tap wouldn't run. He looked in to see what stopped it, and pulled out a big mortgage. "Sign that," says the overseer; "it's only a formality." "All right," says the judge, and away went a thousand acres; so at the end of eight years, Jacob M'Closky, Esquire, finds himself proprietor of the richest half of Terrebonne—

GEORGE. But the other half is free.

SCUDDER. No, it ain't; because, just then, what does the judge do, but hire another overseer—a Yankee—a Yankee named Salem Scudder.

MRS. PEYTON. O, no, it was—

SCUDDER. Hold on, now! I'm going to straighten this account clear out. What was this here Scudder? Well, he lived in New York by sittin' with his heels up in front of French's Hotel, and inventin'—

GEORGE. Inventing what?

SCUDDER. Improvements—anything, from a stay-lace to a fire-engine. Well, he cut that for the photographing line. He and his apparatus arrived here, took the judge's likeness and his fancy, who made him overseer right off. Well, sir, what does this Scudder do but introduces his inventions and improvements on this estate. His new cotton gins broke down, the steam sugar-mills burst up, until he finished off with his folly what Mr. M'Closky with his knavery began.

MRS. PEYTON. O, Salem! how can you say so? Haven't you worked like a horse?

SCUDDER. No, ma'am, I worked like an ass, an honest one, and that's all. Now, Mr. George, between the two overseers, you and that good old lady have come to the ground; that is the state of things, just as near as I can fix it.

(ZOE *sings without.*)

GEORGE. 'Tis Zoe.

SCUDDER. O, I have not spoiled that anyhow. I can't introduce any darned improvement there. Ain't that a cure for old age; it kinder lifts the heart up, don't it?

MRS. PEYTON. Poor child! what will become of her when I am gone? If you haven't spoiled her, I fear I have. She has had the education of a lady.

GEORGE. I have remarked that she is treated by the neighbors with a kind of familiar condescension that annoyed me.

SCUDDER. Don't you know that she is the natural daughter of the judge, your uncle, and that old lady thar just adored anything her husband cared for; and this girl, that another woman would a hated, she loves as if she'd been her own child.

GEORGE. Aunt, I am prouder and happier to be your nephew and heir to the ruins of Terrebonne, than I would have been to have had half Louisiana without you.

(*Enter* ZOE, *from house.*)

ZOE. Am I late? Ah! Mr. Scudder, good morning.

SCUDDER. Thank'ye. I'm from fair to middlin', like a bamboo cane, much the same all the year round.

ZOE. No; like a sugar cane; so dry outside, one would never think there was so much sweetness within.

SCUDDER. Look here; I can't stand that gal! if I stop here, I shall hug her right off. (*Sees* PETE, *who has set his pail down up stage, and goes to sleep on it.*) If that old nigger ain't asleep, I'm blamed. Hillo! (*Kicks pail from under* PETE, *and lets him down. Exit* [SCUDDER].)

PETE. Hi! Debbel's in de pail! Whar's breakfass?

(*Enter* SOLON *and* DIDO *with coffee-pot, dishes, &c.*)

DIDO. Bless'ee, Missy Zoe, here it be. Dere's a dish of penpans—jess taste, Mas'r George—and here's fried bananas; smell 'em, do, sa glosh.

PETE. Hole yer tongue, Dido. Whar's de coffee? (*Pours out.*) If it don't stain de cup, your wicked ole life's in danger, sure! dat right! black as nigger; clar as ice.

You may drink dat, Mas'r George. (*Looks off.*) Yah! here's Mas'r Sunnyside, and Missy Dora, jist drov up. Some of you niggers run and hole de hosses; and take dis, Dido. (*Gives her coffee-pot to hold, and hobbles off, followed by* SOLON *and* DIDO.)

(*Enter* SUNNYSIDE *and* DORA.)

SUNNYSIDE. Good day, ma'am. (*Shakes hands with* GEORGE.) I see we are just in time for breakfast. (*Sits.*)

DORA. O, none for me; I never eat. (*Sits.*)

GEORGE (*aside*). They do not notice Zoe.—(*aloud*) You don't see Zoe, Mr. Sunnyside.

SUNNYSIDE. Ah! Zoe, girl; are you there?

DORA. Take my shawl, Zoe. (ZOE *helps her.*) What a good creature she is.

SUNNYSIDE. I dare say, now, that in Europe you have never met any lady more beautiful in person, or more polished in manners, than that girl.

GEORGE. You are right, sir; though I shrank from expressing that opinion in her presence, so bluntly.

SUNNYSIDE. Why so?

GEORGE. It may be considered offensive.

SUNNYSIDE (*astonished*). What? I say, Zoe, do you hear that?

DORA. Mr. Peyton is joking.

MRS. PEYTON. My nephew is not acquainted with our customs in Louisiana, but he will soon understand.

GEORGE. Never, Aunt! I shall never understand how to wound the feelings of any lady; and, if that is the custom here, I shall never acquire it.

DORA. Zoes, my dear, what does he mean?

ZOE. I don't know.

GEORGE. Excuse me, I'll light a cigar. (*Goes up.*)

DORA (*aside to* ZOE). Isn't he sweet! O, dear Zoe, is he in love with anybody?

ZOE. How can I tell?

DORA. Ask him, I want to know; don't say I told you to inquire, but find out. Minnie, fan me, it is so nice— and his clothes are French, ain't they?

ZOE. I think so; shall I ask him that too?

DORA. No, dear. I wish he would make love to me. When he speaks to one he does it so easy, so gentle; it isn't bar-room style; love lined with drinks, sighs tinged with tobacco—and they say all the women in Paris were in love with him, which I feel *I* shall be: stop fanning me; what nice boots he wears.

SUNNYSIDE (*To* MRS. PEYTON). Yes, ma'am, I hold the mortgage over Terrebonne; mine's a ninth, and pretty near covers all the property, except the slaves. I believe Mr. M'Closky has a bill of sale on them. O, here he is.

(*Enter* M'CLOSKY.)

SUNNYSIDE. Good morning, Mr. M'Closky.

M'CLOSKY. Good morning, Mr. Sunnyside; Miss Dora, your servant.

DORA. Fan me, Minnie.—(*aside*) I don't like that man.

M'CLOSKY (*aside*). Insolent as usual.—(*aloud*) You begged me to call this morning. I hope I'm not intruding.

MRS. PEYTON. My nephew, Mr. Peyton.

M'CLOSKY. O, how d'ye do, sir? (*Offers hand,* GEORGE *bows coldly. Aside.*) A puppy, if he brings any of his European airs here we'll fix him.—(*aloud.*) Zoe, tell Pete to give my mare a feed, will ye?

GEORGE (*angrily*). Sir.

M'CLOSKY. Hillo! Did I tread on ye?

MRS. PEYTON. What is the matter with George?

ZOE (*Takes fan from* MINNIE). Go, Minnie, tell Pete; run!

(*Exit* MINNIE.)

MRS. PEYTON. Grace, attend to Mr. M'Closky.

M'CLOSKY. A julep, gal, that's my breakfast, and a bit of cheese.

GEORGE (*aside to* MRS. PEYTON). How can you ask that vulgar ruffian to your table?

MRS. PEYTON. Hospitality in Europe is a courtesy; here, it is an obligation. We tender food to a stranger, not because he is a gentleman, but because he is hungry.

GEORGE. Aunt, I will take my rifle down to the Atchafalaya. Paul has promised me a bear and a deer or two. I see my little Nimrod yonder, with his Indian companion. Excuse me, ladies. Ho! Paul! (*Enters house.*)

PAUL (*outside*). I'ss, Mas'r George.

(*Enter* PAUL, *with* INDIAN.)

SUNNYSIDE. It's a shame to allow that young cub to run over the swamps and woods, hunting and fishing his life away instead of hoeing cane.

MRS. PEYTON. The child was a favorite of the judge, who encouraged his gambols. I couldn't bear to see him put to work.

GEORGE (*returning with rifle*). Come, Paul, are you ready?

PAUL. I'ss, Mas'r George. O, golly! ain't that a pooty gun.

M'CLOSKY. See here, you imps; if I catch you, and your red skin yonder, gunning in my swamps, I'll give you rats,[1] mind; them vagabonds, when the game's about, shoot my pigs.

(*Exit* GEORGE *into house.*)

PAUL. You gib me rattan, Mas'r Clostry, but I guess you take a berry long stick to Wahnotee; ugh, he make bacon of you.

M'CLOSKY. Make bacon of me, you young whelp. Do you mean that I'm a pig? Hold on a bit. (*Seizes whip, and holds* PAUL.)

ZOE. O, sir! don't, pray, don't.

M'CLOSKY (*slowly lowering his whip*). Darn you, red skin, I'll pay you off some day, both of ye. (*Returns to table and drinks.*)

SUNNYSIDE. That Indian is a nuisance. Why don't he return to his nation out West.

M'CLOSKY. He's too fond of thieving and whiskey.

ZOE. No; Wahnotee is a gentle, honest creature, and remains here because he loves that boy with the tenderness of a woman. When Paul was taken down with the swamp fever the Indian sat outside the hut, and neither ate, slept, or spoke for five days, till the child could recognize and call him to his bedside. He who can love so well is honest—don't speak ill of poor Wahnotee.

MRS. PEYTON. Wahnotee, will you go back to your people?

WAHNOTEE. Sleugh.

PAUL. He don't understand; he speaks a mash-up of Indian and Mexican. Wahnotee, Patira na sepau assa wigiran?

WAHNOTEE. Weal, Omenee.

PAUL. Says he'll go if I'll go with him. He calls me Omenee, the Pigeon, and Miss Zoe is Ninemoosha, the Sweetheart.

WAHNOTEE (*pointing to* ZOE). Ninemoosha.

[1] Make trouble for you.

ZOE. No, Wahnotee, we can't spare Paul.

PAUL. If Omenee remain, Wahnotee will die in Terrebonne.

(*During the dialogue* WAHNOTEE *has taken* GEORGE's *gun.*)

(*Enter* GEORGE.)

GEORGE. Now I'm ready.

(GEORGE *tries to regain his gun;* WAHNOTEE *refuses to give it up;* PAUL *quietly takes it from him and remonstrates with him.*)

DORA. Zoe, he's going; I want him to stay and make love to me, that's what I came for to-day.

MRS. PEYTON. George, I can't spare Paul for an hour or two; he must run over to the landing; the steamer from New Orleans passed up the river last night, and if there's a mail they have thrown it ashore.

SUNNYSIDE. I saw the mail-bags lying in the shed this morning.

MRS. PEYTON. I expect an important letter from Liverpool; away with you, Paul; bring the mail-bags here.

PAUL. I'm 'most afraid to take Wahnotee to the shed, there's rum there.

WAHNOTEE. Rum!

PAUL. Come, then, but if I catch you drinkin', O, laws a mussey, you'll get snakes! I'll gib it you! now mind. (*Exit with* INDIAN.)

GEORGE. Come, Miss Dora, let me offer you my arm.

DORA. Mr. George, I am afraid, if all we hear is true, you have led a dreadful life in Europe.

GEORGE. That's a challenge to begin a description of my feminine adventures.

DORA. You have been in love, then?

GEORGE. Two hundred and forty-nine times! Let me relate you the worst cases.

DORA. No! no!

GEORGE. I'll put the naughty parts in French.

DORA. I won't hear a word! O, you horrible man! Go on.

(*Exit* GEORGE *and* DORA *to house.*)

M'CLOSKY. Now, ma'am, I'd like a little business, if agreeable. I bring you news: your banker, old Lafouche, of New Orleans, is dead; the executors are winding up his affairs, and have foreclosed on all overdue mortgages, so Terrebonne is for sale. Here's the *Picayune* (*producing paper*) with the advertisement.

ZOE. Terrebonne for sale!

MRS. PEYTON. Terrebonne for sale, and you, sir, will doubtless become its purchaser.

M'CLOSKY. Well, ma'am, I spose there's no law agin my bidding for it. The more bidders, the better for you. You'll take care, I guess, it don't go too cheap.

MRS. PEYTON. O, sir, I don't value the place for its price, but for the many happy days I've spent here: that landscape, flat and uninteresting though it may be, is full of charm for me; those poor people, born around me, growing up about my heart, have bounded my view of life; and now to lose that homely scene, lose their black, ungainly faces: O, sir, perhaps you should be as old as I am, to feel as I do, when my past life is torn away from me.

M'CLOSKY. I'd be darned glad if somebody would tear my past life away from *me*. Sorry I can't help you, but the fact is, you're in such an all-fired mess that you couldn't be pulled out without a derrick.

MRS. PEYTON. Yes, there is a hope left yet, and I cling to it. The house of Mason Brothers, of Liverpool, failed some twenty years ago in my husband's debt.

M'CLOSKY. They owed him over fifty thousand dollars.

MRS. PEYTON. I cannot find the entry in my husband's accounts; but you, Mr. M'Closky, can doubtless detect it. Zoe, bring here the judge's old desk; it is in the library.

(*Exit* ZOE *to house.*)

M'CLOSKY. You don't expect to recover any of this old debt, do you?

MRS. PEYTON. Yes; the firm has recovered itself, and I received a notice two months ago that some settlement might be anticipated.

SUNNYSIDE. Why, with principal and interest this debt has been more than doubled in twenty years.

MRS. PEYTON. But it may be years yet before it will be paid off, if ever.

SUNNYSIDE. If there's a chance of it, there's not a planter round here who wouldn't lend you the whole cash, to keep your name and blood amongst us. Come, cheer up, old friend.

MRS. PEYTON. Ah! Sunnyside, how good you are; so like my poor Peyton.

(*Exit* MRS. PEYTON *and* SUNNYSIDE *to house.*)

M'CLOSKY. Curse their old families—they cut me—a bilious, conceited, thin lot of dried up aristocracy. I hate 'em. Just because my grandfather wasn't some broken-down Virginia transplant, or a stingy old Creole, I ain't fit to sit down with the same meat with them. It makes my blood so hot I feel my heart hiss. I'll sweep these Peytons from this section of the country. Their presence keeps alive the reproach against me that I ruined them; yet, if this money should come. Bah! There's no chance of it. Then, if they go, they'll take Zoe—she'll follow them. Darn that girl; she makes me quiver when I think of her; she's took me for all I'm worth.

(*Enter* ZOE *from house, with the desk.*)

O, here, do you know what the annuity the old judge left you is worth today? Not a picayune.

ZOE. It's surely worth the love that dictated it; here are the papers and accounts. (*putting it on the table*)

M'CLOSKY. Stop, Zoe; come here! How would you like to rule the house of the richest planter on Atchapalaga—eh? or say the word, and I'll buy this old barrack, and you shall be mistress of Terrebonne.

ZOE. O, sir, do not speak so to me!

M'CLOSKY. Why not! Look here, these Peytons are bust; cut 'em; I am rich, jine me; I'll set you up grand, and we'll give these first families here our dust, until you'll see their white skins shrivel up with hate and rage; what do'ye say?

ZOE. Let me pass! O, pray, let me go!

M'CLOSKY. What, you won't, won't ye? If young George Peyton was to make the same offer, you'd jump at it, pretty darned quick, I guess. Come, Zoe, don't be a fool; I'd marry you if I could, but you know I can't;[2] so just say what you want. Here, then, I'll put back these Peytons in Terrebonne, and they shall know you

2 Blacks and whites could not legally marry in the southern states.

done it; yes, they'll have you to thank for saving them from ruin.

ZOE. Do you think they would live here on such terms?

M'CLOSKY. Why not? We'll hire out our slaves, and live on their wages.

ZOE. But I'm not a slave.

M'CLOSKY. No; if you were I'd buy you, if you cost all I'm worth.

ZOE. Let me pass!

M'CLOSKY. Stop.

(*Enter* SCUDDER.)

SCUDDER. Let her pass.

M'CLOSKY. Eh?

SCUDDER. Let her pass! (*Takes out his knife.*)

(*Exit* ZOE *to house.*)

M'CLOSKY. Is that you, Mr. Overseer? (*Examines paper.*)

SCUDDER. Yes, I'm here, somewhere, interferin'.

M'CLOSKY (*sitting*). A pretty mess you've got this estate in—

SCUDDER. Yes—me and Co.—we done it; but, as you were senior partner in the concern, I reckon you got the big lick.

M'CLOSKY. What d'ye mean.

SCUDDER. Let me proceed by illustration. (*Sits.*) Look thar! (*Points with knife offstage.*) D'ye see that tree?—It's called a live oak, and is a native here; beside it grows a creeper; year after year that creeper twines its long arms round and round the tree—sucking the earth dry all about its roots—living on its life—over-running its branches, until at last the live oak withers and dies out. Do you know what the niggers round here call that sight? they call it the Yankee hugging the Creole.

M'CLOSKY. Mr. Scudder, I've listened to a great many of your insinuations, and now I'd like to come to an understanding what they mean. If you want a quarrel—

SCUDDER. No, I'm the skurriest crittur at a fight you ever see; my legs have been too well brought up to stand and see my body abused; I take good care of myself, I can tell you.

M'CLOSKY. Because I heard that you had traduced my
　　character.

SCUDDER. Traduced! Whoever said so lied. I always said
　　you were the darndest thief that ever escaped a white
　　jail to misrepresent the North to the South.

M'CLOSKY (*raises hand to back of his neck*). What!

SCUDDER. Take your hand down—take it down.

　　(M'CLOSKY *lowers his hand.*)

　　Whenever I gets into company like yours, I *always*
　　start with the advantage on my side.

M'CLOSKY. What d'ye mean?

SCUDDER. I mean that before you could draw that bowie-
　　knife, you wear down your back, I'd cut you into
　　shingles. Keep quiet, and let's talk sense. You wanted
　　to come to an understanding, and I'm coming thar as
　　quick as I can. Now, Jacob M'Closky, you despise
　　me because you think I'm a fool; I despise you be-
　　cause I know you to be a knave. Between us we've
　　ruined these Peytons; you fired the judge, and I
　　finished off the widow. Now, I feel bad about my
　　share in the business. I'd give half the balance of my
　　life to wipe out my part of the work. Many a night
　　I've laid awake and thought how to pull them through,
　　till I've cried like a child over the sum I couldn't do;
　　and you know how darned hard 'tis to make a
　　Yankee cry.

M'CLOSKY. Well, what's that to me?

SCUDDER. Hold on, Jacob, I'm coming to that—I tell ye,
　　I'm such a fool—I can't bear the feeling, it keeps at
　　me like a skin complaint, and if this family is sold
　　up—

M'CLOSKY. What then?

SCUDDER (*rising*). I'd cut my throat—or yours—yours I'd
　　prefer.

M'CLOSKY. Would you now? why don't you do it?

SCUDDER. 'Cos I's skeered to try! I never killed a man in
　　my life—and civilization is so strong in me I guess I
　　couldn't do it—I'd like to, though!

M'CLOSKY. And all for the sake of that old woman and
　　that young puppy—eh? No other cause to hate—to
　　envy me—to be jealous of me—eh?

SCUDDER. Jealous! what for?

M'CLOSKY. Ask the color in your face: d'ye think I can't

read you, like a book? With your New England
hypocrisy, you would persuade yourself it was this
family alone you cared for: it ain't—you know it
ain't—'tis the "Octoroon"; and you love her as I do;
and you hate me because I'm your rival—that's where
the tears come from, Salem Scudder, if you ever shed
any—that's where the shoe pinches.

SCUDDER. Wal, I do like the gal; she's a—

M'CLOSKY. She's in love with young Peyton; it made me
curse, whar it made you cry, as it does now; I see
the tears on your cheeks now.

SCUDDER. Look at 'em, Jacob, for they are honest water
from the well of truth. I ain't ashamed of it—I do
love the gal; but I ain't jealous of you, because I
believe the only sincere feeling about you is your love
for Zoe, and it does your heart good to have her
image thar; but I believe you put it thar to spile. By
fair means I don't think you can get her, and don't
you try foul with her, 'cause if you do, Jacob, civilization be darned. I'm on you like a painter,[3] and when
I'm drawed out I'm pizin. (*Exit* SCUDDER *to house.*)

M'CLOSKY. Fair or foul, I'll have her—take that home with
you! (*Opens desk.*) What's here—judgments? yes,
plenty of 'em; bill of costs; account with Citizens'
Bank—what's this? "Judgment, 40,000, 'Thibodeaux
against Peyton,' "—surely, that is the judgment under
which this estate is now advertised for sale—(*Takes
up paper and examines it.*): yes, "Thibodeaux against
Peyton, 1838." Hold on! whew! this is worth taking
to—in this desk the judge used to keep one paper I
want—this should be it. (*Reads.*) "The free papers of
my daughter, Zoe, registered February 4th, 1841."
Why, judge, wasn't you lawyer enough to know that
while a judgment stood against you it was a lien on
your slaves? Zoe is your child by a quadroon slave,
and you didn't free her; blood! if this is so, she's mine!
this old Liverpool debt—that may cross me—if it only
arrive too late—if it don't come by this mail—Hold
on! this letter the old lady expects—that's it; let me
only head off that letter, and Terrebonne will be sold
before they can recover it. That boy and the Indian
have gone down to the landing for the post-bags;

---

[3] Mountain lion (Western dialect).

they'll idle on the way as usual; my mare will take me across the swamp, and before they can reach the shed, I'll have purified them bags—ne'er a letter shall show this mail. Ha, ha!—(*Calls.*) Pete, you old turkey-buzzard, saddle my mare. Then, if I sink every dollar I'm worth in her purchase, I'll own that Octoroon. (*Stands with his hand extended towards the house and tableau.*)

ACT II

THE WHARF—*goods, boxes and bales scattered about— a camera on stand.*

(SCUDDER, DORA, GEORGE and PAUL *discovered;* DORA *being photographed by* SCUDDER, *who is arranging photographic apparatus,* GEORGE and PAUL *looking on at back.*)

SCUDDER. Just turn your face a leetle this way—fix your—let's see—look here.

DORA. So?

SCUDDER. That's right. (*Puts his hand under the darkening apron.*) It's such a long time since I did this sort of thing, and this old machine has got so dirty and stiff, I'm afraid it won't operate. That's about right. Now don't stir.

PAUL. Ugh! she look as though she war gwine to have a tooth drawed.

SCUDDER. I've got four plates ready, in case we miss the first shot. One of them is prepared with a self-developing liquid that I've invented. I hope it will turn out better than most of my notions. Now fix yourself. Are you ready?

DORA. Ready!

SCUDDER. Fire!—one, two, three. (SCUDDER *takes out watch.*)

PAUL. Now it's cooking, laws mussey, I feel it all inside, as if it was at a lottery.

SCUDDER. So! (*Throws down apron.*) That's enough. (*Withdraws slide, turns and sees* PAUL.) What! what are you doing there, you young varmint! Ain't you took them bags to the house yet?

PAUL. Now, it ain't no use trying to get mad, Mas'r

Scudder. I'm gwine! I only come back to find Wahnotee; whar is dat ign'ant Ingiun?

SCUDDER. You'll find him scenting round the rum store, hitched up by the nose. (*Exit into room.*)

PAUL (*calling at door*). Say, Mas'r Scudder, take me in dat telescope?

SCUDDER (*inside room*). Get out, you cub! clar out!

PAUL. You got four of dem dishes ready. Gosh, wouldn't I like to hab myself took! What's de charge, Mas'r Scudder? (*Runs off.*)

(*Enter* SCUDDER, *from room.*)

SCUDDER. Job had none of them critters on his plantation, else he'd never ha' stood through so many chapters. Well, that has come out clear, ain't it? (*Shows plate.*)

DORA. O, beautiful! Look, Mr. Peyton.

GEORGE (*looking*). Yes, very fine!

SCUDDER. The apparatus can't mistake. When I travelled round with this machine, the homely folks used to sing out, "Hillo, mister, this ain't like me!" "Ma'am," says I, "the apparatus can't mistake." "But, mister, that ain't my nose." "Ma'am, your nose drawed it. The machine can't err—you may mistake your phiz but the apparatus don't." "But, sir, it ain't agreeable." "No, ma'am, the truth seldom is."

(*Enter* PETE, *puffing.*)

PETE. Mas'r Scudder! Mas'r Scudder!

SCUDDER. Hillo! what are you blowing about like a steamboat with one wheel for?

PETE. *You* blow, Mas'r Scudder, when I tole you: dere's a man from Noo Aleens just arriv' at de house, and he's stuck up two papers on de gates: "For sale—dis yer property," and a heap of oder tings—and he seen missus, and arter he shown some papers she burst out crying—I yelled; den de corious of little niggers dey set up, den de hull plantation children—de live stock reared up and created a purpiration of lamentation as did de ole heart good to har.

DORA. What's the matter?

SCUDDER. He's come.

PETE. Dass it—I saw'm!

SCUDDER. The sheriff from New Orleans has taken possession—Terrebonne is in the hands of the law.

(*Enter* ZOE.)

ZOE. O, Mr. Scudder! Dora! Mr. Peyton! come home—
there are strangers in the house.

DORA. Stay, Mr. Peyton: Zoe, a word! (*Leads her forward
—aside.*) Zoe, the more I see of George Peyton the
better I like him; but he is too modest—that is a very
impertinent virtue in a man.

ZOE. I'm no judge, dear.

DORA. Of course not, you little fool; no one ever made
love to you, and you can't understand; I mean, that
George knows I am an heiress; my fortune would
release this estate from debt.

ZOE. O, I see!

DORA. If he would only propose to marry me I would
accept him, but he don't know that, and will go on
fooling, in his slow European way, until it is too late.

ZOE. What's to be done?

DORA. You tell him.

ZOE. What? that he isn't to go on fooling in his slow—

DORA. No, you goose! twit him on his silence and abstraction—I'm sure it's plain enough, for he has not spoken
two words to me all the day; then joke round the
subject, and at last speak out.

SCUDDER. Pete, as you came here, did you pass Paul and
the Indian with the letter-bags?

PETE. No, sar; but dem vagabonds neber take de 'specable
straight road, dey goes by de swamp. (*Exit up path.*)

SCUDDER. Come, sir!

DORA (*To* ZOE). Now's your time—(*aloud*) Mr. Scudder,
take us with you—Mr. Peyton is so slow, there's no
getting him on.

(*Exit* DORA *and* SCUDDER.)

ZOE. They are gone!—(*glancing at* GEORGE) Poor fellow,
he has lost all.

GEORGE. Poor child! how sad she looks now she has no
resource.

ZOE. How shall I ask him to stay?

GEORGE. Zoe, will you remain here? I wish to speak to you.

ZOE (*aside*). Well, that saves trouble.

GEORGE. By our ruin, you lose all.

ZOE. O, I'm nothing; think of yourself.

GEORGE. I can think of nothing but the image that remains

face to face with me; so beautiful, so simple, so confiding, that I dare not express the feelings that have grown up so rapidly in my heart.

ZOE (*aside*). He means Dora.

GEORGE. If I dared to speak!

ZOE. That's just what you must do, and do it at once, or it will be too late.

GEORGE. Has my love been divined?

ZOE. It has been more than suspected.

GEORGE. Zoe, listen ot me, then. I shall see this estate pass from me without a sigh, for it possesses no charm for me; the wealth I covet is the love of those around me—eyes that are rich in fond looks, lips that breathe endearing words; the only estate I value is the heart of one true woman, and the slaves I'd have are her thoughts.

ZOE. George, George, your words take away my breath!

GEORGE. The world, Zoe, the free struggle of minds and hands, is before me; the education bestowed on me by my dear uncle is a noble heritage which no sheriff can seize; with that I can build up a fortune, spread a roof over the heads I love, and place before them the food I have earned; I will work—

ZOE. Work! I thought none but colored people worked.

GEORGE. Work, Zoe, is the salt that gives savor to life.

ZOE. Dora said you were slow: if she could hear you now—

GEORGE. Zoe, you are young; your mirror must have told you that you are beautiful. Is your heart free?

ZOE. Free? of course it is!

GEORGE. We have known each other but a few days, but to me those days have been worth all the rest of my life. Zoe, you have suspected the feeling that now commands an utterance—you have seen that I love you.

ZOE. Me! You love *me*?

GEORGE. As my wife,—the sharer of my hopes, my ambitions, and my sorrows: under the shelter of your love I could watch the storms of fortune pass unheeded by.

ZOE. *My* love! *My* love? George, you know not what you say. *I* the sharer of your sorrows—your wife. Do you know what I am?

GEORGE. Your birth—I know it. Has not my dear aunt forgotten it—she who had the most right to remember it? You are illegitimate, but love knows no prejudice.

ZOE (*aside*). Alas! he does not know, he does not know! and will despise me, spurn me, loathe me, when he learns who, what, he has so loved.—(*aloud.*) George, O, forgive me! Yes, I love you—I did not know it until your words showed me what has been in my heart; each of them awoke a new sense, and now I know how unhappy—how very unhappy I am.

GEORGE. Zoe, what have I said to wound you?

ZOE. Nothing; but you must learn what I thought you already knew. George, you cannot marry me; the laws forbid it!

GEORGE. Forbid it?

ZOE. There is a gulf between us, as wide as your love, as deep as my despair; but, O, tell me, say you will pity me! that you will not throw me from you like a poisoned thing!

GEORGE. Zoe, explain yourself—your language fills me with shapeless fears.

ZOE. And what shall I say? I—my mother was—no, no,—not her! Why should I refer the blame to her? George, do you see that hand you hold? look at these fingers; do you see the nails are of a bluish tinge?

GEORGE. Yes, near the quick there is a faint blue mark.

ZOE. Look in my eyes; is not the same color in the white?

GEORGE. It is their beauty.

ZOE. Could you see the roots of my hair you would see the same dark, fatal mark. Do you know what that is?

GEORGE. No.

ZOE. That is the ineffaceable curse of Cain. Of the blood that feeds my heart, one drop in eight is black—bright red as the rest may be, that one drop poisons all the flood; those seven bright drops give me love like yours—hope like yours—ambition like yours—life hung with passions like dew-drops on the morning flowers; but the one black drop gives me despair, for I'm an unclean thing—forbidden by the laws—I'm an Octoroon!

GEORGE. Zoe, I love you none the less; this knowledge brings no revolt to my heart, and I can overcome the obstacle.

ZOE. But *I* cannot.

GEORGE. We can leave this country, and go far away where none can know.

ZOE. And our mother, she who from infancy treated me

with such fondness, she who, as you said, had most reason to spurn me, can she forget what I am? Will she gladly see you wedded to the child of her husband's slave? No! she would revolt from it, as all but you would; and if I consented to hear the cries of my heart, if I did not crush out my infant love, what would she say to the poor girl on whom she had bestowed so much? No, no!

GEORGE. Zoe, must we immolate our lives on her prejudice?

ZOE. Yes, for I'd rather be black than ungrateful! Ah, George, our race has at least one virtue—it knows how to suffer!

GEORGE. Each word you utter makes my love sink deeper into my heart.

ZOE. And I remained here to induce you to offer that heart to Dora!

GEORGE. If you bid me do so I will obey you—

ZOE. No, no! if you cannot be mine, O, let me not blush when I think of you.

GEORGE. Dearest Zoe!

(*Exit* GEORGE *and* ZOE. *As they exit,* M'CLOSKY *rises from behind rock and looks after them.*)

M'CLOSKY. She loves him! I felt it—and how she can love! (*Advances.*) That one black drop of blood burns in her veins and lights up her heart like a foggy sun. O, how I lapped up her words, like a thirsty bloodhound! I'll have her, if it costs me my life. Yonder the boy still lurks with those mail-bags; the devil still keeps him here to tempt me, darn his yellow skin. I arrived just too late, he had grabbed the prize as I came up. Hillo! he's coming this way, fighting with his Injiun. (*Conceals himself.*)

(*Enter* PAUL, *wrestling with* WAHNOTEE.)

PAUL. It ain't no use now; you got to gib it up!

WAHNOTEE. Ugh!

PAUL. It won't do! You got dat bottle of rum hid under your blanket—gib it up now, you—. Yar! (*Wrenches it from him.*) You nasty, lying Injiun! It's no use you putting on airs; I ain't gwine to sit up wid you all night and you drunk. Hillo! war's de crowd gone? And dar's de 'paratus—O, gosh, if I could take a likeness ob dis child! Uh—uh, let's have a peep. (*Looks

through camera.) O, golly! yar, you Wahnotee! you
stan' dar, I see you. Ta demine usti. (*Looks at*
WAHNOTEE *through the camera;* WAHNOTEE *springs
back with an expression of alarm.*)

WAHNOTEE. No tue Wahnotee.

PAUL. Ha, ha! he tinks it's a gun. You ign'ant Injiun, it
can't hurt you! Stop, here's dem dishes—plates—
dat's what he call 'em, all fix: I see Mas'r Scudder
do it often—tink I can take likeness—stay dere,
Wahnotee.

WAHNOTEE. No, carabine tue.

PAUL. I must operate and take my own likeness too—how
debbel I do dat? Can't be ober dar an' here too—I
ain't twins. Ugh! ach! 'Top; you look, you Wahnotee;
do you see dis rag, eh? Well when I say go, den lift
dis rag like dis, see! den run to dat pine tree up dar
(*points*) and back agin, and den pull down de rag
so, d'ye see?

WAHNOTEE. Hugh!

PAUL. Den you hab glass ob rum.

WAHNOTEE. Rum!

PAUL. Dat wakes him up. Coute Wahnotee in omenee dit
go Wahnotee, poina la fa, comb a pine tree, la
revieut sala, la fa.

WAHNOTEE. Fire-water!

PAUL. Yes, den a glass ob fire-water; now den. (*Throws
mail-bags down and sits on them.*) Pret, now den go.

(WAHNOTEE *raises apron and runs off.* PAUL *sits for his
picture*—M'CLOSKY *appears.*)

M'CLOSKY. Where are they? Ah, yonder goes the Indian!

PAUL. De time he gone just 'bout enough to cook dat
dish plate.

M'CLOSKY. Yonder is the boy—now is my time! What's he
doing; is he asleep? (*Advances.*) He is sitting on my
prize! darn his carcass! I'll clear him off there—he'll
never know what stunned him. (*Takes Indian's tomahawk and steals to* PAUL.)

PAUL. Dam dat Injiun! is dat him creeping dar? I daren't
move fear to spile myself.

(M'CLOSKY *strikes him on the head—he falls dead.*)

M'CLOSKY. Horraw! the bags are mine—now for it!—
(*Opens mail-bags.*) What's here? Sunnyside, Point-

dexter, Jackson, Peyton; here it is—the Liverpool post-mark, sure enough!—(*Opens letter—reads.*) "Madam, we are instructed by the firm of Mason and Co., to inform you that a dividend of forty per cent is payable on the 1st proximo, this amount in consideration of position, they send herewith, and you will find en-closed by draft to your order on the Bank of Louisiana, which please acknowledge—the balance will be paid in full, with interest, in three, six, and nine months—your drafts on Mason Brothers at those dates will be accepted by La Palisse and Compagnie, N. O., so that you may command immediate use of the whole amount at once, if required. Yours, &c., James Brown." What a find! this infernal letter would have saved all. (*During the reading of letter he re-mains nearly motionless under the focus of the camera.*) But now I guess it will arrive too late—these darned U. S. mails are to blame. The Injiun! he must not see me. (*Exit rapidly.*)

(WAHNOTEE *runs on, pulls down apron—sees* PAUL *lying on ground—speaks to him—thinks he's shamming sleep —gesticulates and jabbers—goes to him—moves him with feet, then kneels down to rouse him—to his horror finds him dead—expresses great grief—raises his eyes— they fall upon the camera—rises with savage growl, seizes tomahawk and smashes camera to pieces, then goes to* PAUL—*expresses grief, sorrow, and fondness, and takes him in his arms to carry him away.—Tableau.*)

ACT III

A Room in MRS. PEYTON's *house. An Auction Bill stuck up, chairs and tables.*

(SOLON *and* GRACE *discovered.*)

PETE (*outside*). Dis way—dis way.

(*Enter* PETE, POINTDEXTER, JACKSON, LAFOUCHE, *and* CAILLOU.)

PETE. Dis way, gen'l'men; now Solon—Grace—dey's hot and tirsty—sangaree, brandy, rum.

JACKSON. Well, what d'ye say, Lafouche—d'ye smile?

(*Enter* THIBODEAUX *and* SUNNYSIDE.)

THIBODEAUX. I hope we don't intrude on the family.

PETE. You see dat hole in dar, sar. I was raised on dis har
plantation—neber see no door in it—always open,
sar, for stranger to walk in.

SUNNYSIDE. And for substance to walk out.

(*Enter* RATTS.)

RATTS. Fine southern style that, eh!

LAFOUCHE (*reading bill*). "A fine, well-built old family
mansion, replete with every comfort."

RATTS. There's one name on the list of slaves scratched,
I see.

LAFOUCHE. Yes; No. 49, Paul, a quadroon boy, aged
thirteen.

SUNNYSIDE. He's missing.

POINTDEXTER. Run away, I suppose.

PETE (*indignantly*). No, sar; nigger nebber cut stick on
Terrebonne; dat boy's dead, sure.

RATTS. What, Picayune Paul, as we called him, that used
to come aboard my boat?—poor little darky, I hope
not; many a picayune he picked up for his dance and
nigger songs, and he supplied our table with fish and
game from the bayous.

PETE. Nebber supply no more, sar—nebber dance again.
Mas'r Ratts, you hard him sing about de place where
de good niggers go, de last time.

RATTS. Well!

PETE. Well, he gone dar hisself; why, I tink so—'cause
we missed Paul for some days, but nebber tought
nothin' till one night dat Injiun Wahnotee suddenly
stood right dar 'mongst us—was in his war paint, and
mighty cold and grave—he sit down by de fire.
"Whar's Paul?" I say—he smoke and smoke, but
nebber look out ob de fire; well knowing dem critters,
I wait a long time—den he say, "Wahnotee, great
chief"; den I say nothing—smoke anoder time—last,
rising to go, he turn round at door, and say berry low
—O, like a woman's voice, he say, "Omenee Pangeuk,"
—dat is, Paul is dead—nebber see him since.

RATTS. That red-skin killed him.

SUNNYSIDE. So we believe; and so mad are the folks

around, if they catch the red-skin they'll lynch him sure.

RATTS. Lynch him! Darn his copper carcass, I've got a set of Irish deck-hands aboard that just loved that child; and after I tell them this, let them get a sight of the red-skin, I believe they would eat him, tomahawk and all. Poor little Paul!

THIBODEAUX. What was he worth?

RATTS. Well, near on five hundred dollars.

PETE (*scandalized*). What, sar! You p'tend to be sorry for Paul, and prize him like dat. Five hundred dollars!—

(*To* THIBODEAUX): Tousand dollars, Massa Thibodeaux.

(*Enter* SCUDDER.)

SCUDDER. Gentlemen, the sale takes place at three. Good morning, Colonel. It's near that now, and there's still the sugar-houses to be inspected. Good day, Mr. Thibodeaux—shall we drive down that way? Mr. Lafouche, why, how do you do, sir? you're looking well.

LAFOUCHE. Sorry I can't return the compliment.

RATTS. Salem's looking a kinder hollowed out.

SCUDDER. What, Mr. Ratts, are you going to invest in swamps?

RATTS. No; I want a nigger.

SCUDDER. Hush.

PETE. Eh! wass dat?

SCUDDER. Mr. Sunnyside, I can't do this job of showin' round the folks; my stomach goes agin it. I want Pete here a minute.

SUNNYSIDE. I'll accompany them certainly.

SCUDDER (*eagerly*). Will ye? Thank ye; thank ye.

SUNNYSIDE. We must excuse Scudder, friends. I'll see you round the estate.

(*Enter* GEORGE *and* MRS. PEYTON.)

LAFOUCHE. Good morning, Mrs. Peyton. (*All salute.*)

SUNNYSIDE. This way, gentlemen.

RATTS (*aside to* SUNNYSIDE). I say, I'd like to say summit soft to the old woman; perhaps it wouldn't go well, would it?

THIBODEAUX. No; leave it alone.

RATTS. Darn it, when I see a woman in trouble, I feel like selling the skin off my back.

(*Exit* THIBODEAUX, SUNNYSIDE, RATTS, POINTDEXTER, GRACE, JACKSON, LAFOUCHE, CAILLOU, SOLON.)

SCUDDER (*aside to* PETE). Go outside, there; listen to what you hear, then go down to the quarters and tell the boys, for I can't do it. O, get out.

PETE. He said I want a nigger. Laws, mussey! What am goin' to cum ob us!

(*Exit slowly, as if concealing himself.*)

GEORGE. My dear aunt, why do you not move from this painful scene? Go with Dora to Sunnyside.

MRS. PEYTON. No, George; your uncle said to me with his dying breath, "Nellie, never leave Terrebonne," and I never *will* leave it, till the law compels me.

SCUDDER. Mr. George, I'm going to say somethin' that has been chokin' me for some time. I know you'll excuse it. Thar's Miss Dora—that girl's in love with you; yes, sir, her eyes are startin' out of her head with it; now her fortune would redeem a good part of this estate.

MRS. PEYTON. Why, George, I never suspected this!

GEORGE. I did, Aunt, I confess, but—

MRS. PEYTON. And you hesitated from motives of delicacy?

SCUDDER. No, ma'am; here's the plan of it. Mr. George is in love with Zoe.

GEORGE. Scudder!

MRS. PEYTON. George!

SCUDDER. Hold on now! things have got so jammed in on top of us, we ain't got time to put kid gloves on to handle them. He loves Zoe, and has found out that she loves him. (*sighing*) Well, that's all right; but as he can't marry her, and as Miss Dora would jump at him—

MRS. PEYTON. Why didn't you mention this before?

SCUDDER. Why, because *I* love Zoe too, and I couldn't take that young feller from her; and she's jist living on the sight of him, as I saw her do; and they so happy in spite of this yer misery around them, and they reproachin' themselves with not feeling as they ought. I've seen it, I tell you; and darn it, ma'am, can't you see that's what's been a hollowing me out so—I beg your pardon.

MRS. PEYTON. O, George,—my son, let me call you,—I do
not speak for my own sake, nor for the loss of the
estate, but for the poor people here: they will be sold,
divided, and taken away—they have been born here.
Heaven has denied me children; so all the strings of
my heart have grown round and amongst them, like
the fibres and roots of an old tree in its native earth.
O, let all go, but save them! With them around us, if
we have not wealth, we shall at least have the home
that they alone can make—

GEORGE. My dear mother—Mr. Scudder—you teach me
what I ought to do; if Miss Sunnyside will accept me
as I am, Terrebonne shall be saved: I will sell myself,
but the slaves shall be protected.

MRS. PEYTON. *Sell* yourself, George! Is not Dora worth any
man's—

SCUDDER. Don't say that, ma'am; don't say that to a man
that loves another gal. He's going to do an heroic
act; don't spile it.

MRS. PEYTON. But Zoe is only an Octoroon.

SCUDDER. She's won this race agin the white, anyhow; it's
too late now to start her pedigree.

(*Enter* DORA.)

SCUDDER (*seeing* DORA). Come, Mrs. Peyton, take my arm.
Hush! here's the other one: she's a little too thorough-
bred—too much of a greyhound; but the heart's there,
I believe.

(*Exit* SCUDDER *and* MRS. PEYTON.)

DORA. Poor Mrs. Peyton.

GEORGE. Miss Sunnyside, permit me a word: a feeling of
delicacy has suspended upon my lips an avowal,
which—

DORA (*aside*). O, dear, has he suddenly come to his senses?

(*Enter* ZOE; *she stops at back.*)

GEORGE. In a word, I have seen and admired you!

DORA (*aside*). He has a strange way of showing it. European, I suppose.

GEORGE. If you would pardon the abruptness of the question, I would ask you, Do you think the sincere

devotion of my life to make yours happy would
succeed?

DORA (*aside*). Well, he has the oddest way of making love.

GEORGE. You are silent?

DORA. Mr. Peyton, I presume you have hesitated to make
this avowal because you feared, in the present condition of affairs here, your object might be miscon-
strued, and that your attention was rather to my
fortune than myself. (*a pause*) Why don't he speak?—
I mean, you feared I might not give you credit for
sincere and pure feelings. Well, you wrong me. I don't
think you capable of anything else than—

GEORGE. No, I hesitated because an attachment I had
formed before I had the pleasure of seeing you had
not altogether died out.

DORA (*smiling*). Some of those sirens of Paris, I presume.
(*pause*) I shall endeavor not to be jealous of the past;
perhaps I have no right to be. (*pause*) But now that
vagrant love is—eh? faded—is it not? Why don't you
speak, sir?

GEORGE. Because, Miss Sunnyside, I have not learned to lie.

DORA. Good gracious—who wants you to?

GEORGE. I do, but I can't do it. No, the love I speak of is
not such as you suppose,—it is a passion that has
grown up here since I arrived; but it is a hopeless,
mad, wild feeling, that must perish.

DORA. Here! since you arrived! Impossible: you have seen
no one; whom can you mean?

ZOE (*advancing*). Me.

GEORGE. Zoe!

DORA. You!

ZOE. Forgive him, Dora; for he knew no better until I told
him. Dora, you are right. He is incapable of any but
sincere and pure feelings—so are you. He loves me—
what of that? You know you can't be jealous of a poor
creature like me. If he caught the fever, were stung
by a snake, or possessed of any other poisonous or
unclean thing, you could pity, tend, love him through
it, and for your gentle care he would love you in
return. Well, is he not thus afflicted now? I am his
love—he loves an Octoroon.

GEORGE. O, Zoe, you break my heart!

DORA. At college they said I was a fool—I must be. At
New Orleans, they said, "She's pretty, very pretty, but

no brains." I'm afraid they must be right; I can't understand a word of all this.

ZOE. Dear Dora, try to understand it with your heart. You love George; you love him dearly; I know it: and you deserve to be loved by him. He will love you—he must. His love for me will pass away—it shall. You heard him say it was hopeless. O, forgive him and me!

DORA (*weeping*). O, why did he speak to me at all then? You've made me cry, then, and I hate you both! (*Exit, through room.*)

(*Enter* MRS. PEYTON *and* SCUDDER, M'CLOSKY *and* POINTDEXTER.)

M'CLOSKY. I'm sorry to intrude, but the business I came upon will excuse me.

MRS. PEYTON. Here is my nephew, sir.

ZOE. Perhaps I had better go.

M'CLOSKY. Wal, as it consarns you, perhaps you better had.

SCUDDER. Consarns Zoe?

M'CLOSKY. I don't know; she may as well hear the hull of it. Go on, Colonel—Colonel Pointdexter, ma'am—the mortgagee, auctioneer, and general agent.

POINTDEXTER. Pardon me, madam, but do you know these papers? (*Hands papers to* MRS. PEYTON.)

MRS. PEYTON (*takes them*). Yes, sir; they were the free papers of the girl Zoe; but they were in my husband's secretary. How came they in your possession?

M'CLOSKY. I—I found them.

GEORGE. And you purloined them?

M'CLOSKY. Hold on, you'll see. Go on, Colonel.

POINTDEXTER. The list of your slaves is incomplete—it wants one.

SCUDDER. The boy Paul—we know it.

POINTDEXTER. No, sir; you have omitted the Octoroon girl, Zoe.

MRS. PEYTON. } { Zoe!
ZOE. } { Me!

POINTDEXTER. At the time the judge executed those free papers to his infant slave, a judgment stood recorded against him; while that was on record he had no right to make away with his property. That judgment still exists; under it and others this estate is sold today. Those free papers ain't worth the sand that's on 'em.

MRS. PEYTON. Zoe a slave! It is impossible.

POINTDEXTER. It is certain, madam: the judge was negligent, and doubtless forgot this small formality.

SCUDDER. But the creditors will not claim the gal?

M'CLOSKY. Excuse me; one of the principal mortgagees has made the demand.

(*Exit* M'CLOSKY *and* POINTDEXTER.)

SCUDDER. Hold on yere, George Peyton; you sit down there. You're trembling so, you'll fall down directly. This blow has staggered me some.

MRS. PEYTON. O, Zoe, my child! don't think too hardly of your poor father.

ZOE. I shall do so if you weep. See, I'm calm.

SCUDDER. Calm as a tombstone, and with about as much life. I see it in your face.

GEORGE. It cannot be! It shall not be!

SCUDDER. Hold your tongue—it must. Be calm—darn the things; the proceeds of this sale won't cover the debts of the estate. Consarn those Liverpool English fellers, why couldn't they send something by the last mail? Even a letter, promising something—such is the feeling amongst the planters. Darn me, if I couldn't raise thirty thousand on the envelope alone, and ten thousand more on the post-mark.

GEORGE. Zoe, they shall not take you from us while I live.

SCUDDER. Don't be a fool; they'd kill you, and then take her, just as soon as—stop: Old Sunnyside, he'll buy her! that'll save her.

ZOE. No, it won't; we have confessed to Dora that we love each other. How can she then ask her father to free me?

SCUDDER. What in thunder made you do that?

ZOE. Because it was the truth; and I had rather be a slave with a free soul, than remain free with a slavish, deceitful heart. My father gives me freedom—at least he thought so. May Heaven bless him for the thought, bless him for the happiness he spread around my life. You say the proceeds of the sale will not cover his debts. Let me be sold then, that I may free his name. I give him back the liberty he bestowed upon me; for I can never repay him the love he bore his poor Octoroon child, on whose breast his last sigh was drawn, into whose eyes he looked with the last gaze of affection.

MRS. PEYTON. O, my husband! I thank Heaven you have not lived to see this day.

ZOE. George, leave me! I would be alone a little while.

GEORGE. Zoe! (*Turns away overpowered.*)

ZOE. Do not weep, George. Dear George, you now see what a miserable thing I am.

GEORGE. Zoe!

SCUDDER. I wish they could sell *me*! I brought half this ruin on this family, with my all-fired improvements. I deserve to be a nigger this day—I feel like one, inside. (*Exit* SCUDDER.)

ZOE. Go now, George—leave me—take her with you.

(*Exit* MRS. PEYTON *and* GEORGE.)

A slave! a slave! Is this a dream—for my brain reels with the blow? He said so. What! then I shall be sold! —sold! and my master—O! (*Falls on her knees, with her face in her hands.*) no—no master, but one. George—George—hush—they come! save me! No, (*Looks off.*) 'tis Pete and the servants—they come this way. (*Enters inner room.*)

(*Enter* PETE, GRACE, MINNIE, SOLON, DIDO, *and all* NIGGERS.)

PETE. Cum yer now—stand round, cause I've got to talk to you darkies—keep dem chil'n quiet—don't make no noise, de missus up dar har us.

SOLON. Go on, Pete.

PETE. Gen'l'men, my colored frens and ladies, dar's mighty bad news gone round. Dis yer prop'ty to be sold—old Terrebonne—whar we all been raised, is gwine—dey's gwine to tak it away—can't stop here no how.

OMNES. O-o!—O-o!

PETE. Hold quiet, you trash o'niggers! tink anybody wants you to cry? Who's you to set up screeching?—be quiet! But dis ain't all. Now, my culled brethren, gird up your lines, and listen—hold on yer bref—it's a comin. We tought dat de niggers would belong to de ole missus, and if she lost Terrebonne, we must live dere allers, and we would hire out, and bring our wages to ole Missus Peyton.

OMNES. Ya! Ya! Well—

PETE. Hush! I tell ye, t'ain't so—we can't do it—we've got to be sold—

OMNES. Sold!

PETE. Will you hush? she will har you. Yes! I listen dar jess now—dar was old lady cryin'—Mas'r George—ah! you seen dem big tears in his eyes. O, Mas'r Scudder, he didn't cry zackly; both ob his eyes and cheeks look like de bad Bayou in low season—so dry dat I cry for him. (*raising his voice*) Den say de missus, "Tain't for de land I keer, but for dem poor niggers—dey'll be sold—dat wot stagger me." "No," say Mas'r George, "I'd rather sell myself fuss; but dey shan't suffer, nohow,—I see 'em dam fuss."

OMNES. O, bless um! Bless Mas'r George.

PETE. Hole yer tongues. Yes, for you, for me, for dem little ones, dem folks cried. Now, den, if Grace dere wid her chil'n were all sold, she'll begin screechin' like a cat. She didn't mind how kind old judge was to her; and Solon, too, he'll holler, and break de ole lady's heart.

GRACE. No, Pete; no, I won't. I'll bear it.

PETE. I don't tink you will any more, but dis here will; 'cause de family spile Dido, dey has. She nebber was worth much a' dat nigger.

DIDO. How dar you say dat, you black nigger, you? I fetch as much as any odder cook in Louisiana.

PETE. What's de use of your takin' it kind, and comfortin' de missus heart, if Minnie dere, and Louise, and Marie, and Julie is to spile it?

MINNIE. We won't, Pete; we won't.

PETE (*To the men*). Dar, do ye hear dat, ye mis'able darkies, dem gals is worth a boat load of kinder men dem is. Cum, for de pride of de family, let every darky look his best for the judge's sake—dat ole man so good to us, and dat ole woman—so dem strangers from New Orleans shall say, Dem's happy darkies, dem's a fine set of niggers; every one say when he's sold, "Lor' bless dis yer family I'm gwine out of, and send me as good a home."

OMNES. We'll do it, Pete; we'll do it.

PETE. Hush! hark! I tell ye dar's somebody in dar. Who is it?

GRACE. It's Missy Zoe. See! see!

PETE. Come along; she har what we say, and she's cryin' for us. None o' ye ign'rant niggers could cry for yerselves like dat. Come here quite: now quite.

(*Exit* PETE *and all the* NEGROES, *slowly. Enter* ZOE, *supposed to have overheard the last scene.*)

ZOE. O! must I learn from these poor wretches how much I owe, and how I ought to pay the debt? Have I slept upon the benefits I received, and never saw, never felt, never knew that I was forgetful and ungrateful? O, my father! my dear, dear father! forgive your poor child. You made her life too happy, and now these tears will flow. Let me hide them till I teach my heart. O, my—my heart! (*Exit, with a low, wailing, suffocating cry.*)

(*Enter* M'CLOSKY, LAFOUCHE, JACKSON, SUNNYSIDE, *and* POINTDEXTER.)

POINTDEXTER (*looking at watch*). Come, the hour is past. I think we may begin business. Where is Mr. Scudder?

JACKSON. I want to get to Ophelensis to-night.

(*Enter* DORA.)

DORA. Father, come here.

SUNNYSIDE. Why, Dora, what's the matter? Your eyes are red.

DORA. Are they? I thank you. I don't care, they were blue this morning, but it don't signify now.

SUNNYSIDE. My darling! who has been teasing you?

DORA. Never mind. I want you to buy Terrebonne.

SUNNYSIDE. Buy Terrebonne! What for?

DORA. No matter—buy it!

SUNNYSIDE. It will cost me all I'm worth. This is folly, Dora.

DORA. Is my plantation at Comptableau worth this?

SUNNYSIDE. Nearly—perhaps.

DORA. Sell it, then, and buy this.

SUNNYSIDE. Are you mad, my love?

DORA. Do you want *me* to stop here and *bid* for it?

SUNNYSIDE. Good gracious! no.

DORA. Then I'll do it, if you don't.

SUNNYSIDE. I will! I will! But for Heaven's sake go—here comes the crowd.

(*Exit* DORA.)

What on earth does that child mean or want?

(*Enter* SCUDDER, GEORGE, RATTS, CAILLOU, PETE, GRACE, MINNIE, *and all the* NEGROES. *A large table is in the center, at back.* POINTDEXTER *mounts the table with his hammer, his* CLERK *sits at his feet. The* NEGRO *mounts the table from behind. The* COMPANY *sit.*)

POINTDEXTER. Now, gentlemen, we shall proceed to business. It ain't necessary for me to dilate, describe, or enumerate; Terrebonne is known to you as one of the richest bits of sile in Louisiana, and its condition reflects credit on them as had to keep it. I'll trouble you for that piece of baccy, Judge—thank you—so, gentlemen, as life is short, we'll start right off. The first lot on here is the estate in block, with its sugar-houses, stock, machines, implements, good dwelling-houses and furniture. If there is no bid for the estate and stuff, we'll sell it in smaller lots. Come, Mr. Thibodeaux, a man has a chance once in his life— here's yours.

THIBODEAUX. Go on. What's the reserve bid?

POINTDEXTER. The first mortgagee bids forty thousand dollars.

THIBODEAUX. Forty-five thousand.

SUNNYSIDE. Fifty thousand.

POINTDEXTER. When you have done joking, gentlemen, you'll say one hundred and twenty thousand. It carried that easy on mortgage.

LAFOUCHE. Then why don't you buy it yourself, Colonel?

POINTDEXTER. I'm waiting on your fifty thousand bid.

CAILLOU. Eighty thousand.

POINTDEXTER. Don't be afraid: it ain't going for that, Judge.

SUNNYSIDE. Ninety thousand.

POINTDEXTER. We're getting on.

THIBODEAUX. One hundred—

POINTDEXTER. One hundred thousand bid for this mag—

CAILLOU. One hundred and ten thousand—

POINTDEXTER. Good again—one hundred and—

SUNNYSIDE. Twenty.

POINTDEXTER. And twenty thousand bid. Squire Sunnyside is going to sell this at fifty thousand advance to-morrow.—(*Looks round.*) Where's that man from Mobile that wanted to give one hundred and eighty thousand?

THIBODEAUX. I guess he ain't left home yet, Colonel.

POINTDEXTER. I shall knock it down to the Squire—going

—gone—for one hundred and twenty thousand dollars. (*Raises hammer.*) Judge, you can raise the hull on mortgage—going for half its value. (*Knocks.*) Squire Sunnyside, you've got a pretty bit o' land, Squire. Hillo, darky, hand me a smash dar.

SUNNYSIDE. I got more than I can work now.

POINTDEXTER. Then buy the hands along with the property. Now, gentlemen, I'm proud to submit to you the finest lot of field hands and house servants that was ever offered for competition: they speak for themselves, and do credit to their owners.—(*Reads.*) "No. 1, Solon, a guest boy, and good waiter."

PETE. That's my son—buy him, Mas'r Ratts; he's sure to sarve you well.

POINTDEXTER. Hold your tongue!

RATTS. Let the old darky alone—eight hundred for that boy.

CAILLOU. Nine.

RATTS. A thousand.

SOLON. Thank you, Mas'r Ratts: I die for you, sar; hold up for me, sar.

RATTS. Look here, the boy knows and likes me, Judge; let him come my way?

CAILLOU. Go on—I'm dumb.

POINTDEXTER. One thousand bid. (*Knocks.*) He's yours, Captain Ratts, Magnolia steamer.

(SOLON *goes down and stands behind* RATTS.)

"No. 2, the yellow girl Grace, with two children.— Saul, aged four, and Victoria five." (*They get on table.*)

SCUDDER. That's Solon's wife and children, Judge.

GRACE (*To* RATTS). Buy me, Mas'r Ratts, do buy me, sar?

RATTS. What in thunder should I do with you and those devils on board my boat?

GRACE. Wash, sar—cook, sar—anyting.

RATTS. Eight hundred agin, then—I'll go it.

JACKSON. Nine.

RATTS. I'm broke, Solon—I can't stop the Judge.

THIBODEAUX. What's the matter, Ratts? I'll lend you all you want. Go it, if you're a mind to.

RATTS. Eleven.

JACKSON. Twelve.

SUNNYSIDE. O, O!

SCUDDER (*To* JACKSON). Judge, my friend. The Judge is a little deaf. Hello! (*speaking in his ear-trumpet*) This gal and them children belong to that boy Solon there. You're bidding to separate them, Judge.

JACKSON. The devil I am! (*Rises.*) I'll take back my bid, Colonel.

POINTDEXTER. All right, Judge: I thought there was a mistake. I must keep you, Captain, to the eleven hundred.

RATTS. Go it.

POINTDEXTER. Eleven hundred—going—going—sold! "No. 3, Pete, a house servant."

PETE. Dat's me—yer, I'm comin'—stand around dar. (*Tumbles upon the table.*)

POINTDEXTER. Aged seventy-two.

PETE. What's dat? A mistake, sar—forty-six.

POINTDEXTER. Lame.

PETE. But don't mount to nuffin—kin work cannel. Come, Judge, pick up. Now's your time, sar.

JACKSON. One hundred dollars.

PETE. What, sar? me! for me—look ye here! (*Dances.*)

GEORGE. Five hundred.

PETE. Mas'r George—ah, no, sar—don't buy me—keep your money for some udder dat is to be sold. I ain't no count, sar.

POINTDEXTER. Five hundred bid—it's a good price. (*Knocks.*) He's yours, Mr. George Peyton. (PETE *goes down.*) "No. 4, the Octoroon girl, Zoe."

(*Enter* ZOE, *very pale, and stands on table.*—M'CLOSKY *hitherto has taken no interest in the sale, now turns his chair.*)

SUNNYSIDE (*rising*). Gentlemen, we are all acquainted with the circumstances of this girl's position and I feel sure that no one here will oppose the family who desires to redeem the child of our esteemed and noble friend, the late Judge Peyton.

OMNES. Hear! bravo! hear!

POINTDEXTER. While the proceeds of this sale promises to realize less than the debts upon it, it is my duty to prevent any collusion for the depreciation of the property.

RATTS. Darn ye! You're a man as well as an auctioneer, ain't ye?

POINTDEXTER. What is offered for this slave?

SUNNYSIDE. One thousand dollars.

M'CLOSKY. Two thousand.

SUNNYSIDE. Three thousand.

M'CLOSKY. Five thousand.

GEORGE. Demon!

SUNNYSIDE. I bid seven thousand, which is the last dollar this family possesses.

M'CLOSKY. Eight.

THIBODEAUX. Nine.

OMNES. Bravo!

M'CLOSKY. Ten. It's no use, Squire.

SCUDDER. Jacob M'Closky, you shan't have that girl. Now take care what you do. Twelve thousand.

M'CLOSKY. Shan't I! Fifteen thousand. Beat that any of ye.

POINTDEXTER. Fifteen thousand bid for the Octoroon.

(*Enter* DORA.)

DORA. Twenty thousand.

OMNES. Bravo!

M'CLOSKY. Twenty-five thousand.

OMNES (*groan*). O! O!

GEORGE. Yelping hound—take that.

(*Rushes on* M'CLOSKY—M'CLOSKY *draws his knife.*)

SCUDDER (*darts between them*). Hold on, George Peyton —stand back. This is your own house; we are under your uncle's roof; recollect yourself. And, strangers, ain't we forgetting there's a lady present. (*The knives disappear.*) If we can't behave like Christians, let's try and act like gentlemen. Go on, Colonel.

LAFOUCHE. He didn't ought to bid against a lady.

M'CLOSKY. O, that's it, is it? Then I'd like to hire a lady to go to auction and buy my hands.

POINTDEXTER. Gentlemen, I believe none of us have two feelings about the conduct of that man; but he has the law on his side—we may regret, but we must respect it. Mr. M'Closky has bid twenty-five thousand dollars for the Octoroon. Is there any other bid? For the first time, twenty-five thousand—last time. (*Brings hammer down.*) To Jacob M'Closky, the Octoroon girl, Zoe, twenty-five thousand dollars.

(*Tableau.*)

ACT IV

[SCENE.]—*The Wharf. The Steamer "Magnolia," alongside;*
a bluff rock.

(RATTS *discovered, superintending the loading of ship.*
Enter LAFOUCHE *and* JACKSON.)

JACKSON. How long before we start, Captain?

RATTS. Just as soon as we put this cotton on board.

(*Enter* PETE, *with lantern, and* SCUDDER, *with note*
book.)

SCUDDER. One hundred and forty-nine bales. Can you
take any more?

RATTS. Not a bale. I've got engaged eight hundred bales at
the next landing, and one hundred hogsheads of sugar
at Patten's Slide—that'll take my guards under[4]—
hurry up thar.

VOICE (*outside*). Wood's aboard.

RATTS. All aboard then.

(*Enter* M'CLOSKY.)

SCUDDER. Sign that receipt, Captain, and save me going
up to the clerk.

M'CLOSKY. See here—there's a small freight of turpentine
in the fore hold there, and one of the barrels leaks;
a spark from your engines might set the ship on fire,
and you'd go with it.

RATTS. You be darned! Go and try it, if you've a mind to.

LAFOUCHE. Captain, you've loaded up here until the boat
is sunk so deep in the mud she won't float.

RATTS (*calls off*). Wood up thar, you Pollo—hang on to
the safety valve—guess she'll crawl off on her paddles.
(*Shouts heard.*)

JACKSON. What's the matter?

(*Enter* SOLON.)

---

[4] Weigh down the boat until its deck is almost at water level; guards
were protective timbers extending out from the deck.

SOLON. We got him!

SCUDDER. Who?

SOLON. The Injiun!

SCUDDER. Wahnotee? Where is he? D'ye call running away from a fellow catching him?

RATTS. Here he comes.

OMNES. Where? Where?

(*Enter* WAHNOTEE. *They are all about to rush on him.*)

SCUDDER. Hold on! stan' round thar! no violence—the critter don't know what we mean.

JACKSON. Let him answer for the boy, then.

M'CLOSKY. Down with him—lynch him.

OMNES. Lynch him!

(*Exit* LAFOUCHE.)

SCUDDER. Stay back, I say! I'll nip the first that lays a finger on him. Pete, speak to the red-skin.

PETE. Whar's Paul, Wahnotee? What's come ob de child?

WAHNOTEE. Paul wunce—Paul pangeuk.

PETE. Pangeuk—dead.

WAHNOTEE. Mort!

M'CLOSKY. And you killed him?

(*They approach again.*)

SCUDDER. Hold on!

PETE. Um, Paul reste?

WAHNOTEE. Hugh vieu. Paule reste ci!

SCUDDER. Here, stay! (*Examines the ground.*) The earth has been stirred here lately.

WAHNOTEE. Weenee Paul. (*Points down and shows by pantomine how he buried* PAUL.)

SCUDDER. The Injiun means that he buried him there! Stop! here's a bit of leather; (*Draws out mail-bags.*) the mail-bags that were lost! (*Sees tomahawk in* WAHNOTEE's *belt—draws it out and examines it.*) Look! here are marks of blood—look thar, red-skin, what's that?

WAHNOTEE. Paul! (*Makes sign that* PAUL *was killed by a blow on the head.*)

M'CLOSKY. He confesses it; the Indian got drunk, quarrelled with him, and killed him.

(*Re-enter* LAFOUCHE, *with smashed apparatus.*)

LAFOUCHE. Here are evidences of the crime; this rum-bottle
    half emptied—this photographic apparatus smashed
    —and there are marks of blood and footsteps around
    the shed.

M'CLOSKY. What more d'ye want—ain't that proof enough?
    Lynch him.

OMNES. Lynch him! Lynch him!

SCUDDER. Stan' back, boys! He's an Injiun—fair play.

JACKSON. Try him, then—try him on the spot of his crime.

OMNES. Try him! Try him!

LAFOUCHE. Don't let him escape!

RATTS. I'll see to that. (*Draws revolver.*) If he stirs, I'll put
    a bullet through his skull, mighty quick.

M'CLOSKY. Come, form a court then, choose a jury—we'll
    fix this varmin.

(*Enter* THIBODEAUX *and* CAILLOU.)

THIBODEAUX. What's the matter?

LAFOUCHE. We've caught this murdering Injiun, and we are
    going to try him.

(WAHNOTEE *sits, rolled in blanket.*)

PETE. Poor little Paul—poor little nigger!

SCUDDER. This business goes agin me, Ratts—'tain't right.

LAFOUCHE. We're ready; the jury's impanelled—go ahead
    —who'll be accuser?

RATTS. M'Closky.

M'CLOSKY. Me?

RATTS. Yes; you was the first to hail Judge Lynch.

M'CLOSKY. Well, what's the use of argument whar guilt
    sticks out so plain; the boy and Injiun were alone
    when last seen.

SCUDDER. Who says that?

M'CLOSKY. Everybody—that is, I heard so.

SCUDDER. Say what you know—not what you heard.

M'CLOSKY. I know then that the boy was killed with that
    tomahawk—the red-skin owns it—the signs of violence
    are all round the shed—this apparatus smashed—ain't
    it plain that in a drunken fit he slew the boy, and
    when sober concealed the body yonder?

OMNES. That's it—that's it.

RATTS. Who defends the Injiun?

SCUDDER. I will; for it is agin my natur' to believe him guilty; and if he be, this ain't the place, nor you the authority to try him. How are we sure the boy is dead at all? There are no witnesses but a rum bottle and an old machine. Is it on such evidence you'd hang a human being?

RATTS. His own confession.

SCUDDER. I appeal against your usurped authority. That lynch law is a wild and lawless proceeding. Here's a pictur' for a civilized community to afford: yonder a poor, ignorant savage, and round him a circle of hearts, white with revenge and hate, thirsting for his blood: you call yourselves judges—you ain't—you're a jury of executioners. It is such scenes as these that bring disgrace upon our Western life.

M'CLOSKY. Evidence! Evidence! Give us evidence. We've had talk enough; now for proof.

OMNES. Yes, yes! Proof, proof.

SCUDDER. Where am I to get it? The proof is here, in my heart.

PETE (*who has been looking about the camera*). 'Top, sar! 'Top a bit! O, laws-a-mussey, see dis: Here's a pictur' I found stickin' in that yar telescope machine, sar! look sar!

SCUDDER. A photographic plate.

(PETE *holds lantern up.*)

What's this, eh? two forms! The child—'tis he! dead —and above him—Ah, ah! Jacob M'Closky, 'twas you murdered that boy!

M'CLOSKY. Me?

SCUDDER. You! You slew him with that tomahawk; and as you stood over his body with the letter in your hand, you thought that no witness saw the deed, that no eye was on you—but there was, Jacob M'Closky, there was. The eye of the Eternal was on you—the blessed sun in heaven, that, looking down, struck upon this plate the image of the deed. Here you are, in the very attitude of your crime!

M'CLOSKY. 'Tis false.

SCUDDER. 'Tis true! the apparatus can't lie. Look there, jurymen. (*Shows plate to jury.*) Look there. O, you wanted evidence—you called for proof—Heaven has answered and convicted you.

M'CLOSKY. What court of law would receive such evidence? (*going*)

RATTS. Stop; *this* would. You called it yourself; you wanted to make us murder this Injiun; and since we've got our hands in for justice, we'll try it on *you*. What say ye? shall we have one law for the red-skin and another for the white?

OMNES. Try him! Try him!

RATTS. Who'll be the accuser?

SCUDDER. I will! Fellow-citizens, you are convened and assembled here under a higher power than the law. What's the law? When the ship's abroad on the ocean, when the army is before the enemy, where in thunder is the law? It is in the hearts of brave men, who can tell right from wrong, and from whom justice can't be bought. So it is here, in the wilds of the West, where our hatred of crime is measured by the speed of our executions—where necessity is law! I say, then, air you honest men? air you true? Put your hands on your naked breasts, and let every man as don't feel a real American heart there, bustin' up with freedom, truth, and right, let that man step out—that's the oath I put to ye—and then say, Darn ye, go it!

OMNES. Go on. Go on.

SCUDDER. No! I won't go on; that man's down. I won't strike him, even with words. Jacob, your accuser is that picter of the crime—let that speak—defend yourself.

M'CLOSKY (*draws knife*). I will, quicker than lightning.

RATTS. Seize him, then!

(*They rush on* M'CLOSKY, *and disarm him.*)

He can fight though he's a painter: claws all over.

SCUDDER. Stop! Search him, we may find more evidence.

M'CLOSKY. Would you rob me first, and murder me afterwards?

RATTS (*searching him*). That's his program—here's a pocketbook.

SCUDDER (*opens it*). What's here? Letters! Hello! To "Mrs. Peyton, Terrebonne, Louisiana, United States." Liverpool post mark. Ho! I've got hold of the tail of a rat —come out. (*Reads.*) What's this? A draft for eighty-five thousand dollars, and credit on Palisse and Co., of New Orleans, for the balance. Hi! the rat's out.

You killed the boy to steal this letter from the mail-bags—you stole this letter, that the money should not arrive in time to save the Octoroon; had it done so, the lien on the estate would have ceased, and Zoe be free.

OMNES. Lynch him! Lynch him! Down with him!

SCUDDER. Silence in the court: stand back, let the gentlemen of the jury retire, consult, and return their verdict.

RATTS. I'm responsible for the crittur—go on.

PETE (*To* WAHNOTEE). See Injiun; look dar (*Shows him plate.*) see dat innocent: Look, dar's de murderer of poor Paul.

WAHNOTEE. Ugh! (*Examines plate.*)

PETE. Ya! as he? Closky tue Paul—kill de child with your tomahawk dar: 'twasn't you, no—ole Pete allus say so. Poor Injiun lub our little Paul.

(WAHNOTEE *rises and looks at* M'CLOSKY—*he is in his war paint and fully armed.*)

SCUDDER. What say ye, gentlemen? Is the prisoner guilty, or is he not guilty?

OMNES. Guilty!

SCUDDER. And what is to be his punishment?

OMNES. Death! (*All advance.*)

WAHNOTEE (*crosses to* M'CLOSKY). Ugh!

SCUDDER. No, Injiun; we deal out justice here, not revenge. 'Tain't you he has injured, 'tis the white man, whose laws he has offended.

RATTS. Away with him—put him down the aft hatch, till we rig his funeral.

M'CLOSKY. Fifty against one! O! if I had you one by one, alone in the swamp, I'd rip ye all. (*He is borne off in boat, struggling.*)

SCUDDER. Now then to business.

PETE (*re-enters from boat*). O, law, sir, dat debil Closky, he tore hisself from de gen'lam, knock me down, take my light, and trows it on de turpentine barrels, and de shed's all afire! (*Fire seen.*)

JACKSON (*re-entering*). We are catching fire forward: quick, cut free from the shore.

RATTS. All hands aboard there—cut the stern ropes—give her headway!

ALL. Ay, ay!

(*Cry of "fire" heard—Engine bells heard—steam whistle noise.*)

RATTS. Cut all away for'ard—overboard with every bale afire.

(*The steamer moves off—fire kept up—*M'CLOSKY *re-enters, swimming on.*)

M'CLOSKY. Ha! have I fixed ye? Burn! burn! that's right. You thought you had cornered me, did ye? As I swam down, I thought I heard something in the water, as if pursuing me—one of them darned alligators, I suppose—they swarm hereabout—may they crunch every limb of ye! (*Exit.*)

(WAHNOTEE *swims on—finds trail—follows him. The Steamer floats on at back, burning. Tableau.*)

ACT V

[SCENE I.] *Negroes' Quarters.*

(*Enter* ZOE.)

ZOE. It wants an hour yet to daylight—here is Pete's hut —(*Knocks.*) He sleeps—no; I see a light.

DIDO (*enters from hut*). Who dat?

ZOE. Hush, Aunty! 'Tis I—Zoe.

DIDO. Missy Zoe! Why you out in de swamp dis time ob night, you catch de fever sure—you is all wet.

ZOE. Where's Pete?

DIDO. He gone down to de landing last night wid Mas'r Scudder: not come back since—kint make it out.

ZOE. Aunty, there is sickness up at the house: I have been up all night beside one who suffers, and I remembered that when I had the fever you gave me a drink, a bitter drink, that made me sleep—do you remember it?

DIDO. Didn't I? Dem doctors ain't no 'count; dey don't know nuffin.

ZOE. No; but you, Aunty, you are wise—you know every plant, don't you, and what it is good for?

DIDO. Dat you drink is fust rate for red fever. Is de folks' head bad?

ZOE. Very bad, Aunty; and the heart aches worse, so they can get no rest.

DIDO. Hold on a bit, I get you de bottle. (*Exit.*)

ZOE. In a few hours that man, my master, will come for me: he has paid my price, and he only consented to let me remain here this one night, because Mrs. Peyton promised to give me up to him today.

DIDO (*re-enters with phial*). Here 'tis—now you give one timble-full—dat's nuff.

ZOE. All there is there would kill one, wouldn't it?

DIDO. Guess it kill a dozen—nebber try.

ZOE. It's not a painful death, Aunty, is it? You told me it produced a long, long sleep.

DIDO. Why you tremble so? Why you speak so wild? What you's gwine to do, missy?

ZOE. Give me the drink.

DIDO. No. Who dat sick at de house?

ZOE. Give it to me.

DIDO. No, you want to hurt yourself. O, Miss Zoe, why you ask old Dido for dis pison?

ZOE. Listen to me. I love one who is here, and he loves me—George. I sat outside his door all night—I heard his sighs—his agony—torn from him by my coming fate; and he said, "I'd rather see her dead than his!"

DIDO. Dead!

ZOE. He said so—then I rose up, and stole from the house, and ran down to the bayou; but its cold, black, silent stream terrified me—drowning must be so horrible a death. I could not do it. Then, as I knelt there, weeping for courage, a snake rattled beside me. I shrunk from it and fled. Death was there beside me, and I dared not take it. O! I'm afraid to die; yet I am more afraid to live.

DIDO. Die!

ZOE. So I came here to you; to you, my own dear nurse; to you, who so often hushed me to sleep when I was a child; who dried my eyes and put your little Zoe to rest. Ah! give me the rest that no master but One can disturb—the sleep from which I shall awake free! You can protect me from that man—do let me die without pain. (*Music.*)

DIDO. No, no—life is good for young ting like you.

ZOE. O! good, good nurse: you will, you will.

DIDO. No—g'way.

ZOE. Then I shall never leave Terrebonne—the drink,
nurse; the drink; that I may never leave my home—
my dear, dear home. You will not give me to that
man? Your own Zoe, that loves you, Aunty, so much,
so much.—(*Gets phial.*) Ah! I have it.

DIDO. No, missy. O! no—don't.

ZOE. Hush! (*Runs off.*)

DIDO. Here, Solon, Minnie, Grace.

(*They enter.*)

ALL. Was de matter?

DIDO. Miss Zoe got de pison.

ALL. O! O!

(*Exeunt.*)

[SCENE II.] *Cane-brake Bayou: Bank, Triangle Fire,—Canoe.*

(M'CLOSKY *discovered asleep.*)

M'CLOSKY. Burn, burn! blaze away! How the flames crack.
I'm not guilty; would ye murder me? Cut, cut the
rope—I choke—choke! Ah! (*Wakes.*) Hello! where
am I? Why, I was dreaming—curse it! I can never
sleep now without dreaming. Hush! I thought I heard
the sound of a paddle in the water. All night, as I
fled through the cane-brake, I heard footsteps behind
me. I lost them in the cedar swamp—again they
haunted my path down the bayou, moving as I moved,
resting when I rested—hush! there again!—no; it was
only the wind over the canes. The sun is rising. I
must launch my dug-out, and put for the bay, and in
a few hours I shall be safe from pursuit on board of
one of the coasting schooners that run from Galveston
to Matagorda. In a little time this darned business will
blow over, and I can show again. Hark! there's that
noise again! If it was the ghost of that murdered boy
haunting me! Well—I didn't mean to kill him, did I?
Well, then, what has my all-cowardly heart got to
skeer me so for? (*Music.*)

(*Gets in canoe and rows off.* WAHNOTEE *paddles canoe
on, gets out and finds trail—paddles off after him.*)

[SCENE III.] *Cedar swamp.*

(*Enter* SCUDDER *and* PETE.)

SCUDDER. Come on, Pete, we shan't reach the house before mid-day.

PETE. Nebber mind, sa, we bring good news—it won't spile for de keeping.

SCUDDER. Ten miles we've had to walk, because some blamed varmin onhitched our dug-out. I left it last night all safe.

PETE. P'r'aps it floated away itself.

SCUDDER. No; the hitching line was cut with a knife.

PETE. Say, Mas'r Scudder, s'pose we go in round by de quarters and raise de darkies, den dey cum long wid us, and we 'proach dat ole house like Gin'ral Jackson when he took London out dar.

SCUDDER. Hello, Pete, I never heard of that affair.

PETE. I tell you, sa—hush!

SCUDDER. What? (*Music.*)

PETE. Was dat?—a cry out dar in de swamp—dar agin!

SCUDDER. So it is. Something forcing its way through the undergrowth—it comes this way—it's either a bear or a runaway nigger.

(*Draws pistol*—M'CLOSKY *rushes on and falls at* SCUDDER'S *feet.*)

SCUDDER. Stand off—what are ye?

PETE. Mas'r Closky.

M'CLOSKY. Save me—save me! I can go no farther. I heard voices.

SCUDDER. Who's after you?

M'CLOSKY. I don't know, but I feel it's death! In some form, human, or wild beast, or ghost, it has tracked me through the night. I fled; it followed. Hark! there it comes—it comes—don't you hear a footstep on the dry leaves?

SCUDDER. Your crime has driven you mad.

M'CLOSKY. D'ye hear it—nearer—nearer—ah!

(WAHNOTEE *rushes on, and at* M'CLOSKY.)

SCUDDER. The Injiun! by thunder.

PETE. You'se a dead man, Mas'r Closky—you got to b'lieve dat.

M'CLOSKY. No—no. If I must die, give me up to the law; but save me from the tomahawk. You are a white man; you'll not leave one of your own blood to be butchered by the red-skin?

SCUDDER. Hold on now, Jacob; we've got to figure on that —let us look straight at the thing. Here we are on the selvage of civilization. It ain't our side, I believe, rightly; but Nature has said that where the white man sets his foot, the red man and the black man shall up sticks and stand around. But what do we pay for that possession? In cash? No—in kind—that is, in protection, forbearance, gentleness, in all them goods that show the critters the difference between the Christian and the savage. Now, what have you done to show them the distinction? for, darn me, if I can find out.

M'CLOSKY. For what I have done, let me be tried.

SCUDDER. You have been tried—honestly tried and convicted. Providence has chosen your executioner. I shan't interfere.

PETE. O, no; Mas'r Scudder, don't leave Mas'r Closky like dat—don't, sa—'taint what good Christian should do.

SCUDDER. D'ye hear that, Jacob? This old nigger, the grandfather of the boy you murdered, speaks for you—don't that go through you? D'ye feel it? Go on, Pete, you've waked up the Christian here, and the old hoss responds. (*Throws bowie-knife to* M'CLOSKY.) Take that, and defend yourself.

(*Exit* SCUDDER *and* PETE.—WAHNOTEE *faces him.— Fight.* M'CLOSKY *runs off.*—WAHNOTEE *follows him.— Screams outside.*)

[SCENE IV.] *Parlor at Terrebonne.*
(*Enter* ZOE. *Music.*)

ZOE. My home, my home! I must see you no more. Those little flowers can live, but I cannot. Tomorrow they'll bloom the same—all will be here as now, and I shall be cold. O! my life, my happy life, why has it been so bright?

(*Enter* MRS. PEYTON *and* DORA.)

DORA. Zoe, where have you been?
MRS. PEYTON. We felt quite uneasy about you.
ZOE. I've been to the Negro quarters. I suppose I shall go

before long, and I wished to visit all the places, once again, to see the poor people.

MRS. PEYTON. Zoe, dear, I'm glad to see you more calm this morning.

DORA. But how pale she looks, and she trembles so.

ZOE. Do I?

(*Enter* GEORGE.)

Ah! he is here.

DORA. George, here she is.

ZOE. I have come to say good-by, sir; two hard words—so hard, they might break many a heart; mightn't they?

GEORGE. O, Zoe! can you smile at this moment?

ZOE. You see how easily I have become reconciled to my fate—so it will be with you. You will not forget poor Zoe! but her image will pass away like a little cloud that obscured your happiness a while—you will love each other; you are both too good not to join your hearts. Brightness will return amongst you. Dora, I once made you weep; those were the only tears I caused anybody. Will you forgive me?

DORA. Forgive you—(*Kisses her.*)

ZOE. I feel you do, George.

GEORGE. Zoe, you are pale. Zoe!—she faints!

ZOE. No; a weakness, that's all—a little water. (DORA *gets water.*) I have a restorative here—will you pour it in the glass? (DORA *attempts to take it.*) No; not you —George. (GEORGE *pours contents of phial in glass.*) Now, give it to me. George, dear George, do you love me?

GEORGE. Do you doubt it, Zoe?

ZOE. No! (*Drinks.*)

DORA. Zoe, if all I possess would buy your freedom, I would gladly give it.

ZOE. I am free! I had but one Master on earth, and he has given me my freedom!

DORA. Alas! but the deed that freed you was not lawful.

ZOE. Not lawful—no—but I am going to where there is no law—where there is only justice.

GEORGE. Zoe, you are suffering—your lips are white—your cheeks are flushed.

ZOE. I must be going—it is late. Farewell, Dora. (*Retires.*)

PETE (*outside*). Whar's Missus—whar's Mas'r George?

GEORGE. They come.

(*Enter* SCUDDER.)

SCUDDER. Stand around and let me pass—room thar! I feel so big with joy, creation ain't wide enough to hold me. Mrs. Peyton, George Peyton, Terrebonne is yours. It was that rascal M'Closky—but he got rats, I swow[5] —he killed the boy, Paul, to rob this letter from the mail-bags—the letter from Liverpool you know—he sot fire to the shed—that was how the steamboat got burned up.

MRS. PEYTON. What d'ye mean?

SCUDDER. Read—read that. (*Gives letter.*)

GEORGE. Explain yourself.

(*Enter* SUNNYSIDE.)

SUNNYSIDE. Is it true?

SCUDDER. Every word of it, Squire. Here, you tell it, since you know it. If I was to try, I'd bust.

MRS. PEYTON. Read, George. Terrebonne is yours.

(*Enter* PETE, DIDO, SOLON, MINNIE, *and* GRACE.)

PETE. Whar is she—whar is Miss Zoe?

SCUDDER. What's the matter?

PETE. Don't ax me. Whar's de gal? I say.

SCUDDER. Here she is—Zoe!—water—she faints.

PETE. No—no. 'Tain't no faint—she's a dying, sa: she got pison from old Dido here, this mornin'.

GEORGE. Zoe.

SCUDDER. Zoe! is this true?—no, it ain't—darn it, say it ain't. Look here, you're free, you know—nary a master to hurt you now: you will stop here as long as you're a mind to, only don't look so.

DORA. Her eyes have changed color.

PETE. Dat's what her soul's gwine to do. It's going up dar, whar dere's no line atween folks.

GEORGE. She revives.

ZOE (*on sofa*). George—where—where—

GEORGE. O, Zoe! what have you done?

ZOE. Last night I overheard you weeping in your room, and you said, "I'd rather see her dead than so!"

GEORGE. Have I then prompted you to this?

ZOE. No; but I loved you so, I could not bear my fate; and then I stood between your heart and hers. When I am

---

[5] He was crazy, I declare.

dead she will not be jealous of your love for me, no laws will stand between us. Lift me; so—(GEORGE *raises her head.*)—let me look at you, that your face may be the last I see of this world. O! George, you may, without a blush, confess your love for the Octoroon!

(*Dies.*—GEORGE *lowers her head gently.*—*Kneels.*—*Others form picture.*)

(*Darken front of house and stage.*)

(*Light fires.*—*Draw flats and discover* PAUL'*s grave.*—M'CLOSKY *dead on it.*—WAHNOTEE *standing triumphantly over him.*)

RUDDIGORE

OR,

THE WITCH'S CURSE

～ 1887 ～

William Schwenck Gilbert

INTRODUCTORY NOTE

WILLIAM SCHWENCK GILBERT (1836–1911) spent years as an unhappy clerk and an unsuccessful lawyer before becoming a professional writer. His most significant early works were *The Bab Ballads*, written for *Fun* magazine from 1861, in which he developed the topsy-turvy world of his light operas. Turning to the stage in 1866, he wrote many serious and comic plays, of which the best is *Engaged* (1877). Although he met Arthur Sullivan in 1869 and they collaborated on *Thespis* in 1871, their first real success was *Trial by Jury* (1875). Richard D'Oyly Carte, a theater manager, brought them into a partnership to supply light operas for a native English company, which they recruited and trained. For fourteen years, Gilbert and Sullivan worked together in a unique partnership, with librettist and composer functioning as equals. Gilbert meticulously directed all the productions, and the two shared expenses and profits with D'Oyly Carte. They produced one success after another, the most spectacular being *The Mikado* (1885), which had an initial run of 672 performances. There were constant strains in the relationship, however, resulting from Gilbert's irascibility and Sullivan's aspirations to compose more serious music. They quarreled bitterly after writing *The Gondoliers* (1889).

Ruddigore; or, The Witch's Curse (1887) was not particularly successful by Savoyard standards, partly because of its provocative title; for *bloody* is a vulgar expletive in England. But it was one of Gilbert's favorite librettos and, as he said later, it was hardly a failure since it ran for over nine months and put £7,000 in his pocket. Although *Ruddigore* makes fun of the perennial falsifications of melodramatic and sentimental literature, its satire applies particularly to the popular melodrama of the nineteenth century, as exemplified by such a work as Douglas Jerrold's highly popular *Black Ey'd Susan* (1829). Jerrold's play shamelessly appeals to sympathy and chauvinism with its virtuous victimized hero and heroine and its glorification of the British Navy. William, the sailor hero, is as nobly forthright as Gilbert's Dick Dauntless appears to be, and his nautical metaphors are hardly less exaggerated and absurd.

As in *The Beggar's Opera*, the music of *Ruddigore* softens its cynical presentation of human nature: Rose, warbling her delightful songs, does not seem as calculating as she really is. The ghost music in Act II is genuinely impressive—too much so, Gilbert felt, for a light opera. Often, however, Sullivan's music accentuates the fun, as in the little sliding note he added to the end of the bridesmaids' chorus ("Hail the Bridegroom—hail the Bride?"), which makes audible the derisive question mark. In the duet where Sir Despard agrees with Dick to pin the Ruddigore title on Robin, the lively music which expresses their real feelings emphasizes the hypocrisy of their pretended regret that "duty, duty must be done."

BIBLIOGRAPHY

❧ ❧

Major Works:

The Bab Ballads, 1861–; book form, 1869

Trial by Jury, 1875 (light opera, with Sullivan)

The Sorcerer, 1877 (light opera, with Sullivan)

Engaged, 1877 (comedy)

H.M.S. Pinafore; or, The Lass That Loved a Sailor, 1878 (light opera, with Sullivan)

The Pirates of Penzance; or, The Slave of Duty, 1879 (light opera, with Sullivan)

Patience; or, Bunthorne's Bride, 1881 (light opera, with Sullivan)

Iolanthe; or, The Peer and the Peri, 1882 (light opera, with Sullivan)

Princess Ida; or, Castle Adamant, 1884 (light opera, with Sullivan)

The Mikado; or, The Town of Titipu, 1885 (light opera, with Sullivan)

Ruddigore; or, The Witch's Curse, 1887 (light opera, with Sullivan)

The Yeomen of the Guard; or, The Merryman and His Maid, 1888 (light opera, with Sullivan)

The Gondoliers; or, The King of Barataria, 1889 (light opera, with Sullivan)

Utopia, Limited; or, The Flowers of Progress, 1893 (light opera, with Sullivan)

The Grand Duke; or, The Statutory Duel, 1896 (light opera, with Sullivan)

Gilbert's essay "A Stage Play," reprinted in *Papers on Playmaking*, ed. Brander Matthews (New York: Hill and Wang, 1957), gives an entertaining account of his methods.

Works About:

Baily, Leslie. *Gilbert and Sullivan: Their Lives and Times.* New York: Viking Press, 1974.

Gilbert and Sullivan: Papers Presented at the International Conference Held at the University of Kansas in May 1970: University of Kansas Publications Library Series, 37. Lawrence, Kansas: University of Kansas Libraries, 1971.

Goldberg, Isaac. *The Story of Gilbert and Sullivan, or The "Compleat" Savoyard.* New York: Crown, 1935.

Williamson, Audrey. *Gilbert and Sullivan Opera: A New Assessment.* New York: Macmillan, 1953.

RUDDIGORE

Dramatis Personae

MORTALS

SIR RUTHVEN MURGATROYD, *disguised as Robin Oakapple, a young farmer*

RICHARD DAUNTLESS, *his foster-brother—a man-o'-war's-man*

SIR DESPARD MURGATROYD, OF RUDDIGORE, *a wicked baronet*

OLD ADAM GOODHEART, *Robin's faithful servant*

ROSE MAYBUD, *a village maiden*

MAD MARGARET

DAME HANNAH, *Rose's aunt*

ZORAH }
RUTH } *professional bridesmaids*

GHOSTS

SIR RUPERT MURGATROYD, *the First Baronet*

SIR JASPER MURGATROYD, *the Third Baronet*

SIR LIONEL MURGATROYD, *the Sixth Baronet*

SIR CONRAD MURGATROYD, *the Twelfth Baronet*

SIR DESMOND MURGATROYD, *the Sixteenth Baronet*

SIR GILBERT MURGATROYD, *the Eighteenth Baronet*

SIR MERVYN MURGATROYD, *the Twentieth Baronet*
  and

SIR RODERIC MURGATROYD, *the Twenty-first Baronet*

Chorus of officers, ancestors, professional bridesmaids, and villagers

ACT I
The fishing village of Rederring,[1] in Cornwall

---

1 Probably pronounced "red herring"—i.e., something used to confuse an issue.

ACT II
The picture gallery in Ruddigore Castle

TIME
Early in the 19th century

ACT I

[SCENE.] *The fishing village of Rederring (in Cornwall).*
ROSE MAYBUD's *cottage is seen left.*

(Enter Chorus of Bridesmaids. They range themselves in front of ROSE's *cottage.)*

Chorus of Bridesmaids

Fair is Rose as the bright May-day;
   Soft is Rose as the warm west-wind;
Sweet is Rose as the new-mown hay—
   Rose is the queen of maiden-kind!
      Rose, all glowing
         With virgin blushes, say—
      Is anybody going
         To marry you to-day?

Solo—ZORAH

Every day, as the days roll on,
Bridesmaids' garb we gaily don,
Sure that a maid so fairly famed
Can't long remain unclaimed.
Hour by hour and day by day,
Several months have passed away,
Though she's the fairest flower that blows,
No one has married Rose!

Chorus

      Rose, all glowing
         With virgin blushes, say—
      Is anybody going
         To marry you to-day?

(*Enter* DAME HANNAH, *from cottage.*)

HANNAH. Nay, gentle maidens, you sing well but vainly, for Rose is still heart-free, and looks but coldly upon her many suitors.

ZORAH. It's very disappointing. Every young man in the village is in love with her, but they are appalled by her beauty and modesty, and won't declare themselves; so, until she makes her own choice, there's no chance for anybody else.

RUTH. This is, perhaps, the only village in the world that possesses an endowed corps of professional brides-maids who are bound to be on duty every day from ten to four—and it is at least six months since our services were required. The pious charity by which we exist is practically wasted!

ZORAH. We shall be disendowed—that will be the end of it! Dame Hannah—you're a nice old person—*you* could marry if you liked. There's old Adam—Robin's faithful servant—he loves you with all the frenzy of a boy of fourteen.

HANNAH. Nay—that may never be, for I am pledged!

ALL. To whom?

HANNAH. To an eternal maidenhood! Many years ago I was betrothed to a god-like youth who woo'd me under an assumed name. But on the very day upon which our wedding was to have been celebrated, I discovered that he was no other than Sir Roderic Murgatroyd, one of the bad Baronets of Ruddigore, and the uncle of the man who now bears that title. As a son of that accursed race he was no husband for an honest girl, so, madly as I loved him, I left him then and there. He died but ten years since, but I never saw him again.

ZORAH. But why should you not marry a bad Baronet of Ruddigore?

RUTH. All baronets are bad; but was he worse than other baronets?

HANNAH. My child, he was accursed.

ZORAH. But who cursed him? Not you, I trust!

HANNAH. The curse is on all his line and has been, ever since the time of Sir Rupert, the first Baronet. Listen, and you shall hear the legend:

Legend—HANNAH

Sir Rupert Murgatroyd
  His leisure and his riches
He ruthlessly employed
  In persecuting witches.
With fear he'd make them quake—
He'd duck them in his lake—
    He'd break their bones
    With sticks and stones,
And burn them at the stake!

CHORUS   This sport he much enjoyed,
Did Rupert Murgatroyd—
    No sense of shame
    Or pity came
To Rupert Murgatroyd!

Once, on the village green,
  A palsied hag he roasted,
And what took place, I ween,
  Shook his composure boasted;
For, as the torture grim
Seized on each withered limb,
    The writhing dame
    'Mid fire and flame
Yelled forth this curse on him:

"Each lord of Ruddigore,
  Despite his best endeavour,
Shall do one crime, or more,
  Once, every day, for ever!
This doom he can't defy,
However he may try,
    For should he stay
    His hand, that day
In torture he shall die!"

The prophecy came true:
  Each heir who held the title
Had, every day, to do
  Some crime of import vital;
Until, with guilt o'erplied,
"I'll sin no more!" he cried,
    And on the day
    He said that say,
In agony he died!

CHORUS   And thus, with sinning cloyed,
            Has died each Murgatroyd,
                And so shall fall,
                Both one and all,
            Each coming Murgatroyd!

(*Exeunt Chorus of Bridesmaids.*)

(*Enter* ROSE MAYBUD *from cottage, with small basket on her arm.*)

HANNAH. Whither away, dear Rose? On some errand of charity, as is thy wont?

ROSE. A few gifts, dear aunt, for deserving villagers. Lo, here is some peppermint rock for old gaffer Gadderby, a set of false teeth for pretty little Ruth Rowbottom, and a pound of snuff for the poor orphan girl on the hill.

HANNAH. Ah, Rose, pity that so much goodness should not help to make some gallant youth happy for life! Rose, why dost thou harden that little heart of thine? Is there none hereaway whom thou couldst love?

ROSE. And if there were such an one, verily it would ill become me to tell him so.

HANNAH. Nay, dear one, where true love is, there is little need of prim formality.

ROSE. Hush, dear aunt, for thy words pain me sorely. Hung in a plated dish-cover to the knocker of the workhouse door, with naught that I could call mine own, save a change of baby-linen and a book of etiquette, little wonder if I have always regarded that work as a voice from a parent's tomb. This hallowed volume [*producing a book of etiquette*], composed, if I may believe the title-page, by no less an authority than the wife of a Lord Mayor, has been, through life, my guide and monitor. By its solemn precepts I have learnt to test the moral worth of all who approach me. The man who bites his bread, or eats peas with a knife, I look upon as a lost creature, and he who has not acquired the proper way of entering and leaving a room is the object of my pitying horror. There are those in this village who bite their nails, dear aunt, and nearly all are wont to use their pocket combs in public places. In truth I could pursue this painful theme much further, but behold, I have said enough.

HANNAH. But is there not one among them who is faultless,
in thine eyes? For example—young Robin. He combines the manners of a Marquis with the morals of a
Methodist. Couldst thou not love *him?*

ROSE. And even if I could, how should I confess it unto
him? For lo, he is shy, and sayeth naught!

Ballad—ROSE

> If somebody there chanced to be
>   Who loved me in a manner true,
> My heart would point him out to me,
>   And I would point him out to you.
> *(referring to book)*
>   But here it says of those who point—
>   Their manners must be out of joint—
>   You *may* not point—
>   You *must* not point—
>   It's manners out of joint, to point!
> Had I the love of such as he,
>   Some quiet spot he'd take me to,
> Then he could whisper it to me,
>   And I could whisper it to you.
> *(referring to book)*
>   But whispering, I've somewhere met,
>   Is contrary to etiquette:
>   Where can it be? *(searching book)*
>   Now let me see—*(finding reference)*
>   Yes, yes!
>   It's contrary to etiquette!

(Showing it to HANNAH.)

> If any well-bred youth I knew,
>   Polite and gentle, neat and trim,
> Then I would hint as much to you,
>   And you could hint as much to him.
> *(referring to book)*
>   But here it says, in plainest print,
>   "It's most unladylike to hint"—
>   You *may* not hint,
>   You *must* not hint—
>   It says you mustn't hint, in print!
> And if I loved him through and through—

> · (True love and not a passing whim),
> Then I could speak of it to you,
>   And you could speak of it to him.
> (*referring to book*)
>   But here I find it doesn't do
>   To speak until you're spoken to.
>   Where can it be? (*searching book*)
>   Now let me see—(*finding reference*)
>   Yes, yes!
>   "Don't speak until you're spoken to!"

(*Exit* HANNAH.)

ROSE. Poor aunt! Little did the good soul think, when she breathed the hallowed name of Robin, that he would do even as well as another. But he resembleth all the youths in this village, in that he is unduly bashful in my presence, and lo, it is hard to bring him to the point. But soft, he is here!

(ROSE *is about to go when* ROBIN *enters and calls her.*)

ROBIN. Mistress Rose!
ROSE (*surprised*). Master Robin!
ROBIN. I wished to say that—it is fine.
ROSE. It is passing fine.
ROBIN. But we do want rain.
ROSE. Aye, sorely! Is that all?
ROBIN (*sighing*). That is all.
ROSE. Good day, Master Robin!
ROBIN. Good day, Mistress Rose! (*Both going—both stop.*)
ROSE. } {I crave pardon, I—
ROBIN.} {I beg pardon, I—
ROSE. You were about to say?—
ROBIN. I would fain consult you—
ROSE. Truly?
ROBIN. It is about a friend.
ROSE. In truth I have a friend myself.
ROBIN. Indeed? I mean, of course—
ROSE. And I would fain consult you—
ROBIN (*anxiously*). About him?
ROSE (*prudishly*). About *her*.
ROBIN (*relieved*). Let us consult one another.

Duet—ROBIN *and* ROSE

ROBIN. I know a youth who loves a little maid—
    (Hey, but his face is a sight to see!)
    Silent is he, for he's modest and afraid—
       (Hey, but he's timid as a youth can be!)

ROSE. I know a maid who loves a gallant youth,
       (Hey, but she sickens as the days go by!)
    She cannot tell him all the sad, sad truth—
       (Hey, but I think that little maid will die!)

ROBIN. Poor little man!

ROSE. Poor little maid!

ROBIN. Poor little man!

ROSE. Poor little maid!

BOTH. Now tell me pray, and tell me true,

    What in the world should the $\left\{ \begin{matrix} \text{young man} \\ \text{maiden} \end{matrix} \right\}$ do?

ROBIN. He cannot eat and he cannot sleep—
    (Hey, but his face is a sight for to see!)
    Daily he goes for to wail—for to weep
    (Hey, but he's wretched as a youth can be!)

ROSE. She's very thin and she's very pale—
    (Hey, but she sickens as the days go by!)
    Daily she goes for to weep—for to wail—
    (Hey, but I think that little maid will die!)

ROBIN. Poor little maid!

ROSE. Poor little man!

ROBIN. Poor little maid!

ROSE. Poor little man!

BOTH. Now tell me pray, and tell me true,

    What in the world should the $\left\{ \begin{matrix} \text{young man} \\ \text{maiden} \end{matrix} \right\}$ do?

ROSE. If I were the youth I should offer her my name—
    (Hey, but her face is a sight for to see!)

ROBIN. If I were the maid I should fan his honest flame—
    (Hey, but he's bashful as a youth can be!)

ROSE. If I were the youth I should speak to her to-day—
      (Hey, but she sickens as the days go by!)

ROBIN. If I were the maid I should meet the lad half way—
      (For I really do believe that timid youth will die!)

ROSE. Poor little man!

ROBIN. Poor little maid!

ROSE. Poor little man!

ROBIN. Poor little maid!

BOTH. I thank you, $\begin{Bmatrix} \text{miss,} \\ \text{sir,} \end{Bmatrix}$ for your counsel true;

    I'll tell that $\begin{Bmatrix} \text{youth} \\ \text{maid} \end{Bmatrix}$ what $\begin{Bmatrix} \text{he} \\ \text{she} \end{Bmatrix}$ ought to do!

(*Exit* ROSE.)

ROBIN. Poor child! I sometimes think that if she wasn't quite so particular I might venture—but no, no— even then I should be unworthy of her!

(*He sits desponding. Enter* OLD ADAM.)

ADAM. My kind master is sad! Dear Sir Ruthven Murgatroyd—

ROBIN. Hush! As you love me, breathe not that hated name. Twenty years ago, in horror at the prospect of inheriting that hideous title, and with it the ban that compels all who succeed to the baronetcy to commit at least one deadly crime per day, for life, I fled my home, and concealed myself in this innocent village under the name of Robin Oakapple. My younger brother, Despard, believing me to be dead, succeeded to the title and its attendant curse. For twenty years I have been dead and buried. Don't dig me up now.

ADAM. Dear master, it shall be as you wish, for have I not sworn to obey you for ever in all things? Yet, as we are here alone, and as I belong to that particular description of good old man to whom the truth is a refreshing novelty, let me call you by your own right title once more! (ROBIN *assents*.) Sir Ruthven Murgatroyd! Baronet! Of Ruddigore! Whew! It's like eight hours at the seaside!

ROBIN. My poor old friend! Would there were more like you!

ADAM. Would there were indeed! But I bring you good
    tidings. Your foster-brother, Richard, has returned
    from sea—his ship the *Tom-Tit* rides yonder at
    anchor, and he himself is even now in this very
    village!

ROBIN. My beloved foster-brother? No, no—it cannot be!

ADAM. It is even so—and see, he comes this way!

(*Exeunt together.*)

(*Enter Chorus of Bridesmaids.*)

CHORUS.   From the briny sea
            Comes young Richard, all victorious!
        Valorous is he—
            His achievements all are glorious

            Let the welkin ring
            With the news we bring
                Sing it—shout it—
                Tell about it—
            Safe and sound returneth he,
            All victorious from the sea!

(*Enter* RICHARD. *The girls welcome him as he greets old
acquaintances.*)

Ballad—RICHARD

I shipped, d'ye see, in a Revenue sloop,
    And, off Cape Finistere,
        A merchantman we see,
        A Frenchman, going free,
    So we made for the bold Mounseer,
        D'ye see?
    We made for the bold Mounseer.
But she proved to be a Frigate[2]—and she up with her ports,
    And fires with a thirty-two!
        It come uncommon near,
        But we answered with a cheer,
    Which paralysed the Parley-voo,
        D'ye see?
    Which paralysed the Parley-voo!

2 Warship.

Then our Captain he up and he says, says he,
"That chap we need not fear,—
    We can take her, if we like,
    She is sartin for to strike,
For she's only a darned Mounseer,
        D'ye see?
She's only a darned Mounseer!
But to fight a French fal-lal—it's like hittin' of a gal!
    It's a lubberly thing for to do;
    For we, with our faults,
    Why we're sturdy British salts,
While she's only a Parley-voo,
        D'ye see?
While she's only a Parley-voo!"

So we up with our helm, and we scuds before the breeze
    As we gives a compassionating cheer;
        Froggee answers with a shout
        As he sees us go about,
    Which was grateful of the poor Mounseer,
        D'ye see?
    Which was grateful of the poor Mounseer!
And I'll wager in their joy they kissed each other's cheek
    (Which is what them furriners do),
        And they blessed their lucky stars
        We were hardy British tars
    Who had pity on a poor Parley-voo,
        D'ye see?
    Who had pity on a poor Parley-voo!

[HORNPIPE]

(*Exeunt* CHORUS. *Enter* ROBIN.)

ROBIN. Richard!

RICHARD. Robin!

ROBIN. My beloved foster-brother, and very dearest friend,
    welcome home again after ten long years at sea! It is
    such deeds as yours that cause our flag to be loved and
    dreaded throughout the civilized world!

RICHARD. Why, lord love ye, Rob, that's but a trifle to what
    we *have* done in the way of sparing life! I believe I
    may say, without exaggeration, that the marciful little
    Tom-Tit has spared more French frigates than any
    craft afloat! But 'tain't for a British seaman to brag, so

I'll just stow my jawin' tackle and belay. (ROBIN
sighs.) But 'vast heavin', messmate, what's brought
you all a-cockbill?

ROBIN. Alas, Dick, I love Rose Maybud, and love in vain!

RICHARD. *You* love in vain? Come, that's too good! Why,
you're a fine strapping muscular young fellow—tall
and strong as a to'-gall'n'-m'st—taut as a forestay—
aye, and a barrowknight[3] to boot, if all had their
rights!

ROBIN. Hush, Richard—not a word about my true rank,
which none here suspect. Yes, I know well enough
that few men are better calculated to win a woman's
heart than I. I'm a fine fellow, Dick, and worthy any
woman's love—happy the girl who gets me, say I. But
I'm timid, Dick; shy—nervous—modest—retiring—
diffident—and I cannot tell her, Dick, I cannot tell
her! Ah, you've no idea what a poor opinion I have of
myself, and how little I deserve it.

RICHARD. Robin, do you call to mind how, years ago, we
swore that, come what might, we would always act
upon our hearts' dictates?

ROBIN. Aye, Dick, and I've always kept that oath. In doubt,
difficulty, and danger I've always asked my heart what
I should do, and it has never failed me.

RICHARD. Right! Let your heart be your compass, with a
clear conscience for your binnacle light, and you'll
sail ten knots on a bowline, clear of shoals, rocks, and
quicksands! Well, now, what does my heart say in
this here difficult situation? Why, it says, "Dick," it
says—(it calls me Dick acos it's known me from a
babby)—"Dick," it says, "*you* ain't shy—*you* ain't
modest—speak you up for him as is!" Robin, my lad,
just you lay me alongside, and when she's becalmed
under my lee, I'll spin her a yarn that shall sarve to
fish you two together for life!

ROBIN. Will you do this thing for me? Can you, do you
think? Yes. (*feeling his pulse*) There's no false
modesty about *you*. Your—what I would call bump-
tious self-assertiveness (I mean the expression in its
complimentary sense) has already made you a bo's'n's
mate, and it will make an admiral of you in time, if

---

3 Richard's mispronunciation of "baronet."

you work it properly, you dear, incompetent old impostor! My dear fellow, I'd give my right arm for one tenth of your modest assurance!

Song—ROBIN

My boy, you may take it from me,
    That of all the afflictions accurst
        With which a man's saddled
        And hampered and addled,
    A diffident nature's the worst.
Though clever as clever can be—
    A Crichton of early romance—
        You must stir it and stump it,
        And blow your own trumpet,
Or, trust me, you haven't a chance!

    If you wish in the world to advance,
    Your merits you're bound to enhance,
        You must stir it and stump it,
        And blow your own trumpet,
    Or, trust me, you haven't a chance!

Now take, for example, *my* case:
    I've a bright intellectual brain—
        In all London city
        There's no one so witty—
    I've thought so again and again.
I've a highly intelligent face—
    My features cannot be denied—
        But, whatever I try, sir,
        I fail in—and why, sir?
I'm modesty personified!

    If you wish in the world to advance, etc.

As a poet, I'm tender and quaint—
    I've passion and fervour and grace—
        From Ovid and Horace
        To Swinburne and Morris,
    They all of them take a back place.
Then I sing and I play and I paint:
    Though none are accomplished as I,
        To say so were treason:
        You ask me the reason?
I'm diffident, modest, and shy!

If you wish in the world to advance, etc.

(*Exit* ROBIN.)

RICHARD (*looking after him*). Ah, it's a thousand pities he's such a poor opinion of himself, for a finer fellow don't walk! Well, I'll do my best for him. "Plead for him as though it was for your own father"—that's what my heart's a-remarkin' to me just now. But here she comes! Steady! Steady it is!

(*Enter* ROSE—*he is much struck by her.*)

By the Port Admiral, but she's a tight little craft! Come, come, she's not for you, Dick, and yet—she's fit to marry Lord Nelson! By the Flag of Old England, I can't look at her unmoved.

ROSE. Sir, you are agitated—

RICHARD. Aye, aye, my lass, well said! I am agitated, true enough!—took flat aback, my girl; but 'tis naught— —'twill pass. (*aside*) This here heart of mine's a-dictatin' to me like anythink. Question is, Have I a right to disregard its promptings?

ROSE. Can I do aught to relieve thine anguish, for it seemeth to me that thou art in sore trouble? This apple—(*offering a damaged apple*)

RICHARD (*looking at it and returning it*). No, my lass, 'tain't that: I'm—I'm took flat aback—I never see anything like you in all my born days. Parbuckle me, if you ain't the loveliest gal I've ever set eyes on. There—I can't say fairer than that, can I?

ROSE. No. (*aside*) The question is, Is it meet that an utter stranger should thus express himself? (*Refers to book.*) Yes—"Always speak the truth."[4]

RICHARD. I'd no thoughts of sayin' this here to you on my own account, for, truth to tell, I was chartered by another; but when I see you my heart it up and it says, says it, "This is the very lass for *you*, Dick,"—"speak up to her, Dick," it says—it calls me Dick acos we was at school together—"tell her all, Dick," it says, "never sail under false colours—it's mean!" *That's* what my

---

[4] A note in Gilbert's prompt-book directs Rose to kiss the book at this point, thus parodying the oath taken on the Bible by a witness in a law court. The gesture emphasizes Gilbert's satire on the excessive gentility which makes her equate etiquette with ethics.

heart tells me to say, and in my rough, common-sailor fashion, I've said it, and I'm a-waiting for your reply. I'm a-tremblin', miss. Lookye here—(*holding out his hand*) That's narvousness!

ROSE (*aside*). Now, how should a maiden deal with such an one? (*Consults book.*) "Keep no one in unnecessary suspense." (*aloud*) Behold I will not keep you in un-necessary suspense. (*Refers to book.*) "In accepting an offer of marriage, do so with apparent hesitation." (*aloud*) I take you, but with a certain show of reluc-tance. (*Refers to book.*) "Avoid any appearance of eagerness." (*aloud*) Though you will bear in mind that I am far from anxious to do so. (*Refers to book.*) "A little show of emotion will not be misplaced!" (*aloud*) Pardon this tear! (*Wipes her eye.*)

RICHARD. Rose, you've made me the happiest blue-jacket in England! I wouldn't change places with the Admiral of the Fleet, no matter who he's a-huggin' of at this present moment! But, axin' your pardon, miss (*wiping his lips with his hand*), might I be permitted to salute the flag I'm goin' to sail under?

ROSE (*referring to book*). "An engaged young lady should not permit too many familiarities." (*aloud*) Once! (RICHARD *kisses her.*)

Duet—RICHARD and ROSE

RICHARD.   The battle's roar is over,
          O my love!
      Embrace thy tender lover,
          O my love!
      From tempests' welter,
          From war's alarms,
      O give me shelter
          Within those arms!
      Thy smile alluring,
      All heart-ache curing,
      Gives peace enduring,
          O my love!

ROSE.   If heart both true and tender,
          O my love!
      A life-love can engender,
          O my love!

> A truce to sighing
>   And tears of brine,
> For joy undying
>   Shall aye be mine,
> And thou and I, love,
> Shall live and die, love,
> Without a sigh, love—
>   My own, my love!

(*Enter* ROBIN, *with Chorus of Bridesmaids.*)

Chorus

> If well his suit has sped,
> Oh, may they soon be wed!
> Oh, tell us, tell us, pray,
> What doth the maiden say?
> In singing are we justified,
>   Hail the Bridegroom—hail the Bride!
> Let the nuptial knot be tied:
>   In fair phrases,
>   Hymn their praises,
> Hail the Bridegroom—hail the Bride?

ROBIN. Well—what news? Have you spoken to her?

RICHARD. Aye, my lad, I have—so to speak—spoke her.

ROBIN. And she refuses?

RICHARD. Why no, I can't truly say she do.

ROBIN. Then she accepts! My darling! (*Embraces her.*)

BRIDESMAIDS

Hail the Bridegroom—hail the Bride! etc.

ROSE (*aside, referring to her book*). Now, what should a maiden do when she is embraced by the wrong gentleman?

RICHARD. Belay, my lad, belay. You don't understand.

ROSE. Oh, sir, belay,[5] I beseech you!

RICHARD. You see, it's like this: she accepts—but it's *me!*

ROBIN. You! (RICHARD *embraces* ROSE.)

---

[5] In nautical usage, to make a rope secure by winding it around a belaying pin; hence, to hold or stop. Dick's nautical language, conventional for the stage sailor, becomes more obviously ridiculous when taken up by a non-nautical character.

BRIDESMAIDS

Hail the Bridegroom—hail the Bride!
When the nuptial knot is tied—

ROBIN (*interrupting angrily*). Hold your tongues, will you!
Now then, what does this mean?

RICHARD. My poor lad, my heart grieves for thee, but it's
like this: the moment I see her, and just as I was
a-goin' to mention your name, my heart it up and it
says, says it—"Dick, you've fell in love with her yourself," it says; "Be honest and sailor-like—don't skulk
under false colours—speak up," it says, "take her, you
dog, and with her my blessin'!"

BRIDESMAIDS

Hail the Bridegroom—hail the Bride!—

ROBIN. Will you be quiet! Go away! (CHORUS *make faces
at him and exeunt.*) Vulgar girls!

RICHARD. What could I do? I'm bound to obey my heart's
dictates.

ROBIN. Of course—no doubt. It's quite right—I don't mind
—that is, not particularly—only it's—it *is* disappointing, you know.

ROSE (*To* ROBIN). Oh, but, sir, I knew not that thou didst
seek me in wedlock, or in very truth I should not have
hearkened unto this man, for behold, he is but a lowly
mariner, and very poor withal, whereas thou art a
tiller of the land, and thou hast fat oxen, and many
sheep and swine, a considerable dairy farm and much
corn and oil!

RICHARD. That's true, my lass, but it's done now, ain't it,
Rob?

ROSE. Still it may be that I should not be happy in thy
love. I am passing young and little able to judge. Moreover, as to thy character I know naught!

ROBIN. Nay, Rose, I'll answer for that. Dick has won thy
love fairly. Broken-hearted as I am, I'll stand up for
Dick through thick and thin!

RICHARD (*with emotion*). Thankye, messmate! that's well
said. That's spoken honest: Thankye, Rob! (*Grasps
his hand.*)

ROSE. Yet methinks I have heard that sailors are but worldly men, and little prone to lead serious and thoughtful lives!

ROBIN. And what then? Admit that Dick is *not* a steady character, and that when he's excited he uses language that would make your hair curl. Grant that— he does. It's the truth, and I'm not going to deny it. But look at his *good* qualities. He's as nimble as a pony, and his hornpipe is the talk of the Fleet!

RICHARD. Thankye, Rob! That's well spoken. Thankye, Rob!

ROSE. But it may be that he drinketh strong waters which do bemuse a man, and make him even as the wild beasts of the desert!

ROBIN. Well, suppose he does, and I don't say he don't, for rum's his bane, and ever has been. He *does* drink—I won't deny it. But what of that? Look at his arms— tattooed to the shoulder! (RICHARD *rolls up his sleeves.*) No, no—I won't hear a word against Dick!

ROSE. But they say that mariners are but rarely true to those whom they profess to love!

ROBIN. Granted—granted—and I don't say that Dick isn't as bad as any of 'em. (RICHARD *chuckles*) You are, you know you are, you dog! a devil of a fellow—a regular out-and-out Lothario! But what then? You can't have everything, and a better hand at turning-in a dead-eye[6] don't walk a deck! And what an accomplishment *that* is in a family man! No, no—not a word against Dick. I'll stick up for him through thick and thin!

RICHARD. Thankye, Rob, thankye. You're a true friend. I've acted accordin' to my heart's dictates, and such orders as them no man should disobey.

Ensemble—RICHARD, ROBIN, ROSE

In sailing o'er life's ocean wide
Your heart should be your only guide;
With summer sea and favouring wind,
Yourself in port you'll surely find.

6 Fastening a rope to a fitting.

Solo—RICHARD

My heart says, "To this maiden strike—
    She's captured you.
She's just the sort of girl you like—
    You know you do.
If other man her heart should gain,
    I shall resign."
That's what it says to me quite plain,
    This heart of mine.

Solo—ROBIN

My heart says, "You've a prosperous lot,
    With acres wide;
You mean to settle all you've got
    Upon your bride."
It don't pretend to shape my acts
    By word or sign;
It merely states these simple facts,
    This heart of mine!

Solo—ROSE

Ten minutes since my heart said "white"—
    It now says "black."
It then said "left"—it now says "right"—
    Hearts often tack.

I must obey its latest strain—
    You tell me so. (*To* RICHARD)
But should it change its mind again,
    I'll let you know.

(*Turning from* RICHARD *to* ROBIN, *who embraces her.*)

Ensemble

In sailing o'er life's ocean wide
No doubt the heart should be your guide;
But it is awkward when you find
A heart that does not know its mind!

(*Exeunt* ROBIN *with* ROSE L., *and* RICHARD *weeping,* R.)

(*Enter* MAD MARGARET. *She is wildly dressed in picturesque tatters, and is an obvious caricature of theatrical madness.*)

Scena—MARGARET

Cheerily carols the lark
   Over the cot.
Merrily whistles the clerk
   Scratching a blot.
     But the lark
     And the clerk,
     I remark,
    Comfort me not!

Over the ripening peach
   Buzzes the bee.
Splash on the billowy beach
   Tumbles the sea.
     But the peach
     And the beach
     They are each
    Nothing to me!
     And why?
     Who am I?
Daft Madge! Crazy Meg!
Mad Margaret! Poor Peg!
   He! he! he! he! he! (*chuckling*)

   Mad, I?
     Yes, very!
   But why?
     Mystery!
       Don't call!
         Whisht! whisht!
   No crime—
     'Tis only
   That I'm
     Love-lonely!
      That's all!

Ballad

To a garden full of posies
   Cometh one to gather flowers,
   And he wanders through its bowers
Toying with the wanton roses,
   Who, uprising from their beds,
   Hold on high their shameless heads

With their pretty lips a-pouting,
Never doubting—never doubting
   That for Cytherean posies
   He would gather aught but roses!

In a nest of weeds and nettles
   Lay a violet, half-hidden,
   Hoping that his glance unbidden
Yet might fall upon her petals.
   Though she lived alone, apart,
   Hope lay nestling at her heart,
But, alas, the cruel awaking
Set her little heart a-breaking,
   For he gathered for his posies
   Only roses—only roses!

(*Bursts into tears.*)

(*Enter* ROSE.)

ROSE. A maiden, and in tears? Can I do aught to soften
   thy sorrow? This apple—(*offering apple*)
MARGARET (*examines it and rejects it*). No! (*mysteriously*)
   Tell me, are you mad?
ROSE. I? No! That is, I think not.
MARGARET. That's well! Then you don't love Sir Despard
   Murgatroyd? All mad girls love him. *I* love him. I'm
   poor Mad Margaret—Crazy Meg—Poor Peg! He!
   he! he! he! (*chuckling*)
ROSE. Thou lovest the bad Baronet of Ruddigore? Oh,
   horrible—too horrible!
MARGARET. You pity me? Then be my mother! The squirrel
   had a mother, but she drank and the squirrel fled!
   Hush! They sing a brave song in our parts—it runs
   somewhat thus: (*Sings*)

   "The cat and the dog and the little puppee
   Sat down in a—down in a—in a—"

I forget what they sat down in, but so the song goes!
Listen—I've come to pinch her!
ROSE. Mercy, whom?
MARGARET. You mean "who."
ROSE. Nay! it is the accusative after the verb.
MARGARET. True (*Whispers melodramatically*) I have come
   to pinch Rose Maybud!

ROSE (*aside, alarmed*). Rose Maybud!

MARGARET. Aye! I love him—he loved me once. But that's all gone, fisht! He' gave me an Italian glance—thus (*business*)—and made me his. He will give *her* an Italian glance, and make *her* his. But it shall not be, for I'll stamp on her—stamp on her—stamp on her! Did you ever kill anybody? No? Why not? Listen— I killed a fly this morning! It buzzed, and I wouldn't have it. So it died—pop! So shall she!

ROSE. But, behold, *I* am Rose Maybud, and I would fain not die "pop."

MARGARET. You are Rose Maybud?

ROSE. Yes, sweet Rose Maybud!

MARGARET. Strange! They told me she was beautiful. And *he* loves *you!* No, no! If I thought that, I would treat you as the auctioneer and land-agent treated the lady-bird—I would rend you asunder!

ROSE. Nay, be pacified, for behold I am pledged to another, and lo, we are to be wedded this very day!

MARGARET. Swear me that! Come to a Commissioner and let me have it on affidavit! *I* once made an affidavit— but it died—it died—it died! But, see, they come— Sir Despard and his evil crew! Hide, hide—they are all mad—quite mad!

ROSE. What makes you think that?

MARGARET. Hush! They sing choruses in public. That's mad enough, I think! Go—hide away, or they will seize you! Hush! Quite softly—quite, quite softly!

(*Exeunt together, on tiptoe.*)

(*Enter Chorus of Bucks and Blades,[7] heralded by Chorus of Bridesmaids.*)

Chorus of Bridesmaids

Welcome, gentry,
For your entry
Sets our tender hearts a-beating.
Men of station,
Admiration
Prompts this unaffected greeting.
Hearty greeting offer we!

[7] Dashing young men, dandies.

Chorus of Bucks and Blades

When thoroughly tired
Of being admired
By ladies of gentle degree—degree,
With flattery sated,
High-flown and inflated,
Away from the city we flee—we flee!
From charms intramural
To prettiness rural
The sudden transition
Is simply Elysian,
So come, Amaryllis,
Come, Chloe and Phyllis,
Your slaves, for the moment, are we!

ALL.   From charms intramural, etc.

Chorus of Bridesmaids

The sons of the tillage
Who dwell in this village
Are people of lowly degree—degree.
Though honest and active,
They're most unattractive,
And awkward as awkward can be—can be.
They're clumsy clodhoppers
With axes and choppers,
And shepherds and ploughmen
And drovers and cowmen
And hedgers and reapers
And carters and keepers,
And never a lover for me!

Bridesmaids

So, welcome, gentry, etc.

Bucks and Blades

When thoroughly tired, etc.

(*Enter* SIR DESPARD MURGATROYD.)

Song and Chorus—SIR DESPARD

SIR DESPARD. Oh, why am I moody and sad?
CHORUS.   Can't guess!

SIR DESPARD. And why am I guiltily mad?

CHORUS. Confess!

SIR DESPARD. Because I am thoroughly bad!

CHORUS. Oh yes—

SIR DESPARD. You'll see it at once in my face.
Oh, why am I husky and hoarse?

CHORUS. Ah, why?

SIR DESPARD. It's the workings of conscience, of course.

CHORUS. Fie, fie!

SIR DESPARD. And huskiness stands for remorse,

CHORUS. Oh my!

SIR DESPARD. At least it does so in my case!
When in crime one is fully employed—

CHORUS. Like you—

SIR DESPARD. Your expression gets warped and destroyed:

CHORUS. It do.

SIR DESPARD. It's a penalty none can avoid;

CHORUS. How true!

SIR DESPARD. I once was a nice-looking youth;
But like stone from a strong catapult—

CHORUS (*explaining to each other*). A trice—

SIR DESPARD. I rushed at my terrible cult—

CHORUS (*explaining to each other*). That's vice—

SIR DESPARD. Observe the unpleasant result!

CHORUS. Not nice.

SIR DESPARD. Indeed I am telling the truth!
Oh, innocent, happy though poor!

CHORUS. That's we—

SIR DESPARD. If I had been virtuous, I'm sure—

CHORUS. Like me—

SIR DESPARD. I should be as nice-looking as you're!

CHORUS. May be.

SIR DESPARD. You are very nice-looking indeed!
Oh, innocents, listen in time—

CHORUS. We *doe*,

SIR DESPARD. Avoid an existence of crime—

CHORUS. Just so—

SIR DESPARD. Or you'll be as ugly as I'm—

CHORUS (*loudly*). No! No!

SIR DESPARD. And now, if you please, we'll proceed.

(*All the girls express their horror of* SIR DESPARD. *As he approaches them they fly from him, terror-stricken, leaving him alone on the stage.*)

SIR DESPARD. Poor children, how they loathe me—me whose hands are certainly steeped in infamy, but whose heart is as the heart of a little child. But what *is* a poor baronet to do, when a whole picture gallery of ancestors step down from their frames and threaten him with an excruciating death if he hesitate to commit his daily crime? But ha! ha! I am even with them! (*mysteriously*) I get my crime over the first thing in the morning, and then, ha! ha! for the rest of the day I do good—I do good—I do good! (*melodramatically*) Two days since, I stole a child and built an orphan asylum. Yesterday I robbed a bank and endowed a bishopric. To-day I carry off Rose Maybud and atone with a cathedral! This is what it is to be the sport and toy of a Picture Gallery! But I will be bitterly revenged upon them! I will give them all to the Nation, and nobody shall ever look upon their faces again!

(*Enter* RICHARD.)

RICHARD. Ax your honour's pardon, but—

SIR DESPARD. Ha! observed! And by a mariner! What would you with me, fellow?

RICHARD. Your honour, I'm a poor man-o'war's man, becalmed in the doldrums—

SIR DESPARD. I don't know them.

RICHARD. And I make bold to ax your honour's advice. Does your honour know what it is to have a heart?

SIR DESPARD. My honour knows what it is to have a complete apparatus for conducting the circulation of the blood through the veins and arteries of the human body.

RICHARD. Aye, but has your honour a heart that ups and looks you in the face, and gives you quarter-deck orders that it's life and death to disobey?

SIR DESPARD. I have not a heart of that description, but I have a Picture Gallery that presumes to take that liberty.

RICHARD. Well, your honour, it's like this—Your honour had an elder brother—

SIR DESPARD. It had.

RICHARD. Who should have inherited your title and, with it, its cuss.

SIR DESPARD. Aye, but he died. Oh, Ruthven!—

RICHARD. He didn't.

SIR DESPARD. He did *not*?

RICHARD. He didn't. On the contrary, he lives in this here very village, under the name of Robin Oakapple, and he's a-going to marry Rose Maybud this very day.

SIR DESPARD. Ruthven alive, and going to marry Rose Maybud! Can this be possible?

RICHARD. Now the question I was going to ask your honour is—Ought I to tell your honour this?

SIR DESPARD. I don't know. It's a delicate point. I think you ought. Mind, I'm not sure, but I think so.

RICHARD. That's what my heart says. It says, "Dick," it says (it calls me Dick acos it's entitled to take that liberty), "that there young gal would recoil from him if she knowed what he really were. Ought you to stand off and on, and let this young gal take this false step and never fire a shot across her bows to bring her to? No," it says, "you did *not* ought." And I won't ought, accordin'.

SIR DESPARD. Then you really feel yourself at liberty to tell me that my elder brother lives—that I may charge him with his cruel deceit, and transfer to his shoulders the hideous thraldom under which I have laboured for so many years! Free—free at last! Free to live a blameless life, and to die beloved and regretted by all who knew me!

Duet—SIR DESPARD and RICHARD

RICHARD.	You understand?
SIR DESPARD.	I think I do;
	With vigour unshaken
	This step shall be taken.
	It's neatly planned.
RICHARD.	I think so too;
	I'll readily bet it
	You'll never regret it!
BOTH.	For duty, duty must be done;
	The rule applies to every one,
	And painful though that duty be,
	To shirk the task were fiddle-de-dee!
SIR DESPARD.	The bridegroom comes—
RICHARD.	Likewise the bride—
	The maidens are very

Elated and merry;
They are her chums.

SIR DESPARD.   To lash their pride
                Were almost a pity,
                The pretty committee!

BOTH.   But duty, duty must be done;
            The rule applies to every one,
            And painful though that duty be,
            To shirk the task were fiddle-de-dee!

(*Exeunt* RICHARD *and* SIR DESPARD.)

(*Enter Chorus of Bridesmaids and Bucks.*)

Chorus of Bridesmaids

Hail the bride of seventeen summers:
            In fair phrases
            Hymn her praises;
Lift your song on high, all comers.
            She rejoices
            In your voices.
Smiling summer beams upon her,
Shedding every blessing on her:
            Maidens greet her—
            Kindly treat her—
You may all be brides some day!

Chorus of Bucks

Hail the bridegroom who advances,
            Agitated,
            Yet elated.
He's in easy circumstances,
            Young and lusty,
            True and trusty.

(*Enter* ROBIN, *attended by* RICHARD *and* OLD ADAM, *meeting* ROSE, *attended by* ZORAH *and* DAME HANNAH. ROSE *and* ROBIN *embrace*.)

Madrigal

ROSE.   When the buds are blossoming,
            Smiling welcome to the spring,
            Lovers choose a wedding day—
            Life is love in merry May!

GIRLS.	Spring is green—Fal lal la!
	Summer's rose—Fal lal la!
ALL.	It is sad when summer goes,
	Fal la!
MEN.	Autumn's gold—Fal lal la!
	Winter's gray—Fal lal la!
ALL.	Winter still is far away—
	Fal la!

Leaves in autumn fade and fall,
Winter is the end of all.
Spring and summer teem with glee:
Spring and summer, then, for me!
Fal la!

HANNAH.	In the spring-time seed is sown:
In the summer grass is mown:
In the autumn you may reap:
Winter is the time for sleep.

GIRLS.	Spring is hope—Fal lal la!
	Summer's joy—Fal lal la!
ALL.	Spring and summer never cloy.
	Fal la!
MEN.	Autumn, toil—Fal lal la!
	Winter, rest—Fal lal la!
ALL.	Winter, after all, is best—
	Fal la!

ALL.	Spring and summer pleasure you,
Autumn, aye, and winter too—
Every season has its cheer,
Life is lovely all the year!
Fal la!

[*Gavotte*]

(*After Gavotte, enter* SIR DESPARD.)

SIR DESPARD. Hold, bride and bridegroom, ere you wed
each other,
I claim young Robin as my elder brother!
His rightful title I have long enjoyed:
I claim him as Sir Ruthven Murgatroyd!

ALL.	O wonder!

ROSE (*wildly*). Deny the falsehood, Robin, as you should,
It is a plot!

ROBIN.	I would, if conscientiously I could,
But I cannot!

ALL.	Ah, base one!

Solo—ROBIN

As pure and blameless peasant,
　I cannot, I regret,
Deny a truth unpleasant,
　I am that Baronet!

ALL. 　　He is that Baronet!
But when completely rated
　Bad Baronet am I,
That I am what he's stated
　I'll recklessly deny!

ALL. 　　He'll recklessly deny!
ROBIN. 　When I'm a bad Bart.[8] I will tell taradiddles!
ALL. 　　He'll tell taradiddles when he's a bad Bart.
ROBIN. 　I'll play a bad part on the falsest of fiddles.
ALL. 　　On very false fiddles he'll play a bad part!
ROBIN. 　But until that takes place I must be con-
　　　　scientious—
ALL. 　　He'll be conscientious until that takes place.
ROBIN. 　Then adieu with good grace to my morals
　　　　sententious!
ALL. 　　To morals sententious adieu with good grace!
ZORAH. 　　Who is the wretch who hath betrayed thee?
　　　　　Let him stand forth!
RICHARD (*coming forward*). 'Twas I!
ALL. 　　Die, traitor!
RICHARD. 　Hold! my conscience made me!
　　　　Withhold your wrath!

Solo—RICHARD

Within this breast there beats a heart
　Whose voice can't be gainsaid.
It bade me thy true rank impart,
　And I at once obeyed.
I knew 'twould blight thy budding fate—
I knew 'twould cause thee anguish great—
But did I therefore hesitate?
　No! I at once obeyed!

ALL. 　　Acclaim him who, when his true heart
Bade him young Robin's rank impart,
　　Immediately obeyed!

---

[8] Standard abbreviation for baronet, as in Sir Ruthven Murgatroyd,
Bart.

Solo—ROSE (*addressing* ROBIN)

Farewell!
Thou hadst my heart—
'Twas quickly won!
But now we part—
Thy face I shun!
Farewell!

Go bend the knee
At Vice's shrine,
Of life with me
All hope resign.
Farewell!

(*To* SIR DESPARD): Take me—I am thy bride!

Bridesmaids

Hail the Bridegroom—hail the Bride!
When the nuptial knot is tied;
Every day will bring some joy
That can never, never cloy!

(*Enter* MARGARET, *who listens.*)

SIR DESPARD. Excuse me, I'm a virtuous person now—
ROSE.   That's why I wed you!
SIR DESPARD. And I to Margaret must keep my vow!
MARGARET.   Have I misread you?
Oh, joy! with newly kindled rapture warmed,
I kneel before you! (*Kneels.*)
SIR DESPARD. I once disliked you; now that I've reformed,
How I adore you! (*They embrace.*)

Bridesmaids

Hail the Bridegroom—hail the Bride!
When the nuptial knot is tied;
Every day will bring some joy
That can never, never cloy!

ROSE.   Richard, of him I love bereft,
Through thy design,
Thou art the only one that's left,
So I am thine! (*They embrace.*)

Bridesmaids

Hail the Bridegroom—hail the Bride!
Let the nuptial knot be tied!

Duet—ROSE and RICHARD

Oh, happy the lily
    When kissed by the bee;
And, sipping tranquilly,
    Quite happy is he;
And happy the filly
    That neighs in her pride;
But happier than any,
A pound to a penny,
A lover is, when he
    Embraces his bride!

Duet—SIR DESPARD and MARGARET

Oh, happy the flowers
    That blossom in June,
And happy the bowers
    That gain by the boon,
But happier by hours
    The man of descent,
Who, folly regretting,
Is bent on forgetting
His bad baronetting,
    And means to repent!

Trio—HANNAH, ADAM, and ZORAH

Oh, happy the blossom
    That blooms on the lea,
Likewise the opossum
    That sits on a tree,
But when you come across 'em,
    They cannot compare
With those who are treading
The dance at a wedding,
While people are spreading
    The best of good fare!

Solo—ROBIN

Oh, wretched the debtor
    Who's signing a deed!
And wretched the letter
    That no one can read!
But very much better
    Their lot it must be
Than that of the person
I'm making this verse on,
Whose head there's a curse on—
    Alluding to me!

Repeat ensemble with Chorus

(*Dance*)

(*At the end of the dance* ROBIN *falls senseless on the stage. Picture.*)

END OF ACT I

ACT II

[SCENE.] *Picture Gallery in Ruddigore Castle. The walls are covered with full-length portraits of the Baronets of Ruddigore from the time of* JAMES I.—*the first being that of* SIR RUPERT, *alluded to in the legend; the last that of the last deceased Baronet,* SIR RODERIC.

(*Enter* ROBIN *and* ADAM *melodramatically. They are greatly altered in appearance,* ROBIN *wearing the haggard aspect of a guilty roué;* ADAM, *that of the wicked steward to such a man.*)

Duet—ROBIN *and* ADAM

ROBIN. I once was as meek as a new-born lamb,
    I'm now Sir Murgatroyd—ha! ha!
      With greater precision
      (Without the elision),
    Sir Ruthven Murgatroyd—ha! ha!

ADAM.   And I, who was once his *valley-de-sham*,
            As steward I'm now employed—ha! ha!
            The dickens may take him—
            I'll never forsake him!
            As steward I'm now employed—ha! ha!

BOTH.   How dreadful when an innocent heart
            Becomes, perforce, a bad young Bart.,
            And still more hard on old Adam,
            His former faithful *valley-de-sham!*

ROBIN. This is a painful state of things, old Adam!

ADAM.   Painful, indeed! Ah, my poor master, when I swore
            that, come what would, I would serve you in all things
            for ever, I little thought to what a pass it would
            bring me! The confidential adviser to the greatest
            villain unhung! Now, sir, to business. What crime do
            you propose to commit to-day?
ROBIN. How should I know? As my confidential adviser, it's
            your duty to suggest something.
ADAM.   Sir, I loathe the life you are leading, but a good old
            man's oath is paramount, and I obey. Richard Daunt-
            less is here with pretty Rose Maybud, to ask your
            consent to their marriage. Poison their beer.
ROBIN. No—not that—I know I'm a bad Bart., but I'm not
            as bad a Bart. as all that.
ADAM.   Well, there you are, you see! It's no use my making
            suggestions if you don't adopt them.
ROBIN. (*melodramatically*). How would it be, do you think,
            were I to lure him here with cunning wile—bind him
            with good stout rope to yonder post—and then, by
            making hideous faces at him, curdle the heart-blood
            in his arteries, and freeze the very marrow in his
            bones? How say you, Adam, is not the scheme well
            planned?
ADAM.   It would be simply rude—nothing more. But soft—
            they come!

(ADAM *and* ROBIN *retire up* [*stage*] *as* RICHARD *and* ROSE
enter, preceded by Chorus of Bridesmaids.)

Duet—RICHARD and ROSE

RICHARD. Happily coupled are we,
              You see—
        I am a jolly Jack Tar,
              My star,
          And you are the fairest,
          The richest and rarest
        Of innocent lasses you are,
              By far—
        Of innocent lasses you are!
        Fanned by a favouring gale,
              You'll sail
        Over life's treacherous sea
              With me,
          And as for bad weather,
          We'll brave it together,
        And you shall creep under my lee,
              My wee!
        And you shall creep under my lee!
        For you are such a smart little craft—
        Such a neat little, sweet little craft,
          Such a bright little, tight little,
          Slight little, light little,
        Trim little, prim little craft!

CHORUS.   For she is such, etc.

ROSE.   My hopes will be blighted, I fear,
              My dear;
        In a month you'll be going to sea,
              Quite free,
          And all of my wishes
          You'll throw to the fishes
        As though they were never to be;
              Poor me!
        As though they were never to be.
        And I shall be left all alone
              To moan,
        And weep at your cruel deceit,
              Complete;
          While you'll be asserting
          Your freedom by flirting

With every woman you meet,
      You cheat—
With every woman you meet!

Though I am such a smart little craft—
Such a neat little, sweet little craft,
      Such a bright little, tight little,
      Slight little, light little,
Trim little, prim little craft!

CHORUS. For she is such, etc.

(*Enter* ROBIN.)

ROBIN. Soho! pretty one—in my power at last, eh? Know
ye not that I have those within my call who, at my
lightest bidding, would immure ye in an uncomfortable
dungeon? (*calling*) What ho! within there!

RICHARD. Hold—we are prepared for this. (*producing a
Union Jack*) Here is a flag that none dare defy (*All
kneel.*), and while this glorious rag floats over Rose
Maybud's head, the man does not live who would dare
to lay unlicensed hand upon her!

ROBIN. Foiled—and by a Union Jack! But a time will come,
and then—

ROSE. Nay, let me plead with him. (*To* ROBIN) Sir Ruthven,
have pity. In my book of etiquette the case of a maiden
about to be wedded to one who unexpectedly turns
out to be a baronet with a curse on him is not considered. Time was when you loved me madly. Prove
that this was no selfish love by according your consent
to my marriage with one who, if he be not you yourself, is the next best thing—your dearest friend!

Ballad—ROSE

In bygone days I had thy love—
      Thou hadst my heart.
But Fate, all human vows above,
      Our lives did part!
By the old love thou hadst for me—
By the fond heart that beat for thee—
By joys that never now can be,
      Grant thou my prayer!

ALL (*kneeling*). Grant thou her prayer!

ROBIN (*recit.*). Take her—I yield!

ALL (*recit.*).   Oh, rapture!

CHORUS. Away to the parson we go—
             Say we're solicitious very
         That he will turn two into one—
             Singing hey, derry down derry!

RICHARD. For she *is* such a smart little craft—
ROSE.   Such a neat little, sweet little craft—
RICHARD.   Such a bright little—
ROSE.   Tight little—
RICHARD.   Slight little—
ROSE.   Light little—
BOTH.   Trim little, slim little craft!

CHORUS. For she *is* such a smart little craft, etc.

(*Exeunt all but* ROBIN.)

ROBIN. For a week I have fulfilled my accursed doom! I
    have duly committed a crime a day! Not a great
    crime, I trust, but still, in the eyes of one as strictly
    regulated as I used to be, a crime. But will my ghostly
    ancestors be satisfied with what I have done, or will
    they regard it as an unworthy subterfuge? (*addressing
    Pictures*) Oh, my forefathers, wallowers in blood, there
    came at last a day when, sick of crime, you, each
    and every, vowed to sin no more, and so, in agony,
    called welcome Death to free you from your cloying
    guiltiness. Let the sweet psalm of that repentant hour
    soften your long-dead hearts, and tune your souls to
    mercy on your poor posterity! (*kneeling*)

(*The stage darkens for a moment. It becomes light again,
and the pictures are seen to have become animated.*)

Chorus of Family Portraits

    Painted emblems of a race,
        All accurst in days of yore,
    Each from his accustomed place
        Steps into the world once more.

(*The Pictures step from their frames and march round
the stage.*)

Baronet of Ruddigore,
 Last of our accursèd line,
Down upon the oaken floor—
 Down upon those knees of thine.

 Coward, poltroon, shaker, squeamer,
 Blockhead, sluggard, dullard, dreamer,
 Shirker, shuffler, crawler, creeper,
 Sniffler, snuffler, wailer, weeper,
 Earthworm, maggot, tadpole, weevil!
 Set upon thy course of evil,
 Lest the king of Spectre-Land
 Set on thee his grisly hand!

(*The Spectre of* SIR RODERIC *descends from his frame.*)

SIR RODERIC. Beware! beware! beware!
ROBIN.   Gaunt vision, who are thou
    That thus, with icy glare
     And stern relentless brow,
     Appearest, who knows how?

SIR RODERIC. I am the spectre of the late
    Sir Roderic Murgatroyd,
   Who comes to warn thee that thy fate
    Thou canst not now avoid.

ROBIN.   Alas, poor ghost!
SIR RODERIC.   The pity you
   Express for nothing goes:
   We spectres are a jollier crew
    Than you, perhaps, suppose!
CHORUS.   We spectres are a jollier crew
    Than you, perhaps, suppose!

Song—SIR RODERIC

When the night wind howls in the chimney cowls,[9] and the
 bat in the moonlight flies,
And inky clouds, like funeral shrouds, sail over the mid-
 night skies—
When the footpads quail at the night-bird's wail, and black
 dogs bay at the moon,
Then is the spectre's holiday—then is the ghosts' high-noon!
 CHORUS.   Ha! ha!
   Then is the ghosts' high-noon!

9 Covers.

As the sob of the breeze sweeps over the trees, and the
  mists lie low on the fen,
From grey tomb-stones are gathered the bones that once
  were women and men,
And away they go, with a mop and a mow, to the revel that
  ends too soon,
For cockcrow limits our holiday—the dead of the night's
  high-noon!

CHORUS.   Ha! ha!
          The dead of the night's high-noon!

And then each ghost with his ladye-toast to their church-
  yard beds takes flight,
With a kiss, perhaps, on her lantern chaps, and a grisly
  grim "good-night";
Till the welcome knell of the midnight bell rings forth its
  jolliest tune,
And ushers in our next high holiday—the dead of the
  night's high-noon!

CHORUS.   Ha! ha!
          The dead of the night's high-noon!

ROBIN. I recognize you now—you are the picture that
  hangs at the end of the gallery.

SIR RODERIC. In a bad light. I am.

ROBIN. Are you considered a good likeness?

SIR RODERIC. Pretty well. Flattering.

ROBIN. Because as a work of art you are poor.

SIR RODERIC. I am crude in colour, but I have only been
  painted ten years. In a couple of centuries I shall
  be an Old Master, and then you will be sorry you
  spoke lightly of me.

ROBIN. And may I ask why you have left your frames?

SIR RODERIC. It is our duty to see that our successors commit their daily crimes in a conscientious and workman-
  like fashion. It is our duty to remind you that you
  are evading the conditions under which you are permitted to exist.

ROBIN. Really, I don't know what you'd have. I've only
  been a bad baronet a week, and I've committed a
  crime punctually every day.

SIR RODERIC. Let us inquire into this. Monday?

ROBIN. Monday was a Bank Holiday.

SIR RODERIC. True. Tuesday?

ROBIN. On Tuesday I made a false income-tax return.

ALL. Ha! ha!

1ST GHOST. That's nothing.

2ND GHOST. Nothing at all.

3RD GHOST. Everybody does that.

4TH GHOST. It's expected of you.

SIR RODERIC. Wednesday?

ROBIN (*melodramatically*). On Wednesday I forged a will.

SIR RODERIC. Whose will?

ROBIN. My own.

SIR RODERIC. My good sir, you can't forge your own will!

ROBIN. Can't I, though! I like that! I *did!* Besides, if a man can't forge his own will, whose will can he forge?

1ST GHOST. There's something in that.

2ND GHOST. Yes, it seems reasonable.

3RD GHOST. At first sight it does.

4TH GHOST. Fallacy somewhere, I fancy!

ROBIN. A man can do what he likes with his own?

SIR RODERIC. I suppose he can.

ROBIN. Well, then, he can forge his own will, stoopid! On Thursday I shot a fox.[10]

1ST GHOST. Hear, hear!

SIR RODERIC. That's better. (*addressing Ghosts*) Pass the fox, I think? (*They assent.*) Yes, pass the fox. Friday?

ROBIN. On Friday I forged a cheque.

SIR RODERIC. Whose cheque?

ROBIN. Old Adam's.

SIR RODERIC. But Old Adam hasn't a banker.

ROBIN. I didn't say I forged his banker—I said I forged his cheque. On Saturday I disinherited my only son.

SIR RODERIC. But you haven't got a son.

ROBIN. No—not yet. I disinherited him in advance, to save time. You see—by this arrangement—he'll be born ready disinherited.

SIR RODERIC. I see. But I don't think you can do that.

ROBIN. My good sir, if I can't disinherit my own unborn son, whose unborn son can I disinherit?

SIR RODERIC. Humph! These arguments sound very well, but I can't help thinking that, if they were reduced to syllogistic form, they wouldn't hold water. Now quite understand us. We are foggy, but we don't permit our

---

[10] Since fox-hunting was the principal aristocratic sport, the aristocrats were horrified at shooting a fox, rather than running it down with hounds in a "sporting" way.

fogginess to be presumed upon. Unless you undertake to—well, suppose we say, carry off a lady? (*addressing Ghosts*) Those who are in favour of his carrying off a lady? (*All hold up their hands except a Bishop.*) Those of the contrary opinion? (*Bishop holds up his hand.*) Oh, you're never satisfied! Yes, unless you undertake to carry off a lady at once—I don't care what lady—any lady—choose your lady—you perish in inconceivable agonies.

ROBIN. Carry off a lady? Certainly not, on any account. I've the greatest respect for ladies, and I wouldn't do anything of the kind for worlds! No, no. I'm not that kind of baronet, I assure you! If that's all you've got to say, you'd better go back to your frames.

SIR RODERIC. Very good—then let the agonies commence.

(*Ghosts make passes.* ROBIN *begins to writhe in agony.*)

ROBIN. Oh! Oh! Don't do that! I can't stand it!

SIR RODERIC. Painful, isn't it? It gets worse by degrees.

ROBIN. Oh—Oh! Stop a bit! Stop it, will you? I want to speak.

(SIR RODERIC *makes signs to Ghosts, who resume their attitudes.*)

SIR RODERIC. Better?

ROBIN. Yes—better now! Whew!

SIR RODERIC. Well, do you consent?

ROBIN. But it's such an ungentlemanly thing to do!

SIR RODERIC. As you please. (*To* GHOSTS) Carry on!

ROBIN. Stop—I can't stand it! I agree! I promise! It shall be done!

SIR RODERIC. To-day?

ROBIN. To-day!

SIR RODERIC. At once?

ROBIN. At once! I retract! I apologize! I had no idea it was anything like that!

Chorus

He yields! He answers to our call!
　　We do not ask for more.
A sturdy fellow, after all,
　　This latest Ruddigore!
All perish in unheard-of woe
　　Who dare our wills defy;

We want your pardon, ere we go.
For having agonized you so—
　　So pardon us—
　　So pardon us—
　　So pardon us—
　　　　Or die!

ROBIN. I pardon you!
　　　　I pardon you!
ALL. He pardons us—
　　　　Hurrah!

(*The Ghosts return to their frames.*)

CHORUS. Painted emblems of a race,
　　　　All accurst in days of yore,
　　　　Each to his accustomed place
　　　　Steps unwillingly once more!

(*By this time the Ghosts have changed to pictures again.*
ROBIN *is overcome by emotion.*)

(*Enter* ADAM.)

ADAM. My poor master, you are not well—
ROBIN. Gideon Crawle,[11] it won't do—I've seen 'em—all
　　my ancestors—they're just gone. They say that I must
　　do something desperate at once, or perish in horrible
　　agonies. Go—go to yonder village—carry off a maiden
　　—bring her here at once—any one—I don't care
　　which.
ADAM. But—
ROBIN. Not a word, but obey! Fly!

(*Exit* ADAM.)

Recitative and Song—ROBIN

Away, Remorse!
　　　　Compunction, hence!
Go, Moral Force!
　　　　Go, Penitence!
To Virtue's plea
　　　　A long farewell—

---

[11] A reference back to a now-omitted exchange between Robin and
Old Adam at the opening of Act II, in which he states that a bad
Bart.'s valley-de-sham (valet-de-chambre) was conventionally named
something like Gideon Crawle.

Propriety,
            I ring your knell!
Come, guiltiness of deadliest hue!
Come, desperate deeds of derring-do!

Henceforth all the crimes that I find in the *Times*,
        I've promised to perpetrate daily;
To-morrow I start, with a petrified heart,
        On a regular course of Old Bailey.
There's confidence tricking, bad coin, pocket-picking,
        And several other disgraces—
There's postage-stamp prigging, and then, thimble-rigging,
        The three-card delusion at races!
Oh! a baronet's rank is exceedingly nice,
But the title's uncommonly dear at the price!

Ye well-to-do squires, who live in the shires,
        Where petty distinctions are vital,
Who found Athenæums and local museums,
        With views to a baronet's title—
Ye butchers and bakers and candlestick makers
        Who sneer at all things that are tradey—
Whose middle-class lives are embarassed by wives
        Who long to parade as "My Lady,"
Oh! allow me to offer a word of advice,
The title's uncommonly dear at the price!

Ye supple M.P.'s who go down on your knees,
        Your precious identity sinking,
And vote black or white as your leaders indite
    (Which saves you the trouble of thinking),
For your country's good fame, her repute, or her shame,
        You don't care the snuff of a candle—
But you're paid for your game when you're told that your
    name
        Will be graced by a baronet's handle—
Oh! allow me to give *you* a word of advice—
The title's uncommonly dear at the price!

(*Exit* ROBIN.)

(*Enter* DESPARD *and* MARGARET. *They are both dressed
in sober black of formal cut, and present a strong contrast to their appearance in Act I.*)

Duet

DESPARD.	I once was a very abandoned person—
MARGARET.	Making the most of evil chances.
DESPARD.	Nobody could conceive a worse 'un—
MARGARET.	Even in all the old romances.
DESPARD.	I blush for my wild extravagances,
	But be so kind
	To bear in mind,
MARGARET.	We were the victims of circumstances!

(*Dance.*)

That is one of our blameless dances.

MARGARET.	I was once an exceedingly odd young lady—
DESPARD.	Suffering much from spleen and vapours.
MARGARET.	Clergymen thought my conduct shady—
DESPARD.	She didn't spend much upon linen-drapers.
MARGARET.	It certainly entertained the gapers.
	My ways were strange
	Beyond all range—
DESPARD.	Paragraphs got into all the papers.

(*Dance.*)

DESPARD.	We only cut respectable capers.

DESPARD.	I've given up all my wild proceedings.
MARGARET.	My taste for a wandering life is waning.
DESPARD.	Now I'm a dab at penny readings.
MARGARET.	They are not remarkably entertaining.
DESPARD.	A moderate livelihood we're gaining.
MARGARET.	In fact we rule
	A National School.[12]
DESPARD.	The duties are dull, but I'm not complaining.

(*Dance.*)

This sort of thing takes a deal of training!

DESPARD. We have been married a week.
MARGARET. One happy, happy week!
DESPARD. Our new life—
MARGARET. Is delightful indeed!

[12] A public school, established by the Elementary Education Act of 1870.

DESPARD. So calm!

MARGARET. So unimpassioned! (*wildly*) Master, all this I owe to you! See, I am no longer wild and untidy. My hair is combed. My face is washed. My boots fit!

DESPARD. Margaret, don't. Pray restrain yourself. Remember you are now a district visitor.[13]

MARGARET. A gentle district visitor!

DESPARD. You are orderly, methodical, neat; you have your emotions well under control.

MARGARET. I have. (*wildly*) Master, when I think of all you have done for me, I fall at your feet. I embrace your ankles. I hug your knees! (*doing so*)

DESPARD. Hush. This is not well. This is calculated to provoke remark. Be composed, I beg!

MARGARET. Ah! you are angry with poor little Mad Margaret!

DESPARD. No, not angry; but a district visitor should learn to eschew melodrama. Visit the poor, by all means, and give them tea and barley-water, but don't do it as if you were administering a bowl of deadly nightshade. It upsets them. Then when you nurse sick people, and find them not as well as could be expected, why go into hysterics?

MARGARET. Why not?

DESPARD. Because it's too jumpy for a sick-room.

MARGARET. How strange! Oh, Master! Master!—how shall I express the all-absorbing gratitude that—(*about to throw herself at his feet*)

DESPARD. Now! (*warningly*)

MARGARET. Yes, I know, dear—it shan't occur again. (*He is seated—she sits on the ground by him.*) Shall I tell you one of poor Mad Margaret's odd thoughts? Well, then, when I am lying awake at night, and the pale moonlight streams through the latticed casement, strange fancies crowd upon my poor mad brain, and I sometimes think that if we could hit upon some word for you to use whenever I am about to relapse—some word that teems with hidden meaning—like "Basingstoke"—it might recall me to my saner self. For, after all, I am only Mad Margaret! Daft Meg! Poor Meg! He! he! he!

---

13 An inspector, working under a clergyman, who investigated the welfare and morals of his parishioners.

DESPARD. Poor child, she wanders! But soft—some one comes—Margaret—pray recollect yourself—Basingstoke, I beg! Margaret, if you don't Basingstoke at once, I shall be seriously angry.

MARGARET (*recovering herself*). Basingstoke it is!

DESPARD. Then make it so.

(*Enter* ROBIN. *He starts on seeing them.*)

ROBIN. Despard! And his young wife! This visit is unexpected.

MARGARET. Shall I fly at him? Shall I tear him limb from limb? Shall I rend him asunder? Say but the word and—

DESPARD. Basingstoke!

MARGARET (*suddenly demure*). Basingstoke it is!

DESPARD (*aside*). Then make it so. (*aloud*) My brother—I call you brother still, despite your horrible profligacy—we have come to urge you to abandon the evil courses to which you have committed yourself, and at any cost to become a pure and blameless ratepayer.[14]

ROBIN. But I've done no wrong yet.

MARGARET (*wildly*). No wrong! He has done no wrong! Did you hear that!

DESPARD. Basingstoke!

MARGARET (*recovering herself*). Basingstoke it is!

DESPARD. My brother—I still call you brother, you observe—you forget that you have been, in the eye of the law, a Bad Baronet of Ruddigore for ten years—and you are therefore responsible—in the eye of the law—for all the misdeeds committed by the unhappy gentleman who occupied your place.

ROBIN. I see! Bless my heart, I never thought of that! Was I very bad?

DESPARD. Awful. Wasn't he? (*To* MARGARET)

ROBIN. And I've been going on like this for how long?

DESPARD. Ten years! Think of all the atrocities you have committed—by attorney as it were—during that period. Remember how you trifled with this poor child's affections—how you raised her hopes on high (don't cry, my love—Basingstoke, you know), only to trample them in the dust when they were at the

---

[14] Taxpayer.

very zenith of their fullness. Oh fie, sir, fie—she trusted you!

ROBIN. Did she? What a scoundrel I must have been! There, there—don't cry, my dear (*to* MARGARET, *who is sobbing on* ROBIN'*s breast*), it's all right now. Birmingham, you know—Birmingham—

MARGARET (*sobbing*). It's Ba—Ba—Basingstoke!

ROBIN. Basingstoke! of course it is—Basingstoke.

MARGARET. Then make it so!

ROBIN. There, there—it's all right—he's married you now —that is, *I've* married you (*turning to* DESPARD)—I say, which of us has married her?

DESPARD. Oh, *I've* married her.

ROBIN (*aside*). Oh, I'm glad of that. (*To* MARGARET) Yes, *he's* married you now (*passing her over to* DESPARD), and anything more disreputable than my conduct seems to have been I've never even heard of. But my mind is made up—I *will* defy my ancestors. I *will* refuse to obey their behests, thus, by courting death, atone in some degree for the infamy of my career!

MARGARET. I knew it—I knew it—God bless you— (*Hysterically.*)

DESPARD. Basingstoke!

MARGARET. Basingstoke it is! (*Recovers herself.*)

Patter-Trio

ROBIN, DESPARD, and MARGARET

ROBIN.   My eyes are fully open to my awful situation—
I shall go at once to Roderic and make him an oration.
I shall tell him I've recovered my forgotten moral senses,
And I don't care twopence-halfpenny for any consequences.
Now I do not want to perish by the sword or by the dagger,
But a martyr may indulge a little pardonable swagger,
And a word or two of compliment my vanity would flatter,
But I've got to die to-morrow, so it really doesn't matter!

DESPARD.   So it really doesn't matter—

MARGARET.   So it really doesn't matter—

ALL.   So it really doesn't matter, matter, matter,
           matter, matter!

MARGARET. If I were not a little mad and generally silly
           I should give you my advice upon the subject,
               willy-nilly;
           I should show you in a moment how to grapple
               with the question,
           And you'd really be astonished at the force of
               my suggestion.
           On the subject I shall write you a most valuable
               letter,
           Full of excellent suggestions when I feel a little
               better,
           But at present I'm afraid I am as mad as any
               hatter,
           So I'll keep 'em to myself, for my opinion
               doesn't matter!

DESPARD.   Her opinion doesn't matter—

ROBIN.   Her opinion doesn't matter—

ALL.   Her opinion doesn't matter, matter, matter,
           matter, matter!

DESPARD.   If I had been so lucky as to have a steady
               brother
           Who could talk to me as we are talking now
               to one another—
           Who could give me good advice when he dis-
               covered I was erring
           (Which is just the very favour which on you
               I am conferring),
           My story would have made a rather interest-
               ing idyll,
           And I might have lived and died a very decent
               indiwiddle.
           This particularly rapid, unintelligible patter
           Isn't generally heard, and if it is it doesn't
               matter!

ROBIN.   If it is it doesn't matter—

MARGARET.   If it ain't it doesn't matter—

ALL.   If it is it doesn't matter, matter, matter, matter, matter!

(*Exeunt* DESPARD *and* MARGARET.)

(*Enter* ADAM.)

ADAM (*guiltily*). Master—the deed is done!

ROBIN. What deed?

ADAM. She is here—alone, unprotected—

ROBIN. Who?

ADAM. The maiden. I've carried her off—I had a hard task, for she fought like a tiger-cat!

ROBIN. Great heaven, I had forgotten her! I had hoped to have died unspotted by crime, but I am foiled again —and by a tiger-cat! Produce her—and leave us!

(ADAM *introduces* DAME HANNAH, *very much excited, and exit.*)

ROBIN. Dame Hannah! This is—this is not what I expected.

HANNAH. Well, sir, and what would you with me? Oh, you have begun bravely—bravely indeed! Unappalled by the calm dignity of blameless womanhood, your minion has torn me from my spotless home, and dragged me, blindfold and shrieking, through hedges, over stiles, and across a very difficult country, and left me, helpless and trembling, at your mercy! Yet not helpless, coward sir, for approach one step—nay, but the twentieth part of one poor inch—and this poniard (*Produces a very small dagger.*) shall teach ye what it is to lay unholy hands on old Stephen Trusty's daughter!

ROBIN. Madam, I am extremely sorry for this. It is not at all what I intended—anything, more correct—more deeply respectful than my intentions towards you, it would be impossible for any one—however particular —to desire.

HANNAH. Bah, I am not to be tricked by smooth words, hypocrite! But be warned in time, for there are, without, a hundred gallant hearts whose trusty blades would hack him limb from limb who dared to lay unholy hands on old Stephen Trusty's daughter!

ROBIN. And this is what it is to embark upon a career of unlicensed pleasure!

(HANNAH, *who has taken a formidable dagger from one of the armed figures, throws her small dagger to* ROBIN.)

HANNAH. Harkye, miscreant, you have secured me, and I am your poor prisoner; but if you think I cannot take care of myself you are very much mistaken. Now then, it's one to one, and let the best man win! (*making for him*)

ROBIN (*in an agony of terror*). Don't! don't look at me like that! I can't bear it! Roderic! Uncle! Save me!

(RODERIC *enters, from his picture. He comes down the stage.*)

RODERIC. What is the matter? Have you carried her off?

ROBIN. I have—she is there—look at her—she terrifies me!

RODERIC (*looking at* HANNAH). Little Nannikin!

HANNAH (*amazed*). Roddy-doddy!

RODERIC. My own old love! Why, how came *you* here?

HANNAH. This brute—he carried me off! Bodily! But I'll show him! (*about to rush at* ROBIN)

RODERIC. Stop! (*To* ROBIN). What do you mean by carrying off this lady? Are you aware that once upon a time she was engaged to be married to me? I'm very angry —very angry indeed.

ROBIN. Now I hope this will be a lesson to you in future not to—

RODERIC. Hold your tongue, sir.

ROBIN. Yes, uncle.

RODERIC. Have you given him any encouragement?

HANNAH (*to* ROBIN). Have I given you any encouragement? Frankly now, have I?

ROBIN. No. Frankly, you have not. Anything more scrupulously correct than your conduct, it would be impossible to desire.

RODERIC. You go away.

ROBIN. Yes, uncle. (*Exit* ROBIN.)

RODERIC. This is a strange meeting after so many years!

HANNAH. Very. I thought you were dead.

RODERIC. I am. I died ten years ago.

HANNAH. And are you pretty comfortable?

RODERIC. Pretty well—that is—yes, pretty well.

HANNAH. You don't deserve to be, for I loved you all the while, dear; and it made me dreadfully unhappy to hear of all your goings-on, you bad, bad boy!

Ballad—HANNAH

There grew a little flower
    'Neath a great oak tree:
When the tempest 'gan to lower
    Little heeded she:
No need had she to cower,
For she dreaded not its power—
She was happy in the bower
    Of her great oak tree!
      Sing hey,
      Lackaday!
    Let the tears fall free
For the pretty little flower and the great oak tree!

BOTH.   Sing hey,
        Lackaday! etc.

When she found that he was fickle,
    Was that great oak tree,
She was in a pretty pickle,
    As she well might be—
But his gallantries were mickle,
For Death followed with his sickle,
And her tears began to trickle
    For her great oak tree!

BOTH.   Sing hey,
        Lackaday! etc.

Said she, "He loved me never,
    Did that great oak tree,
But I'm neither rich nor clever,
    And so why should he?
But though fate our fortunes sever,
To be constant I'll endeavour,
Aye, for ever and for ever,
    To my great oak tree!"

BOTH.   Sing hey,
        Lackaday! etc.

(*Falls weeping on* RODERIC's *bosom.*)

(*Enter* ROBIN, *excitedly, followed by all the characters and Chorus of Bridesmaids.*)

ROBIN. Stop a bit—both of you.

RODERIC. This intrusion is unmannerly.

HANNAH. I'm surprised at you.

ROBIN. I can't stop to apologize—an idea has just occurred to me. A Baronet of Ruddigore can only die through refusing to commit his daily crime.

RODERIC. No doubt.

ROBIN. Therefore, to refuse to commit a daily crime is tantamount to suicide!

RODERIC. It would seem so.

ROBIN. But suicide is, itself, a crime—and so, by your own showing, you ought never to have died at all!

RODERIC. I see—I understand! Then I'm practically alive!

ROBIN. Undoubtedly! (SIR RODERIC *embraces* HANNAH.) Rose, when you believed that I was a simple farmer, I believe you loved me?

ROSE. Madly, passionately!

ROBIN. But when I became a bad baronet, you very properly loved Richard instead?

ROSE. Passionately, madly!

ROBIN. But if I should turn out *not* to be a bad baronet after all, how would you love me then?

ROSE. Madly, passionately!

ROBIN. As before?

ROSE. Why, of course!

ROBIN. My darling! (*They embrace.*)

RICHARD. Here, I say, belay!

ROSE. Oh sir, belay, if it's absolutely necessary!

ROBIN. Belay? Certainly not!

Finale

ROBIN.
> Having been a wicked baronet a week,
> Once again a modest livelihood I seek,
>   Agricultural employment
>   Is to me a keen enjoyment,
> For I'm naturally diffident and meek!

ROSE.
> When a man has been a naughty baronet,
> And expresses his repentance and regret,
>   You should help him, if you're able,
>   Like the mousie in the fable,
> That's the teaching of my Book of Etiquette.

RICHARD.   If you ask me why I do not pipe my eye,
            Like an honest British sailor, I reply,
                That with Zorah for my missis,
                There'll be bread and cheese and kisses,
            Which is just the sort of ration I enjye!

DESPARD   Prompted by a keen desire to evoke,
   and   All the blessed calm of matrimony's yoke,
MARGARET.   We shall toddle off to-morrow,
                From this scene of sin and sorrow,
            For to settle in the town of Basingstoke!

ALL.   For happy the lily
                           That's kissed by the bee;
                       And, sipping tranquilly,
                           Quite happy is he;
                       And happy the filly
                           That neighs in her pride;
                       But happier than any,
                       A pound to a penny,
                       A lover is, when he
                           Embraces his bride!

                       CURTAIN

THE IMPORTANCE OF BEING EARNEST

A TRIVIAL COMEDY FOR SERIOUS PEOPLE

～ 1895 ～

Oscar Wilde

INTRODUCTORY NOTE

OSCAR WILDE (1854–1900), born in Dublin to a woman nationalist poet and a well-known doctor, was raised in a cultured home but exposed to scandal as a child when his father was sued for rape. After solid scholarly achievement at Trinity College, Dublin and at Oxford, Wilde established himself in London society as a brilliant conversationalist. His constant flow of paradoxes and fables, superbly delivered, impressed everyone. William Butler Yeats described in his *Autobiography* how Wilde talked "with perfect sentences, as if he had written them all overnight with labour and yet all spontaneous."

Wilde supported himself as a poet, editor, critic, and fiction writer, but won great financial success only with his comedies, starting with *Lady Windermere's Fan* in 1892. Though he had married in 1884, he became increasingly involved in homosexual affairs, ultimately with the beautiful Lord Alfred Douglas. A few days after the triumphant opening of *The Importance of Being Earnest* (1895), Douglas' father accused him of sodomy. Wilde imprudently sued him for libel, lost his case, and was promptly tried for homosexual practices, convicted, and sentenced to two years at hard labor. All the while, *The Importance of Being Earnest* continued its successful run, though his name was removed from the playbills and programs.

With this play, Wilde attained his distinctive manner in comedy. He eliminated the sentimental and melodramatic

elements of his earlier plays—concessions to popular taste
as well as expression of the sentimental side of his own
nature—transmuting them into intellectual farce. The
woman with a past, for example, seriously presented in two
earlier comedies, here reappears absurdly as respectable
Miss Prism. Wilde's apparently irresponsible paradoxes,
however, generally express truth—not the whole truth, but
a half truth which provokes scrutiny of the platitude it
mocks. Algy's "Divorces are made in Heaven" suggests by
its incongruity that it is equally absurd to say marriages
are made in Heaven. Also it points to the actual truth that
divorce from an unhappy marriage can be even more of a
blessing than achievement of a happy one.

Lady Bracknell's absurdity consists in her flat statements
of the tacit assumptions of a ruling class which took for
granted its rightness, privileges, and central importance.
Utterly sure of herself and sublimely oblivious to other
people's points of view, she is the comic but awesome and
awful embodiment of the Establishment which Wilde admired and challenged, and which ultimately was to
crush him.

BIBLIOGRAPHY

Major Works:

The Happy Prince and Other Tales, 1888 (fairy tales for adults)
"The Decay of Lying," 1889 (criticism)
"The Critic as Artist," 1890 (criticism)
The Picture of Dorian Gray, 1891 (novel)
Lady Windermere's Fan, 1892 (comedy)
Salomé, 1892 (tragedy)
A Woman of No Importance, 1893 (comedy)
An Ideal Husband, 1895 (comedy)
The Importance of Being Earnest, 1895 (comedy)
"The Ballad of Reading Gaol," 1898 (poem)

Editions:

The Artist as Critic: Critical Writings of Oscar Wilde. Ed. Richard Ellmann. New York: Random House, 1968.
The Letters of Oscar Wilde. Ed. Rupert Hart-Davis. New York: Harcourt, Brace and World, 1962.
Literary Criticism of Oscar Wilde. Ed. Stanley Weintraub. Lincoln: University of Nebraska Press, 1968.

Works About:

Auden, W. H. "An Improbable Life" (review of *Letters of Oscar Wilde*), *New Yorker*, 39 (March 9, 1963), 155–77.
Bentley, Eric. *The Playwright as Thinker*. New York: Harcourt, Brace, and World, 1967, pp. 140–45.
Ellmann, Richard. "Romantic Pantomime in Oscar Wilde," *Partisan Review*, 30 (Fall 1963), 342–55.

Jullian, Philippe. *Oscar Wilde*. Trans. Violet Wyndham. New York: Viking Press, 1969.

McCarthy, Mary. "The Unimportance of Being Oscar," *Theatre Chronicles 1937–1962*. New York: Farrar, Straus, 1963, pp. 106–10.

San Juan, Epifanio, Jr. *The Art of Oscar Wilde*. Princeton: Princeton University Press, 1967.

THE IMPORTANCE OF
BEING EARNEST

The Persons of the Play

JOHN WORTHING, J.P.
ALGERNON MONCRIEFF
REV. CANON CHASUBLE, D.D.
MERRIMAN, *butler*
LANE, *manservant*
LADY BRACKNELL
HON. GWENDOLEN FAIRFAX
CECILY CARDEW
MISS PRISM, *governess*

THE SCENES OF THE PLAY

ACT I
Algernon Moncrieff's flat in Half-Moon Street, W.
ACT II
The garden at the Manor House, Woolton
ACT III
Drawing-room at the Manor House, Woolton
TIME
The Present

FIRST ACT

[SCENE.] *Morning-room in* ALGERNON'S *flat in Half-Moon Street. The room is luxuriously and artistically furnished. The sound of a piano is heard in the adjoining room.*

(LANE *is arranging afternoon tea on the table and, after the music has ceased,* ALGERNON *enters.*)

ALGERNON. Did you hear what I was playing, Lane?

LANE. I didn't think it polite to listen, sir.

ALGERNON. I'm sorry for that, for your sake. I don't play accurately—anyone can play accurately—but I play with wonderful expression. As far as the piano is concerned, sentiment is my forte. I keep science for Life.

LANE. Yes, sir.

ALGERNON. And, speaking of the science of Life, have you got the cucumber sandwiches cut for Lady Bracknell?

LANE. Yes, sir. (*Hands them on a salver.*)

ALGERNON (*inspects them, takes two, and sits down on the sofa*). Oh! . . . by the way, Lane, I see from your book that on Thursday night, when Lord Shoreman and Mr. Worthing were dining with me, eight bottles of champagne are entered as having been consumed.

LANE. Yes, sir; eight bottles and a pint.

ALGERNON. Why is it that at a bachelor's establishment the servants invariably drink the champagne? I ask merely for information.

LANE. I attribute it to the superior quality of the wine, sir. I have often observed that in married households the champagne is rarely of a first-rate brand.

ALGERNON. Good heavens! Is marriage so demoralizing as that?

LANE. I believe it *is* a very pleasant state, sir. I have had very little experience of it myself up to the present.

I have only been married once. That was in consequence of a misunderstanding between myself and a young person.

ALGERNON (*languidly*). I don't know that I am much interested in your family life, Lane.

LANE. No, sir; it is not a very interesting subject. I never think of it myself.

ALGERNON. Very natural, I am sure. That will do, Lane, thank you.

LANE. Thank you, sir.

(LANE *goes out.*)

ALGERNON. Lane's views on marriage seem somewhat lax. Really, if the lower orders don't set us a good example, what on earth is the use of them? They seem, as a class, to have absolutely no sense of moral responsibility.

(*Enter* LANE.)

LANE. Mr. Ernest Worthing.

(*Enter* JACK. LANE *goes out.*)

ALGERNON. How are you, my dear Ernest? What brings you up to town?

JACK. Oh, pleasure, pleasure! What else should bring one anywhere? Eating as usual, I see, Algy!

ALGERNON (*stiffly*). I believe it is customary in good society to take some slight refreshment at five o'clock. Where have you been since last Thursday?

JACK (*sitting down on the sofa*). In the country.

ALGERNON. What on earth do you do there?

JACK (*pulling off his gloves*). When one is in town one amuses oneself. When one is in the country one amuses other people. It is excessively boring.

ALGERNON. And who are the people you amuse?

JACK (*airily*). Oh, neighbours, neighbours.

ALGERNON. Got nice neighbours in your part of Shropshire?

JACK. Perfectly horrid! Never speak to one of them.

ALGERNON. How immensely you must amuse them! (*Goes over and takes sandwich.*) By the way, Shropshire is your county, is it not?

JACK. Eh? Shropshire? Yes, of course. Hallo! Why all these

cups? Why cucumber sandwiches? Why such reckless
extravagance in one so young? Who is coming to tea?

ALGERNON. Oh! merely Aunt Augusta and Gwendolen.

JACK. How perfectly delightful!

ALGERNON. Yes, that is all very well; but I am afraid Aunt
Augusta won't quite approve of your being here.

JACK. May I ask why?

ALGERNON. My dear fellow, the way you flirt with Gwendolen is perfectly disgraceful. It is almost as bad as the
way Gwendolen flirts with you.

JACK. I am in love with Gwendolen. I have come up to
town expressly to propose to her.

ALGERNON. I thought you had come up for pleasure? . . .
I call that business.

JACK. How utterly unromantic you are!

ALGERNON. I really don't see anything romantic in proposing. It is very romantic to be in love. But there is
nothing romantic about a definite proposal. Why, one
may be accepted. One usually is, I believe. Then the
excitement is all over. The very essence of romance
is uncertainty. If ever I get married, I'll certainly try
to forget the fact.

JACK. I have no doubt about that, dear Algy. The Divorce
Court was specially invented for people whose memories are so curiously constituted.

ALGERNON. Oh, there is no use speculating on that subject.
Divorces are made in Heaven—(JACK *puts out his
hand to take a sandwich.* ALGERNON *at once inter-
feres.*) Please don't touch the cucumber sandwiches.
They are ordered specially for Aunt Augusta. (*Takes
one and eats it.*)

JACK. Well, you have been eating them all the time.

ALGERNON. That is quite a different matter. She is my aunt.
(*Takes plate from below.*) Have some bread and butter.
The bread and butter is for Gwendolen. Gwendolen is
devoted to bread and butter.

JACK (*advancing to table and helping himself*). And very
good bread and butter it is too.

ALGERNON. Well, my dear fellow, you need not eat as if
you were going to eat it all. You behave as if you
were married to her already. You are not married
to her already, and I don't think you ever will be.

JACK. Why on earth do you say that?

ALGERNON. Well, in the first place, girls never marry the men they flirt with. Girls don't think it right.

JACK. Oh, that is nonsense!

ALGERNON. It isn't. It is a great truth. It accounts for the extraordinary number of bachelors that one sees all over the place. In the second place, I don't give my consent.

JACK. Your consent!

ALGERNON. My dear fellow, Gwendolen is my first cousin. And before I allow you to marry her, you will have to clear up the whole question of Cecily. (*Rings bell.*)

JACK. Cecily! What on earth do you mean? What do you mean, Algy, by Cecily! I don't know any one of the name of Cecily.

(*Enter* LANE.)

ALGERNON. Bring me that cigarette case Mr. Worthing left in the smoking-room the last time he dined here.

LANE. Yes, sir.

(*LANE goes out.*)

JACK. Do you mean to say you have had my cigarette case all this time? I wish to goodness you had let me know. I have been writing frantic letters to Scotland Yard about it. I was very nearly offering a large reward.

ALGERNON. Well, I wish you would offer one. I happen to be more than usually hard up.

JACK. There is no good offering a large reward now that the thing is found.

(*Enter* LANE *with the cigarette case on a salver.* ALGERNON *takes it at once.* LANE *goes out.*)

ALGERNON. I think that is rather mean of you, Ernest, I must say. (*Opens case and examines it.*) However, it makes no matter, for, now that I look at the inscription inside, I find that the thing isn't yours after all.

JACK. Of course it's mine. (*moving to him*) You have seen me with it a hundred times, and you have no right whatsoever to read what is written inside. It is a very ungentlemanly thing to read a private cigarette case.

ALGERNON. Oh! it is absurd to have a hard and fast rule about what one should read and what one shouldn't.

More than half of modern culture depends on what one shouldn't read.

JACK. I am quite aware of the fact, and I don't propose to discuss modern culture. It isn't the sort of thing one should talk of in private. I simply want my cigarette case back.

ALGERNON. Yes; but this isn't your cigarette case. This cigarette case is a present from someone of the name of Cecily, and you said you didn't know anyone of that name.

JACK. Well, if you want to know, Cecily happens to be my aunt.

ALGERNON. Your aunt!

JACK. Yes. Charming old lady she is, too. Lives at Tunbridge Wells. Just give it back to me, Algy.

ALGERNON (*retreating to back of sofa*). But why does she call herself little Cecily if she is your aunt and lives at Tunbridge Wells? (*reading*) "From little Cecily with her fondest love."

JACK (*moving to sofa and kneeling upon it*). My dear fellow, what on earth is there in that? Some aunts are tall, some aunts are not tall. That is a mattter that surely an aunt may be allowed to decide for herself. You seem to think that every aunt should be exactly like your aunt! That is absurd. For Heaven's sake give me back my cigarette case. (*follows* ALGERNON *round the room*)

ALGERNON. Yes. But why does your aunt call you her uncle? "From little Cecily, with her fondest love to her dear Uncle Jack." There is no objection, I admit, to an aunt being a small aunt, but why an aunt, no matter what her size may be, should call her own nephew her uncle, I can't quite make out. Besides, your name isn't Jack at all; it is Ernest.

JACK. It isn't Ernest; it's Jack.

ALGERNON. You have always told me it was Ernest. I have introduced you to every one as Ernest. You answer to the name of Ernest. You look as if your name was Ernest. You are the most earnest-looking person I ever saw in my life. It is perfectly absurd your saying that your name isn't Ernest. It's on your cards. Here is one of them. (*taking it from case*) "Mr. Ernest Worthing, B.4, The Albany." I'll keep this as a proof that your name is Ernest if ever you attempt to deny it to me, or to Gwendolen, or to anyone else. (*Puts the card in his pocket.*)

JACK. Well, my name is Ernest in town and Jack in the country, and the cigarette case was given to me in the country.

ALGERNON. Yes, but that does not account for the fact that your small Aunt Cecily, who lives at Tunbridge Wells, calls you her dear uncle. Come, old boy, you had much better have the thing out at once.

JACK. My dear Algy, you talk exactly as if you were a dentist. It is very vulgar to talk like a dentist when one isn't a dentist. It produces a false impression.

ALGERNON. Well, that is exactly what dentists always do. Now, go on! Tell me the whole thing. I may mention that I have always suspected you of being a confirmed and secret Bunburyist; and I am quite sure of it now.

JACK. Bunburyist? What on earth do you mean by a Bunburyist?

ALGERNON. I'll reveal to you the meaning of that incomparable expression as soon as you are kind enough to inform me why you are Ernest in town and Jack in the country.

JACK. Well, produce my cigarette case first.

ALGERNON. Here it is. (*Hands cigarette case.*) Now produce your explanation, and pray make it improbable. (*Sits on sofa.*)

JACK. My dear fellow, there is nothing improbable about my explanation at all. In fact it's perfectly ordinary. Old Mr. Thomas Cardew, who adopted me when I was a little boy, made me in his will guardian to his granddaughter, Miss Cecily Cardew. Cecily, who addresses me as her uncle from motives of respect that you could not possibly appreciate, lives at my place in the country under the charge of her admirable governess, Miss Prism.

ALGERNON. Where is that place in the country, by the way?

JACK. That is nothing to you, dear boy. You are not going to be invited. . . . I may tell you candidly that the place is not in Shropshire.

ALGERNON. I suspected that, my dear fellow! I have Bunburyed all over Shropshire on two separate occasions. Now, go on. Why are you Ernest in town and Jack in the country?

JACK. My dear Algy, I don't know whether you will be able

to understand my real motives. You are hardly serious enough. When one is placed in the position of guardian, one has to adopt a very high moral tone on all subjects. It's one's duty to do so. And as a high moral tone can hardly be said to conduce very much to either one's health or one's happiness, in order to get up to town I have always pretended to have a younger brother of the name of Ernest, who lives in the Albany, and gets into the most dreadful scrapes. That, my dear Algy, is the whole truth pure and simple.

ALGERNON. The truth is rarely pure and never simple. Modern life would be very tedious if it were either, and modern literature a complete impossibility!

JACK. That wouldn't be at all a bad thing.

ALGERNON. Literary criticism is not your forte, my dear fellow. Don't try it. You should leave that to people who haven't been at a University. They do it so well in the daily papers. What you really are is a Bunburyist. I was quite right in saying you were a Bunburyist. You are one of the most advanced Bunburyists I know.

JACK. What on earth do you mean?

ALGERNON. You have invented a very useful younger brother called Ernest, in order that you may be able to come up to town as often as you like. I have invented an invaluable permanent invalid called Bunbury, in order that I may be able to go down into the country whenever I choose. Bunbury is perfectly invaluable. If it wasn't for Bunbury's extraordinary bad health, for instance, I wouldn't be able to dine with you at Willis's to-night, for I have been really engaged to Aunt Augusta for more than a week.

JACK. I haven't asked you to dine with me anywhere to-night.

ALGERNON. I know. You are absurdly careless about sending out invitations. It is very foolish of you. Nothing annoys people so much as not receiving invitations.

JACK. You had much better dine with your Aunt Augusta.

ALGERNON. I haven't the smallest intention of doing anything of the kind. To begin with, I dined there on Monday, and once a week is quite enough to dine with one's own relations. In the second place, whenever I do dine there I am always treated as a member of the family, and sent down with either no woman at all, or two. In the third place, I know perfectly well whom she will place me next to, to-night. She will place me next Mary Farquhar, who always flirts with her own husband across the dinner-table. That is not very pleasant. Indeed, it is not even decent . . . and that sort of thing is enormously on the increase. The amount of women in London who flirt with their own husbands is perfectly scandalous. It looks so bad. It is simply washing one's clean linen in public. Besides, now that I know you to be a confirmed Bunburyist I naturally want to talk to you about Bunburying. I want to tell you the rules.

JACK. I'm not a Bunburyist at all. If Gwendolen accepts me, I am going to kill my brother, indeed I think I'll kill him in any case. Cecily is a little too much interested in him. It is rather a bore. So I am going to get rid of Ernest. And I strongly advise you to do the same with Mr. . . . with your invalid friend who has the absurd name.

ALGERNON. Nothing will induce me to part with Bunbury, and if you ever get married, which seems to me extremely problematic, you will be very glad to know Bunbury. A man who marries without knowing Bunbury has a very tedious time of it.

JACK. That is nonsense. If I marry a charming girl like Gwendolen, and she is the only girl I ever saw in my life that I would marry, I certainly won't want to know Bunbury.

ALGERNON. Then your wife will. You don't seem to realize, that in married life three is company and two is none.

JACK (*sententiously*). That, my dear young friend, is the theory that the corrupt French Drama has been propounding for the last fifty years.

ALGERNON. Yes; and that the happy English home has proved in half the time.

JACK. For heaven's sake, don't try to be cynical. It's perfectly easy to be cynical.

ALGERNON. My dear fellow, it isn't easy to be anything nowadays. There's such a lot of beastly competition about. (*The sound of an electric bell is heard.*) Ah! that must be Aunt Augusta. Only relatives, or creditors, ever ring in that Wagnerian manner. Now, if I get

her out of the way for ten minutes, so that you can
have an opportunity for proposing to Gwendolen, may
I dine with you tonight at Willis's?

JACK. I suppose so, if you want to.

ALGERNON. Yes, but you must be serious about it. I hate
people who are not serious about meals. It is so shallow
of them.

(*Enter* LANE.)

LANE. Lady Bracknell and Miss Fairfax.

(ALGERNON *goes forward to meet them. Enter* LADY
BRACKNELL *and* GWENDOLEN.)

LADY BRACKNELL. Good afternoon, dear Algernon, I hope
you are behaving very well.

ALGERNON. I'm feeling very well, Aunt Augusta.

LADY BRACKNELL. That's not quite the same thing. In fact
the two things rarely go together. (*Sees* JACK *and
bows to him with icy coldness.*)

ALGERNON (*To* GWENDOLEN). Dear me, you are smart!

GWENDOLEN. I am always smart! Am I not, Mr. Worthing?

JACK. You're quite perfect, Miss Fairfax.

GWENDOLEN. Oh! I hope I am not that. It would leave no
room for developments, and I intend to develop in
many directions. (GWENDOLEN *and* JACK *sit down together in the corner.*)

LADY BRACKNELL. I'm sorry if we are a little late, Algernon,
but I was obliged to call on dear Lady Harbury. I
hadn't been there since her poor husband's death. I
never saw a woman so altered; she looks quite twenty
years younger. And now I'll have a cup of tea, and
one of those cucumber sandwiches you promised me.

ALGERNON. Certainly, Aunt Augusta. (*Goes over to tea-
table.*)

LADY BRACKNELL. Won't you come and sit here,
Gwendolen?

GWENDOLEN. Thanks, mamma, I'm quite comfortable
where I am.

ALGERNON (*picking up empty plate in horror*). Good
heavens! Lane! Why are there no cucumber sandwiches? I ordered them specially.

LANE (*gravely*). There were no cucumbers in the market
this morning, sir. I went down twice.

ALGERNON. No cucumbers!

LANE. No, sir. Not even for ready money.

ALGERNON. That will do, Lane, thank you.

LANE. Thank you, sir. (*Goes out.*)

ALGERNON. I am greatly distressed, Aunt Augusta, about there being no cucumbers, not even for ready money.

LADY BRACKNELL. It really makes no matter, Algernon. I had some crumpets with Lady Harbury, who seems to me to be living entirely for pleasure now.

ALGERNON. I hear her hair has turned quite gold from grief.

LADY BRACKNELL. It certainly has changed its colour. From what cause I, of course, cannot say. (ALGERNON *crosses and hands tea.*) Thank you. I've quite a treat for you tonight, Algernon. I am going to send you down with Mary Farquhar. She is such a nice woman, and so attentive to her husband. It's delightful to watch them.

ALGERNON. I am afraid, Aunt Augusta, I shall have to give up the pleasure of dining with you tonight after all.

LADY BRACKNELL (*frowning*). I hope not, Algernon. It would put my table completely out. Your uncle would have to dine upstairs. Fortunately he is accustomed to that.

ALGERNON. It is a great bore, and, I need hardly say, a terrible disappointment to me, but the fact is I have just had a telegram to say that my poor friend Bunbury is very ill again. (*Exchanges glances with* JACK). They seem to think I should be with him.

LADY BRACKNELL. It is very strange. This Mr. Bunbury seems to suffer from curiously bad health.

ALGERNON. Yes; poor Bunbury is a dreadful invalid.

LADY BRACKNELL. Well, I must say, Algernon, that I think it is high time that Mr. Bunbury made up his mind whether he was going to live or to die. This shilly-shallying with the question is absurd. Nor do I in any way approve of the modern sympathy with invalids. I consider it morbid. Illness of any kind is hardly a thing to be encouraged in others. Health is the primary duty of life. I am always telling that to your poor uncle, but he never seems to take much notice . . . as far as any improvement in his ailment goes. I should be much obliged if you would ask Mr. Bunbury, from me, to be kind enough not to have a relapse on Saturday, for I rely on you to arrange my music for me. It is my last reception, and one wants something that will encourage conversation, particularly at the end of the season when everyone has practically said whatever they had to say, which, in most cases, was probably not much.

ALGERNON. I'll speak to Bunbury, Aunt Augusta, if he is still conscious, and I think I can promise you he'll be all right by Saturday. Of course the music is a great difficulty. You see, if one plays good music, people don't listen, and if one plays bad music people don't talk. But I'll run over the programme I've drawn out, if you will kindly come into the next room for a moment.

LADY BRACKNELL. Thank you, Algernon. It is very thoughtful of you. (*rising, and following* ALGERNON) I'm sure the programme will be delightful, after a few expurgations. French songs I cannot possibly allow. People always seem to think that they are improper, and either look shocked, which is vulgar, or laugh, which is worse. But German sounds a thoroughly respectable language, and, indeed I believe is so. Gwendolen, you will accompany me.

GWENDOLEN. Certainly, mamma.

(LADY BRACKNELL *and* ALGERNON *go into the music-room*, GWENDOLEN *remains behind.*)

JACK. Charming day it has been, Miss Fairfax.

GWENDOLEN. Pray don't talk about the weather, Mr. Worthing. Whenever people talk to me about the weather, I always feel quite certain that they mean something else. And that makes me so nervous.

JACK. I do mean something else.

GWENDOLEN. I thought so. In fact, I am never wrong.

JACK. And I would like to be allowed to take advantage of Lady Bracknell's temporary absence. . . .

GWENDOLEN. I would certainly advise you to do so. Mamma has a way of coming back suddenly into a room that I have often had to speak to her about.

JACK (*nervously*). Miss Fairfax, ever since I met you I have admired you more than any girl . . . I have ever met since . . . I met you.

GWENDOLEN. Yes, I am quite well aware of the fact. And I often wish that in public, at any rate, you had been more demonstrative. For me you have always had an irresistible fascination. Even before I met you I was far from indifferent to you. (JACK *looks at her in amazement*.) We live, as I hope you know, Mr. Worthing, in an age of ideals. The fact is constantly mentioned in the more expensive monthly magazines, and has reached the provincial pulpits, I am told; and my ideal has always been to love someone of the name of Ernest. There is something in that name that inspires absolute confidence. The moment Algernon first mentioned to me that he had a friend called Ernest, I knew I was destined to love you.

JACK. You really love me, Gwendolen?

GWENDOLEN. Passionately!

JACK. Darling! You don't know how happy you've made me.

GWENDOLEN. My own Ernest!

JACK. But you don't really mean to say that you couldn't love me if my name wasn't Ernest?

GWENDOLEN. But your name is Ernest.

JACK. Yes, I know it is. But supposing it was something else? Do you mean to say you couldn't love me then?

GWENDOLEN (*glibly*). Ah! that is clearly a metaphysical speculation, and like most metaphysical speculations has very little reference at all to the actual facts of real life, as we know them.

JACK. Personally, darling, to speak quite candidly, I don't much care about the name of Ernest. . . . I don't think the name suits me at all.

GWENDOLEN. It suits you perfectly. It is a divine name. It has music of its own. It produces vibrations.

JACK. Well, really, Gwendolen, I must say that I think there are lots of other much nicer names. I think Jack, for instance, a charming name.

GWENDOLEN. Jack? . . . No, there is very little music in the name Jack, if any at all, indeed. It does not thrill. It produces absolutely no vibrations. . . . I have known several Jacks, and they all, without exception, were more than usually plain. Besides, Jack is a notorious domesticity for John! And I pity any woman who is married to a man called John. She would probably never be allowed to know the entrancing pleasure of a single moment's solitude. The only really safe name is Ernest.

JACK. Gwendolen, I must get christened at once—I mean

we must get married at once. There is no time to be lost.

GWENDOLEN. Married, Mr. Worthing?

JACK (*astounded*). Well . . . surely. You know that I love you, and you led me to believe, Miss Fairfax, that you were not absolutely indifferent to me.

GWENDOLEN. I adore you. But you haven't proposed to me yet. Nothing has been said at all about marriage. The subject has not even been touched on.

JACK. Well . . . may I propose to you now?

GWENDOLEN. I think it would be an admirable opportunity. And to spare you any possible disappointment, Mr. Worthing, I think it only fair to tell you quite frankly beforehand that I am fully determined to accept you.

JACK. Gwendolen!

GWENDOLEN. Yes, Mr. Worthing, what have you got to say to me?

JACK. You know what I have got to say to you.

GWENDOLEN. Yes, but you don't say it.

JACK. Gwendolen, will you marry me? (*Goes on his knees.*)

GWENDOLEN. Of course I will, darling. How long you have been about it! I am afraid you have had very little experience in how to propose.

JACK. My own one, I have never loved any one in the world but you.

GWENDOLEN. Yes, but men often propose for practice. I know my brother Gerald does. All my girl-friends tell me so. What wonderfully blue eyes you have, Ernest! They are quite, quite blue. I hope you will always look at me just like that, especially when there are other people present.

(*Enter* LADY BRACKNELL.)

LADY BRACKNELL. Mr. Worthing! Rise, sir, from this semi-recumbent posture. It is most indecorous.

GWENDOLEN. Mamma! (*He tries to rise; she restrains him.*) I must beg you to retire. This is no place for you. Besides, Mr. Worthing has not quite finished yet.

LADY BRACKNELL. Finished what, may I ask?

GWENDOLEN. I am engaged to Mr. Worthing, mamma. (*They rise together.*)

LADY BRACKNELL. Pardon me, you are not engaged to any one. When you do become engaged to some one, I, or your father, should his health permit him, will inform you of the fact. An engagement should come on a young girl as a surprise, pleasant or unpleasant, as the case may be. It is hardly a matter that she could be allowed to arrange for herself. . . . And now I have a few questions to put to you, Mr. Worthing. While I am making these inquiries, you, Gwendolen, will wait for me below in the carriage.

GWENDOLEN (*reproachfully*). Mamma!

LADY BRACKNELL. In the carriage, Gwendolen!

(GWENDOLEN *goes to the door. She and* JACK *blow kisses to each other behind* LADY BRACKNELL'*s back.* LADY BRACKNELL *looks vaguely about as if she could not understand what the noise was. Finally turns round.*)

Gwendolen, the carriage!

GWENDOLEN. Yes, mamma. (*Goes out, looking back at* JACK.)

LADY BRACKNELL (*sitting down*). You can take a seat, Mr. Worthing. (*Looks in her pocket for note-book and pencil.*)

JACK. Thank you, Lady Bracknell, I prefer standing.

LADY BRACKNELL (*pencil and note-book in hand*). I feel bound to tell you that you are not down on my list of eligible young men, although I have the same list as the dear Duchess of Bolton has. We work together, in fact. However, I am quite ready to enter your name, should your answers be what a really affectionate mother requires. Do you smoke?

JACK. Well, yes, I must admit I smoke.

LADY BRACKNELL. I am glad to hear it. A man should always have an occupation of some kind. There are far too many idle men in London as it is. How old are you?

JACK. Twenty-nine.

LADY BRACKNELL. A very good age to be married at. I have always been of opinion that a man who desires to get married should know either everything or nothing. Which do you know?

JACK (*after some hesitation*). I know nothing, Lady Bracknell.

LADY BRACKNELL. I am pleased to hear it. I do not approve of anything that tampers with natural ignorance. Ignorance is like a delicate exotic fruit; touch it and the bloom is gone. The whole theory of modern education is radically unsound. Fortunately in England, at any rate, education produces no effect whatsoever. If it did, it would prove a serious danger to the upper classes, and probably lead to acts of violence in Grosvenor Square. What is your income?

JACK. Between seven and eight thousand a year.

LADY BRACKNELL (*makes a note in her book*). In land, or in investments?

JACK. In investments, chiefly.

LADY BRACKNELL. That is satisfactory. What between the duties expected of one during one's lifetime, and the duties exacted from one after one's death, land has ceased to be either a profit or a pleasure. It gives one position, and prevents one from keeping it up. That's all that can be said about land.

JACK. I have a country house with some land, of course, attached to it, about fifteen hundred acres, I believe; but I don't depend on that for my real income. In fact, as far as I can make out, the poachers are the only people who make anything out of it.

LADY BRACKNELL. A country house! How many bedrooms? Well, that point can be cleared up afterwards. You have a town house, I hope? A girl with a simple, unspoiled nature, like Gwendolen, could hardly be expected to reside in the country.

JACK. Well, I own a house in Belgrave Square, but it is let by the year to Lady Bloxham. Of course, I can get it back whenever I like, at six months' notice.

LADY BRACKNELL. Lady Bloxham? I don't know her.

JACK. Oh, she goes about very little. She is a lady considerably advanced in years.

LADY BRACKNELL. Ah, nowadays that is no guarantee of respectability of character. What number in Belgrave Square?

JACK. 149.

LADY BRACKNELL (*shaking her head*). The unfashionable side. I thought there was something. However, that could easily be altered.

JACK. Do you mean the fashion, or the side?

LADY BRACKNELL (*sternly*). Both, if necessary, I presume. What are your politics?

JACK. Well, I am afraid I really have none. I am a Liberal Unionist.

LADY BRACKNELL. Oh, they count as Tories. They dine with us. Or come in the evening, at any rate. Now to minor matters. Are your parents living?

JACK. I have lost both my parents.

LADY BRACKNELL. To lose one parent, Mr. Worthing, may be regarded as a misfortune; to lose both looks like carelessness. Who was your father? He was evidently a man of some wealth. Was he born in what the Radical papers call the purple of commerce, or did he rise from the ranks of the aristocracy?

JACK. I am afraid I really don't know. The fact is, Lady Bracknell, I said I had lost my parents. It would be nearer the truth to say that my parents seem to have lost me. . . . I don't actually know who I am by birth. I was . . . well, I was found.

LADY BRACKNELL. Found!

JACK. The late Mr. Thomas Cardew, an old gentleman of a very charitable and kindly disposition, found me, and gave me the name of Worthing, because he happened to have a first-class ticket for Worthing in his pocket at the time. Worthing is a place in Sussex. It is a seaside resort.

LADY BRACKNELL. Where did the charitable gentleman who had a first-class ticket for this seaside resort find you?

JACK (*gravely*). In a hand-bag.

LADY BRACKNELL. A hand-bag?

JACK (*very seriously*). Yes, Lady Bracknell. I was in a hand-bag—a somewhat large, black leather hand-bag, with handles to it—an ordinary hand-bag in fact.

LADY BRACKNELL. In what locality did this Mr. James, or Thomas, Cardew come across this ordinary hand-bag?

JACK. In the cloak-room at Victoria Station. It was given to him in mistake for his own.

LADY BRACKNELL. The cloak-room at Victoria Station?

JACK. Yes. The Brighton line.

LADY BRACKNELL. The line is immaterial. Mr. Worthing, I confess I feel somewhat bewildered by what you have just told me. To be born, or at any rate bred, in a hand-bag, whether it had handles or not, seems to me to display a contempt for the ordinary decencies of family life that reminds one of the worst excesses of the French Revolution. And I presume you know what that unfortunate movement led to? As for the particular locality in which the hand-bag was found, a cloak-room at a railway station might serve to conceal a social indiscretion—has probably, indeed, been used for that purpose before now—but it could hardly be regarded as an assured basis for a recognized position in good society.

JACK. May I ask you then what you would advise me to do? I need hardly say I would do anything in the world to ensure Gwendolen's happiness.

LADY BRACKNELL. I would strongly advise you, Mr. Worthing, to try and acquire some relations as soon as possible, and to make a definite effort to produce at any rate one parent, of either sex, before the season is quite over.

JACK. Well, I don't see how I could possibly manage to do that. I can produce the hand-bag at any moment. It is in my dressing-room at home. I really think that should satisfy you, Lady Bracknell.

LADY BRACKNELL. Me, sir! What has it to do with me? You can hardly imagine that I and Lord Bracknell would dream of allowing our only daughter—a girl brought up with the utmost care—to marry into a cloak-room, and form an alliance with a parcel. Good morning, Mr. Worthing!

(LADY BRACKNELL *sweeps out in majestic indignation.*)

JACK. Good morning! (ALGERNON, *from the other room, strikes up the Wedding March.* JACK *looks perfectly furious, and goes to the door.*) For goodness' sake don't play that ghastly tune, Algy! How idiotic you are!

(*The music stops and* ALGERNON *enters cheerily.*)

ALGERNON. Didn't it go off all right, old boy? You don't mean to say Gwendolen refused you? I know it is a way she has. She is always refusing people. I think it is most ill-natured of her.

JACK. Oh, Gwendolen is as right as a trivet. As far as she is concerned, we are engaged. Her mother is perfectly unbearable. Never met such a Gorgon. . . . I don't really know what a Gorgon is like, but I am quite sure that Lady Bracknell is one. In any case, she is a monster, without being a myth, which is rather unfair. . . . I beg your pardon, Algy, I suppose I shouldn't talk about your own aunt in that way before you.

ALGERNON. My dear boy, I love hearing my relations abused. It is the only thing that makes me put up with them at all. Relations are simply a tedious pack of people, who haven't got the remotest knowledge of how to live, nor the smallest instinct about when to die.

JACK. Oh, that is nonsense!

ALGERNON. It isn't!

JACK. Well, I won't argue about the matter. You always want to argue about things.

ALGERNON. That is exactly what things were originally made for.

JACK. Upon my word, if I thought that, I'd shoot myself. . . . (a pause) You don't think there is any chance of Gwendolen becoming like her mother in about a hundred and fifty years, do you, Algy?

ALGERNON. All women become like their mothers. That is their tragedy. No man does. That's his.

JACK. Is that clever?

ALGERNON. It is perfectly phrased! and quite as true as any observation in civilized life should be.

JACK. I am sick to death of cleverness. Everybody is clever nowadays. You can't go anywhere without meeting clever people. The thing has become an absolute public nuisance. I wish to goodness we had a few fools left.

ALGERNON. We have.

JACK. I should extremely like to meet them. What do they talk about?

ALGERNON. The fools? Oh! about the clever people, of course.

JACK. What fools.

ALGERNON. By the way, did you tell Gwendolen the truth about your being Ernest in town, and Jack in the country?

JACK (in a very patronizing manner). My dear fellow, the truth isn't quite the sort of thing one tells to a nice, sweet, refined girl. What extraordinary ideas you have about the way to behave to a woman!

ALGERNON. The only way to behave to a woman is to make love to her, if she is pretty, and to someone else, if she is plain.

JACK. Oh, that is nonsense.

ALGERNON. What about your brother? What about the profligate Ernest?

JACK. Oh, before the end of the week I shall have got rid of him. I'll say he died in Paris of apoplexy. Lots of people die of apoplexy, quite suddenly, don't they?

ALGERNON. Yes, but it's hereditary, my dear fellow. It's a sort of thing that runs in families. You had much better say a severe chill.

JACK. You are sure a severe chill isn't hereditary, or anything of that kind?

ALGERNON. Of course it isn't!

JACK. Very well, then. My poor brother Ernest is carried off suddenly, in Paris, by a severe chill. That gets rid of him.

ALGERNON. But I thought you said that . . . Miss Cardew was a little too much interested in your poor brother Ernest? Won't she feel his loss a good deal?

JACK. Oh, that is all right. Cecily is not a silly romantic girl, I am glad to say. She has got a capital appetite, goes long walks, and pays no attention at all to her lessons.

ALGERNON. I would rather like to see Cecily.

JACK. I will take very good care you never do. She is excessively pretty, and she is only just eighteen.

ALGERNON. Have you told Gwendolen yet that you have an excessively pretty ward who is only just eighteen?

JACK. Oh! one doesn't blurt these things out to people. Cecily and Gwendolen are perfectly certain to be extremely great friends. I'll bet you anything you like that half an hour after they have met, they will be calling each other sister.

ALGERNON. Women only do that when they have called each other a lot of other things first. Now, my dear boy, if we want to get a good table at Willis's, we really must go and dress. Do you know it is nearly seven?

JACK (*irritably*). Oh! it always is nearly seven.

ALGERNON. I'm hungry.

JACK. I never knew you when you weren't. . . .

ALGERNON. What shall we do after dinner? Go to a theatre?

JACK. Oh, no! I loathe listening.

ALGERNON. Well, let us go to the Club?

JACK. Oh, no! I hate talking.

ALGERNON. Well, we might trot round to the Empire[1] at ten?

JACK. Oh, no! I can't bear looking at things. It is so silly.

ALGERNON. Well, what shall we do?

JACK. Nothing!

ALGERNON. It is awfully hard work doing nothing. However, I don't mind hard work where there is no definite object of any kind.

(*Enter* LANE.)

LANE. Miss Fairfax.

(*Enter* GWENDOLEN. LANE *goes out.*)

ALGERNON. Gwendolen, upon my word!

GWENDOLEN. Algy, kindly turn your back. I have something very particular to say to Mr. Worthing.

ALGERNON. Really, Gwendolen, I don't think I can allow this at all.

GWENDOLEN. Algy, you always adopt a strictly immoral attitude towards life. You are not quite old enough to do that.

(ALGERNON *retires to the fireplace.*)

JACK. My own darling!

GWENDOLEN. Ernest, we may never be married. From the expression on mamma's face I fear we never shall. Few parents nowadays pay any regard to what their children say to them. The old-fashioned respect for the young is fast dying out. Whatever influence I ever had over mamma, I lost at the age of three. But although she may prevent us from becoming man and wife, and I may marry someone else, and marry often, nothing that she can possibly do can alter my eternal devotion to you.

JACK. Dear Gwendolen!

GWENDOLEN. The story of your romantic origin, as related to me by mamma, with unpleasing comments, has naturally stirred the deeper fibres of my nature. Your Christian name has an irresistible fascination. The simplicity of your character makes you exquisitely incomprehensible to me. Your town address at the Albany I have. What is your address in the country?

[1] The Empire Theatre of Varieties, a music-hall.

JACK. The Manor House, Woolton, Hertfordshire.

(ALGERNON, *who has been carefully listening, smiles to himself, and writes the address on his shirt-cuff. Then picks up the Railway Guide.*)

GWENDOLEN. There is a good postal service, I suppose? It may be necessary to do something desperate. That of course will require serious consideration. I will communicate with you daily.

JACK. My own one!

GWENDOLEN. How long do you remain in town?

JACK. Till Monday.

GWENDOLEN. Good! Algy, you may turn round now.

ALGERNON. Thanks, I've turned round already.

GWENDOLEN. You may also ring the bell.

JACK. You will let me see you to your carriage, my own darling?

GWENDOLEN. Certainly.

JACK (*To* LANE, *who now enters*). I will see Miss Fairfax out.

LANE. Yes, sir. (JACK *and* GWENDOLEN *go off.*)

(LANE *presents several letters on a salver, to* ALGERNON. *It is to be surmised that they are bills, as* ALGERNON, *after looking at the envelopes, tears them up.*)

ALGERNON. A glass of sherry, Lane.

LANE. Yes, sir.

ALGERNON. Tomorrow, Lane, I'm going Bunburying.

LANE. Yes, sir.

ALGERNON. I shall probably not be back till Monday. You can put up my dress clothes, my smoking jacket, and all the Bunbury suits . . .

LANE. Yes, sir. (*handing sherry*)

ALGERNON. I hope tomorrow will be a fine day, Lane.

LANE. It never is, sir.

ALGERNON. Lane, you're a perfect pessimist.

LANE. I do my best to give satisfaction, sir.

(*Enter* JACK. LANE *goes off.*)

JACK. There's a sensible, intellectual girl! the only girl I ever cared for in my life. (ALGERNON *is laughing immoderately.*) What on earth are you so amused at?

ALGERNON. Oh, I'm a little anxious about poor Bunbury, that is all.

JACK. If you don't take care, your friend Bunbury will get you into a serious scrape some day.

ALGERNON. I love scrapes. They are the only things that are never serious.

JACK. Oh, that's nonsense, Algy. You never talk anything but nonsense.

ALGERNON. Nobody ever does.

(JACK *looks indignantly at him, and leaves the room.* ALGERNON *lights a cigarette, reads his shirt-cuff, and smiles.*)

SECOND ACT

[SCENE.] *Garden at the Manor House. A flight of grey stone steps leads up to the house. The garden, an old-fashioned one, full of roses. Time of year, July. Basket chairs, and a table covered with books, are set under a large yew-tree.*

(MISS PRISM *discovered seated at the table.* CECILY *is at the back, watering flowers.*)

MISS PRISM (*calling*). Cecily, Cecily! Surely such a utilitarian occupation as the watering of flowers is rather Moulton's duty than yours? Especially at a moment when intellectual pleasures await you. Your German grammar is on the table. Pray open it at page fifteen. We will repeat yesterday's lesson.

CECILY (*coming over very slowly*). But I don't like German. It isn't at all a becoming language. I know perfectly well that I look quite plain after my German lesson.

MISS PRISM. Child, you know how anxious your guardian is that you should improve yourself in every way. He laid particular stress on your German, as he was leaving for town yesterday. Indeed, he always lays stress on your German when he is leaving for town.

CECILY. Dear Uncle Jack is so very serious! Sometimes he is so serious that I think he cannot be quite well.

MISS PRISM (*drawing herself up*). Your guardian enjoys the best of health, and his gravity of demeanour is especially to be commended in one so comparatively young as he is. I know no one who has a higher sense of duty and responsibility.

CECILY. I suppose that is why he often looks a little bored
   when we three are together.

MISS PRISM. Cecily! I am surprised at you. Mr. Worthing
   has many troubles in his life. Idle merriment and
   triviality would be out of place in his conversation.
   You must remember his constant anxiety about that
   unfortunate young man his brother.

CECILY. I wish Uncle Jack would allow that unfortunate
   young man, his brother, to come down here sometimes. We might have a good influence over him, Miss
   Prism. I am sure you certainly would. You know
   German, and geology, and things of that kind influence
   a man very much. (CECILY *begins to write in her
   diary.*)

MISS PRISM (*shaking her head*). I do not think that even
   I could produce any effect on a character that according to his own brother's admission is irretrievably
   weak and vacillating. Indeed I am not sure that I
   would desire to reclaim him. I am not in favour of
   this modern mania for turning bad people into good
   people at a moment's notice. As a man sows so let
   him reap. You must put away your diary, Cecily. I
   really don't see why you should keep a diary at all.

CECILY. I keep a diary in order to enter the wonderful
   secrets of my life. If I didn't write them down, I should
   probably forget all about them.

MISS PRISM. Memory, my dear Cecily, is the diary that we
   all carry about with us.

CECILY. Yes, but it usually chronicles the things that have
   never happened, and couldn't possibly have happened.
   I believe that Memory is responsible for nearly all the
   three-volume novels that Mudie[2] sends us.

MISS PRISM. Do not speak slightingly of the three-volume
   novel, Cecily. I wrote one myself in earlier days.

CECILY. Did you really, Miss Prism? How wonderfully
   clever you are! I hope it did not end happily? I don't
   like novels that end happily. They depress me so much.

MISS PRISM. The good ended happily, and the bad un-
   happily. That is what Fiction means.

CECILY. I suppose so. But it seems very unfair. And was
   your novel ever published?

MISS PRISM. Alas! no. The manuscript unfortunately was

---

[2] Mudie's was a nationwide system of lending libraries.

abandoned. (CECILY *starts*.) I used the word in the sense of lost or mislaid. To your work, child, these speculations are profitless.

CECILY (*smiling*). But I see dear Dr. Chasuble coming up through the garden.

MISS PRISM (*rising and advancing*). Dr. Chasuble! This is indeed a pleasure.

(*Enter* CANON CHASUBLE.)

CHASUBLE. And how are we this morning? Miss Prism, you are, I trust, well?

CECILY. Miss Prism has just been complaining of a slight headache. I think it would do her so much good to have a short stroll with you in the Park, Dr. Chasuble.

MISS PRISM. Cecily, I have not mentioned anything about a headache.

CECILY. No, dear Miss Prism, I know that, but I felt instinctively that you had a headache. Indeed I was thinking about that, and not about my German lesson, when the Rector came in.

CHASUBLE. I hope, Cecily, you are not inattentive.

CECILY. Oh, I am afraid I am.

CHASUBLE. That is strange. Were I fortunate enough to be Miss Prism's pupil, I would hang upon her lips. (MISS PRISM *glares*.) I spoke metaphorically.—My metaphor was drawn from bees. Ahem! Mr. Worthing, I suppose, has not returned from town yet?

MISS PRISM. We do not expect him till Monday afternoon.

CHASUBLE. Ah yes, he usually likes to spend his Sunday in London. He is not one of those whose sole aim is enjoyment, as, by all accounts, that unfortunate young man his brother seems to be. But I must not disturb Egeria and her pupil any longer.

MISS PRISM. Egeria? My name is Laetitia, Doctor.

CHASUBLE (*bowing*). A classical allusion merely, drawn from the Pagan authors. I shall see you both no doubt at Evensong?

MISS PRISM. I think, dear Doctor, I will have a stroll with you. I find I have a headache after all, and a walk might do it good.

CHASUBLE. With pleasure, Miss Prism, with pleasure. We might go as far as the schools and back.

MISS PRISM. That would be delightful. Cecily, you will read your Political Economy in my absence. The chapter

on the Fall of the Rupee you may omit. It is somewhat too sensational. Even these metallic problems
have their melodramatic side.

(*Goes down the garden with* DR. CHASUBLE.)

CECILY (*picks up books and throws them back on table*).
Horrid Political Economy! Horrid Geography! Horrid,
horrid German!

(*Enter* MERRIMAN *with a card on a salver.*)

MERRIMAN. Mr. Ernest Worthing has just driven over from
the station. He has brought his luggage with him.

CECILY (*takes the card and reads it*). "Mr. Ernest Worthing, B.4, The Albany, W." Uncle Jack's brother! Did
you tell him Mr. Worthing was in town?

MERRIMAN. Yes, Miss. He seemed very much disappointed.
I mentioned that you and Miss Prism were in the
garden. He said he was anxious to speak to you
privately for a moment.

CECILY. Ask Mr. Ernest Worthing to come here. I suppose you had better talk to the housekeeper about a
room for him.

MERRIMAN. Yes, Miss. (MERRIMAN *goes off.*)

CECILY. I have never met any really wicked person before.
I feel rather frightened. I am so afraid he will look
just like every one else.

(*Enter* ALGERNON, *very gay and debonair.*)

He does!

ALGERNON (*raising his hat*). You are my little cousin
Cecily, I'm sure.

CECILY. You are under some strange mistake. I am not
little. In fact, I believe I am more than usually tall for
my age. (ALGERNON *is rather taken aback.*) But I am
your cousin Cecily. You, I see from your card, are
Uncle Jack's brother, my cousin Ernest, my wicked
cousin Ernest.

ALGERNON. Oh! I am not really wicked at all, Cousin
Cecily. You mustn't think that I am wicked.

CECILY. If you are not, then you have certainly been deceiving us all in a very inexcusable manner. I hope
you have not been leading a double life, pretending
to be wicked and being really good all the time. That
would be hypocrisy.

ALGERNON (*looks at her in amazement*). Oh! Of course I have been rather reckless.

CECILY. I am glad to hear it.

ALGERNON. In fact, now you mention the subject, I have been very bad in my own small way.

CECILY. I don't think you should be so proud of that, though I am sure it must have been very pleasant.

ALGERNON. It is much pleasanter being here with you.

CECILY. I can't understand how you are here at all. Uncle Jack won't be back till Monday afternoon.

ALGERNON. That is a great disappointment. I am obliged to go up by the first train on Monday morning. I have a business appointment that I am anxious . . . to miss!

CECILY. Couldn't you miss it anywhere but in London?

ALGERNON. No: the appointment is in London.

CECILY. Well, I know, of course, how important it is not to keep a business engagement, if one wants to retain any sense of the beauty of life, but still I think you had better wait till Uncle Jack arrives. I know he wants to speak to you about your emigrating.

ALGERNON. About my what?

CECILY. Your emigrating. He has gone up to buy your outfit.

ALGERNON. I certainly wouldn't let Jack buy my outfit. He has no taste in neckties at all.

CECILY. I don't think you will require neckties. Uncle Jack is sending you to Australia.

ALGERNON. Australia! I'd sooner die.

CECILY. Well, he said at dinner on Wednesday night, that you would have to choose between this world, the next world, and Australia.

ALGERNON. Oh, well! The accounts I have received of Australia and the next world are not particularly encouraging. This world is good enough for me, Cousin Cecily.

CECILY. Yes, but are you good enough for it?

ALGERNON. I'm afraid I'm not that. That is why I want you to reform me. You might make that your mission, if you don't mind, Cousin Cecily.

CECILY. I'm afraid I've no time, this afternoon.

ALGERNON. Well, would you mind my reforming myself this afternoon?

CECILY. It is rather Quixotic of you. But I think you should try.

ALGERNON. I will. I feel better already.

CECILY. You are looking a little worse.

ALGERNON. That is because I am hungry.

CECILY. How thoughtless of me. I should have remembered that when one is going to lead an entirely new life, one requires regular and wholesome meals. Won't you come in?

ALGERNON. Thank you. Might I have a buttonhole first? I have never any appetite unless I have a buttonhole first.

CECILY. A Maréchal Neil? (*Picks up scissors.*)

ALGERNON. No, I'd sooner have a pink rose.

CECILY. Why? (*Cuts a flower.*)

ALGERNON. Because you are like a pink rose, Cousin Cecily.

CECILY. I don't think it can be right for you to talk to me like that. Miss Prism never says such things to me.

ALGERNON. Then Miss Prism is a short-sighted old lady. (CECILY *puts the rose in his buttonhole.*) You are the prettiest girl I ever saw.

CECILY. Miss Prism says that all good looks are a snare.

ALGERNON. They are a snare that every sensible man would like to be caught in.

CECILY. Oh, I don't think I would care to catch a sensible man. I shouldn't know what to talk to him about.

(*They pass into the house.* MISS PRISM *and* DR. CHASUBLE *return.*)

MISS PRISM. You are too much alone, dear Dr. Chasuble. You should get married. A misanthrope I can understand—a womanthrope, never!

CHASUBLE (*with a scholar's shudder*). Believe me, I do not deserve so neologistic a phrase. The precept as well as the practice of the Primitive Church was distinctly against matrimony.

MISS PRISM (*sententiously*). That is obviously the reason why the Primitive Church has not lasted up to the present day. And you do not seem to realize, dear Doctor, that by persistently remaining single, a man converts himself into a permanent public temptation. Men should be more careful; this very celibacy leads weaker vessels astray.

CHASUBLE. But is a man not equally attractive when married?

MISS PRISM. No married man is ever attractive except to his wife.

CHASUBLE. And often, I've been told, not even to her.

MISS PRISM. That depends on the intellectual sympathies of the woman. Maturity can always be depended on. Ripeness can be trusted. Young women are green. (DR. CHASUBLE *starts*.) I spoke horticulturally. My metaphor was drawn from fruits. But where is Cecily?

CHASUBLE. Perhaps she followed us to the schools.

(*Enter* JACK *slowly from the back of the garden. He is dressed in the deepest mourning, with crepe hatband and black gloves.*)

MISS PRISM. Mr. Worthing!

CHASUBLE. Mr. Worthing?

MISS PRISM. This is indeed a surprise. We did not look for you till Monday afternoon.

JACK (*shakes* MISS PRISM's *hand in a tragic manner*). I have returned sooner than I expected. Dr. Chasuble, I hope you are well?

CHASUBLE. Dear Mr. Worthing, I trust this garb of woe does not betoken some terrible calamity?

JACK. My brother.

MISS PRISM. More shameful debts and extravagance?

CHASUBLE. Still leading his life of pleasure?

JACK (*shaking his head*). Dead!

CHASUBLE. Your brother Ernest dead?

JACK. Quite dead.

MISS PRISM. What a lesson for him! I trust he will profit by it.

CHASUBLE. Mr. Worthing, I offer you my sincere condolence. You have at least the consolation of knowing that you were always the most generous and forgiving of brothers.

JACK. Poor Ernest! He had many faults, but it is a sad, sad blow.

CHASUBLE. Very sad indeed. Were you with him at the end?

JACK. No. He died abroad; in Paris, in fact. I had a telegram last night from the manager of the Grand Hotel.

CHASUBLE. Was the cause of death mentioned?

JACK. A severe chill, it seems.

MISS PRISM. As a man sows, so shall he reap.

CHASUBLE (*raising his hand*). Charity, dear Miss Prism,

charity! None of us are perfect. I myself am peculiarly
susceptible to draughts. Will the interment take place
here?

JACK. No. He seems to have expressed a desire to be
buried in Paris.

CHASUBLE. In Paris! (*Shakes his head.*) I fear that hardly
points to any very serious state of mind at the last.
You would no doubt wish me to make some slight
allusion to this tragic domestic affliction next Sunday.
(JACK *presses his hand convulsively.*) My sermon on
the meaning of the manna in the wilderness can be
adapted to almost any occasion, joyful, or, as in the
present case, distressing. (*All sigh.*) I have preached
it at harvest celebrations, christenings, confirmations,
on days of humiliation and festal days. The last time
I delivered it was in the Cathedral, as a charity sermon
on behalf of the Society for the Prevention of Dis-
content among the Upper Orders. The Bishop, who
was present, was much struck by some of the anologies
I drew.

JACK. Ah! that reminds me, you mentioned christenings I
think, Dr. Chasuble? I suppose you know how to
christen all right? (DR. CHASUBLE *looks astounded.*)
I mean, of course, you are continually christening,
aren't you?

MISS PRISM. It is, I regret to say, one of the Rector's most
constant duties in this parish. I have often spoken to
the poorer classes on the subject. But they don't seem
to know what thrift is.

CHASUBLE. But is there any particular infant in whom you
are interested, Mr. Worthing? Your brother was, I
believe, unmarried, was he not?

JACK. Oh yes.

MISS PRISM (*bitterly*). People who live entirely for pleasure
usually are.

JACK. But it is not for any child, dear Doctor. I am very
fond of children. No! the fact is, I would like to be
christened myself, this afternoon, if you have nothing
better to do.

CHASUBLE. But surely, Mr. Worthing, you have been christened already?

JACK. I don't remember anything about it.

CHASUBLE. But have you any grave doubts on the subject?

JACK. I certainly intend to have. Of course I don't know if the thing would bother you in any way, or if you think I am a little too old now.

CHASUBLE. Not at all. The sprinkling, and, indeed, the immersion of adults is a perfectly canonical practice.

JACK. Immersion!

CHASUBLE. You need have no apprehensions. Sprinkling is all that is necessary, or indeed I think advisable. Our weather is so changeable. At what hour would you wish the ceremony performed?

JACK. Oh, I might trot round about five if that would suit you.

CHASUBLE. Perfectly, perfectly! In fact I have two similar ceremonies to perform at that time. A case of twins that occurred recently in one of the outlying cottages on your own estate. Poor Jenkins the carter, a most hard-working man.

JACK. Oh! I don't see much fun in being christened along with other babies. It would be childish. Would half-past five do?

CHASUBLE. Admirably! Admirably! (*Takes out watch.*) And now, dear Mr. Worthing, I will not intrude any longer into a house of sorrow. I would merely beg you not to be too much bowed down by grief. What seem to us bitter trials are often blessings in disguise.

MISS PRISM. This seems to me a blessing of an extremely obvious kind.

(*Enter* CECILY *from the house.*)

CECILY. Uncle Jack! Oh, I am pleased to see you back. But what horrid clothes you have got on. Do go and change them.

MISS PRISM. Cecily!

CHASUBLE. My child! my child. (CECILY *goes toward* JACK; *he kisses her brow in a melancholy manner.*)

CECILY. What is the matter, Uncle Jack? Do look happy! You look as if you had toothache, and I have got such a surprise for you. Who do you think is in the dining-room? Your brother!

JACK. Who?

CECILY. Your brother Ernest. He arrived about half an hour ago.

JACK. What nonsense! I haven't got a brother.

CECILY. Oh, don't say that. However badly he may have behaved to you in the past he is still your brother. You couldn't be so heartless as to disown him. I'll tell him to come out. And you will shake hands with him, won't you, Uncle Jack? (*Runs back into the house.*)

CHASUBLE. These are very joyful tidings.

MISS PRISM. After we had all been resigned to his loss, his sudden return seems to me particularly distressing.

JACK. My brother is in the dining-room? I don't know what it all means. I think it is perfectly absurd.

(*Enter* ALGERNON *and* CECILY *hand in hand. They come slowly up to* JACK.)

JACK. Good heavens! (*Motions* ALGERNON *away.*)

ALGERNON. Brother John, I have come down from town to tell you that I am very sorry for all the trouble I have given you, and that I intend to lead a better life in the future. (JACK *glares at him and does not take his hand.*)

CECILY. Uncle Jack, you are not going to refuse your own brother's hand?

JACK. Nothing will induce me to take his hand. I think his coming down here disgraceful. He knows perfectly well why.

CECILY. Uncle Jack, do be nice. There is some good in everyone. Ernest has just been telling me about his poor invalid friend Mr. Bunbury whom he goes to visit so often. And surely there must be much good in one who is kind to an invalid, and leaves the pleasures of London to sit by a bed of pain.

JACK. Oh! he has been talking about Bunbury, has he?

CECILY. Yes, he has told me all about poor Mr. Bunbury, and his terrible state of health.

JACK. Bunbury! Well, I won't have him talk to you about Bunbury or about anything else. It is enough to drive one perfectly frantic.

ALGERNON. Of course I admit that the faults were all on my side. But I must say that I think that Brother John's coldness to me is peculiarly painful. I expected a more enthusiastic welcome especially considering it is the first time I have come here.

CECILY. Uncle Jack, if you don't shake hands with Ernest, I will never forgive you.

JACK. Never forgive me?

CECILY. Never, never, never!

JACK. Well, this is the last time I shall ever do it. (*Shakes hands with* ALGERNON *and glares.*)

CHASUBLE. It's pleasant, is it not, to see so perfect a reconciliation? I think we might leave the two brothers together.

MISS PRISM. Cecily, you will come with us.

CECILY. Certainly, Miss Prism. My little task of reconciliation is over.

CHASUBLE. You have done a beautiful action today, dear child.

MISS PRISM. We must not be premature in our judgements.

CECILY. I feel very happy. (*They all go off except* JACK *and* ALGERNON.)

JACK. You young scoundrel, Algy, you must get out of this place as soon as possible. I don't allow any Bunburying here.

(*Enter* MERRIMAN.)

MERRIMAN. I have put Mr. Ernest's things in the room next to yours, sir. I suppose that is all right?

JACK. What?

MERRIMAN. Mr. Ernest's luggage, sir. I have unpacked it and put it in the room next to your own.

JACK. His luggage?

MERRIMAN. Yes, sir. Three portmanteaus, a dressing-case, two hatboxes, and a large luncheon-basket.

ALGERNON. I am afraid I can't stay more than a week this time.

JACK. Merriman, order the dog-cart[3] at once. Mr. Ernest has been suddenly called back to town.

MERRIMAN. Yes, sir. (*Goes back into the house.*)

ALGERNON. What a fearful liar you are, Jack. I have not been called back to town at all.

JACK. Yes, you have.

ALGERNON. I haven't heard any one call me.

JACK. Your duty as a gentleman calls you back.

ALGERNON. My duty as a gentleman has never interfered with my pleasures in the smallest degree.

JACK. I can quite understand that.

---

[3] A small two-seated carriage, so called because it originally had a box under the seat for a sportsman's dogs.

ALGERNON. Well, Cecily is a darling.

JACK. You are not to talk of Miss Cardew like that. I don't like it.

ALGERNON. Well, I don't like your clothes. You look perfectly ridiculous in them. Why on earth don't you go up and change? It is perfectly childish to be in deep mourning for a man who is actually staying for a whole week with you in your house as a guest. I call it grotesque.

JACK. You are certainly not staying with me for a whole week as a guest or anything else. You have got to leave . . . by the four-five train.

ALGERNON. I certainly won't leave you so long as you are in mourning. It would be most unfriendly. If I were in mourning you would stay with me, I suppose. I should think it very unkind if you didn't.

JACK. Well, will you go if I change my clothes?

ALGERNON. Yes, if you are not too long. I never saw anybody take so long to dress, and with such little result.

JACK. Well, at any rate, that is better than being always over-dressed as you are.

ALGERNON. If I am occasionally a little over-dressed, I make up for it by being always immensely over-educated.

JACK. Your vanity is ridiculous, your conduct an outrage, and your presence in my garden utterly absurd. However, you have got to catch the four-five, and I hope you will have a pleasant journey back to town. This Bunburying, as you call it, has not been a great success for you.

(*Goes into the house.*)

ALGERNON. I think it has been a great success. I'm in love with Cecily, and that is everything.

(*Enter* CECILY *at the back of the garden. She picks up the can and begins to water the flowers.*)

But I must see her before I go, and make arrangements for another Bunbury. Ah, there she is.

CECILY. Oh, I merely came back to water the roses. I thought you were with Uncle Jack.

ALGERNON. He's gone to order the dog-cart for me.

CECILY. Oh, is he going to take you for a nice drive?

ALGERNON. He's going to send me away.

CECILY. Then have we got to part?

ALGERNON. I am afraid so. It's a very painful parting.

CECILY. It is always painful to part from people whom one
has known for a very brief space of time. The absence
of old friends one can endure with equanimity. But
even a momentary separation from any one to whom
one has just been introduced is almost unbearable.

ALGERNON. Thank you.

(*Enter* MERRIMAN.)

MERRIMAN. The dog-cart is at the door, sir.

(ALGERNON *looks appealingly at* CECILY.)

CECILY. It can wait, Merriman . . . for . . . five minutes.

MERRIMAN. Yes, Miss.

(*Exit* MERRIMAN.)

ALGERNON. I hope, Cecily, I shall not offend you if I state
quite frankly and openly that you seem to me to be in
every way the visible personification of absolute
perfection.

CECILY. I think your frankness does you great credit,
Ernest. If you will allow me, I will copy your remarks
into my diary. (*Goes over to table and begins writing
in diary.*)

ALGERNON. Do you really keep a diary? I'd give anything
to look at it. May I?

CECILY. Oh no. (*Puts her hand over it.*) You see, it is
simply a very young girl's record of her own thoughts
and impressions, and consequently meant for publication. When it appears in volume form I hope you will
order a copy. But pray, Ernest, don't stop. I delight
in taking down from dictation. I have reached "absolute perfection." You can go on. I am quite ready
for more.

ALGERNON (*somewhat taken aback*). Ahem! Ahem!

CECILY. Oh, don't cough, Ernest. When one is dictating
one should speak fluently and not cough. Besides, I
don't know how to spell a cough. (*Writes as* ALGERNON
speaks.)

ALGERNON (*speaking very rapidly*). Cecily, ever since I first
looked upon your wonderful and incomparable beauty,
I have dared to love you wildly, passionately, devotedly, hopelessly.

CECILY. I don't think that you should tell me that you love me wildly, passionately, devotedly, hopelessly. Hopelessly doesn't seem to make much sense, does it?

ALGERNON. Cecily.

(*Enter* MERRIMAN.)

MERRIMAN. The dog-cart is waiting, sir.

ALGERNON. Tell it to come round next week, at the same hour.

MERRIMAN (*looks at* CECILY, *who makes no sign*). Yes, sir.

(MERRIMAN *retires*.)

CECILY. Uncle Jack would be very much annoyed if he knew you were staying on till next week, at the same hour.

ALGERNON. Oh, I don't care about Jack. I don't care for anybody in the whole world but you. I love you, Cecily. You will marry me, won't you?

CECILY. You silly boy! Of course. Why, we have been engaged for the last three months.

ALGERNON. For the last three months?

CECILY. Yes, it will be exactly three months on Thursday.

ALGERNON. But how did we become engaged?

CECILY. Well, ever since dear Uncle Jack first confessed to us that he had a younger brother who was very wicked and bad, you of course have formed the chief topic of conversation between myself and Miss Prism. And of course a man who is much talked about is always very attractive. One feels there must be something in him, after all. I daresay it was foolish of me, but I fell in love with you, Ernest.

ALGERNON. Darling. And when was the engagement actually settled?

CECILY. On the 14th of February last. Worn out by your entire ignorance of my existence, I determined to end the matter one way or the other, and after a long struggle with myself I accepted you under this dear old tree here. The next day I bought this little ring in your name, and this is the little bangle with the true lover's knot I promised you always to wear.

ALGERNON. Did I give you this? It's very pretty, isn't it?

CECILY. Yes, you've wonderfully good taste, Ernest. It's the excuse I've always given for your leading such a bad life. And this is the box in which I keep all your dear letters. (*Kneels at table, opens box, and produces letters tied up with blue ribbon.*)

ALGERNON. My letters! But, my own sweet Cecily, I have never written you any letters.

CECILY. You need hardly remind me of that, Ernest. I remember only too well that I was forced to write your letters for you. I wrote always three times a week, and sometimes oftener.

ALGERNON. Oh, do let me read them, Cecily?

CECILY. Oh, I couldn't possibly. They would make you far too conceited. (*Replaces box.*) The three you wrote me after I had broken off the engagement are so beautiful, and so badly spelled, that even now I can hardly read them without crying a little.

ALGERNON. But was our engagement ever broken off?

CECILY. Of course it was. On the 22nd of last March. You can see the entry if you like. (*Shows diary.*) "Today I broke off my engagement with Ernest. I feel it is better to do so. The weather still continues charming."

ALGERNON. But why on earth did you break it off? What had I done? I had done nothing at all. Cecily, I am very much hurt indeed to hear you broke it off. Particularly when the weather was so charming.

CECILY. It would hardly have been a really serious engagement if it hadn't been broken off at least once. But I forgave you before the week was out.

ALGERNON (*crossing to her, and kneeling*). What a perfect angel you are, Cecily.

CECILY. You dear romantic boy. (*He kisses her, she puts her fingers through his hair.*) I hope your hair curls naturally, does it?

ALGERNON. Yes, darling, with a little help from others.

CECILY. I am so glad.

ALGERNON. You'll never break off our engagement again, Cecily?

CECILY. I don't think I could break it off now that I have actually met you. Besides, of course, there is the question of your name.

ALGERNON. Yes, of course. (*nervously*)

CECILY. You must not laugh at me, darling, but it had always been a girlish dream of mine to love some one whose name was Ernest. (ALGERNON *rises*, CECILY *also.*) There is something in that name that seems to inspire absolute confidence. I pity any poor married woman whose husband is not called Ernest.

ALGERNON. But, my dear child, do you mean to say you could not love me if I had some other name?

CECILY. But what name?

ALGERNON. Oh, any name you like—Algernon—for instance . . .

CECILY. But I don't like the name of Algernon.

ALGERNON. Well, my own dear, sweet, loving little darling, I really can't see why you should object to the name of Algernon. It is not at all a bad name. In fact, it is rather an aristocratic name. Half of the chaps who get into the Bankruptcy Court are called Algernon. But seriously, Cecily . . . (*moving to her*) if my name was Algy, couldn't you love me?

CECILY (*rising*). I might respect you, Ernest, I might admire your character, but I fear that I should not be able to give you my undivided attention.

ALGERNON. Ahem! Cecily! (*picking up hat*) Your Rector here is, I suppose, thoroughly experienced in the practice of all the rites and ceremonials of the Church?

CECILY. Oh, yes. Dr. Chasuble is a most learned man. He has never written a single book, so you can imagine how much he knows.

ALGERNON. I must see him at once on a most important christening—I mean on most important business.

CECILY. Oh!

ALGERNON. I shan't be away more than half an hour.

CECILY. Considering that we have been engaged since February the 14th, and that I only met you to-day for the first time, I think it is rather hard that you should leave me for so long a period as half an hour. Couldn't you make it twenty minutes?

ALGERNON. I'll be back in no time. (*Kisses her and rushes down the garden.*)

CECILY. What an impetuous boy he is! I like his hair so much. I must enter his proposal in my diary.

(*Enter* MERRIMAN.)

MERRIMAN. A Miss Fairfax has just called to see Mr. Worthing. On very important business, Miss Fairfax states.

CECILY. Isn't Mr. Worthing in his library?

MERRIMAN. Mr. Worthing went over in the direction of the rectory some time ago.

CECILY. Pray ask the lady to come out here; Mr. Worthing is sure to be back soon. And you can bring tea.

MERRIMAN. Yes, Miss.

(*Goes out.*)

CECILY. Miss Fairfax! I suppose one of the many good elderly women who are associated with Uncle Jack in some of his philanthropic work in London. I don't quite like women who are interested in philanthropic work. I think it is so forward of them.

(*Enter* MERRIMAN.)

MERRIMAN. Miss Fairfax.

(*Enter* GWENDOLEN. *Exit* MERRIMAN.)

CECILY (*advancing to meet her*). Pray let me introduce myself to you. My name is Cecily Cardew.

GWENDOLEN. Cecily Cardew? (*moving to her and shaking hands*) What a very sweet name! Something tells me that we are going to be great friends. I like you already more than I can say. My first impressions of people are never wrong.

CECILY. How nice of you to like me so much after we have known each other such a comparatively short time. Pray sit down.

GWENDOLEN (*still standing up*). I may call you Cecily, may I not?

CECILY. With pleasure!

GWENDOLEN. And you will always call me Gwendolen, won't you?

CECILY. If you wish.

GWENDOLEN. Then that is all quite settled, is it not?

CECILY. I hope so. (*A pause. They both sit down together.*)

GWENDOLEN. Perhaps this might be a favourable opportunity for my mentioning who I am. My father is Lord Bracknell. You have never heard of papa, I suppose?

CECILY. I don't think so.

GWENDOLEN. Outside the family circle, papa, I am glad to say, is entirely unknown. I think that is quite as it should be. The home seems to me to be the proper sphere for the man. And certainly once a man begins to neglect his domestic duties he becomes painfully effeminate, does he not? And I don't like that. It makes men so very attractive. Cecily, mamma, whose views on education are remarkably strict, has brought me up to be extremely short-sighted; it is part of her system; so do you mind my looking at you through my glasses?

CECILY. Oh! not at all, Gwendolen. I am very fond of being looked at.

GWENDOLEN (*after examining* CECILY *carefully through a lorgnette*). You are here on a short visit, I suppose.

CECILY. Oh no! I live here.

GWENDOLEN (*severely*). Really? Your mother, no doubt, or some female relative of advanced years, resides here also?

CECILY. Oh no! I have no mother, nor, in fact, any relations.

GWENDOLEN. Indeed?

CECILY. My dear guardian, with the assistance of Miss Prism, has the arduous task of looking after me.

GWENDOLEN. Your guardian?

CECILY. Yes, I am Mr. Worthing's ward.

GWENDOLEN. Oh! It is strange he never mentioned to me that he had a ward. How secretive of him! He grows more interesting hourly. I am not sure, however, that the news inspires me with feelings of unmixed delight. (*rising and going to her*) I am very fond of you, Cecily; I have liked you ever since I met you! But I am bound to state that now that I know that you are Mr. Worthing's ward, I cannot help expressing a wish you were—well, just a little older than you seem to be—and not quite so very alluring in appearance. In fact, if I may speak candidly—

CECILY. Pray do! I think that whenever one has anything unpleasant to say, one should always be quite candid.

GWENDOLEN. Well, to speak with perfect candour, Cecily, I wish that you were fully forty-two, and more than usually plain for your age. Ernest has a strong upright nature. He is the very soul of truth and honour. Disloyalty would be as impossible to him as deception. But even men of the noblest possible moral character are extremely susceptible to the influence of the physical charms of others. Modern, no less than

Ancient History, supplies us with many most painful examples of what I refer to. If it were not so, indeed, History would be quite unreadable.

CECILY. I beg your pardon, Gwendolen, did you say Ernest?

GWENDOLEN. Yes.

CECILY. Oh, but it is not Mr. Ernest Worthing who is my guardian. It is his brother—his elder brother.

GWENDOLEN (*sitting down again*). Ernest never mentioned to me that he had a brother.

CECILY. I am sorry to say that they have not been on good terms for a long time.

GWENDOLEN. Ah! that accounts for it. And now that I think of it I have never heard any man mention his brother. The subject seems distasteful to most men. Cecily, you have lifted a load from my mind. I was growing almost anxious. It would have been terrible if any cloud had come across a friendship like ours, would it not? Of course you are quite, quite sure that it is not Mr. Ernest Worthing who is your guardian?

CECILY. Quite sure. (*a pause*) In fact, I am going to be his.

GWENDOLEN (*inquiringly*). I beg your pardon?

CECILY (*rather shy and confidingly*). Dearest Gwendolen, there is no reason why I should make a secret of it to you. Our little county newspaper is sure to chronicle the fact next week. Mr. Ernest Worthing and I are engaged to be married.

GWENDOLEN (*quite politely, rising*). My darling Cecily, I think there must be some slight error. Mr. Ernest Worthing is engaged to me. The announcement will appear in the *Morning Post* on Saturday at the latest.

CECILY (*very politely, rising*). I am afraid you must be under some misconception. Ernest proposed to me exactly ten minutes ago. (*Shows diary.*)

GWENDOLEN (*examines diary through her lorgnette carefully*). It is very curious, for he asked me to be his wife yesterday afternoon at 5.30. If you would care to verify the incident, pray do so. (*Produces diary of her own.*) I never travel without my diary. One should always have something sensational to read in the train. I am so sorry, dear Cecily, if it is any disappointment to you, but I am afraid I have the prior claim.

CECILY. It would distress me more than I can tell you, dear

Gwendolen, if it caused you any mental or physical anguish, but I feel bound to point out that since Ernest proposed to you he clearly has changed his mind.

GWENDOLEN (*meditatively*). If the poor fellow has been entrapped into any foolish promise, I shall consider it my duty to rescue him at once, and with a firm hand.

CECILY (*thoughtfully and sadly*). Whatever unfortunate entanglement my dear boy may have got into, I will never reproach him with it after we are married.

GWENDOLEN. Do you allude to me, Miss Cardew, as an entanglement? You are presumptuous. On an occasion of this kind it becomes more than a moral duty to speak one's mind. It becomes a pleasure.

CECILY. Do you suggest, Miss Fairfax, that I entrapped Ernest into an engagement? How dare you? This is no time for wearing the shallow mask of manners. When I see a spade I call it a spade.

GWENDOLEN (*satirically*). I am glad to say that I have never seen a spade. It is obvious that our social spheres have been widely different.

(*Enter* MERRIMAN, *followed by the footman. He carries a salver, table cloth, and plate stand.* CECILY *is about to retort. The presence of the servants exercises a restraining influence, under which both girls chafe.*)

MERRIMAN. Shall I lay tea here as usual, Miss?

CECILY (*sternly, in a calm voice*). Yes, as usual.

(MERRIMAN *begins to clear table and lay cloth. A long pause.* CECILY *and* GWENDOLEN *glare at each other.*)

GWENDOLEN. Are there many interesting walks in the vicinity, Miss Cardew?

CECILY. Oh! yes! a great many. From the top of one of the hills quite close one can see five counties.

GWENDOLEN. Five counties! I don't think I should like that; I hate crowds.

CECILY (*sweetly*). I suppose that is why you live in town?

(GWENDOLEN *bites her lip, and beats her foot nervously with her parasol.*)

GWENDOLEN (*looking around*). Quite a well-kept garden this is, Miss Cardew.

CECILY. So glad you like it, Miss Fairfax.

GWENDOLEN. I had no idea there were any flowers in the country.

CECILY. Oh, flowers are as common here, Miss Fairfax, as people are in London.

GWENDOLEN. Personally I cannot understand how anybody manages to exist in the country, if anybody who is anybody does. The country always bores me to death.

CECILY. Ah! this is what the newspapers call agricultural depression, is it not? I believe the aristocracy are suffering very much from it just at present. It is almost an epidemic amongst them, I have been told. May I offer you some tea, Miss Fairfax?

GWENDOLEN (*with elaborate politeness*). Thank you. (*aside*) Detestable girl! But I require tea!

CECILY (*sweetly*). Sugar?

GWENDOLEN (*superciliously*). No, thank you. Sugar is not fashionable any more. (CECILY *looks angrily at her, takes up the tongs and puts four lumps of sugar into the cup.*)

CECILY (*severely*). Cake or bread and butter?

GWENDOLEN (*in a bored manner*). Bread and butter, please. Cake is rarely seen at the best houses nowadays.

CECILY (*cuts a very large slice of cake and puts it on the tray*). Hand that to Miss Fairfax.

(MERRIMAN *does so, and goes out with footman.* GWENDOLEN *drinks the tea and makes a grimace. Puts down cup at once, reaches out her hand to the bread and butter, looks at it, and finds it is cake. Rises in indignation.*)

GWENDOLEN. You have filled my tea with lumps of sugar, and though I asked most distinctly for bread and butter, you have given me cake. I am known for the gentleness of my disposition, and the extraordinary sweetness of my nature, but I warn you, Miss Cardew, you may go too far.

CECILY (*rising*). To save my poor, innocent, trusting boy from the machinations of any other girl there are no lengths to which I would not go.

GWENDOLEN. From the moment I saw you I distrusted you. I felt that you were false and deceitful. I am never deceived in such matters. My first impressions of people are invariably right.

CECILY. It seems to me, Miss Fairfax, that I am trespassing on your valuable time. No doubt you have many other calls of a similar character to make in the neighbourhood.

(*Enter* JACK.)

GWENDOLEN (*catching sight of him*). Ernest! My own Ernest!

JACK. Gwendolen! Darling! (*Offers to kiss her.*)

GWENDOLEN (*drawing back*). A moment! May I ask if you are engaged to be married to this young lady? (*Points to* CECILY.)

JACK (*laughing*). To dear little Cecily! Of course not! What could have put such an idea into your pretty little head?

GWENDOLEN. Thank you. You may! (*Offers her cheek.*)

CECILY (*very sweetly*). I knew there must be some misunderstanding, Miss Fairfax. The gentleman whose arm is at present round your waist is my guardian, Mr. John Worthing.

GWENDOLEN. I beg your pardon?

CECILY. This is Uncle Jack.

GWENDOLEN (*receding*). Jack! Oh!

(*Enter* ALGERNON.)

CECILY. Here is Ernest.

ALGERNON (*goes straight over to* CECILY *without noticing anyone else*). My own love! (*Offers to kiss her.*)

CECILY (*drawing back*). A moment, Ernest! May I ask you —are you engaged to be married to this young lady?

ALGERNON (*looking round*). To what young lady? Good heavens! Gwendolen!

CECILY. Yes: to good heavens, Gwendolen, I mean to Gwendolen.

ALGERNON (*laughing*). Of course not! What could have put such an idea into your pretty little head?

CECILY. Thank you. (*Presenting her cheek to be kissed.*) You may. (ALGERNON *kisses her.*)

GWENDOLEN. I felt there was some slight error, Miss Cardew. The gentleman who is now embracing you is my cousin, Mr. Algernon Moncrieff.

CECILY (*breaking away from* ALGERNON). Algernon Moncrieff! Oh! (*The two girls move towards each other and put their arms round each other's waists as if for protection.*)

CECILY. Are you called Algernon?

ALGERNON. I cannot deny it.

CECILY. Oh!

GWENDOLEN. Is your name really John?

JACK (*standing rather proudly*). I could deny it if I liked. I could deny anything if I liked. But my name certainly is John. It has been John for years.

CECILY (*To* GWENDOLEN). A gross deception has been practised on both of us.

GWENDOLEN. My poor wounded Cecily!

CECILY. My sweet wronged Gwendolen!

GWENDOLEN (*slowly and seriously*). You will call me sister, will you not? (*They embrace.* JACK *and* ALGERNON *groan and walk up and down.*)

CECILY (*rather brightly*). There is just one question I would like to be allowed to ask my guardian.

GWENDOLEN. An admirable idea! Mr. Worthing, there is just one question I would like to be permitted to put to you. Where is your brother Ernest? We are both engaged to be married to your brother Ernest, so it is a matter of some importance to us to know where your brother Ernest is at present.

JACK (*slowly and hesitatingly*). Gwendolen—Cecily—it is very painful for me to be forced to speak the truth. It is the first time in my life that I have ever been reduced to such a painful position, and I am really quite inexperienced in doing anything of the kind. However, I will tell you quite frankly that I have no brother Ernest. I have no brother at all. I never had a brother in my life, and I certainly have not the smallest intention of ever having one in the future.

CECILY (*surprised*). No brother at all?

JACK (*cheerily*). None!

GWENDOLEN (*severely*). Had you never a brother of any kind?

JACK (*pleasantly*). Never. Not even of any kind.

GWENDOLEN. I am afraid it is quite clear, Cecily, that neither of us is engaged to be married to anyone.

CECILY. It is not a very pleasant position for a young girl suddenly to find herself in. Is it?

GWENDOLEN. Let us go into the house. They will hardly venture to come after us there.

CECILY. No, men are so cowardly, aren't they?

(*They retire into the house with scornful looks.*)

JACK. This ghastly state of things is what you call Bunburying, I suppose?

ALGERNON. Yes, and a perfectly wonderful Bunbury it is. The most wonderful Bunbury I have ever had in my life.

JACK. Well, you've no right whatsoever to Bunbury here.

ALGERNON. That is absurd. One has a right to Bunbury anywhere one chooses. Every serious Bunburyist knows that.

JACK. Serious Bunburyist? Good heavens!

ALGERNON. Well, one must be serious about something, if one wants to have any amusement in life. I happen to be serious about Bunburying. What on earth you are serious about I haven't got the remotest idea. About everything, I should fancy. You have such an absolutely trivial nature.

JACK. Well, the only small satisfaction I have in the whole of this wretched business is that your friend Bunbury is quite exploded. You won't be able to run down to the country quite so often as you used to do, dear Algy. And a very good thing too.

ALGERNON. Your brother is a little off colour, isn't he, dear Jack? You won't be able to disappear to London quite so frequently as your wicked custom was. And not a bad thing either.

JACK. As for your conduct towards Miss Cardew, I must say that your taking in a sweet, simple, innocent girl like that is quite inexcusable. To say nothing of the fact that she is my ward.

ALGERNON. I can see no possible defence at all for your deceiving a brilliant, clever, thoroughly experienced young lady like Miss Fairfax. To say nothing of the fact that she is my cousin.

JACK. I wanted to be engaged to Gwendolen, that is all. I love her.

ALGERNON. Well, I simply wanted to be engaged to Cecily. I adore her.

JACK. There is certainly no chance of your marrying Miss Cardew.

ALGERNON. I don't think there is much likelihood, Jack, of you and Miss Fairfax being united.

JACK. Well, that is no business of yours.

ALGERNON. If it was my business, I wouldn't talk about it. (*Begins to eat muffins.*) It is very vulgar to talk about one's business. Only people like stockbrokers do that, and then merely at dinner parties.

JACK. How you can sit there, calmly eating muffins when we are in this horrible trouble, I can't make out. You seem to me to be perfectly heartless.

ALGERNON. Well, I can't eat muffins in an agitated manner. The butter would probably get on my cuffs. One should always eat muffins quite calmly. It is the only way to eat them.

JACK. I say it's perfectly heartless your eating muffins at all, under the circumstances.

ALGERNON. When I am in trouble, eating is the only thing that consoles me. Indeed, when I am in really great trouble, as any one who knows me intimately will tell you, I refuse everything except food and drink. At the present moment I am eating muffins because I am unhappy. Besides, I am particularly fond of muffins. (*rising*)

JACK (*rising*). Well, there is no reason why you should eat them all in that greedy way. (*Takes muffins from* ALGERNON.)

ALGERNON (*offering tea-cake*). I wish you would have tea-cake instead. I don't like tea-cake.

JACK. Good heavens! I suppose a man may eat his own muffins in his own garden.

ALGERNON. But you have just said it was perfectly heartless to eat muffins.

JACK. I said it was perfectly heartless of you, under the circumstances. That is a very different thing.

ALGERNON. That may be. But the muffins are the same. (*He seizes the muffin-dish from* JACK.)

JACK. Algy, I wish to goodness you would go.

ALGERNON. You can't possibly ask me to go without having some dinner. It's absurd. I never go without my dinner. No one ever does, except vegetarians and people like that. Besides I have just made arrangements with Dr. Chasuble to be christened at a quarter to six under the name of Ernest.

JACK. My dear fellow, the sooner you give up that nonsense the better. I made arrangements this morning with Dr. Chasuble to be christened myself at 5.30, and I naturally will take the name of Ernest. Gwendolen would wish it. We can't both be christened Ernest. It's absurd. Besides, I have a perfect right to be christened if I like. There is no evidence at all that I have ever been christened by anybody. I should think it extremely probable I never was, and so does Dr. Chasuble. It is entirely different in your case. You have been christened already.

ALGERNON. Yes, but I have not been christened for years.

JACK. Yes, but you have been christened. That is the important thing.

ALGERNON. Quite so. So I know my constitution can stand it. If you are not quite sure about your ever having been christened, I must say I think it rather dangerous your venturing on it now. It might make you very unwell. You can hardly have forgotten that someone very closely connected with you was very nearly carried off this week in Paris by a severe chill.

JACK. Yes, but you said yourself that a severe chill was not hereditary.

ALGERNON. It usen't to be, I know—but I daresay it is now. Science is always making wonderful improvements in things.

JACK (*picking up the muffin-dish*). Oh, that is nonsense; you are always talking nonsense.

ALGERNON. Jack, you are at the muffins again! I wish you wouldn't. There are only two left. (*Takes them.*) I told you I was particularly fond of muffins.

JACK. But I hate tea-cake.

ALGERNON. Why on earth then do you allow tea-cake to be served up for your guests? What ideas you have of hospitality!

JACK. Algernon! I have already told you to go. I don't want you here. Why don't you go!

ALGERNON. I haven't quite finished my tea yet! and there is still one muffin left.

(JACK *groans, and sinks into a chair.* ALGERNON *continues eating.*)

THIRD ACT

[SCENE.] *Drawing-room at the Manor House*

(GWENDOLEN *and* CECILY *are at the window, looking out into the garden.*)

GWENDOLEN. The fact that they did not follow us at once into the house, as anyone else would have done, seems to me to show that they have some sense of shame left.

CECILY. They have been eating muffins. That looks like repentance.

GWENDOLEN (*after a pause*). They don't seem to notice us at all. Couldn't you cough?

CECILY. But I haven't got a cough.

GWENDOLEN. They're looking at us. What effrontery!

CECILY. They're approaching. That's very forward of them.

GWENDOLEN. Let us preserve a dignified silence.

CECILY. Certainly. It's the only thing to do now.

(*Enter* JACK *followed by* ALGERNON. *They whistle some dreadful popular air from a British Opera.*)

GWENDOLEN. This dignified silence seems to produce an unpleasant effect.

CECILY. A most distasteful one.

GWENDOLEN. But we will not be the first to speak.

CECILY. Certainly not.

GWENDOLEN. Mr. Worthing, I have something very particular to ask you. Much depends on your reply.

CECILY. Gwendolen, your common sense is invaluable. Mr. Moncrieff, kindly answer me the following question. Why did you pretend to be my guardian's brother?

ALGERNON. In order that I might have an opportunity of meeting you.

CECILY (*To* GWENDOLEN). That certainly seems a satisfactory explanation, does it not?

GWENDOLEN. Yes, dear, if you can believe him.

CECILY. I don't. But that does not affect the wonderful beauty of his answer.

GWENDOLEN. True. In matters of grave importance, style, not sincerity, is the vital thing. Mr. Worthing, what explanation can you offer to me for pretending to have a brother? Was it in order that you might have an opportunity of coming up to town to see me as often as possible?

JACK. Can you doubt it, Miss Fairfax?

GWENDOLEN. I have the gravest doubts upon the subject. But I intend to crush them. This is not the moment for German scepticism. (*moving to* CECILY) Their explanations appear to be quite satisfactory, especially Mr. Worthing's. That seems to me to have the stamp of truth upon it.

CECILY. I am more than content with what Mr. Moncrieff said. His voice alone inspires one with absolute credulity.

GWENDOLEN. Then you think we should forgive them?

CECILY. Yes. I mean no.

GWENDOLEN. True! I had forgotten. There are principles at stake that one cannot surrender. Which of us should tell them? The task is not a pleasant one.

CECILY. Could we not both speak at the same time?

GWENDOLEN. An excellent idea! I nearly always speak at the same time as other people. Will you take the time from me?

CECILY. Certainly. (GWENDOLEN *beats time with uplifted finger.*)

GWENDOLEN and CECILY (*speaking together*). Your Christian names are still an insuperable barrier. That is all!

JACK and ALGERNON (*speaking together*). Our Christian names! Is that all? But we are going to be christened this afternoon.

GWENDOLEN (*To* JACK). For my sake you are prepared to do this terrible thing?

JACK. I am.

CECILY (*To* ALGERNON). To please me you are ready to face this fearful ordeal?

ALGERNON. I am!

GWENDOLEN. How absurd to talk of the equality of the sexes! Where questions of self-sacrifice are concerned, men are infinitely beyond us.

JACK. We are. (*Clasps hands with* ALGERNON.)

CECILY. They have moments of physical courage of which we women know absolutely nothing.

GWENDOLEN (*To* JACK). Darling!

ALGERNON (*To* CECILY). Darling! (*They fall into each other's arms.*)

(*Enter* MERRIMAN. *When he enters he coughs loudly, seeing the situation.*)

MERRIMAN. Ahem! Ahem! Lady Bracknell.

JACK. Good heavens!

(*Enter* LADY BRACKNELL. *The couples separate in alarm. Exit* MERRIMAN.)

LADY BRACKNELL. Gwendolen! What does this mean?

GWENDOLEN. Merely that I am engaged to be married to Mr. Worthing, mamma.

LADY BRACKNELL. Come here. Sit down. Sit down immediately. Hesitation of any kind is a sign of mental decay in the young, of physical weakness in the old. (*Turns to* JACK.) Apprised, sir, of my daughter's sudden flight by her trusty maid, whose confidence I purchased by means of a small coin, I followed her at once by a luggage train. Her unhappy father is, I am glad to say, under the impression that she is attending a more than usually lengthy lecture by the University Extension Scheme on the Influence of a Permanent Income on Thought. I do not propose to undeceive him. Indeed I have never undeceived him on any question. I would consider it wrong. But of course, you will clearly understand that all communication between yourself and my daughter must cease immediately from this moment. On this point, as indeed on all points, I am firm.

JACK. I am engaged to be married to Gwendolen, Lady Bracknell!

LADY BRACKNELL. You are nothing of the kind, sir. And now as regards Algernon! . . . Algernon!

ALGERNON. Yes, Aunt Augusta.

LADY BRACKNELL. May I ask if it is in this house that your invalid friend Mr. Bunbury resides?

ALGERNON (*stammering*). Oh! No! Bunbury doesn't live here. Bunbury is somewhere else at present. In fact, Bunbury is dead.

LADY BRACKNELL. Dead! When did Mr. Bunbury die? His death must have been extremely sudden.

ALGERNON (*airily*). Oh! I killed Bunbury this afternoon. I mean poor Bunbury died this afternoon.

LADY BRACKNELL. What did he die of?

ALGERNON. Bunbury? Oh, he was quite exploded.

LADY BRACKNELL. Exploded! Was he the victim of a revolutionary outrage? I was not aware that Mr. Bunbury was interested in social legislation. If so, he is well punished for his morbidity.

ALGERNON. My dear Aunt Augusta, I mean he was found out! The doctors found out that Bunbury could not live, that is what I mean—so Bunbury died.

LADY BRACKNELL. He seems to have had great confidence in the opinion of his physicians. I am glad, however, that he made up his mind at the last to some definite course of action, and acted under proper medical advice. And now that we have finally got rid of this Mr. Bunbury, may I ask, Mr. Worthing, who is that young person whose hand my nephew Algernon is now holding in what seems to me a peculiarly unnecessary manner?

JACK. That lady is Miss Cecily Cardew, my ward. (LADY BRACKNELL *bows coldly to* CECILY.)

ALGERNON. I am engaged to be married to Cecily, Aunt Augusta.

LADY BRACKNELL. I beg your pardon?

CECILY. Mr. Moncrieff and I are engaged to be married, Lady Bracknell.

LADY BRACKNELL (*with a shiver, crossing to the sofa and sitting down*). I do not know whether there is anything peculiarly exciting in the air of this particular part of Hertfordshire, but the number of engagements that go on seem to me considerably above the proper average that statistics have laid down for our guidance. I think some preliminary inquiry on my part would not be out of place. Mr. Worthing, is Miss Cardew at all connected with any of the larger railway stations in London? I merely desire information. Until yesterday I had no idea that there were any families or persons whose origin was a Terminus. (JACK *looks perfectly furious, but restrains himself.*)

JACK (*in a cold, clear voice*). Miss Cardew is the granddaughter of the late Mr. Thomas Cardew of 149 Belgrave Square, S.W.; Gervase Park, Dorking, Surrey; and the Sporran, Fifeshire, N.B.

LADY BRACKNELL. That sounds not unsatisfactory. Three addresses always inspire confidence, even in tradesmen. But what proof have I of their authenticity?

JACK. I have carefully preserved the Court Guides[4] of the period. They are open to your inspection, Lady Bracknell.

LADY BRACKNELL (*grimly*). I have known strange errors in that publication.

JACK. Miss Cardew's family solicitors are Messrs. Markby, Markby, and Markby.

LADY BRACKNELL. Markby, Markby, and Markby? A firm of the very highest position in their profession. Indeed I am told that one of the Mr. Markby's is occasionally to be seen at dinner parties. So far I am satisfied.

JACK (*very irritably*). How extremely kind of you, Lady Bracknell! I have also in my possession, you will be pleased to hear, certificates of Miss Cardew's birth, baptism, whooping cough, registration, vaccination, confirmation, and the measles; both the German and the English variety.

LADY BRACKNELL. Ah! A life crowded with incident, I see; though perhaps somewhat too exciting for a young girl. I am not myself in favour of premature experiences. (*Rises, looks at her watch.*) Gwendolen! the time approaches for our departure. We have not a moment to lose. As a matter of form, Mr. Worthing, I had better ask you if Miss Cardew has any little fortune?

JACK. Oh! about a hundred and thirty thousand pounds in the Funds. That is all. Good-bye, Lady Bracknell. So pleased to have seen you.

LADY BRACKNELL (*sitting down again*). A moment, Mr. Worthing. A hundred and thirty thousand pounds! And in the Funds! Miss Cardew seems to me a most attractive young lady, now that I look at her. Few girls of the present day have any really solid qualities, any of the qualities that last, and improve with time. We live, I regret to say, in an age of surfaces. (*To* CECILY.) Come over here, dear. (CECILY *goes across.*) Pretty child! your dress is sadly simple, and your hair seems almost as Nature might have left it. But we can soon alter all that. A thoroughly experienced French maid produces a really marvellous result in

---

[4] Directories containing the names and addresses of people in "society," supposed to contain the names of all persons who have been presented at Court.

a very brief space of time. I remember recommending one to young Lady Lancing, and after three months her own husband did not know her.

JACK. And after six months nobody knew her.

LADY BRACKNELL (*glares at* JACK *for a few moments. Then bends, with a practised smile, to* CECILY). Kindly turn round, sweet child. (CECILY *turns completely round.*) No, the side view is what I want. (CECILY *presents her profile.*) Yes, quite as I expected. There are distinct social possibilities in your profile. The two weak points in our age are its want of principle and its want of profile. The chin a little higher, dear. Style largely depends on the way the chin is worn. They are worn very high, just at present. Algernon!

ALGERNON. Yes, Aunt Augusta!

LADY BRACKNELL. There are distinct social possibilities in Miss Cardew's profile.

ALGERNON. Cecily is the sweetest, dearest, prettiest girl in the whole world. And I don't care twopence about social possibilities.

LADY BRACKNELL. Never speak disrespectfully of Society, Algernon. Only people who can't get into it do that. (*To* CECILY.) Dear child, of course you know that Algernon has nothing but his debts to depend upon. But I do not approve of mercenary marriages. When I married Lord Bracknell I had no fortune of any kind. But I never dreamed for a moment of allowing that to stand in my way. Well, I suppose I must give my consent.

ALGERNON. Thank you, Aunt Augusta.

LADY BRACKNELL. Cecily, you may kiss me!

CECILY (*kisses her*). Thank you, Lady Bracknell.

LADY BRACKNELL. You may also address me as Aunt Augusta for the future.

CECILY. Thank you, Aunt Augusta.

LADY BRACKNELL. The marriage, I think, had better take place quite soon.

ALGERNON. Thank you, Aunt Augusta.

CECILY. Thank you, Aunt Augusta.

LADY BRACKNELL. To speak frankly, I am not in favour of long engagements. They give people the opportunity of finding out each other's character before marriage, which I think is never advisable.

JACK. I beg your pardon for interrupting you, Lady Bracknell, but this engagement is quite out of the question. I am Miss Cardew's guardian, and she cannot marry without my consent until she comes of age. That consent I absolutely decline to give.

LADY BRACKNELL. Upon what grounds, may I ask? Algernon is an extremely, I may almost say an ostentatiously, eligible young man. He has nothing, but he looks everything. What more can one desire?

JACK. It pains me very much to have to speak frankly to you, Lady Bracknell, about your nephew, but the fact is that I do not approve at all of his moral character. I suspect him of being untruthful. (ALGERNON *and* CECILY *look at him in indignant amazement.*)

LADY BRACKNELL. Untruthful! My nephew Algernon? Impossible! He is an Oxonian.

JACK. I fear there can be no possible doubt about the matter. This afternoon during my temporary absence in London on an important question of romance, he obtained admission to my house by means of the false pretence of being my brother. Under an assumed name he drank, I've just been informed by my butler, an entire pint bottle of my Perrier-Jouet, Brut, '89; wine I was specially reserving for myself. Continuing his disgraceful deception, he succeeded in the course of the afternoon in alienating the affections of my only ward. He subsequently stayed to tea, and devoured every single muffin. And what makes his conduct all the more heartless is, that he was perfectly well aware from the first that I have no brother, that I never had a brother, and that I don't intend to have a brother, not even of any kind. I distinctly told him so myself yesterday afternoon.

LADY BRACKNELL. Ahem! Mr. Worthing, after careful consideration I have decided entirely to overlook my nephew's conduct to you.

JACK. That is very generous of you, Lady Bracknell. My own decision, however, is unalterable. I decline to give my consent.

LADY BRACKNELL (*To* CECILY). Come here, sweet child. (CECILY *goes over.*) How old are you, dear?

CECILY. Well, I am really only eighteen, but I always admit to twenty when I go to evening parties.

LADY BRACKNELL. You are perfectly right in making some slight alteration. Indeed, no woman should ever be quite accurate about her age. It looks so calculating. ... (*in a meditative manner*) Eighteen, but admitting to twenty at evening parties. Well, it will not be very long before you are of age and free from the restraints of tutelage. So I don't think your guardian's consent is, after all, a matter of any importance.

JACK. Pray excuse me, Lady Bracknell, for interrupting you again, but it is only fair to tell you that according to the terms of her grandfather's will Miss Cardew does not come legally of age till she is thirty-five.

LADY BRACKNELL. That does not seem to me to be a grave objection. Thirty-five is a very attractive age. London society is full of women of the very highest birth who have, of their own free choice, remained thirty-five for years. Lady Dumbleton is an instance in point. To my own knowledge she has been thirty-five ever since she arrived at the age of forty, which was many years ago now. I see no reason why our dear Cecily should not be even still more attractive at the age you mention than she is at present. There will be a large accumulation of property.

CECILY. Algy, could you wait for me till I was thirty-five?

ALGERNON. Of course I could, Cecily. You know I could.

CECILY. Yes, I felt it instinctively, but I couldn't wait all that time. I hate waiting even five minutes for anybody. It always makes me rather cross. I am not punctual myself, I know, but I do like punctuality in others, and waiting, even to be married, is quite out of the question.

ALGERNON. Then what is to be done, Cecily?

CECILY. I don't know, Mr. Moncrieff.

LADY BRACKNELL. My dear Mr. Worthing, as Miss Cardew states positively that she cannot wait till she is thirty-five—a remark which I am bound to say seems to me to show a somewhat impatient nature—I would beg of you to reconsider your decision.

JACK. But my dear Lady Bracknell, the matter is entirely in your own hands. The moment you consent to my marriage with Gwendolen, I will most gladly allow your nephew to form an alliance with my ward.

LADY BRACKNELL (*rising and drawing herself up*). You must be quite aware that what you propose is out of the question.

JACK. Then a passionate celibacy is all that any of us can look forward to.

LADY BRACKNELL. That is not the destiny I propose for Gwendolen. Algernon, of course, can choose for himself. (*Pulls out her watch.*) Come, dear (GWENDOLEN *rises.*), we have already missed five, if not six, trains. To miss any more might expose us to comment on the platform.

(*Enter* DR. CHASUBLE.)

CHASUBLE. Everything is quite ready for the christenings.

LADY BRACKNELL. The christenings, sir! Is not that somewhat premature?

CHASUBLE (*looking rather puzzled, and pointing to* JACK *and* ALGERNON). Both these gentlemen have expressed a desire for immediate baptism.

LADY BRACKNELL. At their age? The idea is grotesque and irreligious! Algernon, I forbid you to be baptized. I will not hear of such excesses. Lord Bracknell would be highly displeased if he learned that that was the way in which you wasted your time and money.

CHASUBLE. Am I to understand then that there are to be no christenings at all this afternoon?

JACK. I don't think that, as things are now, it would be of much practical value to either of us, Dr. Chasuble.

CHASUBLE. I am grieved to hear such sentiments from you, Mr. Worthing. They savour of the heretical views of the Anabaptists, views that I have completely refuted in four of my unpublished sermons. However, as your present mood seems to be one peculiarly secular, I will return to the church at once. Indeed, I have just been informed by the pew-opener that for the last hour and a half Miss Prism has been waiting for me in the vestry.

LADY BRACKNELL (*starting*). Miss Prism! Did I hear you mention a Miss Prism?

CHASUBLE. Yes, Lady Bracknell. I am on my way to join her.

LADY BRACKNELL. Pray allow me to detain you for a moment. This matter may prove to be one of vital importance to Lord Bracknell and myself. Is this Miss Prism a female of repellent aspect, remotely connected with education?

CHASUBLE (*somewhat indignantly*). She is the most cultivated of ladies, and the very picture of respectability.

LADY BRACKNELL. It is obviously the same person. May I
ask what position she holds in your household?

CHASUBLE (*severely*). I am a celibate, madam.

JACK (*interposing*). Miss Prism, Lady Bracknell, has been
for the last three years Miss Cardew's esteemed governess and valued companion.

LADY BRACKNELL. In spite of what I hear of her, I must see
her at once. Let her be sent for.

CHASUBLE (*looking off*). She approaches; she is nigh.

(*Enter* MISS PRISM *hurriedly.*)

MISS PRISM. I was told you expected me in the vestry, dear
Canon. I have been waiting for you there for an hour
and three-quarters. (*Catches sight of* LADY BRACKNELL,
who has fixed her with a stony glare. MISS PRISM *grows
pale and quails. She looks anxiously round as if desirous to escape.*)

LADY BRACKNELL (*in a severe, judicial voice*). Prism!
(MISS PRISM *bows her head in shame.*) Come here,
Prism! (MISS PRISM *approaches in a humble manner.*)
Prism! Where is that baby? (*General consternation.
The Canon starts back in horror.* ALGERNON *and* JACK
pretend to be anxious to shield CECILY *and* GWEN-
DOLEN *from hearing the details of a terrible public
scandal.*) Twenty-eight years ago, Prism, you left
Lord Bracknell's house, Number 104, Upper Grosvenor Street, in charge of a perambulator that contained a baby of the male sex. You never returned.
A few weeks later, through the elaborate investigations
of the Metropolitan police, the perambulator was discovered at midnight standing by itself in a remote
corner of Bayswater. It contained the manuscript of
a three-volume novel of more than usually revolting
sentimentality. (MISS PRISM *starts in involuntary
indignation.*) But the baby was not there. (*Every one
looks at* MISS PRISM.) Prism! Where is that baby? (*A
pause.*)

MISS PRISM. Lady Bracknell, I admit with shame that I do
not know. I only wish I did. The plain facts of the case
are these. On the morning of the day you mention,
a day that is for ever branded on my memory, I prepared as usual to take the baby out in its perambu-

lator. I had also with me a somewhat old, but capacious hand-bag in which I had intended to place the manuscript of a work of fiction that I had written during my few unoccupied hours. In a moment of mental abstraction, for which I can never forgive myself, I deposited the manuscript in the bassinette and placed the baby in the hand-bag.

JACK (*who has been listening attentively*). But where did you deposit the hand-bag?

MISS PRISM. Do not ask me, Mr. Worthing.

JACK. Miss Prism, this is a matter of no small importance to me. I insist on knowing where you deposited the hand-bag that contained that infant.

MISS PRISM. I left it in the cloak-room of one of the larger railway stations in London.

JACK. What railway station?

MISS PRISM (*quite crushed*). Victoria. The Brighton line. (*Sinks into a chair.*)

JACK. I must retire to my room for a moment. Gwendolen, wait here for me.

GWENDOLEN. If you are not too long, I will wait here for you all my life. (*Exit* JACK *in great excitement.*)

CHASUBLE. What do you think this means, Lady Bracknell?

LADY BRACKNELL. I dare not even suspect, Dr. Chasuble. I need hardly tell you that in families of high position strange coincidences are not supposed to occur. They are hardly considered the thing.

(*Noises heard overhead as if some one was throwing trunks about. Every one looks up.*)

CECILY. Uncle Jack seems strangely agitated.

CHASUBLE. Your guardian has a very emotional nature.

LADY BRACKNELL. This noise is extremely unpleasant. It sounds as if he was having an argument. I dislike arguments of any kind. They are always vulgar, and often convincing.

CHASUBLE (*looking up*). It has stopped now. (*The noise is redoubled.*)

LADY BRACKNELL. I wish he would arrive at some conclusion.

GWENDOLEN. This suspense is terrible. I hope it will last.

(*Enter* JACK *with a hand-bag of black leather in his hand.*)

JACK (*rushing over to* MISS PRISM). Is this the hand-bag, Miss Prism? Examine it carefully before you speak. The happiness of more than one life depends on your answer.

MISS PRISM (*calmly*). It seems to be mine. Yes, here is the injury it received through the upsetting of a Gower Street omnibus in younger and happier days. Here is the stain on the lining caused by the explosion of a temperance beverage, an incident that occurred at Leamington. And here, on the lock, are my initials. I had forgotten that in an extravagant mood I had had them placed there. The bag is undoubtedly mine. I am delighted to have it so unexpectedly restored to me. It has been a great inconvenience being without it all these years.

JACK (*in a pathetic voice*). Miss Prism, more is restored to you than this hand-bag. I was the baby you placed in it.

MISS PRISM (*amazed*). You?

JACK (*embracing her*). Yes . . . mother!

MISS PRISM (*recoiling in indignant astonishment*). Mr. Worthing. I am unmarried!

JACK. Unmarried! I do not deny that is a serious blow. But after all, who has the right to cast a stone against one who has suffered? Cannot repentance wipe out an act of folly? Why should there be one law for men, and another for women? Mother, I forgive you. (*Tries to embrace her again.*)

MISS PRISM (*still more indignant*). Mr. Worthing, there is some error. (*pointing to* LADY BRACKNELL) There is the lady who can tell you who you really are.

JACK (*after a pause*). Lady Bracknell, I hate to seem inquisitive, but would you kindly inform me who I am?

LADY BRACKNELL. I am afraid that the news I have to give you will not altogether please you. You are the son of my poor sister, Mrs. Moncrieff, and consequently Algernon's elder brother.

JACK. Algy's elder brother! Then I have a brother after all. I knew I had a brother! I always said I had a brother! Cecily—how could you have ever doubted that I had a brother? (*Seizes hold of* ALGERNON.) Dr. Chasuble, my unfortunate brother. Miss Prism, my unfortunate brother. Gwendolen, my unfortunate brother. Algy, you young scoundrel, you will have to treat me with

more respect in the future. You have never behaved
to me like a brother in all your life.

ALGERNON. Well, not till to-day, old boy, I admit. I did
my best, however, though I was out of practice.
(*Shakes hands.*)

GWENDOLEN (*To* JACK). My own! But what own are you?
What is your Christian name, now that you have become some one else?

JACK. Good heavens! . . . I had quite forgotten that point.
Your decision on the subject of my name is irrev-
ocable, I suppose?

GWENDOLEN. I never change, except in my affections.

CECILY. What a noble nature you have, Gwendolen!

JACK. Then the question had better be cleared up at once.
Aunt Augusta, a moment. At the time when Miss
Prism left me in the hand-bag, had I been christened
already?

LADY BRACKNELL. Every luxury that money could buy, including christening, had been lavished on you by
your fond and doting parents.

JACK. Then I was christened! That is settled. Now, what
name was I given? Let me know the worst.

LADY BRACKNELL. Being the eldest son you were naturally
christened after your father.

JACK (*irritably*). Yes, but what was my father's Christian
name?

LADY BRACKNELL (*meditatively*). I cannot at the present
moment recall what the General's Christian name was.
But I have no doubt he had one. He was eccentric, I
admit. But only in later years. And that was the result
of the Indian climate, and marriage, and indigestion,
and other things of that kind.

JACK. Algy! Can't you recollect what our father's Christian
name was?

ALGERNON. My dear boy, we were never even on speaking
terms. He died before I was a year old.

JACK. His name would appear in the Army Lists of the
period, I suppose, Aunt Augusta?

LADY BRACKNELL. The General was essentially a man of
peace, except in his domestic life. But I have no doubt
his name would appear in any military directory.

JACK. The Army Lists of the last forty years are here. These
delightful records should have been my constant study.
(*Rushes to bookcase and tears the books out.*) M. Gen-

erals . . . Mallam, Maxbohm, Magley—what ghastly
names they have—Markby, Migsby, Mobbs, Moncrieff! Lieutenant 1840, Captain, Lieutenant-Colonel,
Colonel, General 1869, Christian names, Ernest John.
(*Puts book very quietly down and speaks quite
calmly.*) I always told you, Gwendolen, my name was
Ernest, didn't I? Well, it is Ernest after all. I mean it
naturally is Ernest.

LADY BRACKNELL. Yes, I remember now that the General
was called Ernest. I knew I had some particular reason
for disliking the name.

GWENDOLEN. Ernest! My own Ernest! I felt from the first
that you could have no other name!

JACK. Gwendolen, it is a terrible thing for a man to find
out suddenly that all his life he has been speaking
nothing but the truth. Can you forgive me?

GWENDOLEN. I can. For I feel that you are sure to change.

JACK. My own one!

CHASUBLE (*To* MISS PRISM). Laetitia! (*Embraces her.*)

MISS PRISM (*enthusiastically*). Frederick! At last!

ALGERNON. Cecily! (*Embraces her.*) At last!

JACK. Gwendolen! (*Embraces her.*) At last!

LADY BRACKNELL. My nephew, you seem to be displaying
signs of triviality.

JACK. On the contrary, Aunt Augusta, I've now realized
for the first time in my life the vital Importance of
Being Earnest.

TABLEAU

CURTAIN